FOUR GREAT SF NOVELS

Arthur C. Clarke

FOUR GREAT S F NOVELS

The City and the Stars
The Deep Range
A Fall of Moondust
Rendezvous With Rama

LONDON
VICTOR GOLLANCZ LTD
1978

This edition © Victor Gollancz Ltd 1978

THE CITY AND THE STARS © Arthur C. Clarke 1956

THE DEEP RANGE © Arthur C. Clarke 1957

A FALL OF MOONDUST © Arthur C. Clarke 1961

RENDEZVOUS WITH RAMA © Arthur C. Clarke 1973

ISBN 0 575 02409 7

MADE AND PRINTED IN GREAT BRITAIN BY
THE GARDEN CITY PRESS LIMITED
LETCHWORTH, HERTFORDSHIRE
SG6 1JS

Contents

THE CITY
AND THE STARS

TO VAL

PROLOGUE

LIKE A GLOWING jewel, the city lay upon the breast of the desert. Once it had known change and alteration, but now Time passed it by. Night and day fled across the desert's face, but in the streets of Diaspar it was always afternoon, and darkness never came. The long winter nights might dust the desert with frost, as the last moisture left in the thin air of Earth congealed— but the city knew neither heat nor cold. It had no contact with the outer world; it was a universe itself.

Men had built cities before, but never a city such as this. Some had lasted for centuries, some for millennia, before Time had swept away even their names. Diaspar alone had challenged Eternity, defending itself and all it sheltered against the slow attrition of the ages, the ravages of decay, and the corruption of rust.

Since the city was built, the oceans of Earth had passed away and the desert had encompassed all the globe. The last mountains had been ground to dust by the winds and the rain, and the world was too weary to bring forth more. The city did not care; Earth itself could crumble and Diaspar would still protect the children of its makers, bearing them and their treasures safely down the stream of time.

They had forgotten much, but they did not know it. They were as perfectly fitted to their environment as it was to them—for both had been designed together. What was beyond the walls of the city was no concern of theirs; it was something that had been shut out of their minds. Diaspar was all that existed, all that they needed, all that they could imagine. It mattered nothing to them that Man had once possessed the stars.

Yet sometimes the ancient myths rose up to haunt them, and they stirred uneasily as they remembered the legends of the Empire, when Diaspar was young and drew its life-blood from the commerce of many suns. They did not wish to bring back the old days, for they were content in their eternal autumn. The glories of the Empire belonged to the past, and could remain there—for they remembered how the Empire had met its end, and at the thought of the Invaders the chill of space itself came seeping into their bones.

Then they would turn once more to the life and warmth of the city, to the long golden age whose beginning was already lost and whose end was yet more distant. Other men had dreamed of such an age, but they alone had achieved it.

For they had lived in the same city, had walked the same miraculously unchanging streets, while more than a thousand million years had worn away.

CHAPTER I

IT HAD TAKEN them many hours to fight their way out of the Cave of the White Worms. Even now, they could not be sure that some of the pallid monsters were not pursuing them—and the power of their weapons was almost exhausted. Ahead, the floating arrows of light that had been their mysterious guide through the labyrinths of the Crystal Mountain still beckoned them on. They had no choice but to follow it, though as it had done so many times before it might lead them into yet more frightful dangers.

Alvin glanced back to see if all his companions were still with him. Alystra was close behind, carrying the sphere of cold but ever-burning light which had revealed such horrors and such beauty since their adventure had begun. The pale white radiance flooded the narrow corridor and splashed from the glittering walls; while its power lasted, they could see where they were going and could detect the presence of any visible dangers. But the greatest dangers in these caves, Alvin knew too well, were not the visible ones at all.

Behind Alystra, struggling with the weight of their projectors, came Narillian and Floranus. Alvin wondered briefly why those projectors were so heavy, since it would have been such a simple matter to provide them with gravity neutralisers. He was always thinking of points like this, even in the midst of the most desperate adventures. When such thoughts crossed his mind, it seemed as if the structure of reality trembled for an instant, and that behind the world of the senses he caught a glimpse of another and totally different universe. . . .

The corridor ended in a blank wall. Had the arrow betrayed them again? No—even as they approached, the rock began to crumble into dust. Through the wall pierced a spinning metal spear, which broadened rapidly into a giant screw. Alvin and his friends moved back, waiting for the machine to force its way into the cave. With a deafening screech of metal upon rock—which surely must echo through all the recesses of the Mountain, and waken all its nightmare brood!—the subterrene smashed through the wall and came to rest beside them. A massive door opened, and Callistron appeared, shouting to them to hurry. ("Why Callistron?" wondered Alvin. "What's *he* doing here?") A moment later they were in safety, and the machine lurched forward as it began its journey through the depths of the earth.

The adventure was over. Soon, as always happened, they would be home, and all the wonder, the terror, and the excitement would be behind them. They were tired and content.

Alvin could tell from the tilt of the floor that the subterrene was heading down into the earth. Presumably Callistron knew what he was doing, and this was the way that led to home. Yet it seemed a pity. . . .

"Callistron," he said suddenly, "why don't we go upwards? No one knows what the Crystal Mountain really looks like. How wonderful it would be to come out somewhere on its slopes, to see the sky and all the land around it. We've been underground for long enough."

Even as he said these words, he somehow knew that they were wrong. Alystra gave a strangled scream, the interior of the subterrene wavered like an image seen through water, and behind and beyond the metal walls that surrounded him Alvin once more glimpsed that other universe. The two worlds seemed in conflict, first one and then the other predominating. Then, quite suddenly, it was all over. There was a snapping, rending sensation—and the dream had ended. Alvin was back in Diaspar, in his own familiar room, floating a foot or two above the floor as the gravity field protected him from the bruising contact of brute matter.

He was himself again. *This* was reality—and he knew exactly what would happen next.

Alystra was the first to appear. She was more upset than annoyed, for she was very much in love with Alvin.

"Oh, Alvin!" she lamented, as she looked down at him from the wall in which she had apparently materialised. "It was such an exciting adventure! Why did you have to spoil it?"

"I'm sorry. I didn't intend to—I just thought it would be a good idea——"

He was interrupted by the simultaneous arrival of Callistron and Floranus.

"Now listen, Alvin," began Callistron. "This is the *third* time you've interrupted a saga. You broke the sequence yesterday, by wanting to climb out of the Valley of Rainbows. And the day before you upset everything by trying to get back to the Origin in that time-track we were exploring. If you don't keep the rules, you'll have to go by yourself."

He vanished in high dudgeon, taking Floranus with him. Narillian never appeared at all; he was probably too fed up with the whole affair. Only the image of Alystra was left, looking sadly down at Alvin.

Alvin tilted the gravity field, rose to his feet, and walked towards the table he had materialised. A bowl of exotic fruit appeared upon it—not the food he had intended, for in his confusion his thoughts had wandered. Not wishing to reveal his error, he picked up the least dangerous-looking of the fruits and started to suck it cautiously.

"Well," said Alystra at last, "what are you going to do?"

"I can't help it," he said a little sulkily. "I think the rules are stupid. Besides, how can I remember them when I'm living a saga? I just behave in the way that seems natural. Didn't *you* want to look at the mountain?"

Alystra's eyes widened with horror.

"That would have meant going outside!" she gasped.

Alvin knew that it was useless to argue further. Here was the barrier that sundered him from all the people of his world, and which might doom him to a life of frustration. He was always wanting to go outside, both in reality and in dream. Yet to everyone in Diaspar, "outside" was a nightmare that they could not face. They would never talk about it if it could be avoided; it was something unclean and evil. Not even Jeserac, his tutor, would tell him why. . . .

Alystra was still watching him with puzzled but tender eyes. "You're unhappy, Alvin," she said. "No one should be unhappy in Diaspar. Let me come over and talk to you."

Ungallantly, Alvin shook his head. He knew where *that* would lead, and at the moment he wanted to be alone. Doubly disappointed, Alystra faded from view.

In a city of ten million human beings, thought Alvin, there was no one to whom he could really talk. Eriston and Etania were fond of him in their way, but now that their term of guardianship was ending, they were happy enough to leave him to shape his own amusements and his own life. In the last few years, as his divergence from the standard pattern became more and more obvious, he had often felt his parents' resentment. Not with him—that, perhaps, was something he could have faced and fought—but with the sheer bad luck that had chosen them from all the city's millions, to meet him when he walked out of the Hall of Creation twenty years ago.

Twenty years. He could remember its first moment, and the first words he had ever heard: "Welcome, Alvin, I am Eriston, your appointed father. This is Etania, your mother." The words had meant nothing then, but his mind had recorded them with flawless accuracy. He remembered how he had looked down at his body; it was an inch or two taller now, but had scarcely altered since the moment of his birth. He had come almost fully grown into the world, and would have changed little save in height when it was time to leave it a thousand years hence.

Before that first memory, there was nothing. One day, perhaps, that nothingness would come again, but that was a thought too remote to touch his emotions in any way.

He turned his mind once more towards the mystery of his birth. It did not seem strange to Alvin that he might be created, in a single moment of time, by the powers and forces that materialised all the other objects of his everyday life. No; *that* was not the mystery. The enigma he had never been able to solve, and which no one would ever explain to him, was his uniqueness.

Unique. It was a strange, sad word—and a strange, sad thing to be. When it was applied to him—as he had often heard it done when no one thought he was listening—it seemed to possess ominous undertones that threatened more than his own happiness.

His parents—his tutor—everyone he knew—had tried to protect him from the truth, as if anxious to preserve the innocence of his long childhood. The pretence must soon be ended; in a few days he would be a full citizen of Diaspar, and nothing could be withheld from him that he wished to know.

Why, for example, did he not fit into the Sagas? Of all the thousands of forms of recreation in the city, these were the most popular. When you entered a Saga, you were not merely a passive observer, as in the crude entertainments of primitive times which Alvin had sometimes sampled. You were an active participant and possessed—or seemed to possess—free will. The events and scenes which were the raw materials of your adventures might have been prepared beforehand by forgotten artists, but there was enough flexibility to allow of wide variation. You could go into these phantom worlds with your friends, seeking the excitement that did not exist in Diaspar—and as long as the dream lasted there was no way in which it could be distinguished from reality. Indeed, who could be certain that Diaspar itself was not the dream?

No one could ever exhaust all the Sagas that had been conceived and recorded since the city began. They played upon all the emotions and were of infinitely varying subtlety. Some—those popular among the very young—were uncomplicated dramas of adventure and discovery. Others were purely explorations of psychological states, while others again were exercises in logic or mathematics which could provide the keenest of delights to more sophisticated minds.

Yet though the Sagas seemed to satisfy his companions, they left Alvin with a feeling of incompleteness. For all their colour and excitement, their varying *locales* and themes, there was something missing.

The Sagas, he decided, never really got anywhere. They were always painted on such a narrow canvas. There were no great vistas, none of the rolling landscapes for which his soul craved. Above all, there was never a hint of the immensity in which the exploits of ancient man had really taken place—the luminous void between the stars and planets. The artists who had planned the Sagas had been infected by the same strange phobia that ruled all the citizens of Diaspar. Even their vicarious adventures must take place cosily indoors, in subterranean caverns, or in neat little valleys surrounded by mountains which shut out all the rest of the world.

There was only one explanation. Far back in time, perhaps before Diaspar was founded, something had happened that had not only destroyed Man's curiosity and ambition, but had sent him homeward from the stars to cower for shelter in the tiny closed world of Earth's last city. He had renounced the Universe and returned to the artificial womb of Diaspar. The flaming, invincible urge that had once driven him over the Galaxy, and to the islands of mist beyond, had altogether died. No ships had entered the Solar System for countless aeons; out there among the stars the descendants of Man might still be building Empires and wrecking suns—Earth neither knew nor cared.

Earth did not. But Alvin did.

CHAPTER II

T H E R O O M W A S dark save for one glowing wall, upon which the tides of colour ebbed and flowed as Alvin wrestled with his dreams. Part of the pattern satisfied him; he had fallen in love with the soaring lines of the mountains as they leapt out of the sea. There was a power and pride about those ascending curves; he had studied them for a long time, and then fed them into the memory unit of the visualiser, where they would be preserved while he experimented with the rest of the picture. Something was eluding him, though what it was he did not know. Again and again he had tried to fill in the blank spaces, while the instrument read the shifting patterns in his mind and materialised them upon the wall. It was no good. The lines were blurred and uncertain, the colours muddy and dull. If the artist did not know his goal, even the most miraculous of tools could not find it for him.

Alvin cancelled his unsatisfactory scribblings and stared morosely at the three-quarters-empty rectangle he had been trying to fill with beauty. On a sudden impulse, he doubled the size of the existing design and shifted it to the centre of the frame. No—that was a lazy way out, and the balance was all wrong. Worse still, the change of scale had revealed the defects in his construction, the lack of certainty in those at-first-sight confident lines. He would have to start all over again.

"Total erasure," he ordered the machine. The blue of the sea faded; the mountains dissolved like mist, until only the blank wall remained. They were as if they had never been—as if they were lost in the limbo that had taken all Earth's seas and mountains ages before Alvin was born.

The light came flooding back into the room and the luminous rectangle upon which Alvin had projected his dreams merged into its surroundings, to become one with the other walls. But were they walls? To anyone who had never seen such a place before, this was a very peculiar room indeed. It was utterly featureless and completely devoid of furniture, so that it seemed as if Alvin stood at the centre of a sphere. No visible dividing lines separated walls from floor or ceiling. There was nothing on which the eye could focus; the space enclosing Alvin might have been ten feet or ten miles across, for all that the sense of vision could have told. It would have been hard to resist the temptation to walk forward, hands out-stretched, to discover the physical limits of this extraordinary place.

Yet such rooms had been "home" to most of the human race, for the greater part of its history. Alvin had only to frame the appropriate thought, and the walls would become windows opening upon any part of the city he chose. Another wish, and machines which he had never seen would fill the chamber with the projected images of any articles of furniture he might need. Whether they were "real" or not was a problem that had bothered few men for the past billion years. Ceratinly they were no less real than that other impostor, solid matter, and when they were no longer required they could be returned to the phantom world of the city's memory banks. Like everything else in Diaspar, they would never wear out—and they would never change, unless their stored patterns were cancelled by a deliberate act of will.

Alvin had partly reconstructed his room when a persistent, bell-like chime sounded in his ear. He mentally framed the admission signal, and the wall upon which he had just been painting dissolved once more. As he had expected, there stood his parents, with Jeserac a little behind them. The presence of his tutor meant that this was no ordinary family reunion—but he knew that already.

The illusion was perfect, and it was not lost when Eriston spoke. In reality, as Alvin was well aware, Eriston, Etania, and Jeserac were all miles apart, for the builders of the city had conquered space as completely as they had subjugated time. Alvin was not even certain where his parents lived among the multitudinous spires and intricate labyrinths of Diaspar, for they had moved since he had last been physically in their presence.

"Alvin," began Eriston, "it is twenty years since your mother and I first met you. You know what that means. Our guardianship is now ended, and you are free to do as you please."

There was a trace—but merely a trace—of sadness in Eriston's voice. There was considerably more relief, as if Eriston was glad that a state of affairs that had existed for some time in fact now had legal recognition. Alvin had anticipated his freedom by a good many years.

"I understand," he answered. "I thank you for watching over me, and I will remember you in all my lives." That was the formal response; he had heard it so often that all meaning had been leached away from it—it was merely a pattern of sounds with no particular significance. Yet "All my lives" was a strange expression, when one stopped to consider it. He knew vaguely what it meant; now the time had come for him to know exactly. There were many things in Diaspar which he did not understand, and which he would have to learn in the centuries that lay ahead of him.

For a moment it seemed as if Etania wished to speak. She raised one hand, disturbing the iridescent gossamer of her gown, then let it fall back to her side. Then she turned helplessly to Jeserac, and for the first time Alvin realised that his parents were worried. His memory swiftly scanned the events of the past few weeks. No, there was nothing in his recent life that could have caused this faint uncertainty, this air of mild alarm that seemed to surround both Eriston and Etania.

Jeserac, however, appeared to be in command of the situation. He gave an inquiring look at Eriston and Etania, satisfied himself that they had nothing more to say, and launched forth on the dissertation he had waited many years to make.

"Alvin," he began, "for twenty years you have been my pupil, and I have done my best to teach you the ways of the city, and to lead you to the heritage which is yours. You have asked me many questions, and not all of them have

I been able to answer. Some things you were not ready to learn, and some I did not know myself. Now your infancy is over, though your childhood is scarcely begun. It is still my duty to guide you, if you need my help. In two hundred years, Alvin, you may begin to know something of this city and a little of its history. Even I, who am nearing the end of this life, have seen less than a quarter of Diaspar, and perhaps less than a thousandth of its treasures."

There was nothing so far that Alvin did not know, but there was no way of hurrying Jeserac. The old man looked steadfastly at him across the gulf of centuries, his words weighed down with the incomputable wisdom acquired during a long lifetime's contact with men and machines.

"Tell me, Alvin," he said, "have you ever asked yourself *where* you were before you were born—before you found yourself facing Etania and Eriston in the Hall of Creation?"

"I assumed I was nowhere—that I was nothing but a pattern in the mind of the city, waiting to be created—like this."

A low couch glimmered and thickened into reality beside Alvin. He sat down upon it and waited for Jeserac to continue.

"You are correct, of course," came the reply. "But that is merely part of the answer—and a very small part indeed. Until now, you have met only children of your own age, and they have been ignorant of the truth. Soon they will remember, but you will not, so we must prepare you to face the facts.

"For over a thousand million years, Alvin, the human race lived in this city. Since the Galactic Empire fell, and the Invaders went back to the stars, this has been our world. Outside the walls of Diaspar, there is nothing except the desert of which our legends speak.

"We know little about our primitive ancestors, except that they were very short-lived beings and that, strange though it seems, they could reproduce themselves without the aid of memory units or matter organisers. In a complex and apparently uncontrollable process, the key patterns of each human being were preserved in microscopic cell-structures actually created inside the body. If you are interested, the biologists can tell you more about it, but the method is of no great importance as it was abandoned at the dawn of history.

"A human being, like any other object, is defined by its structure—its pattern. The pattern of a man, and still more the pattern which specifies a man's mind, is incredibly complex. Yet Nature was able to pack that pattern into a tiny cell, too small for the eye to see.

"What Nature can do, Man can do also, in his own way. We do not know how long the task took. A million years, perhaps—but what is that? In the end our ancestors learned how to analyse and store the information which would define any specific human being—and to use that information to recreate the original, as you have just created that couch.

"I know that such things interest you, Alvin, but I cannot tell you exactly how it was done. The way in which information is stored is of no importance; all that matters is the information itself. It may be in the form of written words on paper, of varying magnetic fields, or patterns of electric charge. Men have used all these methods of storage, and many others. Suffice it to say that long ago they were able to store themselves—or, to be more precise, the dis-embodied patterns from which they could be called back into existence.

"So much you already know. This is the way our ancestors gave us virtual immortality, yet avoided the problems raised by the abolition of death. A thousand years in one body is long enough for any man; at the end of that time, his mind is clogged with memories, and he asks only for rest—or a new beginning.

"In a little while, Alvin, I shall prepare to leave this life. I shall go back through my memories, editing them and cancelling those I do not wish to keep. Then I shall walk into the Hall of Creation, but through a door which you have never seen. This old body will cease to exist, and so will consciousness itself. Nothing will be left of Jeserac but a galaxy of electrons frozen in the heart of a crystal.

"I shall sleep, Alvin, and without dreams. Then one day, perhaps a hundred thousand years from now, I shall find myself in a new body, meeting those who have been chosen to be my guardians. They will look after me as Eriston and Etania have guided you, for at first I will know nothing of Diaspar and will have no memories of what I was before. Those memories will slowly return, at the end of my infancy, and I will build upon them as I move forward into my new cycle of existence.

"That is the pattern of our lives, Alvin. We have all been here many, many times before, though as the intervals of non-existence vary according to apparently random laws this present population will never repeat itself again. The new Jeserac will have new and different friends and interests, but the old Jeserac—as much of him as I wish to save—will still exist.

"That is not all. At any moment, Alvin, only a hundredth of the citizens of Diaspar live and walk in its streets. The vast majority slumber in the memory banks, waiting for the signal that will call them forth on to the stage of existence once again. So we have continuity, yet change—immortality, but not stagnation.

"I know what you are wondering, Alvin. You want to know when you will recall the memories of your earlier lives, as your companions are already doing.

"There are no such memories, for you are unique. We have tried to keep this knowledge from you as long as we could, so that no shadow should lie across your childhood—though I think you must have guessed part of the truth already. We did not suspect it ourselves until five years ago, but now there is no doubt.

"You, Alvin, are something that has happened in Diaspar only a handful of times since the founding of the city. Perhaps you have been lying dormant in the memory banks through all the ages—or perhaps you were created only twenty years ago by some random permutation. You may have been planned in the beginning by the designers of the city, or you may be a purposeless accident of our own time.

"We do not know. All that we do know is this: you, Alvin, alone of the human race, have never lived before. In literal truth, you are the first child to be born on Earth for at least ten million years."

CHAPTER III

WHEN JESERAC AND his parents had faded from view, Alvin lay for a long time trying to hold his mind empty of thought. He closed his room around him, so that no one could interrupt his trance.

He was not sleeping; sleep was something he had never experienced, for that belonged to a world of night and day, and here there was only day. This was the nearest he could come to that forgotten state, and though it was not really essential to him he knew that it would help compose his mind.

He had learned little new; almost everything that Jeserac had told him he had already guessed. But it was one thing to have guessed it, another to have had that guess confirmed beyond possibility of refutation.

How could it affect his life, if at all? He could not be sure, and uncertainty was a novel sensation to Alvin. Perhaps it would make no difference whatsoever; if he did not adjust completely to Diaspar in this life, he would do so in the next—or the next——

Even as he framed the thought, Alvin's mind rejected it. Diaspar might be sufficient for the rest of humanity, but it was not enough for him. He did not doubt that one could spend a thousand lifetimes without exhausting all its wonders, or sampling all the permutations of experience it could provide. These things he could do—but if he could not do more, he would never be content.

There was only one problem to be faced. What more *was* there to do?

The unanswered question jolted him out of his reverie. He could not stay here while he was in this restless mood, and there was only one place in the city where he could find some peace of mind.

The wall flickered partially out of existence as he stepped through to the corridor, and its polarised molecules resisted his passage like a feeble wind blowing against his face. There were many ways in which he could be carried effortlessly to his goal, but he preferred to walk. His room was almost at the main city level, and a short passage brought him out on to a spiral ramp which led down to the street. He ignored the moving way, and kept to the narrow sidewalk—an eccentric thing to do, since he had several miles to travel. But Alvin liked the exercise, for it soothed his mind. Besides, there was so much to see that it seemed a pity to race past the latest marvels of Diaspar when you had eternity ahead of you.

It was the custom of the city's artists—and everyone in Diaspar was an artist at some time or another—to display their current productions along the side of the moving ways, so that the passers-by could admire their work. In this manner, it was usually only a few days before the entire population had critically examined any noteworthy creation, and also expressed its views upon it. The resulting verdict, recorded automatically by opinion-sampling devices which no one had ever been able to suborn or deceive—and there had been enough attempts—decided the fate of the masterpiece. If there was a sufficiently affirmative vote, its matrix would go into the memory of the city so that anyone who wished, at any future date, could possess a reproduction utterly indistinguishable from the original.

The less successful pieces went the way of all such works. They were either dissolved back into their original elements, or ended up in the homes of the artists' friends.

Alvin saw only one *objet d'art* on his journey that had any appeal to him. It was a creation of pure life, vaguely reminiscent of an unfolding flower. Slowly growing from a minute core of colour, it would expand into complex spirals and curtains, then suddenly collapse and begin the cycle over again. Yet not precisely, for no two cycles were identical. Though Alvin watched through a score of pulsations, each time there were subtle and indefinable differences, even though the basic pattern remained the same.

He knew why he liked this piece of intangible sculpture. Its expanding rhythm gave an impression of space—even of escape. For that reason, it would probably not appeal to many of Alvin's compatriots. He made a note of the artist's name and decided to call him at the earliest opportunity.

All the roads, both moving and stationary, came to an end when they reached the park that was the green heart of the city. Here, in a circular space over three miles across, was a memory of what Earth had been in the days before the desert swallowed all but Diaspar. First there was a wide belt of grass, then low trees which grew thicker and thicker as one walked forward beneath their shade. At the same time the ground sloped gently downwards, so that when at last one emerged from the narrow forest all sign of the city had vanished, hidden by the screen of trees.

The wide stream that lay ahead of Alvin was called, simply, the River. It possessed, and it needed, no other name. At intervals it was spanned by narrow bridges, and it flowed round the Park in a complete, closed circle, broken by occasional lagoons. That a swiftly-moving river could return upon itself after a course of less than six miles had never struck Alvin as at all unusual; indeed, he would not have thought twice about the matter if at some point in its circuit the River had flowed uphill. There were far stranger things than this in Diaspar.

A dozen young people were swimming in one of the little lagoons, and Alvin paused to watch them. He knew most of them by sight, if not by name, and for a moment was tempted to join in their play. Then the secret he was bearing decided him against it, and he contented himself with the role of spectator.

Physically, there was no way of telling which of these young citizens had walked out of the Hall of Creation this year, and which had lived in Diaspar as long as Alvin. Though there were considerable variations in height and weight, they had no correlation with age. People were simply born that way, and although on the average the taller the person, the greater their age, this was not a reliable rule to apply unless one was dealing in centuries.

The face was a safer guide. Some of the new-born were taller than Alvin, but they had a look of immaturity, an expression of wondering surprise at the world in which they now found themselves, that revealed them at once. It was strange to think that, slumbering untapped in their minds, were infinite vistas of lives that they would soon remember. Alvin envied them, yet he was not sure if he should. One's first existence was a precious gift which would never be repeated. It was wonderful to view life for the very first time, as in the freshness of the dawn. If only there were others like him, with whom he could share his thoughts and feelings. . . .

Yet physically he was cast in precisely the same mould as those children playing in the water. The human body had changed not at all in the billion years since the building of Diaspar, since the basic design had been eternally frozen in the memory banks of the city. It had changed, however, a good deal from its original primitive form, though most of the alterations were internal and not visible to the eye. Man had rebuilt himself many times in his long history, in the effort to abolish those ills to which the flesh was once heir.

Such unnecessary appurtenances as nails and teeth had vanished. Hair was confined to the head; not a trace was left on the body. The features that would most have surprised a man of the dawn ages was, perhaps, the disappearance of the navel. Its inexplicable absence would have given him much food for thought, and at first sight he would also have been baffled by the problem of distinguishing male from female. He might even have been tempted to assume that there was no longer any difference, which would have been a grave error. In the appropriate circumstances, there was no doubt about the masculinity of any male in Diaspar. It was merely that his equipment was now more neatly packaged when not required; internal stowage had vastly improved upon Nature's original inelegant and indeed downright hazardous arrangements.

It was true that reproduction was no longer the concern of the body, being far too important a matter to be left to games of chance played with chromosomes as dice. Yet though conception and birth were not even memories, sex remained. Even in ancient times, not one hundredth part of sexual activity had been concerned with reproduction. The disappearance of that mere one per cent had changed the pattern of human society and the meaning of such words as "father" and "mother"—but desire remained, though now its satisfaction had no profounder aim than that of any of the other pleasures of the senses.

Alvin left his playful contemporaries and continued on towards the centre of the Park. There were faintly marked paths here, crossing and criss-crossing through low shrubbery and occasionally diving into narrow ravines between great lichen-covered boulders. Once he came across a small polyhedral machine, no larger than a man's head, floating among the branches of a tree. No one knew how many varieties of robot there were in Diaspar; they kept out of the way and minded their business so effectively that it was quite unusual to see one.

Presently the ground began to rise again; Alvin was approaching the little hill that was at the exact centre of the Park, and therefore of the city itself. There were fewer obstacles and detours, and he had a clear view to the summit of the hill and the simple building that surmounted it. He was a little out of breath by the time he had reached his goal, and was glad to rest against one of the rose-pink columns and to look back over the way he had come.

There are some forms of architecture that can never change because they have reached perfection. The Tomb of Yarlan Zey might have been designed by the temple-builders of the first civilisations man had ever known, though they would have found it impossible to imagine of what material it was made. The roof was open to the sky, and the single chamber was paved with great slabs which only at first sight resembled natural stone. For geological ages human feet had crossed and recrossed that floor and left no trace upon its inconceivably stubborn material.

The creator of the great park—the builder, some said, of Diaspar itself—sat with slightly downcast eyes, as if examining the plans spread across his knees. His face wore that curiously elusive expression that had baffled the world for so many generations. Some had dismissed it as no more than an idle whim of the artist's, but to others it seemed that Yarlan Zey was smiling at some secret jest.

The whole building was enigma, for nothing concerning it could be traced in the historical records of the city. Alvin was not even sure what the word "Tomb" meant; Jeserac could probably tell him, as he was fond of collecting obsolete words and sprinkling his conversation with them, to the confusion of his listeners.

From this central vantage point, Alvin could look clear across the Park, above the screening trees, and out to the city itself. The nearest buildings were almost two miles away, and formed a low belt completely surrounding the Park. Beyond them, rank after rank in ascending height, were the towers and terraces that made up the main bulk of the city. They stretched for mile upon mile, slowly climbing up the sky, becoming ever more complex and monumentally impressive. Diaspar had been planned as an entity; it was a single mighty machine. Yet though its outward appearance was almost overwhelming in its complexity, it merely hinted at the hidden marvels of technology without which all these great buildings would be lifeless sepulchres.

Alvin stared out towards the limits of his world. Ten—twenty miles away, their details lost in distance, were the outer ramparts of the city, upon which seemed to rest the roof of the sky. There was nothing beyond them—nothing at all except the aching emptiness of the desert in which a man would soon go mad.

Then why did that emptiness call to him, as it called to no one else that he had ever met? Alvin did not know. He stared out across the coloured spires and battlements that now enclosed the whole dominion of mankind, as if seeking an answer to his question.

He did not find it. But at that moment, as his heart yearned for the unattainable, he made his decision.

He knew now what he was going to do with life.

CHAPTER IV

J E S E R A C   W A S   N O T very helpful, though he was not as uncooperative
as Alvin had half expected. He had been asked such questions before in his
long career as mentor, and did not believe that even a Unique like Alvin could
produce many surprises, or set him problems which he could not solve.

It was true that Alvin was beginning to show certain minor eccentricities of
behaviour, which might eventually need correction. He did not join as fully as
he should in the incredibly elaborate social life of the city, or in the fantasy
worlds of his companions. He showed no great interest in the higher realms
of thought, though at his age that was hardly surprising. More remarkable was
his erratic love life; he could not be expected to form any relatively stable
partnerships for at least a century, yet the brevity of his affairs was already
famous. They were intense while they lasted—but not one of them had lasted
for more than a few weeks. Alvin, it seemed, could interest himself thoroughly
only in one thing at a time. There were times when he would join whole-
heartedly in the erotic games of his companions, or disappear with the partner
of his choice for several days. But once the mood had passed, there would be
long spells when he seemed totally uninterested in what should have been a
major occupation at his age. This was probably bad for him, and it was
certainly bad for his discarded lovers, who wandered despondently around the
city and took an unusually long time to find consolation elsewhere. Alystra,
Jeserac had noticed, had now arrived at this unhappy stage.

It was not that Alvin was heartless or inconsiderate. In love, as in everything
else, it seemed that he was searching for a goal that Diaspar could not
provide.

None of these characteristics worried Jeserac. A Unique might be expected
to behave in such a manner, and in due course Alvin would conform to the
general pattern of the city. No single individual, however eccentric or brilliant,
could affect the enormous inertia of a society that had remained virtually
unchanged for over a billion years. Jeserac did not merely believe in stability;
he could conceive of nothing else.

"The problem that worries you is a very old one," he told Alvin, "but you
will be surprised how many people take the world so much for granted that it
never worries them or even crosses their mind. It is true that the human race
once occupied an infinitely greater space than this city. You have seen something of what Earth was like before the deserts came and the oceans vanished.
Those records you are so fond of projecting are the earliest we possess; they
are the only ones that show Earth as it was before the Invaders came. I do not
imagine that many people have ever seen them; those limitless, open spaces
are something we cannot bear to contemplate.

"And even Earth, of course, was only a grain of sand in the Galactic

Empire. What the gulfs between the stars must have been like is a nightmare no sane man would try to imagine. Our ancestors crossed them at the dawn of history when they went out to build the Empire. They crossed them again for the last time when the Invaders drove them back to Earth.

"The legend is—and it is only a legend—that we made a pact with the Invaders. They could have the universe if they needed it so badly, and we would be content with the world on which we were born.

"We have kept that pact and forgotten the vain dreams of our childhood, as you too will forget them, Alvin. The men who built this city, and designed the society that went with it, were lords of mind as well as matter. They put everything that the human race would ever need inside these walls—and then made sure that we would never leave them.

"Oh, the physical barriers are the least important ones. Perhaps there are routes that lead out of the city, but I do not think you would go along them for very far, even if you found them. And if you succeeded in the attempt, what good would it do? Your body would not last long in the desert, when the city could no longer protect or nourish it."

"If there is a route out of the city," said Alvin slowly, "then what is there to stop me from leaving?"

"That is a foolish question," answered Jeserac. "I think you already know the answer."

Jeserac was right, but not in the way he imagined. Alvin knew—or, rather, he had guessed. His companions had given him the answer, both in their waking life and in the dream-adventures he had shared with them. They would never be able to leave Diaspar; what Jeserac did not know was that the compulsion which ruled their lives had no power over Alvin. Whether his Uniqueness was due to accident or to an ancient design, he did not know, but this was one of its results. He wondered how many others he had yet to discover.

No one ever hurried in Diaspar, and this was a rule which even Alvin seldom broke. He considered the problem carefully for several weeks, and spent much time searching the earliest of the city's historical memories. For hours on end he would lie, supported by the impalpable arms of an anti-gravity field, while the hypnone projector opened his mind to the past. When the record was finished, the machine would blur and vanish—but still Alvin would lie staring into nothingness before he came back through the ages to meet reality again. He would see again the endless leagues of blue water, vaster than the land itself, rolling their waves against golden shores. His ears would ring with the boom of breakers stilled those thousand million years. He would remember the forests and the prairies, and the strange beasts that had once shared the world with Man.

Very few of these ancient records existed; it was generally accepted, though none knew the reason why, that somewhere between the coming of the Invaders and the building of Diaspar all memories of primitive times had been lost. So complete had been the obliteration that it was hard to believe it could have happened by accident alone. Mankind had lost its past, save for a few chronicles that might be wholly legendary. Before Diaspar there was simply—the Dawn Ages. In that Limbo were merged inextricably together the first men to tame fire and the first to release atomic energy—the first men to build a log canoe and the first to reach the stars. On the far side of this desert of time, they were all neighbours.

Alvin had intended to make his experiment alone, but solitude was not always something that could be arranged in Diaspar. He had barely left his room when he encountered Alystra, who made no attempt to pretend that her presence was accidental.

It had never occurred to Alvin that Alystra was beautiful, for he had never seen human ugliness. When beauty is universal, it loses its power to move the heart, and only its absence can produce any emotional effect.

For a moment Alvin was annoyed by the meeting, with its reminder of passions that no longer moved him. He was still too young and self-reliant to feel the need of any lasting relationships, and when the time came he might find it hard to make them. Even in his most intimate moments, the barrier of his uniqueness came between him and his lovers. For all his fully-formed body, he was still a child and would remain so for decades yet, while his companions one by one recalled the memories of their past lives and left him far behind. He had seen it happen before, and it made him wary of giving himself unreservedly to any other person. Even Alystra, who seemed so *naïve* and artless now, would soon become a complex of memories and talents beyond his imagination.

His mild annoyance vanished almost at once. There was no reason why Alystra should not come with him if she desired. He was not selfish, and did not wish to clutch this new experience to his bosom like a miser. Indeed, he might be able to learn much from her reactions.

She asked no questions, which was unusual, as the express channel swept them out of the crowded heart of the city. Together they worked their way to the central high-speed section, never bothering to glance at the miracle beneath their feet. An engineer of the ancient world would have gone slowly mad trying to understand how an apparently solid roadway could be fixed at the sides, while towards the centre it moved at a steadily increasing velocity. But to Alvin and Alystra, it seemed perfectly natural that types of matter should exist that had the properties of solids in one direction, and of liquids in another.

Around them the buildings rose higher and higher as if the city was strengthening its bulwarks against the outer world. How strange it would be, thought Alvin, if these towering walls became as transparent as glass, and one could watch the life within. Scattered throughout the space around him were friends he knew, friends he would one day know, and strangers he would never meet—though there could be very few of these, since in the course of his lifetime he would meet almost all the people in Diaspar. Most of them would be sitting in their separate rooms, but they would not be alone. They had only to form the wish and they could be, in all but physical fact, in the presence of any other person they chose. They were not bored, for they had access to everything that had happened in the realms of imagination or reality since the days when the city was built. To men whose minds were thus constituted, it was a completely satisfying existence. That it was also a wholly futile one, even Alvin did not yet comprehend.

As Alvin and Alystra moved outwards from the city's heart, the number of people they saw in the streets slowly decreased, and there was no one in sight when they were brought to a smooth halt against a long platform of brightly coloured marble. They stepped across the frozen whirlpool of matter where the substance of the moving way flowed back to its origin, and faced a wall pierced with brightly lit tunnels. Alvin selected one without hesitation and stepped into it, with Alystra close behind. The peristaltic field seized them at once and propelled them forward as they lay back luxuriously, watching their surroundings.

It no longer seemed possible that they were in a tunnel far underground. The art that had used all of Diaspar for its canvas had been busy here, and above them the skies seemed open to the winds of heaven. All around were the spires of the city, gleaming in the sunlight. It was not the city that Alvin knew, but the Diaspar of a much earlier age. Although most of the great buildings were familiar, there were subtle differences that added to the interest of the scene. Alvin wished he could linger, but he had never found any way of retarding his progress through the tunnel.

All too soon they were set gently down in a large elliptical chamber, completely surrounded by windows. Through these they could catch tantalising glimpses of gardens ablaze with brilliant flowers. There were gardens still in Diaspar, but these had existed only in the mind of the artist who conceived them. Certainly there were no such flowers as these in the world today.

Alystra was enchanted by their beauty, and was obviously under the impression that this was what Alvin had brought her to see. He watched her for a while as she ran gaily from scene to scene, enjoying her delight in each new discovery. There were hundreds of such places in the half-deserted buildings round the periphery of Diaspar, kept in perfect order by the hidden powers which watched over them. One day the tide of life might flow this way once more, but until then this ancient garden was a secret which they alone shared.

"We've further to go," said Alvin at last. "This is only the beginning." He stepped through one of the windows and the illusion was shattered. There was no garden behind the glass, but a circular passageway curving steeply upwards. He could still see Alystra a few feet away, though he knew that she could not see him. But she did not hesitate, and a moment later was standing beside him in the passage.

Beneath their feet the floor began to creep slowly forward, as if eager to lead them to their goal. They walked along it for a few paces, until their speed was so great that further effort would be wasted.

The corridor still inclined upwards, and in a hundred feet had curved through a complete right-angle. But only logic knew this; to all the senses it was as if one was now being hurried along an absolutely level corridor. The fact that they were in reality moving straight up a vertical shaft thousands of feet deep gave them no sense of insecurity, for a failure of the polarising field was unthinkable.

Presently the corridor began to slope "downwards" again until once more it had turned through a right-angle. The movement of the floor slowed imperceptibly until it came to rest at the end of a long hall lined with mirrors, and Alvin knew that there was no hope of hurrying Alystra here. It was not merely that some feminine characteristics had survived unchanged since Eve; no one could have resisted the fascination of this place. There was nothing like it, as far as Alvin knew, in the rest of Diaspar. Through some whim of the artist, only a few of the mirrors reflected the scene as it really was—and even these Alvin was convinced, were constantly changing their position. The rest certainly reflected *something*, but it was faintly disconcerting to see oneself walking amid everchanging and quite imaginary surroundings.

Sometimes there were people going to and fro in the world behind the mirror, and more than once Alvin had seen faces that he recognised. He realised well enough that he had not been looking at any friends he knew in this existence. Through the mind of the unknown artist he had been seeing into the past, watching the previous incarnations of people who walked the world today. It saddened him, by reminding him of his own uniqueness, to think that however long he waited before these changing scenes he would never meet any ancient echo of himself.

"Do you know where we are?" Alvin asked Alystra when they had completed the tour of the mirrors. Alystra shook her head. "Somewhere near the edge of the city, I suppose," she answered carelessly. "We seem to have gone a long way, but I've no idea how far."

"We're in the Tower of Loranne," replied Alvin. "This is one of the highest points in Diaspar. Come—I'll show you." He caught Alystra's hand and led her out of the hall. There were no exits visible to the eye, but at various points the pattern on the floor indicated side-corridors, As one approached the mirrors at these points, the reflections seemed to fuse into an archway of light and one could step through into another passage. Alystra lost all conscious track of their twistings and turnings, and at last they emerged into a long, perfectly straight tunnel through which blew a cold and steady wind. It stretched horizontally for hundreds of feet in either direction, and its far ends were tiny circles of light.

"I don't like this place," Alystra complained. "It's cold." She had probably never before experienced real coldness in her life, and Alvin felt somewhat guilty. He should have warned her to bring a cloak—and a good one, for all clothes in Diaspar were purely ornamental and quite useless as a protection.

Since her discomfort was entirely his fault, he handed over his cloak without a word. There was no trace of gallantry in this; the equality of the sexes had been complete for far too long for such conventions to survive. Had matters been the other way round, Alystra would have given Alvin her cloak and he would have as automatically accepted.

It was not unpleasant walking with the wind behind them, and they soon reached the end of the tunnel. A wide-meshed filigree of stone prevented them from going any further, which was just as well, for they stood on the brink of nothingness. The great air-duct opened on the sheer face of the tower, and below them was a vertical drop of at least a thousand feet. They were high upon the outer ramparts of the city, and Diaspar lay spread beneath them as few in their world could ever have seen it.

The view was the obverse of the one that Alvin had obtained from the centre of the Park. He could look down upon the concentric waves of stone and metal as they descended in mile-long sweeps towards the heart of the city. Far away, partly hidden by the intervening towers, he could glimpse the distant fields and trees and the eternally circling river. Further still, the remoter bastions of Diaspar climbed more towards the sky.

Beside him, Alystra was sharing the view with pleasure but with no surprise. She had seen the city countless times before from other, almost equally well-placed vantage points—and in considerably more comfort.

"That's our world—all of it," said Alvin. "Now I want to show you something else." He turned away from the grating and began to walk towards the distant circle of light at the far end of the tunnel. The wind was cold against his lightly-clad body, but he scarcely noticed the discomfort as he walked forward into the air stream.

He had gone only a little way when he realised that Alystra was making no attempt to follow. She stood watching, her borrowed cloak streaming down the wind, one hand half raised to her face. Alvin saw her lips move, but the words did not reach him. He looked back at her first with astonishment, then with an impatience that was not totally devoid of pity. What Jeserac had said was true. She could not follow him. She had realised the meaning of that remote circle of light from which the wind blew for ever into Diaspar. Behind Alystra was the known world, full of wonder yet empty of surprise, drifting like a brilliant but tightly closed bubble down the river of time. Ahead, separated from her by no more than the span of a few footsteps, was the empty wilderness —the world of the desert—the world of the Invaders.

Alvin walked back to join her, and was surprised to find that she was trembling. "Why are you frightened?" he asked. "We're still safely in Diaspar. You've looked out of that window behind us—surely you can look out of this one as well!"

Alystra was staring at him as if he was some strange monster. By her standards, indeed, he was.

"I couldn't do it," she said at last. "Even thinking about it makes me feel colder than this wind. Don't go any further, Alvin!"

"But, there's no logic in it!" Alvin protested remorselessly. "What possible harm would it do you to walk to the end of this corridor and look out? It's strange and lonely out there, but it isn't horrible. In fact, the longer I look the more beautiful I think——"

Alystra did not stay to hear him finish. She turned on her heels and fled back down the long ramp that had brought them up through the floor of this tunnel. Alvin made no attempt to stop her, since that would have involved the bad manners of imposing one's will upon another. Persuasion, he could see, would have been utterly useless. He knew that Alystra would not pause until she had returned to her companions. There was no danger that she would lose herself in the labyrinths of the city, for she would have no difficulty in retracing her footsteps. An instinctive ability to extricate himself from even the most complex of mazes had been merely one of the many accomplishments Man had learned since he started to live in cities. The long-extinct rat had been forced to acquire similar skills when he left the fields and threw in his lot with humanity.

Alvin waited for a moment, as if half-expecting Alystra to return. He was not surprised at her reaction—only at its violence and irrationality. Though he was sincerely sorry that she had gone, he could not help wishing that she had remembered to leave the cloak.

It was not only cold, but it was also hard work moving against the wind which sighed through the lungs of the city. Alvin was fighting both the air-current and whatever force it was that kept it moving. Not until he had reached the stone grille, and could lock his arms around its bars, could he afford to relax. There was just sufficient room for him to force his head through the opening, and even so his view was slightly restricted, as the entrance to the duct was partly recessed into the city's wall.

Yet he could see enough. Thousands of feet below, the sunlight was taking leave of the desert. The almost horizontal rays struck through the grating and threw a weird pattern of gold and shadow far down the tunnel. Alvin shaded his eyes against the glare and peered down at the land upon which no man had walked for unknown ages.

He might have been looking at an eternally frozen sea. For mile after mile, the sand-dunes undulated into the west, their contours grossly exaggerated by the slanting light. Here and there some caprice of the wind had carved curious whirlpools and gullies in the sand, so that it was sometimes hard to realise that none of this sculpture was the work of intelligence. At a very great distance, so far away indeed that he had no way of judging their remoteness, was a range of softly-rounded hills. They had been a disappointment to Alvin; he would have given much to have seen in reality the soaring mountains of the ancient records and of his own dreams.

The sun lay upon the rim of the hills, its light tamed and reddened by the hundreds of miles of atmosphere it was traversing. There were two great black spots upon its disc; Alvin had learned from his studies that such things existed, but he was surprised that he could see them so easily. They seemed almost like a pair of eyes peering back at him as he crouched in his lonely spy-hole with the wind whistling ceaselessly past his ears.

There was no twilight. With the going of the sun, the pools of shadow lying among the sand-dunes flowed swiftly together into one vast lake of darkness. Colour ebbed from the sky; the warm reds and golds drained away leaving an arctic blue that deepened and deepened into night. Alvin waited for that

breathless moment that he alone of all mankind had known—the moment when
the first star shivers into life.

It had been many weeks since he had last come to this place, and he knew
that the pattern of the night sky must have changed meanwhile. Even so, he
was not prepared for this first glimpse of the Seven Suns.

They could have no other name; the phrase leapt unbidden to his lips. They
formed a tiny, very compact and astonishingly symmetrical group against the
afterglow of sunset. Six of them were arranged in a slightly flattened ellipse,
which, Alvin was sure, was in reality a perfect circle, slightly tilted towards
the line of vision. Each star was a different colour; he could pick out red, blue,
gold, and green, but the other tints eluded his eye. At the precise centre of the
formation was a single white giant—the brightest star in all the visible sky.
The whole group looked exactly like a piece of jewellery; it seemed incredible,
and beyond all stretching of the laws of chance, that Nature could ever have
contrived so perfect a pattern.

As his eyes grew slowly accustomed to the darkness, Alvin could make out
the great misty veil that had once been called the Milky Way. It stretched
from the zenith to the horizon and the Seven Suns were entangled in its folds.
The other stars had now emerged to challenge them, and their random groupings only emphasised the enigma of that perfect symmetry. It was almost as if
some power had deliberately opposed the disorders of the natural universe by
setting its sign upon the stars.

Ten times, no more, the Galaxy had turned upon its axis since Man first
walked on Earth. By its own standards, that was but a moment. Yet in that
short period it had changed completely—changed far more than it had any
right to do in the natural course of events. The great suns that had once burnt
so fiercely in the pride of youth were now guttering to their doom. But Alvin
had never seen the heavens in their ancient glory, and so was unaware of all
that had been lost.

The cold, seeping through into his bones, drove him back to the city. He
extricated himself from the grating and rubbed the circulation back into his
limbs. Ahead of him, down the tunnel, the light streaming out from Diaspar
was so brilliant that for a moment he had to avert his eyes. Outside the city
there were such things as day and night, but within it there was only eternal
day. As the sun descended the sky above Diaspar would fill with light and one
would notice when the natural illumination vanished. Even before men had lost
the need for sleep, they had driven darkness from their cities. The only night
that ever came to Diaspar was a rare and unpredictable obscuration that sometimes visited the Park and transformed it into a place of mystery.

Alvin came slowly back through the hall of mirrors, his mind still filled with
night and stars. He felt inspired and yet depressed. There seemed no way in
which he could ever escape out into that enormous emptiness—and no rational
purpose in doing so. Jeserac had said that a man would soon die out in the
desert, and Alvin could well believe him. Perhaps he might one day discover
some way of leaving Diaspar, but if he did, he knew that he must soon return.
To reach the desert would be an amusing game, no more. It was a game he

could share with no one, and it would lead him nowhere. But at least it would be worth doing if it helped to quench the longing in his soul.

As if unwilling to return to the familiar world, Alvin lingered among the reflections from the past. He stood before one of the great mirrors and watched the scenes that came and went within its depths. Whatever mechanism produced these images was controlled by his presence, and to some extent by his thoughts. The mirrors were always blank when he first came into the room, but filled with action as soon as he moved among them.

He seemed to be standing in a large open courtyard which he had never seen in reality but which probably still existed somewhere in Diaspar. It was unusually crowded and some kind of public meeting seemed to be in progress. Two men were arguing politely on a raised platform while their supporters stood round and made interjections from time to time. The complete silence added to the charm of the scene, for imagination immediately went to work supplying the missing sounds. What were they debating? Alvin wondered. Perhaps it was not a real scene from the past, but a purely created episode. The careful balance of figures, the slightly formal movements, all made it seem a little too neat for life.

He studied the faces in the crowd, seeking for anyone he could recognise. There was no one here that he knew, but he might be looking at friends he would not meet for centuries to come. How many possible patterns of human physiognomy were there? The number was enormous, but it was still finite, especially when all the unaesthetic variations had been eliminated.

The people in the mirror world continued their long-forgotten argument, ignoring the image of Alvin which stood motionless among them. Sometimes it was very hard to believe that he was not part of the scene himself, for the illusion was so flawless. When one of the phantoms in the mirror appeared to move behind Alvin, it vanished just as a real object would have done; and when one moved in front of him, he was the one that was eclipsed.

He was preparing to leave when he noticed an oddly-dressed man standing a little apart from the main group. His movements, his clothes—everything about him, seemed slightly out of place in this assembly. He spoilt the pattern; like Alvin, was an anachronism.

He was a good deal more than that. He was real, and he was looking at Alvin with a slightly quizzical smile.

CHAPTER V

I N H I S S H O R T lifetime, Alvin had met less than one thousandth of the inhabitants of Diaspar. He was not surprised, therefore, that the man confronting him was a stranger. What did surprise him was to meet anyone at all here in this deserted tower, so near the frontier of the unknown.

He turned his back on the mirror world, and faced the intruder. Before he could speak, the other had addressed him.

"You are Alvin, I believe. When I discovered that someone was coming here, I should have guessed it was you."

The remark was obviously not intended to give offence; it was a simple statement of fact, and Alvin accepted it as such. He was not surprised to be recognised; whether he liked it or not, the fact of his uniqueness, and its unrevealed potentialities, had made him known to everyone in the city.

"I am Khedron," continued the stranger, as if that explained everything. "They call me the Jester."

Alvin looked blank, and Khedron shrugged his shoulders in mock resignation.

"Ah, such is fame. Still, you are young and there have been no jests in your lifetime. Your ignorance is excused."

There was something refreshingly unusual about Khedron. Alvin searched his mind for the meaning of the strange word "Jester"; it evoked the faintest of memories, but he could not identify it. There were many such titles in the complex social structure of the city, and it took a lifetime to learn them all.

"Do you often come here?" Alvin asked, a little jealously. He had grown to regard the Tower of Loranne as his personal property and felt slightly annoyed that its marvels were known to anyone else. But had Khedron, he wondered, ever looked out across the desert, or seen the stars sinking down into the west?

"No," said Khedron almost as if answering his unspoken thoughts. "I have never been here before. But it is my pleasure to learn of unusual happenings in the city, and it is a very long time since anyone went to the Tower of Loranne."

Alvin wondered fleetingly how Khedron knew of his earlier visits, but quickly dismissed the matter from his mind. Diaspar was full of eyes and ears and other more subtle sense organs which kept the city aware of all that was happening within it. Anyone who was sufficiently interested could no doubt find a way of tapping these channels.

"Even if it is unusual for anyone to come here," said Alvin, still fencing verbally, "why should you be interested?"

"Because in Diaspar," replied Khedron, "the unusual is my prerogative. I had marked you down a long time ago; I knew we should meet some day. After my fashion, I too am unique. Oh, not in the way that you are: this is not my first life. I have walked a thousand times out of the Hall of Creation. But somewhere back at the beginning I was chosen to be Jester, and there is only one Jester at a time in Diaspar. Most people think that is one too many."

There was an irony about Khedron's speech that left Alvin still floundering. It was not the best of manners to ask direct personal questions, but after all Khedron had raised the subject.

"I'm sorry about my ignorance," said Alvin. "But what is a Jester, and what does he do?"

"You ask 'what'," replied Khedron, "so I'll start by telling you 'why'. It's a long story, but I think you will be interested."

"I am interested in everything," said Alvin, truthfully enough.

"Very well. The men—if they were men, which I sometimes doubt—who designed Diaspar had to solve an incredibly complex problem. Diaspar is not merely a machine, you know—it is a living organism, and an immortal one. We are so accustomed to our society that we can't appreciate how strange it would have seemed to our first ancestors. Here we have a tiny, closed world which never changes except in its minor details, and yet which is perfectly stable, age after age. It has probably lasted longer than the rest of human history—yet in *that* history there were, so it is believed, countless thousands of separate cultures and civilisations which endured for a little while and then perished. How did Diaspar achieve its extraordinary stability?"

Alvin was surprised that anyone should ask so elementary a question, and his hopes of learning something new began to wane.

"Through the Memory Banks, of course," he replied. "Diaspar is always composed of the same people, though their actual groupings change as their bodies are created or destroyed."

Khedron shook his head.

"That is only a very small part of the answer. With exactly the same people, you could build many different patterns of society. I can't prove it, and I've no direct evidence of it, but I believe it's true. The designers of the city did not merely fix its population; they fixed the laws governing its behaviour. We're scarcely aware that those laws exist, but we obey them. Diaspar is a frozen culture, which cannot change outside of narrow limits. The Memory Banks store many other things outside the patterns of our bodies and personalities. They store the image of the city itself, holding its every atom rigid against all the changes that Time can bring. Look at this pavement—it was laid down millions of years ago, and countless feet have walked upon it. Can you see any sign of wear? Unprotected matter, however adamant, would have been ground to dust ages ago. But as long as there is power to operate the Memory Banks, and as long as the matrices they contain can still control the patterns of the city, the physical structure of Diaspar will never change."

"But there have been *some* changes," protested Alvin. "Many buildings have been torn down since the city was built, and new ones erected."

"Of course—but only by discharging the information stored in the Memory Banks and then setting up new patterns. In any case I was merely mentioning that as an example of the way the city preserves itself physically. The point I want to make is that in the same way there are machines in Diaspar that preserve our social structure. They watch for any changes and correct them before they become too great. How do they do it? I don't know—perhaps by selecting those who emerge from the Hall of Creation. Perhaps by tampering with our personality patterns we may think we have free-will, but can we be certain of that?

"In any event, the problem was solved. Diaspar has survived and come safely down the ages, like a great ship carrying as its cargo all that is left of the human race. It is a tremendous achievement in social engineering, though whether it is worth doing is quite another matter.

"Stability, however, is not enough. It leads too easily to stagnation, and thence to decadence. The designers of the city took elaborate steps to avoid this, though these deserted buildings suggest that they did not entirely succeed. I, Khedron the Jester, am part of that plan. A very small part, perhaps. I like to think otherwise, but I can never be sure."

"And just what is that part?" asked Alvin, still very much in the dark, and becoming a little exasperated.

"Let us say that I introduce calculated amounts of disorder into the city. To explain my operations would be to destroy their effectiveness. Judge me by my deeds, though they are few, rather than my words, though they are many."

Alvin had never before met anyone quite like Khedron. The Jester was a real personality—a character who stood head and shoulders above the general level of uniformity which was typical of Diaspar. Though there seemed no hope of discovering precisely what his duties were and how he carried them out, that was of minor importance. All that mattered, Alvin sensed, was that here was someone to whom he could talk—when there was a gap in the monologue—and who might give him answers to many of the problems that had puzzled him for so long.

They went back together down through the corridors of the Tower of Loranne, and emerged beside the deserted moving way. Not until they were once more in the streets did it occur to Alvin that Khedron had never asked him what he had been doing out here at the edge of the unknown. He suspected that Khedron knew, and was interested but not surprised. Something told him that it would be very difficult to surprise Khedron.

They exchanged index numbers, so that they could call each other whenever they wished. Alvin was anxious to see more of the Jester, though he fancied that his company might prove exhausting if it was too prolonged. Before they met again, however, he wanted to find what his friends, and particularly Jeserac, could tell him about Khedron.

"Until our next meeting," said Khedron, and promptly vanished. Alvin was somewhat annoyed. If you met anyone when you were merely projecting yourself, and were not present in the flesh, it was good manners to make that clear from the beginning. It could sometimes put the party who was ignorant of the facts at a considerable disadvantage. Probably Khedron had been quietly at home all the time—wherever his home might be. The number that he had given Alvin would ensure that any messages would reach him, but did not reveal where he lived. That at least was according to normal custom. You might be free enough with index numbers, but your actual address was something you disclosed only to your intimate friends.

As he made his way back into the city, Alvin pondered over all that Khedron had told him about Diaspar and its social organisation. It was strange that he had met no one else who had ever seemed dissatisfied with their mode of life. Diaspar and its inhabitants had been designed as part of one master plan; they formed a perfect symbiosis. Throughout their long lives, the people of the city were never bored. Though their world might be a tiny one by the standard of earlier ages, its complexity was overwhelming, its wealth of wonder and treasure beyond calculation. Here Man had gathered all the fruits of his genius, everything that had been saved from the ruin of the past. All the cities that had ever been, so it was said, had given something to Diaspar; before the coming of the Invaders, its name had been known on all the worlds that Man had lost. Into the building of Diaspar had gone all the skill, all the artistry of the Empire. When the great days were coming to an end, men of genius had remoulded the city and given it the machines that made it immortal. Whatever might be forgotten Diaspar would live and bear the descendants of Man safely down the stream of Time.

They had achieved nothing except survival, and were content with that. There were a million things to occupy their lives between the hour when they came, almost full-grown from the Hall of Creation and the hour when, their bodies scarcely older, they returned to the Memory Banks of the city. In a world where all men and women possess an intelligence that would once have been the mark of genius, there can be no danger of boredom. The delights of conversation and argument, the intricate formalities of social intercourse—these alone were enough to occupy a goodly portion of a lifetime. Beyond those were the great formal debates when the whole city would listen entranced while its keenest minds met in combat, or strove to scale those mountain peaks of philosophy which are never conquered yet whose challenge never palls.

No man or woman was without some absorbing intellectual interest. Eriston, for example, spent much of his time in prolonged soliloquies with the Central Computer, which virtually ran the city, yet which had leisure for scores of simultaneous discussions with anyone who cared to match their wits against it. For three hundred years, Eriston had been trying to construct logical paradoxes which the machine could not resolve. He did not expect to make serious progress before he had used up several lifetimes.

Etania's interests were of a more aesthetic nature. She designed and constructed, with the aid of the matter organisers, three-dimensional interlacing patterns of such beautiful complexity that they were really extremely advanced problems in topology. Her work could be seen all over Diaspar, and some of her patterns had been incorporated in the floors of the great halls of choreography, where they were used as the basis for evolving new ballet creations and dance motifs.

Such occupations might have seemed arid to those who did not possess the intellect to appreciate their subtleties. Yet there was no one in Diaspar who could not understand something of what Eriston and Etania were trying to do, and did not have some equally consuming interest of their own.

Athletics and various sports, including many only rendered posible by the control of gravity, made pleasant the first few centuries of youth. For adventure and the exercise of the imagination, the Sagas provided all that anyone could desire. They were the inevitable end-product of that striving for realism which began when men started to reproduce moving images and to record sounds, and then to use these techniques to enact scenes from real or imaginary life. In the Sagas, the illusion was perfect because all the sense-impressions involved were fed directly into the mind and any conflicting sensations were diverted. The entranced spectator was cut off from reality as long as the adventure lasted; it was as if he lived a dream yet believed he was awake.

In a world of order and stability, which in its broad outlines had not changed for a thousand million years, it was perhaps not surprising to find an absorbing interest in games of chance. Humanity had always been fascinated by the mystery of the falling dice, the turn of a card, the spin of the pointer. At its lowest level, this interest was based on mere cupidity—and that was an emotion that could have no place in a world where everyone possessed all that they could reasonably need. Even when this motive was ruled out, however, the purely intellectual fascination of chance remained to seduce the most sophisticated minds. Machines that behaved in a purely random way—events whose outcome could never be predicted, no matter how much information one had —from these philosopher and gambler could derive equal enjoyment.

And there still remained, for all men to share, the linked worlds of Love and Art. Linked, because love without art is merely the slaking of desire, and Art cannot be enjoyed unless it is approached with Love.

Men had sought beauty in many forms—in sequences of sound, in lines upon paper, in surfaces of stone, in the movements of the human body, in colours ranged through space. All these media still survived in Diaspar and down the ages others had been added to them. No one was yet certain if all the possibilities of art had been discovered, or if it had any meaning outside the mind of Man.

CHAPTER VI

J ESERAC SAT MOTIONLESS within a whirlpool of numbers. The first thousand primes, expressed in the binary scale that had been used for all arithmetical operations since electronic computers were invented, marched in order before him. Endless ranks of 1's and 0's paraded past, bringing before Jeserac's eyes the complete sequences of all those numbers that possessed no factors except themselves and unity. There was a mystery about the primes that had always fascinated Man, and they held his imagination still.

Jeserac was no mathematician, though sometimes he liked to believe he was. All he could do was to search among the infinite array of primes for special relationships and rules which more talented men might incorporate in general laws. He could find how numbers behaved, but he could not explain why. It was his pleasure to hack his way through the arithmetical jungle and sometimes he discovered wonders that more skilful explorers had missed.

He set up the matrix of all possible integers, and started his computer stringing the primes across its surface as beads might be arranged at the intersections of a mesh. Jeserac had done this a hundred times before and it had never taught him anything. But he was fascinated by the way in which the numbers he was studying were scattered, apparently according to no laws, across the spectrum of the integers. He knew the laws of distribution that had already been discovered, but always hoped to discover more.

He could scarcely complain about the interruption. If he had wished to remain undisturbed, he should have set his annunciator accordingly. As the gentle chime sounded in his ear, the wall of numbers shivered, the digits blurred together, and Jeserac returned to the world of mere reality.

He recognised Khedron at once, and was none too pleased. Jeserac did not care to be disturbed from his ordered way of life, and Khedron represented the unpredictable. However, he greeted his visitor politely enough and concealed all trace of his mild concern.

When two people met for the first time in Diaspar—or even for the hundredth—it was customary to spend an hour or so in an exchange of courtesies before getting down to business, if any. Khedron somewhat offended Jeserac by racing through these formalities in a mere fifteen minutes and then saying abruptly: "I'd like to talk to you about Alvin. You're his tutor, I believe?"

"That is true," replied Jeserac. "I still see him several times a week—as often as he wishes."

"And would you say that he was an apt pupil?"

Jeserac thought that over; it was a difficult question to answer. The pupil-tutor relationship was extremely important and was, indeed, one of the foundations of life in Diaspar. On the average, ten thousand new minds came into the city every year. Their previous memories were still latent, and for the first twenty years of their existence everything around them was fresh and strange. They had to be taught to use the myriad machines and devices which were the background of everyday life, and they had to learn their way through the most complex society Man had ever built.

Part of this instruction came from the couples chosen to be the parents of the new citizens. The selection was by lot, and the duties were not onerous. Eriston and Etania had devoted no more than a third of their time to Alvin's upbringing, and they had done all that was expected of them.

Jeserac's duties were confined to the more formal aspects of Alvin's education; it was assumed that his parents would teach him how to behave in society, and introduce him to an ever-widening circle of friends. They were responsible for Alvin's character, Jeserac for his mind.

"I find it rather hard to answer your question," Jeserac replied. "Certainly there is nothing wrong with Alvin's intelligence, but many of the things that should concern him seem to be a matter of complete indifference. On the other hand, he shows a morbid curiosity regarding subjects which we do not generally discuss."

"The world outside Diaspar, for example?"

"Yes—but how did you know?"

Khedron hesitated for a moment, wondering how far he should take Jeserac into his confidence. He knew that Jeserac was kindly and well-intentioned, but he knew also that he must be bound by the same taboos that controlled everyone in Diaspar—everyone except Alvin.

"I guessed it," he said at last.

Jeserac settled down more comfortably in the depths of the chair he had just materialised. This was an interesting situation, and he wanted to analyse it as fully as possible. There was not much he could learn, however, unless Khedron was willing to co-operate.

He should have anticipated that Alvin would one day meet the Jester, with unpredictable consequences. Khedron was the only other person in the city who could be called eccentric—and even his eccentricity had been planned by the designers of Diaspar. Long ago it had been discovered that without some crime or disorder, Utopia soon became unbearably dull. Crime, however, from the nature of things, could not be guaranteed to remain at the optimum level which the social equations demanded. If it was licensed and regulated, it ceased to be crime.

The office of Jester was the solution—at first sight *naïve* yet actually profoundly subtle—which the city's designers had evolved. In all the history of Diaspar there were less than two hundred persons whose mental inheritance fitted them for this peculiar role. They had certain privileges which protected them from the consequences of their actions, though there had been Jesters who had overstepped the mark and paid the only penalty that Diaspar could impose—that of being banished into the future before their current incarnation had ended.

On rare and unforeseeable occasions, the Jester would turn the city upside down by some prank which might be no more than an elaborate practical joke, or which might be a calculated assault on some currently cherished belief or way of life. All things considered, the name "Jester" was a highly appropriate one. There had once been men with very similar duties, operating with the same licence, in the days when there were courts and kings.

"It will help," said Jeserac, "if we are frank with one another. We both know that Alvin is Unique—that he has never experienced any earlier life in Diaspar. Perhaps you can guess, better than I can, the implications of that. I doubt if anything that happens in the city is totally unplanned, so there must be a purpose in his creation. Whether he will achieve that purpose—whatever it is

—I do not know. Nor do I know whether it is good or bad. I cannot guess what it is."

"Suppose it concerns something external to the city?"

Jeserac smiled patiently; the Jester was having his little joke, as was only to be expected.

"I have told him what lies there; he knows that there is nothing outside Diaspar except the desert. Take him there if you can; perhaps *you* know a way. When he sees the reality, it may cure the strangeness in his mind."

"I think he has already seen it," said Khedron softly. But he said it to himself, and not to Jeserac.

"I do not believe that Alvin is happy," Jeserac continued. "He has formed no real attachments, and it is hard to see how he can while he still suffers from his obsession. But after all, he is very young. He may grow out of this phase, and become part of the pattern of the city."

Jeserac was talking to reassure himself; Khedron wondered if he really believed what he was saying.

"Tell me, Jeserac," asked Khedron abruptly, "does Alvin know that he is not the first Unique?"

Jeserac looked startled, then a little defiant.

"I might have guessed," he said ruefully, "that *you* would know that. How many Uniques have there been in the whole history of Diaspar? As many as ten?"

"Fourteen," answered Khedron without hesitation. "Not counting Alvin."

"You have better information than I can command," said Jeserac wryly. "Perhaps you can tell me what happened to those Uniques?"

"They disappeared."

"Thank you: I knew that already. That is why I have told Alvin as little as possible about his predecessors: it would hardly help him in his present mood. Can I rely on your co-operation?"

"For the moment—yes. I want to study him myself; mysteries have always intrigued me, and there are too few in Diaspar. Besides, I think that Fate may be arranging a Jest besides which all my efforts will look very modest indeed. In that case, I want to make sure that I am present at its climax."

"You are rather too fond of talking in riddles," complained Jeserac. "Exactly what are you anticipating?"

"I doubt if my guesses will be any better than yours. But I believe this— neither you nor I nor anyone in Diaspar will be able to stop Alvin when he has decided what he wants to do. We have a very interesting few centuries ahead of us."

Jeserac sat motionless for a long time, his mathematics forgotten, after the image of Khedron had faded from sight. A sense of foreboding, the like of which he had never known before, hung heavily upon him. For a fleeting moment he wondered if he should request an audience with the Council—but would that not be making a ridiculous fuss about nothing? Perhaps the whole affair was some complicated and obscure jest of Khedron's, though he could not imagine why he had been chosen to be its butt.

He thought the matter over carefully, examining the problem from every angle. After little more than an hour, he made a characteristic decision.

He would wait and see.

Alvin wasted no time learning all that he could about Khedron. Jeserac, as usual, was his main source of information. The old tutor gave a carefully factual account of his meetings with the Jester, and added what little he knew about the other's mode of life. Insofar as such a thing was possible in Diaspar, Khedron was a recluse: no one knew where he lived or anything about his way of life. The last jest he had contrived had been a rather childish prank involving a general paralysis of the moving ways. That had been fifty years ago; a century earlier he had let loose a particularly revolting dragon which had wandered round the city eating every existing specimen of the works of the currently most popular sculptor. The artist himself, justifiably alarmed when the beast's single-minded diet became obvious, had gone into hiding and not emerged until the monster had vanished as mysteriously as it had appeared.

One thing was obvious from these accounts. Khedron must have a profound understanding of the machines and powers that ruled the city, and could make them obey his will in ways which no one else could do. Presumably there must be some overriding control which prevented any too-ambitious Jester from causing permanent and irreparable damage to the complex structure of Diaspar.

Alvin filed all this information away, but made no move to contact Khedron. Though he had many questions to ask the Jester, his stubborn streak of independence—perhaps the most truly unique of all his qualities—made him determined to discover all he could by his own unaided efforts. He had embarked on a project which might keep him busy for years, but as long as he felt that he was moving towards his goal he was happy.

Like some traveller of old mapping out an unknown land, he had begun the systematic exploration of Diaspar. He spent his weeks and days prowling through the lonely towers at the margin of the city, in the hope that somewhere he might discover a way out into the world beyond. During the course of his search he found a dozen of the great air-vents opening high above the desert, but they were all barred—and even if the bars had not been there, the sheer drop of almost a mile was sufficient obstacle.

He found no other exits, though he explored a thousand corridors and ten thousand empty chambers. All these buildings were in that perfect and spotless condition which the people of Diaspar took for granted as part of the normal order of things. Sometimes Alvin would meet a wandering robot, obviously on a tour of inspection, and he never failed to question the machine. He learnt nothing, because the machines he encountered were not keyed to respond to human speech or thoughts. Though they were aware of his presence, for they floated politely aside to let him pass, they refused to engage in conversation.

There were times when Alvin did not see another human being for days. When he felt hungry, he would go into one of the living compartments and order a meal. Miraculous machines of whose existence he seldom gave a thought would wake to life after aeons of slumber. The patterns they had stored in their memories would flicker on the edge of reality, organising and directing the matter they controlled. And so a meal prepared by a master-chef a hundred million years before would be called again into existence to delight the palate or merely to satisfy the appetite.

The loneliness of this deserted world—the empty shell surrounding the living heart of the city—did not depress Alvin. He was used to loneliness, even when he was among those he called his friends. This ardent exploration, absorbing all his energy and interest, made him forget for the moment the mystery of his heritage and the anomaly that cut him off from all his fellows.

He had explored less than one-hundredth of the city's rim when he decided that he was wasting his time. His decision was not the result of impatience, but of sheer common sense. If need be, he was prepared to come back and finish the task, even if it took him the remainder of his life. He had seen enough, however, to convince him that if a way out of Diaspar did exist, it would not be found as easily as this. He might waste centuries in fruitless search unless he called upon the assistance of wiser men.

Jeserac had told him flatly that he knew no road out of Diaspar, and doubted if one existed. The information machines, when Alvin had questioned them, had searched their almost infinite memories in vain. They could tell him every detail of the city's history back to the beginning of recorded times—back to the barrier beyond which the Dawn Ages lay for ever hidden. But they could not answer Alvin's simple question, or else some higher power had forbidden them to do so.

He would have to see Khedron again.

CHAPTER VII

"YOU TOOK YOUR time," said Khedron, "but I knew you would call sooner or later."

This confidence annoyed Alvin; he did not like to think that his behaviour could be predicted so accurately. He wondered if the Jester had watched all his fruitless searching and knew exactly what he had been doing.

"I am trying to find a way out of the city," he said bluntly. "There *must* be one, and I think you could help me find it."

Khedron was silent for a moment. There was still time, if he wished, to turn back from the road that stretched before him, and which led into a future beyond all his powers of prophecy. No one else would have hesitated; no other man in the city, even if he had the power, would have dared to disturb the ghosts of an age that had been dead for millions of centuries. Perhaps there was no danger, perhaps nothing could alter the perpetual changelessness of Diaspar. But if there was any risk of something strange and new coming into the world, this might be the last chance to ward it off.

Khedron was content with the order of things as it was. True, he might upset that order from time to time—but only by a little. He was a critic, not a revolutionary. On the placidly flowing river of time, he wished only to make a few ripples: he shrank from diverting its course. The desire for adventure, other than that of the mind, had been eliminated from him as carefully and thoroughly as from all the other citizens of Diaspar.

Yet he still possessed, though it was almost extinguished, that spark of curiosity that was once Man's greatest gift. He was still prepared to take a risk.

He looked at Alvin, and tried to remember his own youth, his own dreams of half a thousand years before. Any moment of his past that he cared to choose was still clear and sharp when he turned his memory upon it. Like beads upon a string, this life and all the ones before it stretched back through the ages; he could seize and re-examine any one he wished. Most of those older Khedrons were strangers to him now; the basic patterns might be the same, but the weight of experience separated him from them for ever. If he wished, he could wash his mind clear of all his earlier incarnations, when next he walked back into the Hall of Creation to sleep until the city called him forth again. But that would be a kind of death, and he was not ready for that yet. He was still prepared to go on collecting all that life could offer, like a chambered nautilus patiently adding new cells to its slowly expanding spiral.

In his youth, he had been no different from his companions. It was not until he came of age that the latent memories of this earlier life came flooding back that he had taken up the role for which he had been destined long ago. Sometimes he felt resentment that the intelligence which had contrived Diaspar with such infinite skill could even now, after all these ages, make him move like a puppet across their stage. Here, perhaps, was a chance of obtaining a long-delayed revenge. A new actor had appeared who might ring down the curtain for the last time on a play which already had seen far too many acts.

Sympathy, for one whose loneliness must be even greater than his own; an ennui produced by ages of repetition; and an impish sense of fun—these were the discordant factors which prompted Khedron to act.

"I may be able to help you," he told Alvin, "or I may not. I don't wish to raise any false hopes. Meet me in half an hour at the intersection of Radius 3 and Ring 2. If I cannot do anything else, at least I can promise you an interesting journey."

Alvin was at the rendezvous ten minutes ahead of time, though it was on the other side of the city. He waited impatiently as the moving ways swept eternally past him, bearing the placid and contented people of the city about their unimportant business. At last he saw the tall figure of Khedron appear in the distance, and a moment later he was for the first time in the physical presence of the Jester. This was no projected image; when they touched palms in the ancient greeting Khedron was real enough.

The Jester sat down on one of the marble balustrades and regarded Alvin with a curious intentness.

"I wonder," he said, "if you know what you are asking. And I wonder what you would do if you obtained it. Do you *really* imagine that you could leave the city, even if you found a way?"

"I am sure of it," replied Alvin bravely enough, though Khedron could sense the uncertainty in his voice.

"Then let me tell you something which you may not know. You see those towers there?" Khedron pointed to the twin peaks of Power Central and Council Hall, staring at each other across a canyon a mile deep. "Suppose I was to lay a perfectly firm plank between the two towers—a plank only six inches wide. Could you walk across it?"

Alvin hesitated.

"I don't know," he answered. "I wouldn't like to try."

"I'm quite sure you could never do it. You'd get giddy and fall off before you'd gone a dozen paces. Yet if that same plank was supported just clear of the ground, you'd be able to walk along it without difficulty."

"And what does that prove?"

"A simple point I'm trying to make. In the two experiments I've described, the plank would be exactly the same in both cases. One of those wheeled robots you sometimes meet could cross it just as easily if it was bridging those towers as if it was laid along the ground. *We* couldn't, because we have a fear of heights. It may be irrational, but it's too powerful to be ignored. It is built into us; we are born with it.

"In the same way, we have a fear of space. Show any man in Diaspar a road out of the city—a road that might be just like this road in front of us now—and he could not go far along it. He would have to turn back, as you would turn back if you started to cross a plank between those towers."

"But why?" asked Alvin. "There must have been a time——"

"I know, I know," said Khedron. "Men once went out over the whole world, and to the stars themselves. Something changed them, and gave this fear with which they are now born. You alone imagine that you do not possess it. Well, we shall see. I'm taking you to Council Hall."

The Hall was one of the largest buildings in the city, and was almost entirely given over to the machines which were the real administrators of Diaspar. Not far from this summit was the chamber where the Council met on those infrequent occasions when it had any business to discuss.

The wide entrance swallowed them up, and Khedron strode forward into the golden gloom. Alvin had never entered Council Hall before; there was no rule against it—there were few rules against anything in Diaspar—but like everyone else he had a certain half-religious awe of the place. In a world that had no gods, Council Hall was the nearest thing to a temple.

Khedron never hesitated as he led Alvin along corridors and down ramps that were obviously made for wheeled machines, not human traffic. Some of these ramps zig-zagged down into the depths at such steep angles that it would have been impossible to keep a footing on them had not gravity been twisted to compensate for the slope.

They came at last to a closed door which slid silently open as they approached, then barred their retreat. Ahead was another door, which did not open as they came up to it. Khedron made no move to touch the door, but stood motionless in front of it. After a short pause, a quiet voice said: "Please state your names."

"I am Khedron the Jester. My companion is Alvin."

"And your business?"

"Sheer curiosity."

Rather to Alvin's surprise, the door opened at once. In his experience, if one gave facetious replies to machines it always led to confusion and one had to go back to the beginning. The machine that had interrogated Khedron must have been a very sophisticated one—far up in the hierarchy of the Central Computer.

They met no more barriers, but Alvin suspected that they had passed many tests of which he had no knowledge. A short corridor brought them out abruptly into a huge circular chamber with a sunken floor, and set in that floor was something so astonishing that for a moment Alvin was overwhelmed with wonder. He was looking down upon the entire city of Diaspar, spread out before him with its tallest buildings barely reaching to his shoulder.

He spent so long picking out familiar places and observing unexpected vistas that it was some time before he paid any notice to the rest of the chamber. Its walls were covered with a microscopically detailed pattern of black and white squares; the pattern itself was completely irregular, and when he moved his eyes quickly he got the impression that it was flickering swiftly, though it never changed. At frequent intervals around the chamber were keyboard-operated machines of some type, each complete with a vision screen and a seat for the operator.

Khedron let Alvin look his fill. Then he pointed to the diminutive city and said: "Do you know what that is?"

Alvin was tempted to answer "A model, I suppose," but that answer was so obvious that he was sure it must be wrong. So he shook his head and waited for Khedron to answer his own question.

"You remember," said the Jester, "that I once told you how the city was maintained—how the Memory Banks hold its pattern frozen for ever. Those Banks are all around us, with all their immeasurable store of information, completely defining the city as it is today. Every atom of Diaspar is somehow keyed, by forces we have forgotten, to the matrices buried in these walls."

He waved towards the perfect, infinitely detailed simulacrum of Diaspar that lay below them.

"That is no model; it does not really exist. It is merely the projected image of the pattern held in the Memory Banks, and therefore it is absolutely identical with the city itself. These viewing machines here enable one to magnify any desired portion, to look at it life-size or larger. They are used when it is necessary to make alterations to the design, though it is a very long time since that was done. If you want to know what Diaspar is like, this is the place to come. You can learn more here in a few days than you would in a lifetime of actual exploring."

"It's wonderful," said Alvin. "How many people know that it exists?"

"Oh, a good many, but it seldom concerns them. The Council comes down here from time to time; no alterations to the city can be made unless they are all here. And not even then, if the Central Computer doesn't approve of the proposed change. I doubt if this room is visited more than two or three times a year."

Alvin wanted to know how Khedron had access to it, and then remembered that many of his more elaborate jests must have involved a knowledge of the city's inner mechanisms that could have come only from very profound study. It must be one of the Jester's privileges to go anywhere and learn anything; he could have no better guide to the secrets of Diaspar.

"What you are looking for may not exist," said Khedron, "but if it does, this is where you will find it. Let me show you how to operate the monitors."

For the next hour Alvin sat before one of the vision screens, learning to use the controls. He could select at will any point in the city, and examine it with any degree of magnification. Streets and towers and walls and moving ways flashed across the screen as he changed the co-ordinates; it was as though he was an all-seeing, disembodied spirit that could move effortlessly over the whole of Diaspar, unhindered by any physical obstructions.

Yet it was not, in reality, Diaspar that he was examining. He was moving through the memory cells, looking at the dream image of the city—the dream which had had the power to hold the real Diaspar untouched by time for a thousand million years. He could see only the part of the city which was permanent; the people who walked its streets were no part of this frozen image. For his purpose, that did not matter. His concern now was purely with the creation of stone and metal in which he was imprisoned, and not those who shared—however willingly—his confinement.

He searched for and presently found the Tower of Loranne, and moved swiftly through the corridors and passageways which he had already explored in reality. As the image of the stone grille expanded before his eyes, he could almost feel the cold wind that had blown ceaselessly through it for perhaps half the entire history of mankind, and which was blowing now. He came up to the grille, looked out—and saw nothing. For a moment the shock was so great that he almost doubted his own memory; had his vision of the desert been nothing more than a dream?

Then he remembered the truth. The desert was no part of Diaspar, and therefore no image of it existed in the phantom world he was exploring. Anything might lie beyond the grille in reality; his monitor screen could never show it.

Yet it could show him something that no living man had ever seen. Alvin advanced his viewpoint through the grille, out into the nothingness beyond the city. He turned the control which altered the direction of his vision, so that he looked backwards along the way that he had come. And there behind him lay Diaspar—seen from the outside.

To the computers, the memory circuits, and all the multitudinous mechanisms which created the image at which Alvin was looking, it was merely a simple problem of perspective. They "knew" the form of the city; therefore they could show it as it would appear from the outside. Yet even though he could appreciate how the trick was done, the effect on Alvin was overwhelming. In spirit, if not in reality, he had escaped from the city. He appeared to be hanging in space, a few feet away from the sheer wall of the Tower of Loranne. For a moment he stared at the smooth grey surface before his eyes; then he touched the control and let his viewpoint drop towards the ground.

Now that he knew the possibilities of this wonderful instrument, his plan of action was clear. There was no need to spend months and years exploring Diaspar from the inside, room by room and corridor by corridor. From this new vantage point he could wing his way along the outside of the city, and could see at once any openings that might lead to the desert and the world beyond.

The sense of victory, of achievement, made him feel light-headed and anxious to share his joy. He turned to Khedron, wishing to thank the Jester for having made this possible. But Khedron was gone, and it took only a moment's thought to realise why.

Alvin was perhaps the only man in Diaspar who could look unaffected upon the images that were now drifting across the screen. Khedron could help him in his search, but even the Jester shared the strange terror of the universe which had pinned mankind for so long inside its little world. He had left Alvin to continue his quest alone.

The sense of loneliness, which for a little while had lifted from Alvin's soul, pressed down upon him once more. But this was no time for melancholy; there was too much to do. He turned back to the monitor screen, set the image of the city wall drifting slowly across it, and began his search.

Diaspar saw little of Alvin for the next few weeks, though only a few people noticed his absence. Jeserac, when he discovered that his erstwhile pupil was spending all his time at Council Hall instead of prowling around the frontier of the city, felt slightly relieved, imagining that Alvin could come to no trouble there. Eriston and Etania called his room once or twice, found that he was out and thought nothing of it. Alystra was a little more persistent.

For her own peace of mind, it was a pity that she had become infatuated with Alvin, when there were so many more suitable choices. Alystra had never had any difficulty in finding partners, but by comparison with Alvin all the other men she knew were nonentities, cast from the same featureless mould. She would not lose him without a struggle: his aloofness and indifference set a challenge which she could not resist.

Yet perhaps her motives were not entirely selfish, and were maternal rather than sexual. Though birth had been forgotten the feminine instincts of protection and sympathy still remained. Alvin might appear to be stubborn and self-reliant and determined to have his own way, yet Alystra could sense his inner loneliness.

When she found that Alvin had disappeared, she promptly asked Jeserac what had happened to him. Jeserac, with only a momentary hesitation, told her. If Alvin did not want company, the answer was in his own hands. His tutor neither approved nor disapproved of this relationship. On the whole, he rather liked Alystra and hoped that her influence would help Alvin to adjust himself to life in Diaspar.

The fact that Alvin was spending his time at Council Hall could only mean that he was engaged on some research project, and this knowledge at least served to quell any suspicions Alystra might have concerning possible rivals. But though her jealousy was not aroused, her curiosity was. She sometimes reproached herself for abandoning Alvin in the Tower of Loranne. Though she knew that if the circumstances were repeated she would do exactly the same thing again. There was no way of understanding Alvin's mind, she told herself, unless she could discover what he was trying to do.

She walked purposefully into the main hall, impressed but not overawed by the hush that fell as soon as she passed through the entrance. The information machines were ranged side by side against the far wall, and she chose one at random.

As soon as the recognition signal lit up, she said: "I am looking for Alvin; he is somewhere in this building. Where can I find him?"

Even after a lifetime, one never grew wholly accustomed to the complete absence of time-lag when an information machine replied to an ordinary question. There were people who knew—or claimed to know—how it was done, and talked learnedly of "access time" and "storage space", but that made the final result none the less marvellous. Any question of a purely factual nature, within the city's truly enormous range of available information, could be answered immediately. Only if complex calculations were involved before a reply could be given would there be any appreciable delay.

"He is with the Monitors," came the reply. It was not very helpful, since the name conveyed nothing to Alystra. No machine ever volunteered more information than it was asked for, and learning to frame questions properly was an art which often took a long time to acquire.

"How do I reach him?" asked Alystra. She would find what the monitors were when she got to them.

"I cannot tell you unless you have the permission of the Council."

This was a most unexpected, even a disconcerting, development. There were very few places in Diaspar which could not be visited by anyone who pleased. Alystra was quite certain that Alvin had *not* obtained Council permission, and this could only mean that a higher authority was helping him.

The Council ruled Diaspar, but the Council itself could be overridden by a superior power—the all-but-infinite intellect of the Central Computer. It was difficult to think of the Central Computer as a living entity, localised in a single spot, though actually it was the sum total of all the machines in Diaspar. Even if it was not alive in the biological sense, it certainly possessed at least as much awareness and self-consciousness as a human being. It must know what Alvin was doing—and, therefore, it must approve, otherwise it would have stopped him or referred him to the Council, as the Information Machine had done to Alystra.

There was no point in staying here. Alystra knew that any attempt to find Alvin—even if she knew exactly where he was in this enormous building— would be doomed to failure. Doors would fail to open; slideways would reverse when she stood on them, carrying her backwards instead of forwards; elevator fields would be mysteriously inert, refusing to lift her from one floor to another. If she persisted, she would be gently conveyed out into the street by a polite but firm robot, or else shuttled round and round the Council Hall until she grew fed up and left of her own volition.

She was in a bad temper as she walked out into the street. She was also more than a little puzzled, and for the first time felt that there was some mystery here which made her personal desires and interests seem very trivial indeed. That did not mean that they would be any the less important to her. She had no idea what she was going to do next, but she was sure of one thing. Alvin was not the only person in Diaspar who could be stubborn and persistent.

CHAPTER VIII

THE IMAGE ON the monitor screen faded as Alvin raised his hands from the control panel and cleared the circuits. For a moment he sat quite motionless, looking into the black rectangle which had occupied all his conscious mind for so many weeks. He had circumnavigated his world; across that screen had passed every square foot of the outer wall of Diaspar. He knew the city better than any living man save perhaps Khedron; and he knew now that there was no way through the walls.

The feeling that possessed him was not mere despondency; he had never really expected that it would be as easy as this, that he would find what he sought at the first attempt. What was important was that he had eliminated one possibility. Now he must deal with the others.

He rose to his feet and walked over to the image of the city which almost filled the chamber. It was hard not to think of it as an actual model, though he knew that in reality it was no more than an optical projection of the pattern in the memory cells he had been exploring. When he altered the monitor controls and set his viewpoint moving through Diaspar, a spot of light would travel over the surface of this replica, so that he could see exactly where he was going. It had been a useful guide in the early days, but he had soon grown so skilful at setting the co-ordinates that he had not needed this aid.

The city lay spread out beneath him; he looked down upon it like a god. Yet he scarcely saw it as he considered one by one, the steps he should now take.

If all else failed, there was one solution to the problem. Diaspar might be held in a perpetual stasis by its eternity circuits, frozen for ever according to the pattern in the memory cells. But that pattern could itself be altered, and the city would then change with it. It would be possible to redesign a section of the outer wall so that it contained a doorway, feed this pattern into the monitors, and let the city reshape itself to the new conception.

Alvin suspected that the large areas of the monitor control board whose purpose Khedron had not explained to him were concerned with such alterations. It would be useless to experiment with them; controls which could alter the very structure of the city were firmly locked, and could be operated only with the authority of the Council, and the approval of the Central Computer. There was very little chance that the Council would grant him what he asked, even if he was prepared for decades or even centuries of patient pleading. That was not a prospect that appealed to him in the least.

He turned his thoughts towards the sky. Sometimes he had imagined, in fantasies which he was half-ashamed to recall, that he had regained the freedom of the air which man had renounced so long ago. Once, he knew, the skies of Earth had been filled with strange shapes. Out of space the great ships had come, bearing unknown treasures, to berth at the legendary Port of Diaspar. But the Port had been beyond the limits of the city; aeons ago it had been buried by the drifting sand. He could dream that somewhere in the mazes of Diaspar a flying machine might still be hidden, but he did not really believe it. Even in the days when small, personal flyers had been in common use, it was most unlikely that they had even been allowed to operate inside the limits of the city.

For a moment he lost himself in the old, familiar dream. He imagined that he was master of the sky, that the world lay spread out beneath him. inviting him to travel where he willed. It was not the world of his own time that he saw, but the lost world of the dawn—a rich and living panorama of hills and lakes and forests. He felt a bitter envy of his unknown ancestors, who had flown with such freedom over all the earth, and who had let its beauty die.

This mind-drugging reverie was useless; he tore himself back to the present and to the problem at hand. If the sky was unattainable, and the way by land was barred, what remained?

Once again he had come to the point where he needed help, when he could make no further progress by his own efforts. He disliked admitting the fact, but was honest enough not to deny it. Inevitably, his thoughts turned to Khedron.

Alvin had never been able to decide whether he liked the Jester. He was very glad that they had met, and was grateful to Khedron for the assistance and implicit sympathy he had given him on his quest. There was no one else in Diaspar with whom he had so much in common, yet there was some element in the other's personality which jarred upon him. Perhaps it was Khedron's air of ironic detachment, which sometimes gave Alvin the impression that he was laughing secretly at all his efforts, even while he seemed to be doing his best to help. Because of this, as well as his own natural stubbornness and independence Alvin hesitated to approach the Jester except as a last resort.

They arranged to meet in a small, circular court not far from Council Hall. There were many such secluded spots in the city, perhaps only a few yards from some busy thoroughfare, yet completely cut off from it. Usually they could be reached only on foot after a rather roundabout walk; sometimes, indeed, they were at the centre of skilfully contrived mazes which enhanced their isolation. It was rather typical of Khedron that he should have chosen such a place for a rendezvous.

The court was little more than fifty paces across, and was in reality located deep within the interior of some great building. Yet it appeared to have no definite physical limits, being bounded by a translucent blue-green material which glowed with a faint internal light. However, though there were no visible limits, the court had been so laid out that there was no danger of feeling lost in infinite space. Low walls, less than waist high and broken at intervals so that one could pass through them, managed to give the impression of safe confinement without which no one in Diaspar could ever feel entirely happy.

Khedron was examining one of these walls when Alvin arrived. It was covered with an intricate mosaic of coloured tiles, so fantastically involved that Alvin did not even attempt to unravel it.

"Look at this mosaic, Alvin," said the Jester. "Do you notice anything strange about it?"

"No," confessed Alvin after a brief examination. "I don't care for it—but there's nothing strange about *that*."

Khedron ran his fingers over the coloured tiles. "You are not very observant," he said. "Look at these edges here—see how they have become rounded and softened. This is something that one very seldom sees in Diaspar, Alvin. It is wear—the crumbling away of matter under the assault of time. I can remember when this pattern was new, only eighty thousand years ago, in my last lifetime. If I come back to this spot a dozen lives from now, these tiles will have been worn completely away."

"I don't see anything very surprising about that," answered Alvin. "There are other works of art in the city not good enough to be preserved in the memory circuits, but not bad enough to be destroyed outright. One day, I suppose, some other artist will come along and do a better job. And his work won't be allowed to wear out."

"I knew the man who designed this wall," said Khedron, his fingers still exploring the cracks in the mosaic. "Strange that I can remember that fact, when I don't recall the man himself. I could not have liked him, so I must have erased him from my mind." He gave a short laugh. "Perhaps I designed it myself, during one of my artistic phases, and was so annoyed when the city

refused to make it eternal that I decided to forget the whole affair. There—
I knew that piece was coming loose!"

He managed to pull out a single flake of golden tile, and looked very
pleased at this minor sabotage. He threw the fragment on the ground, adding, "Now the maintenance robots will have to do something about it!"

There was a lesson for him here, Alvin knew. That strange instinct known as
intuition, which seemed to follow short-cuts not accessible to mere logic, told
him that. He looked at the golden shard lying at his feet, trying to link it
somehow to the problem that now dominated his mind.

It was not hard to find the answer, once he realised that it existed.

"I see what you are trying to tell me," he said to Khedron. "There are
objects in Diaspar that aren't preserved in the memory circuits, so I could
never find them through the monitors at Council Hall. If I was to go there
and focus on this court, there would be no sign of the wall we're sitting on."

"I think you might find the wall. But there would be no mosaic on it."

"Yes, I can see that," said Alvin, too impatient now to bother about such
hair-splitting. "And in the same way, parts of the city might exist that had
never been preserved in the eternity circuits, but which hadn't yet worn away.
Still, I don't really see how that helps me. I *know* that the outer wall exists
—and that it has no openings in it."

"Perhaps there is no way out," answered Khedron. "I can promise you
nothing. But I think there is still a great deal that the monitors can teach
us—if the Central Computer will let them. And it seems to have taken rather
a liking to you."

Alvin pondered over this remark on their way to Council Hall. Until now,
he had assumed that it was entirely through Khedron's influence that he had
been able to gain access to the monitors. It had not occurred to him that it
might be through some intrinsic quality of his own. Being a Unique had many
disadvantages; it was only right that it should have some compensations. . . .

The unchanging image of the city still dominated the chamber in which
Alvin had spent so many hours. He looked at it now with a new understanding; all that he saw here existed—but all of Diaspar might not be mirrored
here. Yet, surely, any discordancies must be trivial—and, as far as he could
see, undetectable.

"I attempted to do this many years ago," said Khedron, as he sat down at
the monitor desk, but the controls were locked against me. Perhaps they will
obey me now."

Slowly, and then with mounting confidence as he regained access to long-
forgotten skills, Khedron's fingertips moved over the control desk, resting for
a moment at the nodal points in the sensitive grid buried in the panel before
him.

"I think that's correct," he said at last. "Anyway we'll soon see."

The screen glowed into life, but instead of the picture which Alvin had
expected, there appeared a somewhat baffling message:

REGRESSION WILL COMMENCE AS SOON AS YOU HAVE SET RATE CONTROL

"Foolish of me," muttered Khedron. "I got everything else right, and forgot the most important thing of all." His fingers now moved with a confident assurance over the board, and as the message faded from the screen he swung round in his seat so that he could look at the replica of the city.

"Watch this, Alvin," he said. "I think we are both going to learn something new about Diaspar."

Alvin waited patiently, but nothing happened. The image of the city floated there before his eyes in all its familiar wonder and beauty—though he was conscious of neither now. He was about to ask Khedron what he should look for when a sudden movement caught his attention, and he turned his head quickly to follow it. It had been no more than a half-glimpsed flash or flicker and he was too late to see what had made it. Nothing had altered; Diaspar was just as he had always known it. Then he saw that Khedron was watching him with a sardonic smile, so he looked again at the city. This time, the thing happened before his eyes.

One of the buildings at the edge of the Park suddenly vanished, and was replaced instantly by another of quite different design. The transformation was so abrupt that had Alvin been blinking he would have missed it. He stared in amazement at the subtly altered city, but even during the first shock of astonishment his mind was seeking for the answer. He remembered the words that had appeared on the monitor screen—REGRESSION WILL COMMENCE— and he knew at once what was happening.

"That's the city as it was thousands of years ago," he said to Khedron. "We're going back in time."

"A picturesque but hardly accurate way of putting it," replied the Jester. "What is actually happening is that the monitor is remembering the earlier versions of the city. When any modifications were made, the memory circuits were not simply emptied; the information in them was taken to subsidiary storage units, so that it could be recalled whenever needed. I have set the monitor to regress through those units at the rate of a thousand years a second. Already, we are looking at the Diaspar of half a million years ago. We'll have to go much further back than that to see any real changes—I'll increase the rate."

He turned back to the control board, and even as he did so, not one building but a whole block whipped out of existence and was replaced by a large oval amphitheatre.

"Ah, the Arena!" said Khedron. "I can remember the fuss when we decided to get rid of that. It was hardly ever used, but a great many people felt sentimental about it."

The monitor was now recalling its memories at a far higher rate; the image of Diaspar was receding into the past at millions of years a minute, and changes were occurring so rapidly that the eye could not keep up with them. Alvin noticed that the alterations to the city appeared to come in cycles; there would be a long period of statis, then a whole rash of rebuilding would break out, followed by another pause. It was almost as if Diaspar were a living organism, that had to regain its strength after each explosion of growth.

Through all these changes, the basic design of the city had not altered. Buildings came and went, but the pattern of streets seemed eternal, and the Park remained as the green heart of Diaspar. Alvin wondered how far back the monitor could go. Could it return to the founding of the city, and pass through the veil which sundered known history from the myths and legends of the Dawn?

Already they had gone five hundred million years into the past. Outside the walls of Diaspar, beyond the knowledge of the monitors, it would be a different Earth. Perhaps there might be oceans and forests, even other cities which man had not yet deserted in the long retreat to his final home.

The minutes drifted past, each minute an aeon in the little universe of the monitors. Soon, thought Alvin, the earliest of all these stored memories must be reached and the regression would end. But fascinating though this lesson was, he did not see how it could help him to escape from the city as it was here and now.

With a sudden, soundless implosion, Diaspar contracted to a fraction of its former size. The Park vanished, the boundary wall of linked, titanic towers instantly evaporated. This city was open to the world, for the radial roads stretched out to the limits of the monitor image without obstruction. Here was Diaspar as it had been before the great change came upon mankind.

"We can go no further," said Khedron, pointing to the monitor screen. On it had appeared the words: REGRESSION CONCLUDED. "This must be the earliest version of the city that has been preserved in the memory cells. Before that, I doubt if the eternity units were used, and the buildings were allowed to wear out naturally."

For a long time, Alvin stared at this model of the ancient city. He thought of the traffic those roads had borne, as men came and went freely to all the corners of the world—and to other worlds as well. Those men were his ancestors; he felt a closer kinship to them than to the people who now shared his life. He wished that he could see them and share their thoughts, as they moved through the streets of that billion-year-remote Diaspar. Yet those thoughts could not have been happy ones, for they must have been living then beneath the shadow of the Invaders. In a few more centuries, they were to turn their faces from the glory they had won, and build a wall against the universe.

Khedron ran the monitor backwards and forwards a dozen times through the brief period of history that had wrought the transformation. The change from a small open city to a much larger one had taken little more than a thousand years. In that time, the machines that had served Diaspar so faithfully must have been designed and built, and the knowledge that would enable them to carry out their tasks had been fed into their memory circuits. Into the memory circuits also, must have gone the essential patterns of all the men who were now alive, so that when the right impulse called them forth again they could be clothed in matter and would emerge reborn from the Hall of Creation. In some sense, Alvin realised, he must have existed in that ancient world. It was possible, of course, that he was completely synthetic

—that his entire personality had been designed by artist-technicians who had worked with tools of inconceivable complexity towards some clearly envisaged goal. Yet he thought it more likely that he was a composite of men who had once lived and walked on Earth.

Very little of the old Diaspar had remained when the new city was created; the Park had obliterated it almost completely. Even before the transformation, there had been a small, grass-covered clearing at the the centre of Diaspar, surrounding the junction of all the radial streets. Afterwards it had expanded tenfold, wiping out streets and buildings alike. The Tomb of Yarlan Zey had been brought into existence at this time, replacing a very large circular structure which had previously stood at the meeting point of all the streets. Alvin had never really believed the legends of the Tomb's antiquity but now it seemed that they were true.

"I suppose," said Alvin, struck by a sudden thought, "that we can explore this image, just as we explored the image of today's Diaspar?"

Khedron's fingers flickered over the monitor control board, and the screen answered Alvin's question. The long-vanished city began to expand before his eyes as his viewpoint moved along the curiously narrow streets. This memory of the Diaspar that once had been was still as sharp and clear as the image of the city he lived in today. For a thousand million years, the information circuits had held it in ghostly pseudo-existence, waiting for the moment when someone should call it forth again. And it was not, thought Alvin, merely a memory he was seeing now. It was something more complex than that—it was the memory of a memory. . . .

He did not know what he could learn from it, and whether it could help him in his quest. No matter; it was fascinating to look into the past, and to see a world which had existed in the days when men still roamed among the stars. He pointed to the low, circular building that stood at the city's heart.

"Let's start there," he told Khedron. "That seems as good a place as any to begin."

Perhaps it was sheer luck; perhaps it was some ancient memory; perhaps it was elementary logic. It made no difference, since he would have arrived at this spot sooner or later—this spot upon which all the radial streets of the city converged.

It took him ten minutes to discover that they did not meet here for reasons of symmetry alone—ten minutes to know that his long search had met its reward.

CHAPTER IX

ALYSTRA HAD FOUND it very easy to follow Alvin and Khedron without their knowledge. They seemed in a great hurry—something which in itself was most unusual—and never looked back. It had been an amusing game to pursue them along the moving ways, hiding in the crowds yet always keeping them in sight. Towards the end their goal had been obvious; when they left the pattern of streets and went into the Park, they could only be heading for the Tomb of Yarlan Zey. The Park contained no other buildings, and people in such eager haste as Alvin and Khedron would not be interested merely in enjoying the scenery.

Because there was no way of concealing herself on the last few hundred yards to the Tomb, Alystra waited until Khedron and Alvin had disappeared into the marbled gloom. Then, as soon as they were out of sight, she hurried up the grass-covered slope. She felt fairly sure that she could hide behind one of the great pillars long enough to discover what Alvin and Khedron were doing; it did not matter if they detected her after that.

The Tomb consisted of two concentric rings of columns, enclosing a circular court. Except in one sector, the columns screened off the interior completely, and Alystra avoided approaching through this opening, but entered the Tomb from the side. She cautiously negotiated the first ring of columns, saw that there was no one in sight, and tiptoed across to the second. Through the gaps, she could see Yarlan Zey looking out through the entrance, across the park he had built, and beyond that to the city over which he had watched for so many ages.

And there was no one else in all this marble solitude. The Tomb was empty.

At that moment, Alvin and Khedron were a hundred feet underground, in a small, box-like room whose walls seemed to be flowing steadily upwards. That was the only indication of movement; there was no trace of vibration to show that they were sinking swiftly into the earth, descending towards a goal that even now neither of them fully understood.

It had been absurdly easy, for the way had been prepared for them. (By whom wondered Alvin. By the Central Computer? Or by Yarlan Zey himself, when he transformed the city?) The monitor screen had shown them the long, vertical shaft plunging into the depths, but they had followed its course only a little way when the image had blanked out. That meant, Alvin knew, that they were asking for information that the monitor did not possess, and perhaps had never possessed.

He had scarcely framed this thought when the screen came to life once more. On it appeared a brief message, printed in the simplified script which machines had used to communicate with men ever since they had achieved intellectual equality:

STAND WHERE THE STATUE GAZES—AND REMEMBER:
DIASPAR WAS NOT ALWAYS THUS.

The last five words were in larger type, and the meaning of the entire message was obvious to Alvin at once. Mentally-framed code messages had been used for ages to unlock doors or set machines in action. As for "Stand where the statue gazes"—that was really *too* simple.

"I wonder how many people have read this message?" said Alvin thoughtfully.

"Fourteen, to my knowledge," replied Khedron. "And there may have been others." He did not amplify this rather cryptic remark, and Alvin was in too great a hurry to reach the Park to question him further.

They could not be certain that the mechanisms would still respond to the triggering impulse. When they reached the Tomb, it had taken them only a moment to locate the single slab, among all those paving the floor, upon which the gaze of Yarlan Zey was fixed. It was only at first sight that the statue seemed to be looking out across the city; if one stood directly in front of it, one could see that the eyes were downcast and that the elusive smile was directed towards a spot just inside the entrance to the Tomb. Once the secret was realised, there could be no doubt about it. Alvin moved to the next slab, and found that Yarlan Zey was no longer looking towards him.

He rejoined Khedron, and mentally echoed the words that the Jester spoke aloud: DIASPAR WAS NOT ALWAYS THUS. Instantly, as if the millions of years that had lapsed since their last operation had never existed, the waiting machines responded. The great slab of stone on which they were standing began to carry them smoothly into the depths.

Overhead, the patch of blue suddenly flickered out of existence. The shaft was no longer open; there was no danger that anyone should accidentally stumble into it. Alvin wondered fleetingly if another slab of stone had somehow been materialised to replace the one now supporting him and Khedron, then decided against it. The original slab probably still paved the Tomb; the one upon which they were standing might only exist for infinitesimal fractions of a second, being continuously re-created at greater and greater depths in the earth to give the illusion of steady downward movement.

Neither Alvin nor Khedron spoke as the walls flowed silently past them. Khedron was once again wrestling with his conscience, wondering if this time he had gone too far. He could not imagine where this route might lead, if indeed it led anywhere. For the first time in his life, he began to understand the real meaning of fear.

Alvin was not afraid; he was too excited. This was the sensation he had known in the Tower of Loranne, when he had looked out across the untrodden desert and seen the stars conquering the night sky. He had merely gazed at the unknown then; he was being carried towards it now.

The walls ceased to flow past them. A patch of light appeared at one side of their mysteriously moving room, grew brighter and brighter, and was suddenly a door. They stepped through it, took a few paces along the short corridor beyond—and then were standing in a great, circular cavern whose walls came together in a sweeping curve three hundred feet above their heads.

The column down whose interior they had descended seemed far too slim to support the millions of tons of rock above it; indeed it did not seem to be an integral part of the chamber at all, but gave the impression of being an after-thought. Khedron, following Alvin's gaze, arrived at the same conclusion.

"This column," he said, speaking jerkily, as if anxious to find something to say, "was built simply to house the shaft down which we came. It could never have carried the traffic that must have passed through here when Diaspar was still open to the world. *That* came through those tunnels over there; I suppose you recognise what they are?"

Alvin looked towards the walls of the chamber, more than a hundred yards away. Piercing them at regular intervals were large tunnels—twelve of them, radiating in all directions exactly as the moving ways did today. He could see that they sloped gently upwards, and now he recognised the familiar grey surface of the moving ways. These were only the severed stumps of the great roads; the strange material that gave them life was now frozen into immobility. When the Park had been built, the hub of the moving way system had been buried. But it had never been destroyed.

Alvin began to walk towards the nearest of the tunnels. He had gone only a few paces when he realised that something was happening to the ground beneath his feet. *It was becoming transparent.* A few more yards, and he seemed to be standing in mid-air without visible support. He stopped and stared down into the void beneath him.

"Khedron!" he called. "Come and look at this!"

The other joined him, and together they gazed at the marvel beneath their feet. Faintly visible, at an indefinite depth, lay an enormous map—a great network of lines converging towards a spot beneath the central shaft. They stared at it in silence for a moment; then Khedron said quietly: "You realise what this is?"

"I think so," replied Alvin. "It's a map of the entire transport system, and those little circles must be the other cities of Earth. I can just see names beside them, but they're too faint to read."

"There must have been some form of internal illumination once," said Khedron absently. He was tracing the lines beneath his feet, following them with his eyes out towards the walls of the chamber.

"I thought so!" he exclaimed suddenly. "Do you see how all these radiating lines lead towards the small tunnels?"

Alvin had noticed that besides the great arches of the moving ways there were innumerable smaller tunnels leading out of the chamber—tunnels that sloped *downwards* instead of up.

Khedron continued without waiting for a reply.

"It would be hard to think of a simpler system. People would come down the moving ways, select the place they wished to visit, and then follow the appropriate line on the map."

"And what happened to them after that?" asked Alvin. Khedron was silent, his eyes searching out the mystery of those descending tunnels. There were thirty or forty of them, all looking exactly the same. Only the names on the map would have enabled one to distinguish between them, and those names were indecipherable now.

Alvin had wandered away and was circumnavigating the central pillar. Presently his voice came to Khedron, slightly muffled and overlaid with echoes from the walls of the chamber.

"What is it?" called Khedron, not wishing to move as he had nearly succeeded in reading one of the dimly visible groups of characters. But Alvin's voice was insistent, so he went to join him.

Far beneath was the other half of the great map, its faint web-work radiating to the points of the compass. This time, however, not all of it was too dim to be clearly seen, for one of the lines, and only one—was brilliantly illuminated. It seemed to have no connexion with the rest of the system, and pointed like a gleaming arrow to one of the downward-sloping tunnels. Near its end the line transfixed a circle of golden light, and against that circle was the single word LYS. That was all.

For a long time Alvin and Khedron stood gazing down at that silent symbol. To Khedron it was a challenge he knew he could never accept and which, indeed, he would rather did not exist. But to Alvin it hinted at the fulfilment of all his dreams; though the word LYS meant nothing to him, he let it roll around his mouth, tasting its sibilance like some exotic flavour. The blood was pounding in his veins, and his cheeks were flushed as by a fever. He stared around this great concourse, trying to imagine it as it had been in the ancient days, when air transport had come to an end but the cities of Earth still had contact with one another. He thought of the countless millions of years that had passed with the traffic steadily dwindling and the lights on the great map dying one by one, until at last only this single line remained. How long, he wondered, had it gleamed there among its darkened companions, waiting to guide the steps that never came, until Yarlan Zey had sealed the moving ways and closed Diaspar against the world?

And that had been a thousand million years ago. Even then, Lys must have lost touch with Diaspar. It seemed impossible that it could have survived; perhaps, after all, the map meant nothing now.

Khedron broke into his reverie at last. He seemed nervous and ill at ease, not at all like the confident and self-assured person that he had always been in the city above.

"I do not think that we should go any further now," he said. "It may not be safe until—until we are more prepared."

There was wisdom in this, but Alvin recognised the underlying note of fear in Khedron's voice. Had it not been for that, he might have been sensible, but a too-acute awareness of his own valour, combined with a contempt for

Khedron's timidity, drove Alvin onwards. It seemed foolish to have come so far, only to turn back when the goal might be in sight.

"I'm going down that tunnel," he said stubbornly, as if challenging Khedron to stop him. "I want to see where it leads." He set off resolutely, and after a moment's hesitation the Jester followed him along the arrow of light that burned beneath their feet.

As they stepped into the tunnel, they felt the familiar tug of the peristaltic field, and in a moment were being swept effortlessly into the depths. The journey lasted scarcely a minute; when the field released them they were standing at one end of a long narrow chamber in the form of a half-cylinder. At its distant end, two dimly lit tunnels stretched away towards infinity.

Men of almost every civilisation that had existed since the Dawn would have found their surroundings completely familiar, yet to Alvin and Khedron this was a glimpse of another world. The purpose of the long, streamlined machine that lay aimed like a projectile at the far tunnel was obvious, but that made it none the less novel. Its upper portion was transparent, and looking through the walls Alvin could see rows of luxuriously appointed seats. There was no sign of any entrance, and the entire machine was floating about a foot above a single metal rod that stretched away into the distance, disappearing in one of the tunnels. A few yards away another rod led to the second tunnel, but no machine floated above it. Alvin knew, as surely as if he had been told, that somewhere beneath unknown, far-off Lys, that second machine was waiting in another such chamber as this.

Khedron began to talk, a little too swiftly.

"What a peculiar transport system! It could only handle a hundred people at a time, so they could not have expected much traffic. And why did they go to all this trouble to bury themselves in the Earth, if the skies were still open? Perhaps the Invaders would not even permit them to fly, though I find that hard to believe. Or was this built during the transition period, while men still travelled but did not wish to be reminded of space? They could go from city to city, and never see the sky and the stars." He gave a nervous laugh. "I feel sure of one thing, Alvin. When Lys existed, it was much like Diaspar. All cities must be essentially the same. No wonder that they were all abandoned in the end, and emerged into Diaspar. What was the point of having more than one?"

Alvin scarcely heard him. He was busy examining the long projectile, trying to find the entrance. If the machine was controlled by some mental or verbal order, he might never be able to make it obey him, and it would remain a maddening enigma for the rest of his life.

The silently opening door took him completely unawares. There was no sound, no warning, when a section of the wall simply faded from sight and the beautifully designed interior lay open before his eyes.

This was the moment of choice. Until this instant, he had always been able to turn back if he wished. But if he stepped inside that welcoming door, he knew what would happen, though not where it would lead. He would no longer be in control of his own destiny, but would have placed himself in the keeping of unknown forces.

He scarcely hesitated. He was afraid to hold back, being fearful that if he waited too long this moment might never come again—or that if it did, his courage might not match his desire for knowledge. Khedron opened his mouth in anxious protest, but before he could speak, Alvin had stepped through the entrance. He turned to face Khedron, who was standing framed in the barely visible rectangle of the doorway, and for a moment there was a strained silence while each waited for the other to speak.

The decision was made for them. There was a faint flicker of translucence, and the wall of the machine had closed again. Even as Alvin raised his hand in farewell, the long cylinder started to ease itself forward. Before it had entered the tunnel, it was already moving faster than a man could run.

There had been a time when, every day, millions of men made such journeys, in machines basically the same as this, as they shuttled between their homes and their humdrum jobs. Since that far-off day, Man had explored the Universe and returned again to Earth—had won an empire, and had it wrested from his grasp. Now such a journey was being made again, in a machine wherein legions of forgotten and unadventurous men would have felt completely at home.

And it was to be the most momentous journey any human being had undertaken for a billion years.

Alystra had searched the Tomb a dozen times, though once was quite sufficient, for there was nowhere anyone could hide. After the first shock of surprise, she had wondered if what she had followed across the Park had not been Alvin and Khedron at all, but only their projections. But that made no sense; projections were materialised at any spot one wished to visit, without the trouble of going there in person. No sane person would "walk" his projected image a couple of miles, taking half an hour to reach his destination, when he could be there instantly. No; it was the real Alvin, and the real Khedron, that she had followed into the Tomb.

Somewhere, then, there must be a secret entrance. She might as well look for it while she was waiting for them to come back.

As luck would have it, she missed Khedron's reappearance, for she was examining a column behind the statue when he emerged on the other side of it. She heard his footsteps, turned towards him, and saw at once that he was alone.

"Where is Alvin?" she cried.

It was some time before the Jester answered. He looked distraught and irresolute, and Alystra had to repeat her question before he took any notice of her. He did not seem in the least surprised to find her here.

"I do not know where he is," he answered at last. "I can only tell you that he is on his way to Lys. Now you know as much as I do."

It was never wise to take Khedron's words at their face value. But Alystra needed no further assurance that the Jester was not playing his role today. He was telling her the truth—whatever it might mean.

CHAPTER X

WHEN THE DOOR closed behind him, Alvin slumped into the nearest seat. All strength seemed suddenly to have been drained from his legs: at last he knew, as he had never known before, that fear of the unknown that haunted all his fellow-men. He felt himself trembling in every limb, and his sight became misty and uncertain. Could he have escaped from this speeding machine he would willingly have done so, even at the price of abandoning all his dreams.

It was not fear alone that overwhelmed him, but a sense of unutterable loneliness. All that he knew and loved was in Diaspar; even if he was going into no danger, he might never see his world again. He knew, as no man had known for ages, what it meant to leave one's home for ever. In this moment of desolation, it seemed to him of no importance whether the path he was following led to peril or to safety; all that mattered to him now was that it led away from home.

The mood slowly passed; the dark shadows lifted from his mind. He began to pay attention to his surroundings, and to see what he could learn from the unbelievably ancient vehicle in which he was travelling. It did not strike Alvin as particularly strange or marvellous that this buried transport system should still function perfectly after such aeons of time. It was not preserved in the eternity circuits of the city's own monitors, but there must be similar circuits elsewhere guarding it from change or decay.

For the first time he noticed the indicator board that formed part of the forward wall. It carried a brief but reassuring message:

LYS

35 MINUTES

Even as he watched, the number changed to "34". That, at least, was useful information, though as he had no idea of the machine's speed it told him nothing about the length of the journey. The walls of the tunnel were one continual blur of grey, and the only sensation of movement was a very slight vibration he would never have noticed had he not looked for it.

Diaspar must be many miles away by now, and above him would be the desert with its shifting sand-dunes. Perhaps at this very moment he was racing below the broken hills he had watched so often from the Tower of Loranne.

His imagination sped onwards to Lys, as if impatient to arrive ahead of his body. What sort of city would it be? No matter how hard he tried, he could only picture another and smaller version of Diaspar. He wondered if it still existed, then assured himself that not otherwise would this machine be carrying him swiftly through the earth.

Suddenly there was a distinct change in the vibration underfoot. The vehicle must have passed more swiftly than he had thought; somewhat surprised, Alvin glanced at the indicator.

LYS

23 MINUTES

Feeling puzzled, and a little worried, he pressed his face against the side of the machine. His speed was still blurring the walls of the tunnel into a featureless grey, yet now from time to time he could catch a glimpse of markings that disappeared almost as quickly as they came. And at each disappearance, they seemed to remain in his field of vision for a little longer.

Then, without warning, the walls of the tunnel were snatched away on either side. The machine was passing, still at a very great speed, through an enormously empty space, far larger even than the chamber of the moving ways.

Peering in wonder through the transparent walls, Alvin could glimpse beneath him an intricate network of guiding rods, rods that crossed and crisscrossed to disappear into a maze of tunnels on either side. A flood of bluish light poured down from the arched dome of the ceiling, and silhouetted against the glare he could just make out the frameworks of great machines. The light was so brilliant that it pained the eyes, and Alvin knew that this place had not been intended for man. A moment later, his vehicle flashed past row after row of cylinders, lying motionless above their guide rails. They were much larger than the one in which he was travelling, and Alvin guessed that they must have been used for transporting freight. Around them were grouped incomprehensible, many-joined mechanisms, all silent and stilled.

Almost as quickly as it had appeared, the vast and lonely chamber vanished behind him. Its passing left a feeling of awe in Alvin's mind; for the first time he really understood the meaning of that great, darkened map below Diaspar. The world was more full of wonder than he had ever dreamed.

Alvin glanced again at the indicator. It had not changed; he had taken less than a minute to flash through the great cavern. The machine was accelerating again; though there was little sense of motion, the tunnel walls were flowing past on either side at a speed he could not even guess.

It seemed an age before that indefinable change of vibration occurred again. Now the indicator was reading:

LYS

1 MINUTE

and that minute was the longest that Alvin had ever known. More and more slowly moved the machine; this was no mere slackening of its speed. It was coming at last to rest.

Smoothly and silently the long cylinder slid out of the tunnel into a cavern that might have been the twin of the one below Diaspar. For a moment Alvin was too excited to see anything clearly; the door had been open for a considerable time before he realised that he could leave the vehicle. As he hurried out of the machine, he caught a last glimpse of the indicator. Its wording had now changed and its message was infinitely reassuring:

DIASPAR

35 MINUTES

As he began to search for a way out of the chamber, Alvin found the first hint that he might be in a civilisation different from his own. The way to the surface clearly lay through a low, wide tunnel at one end of the cavern—and leading up through the tunnel was a flight of steps. Such a thing was extremely rare in Diaspar; the architects of the city had built ramps or sloping corridors whenever there was a change of level. This was a survival from the days when most robots had moved on wheels, and so found steps an impossible barrier.

The stairway was very short, and ended against doors that opened automatically at Alvin's approach. He walked into a small room like that which had carried him down the shaft under the Tomb of Yarlan Zey, and was not surprised when a few minutes later the doors opened again to reveal a vaulted corridor rising slowly to an archway that framed a semicircle of sky. There had been no sensation of movement, but Alvin knew that he must have risen many hundreds of feet. He hurried forward up the slope to the sunlit opening, all fear forgotten in his eagerness to see what lay before him.

He was standing at the brow of a low hill, and for an instant it seemed as if he were once again in the central park of Diaspar. Yet if this were indeed a park, it was too enormous for his mind to grasp. The city he had expected to see was nowhere visible. As far as the eye could reach there was nothing but forest and grass-covered plains.

Then Alvin lifted his eyes to the horizon, and there above the trees, sweeping from right to left in a great arc that encircled the world, was a line of stone which would have dwarfed the mightiest giants of Diaspar. It was so far away that its details were blurred by sheer distance, but there was something about its outlines that Alvin found puzzling. Then his eyes became at last accustomed to the scale of that colossal landscape. And he knew that those far-off walls had not been built by man.

Time had not conquered everything; Earth still possessed mountains of which she could be proud.

For a long time Alvin stood at the mouth of the tunnel slowly growing accustomed to the strange world in which he had found himself. He was half stunned by the impact of sheer size and space; that ring of misty mountains could have enclosed a dozen cities as large as Diaspar. Search as he might, however, Alvin could see no trace of human life. Yet the road that led down the hillside seemed well-kept; he could do no better than accept its guidance.

At the foot of the hill, the road disappeared between great trees that almost hid the sun. As Alvin walked into their shadow, a strange medley of scents and sounds greeted him. The rustle of the wind among the leaves he had known before, but underlying that there were a thousand vague noises that conveyed nothing to his mind. Unknown colours assailed him, smells that had been lost even to the memory of his race. The warmth, the profusion of scent and colour, and the unseen presence of a million living things, smote him with almost physical violence.

He came upon the lake without any warning. The trees to the right suddenly ended, and before him was a great expanse of water, dotted with tiny islands. Never in his life had Alvin seen so much water; by comparison, the largest pools in Diaspar were scarcely more than puddles. He walked slowly down to the edge of the lake and cupped the warm water in his hands, letting it trickle through his fingers.

The great silver fish that suddenly forced its way through the underwater reeds was the first non-human creature that Alvin had ever seen. It should have been utterly strange to him, yet its shape teased his mind with a haunting familiarity. As it hung there in the pale green void, its fins a faint blur of motion, it seemed the very embodiment of power and speed. Here incorporated in living flesh, were the graceful lines of the great ships that had once ruled the skies of the Earth. Evolution and science had come to the same answers; and the work of Nature had lasted longer.

At last Alvin broke the lake's enchantment, and continued along the winding road. The forest closed around him once more, but only for a little while. Presently the road ended, in a great clearing half a mile wide and twice as long—and Alvin understood why he had seen no trace of man before.

The clearing was full of low, two-storeyed buildings, coloured in soft shades that rested the eye even in the full glare of the sun. Most were of clean, straight-forward design, but several were built in a complex architectural style involving the use of fluted columns and gracefully fretted stone. In these buildings, which seemed of great age, the immeasurably ancient device of the pointed arch was used.

As he walked slowly towards the village, Alvin was still struggling to grasp his new surroundings. Nothing was familiar; even the air changed, with its hint of throbbing, unknown life. And the tall, golden-haired people going among the buildings with such unconscious grace were obviously of a different stock from the men of Diaspar.

They took no notice of Alvin, and that was strange, for his clothing was totally different from theirs. Since the temperature never changed in Diaspar, dress there was purely ornamental and often extremely elaborate. Here it seemed mainly functional, designed for use rather than display, and frequently consisted of a single sheet draped round the body.

It was not until Alvin was well inside the village that the people of Lys reacted to his presence, and then their response took a somewhat unexpected form. A group of five men emerged from one of the houses and began to walk purposefully towards him—almost as if, indeed, they had been expecting his arrival. Alvin felt a sudden, heady excitement and the blood pounded in his veins. He thought of all the fateful meetings men must have had with other races on far-off worlds. Those he was meeting now were of his own species—but how far had they diverged in the aeons that had sundered them from Diaspar?

The delegation came to a halt a few feet away from Alvin. Its leader smiled, holding out his hand in the ancient gesture of friendship.

"We thought it best to meet you here," he said. "Our home is very different from Diaspar, and the walk from the terminus gives visitors a chance to become—acclimatised."

Alvin accepted the outstretched hand, but for a moment was too surprised to reply. Now he understood why all the other villagers had ignored him so completely.

"You knew I was coming?" he said at length.

"Of course. We always know when the carriers start to move. Tell me— how did you discover the way? It has been such a long time since the last visit that we feared the secret had been lost."

The speaker was interrupted by one of his companions.

"I think we'd better restrain our curiosity, Gerane. Seranis is waiting."

The name "Seranis" was preceded by a word unfamiliar to Alvin, and he assumed that it was a title of some kind. He had no difficulty in understanding the others, and it never occurred to him that there was anything surprising about this. Diaspar and Lys shared the same linguistic heritage, and the ancient invention of sound recording had long ago frozen speech in an unbreakable mould.

Gerane gave a shrug of mock resignation. "Very well," he smiled, "Seranis has few privileges—I should not rob her of this one."

As they walked deeper into the village, Alvin studied the men around him. They appeared kindly and intelligent, but these were virtues he had taken for granted all his life, and he was looking for ways in which they differed from a similar group in Diaspar. There were differences, but it was hard to define them. They were all somewhat taller than Alvin, and two of them showed the unmistakable marks of physical age. Their skins were very brown, and in all their movements they seemed to radiate a vigour and zest which Alvin found refreshing, though at the same time a little bewildering. He smiled as he remembered Khedron's prophecy that, if he ever reached Lys, he would find it exactly the same as Diaspar.

The people of the village now watched with frank curiosity as Alvin followed his guides; there was no longer any pretence that they took him for granted. Suddenly there were shrill, high-pitched shouts from the trees on the right, and a group of small, excited creatures burst out of the woods, and crowded around Alvin. He stopped in utter amazement, unable to believe his eyes. Here was something that his world had lost so long ago that it lay in the realms of mythology. This was the way that life had once begun; these noisy, fascinating creatures were human children.

Alvin watched them with wondering disbelief—and with another sensation which tugged at his heart but which he could not yet identify. No other sight could have brought home to him so vividly his remoteness from the world he knew. Diaspar had paid, and paid in full, the price of immortality.

The party halted before the largest building Alvin had yet seen. It stood in the centre of the village and from a flag-pole on its small circular tower a green pennant floated along the breeze.

All but Gerane dropped behind as he entered the building. Inside it was quiet and cool; sunlight filtering through the translucent walls lit up everything with a soft, restful glow. The floor was smooth and resilient, inlaid with fine mosaics. On the walls, an artist of great ability and power had depicted a set of forest scenes. Mingled with these paintings were other murals which conveyed nothing to Alvin's mind, yet which were attractive and pleasant to look upon. Let into one wall was a rectangular screen filled with a shifting maze of colours—presumably a visiphone receiver, though a rather small one.

They walked together up a short circular stairway that led them out on to the flat roof of the building. From this point, the entire village was visible, and Alvin could see that it consisted of about a hundred buildings. In the distance the trees opened out to enclose wide meadows, where animals of several different types were grazing. Alvin could not imagine what these were; most of them were quadrupeds, but some seemed to have six or eight legs.

Seranis was waiting for him in the shadow of the tower. Alvin wondered how old she was; her long, golden hair was touched with grey, which he guessed must be some indication of age. The presence of children, with all the consequences that implied, had left him very confused. Where there was birth, then surely there must be death, and the life-span here in Lys might be very different from that in Diaspar. He could not tell whether Seranis was fifty, five hundred, or five thousand years old, but looking into her eyes he could sense that wisdom and depth of experience he sometimes felt when he was with Jeserac.

She pointed to a small seat, but though her eyes smiled a welcome she said nothing until Alvin had made himself comfortable—or as comfortable as he could be under that intense though friendly scrutiny. Then she sighed, and addressed Alvin in a low, gentle voice.

"This is an occasion which does not often arise, so you will excuse me if I do not know the correct behaviour. But there are certain rights due to a guest, even if an unexpected one. Before we talk, there is something I should warn you. I can read your mind."

She smiled at Alvin's consternation, and added quickly: "There is no need to let that worry you. No right is respected more strongly than that of mental privacy. I will enter your mind only if you invite me to. But it would not be fair to hide this fact from you, and it will explain why we find speech somewhat slow and difficult. It is not often used here."

This revelation, though slightly alarming, did not surprise Alvin. Once both men and machines had possessed this power, and the unchanging machines could still read their master's orders. But in Diaspar, man himself had lost the gift he had once shared with his slaves.

"I do not know what brought you from your world to ours," continued Seranis, "but if you are looking for life, your search has ended. Apart from Diaspar, there is only desert beyond our mountains."

It was strange that Alvin, who had questioned accepted beliefs so often before, did not doubt the words of Seranis. His only action was one of sadness that all his teaching had been so nearly true.

"Tell me about Lys," he begged. "Why have you been cut off from Diaspar for so long, when you seem to know so much about us?"

Seranis smiled at his eagerness.

"Presently," she said. "But first I would like to know something about you. Tell me how you found the way here, and why you came."

Haltingly at first, and then with growing confidence, Alvin told his story. He had never spoken with such freedom before; here at last was someone who would not laugh at his dreams, because they knew those dreams were true. Once or twice Seranis interrupted him with swift questions when he mentioned some aspect of Diaspar which was unfamiliar to her. It was hard for Alvin to realise that things which were part of his everyday life would be meaningless to someone who had never lived in the city and knew nothing of its complex culture and social organisation. Seranis listened with such understanding that he took her comprehension for granted; not until later did he realise that many other minds besides hers were listening to his words.

When he had finished, there was silence for a while. Then Seranis looked at him and said quickly: "Why did you come to Lys?"

Alvin glanced at her in surprise.

"I've told you," he said. "I wanted to explore the world. Everyone told me that there was only desert beyond the city, but I had to see for myself."

"And that was the only reason?"

Alvin hesitated. When at last he answered, it was not the indomitable explorer who spoke, but the lost child who had been born into an alien world.

"No," he said slowly, "that wasn't the only reason—though I did not know it until now, I was lonely."

"Lonely? In Diaspar?" There was a smile on the lips of Seranis, but sympathy in her eyes, and Alvin knew that she expected no further answer.

Now that he had told his story, he waited for her to keep her share of the bargain. Presently, Seranis rose to her feet, and began to pace to and fro on the roof.

"I know the questions you wish to ask," she said. "Some of them I can answer, but it would be wearisome to do it in words. If you will open your mind to me, I will tell you what you need to know. You can trust me: I will take nothing from you without your permission."

"What do you want me to do?" said Alvin cautiously.

"Will yourself to accept my help—look at my eyes—and forget everything," commanded Seranis.

Alvin was never sure what happened then. There was a total eclipse of all his senses, and though he could never remember acquiring it, when he looked into his mind the knowledge was there.

He saw back into the past, not clearly, but as a man on some high mountain might look out across a misty plain. He understood that Man had not always been a city dweller, and that since the machines gave him freedom from toil there had always been a rivalry between two different types of civilisation. In the Dawn Ages there had been thousands of cities, but a large part of mankind had preferred to live in relatively small communities. Universal transport and instantaneous communications had given them all the contact they required with the rest of the world, and they felt no need to live huddled together with millions of their fellows.

Lys had been little different, in the early days, from hundreds of other communities. But gradually, over the ages, it developed an independent culture which was one of the highest that mankind had ever known. It was a culture based largely upon the direct use of mental power, and this set it apart from the rest of human society, which came to rely more and more upon machines.

Through the aeons, as they advanced along their different roads, the gulf between Lys and the cities widened. It was bridged only in times of great crisis; when the Moon was falling, its destruction was carried out by the scientists of Lys. So also was the defence of Earth against the Invaders, who were held at bay in the final battle of Shalmirane.

The great ordeal exhausted mankind; one by one the cities died and the desert rolled over them. As the population fell, humanity began the migration which was to make Diaspar the last and greatest of all cities.

Most of these changes did not affect Lys, but it had its own battle to fight —the battle against the desert. The natural barrier of the mountains was not enough, and many ages passed before the great oasis was made secure. The picture was blurred here, perhaps deliberately. Alvin could not see what had been done to give Lys the virtual eternity that Diaspar had achieved.

The voice of Seranis seemed to come to him from a great distance—yet it was not her voice alone, for it was merged into a symphony of words, as though many other tongues were chanting in unison with hers.

"That, very briefly, is our history. You will see that even in the Dawn Ages we had little to do with the cities, though their people often came into our land. We never hindered them, for many of our greatest men came from Outside, but when the cities were dying we did not wish to be involved in their downfall. With the ending of air transport, there was only one way into Lys—the carrier system from Diaspar. It was closed at your end, when the Park was built—and you forgot us, though we have never forgotten you.

"Diaspar has surprised us. We expected it to go the way of all other cities, but instead it has achieved a stable culture that may last as long as Earth. It is not a culture that we admire, yet we are glad that those who wish to escape have been able to do so. More than you might think have made the journey, and they have almost always been outstanding men who brought something of value with them when they came to Lys."

The voice faded; the paralysis of Alvin's senses ebbed away and he was himself again. He saw with astonishment that the sun had fallen far below the trees and that the eastern sky already held a hint of night. Somewhere a great bell vibrated with a throbbing boom that pulsed slowly into silence, leaving the air tense with mystery and premonition. Alvin found himself trembling slightly, not with the first touch of the evening's chill, but through sheer awe and wonder at all that he had learned. It was very late, and he was far from home. He had a sudden need to see his friends again, and to be among the familiar sights and screens of Diaspar.

"I must return," he said. "Khedron—my parents—they will be expecting me."

That was not wholly true; Khedron would certainly be wondering what had happened to him, but as far as Alvin was aware no one else knew that he had left Diaspar. He could not have explained the reason for this mild deceit, and was slightly ashamed of himself immediately he had uttered the words.

Seranis looked at him thoughtfully.

"I am afraid it is not as easy as that," she said.

"What do you mean?" asked Alvin. "Won't the carrier that brought me here take me back again?" He still refused to face the fact that he might be held in Lys against his will, though the idea had briefly crossed his mind.

For the first time, Seranis seemed slightly ill at ease.

"We have been talking about you," she said—not explaining who the "we" might be, nor exactly how they had consulted together. "If you return to Diaspar, the whole city will know about us. Even if you promised to say nothing you would find it impossible to keep our secret."

"Why should you wish it kept?" asked Alvin. "Surely it would be a good thing for both our peoples if they could meet again."

Seranis looked displeased.

"We do not think so," she said. "If the gates were opened, our land would be flooded with the idly curious and the sensation seekers. As it is now, only the best of your people have ever reached us."

This reply radiated so much unconscious superiority yet it was based on such false assumptions, that Alvin felt his annoyance quite eclipse his alarm.

"That isn't true," he said flatly. "I do not believe you would find another person in Diaspar who would leave the city, even if he wanted to—even if he knew that there was somewhere to go. If you let me return, it would make no difference to Lys."

"It is not my decision," explained Seranis, "and you underestimate the powers of the mind if you think that the barriers that keep your people inside their city can never be broken. However, we do not wish to hold you here against your will, but if you return to Diaspar we must erase all memories of Lys from your mind." She hesitated for a moment. "This has never arisen before; all your predecessors came here to stay."

Here was a choice that Alvin refused to accept. He wanted to explore Lys, to learn all its secrets, to discover the ways in which it differed from his own home. But equally he was determined to return to Diaspar, so that he could prove to his friends that he had been no idle dreamer. He could not understand the reasons prompting this desire for secrecy; even if he had, it would not have made any difference to his behaviour.

He realised that he must play for time, or else convince Seranis that what she asked him was impossible.

"Khedron knows where I am," he said. "You cannot erase *his* memories."

Seranis smiled. It was a pleasant smile, and one that in any other circumstances would have been friendly enough. But behind it Alvin glimpsed, for the first time, the presence of overwhelming and implacable power.

"You underestimate us, Alvin," she replied. "That would be very easy. I can reach Diaspar more quickly than I can cross Lys. Other men have come here before, and some of them told their friends where they were going. Yet those friends forgot them, and they vanished from the history of Diaspar."

Alvin had been foolish to ignore this possibility, though it was obvious now that Seranis had pointed it out. He wondered how many times, in the millions of years since the two cultures were separated, men from Lys had gone into Diaspar in order to preserve their jealously guarded secret. And he wondered just how extensive were the mental powers which these strange people possessed and did not hesitate to use.

Was it safe to make any plans at all? Seranis had promised that she would not read his mind without his consent, but he wondered if there might be circumstances in which that promise would not be kept. . . .

"Surely," he said, "you don't expect me to make the decision at once. Cannot I see something of your country before I make my choice?"

"Of course," replied Seranis. "You can stay here as long as you wish, and still return to Diaspar eventually if you change your mind. But if you can decide within the next few days, it will be very much easier. You do not want your friends to be worried, and the longer you are missing the harder it will be for us to make the necessary adjustments."

Alvin would appreciate that; he would like to know just what those "adjustments" were. Presumably someone from Lys would contact Khedron—without the Jester ever being aware of it—and tamper with his mind. The fact of Alvin's disappearance could not be concealed, but the information which he and Khedron had discovered could be obliterated. As the ages passed, Alvin's name would join that of the other Uniques who had mysteriously vanished without trace, and had then been forgotten.

There were many mysteries here, and he seemed no closer to solving any of them. Was there any purpose behind the curious, one-sided relationship between Lys and Diaspar, or was it merely an historical accident? Who and what were the Uniques, and if the people from Lys could enter Diaspar, why had they not cancelled the memory circuits that held the clue to their existence? Perhaps that was the only question to which Alvin could give a plausible answer. The Central Computer might be too stubborn an opponent to tackle, and would hardly be affected by even the most advanced of mental techniques. . . .

He put these problems aside; one day, when he had learned a great deal more, he might have some chance of answering them. It was idle to speculate, to build pyramids of surmise on a foundation of ignorance.

"Very well," he said—though not too graciously, for he was still annoyed that this unexpected obstacle had been placed in his path. "I'll give you my answer as soon as I can—if you will show me what your land is like."

"Good," said Seranis, and this time her smile held no hidden threat. "We are proud of Lys, and it will be a pleasure to show you how men can live without the aid of cities. Meanwhile, there is no need for you to worry—your friends will not be alarmed by your absence. We shall see to that, if only for our own protection."

It was the first time Seranis had ever made a promise which she could not keep.

CHAPTER XI

T RY AS SHE would, Alystra could extract no further information from Khedron. The Jester had recovered quickly from his initial shock, and from the panic which had sent him flying back to the surface when he found himself alone in the depths beneath the Tomb. He also felt ashamed of his cowardly behaviour, and wondered if he would ever have the courage to return to the chamber of the Moving Ways and the network of world-ranging tunnels which radiated from it. Although he felt that Alvin had been impatient, if not indeed foolhardy, he did not really believe that he would run into any danger. He would return in his own good time, Khedron was certain of that. Well, almost certain; there was just enough doubt to make him feel the need for caution. It would be wise, he decided, to say as little as possible for the time being, and to pass the whole thing off as another joke.

Unfortunately for this plan, he had not been able to mask his emotions when Alystra encountered him on his return to the surface. She had seen the fear written so unmistakably in his eyes, and had at once interpreted it as meaning that Alvin was in danger. All Khedron's reassurances were in vain, and she became more and more angry with him as they walked together back through the Park. At first Alystra had wanted to remain at the Tomb, waiting for Alvin to return in whatever mysterious manner he had vanished. Khedron had managed to convince her that this would be a waste of time, and was relieved when she followed him back to the city. There was a chance that Alvin might return almost at once, and he did not wish anyone else to discover the secret of Yarlan Zey.

By the time they had reached the city, it was obvious to Khedron that his evasive tactics had failed completely and that the situation was seriously out of hand. It was the first time in his life that he had ever been at a loss, and had not felt himself capable of dealing with any problem that arose. His immediate and irrational fear was being slowly replaced by a profounder and more firmly based alarm. Until now, Khedron had given little thought to the consequences of his actions. His own interests, and a mild but genuine sympathy towards Alvin, had been sufficient motive for all that he had done. Though he had given encouragement and assistance to Alvin, he had never believed that anything like this could ever really happen.

Despite the gulf of years and experience between them, Alvin's will had always been more powerful than his own. It was too late to do anything about it now; Khedron felt that events were sweeping him along towards a climax utterly beyond his control.

In view of this, it was a little unfair that Alystra obviously regarded him as Alvin's evil genius and showed an inclination to blame him for all that had happened. Alystra was not really vindictive, but she was annoyed and part of her annoyance focused on Khedron. If any action of hers caused him trouble, she would be the last person to be sorry.

They parted in stony silence when they had reached the great circular way that surrounded the Park. Khedron watched Alystra disappear into the distance, and wondered wearily what plans were brewing in her mind.

There was only one thing of which he could be certain now. Boredom would not be a serious problem for a considerable time to come. ·

Alystra acted swiftly, and with intelligence. She did not bother to contact Eriston and Etania; Alvin's parents were pleasant nonentities for whom she felt some affection but no respect. They would only waste time in futile arguments, and would then do exactly as Alystra was doing now.

Jeserac listened to her story without apparent emotion. If he was alarmed or surprised, he concealed it well—so well that Alystra was somewhat disappointed. It seemed to her that nothing so extraordinary and important as this had ever happened before, and Jeserac's matter-of-fact behaviour made her feel deflated. When she had finished, he questioned her at some length, and hinted, without actually saying so, that she might have made a mistake. What reason was there for supposing that Alvin had really left the city? Perhaps it had all been a trick at her expense; the fact that Khedron was involved made this seem highly probable. Alvin might be laughing at her, concealed somewhere in Diaspar, at this very moment.

The only positive reaction she got out of Jeserac was a promise to make inquiries and to contact her again within a day. In the meantime she was not to worry, and it would also be best if she said nothing to anyone else about the whole affair. There was no need to spread alarm over an incident which would probably be cleared up in a few hours.

Alystra left Jeserac in a mood of mild frustration. She would have been more satisfied could she have seen his behaviour immediately after she had left.

Jeserac had friends on the Council; he had been a member himself in his long life, and might be again if he was unlucky. He called three of his most influential colleagues, and cautiously aroused their interest. As Alvin's tutor, he was well aware of his own delicate position, and was anxious to safeguard himself. For the present, the fewer who knew what had happened, the better.

It was immediately agreed that the first thing to do was to contact Khedron and ask him for an explanation. There was only one defect in this excellent plan. Khedron had anticipated it, and was nowhere to be found.

If there was any ambiguity about Alvin's position, his hosts were very careful not to remind him of it. He was free to go anywhere he wished in Airlee, the little village over which Seranis ruled—though that was too strong a word to describe her position. Sometimes it seemed to Alvin that she was a benevolent dictator, but at others it appeared that she had no powers at all. So far he had failed completely to understand the social system of Lys, either because it was too simple or else so complex that its ramifications eluded him. All he had discovered for certain was that Lys was divided into innumerable villages, of which Airlee was a quite typical example. Yet in a sense there were no typical examples, for Alvin had been assured that every village tried to be as unlike its neighbours as posible. It was all extremely confusing.

Though it was very small, and contained less than a thousand people, Airlee was full of surprises. There was hardly a single aspect of life which did not differ from its counterpart in Diaspar. The differences extended even to such fundamentals as speech. Only the children used their voices for normal communication; the adults scarcely ever spoke, and after a while Alvin decided that they did so only out of politeness to him. It was a curiously frustrating experience to feel oneself enmeshed in a great net of soundless and undetectable words, but after a while Alvin grew accustomed to it. It seemed surprising that vocal speech had survived at all since there was no longer any use for it, but Alvin later discovered that the people of Lys were very fond of singing, and indeed of all forms of music. Without this incentive, it was very likely that they would long ago have become completely mute.

They were always busy, engaged on tasks or problems which were usually incomprehensible to Alvin. When he could understand what they were doing, much of their work seemed quite unnecessary. A considerable part of their food, for example, was actually grown, and not synthesised in accordance with patterns worked out ages ago. When Alvin commented on this, it was patiently explained to him that the people of Lys liked to watch things grow, to carry out complicated genetic experiments, and to evolve ever more subtle tastes and flavours. Airlee was famous for its fruit, but when Alvin ate some choice samples they seemed to him no better than those he could have conjured up in Diaspar by no more effort than raising a finger.

At first he wondered if the people of Lys had forgotten or had never possessed, the powers and machines which he took for granted and upon which all life in Diaspar was based. He soon found that this was not the case. The tools and the knowledge were there, but they were used only when it was essential. The most striking example of this was provided by the transport system, if it could be dignified by such a name. For short distances, people walked, and seemed to enjoy it. If they were in a hurry, or had small loads to move, they used animals which had obviously been developed for the purpose. The freight-carrying species was a low, six-legged beast, very docile and strong but of poor intelligence. The racing animals were of a different breed altogether, normally walking on four legs but using only their heavily-muscled hind limbs when they really got up speed. They could cross the entire width of Lys in a few hours, and the passenger rode in a pivoted seat strapped on the creature's back. Nothing in the world would have induced Alvin to risk such a ride, though it was a very popular sport among the younger men. Their finely-bred steeds were the aristocrats of the animal world, and were well aware of it. They had fairly large vocabularies and Alvin overheard them talking boastfully among themselves about past and future victories. When he tried to be friendly and attempted to join in the conversation, they pretended that they could not understand him, and if he persisted would go bouncing off in outraged dignity.

These two varieties of animal sufficed for all ordinary needs, and gave their owners a great deal of pleasure which no mechanical contrivances could have done. But when extreme speed was required, or vast loads had to be moved—the machines were there, and were used without hesitation.

Though the animal life of Lys presented Alvin with a whole world of new interests and surprises, it was the two extremes of human population range that fascinated him most of all. The very young and the very old—both were equally strange and equally amazing. Airlee's most senior inhabitant had barely attained his second century, and had only a few more years of life before him. When *he* had reached that age, Alvin reminded himself, his body would scarcely have altered—whereas this old man, who had no chain of future existences to look forward to as compensation, had almost exhausted his physical powers. His hair was completely white and his face an unbelievably intricate mass of wrinkles. He seemed to spend most of his time sitting in the sun, or walking slowly round the village exchanging greetings with everyone he met. As far as Alvin could tell he was completely contented, asking no more of life, and was not distressed by its approaching end.

Here was a philosophy so much at variance with that of Diaspar as to be completely beyond Alvin's comprehension. Why should anyone accept death when it was so unnecessary, when you had the choice of living for a thousand years and then leaping forward through the millennia to make a new start in a world that you had helped to shape? This was one mystery he was determined to solve as soon as he had the chance of discussing it frankly. It was very hard for him to believe that Lys had made this choice of its own free will, if it knew the alternative that existed.

He found part of his answer among the children, those little creatures who were as strange to him as any of the animals of Lys. He spent much of his time among them, watching them at their play and eventually being accepted by them as a friend. Sometimes it seemed to him that they were not human at all, their motives, their logic and even their language were so alien. He would look unbelievably at the adults and ask himself how it was possible that they could have evolved from these extraordinary creatures who seemed to spend most of their lives in a private world of their own.

And yet, even while they baffled him, they aroused within his heart a feeling he had never known before. When—which was not often, but sometimes happened—they burst into tears of frustration or despair, their tiny disappointments seemed to him more tragic than Man's long retreat after the loss of his galactic empire. That was something too huge and remote for comprehension, but the weeping of a child could pierce one to the heart.

Alvin had met love in Diaspar, but now he was learning something equally precious, and without which love itself could never reach its highest fulfilment but must remain ever incomplete. He was learning tenderness.

If Alvin was studying Lys, Lys was also studying him, and was not dissatisfied with what it had found. He had been in Airlee for three days when Seranis suggested that he might like to go further afield and to see something more of her country. It was a proposal he accepted at once—on condition that he was not expected to ride one of the village's prize racing beasts.

"I can assure you," said Seranis, with a rare flash of humour, "that no one here would dream of risking one of their precious animals. Since this is an exceptional case, I will arrange transport in which you will feel more at home. Hilvar will act as your guide, but of course you can go wherever you please."

Alvin wondered if that was strictly true. He imagined that there would be some objection if he tried to return to the little hill from whose summit he had first emerged into Lys. However, that did not worry him for the moment as he was in no hurry to go back to Diaspar, and indeed had given little thought to the problem after his initial meeting with Seranis. Life here was still so interesting and so novel that he was still quite content to live in the present.

He appreciated Seranis' gesture in offering her son as his guide, though doubtless Hilvar had been given careful instructions to see that he did not get into mischief. It had taken Alvin some time to get accustomed to Hilvar, for a reason which he could not very well explain to him without hurting his feelings. Physical perfection was so universal in Diaspar that personal beauty had been completely devalued; men noticed it no more than the air they breathed. This was not the case in Lys, and the most flattering adjective that could be applied to Hilvar was "homely". By Alvin's standards, he was downright ugly, and for a while he had deliberately avoided him. If Hilvar was aware of this, he showed no sign of it, and it was not long before his good-natured friendliness had broken through the barrier between them. The time was to come when Alvin would be so accustomed to Hilvar's broad, twisted smile, his strength and his gentleness that he could scarcely believe he had ever found him unattractive, and would not have had him changed for any consideration in the world.

They left Airlee soon after dawn in a small vehicle which Hilvar called a ground-car, and which apparently worked on the same principle as the machine that had brought Alvin from Diaspar. It floated in the air a few inches above the turf, and although there was no sign of any guide-rail, Hilvar told him that the cars could run only on predetermined routes. All the centres of population were linked together in this fashion, but during his entire stay in Lys Alvin never saw another ground-car in use.

Hilvar had put a great deal of effort into organising this expedition, and was obviously looking forward to it quite as much as Alvin. He had planned the route with his own interests in mind, for natural history was his consuming passion and he hoped to find new types of insect life in the relatively un-inhabited regions of Lys which they would be visiting. He intended to travel as far south as the machine could take them, and the rest of the way they would have to go on foot. Not realising the full implication of this, Alvin made no objections.

They had a companion with them on the journey—Krif, the most spectacular of Hilvar's many pets. When Krif was resting, his six gauzy wings lay folded along his body, which glittered through them like a jewelled sceptre. If some-thing disturbed him, he would rise into the air with a flicker of iridescence and a faint whirring of invisible wings. Though the great insect would come when called and would—sometimes—obey simple orders—it was almost wholly mindless. Yet it had a definite personality of its own, and for some reason was suspicious of Alvin, whose sporadic attempts to gain its confidence always ended in failure.

To Alvin, the journey across Lys had a dreamlike unreality. Silent as a ghost, the machine slid across rolling plains and wound its way through forests, never deviating from its invisible track. It travelled perhaps ten times as fast as a man could comfortably walk; seldom indeed was any inhabitant of Lys in a greater hurry than that.

They passed through many villages, some larger than Airlee but most of them built along very similar lines. Alvin was interested to notice the subtle but significant differences in clothing and even physical appearance that occurred as they moved from one community to the next. The civilisation of Lys was composed of hundreds of distinct cultures, each contributing some special talent towards the whole. The ground-car was well stocked with Airlee's most famous product, a small, yellow peach which was gratefully received whenever Hilvar gave away some samples. He often stopped to talk to friends and to introduce Alvin, who never ceased to be impressed by the simple courtesy with which everyone used vocal speech as soon as they knew who he was. It must often have been very tedious to them, but as far as he could judge they always resisted the temptation to lapse into telepathy and he never felt excluded from their conversation.

They made their longest pause at a tiny village almost hidden in a sea of tall golden grass, which soared high above their heads and which undulated in the gentle wind as if it was endowed with life. As they moved through it, they were continually overtaken by rolling waves as the countless blades bowed in unison above them. At first it was faintly disturbing, for Alvin had a foolish fancy that the grass was bending down to look at him, but after a while he found the continual motion quite restful.

Alvin soon discovered why they had made this stop. Among the little crowd that had already gathered before the car came gliding into the village was a shy, dark girl whom Hilvar introduced as Nyara. They were obviously very pleased to see one another again, and Alvin felt envious of their patent happiness at this brief reunion. Hilvar was clearly torn between his duties as a guide and his desire to have no other company but Nyara, and Alvin soon rescued him from his quandary by setting off on a tour of exploration by himself. There was not much to see in the little village, but he took his time.

When they started on their way again, there were many questions he was anxious to ask Hilvar. He could not imagine what love must be like in a tele-pathic society, and after a discreet interval he broached the subject. Hilvar was willing enough to explain, even though Alvin suspected that he had made his friend interrupt a prolonged and tender mental leave-taking.

In Lys, it seemed, all love began with mental contact, and it might be months or years before a couple actually met. In this way, Hilvar explained, there could be no false impressions, no deceptions, on either side. Two people whose minds were open to one another could hide no secrets. If either attempt-ted it, the other partner would know at once that something was being concealed.

Only very mature and well-balanced minds could afford such honesty; only love based upon absolute unselfishness could survive it. Alvin could well under-stand that such a love would be deeper and richer than anything his people could know; it could be so perfect, in fact, that he found it hard to believe that it could ever occur at all. . . .

Yet Hilvar assured him that it did, and became starry-eyed and lost in his own reveries when Alvin pressed him to be more explicit. There were some things that could not be communicated; one either knew them, or one did not. Alvin decided sadly that he could never attain the kind of mutual under-standing which these fortunate people had made the very basis of their lives.

When the ground-car emerged from the savanna, which ended abruptly as though a frontier had been drawn beyond which the grass was not per-mitted to grow, there was a range of low, heavily-wooded hills ahead of them. This was an outpost, Hilvar explained, of the main rampart guarding Lys. The real mountains lay beyond, but to Alvin even these small hills were an impressive and awe-inspiring sight.

The car came to a halt in a narrow, sheltered valley which was still flooded by the warmth and light of the descending sun. Hilvar looked at Alvin with a kind of wide-eyed candour which, one could have sworn, was totally innocent of any guile.

"This is where we start to walk," he said cheerfully, beginning to throw equipment out of the vehicle. "We can't ride any further."

Alvin looked at the hills surrounding them, then at the comfortable seat in which he had been riding.

"Isn't there a way round?" he asked, not very hopefully.

"Of course," replied Hilvar. "But we're not going round. We're going to the top, which is much more interesting. I'll put the car on automatic so that it will be waiting for us when we get down the other side."

Determined not to give in without a struggle, Alvin made one last effort.

"It will soon be dark," he protested. "We'll never be able to go all that way before sunset."

"Exactly," said Hilvar, sorting packages and equipment with incredible speed. "We'll spend the night on the summit, and finish the journey in the morning."

For once, Alvin knew when he was beaten.

The gear that they were carrying looked very formidable, but though it was bulky it weighed practically nothing. It was all packed in gravity-polarising containers which neutralised its weight, leaving only inertia to be contended with. As long as Alvin moved in a straight line, he was not conscious that he was carrying any load. Dealing with these containers required a little practice, for if he attempted to make a sudden change of direction his pack seemed to develop a stubborn personality and did its best to keep him on to his original course, until he had overcome its momentum.

When Hilvar had adjusted all the straps and satisfied himself that everything was in order, they began to walk slowly up the valley. Alvin looked back wistfully as the ground-car retraced its tracks and disappeared from sight; he wondered how many hours would elapse before he could again relax in its comfort.

Nevertheless, it was very pleasant climbing upwards with the mild sun beating on their backs, and seeing ever-new vistas unfold around them. There was a partly obliterated path which disappeared from time to time but which Hilvar seemed able to follow even when Alvin could see no trace of it. He asked Hilvar what had made the path, and was told that there were many small animals in these hills—some solitary, and some living in primitive communities which echoed many features of human civilisation. A few had even discovered, or been taught, the use of tools and fire. It never occurred to Alvin that such creatures might be other than friendly; both he and Hilvar took this for granted, for it had been so many years since anything on Earth had challenged the supremacy of Man.

They had been climbing for half an hour when Alvin first noticed the faint, reverberating murmur in the air around him. He could not detect its course, for it seemed to come from no particular direction. It never ceased, and it grew steadily louder as the landscape widened around them. He would have asked Hilvar what it was, but it had become necesary to save his breath for more essential purposes.

Alvin was in perfect health; indeed, he had never had an hour's illness in his life. But physical well-being, however important and necessary it might be, was not sufficient for the task he was facing now. He had the body, but he did not possess the skill. Hilvar's easy strides, the effortless surge of power which took him up every slope, filled Alvin with envy—and a determination not to give in while he could still place one foot in front of the other. He knew perfectly well that Hilvar was testing him, and did not resent the fact. It was a good-natured game, and he entered into the spirit of it even while the fatigue spread slowly through his legs.

Hilvar took pity on him when they had completed two-thirds of the ascent, and they rested for a while propped up against a westward-facing bank, letting the mellow sunlight drench their bodies. The throbbing thunder was very strong now, and although Alvin questioned him Hilvar refused to explain it.

It would, he said, spoil the surprise if Alvin knew what to expect at the end of the climb.

They were now racing against the sun, but fortunately the final ascent was smooth and gentle. The trees which had covered the lower part of the hill had now thinned out, as if they were too tired of the fight against gravity, and for the last few hundred yards the ground was carpeted with short, wiry grass on which it was very pleasant to walk. As the summit came in sight, Hilvar put forth a sudden burst of energy and went racing up the slope. Alvin decided to ignore the challenge; indeed, he had no choice. He was quite content to plod steadily onwards, and when he had caught up with Hilvar to collapse in contented exhaustion by his side.

Not until he had regained his breath was he able to appreciate the view spread out beneath him, and to see the origin of the endless thunder which now filled the air. The ground ahead fell away steeply from the crest of the hill—so steeply, indeed, that it soon became an almost vertical cliff. And leaping far out from the face of the cliff was a mighty ribbon of water, which curved out through space to crash into the rocks a thousand feet below. There it was lost in a shimmering mist of spray, while up from the depths rose that ceaseless, drumming thunder that reverberated in hollow echoes from the hills on either side.

Most of the waterfall was now in shadow, but the sunlight streaming past the mountain still illuminated the land beneath, adding the final touch of magic to the scene. For quivering in evanescent beauty above the base of the fall was the last rainbow left on Earth.

Hilvar waved his arm in a sweep which embraced the whole horizon.

"From here," he said, raising his voice so that it could be heard above the thunder of the waterfall, "you can see right across Lys."

Alvin could well believe him. To the north lay mile upon mile of forest, broken here and there by clearings, fields, and the wandering threads of a hundred rivers. Hidden somewhere in that vast panorama was the village of Airlee, but it was hopeless to try to find it. Alvin fancied that he could catch a glimpse of the lake past which the path led to the entrance into Lys, but decided that his eyes had tricked him. Still further north, trees and clearings alike were lost in a mottled carpet of green, rucked here and there by lines of hills. And beyond that, at the very edge of vision, the mountains that hemmed Lys from the desert lay like a bank of distant clouds.

East and west the view was little different, but to the south the mountains seemed only a few miles away. Alvin could see them very clearly, and he realised that they were far higher than the little peak on which he was standing. They were separated from him by country which was much wilder than the land through which he had just passed. In some indefinable way it seemed deserted and empty, as if Man had not lived there for many, many years.

Hilvar answered Alvin's unspoken question.

"Once that part of Lys was inhabited," he said. "I don't know why it was abandoned, and perhaps one day we shall move into it again. Only the animals live there now."

Indeed, there was nowhere any sign of human life—none of the clearings or well-disciplined rivers that spoke of Man's presence. Only in one spot was there any indication that he had ever lived here, for many miles away a solitary white ruin jutted above the forest roof like a broken fang. Elsewhere, the jungle had returned to its own.

The sun was sinking low below the western walls of Lys. For a breathless moment, the distant mountains seemed to burn with golden flames; then the land they guarded was swiftly drowned with shadows and the night had come.

"We should have done this before," said Hilvar, practical as ever, as he started to unload their equipment. "It'll be pitch dark in five minutes—and cold, too."

Curious pieces of apparatus began to cover the grass. A slim tripod extended a vertical rod carrying a pear-shaped bulge at its upper end. Hilvar raised this until the pear was just clear of their heads, and gave some mental signal which Alvin could not intercept. At once their little encampment was flooded with light, and the darkness retreated. The pear gave not only light but also heat, for Alvin could feel a gentle caressing glow that seemed to sink into his very bones.

Carrying the tripod in one hand, and his pack in the other, Hilvar walked down the slope while Alvin hurried behind, doing his best to keep in the circle of light. He finally pitched camp in a small depression a few hundred yards below the crest of the hill, and started to put the rest of his equipment into operation.

First came a large hemisphere of some rigid and almost invisible material which englobed them completely and protected them from the cool breeze which had now begun to blow up the face of the hill. The dome appeared to be generated by a small rectangular box which Hilvar placed on the ground and then ignored completely, even to the extent of burying it beneath the rest of his paraphernalia. Perhaps this also projected the comfortable, semi-transparent couches on which Alvin was so glad to relax. It was the first time he had seen furniture materialised in Lys, where it seemed to him that the houses were terribly cluttered up with permanent artifacts which would be much better kept safely out of the way in memory banks.

The meal which Hilvar produced from yet another of his receptacles was also the first purely synthetic one that Alvin had eaten since reaching Lys. There was a steady blast of air, sucked through some orifice in the dome overhead, as the matter-converter seized its raw material and performed its everyday miracle. On the whole, Alvin was much happier with purely synthetic food. The way in which the other kind was prepared struck him as being appallingly unhygienic, and at least with the matter-converters you knew exactly what you were eating. . . .

They settled down for their evening meal as the night deepened around them and the stars came out. When they had finished, it was completely dark beyond their circle of light, and at the edge of that circle Alvin could see dim shapes moving as the creatures of the forest crept out of their hiding places. From time to time he caught the glint of reflected light as pale eyes stared back at him, but whatever beasts were watching out there would come no closer, so he could see nothing more of them.

It was very peaceful, and Alvin felt utterly content. For a while they lay on their couches and talked about the things that they had seen, the mystery which enmeshed them both, and the many ways in which their two cultures differed. Hilvar was fascinated by the miracle of the Eternity Circuits which had put Diaspar beyond the reach of time, and Alvin found some of his questions very hard to answer.

"What I don't understand," said Hilvar, "is how the designers of Diaspar made certain that nothing would ever go wrong with the memory circuits. You tell me that the information defining the city, and all the people who live in it, is stored as patterns of electric charge inside crystals. Well, crystals will last for ever—but what about all the circuits associated with them? Aren't there ever any failures of *any* kind—"

"I asked Khedron that same question, and he told me that the Memory Banks are virtually triplicated. Any of the three banks can maintain the city, and if anything goes wrong with one of them, the other two automatically correct it. Only if the same failure occurred simultaneosuly in two of the banks would any permanent damage be done—and the chances of that are infinitesimal."

"And how is the relation maintained between the pattern stored in the memory units, and the actual structure of the city? Between the plan, as it were, and the thing it describes?"

Alvin was now completely out of his depth. He knew that the answer involved technologies which relied on the manipulation of space itself—but how one could lock an atom rigidly in the position defined by data stored elsewhere was something he could not begin to explain.

On a sudden inspiration, he pointed to the invisible dome protecting them from the night.

"Tell me how this roof above our heads is created by that box you're sitting on," he answered, "and then I'll explain how the Eternity Circuits work."

Hilvar laughed.

"I suppose it's a fair comparison. You'd have to ask one of our field theory experts if you wanted to know that. I certainly couldn't tell you."

This reply made Alvin very thoughtful. So there were still men in Lys who understood how their machines worked; that was more than could be said of Diaspar.

Thus they talked and argued, until presently Hilvar said: "I'm tired. What about you—are you going to sleep?"

Alvin rubbed his still-weary limbs.

"I'd like to," he confessed, "but I'm not sure if I can. It still seems a strange custom to me."

"It is a good deal more than a custom," smiled Hilvar. "I have been told that it was once a necessity to every human being. We still like to sleep at least once a day even if only for a few hours. During that time the body refreshes itself, and the mind, as well. Does no one in Diaspar *ever* sleep?"

"Only on very rare occasions," said Alvin. "Jeserac, my tutor, has done it once or twice, after he had made some exceptional mental effort. A well-designed body should have no need for such rest periods; we did away with them millions of years ago."

Even as he spoke these rather boastful words, his actions belied them. He felt a weariness such as he had never before known; it seemed to spread from his calves and thighs until it flowed through all his body. There was nothing unpleasant about the sensation—rather the reverse. Hilvar was watching him with an amused smile, and Alvin had enough faculties left to wonder if his companion was exercising any of his mental powers upon him. If so, he did not object in the least.

The light flooding down from the metal pear overhead sank to a faint glow, but the warmth it was radiating continued unabated. By the last flicker of light, Alvin's drowsy mind registered a curious fact which he would have to inquire about in the morning.

Hilvar had stripped off his clothes, and for the first time Alvin saw how much the two branches of the human race had diverged. Some of the changes were merely ones of emphasis of proportion, but others, such as the external genitals and the presence of teeth, nails and definite body-hair, were more fundamental. What puzzled him most of all, however, was the curious small hollow in the pit of Hilvar's stomach.

When, some days later, he suddenly remembered the subject, it took a good deal of explaining. By the time that Hilvar had made the functions of the navel quite clear, he had uttered many thousands of words and drawn half a dozen diagrams.

And both he and Alvin had made a great step forward in understanding the basis of each other's cultures.

CHAPTER XII

THE NIGHT WAS at its deepest when Alvin woke. Something had disturbed him, some whisper of sound that had crept into his mind despite the endless thunder of the falls. He sat up in the darkness, straining his eyes across the hidden land, while with indrawn breath he listened to the drumming roar of the water and the softer, more fugitive sounds of the creatures of the night.

Nothing was visible. The starlight was too dim to reveal the miles of country that lay hundreds of feet below; only a jagged line of darker night eclipsing the stars told of the mountains on the southern horizon. In the darkness beside him Alvin heard his companion roll over and sit up.

"What is it?" came a whispered voice.

"I thought I heard a noise."

"What sort of noise?"

"I don't know: perhaps it was just imagination."

There was a silence while two pairs of eyes peered out into the mystery of the night. Then, suddenly, Hilvar caught Alvin's arm.

"Look!" he whispered.

Far to the south glowed a solitary point of light, too low in the heavens to be a star. It was a brilliant white, tinged with violet, and even as they watched it began to climb the spectrum of intensity, until the eye could no longer bear to look upon it. Then it exploded—and it seemed as if lightning had struck below the rim of the world. For a brief instant the mountains, and the land they encircled were etched with fire against the darkness of the night. Ages later came the ghost of a far-off explosion, and in the woods below a sudden wind stirred among the trees. It died away swiftly, and one by one the routed stars crept back into the sky.

For the second time in his life, Alvin knew fear. It was not as personal and imminent as it had been in the chamber of the Moving Ways, when he had made the decision that took him to Lys. Perhaps it was awe rather than fear; he was looking into the face of the unknown, and it was as if he had already sensed that out there beyond the mountains was something he must go to meet.

"What was that?" he whispered at length.

"I am trying to find out," said Hilvar, and was silent again. Alvin guessed what he was doing, and did not interrupt his friend's silent quest.

Presently Hilvar gave a little sigh of disappointment. "Everyone is asleep," he said. "There was no one who could tell me. We must wait until morning, unless I wake one of my friends. And I would not like to do that unless it is really important."

Alvin wondered what Hilvar would consider a matter of real importance. He was just going to suggest, a little sarcastically, that this might well merit interrupting someone's sleep. Before he could make the proposal Hilvar spoke again.

"I've just remembered," he said, rather apologetically. "It's a long time since I came here, and I'm not quite certain about my bearings. But that must be Shalmirane."

"Shalmirane! Does it still exist?"

"Yes; I'd almost forgotten. Seranis once told me that the fortress lies in those mountains. Of course, it's been in ruins for ages, but perhaps someone still lives there."

Shalmirane! To these children of two races, so widely differing in culture and history, this was indeed a name of magic. In all the long story of Earth, there had been no greater epic than the defence of Shalmirane against an invader who had conquered all the Universe. Though the true facts were utterly lost in the mists which had gathered so thickly round the Dawn Ages, the legends had never been forgotten and would last as long as Man endured.

Presently Hilvar's voice came again out of the darkness.

"The people of the south could tell us more. I have some friends there; I will call them in the morning."

Alvin scarcely heard him; he was deep in his own thoughts, trying to remember all that he had ever heard of Shalmirane. It was little enough; after this immense lapse of time, no one could tell the truth from the legend. All that was certain was that the Battle of Shalmirane marked the end of Man's conquests, and the beginning of his long decline.

Among those mountains, thought Alvin, might lie the answers to all the problems that had tormented him for so many years.

"How long," he said to Hilvar, "would it take us to reach the fortress?"

"I've never been there, but it's much further than I intended to go. I doubt if we could do it in a day."

"Can't we use the ground-car?"

"No; the way lies through the mountains, and no cars can go there."

Alvin thought it over. He was tired, his feet were sore and the muscles of his thighs were still aching from the unaccustomed effort. It was very tempting to leave it for another time. Yet there might be no other time. . . .

Beneath the dim light of the failing stars, not a few of which had died since Shalmirane was built, Alvin wrestled with his thoughts and presently made his decision. Nothing had changed; the mountains resumed their watch over the sleeping land. But a turning-point in history had come and gone, and the human race was moving towards a strange new future.

Alvin and Hilvar slept no more that night, but broke camp with the first glow of dawn. The hill was drenched with dew, and Alvin marvelled at the sparkling jewellery which weighed down each blade and leaf. The "swish" of the wet grass fascinated him as he ploughed through it, and looking back up the hill he could see his path stretching behind him like a dark band across the shining ground.

The sun had just lifted above the eastern wall of Lys when they reached the outsirts of the forest. Here, Nature had returned to her own. Even Hilvar seemed somewhat lost among the gigantic trees that blocked the sunlight and cast pools of shadow on the jungle floor. Fortunately the river from the fall flowed south in a line too straight to be altogether natural, and by keeping to its edge they could avoid the denser undergrowth. A good deal of Hilvar's time was spent in controlling Krif, who disappeared occasionally into the jungle or went skimming wildly across the water. Even Alvin, to whom everything was still so new, could feel that the forest had a fascination not possessed by the smaller, more cultivated woods of nothern Lys. Few trees were alike; most of them were in various stages of devolution and some had reverted through the ages almost to their original natural forms. Many were obviously not of Earth at all—probably not even of the Solar System. Watching like sentinels over the lesser trees were giant sequoias, three or four hundred feet high. Once they had been called the oldest things on Earth; they were still a little older than Man.

The river was widening now; ever and again it opened into small lakes,

THE CITY AND THE STARS

upon which tiny islands lay at anchor. There were insects here, brilliantly coloured creatures swinging to and fro over the surface of the water. Once, despite Hilvar's commands, Krif darted away to join his distant cousins. He disappeared instantly in a cloud of glittering wings, and the sound of angry buzzing floated towards them. A moment later the cloud erupted and Krif came back across the water, almost too quickly for the eye to follow. Thereafter he kept very close to Hilvar and did not stray again.

Towards evening they caught occasional glimpses of the mountains ahead. The river that had been so faithful a guide was flowing sluggishly now, as if it too were nearing the end of its journey. But it was clear that they could not reach the mountains by nightfall; well before sunset the forest had become so dark that further progress was impossible. The great trees lay in pools of shadow, and a cold wind was sweeping through the leaves. Alvin and Hilvar settled down for the night beside a giant redwood whose topmost branches were still ablaze with sunlight.

When at last the hidden sun went down, the light still lingered on the dancing waters. The two explorers—for such they now considered themselves, and such indeed they were—lay in a gathering gloom, watching the river and thinking of all they had seen. Presently Alvin felt once again steal over him that sense of delicious drowsiness he had known for the first time on the previous night, and he gladly resigned himself to sleep. It might not be needed in the effortless life of Diaspar, but he welcomed it here. In the final moment before unconsciousness overcame him, he found himself wondering who last had come this way, and how long since.

The sun was high when they left the forest and stood at last before the mountain walls of Lys. Ahead of them the ground rose steeply to the sky in waves of barren rock. Here the river came to an end as spectacular as its beginning, for the ground opened in its path and it sank roaring from sight. Alvin wondered what happened to it, and through what subterranean caves it travelled before it emerged again into the light of day. Perhaps the lost oceans of Earth still existed, far down in the eternal darkness, and this ancient river still felt the call that drew it to the sea.

For a moment Hilvar stood looking at the whirlpool and the broken land beyond. Then he pointed to a gap in the hills.

"Shalmirane lies in that direction," he said confidently. Alvin did not ask how he knew; he assumed that Hilvar's mind had made brief contact with that of a friend many miles away, and the information he needed had been silently passed to him.

It did not take long to reach the gap, and when they had passed through it they found themselves facing a curious plateau with gently sloping sides. Alvin felt no tiredness now, and no fear—only a taut expectancy and a sense of approaching adventure. What he would discover, he had no conception. That he would discover something he did not doubt at all.

As they approached the summit, the nature of the ground altered abruptly. The lower slopes had consisted of porous, volcanic stone, piled here and there in great mounds of slag. Now the surface turned suddenly to hard, glassy sheets, smooth and treacherous, as if the rock had once run in molten rivers down the mountain.

The rim of the plateau was almost at their feet. Hilvar reached it first, and a few seconds later Alvin overtook him and stood speechless at his side. For they stood on the edge, not of the plateau they had expected, but of a giant bowl half a mile deep and three miles in diameter. Ahead of them the ground plunged steeply downwards, slowly levelling out at the bottom of the valley and rising again, more and more steeply, to the opposite rim. The lowest part of the bowl was occupied by a circular lake, the surface of which trembled continually, as if agitated by incessant waves.

Although it lay in the full glare of the sun, the whole of that great depression was ebon black. What material formed the crater, Alvin and Hilvar could not even guess, but it was black as the rock of a world that had never known a sun. Nor was that all, for lying beneath their feet and ringing the entire crater was a seamless band of metal, some hundred feet wide, tarnished by immeasurable age but still showing no slightest sign of corrosion.

As their eyes grew accustomed to the unearthly scene, Alvin and Hilvar realised that the blackness of the bowl was not as absolute as they had thought. Here and there, so fugitive that they could only see them indirectly, tiny explosions of light were flickering in the ebon walls. They came at random, vanishing as soon as they were born, like the reflections of stars on a broken sea.

"It's wonderful!" gasped Alvin. "But what *is* it?"

"It looks like a reflector of some kind."

"But it's so black!"

"Only to our eyes, remember. We do not know what radiations they used."

"But surely there must be more than this! Where *is* the fortress?"

Hilvar pointed to the lake.

"Look carefully," he said.

Alvin stared through the quivering roof of the lake, trying to plumb the secrets it concealed within its depths. At first he could see nothing; then, in the shallows near its edge, he made out a faint reticulation of light and shade. He was able to trace the pattern out towards the centre of the lake until the deepening water hid all further details.

The dark lake had engulfed the fortress. Down there lay the ruins of once mighty buildings, overthrown by time. Yet not all of them had been submerged, for on the far side of the crater Alvin now noticed piles of jumbled stones, and great blocks that must once have formed part of massive walls. The waters lapped around them, but had not yet risen far enough to complete their victory.

"We'll go around the lake," said Hilvar, speaking softly as if the majestic desolation had struck awe into his soul. "Perhaps we may find something in those ruins over there."

For the first few hundred yards the crater walls were so steep and smooth that it was difficult to stand upright, but after a while they reached the gentler slopes and could walk without difficulty. Near the border of the lake the smooth ebony surface was concealed by a thin layer of soil, which the winds of Lys must have brought here through the ages.

A quarter of a mile away, titanic blocks of stone were piled one upon the other, like the discarded toys of an infant giant. Here, a section of a massive wall was still recognisable; there, two carven obelisks marked what had once been a mighty entrance. Everywhere grew mosses and creeping plants, and tiny stunted trees. Even the wind was hushed.

So Alvin and Hilvar came to the ruins of Shalmirane. Against those walls, and against the energies they had housed, forces that could shatter a world to dust had flamed and thundered and been utterly defeated. Once these peaceful skies had blazed with fires torn from the hearts of suns, and the mountains of Lys must have quailed like living things beneath the fury of their masters.

No one had ever captured Shalmirane. But now the fortress, the impregnable fortress, had fallen at last—captured and destroyed by the patient tendrils of the ivy, the generations of blindly burrowing worms, and the slowly rising waters of the lake.

Overawed by its majesty, Alvin and Hilvar walked in silence towards the colossal wreck. They passed into the shadow of a broken wall, and entered a canyon where the mountains of stone had split asunder. Before them lay the lake, and presently they stood with the dark water lapping at their feet. Tiny waves, no more than a few inches high, broke endlessly upon the narrow shore.

Hilvar was the first to speak, and his voice held a hint of uncertainty which made Alvin glance at him in sudden surprise.

"There's something here I don't understand," he said slowly. "There's no wind, so what causes these ripples? The water should be perfectly still."

Before Alvin could think of any reply, Hilvar dropped to the ground, turned his head on one side, and immersed his right ear in the water. Alvin wondered what he hoped to discover in such a ludicrous position; then he realised that he was listening. With some repugnance—for the rayless waters looked singularly uninviting—he followed Hilvar's example.

The first shock of coldness lasted only for a second; when it passed he could hear, faint but distinct, a steady, rhythmic throbbing. It was as if he could hear, from far down in the depths of the lake, the beating of a giant heart.

They shook the water from their hair, and stared at each other with silent surmise. Neither liked to say what he thought—that the lake was alive.

"It would be best," said Hilvar presently, "if we searched among these ruins, and kept away from the lake."

"Do you think there's something down there?" asked Alvin, pointing to the enigmatic ripples that were still breaking against his feet. "Could it be dangerous?"

"Nothing that possesses a mind is dangerous," Hilvar replied. (Was that true? thought Alvin. What of the Invaders?) "I can detect no thoughts of any kind here, but I do not believe we are alone. It is very strange."

They walked slowly back towards the ruins of the fortress, each carrying in his mind the sound of that steady, muffled pulsing. It seemed to Alvin that mystery was piling upon mystery, and that for all his efforts he was getting further and further from any understanding of the truths he sought.

It did not seem that the ruins could teach them anything, but they searched carefully among the piles of rubble and great mounds of stone. Here, perhaps, lay the graves of buried machines—the machinery that had done their work so long ago. They would be useless now, thought Alvin, if the Invaders returned. Why had they never come back? But that was yet another mystery: he had enough enigmas to deal with—there was no need to seek for any more.

A few yards from the lake they found a small clearing among the rubble. It had been covered with weeds, but they were now blackened and charred by tremendous heat, so that they crumbled to ashes as they approached, smearing their legs with streaks of charcoal. At the centre of the clearing stood a metal tripod, firmly anchored to the ground, and supporting a circular ring which was tilted on its axis so that it pointed to a spot half-way up the sky. At first sight it seemed that the ring enclosed nothing; then, as Alvin looked more carefully, he saw that it was filled with a faint haze that tormented the eye by lurking at the edge of the visible spectrum. It was the glow of power, and from this mechanism, he did not doubt, had come the explosion of light that had lured them to Shalmirane.

They did not venture any closer, but stood looking at the machine from a safe distance. They were on the right track, thought Alvin; now it only remained to discover who—or what—had set this apparatus here, and what their purpose might be. That tilted ring—it was clearly aimed out into Space. Had the flash they had observed been some kind of signal? That was a thought which had breathtaking implications.

"Alvin," said Hilvar suddenly, his voice quiet but urgent, "we have visitors."

Alvin spun on his heels, and found himself staring at a triangle of lidless eyes. That, at least, was his first impression; then behind the staring eyes he saw the outlines of a small but complex machine. It was hanging in the air a few feet above the ground, and it was like no robot he had ever before seen.

Once the initial surprise had worn off, he felt himself the complete master of the situation. All his life he had given orders to machines, and the fact that this one was unfamiliar was of no importance. For that matter, he had never seen more than a few per cent of the robots which provided his daily needs in Diaspar.

"Can you speak?" he asked.

There was silence.

"Is anyone controlling you?"

Still silence.

"Go away. Come here. Rise. Fall."

None of the conventional control thoughts produced any effect. The machine remained contemptuously inactive. That suggested two possibilities. It was either too unintelligent to understand him—or it was very intelligent indeed, with its own powers of choice and volition. In that case, he must treat it as an equal. Even then he might underestimate it—but it would bear him no resentment, for conceit was not a vice from which robots often suffered.

Hilvar could not help laughing at Alvin's obvious discomfiture. He was just about to suggest that he should take over the task of communicating, when the words died on his lips. The stillness of Shalmirane was shattered by an ominous and utterly unmistakable sound—the gurgling splash of a very large body emerging from water.

It was the second time since he had left Diaspar that Alvin wished he were at home. Then he remembered that this was not the spirit in which to meet adventure, and he began to walk slowly but deliberately towards the lake.

The creature now emerging from the dark water seemed a monstrous parody, in living matter, of the robot which was still subjecting them to its silent scrutiny. That same equilateral arrangement of eyes could be no coincidence; even the pattern of tentacles and little jointed limbs had been roughly reproduced. Beyond that, however, the resemblance ceased. The robot did not possess—it obviously did not require—the fringe of delicate, feathery palps which beat the water with a steady rhythm, the stubby multiple legs on which the beast was humping itself ashore, or the ventilating inlets, if that was what they were, which now wheezed fitfully in the thin air.

Most of the creature's body remained in the water; only the first ten feet reared itself into what was clearly an alien element. The entire beast was about fifty feet long, and even anyone with no knowledge of biology would have realised that there was something altogether wrong about it. It had an extraordinary air of improvisation and careless design, as if its components had been manufactured without much forethought and thrown roughly together when the need arose.

Despite its size and their initial doubts, neither Alvin nor Hilvar felt the slightest nervousness once they had had a clear look at the dweller in the lake. There was an engaging clumsiness about the creature which made it quite impossible to regard it as a serious menace, even if there was any reason to suppose it might be dangerous. The human race had long ago overcome its childhood terror of the merely alien in appearance. That was a fear which could no longer survive after the first contact with friendly extraterrestrial races.

"Let me deal with this," said Hilvar quietly. "I'm used to handling animals."

"But this isn't an animal," whispered Alvin in return. "I'm sure it's intelligent, and owns that robot."

"The robot may own *it*. In any case, its mentality must be very strange. I can still detect no sign of thought. Hello—what's happening?"

The monster had not moved from its half-raised position at the water's edge, which it seemed to be maintaining with considerable effort. But a semi-transparent membrane had begun to form at the centre of the triangle of eyes —a membrane which pulsed and quivered and presently started to emit audible sounds. They were low-pitched, resonant boomings which created no intelligible words, though it was obvious that the creature was trying to speak to them.

It was painful to watch this desperate attempt at communication. For several minutes the creature struggled in vain; then, quite suddenly, it seemed to realise that it had made a mistake. The throbbing membrane contracted in size, and the sounds it emitted rose several octaves in frequency until they entered the spectrum of normal speech. Recognisable words began to form, though they were still interspersed with gibberish. It was as if the creature was remembering a vocabulary it had known long ago but had had no occasion to use for many years.

Hilvar tried to give what assistance he could.

"We can understand you now," he said, speaking slowly and distinctly. "Can we help you? We saw the light you made. It brought us here from Lys."

At the word "Lys" the creature seemed to droop as if it had suffered some bitter disappointment.

"Lys," it repeated; it could not manage the "s" very well, so that the word sounded like "Lyd". "Always from Lys. No one else ever comes. We call the Great Ones, but they do not hear."

"Who are the Great Ones?" asked Alvin, leaning forward eagerly. The delicate, ever-moving palps waved briefly towards the sky.

"The Great Ones," he said. "From the planets of eternal day. They will come. The Master promised us."

This did not seem to make matters any clearer. Before Alvin could continue his cross-examination, Hilvar intervened again. His questioning was so patient, so sympathetic and yet so penetrating that Alvin knew better than to interrupt, despite his eagerness. He did not like to admit that Hilvar was his superior in intelligence, but there was no doubt that his flair for handling animals extended even to this fantastic being. What was more, it seemed to respond to him. Its speech became more distinct as the conversation proceeded, and where at first it had been brusque to the point of rudeness, it presently elaborated its answers and volunteered information on its own.

Alvin lost all consciousness of the passage of time as Hilvar pieced together the incredible story. They could not discover the whole truth; there was endless room for conjecture and debate. As the creature answered Hilvar's questions ever more and more willingly, its appearance began to change. It slumped back into the lake, and the stubby legs that had been supporting it seemed to dissolve into the rest of its body. Presently a still more extraordinary change occurred; the three huge eyes slowly closed, shrank to pinpoints, and vanished completely. It was as if the creature had seen all that it wished to for the moment, and therefore had no further use for eyes.

Other and more subtle alterations were continually taking place, and eventually almost all that remained above the surface of the water was the vibrating diaphragm through which the creature spoke. Doubtless this too would be dissolved back into the original amorphous mass of protoplasm when it was no longer required.

Alvin found it hard to believe that intelligence could reside in so unstable a form—and his biggest surprise was yet to come. Though it seemed obvious that the creature was not of terrestrial origin, it was some time before even Hilvar, despite his greater knowledge of biology, realised the type of organism they were dealing with. It was not a single entity; in all their conversations

with it, it always referred to itself as "we". In fact, it was nothing less than a
colony of independent creatures, organised and controlled by unknown forces.

Animals of a remotely similar type—the medusae for example—had once
flourished in the ancient oceans of Earth. Some of them had been of great
size, trailing their translucent bodies and forests of stinging tentacles over fifty
or a hundred feet of water. But none of them had attained even the faintest
flicker of intelligence, beyond the power to react to simple stimuli.

There was certainly intelligence here, though it was a failing, degenerating
intelligence. Never was Alvin to forget this unearthly meeting, as Hilvar slowly
pieced together the story of the Master, while the protean polyp groped for
unfamiliar words, the dark lake lapped at the ruins of Shalmirane, and the
trioptic robot watched them with unwavering eyes.

CHAPTER XIII

THE MASTER HAD come to Earth amid the chaos of the Transition
Centuries, when the Galactic Empire was crumbling but the lines of communication among the stars had not yet completely broken. He had been of
human origin, though his home was a planet circling one of the Seven Suns.
While still a young man, he had been forced to leave his native world, and its
memory had haunted him all his life. His expulsion he blamed on vindictive
enemies, but the fact was that he suffered from an incurable malady which, it
seemed, attacked only *homo sapiens* among all the intelligent races of the
universe. That disease was religious mania.

Throughout the earlier part of its history, the human race had brought forth
an endless succession of prophets, seers, messiahs, and evangelists who convinced themselves and their followers that to them alone were the secrets of the
universe revealed. Some of them succeeded in establishing religions which
survived for many generations and influenced billions of men; others were
forgotten even before their deaths.

The rise of science, which with monotonous regularity refuted the
cosmologies of the prophets and produced miracles which they could never
match, eventually destroyed all these faiths. It did not destroy the awe, nor
the reverence and humility, which all intelligent beings felt as they contemplated the stupendous universe in which they found themselves. What it did
weaken, and finally obliterate, were the countless religions each of which
claimed with unbelievable arrogance, that it was the sole repository of the
truth and that its millions of rivals and predecessors were all mistaken.

Yet though they never possessed any real power, once humanity had reached
a very elementary level of civilisation, all down the ages isolated cults had

continued to appear, and however fantastic their creeds they had always managed to attract some disciples. They thrived with particular strength during the periods of confusion and disorder, and it was not surprising that the Transition Centuries had seen a great outburst of irrationality. When the reality was depressing, men tried to console themselves with myths.

The Master, even if he was expelled from his own world, did not leave it unprovided. The Seven Suns had been the centre of galactic power and science, and he must have possessed influential friends. He had made his Hegira in a small but speedy ship, reputed to be one of the fastest ever built. With him into exile he had taken another of the ultimate products of galactic science— the robot which was looking at Alvin and Hilvar even now.

No one had ever known the full talents and functions of this machine. To some extent, indeed, it had become the Master's *alter ego*; without it, the religion of the Great Ones would probably have collapsed after the Master's death. Together they had roved among the star clouds on a zig-zag trail which led at last, certainly not by accident, back to the world from which the Master's ancestors had sprung.

Entire libraries had been written about that saga, each work therein inspiring a host of commentaries until, by a kind of chain reaction, the original volumes were lost beneath mountains of exegesis and annotation. The Master had stopped at many worlds, and made disciples among many races. His personality must have been an immensely powerful one for it to have inspired humans and non-humans alike, and there was no doubt that a religion of such wide appeal must have contained much that was fine and noble. Probably the Master was the most successful—as he was also the last—of all mankind's messiahs. None of his predecessors could have won so many converts nor had their teachings carried across such gulfs of time and space.

What those teachings were neither Alvin nor Hilvar could ever discover with any accuracy. The great polyp did its best to convey them, but many of the words it used were meaningless and it had a habit of repeating sentences or whole speeches with a kind of swift mechanical delivery which made them very hard to follow. After a while Hilvar did his best to steer the conversation away from these meaningless morasses of theology in order to concentrate on ascertainable facts.

The Master and a band of his most faithful followers had arrived on Earth in the days before the cities had passed away, and while the Port of Diaspar was still open to the stars. They must have come in ships of many kinds; the polyps, for example, in one filled with the waters of the sea which was their natural home. Whether the movement was well received on Earth was not certain; but at least it met no violent opposition, and after further wanderings it set up its final retreat among the forests and mountains of Lys.

At the close of his long life, the Master's thoughts had turned once more towards the home from which he had been exiled, and he had asked his friends to carry him out into the open so that he could watch the stars. He had waited, his strength waning, until the culmination of the Seven Suns, and towards the end he babbled many things which were to inspire yet more libraries of interpretations in future ages. Again and again he spoke of the "Great Ones" who had now left this universe of space and matter but who would surely one day return, and he charged his followers to remain to greet them when they came. Those were his last rational words. He was never again conscious of his surroundings, but just before the end he uttered one phrase that had come down the ages to haunt the minds of all who heard it: *"It is lovely to watch the coloured shadows on the planets of eternal light."* Then he died.

At the Master's death, many of his followers broke away, but others remained faithful to his teachings, which they slowly elaborated through the ages. At first they believed that the Great Ones, whoever they were, would soon return, but that hope faded with the passing centuries. The story here grew very confused, and it seemed that truth and legend were inextricably intertwined. Alvin had only a vague picture of generations of fanatics, waiting for some great event which they did not understand to take place at some unknown future date.

The Great Ones never returned. Slowly the power of the movement failed as death and disillusion robbed it of its disciples. The short-lived human followers were the first to go, and there was something supremely ironic in the fact that the very last adherent of a human prophet was a creature utterly unlike Man.

The great polyp had become the Master's last disciple for a very simple reason. It was immortal. The billions of individual cells from which its body was built up would die, but before that happened they would have reproduced themselves. At long intervals the monster would disintegrate into its myriad separate cells, which would go their own way and multiply by fission if their environment was suitable. During this phase the polyp did not exist as a self-conscious, intelligent entity—and here Alvin was irresistibly reminded of the manner in which the inhabitants of Diaspar spent their quiescent millennia in the city's memory banks.

In due time some mysterious biological force brought the scattered components together again, and the polyp began a new cycle of existence. It returned to awareness and recollected its earlier lives, though often imperfectly as accident sometimes damaged the cells which carried the delicate patterns of memory.

Perhaps no other form of life could have kept faith so long to a creed otherwise forgotten for a thousand million years. In a sense, the great polyp was a helpless victim of its biological nature. Because of its immortality, it could not change, but was forced to repeat eternally the same invariant pattern.

The religion of the Great Ones, in its later stages, had become identified with a veneration of the Seven Suns. When the Great Ones stubbornly refused to appear, attempts were made to signal their distant home. Long ago the signalling had become no more than a meaningless ritual, now maintained by an animal which had forgotten how to learn and a robot which had never known how to forget.

As the immeasurably ancient voice died away into the still air, Alvin found himself overwhelmed by a surge of pity. The misplaced devotion, the loyalty that had held to its futile course while suns and planets passed away—he could never have believed such a tale had he not seen the evidence before his eyes. More than ever before the extent of his ignorance saddened him. A tiny fragment of the past had been illuminated for a little while, but now the darkness had closed over it again.

The history of the Universe must be a mass of such disconnected threads, and no one could say which were important and which were trivial. This fantastic tale of the Master and the Great Ones seemed like another of the countless legends that had somehow survived from the civilisations of the Dawn. Yet the very existence of the huge polyp, and of the silently watching robot, made it impossible for Alvin to dismiss the whole story as a fable built of self-delusion upon a foundation of madness.

What was the relationship, he wondered, between these two entities, which though so different in every possible way had maintained their extraordinary partnership over such aeons of time? He was somehow certain that the robot was much the more important of the two. It had been the confidant of the Master and must still know all his secrets.

Alvin looked at the enigmatic machine that still regarded him steadily. Why would it not speak? What thoughts were passing through its complicated and perhaps alien mind? Yet, surely, if it had been designed to serve the Master, its mind would not be altogether alien, and it should respond to human orders.

As he thought of all the secrets which that stubbornly mute machine must possess, Alvin felt a curiosity so great that it verged upon greed. It seemed unfair that such knowledge should be wasted and hidden from the world; here must lie wonders beyond even the ken of the Central Computer in Diaspar.

"Why won't your robot speak to us?" he asked the polyp, when Hilvar had momentarily run out of questions. The answer was one he had half expected.

"It was against the Master's wishes for it to speak with any voice but his, and his voice is silent now."

"But it will obey you?"

"Yes; the Master placed it in our charge. We can see through its eyes, wherever it goes. It watches over the machines which preserve this lake and keep its water pure. Yet it would be truer to call it our partner than our servant."

Alvin thought this over. An idea, still vague and half-formed, was beginning to take shape in his mind. Perhaps it was inspired by pure lust for knowledge and power; when he looked back on this moment he could never be certain just what his motives were. They might be largely selfish, but they also contained some element of compassion. If he could do so, he would like to break this futile sequence, and release these creatures from their fantastic fate. He was not sure what could be done about the polyp, but it might be possible to cure the robot of his insanity, and at the same time to release its priceless, pent-up memories.

"Are you certain," he said slowly, talking to the polyp but aiming his words at the robot, "that you are really carrying out the Master's wishes by remaining here? He desired the world to know of his teachings, but they have been lost while you hide here in Shalmirane. It was only by chance that we discovered you, and there may be others who would like to hear the doctrine of the Great Ones."

Hilvar glanced at him sharply, obviously uncertain of his intentions. The polyp seemed agitated, and the steady beating of its respiratory equipment faltered for a few seconds. Then it replied, in a voice not altogether under control: "We have discussed this problem for many years. But we cannot leave Shalmirane, so the world must come to us, no matter how long it takes."

"I have a better idea," said Alvin eagerly. "It is true that *you* may have to stay here in the lake, but there is no reason why your companion should not come with us. He can return whenever he wishes, or whenever you need him. Many things have changed since the Master died—things which you should know about, but which you can never understand if you stay here."

The robot never moved, but in its agony of indecision the polyp sank completely below the surface of the lake and remained there for several minutes. Perhaps it was having a soundless argument with its colleague; several times it began to re-emerge, thought better of it, and sank into the water again. Hilvar took this opportunity to exchange a few words with Alvin.

"I'd like to know what you are trying to do," he said softly, his voice half-bantering and half-serious. "Or don't you know yourself?"

"Surely," replied Alvin, "you feel sorry for these poor creatures? Don't you think it would be a kindness to rescue them?"

"I do, but I've learned enough about you to be fairly certain that altruism isn't one of your dominant emotions. You must have some other motive."

Alvin smiled ruefully. Even if Hilvar did not read his mind—and he had no reason to suppose that he did—he could undoubtedly read his character.

"Your people have remarkable mental powers," he replied, trying to divert the conversation from dangerous ground. "I think they might be able to do something for the robot, if not for this animal." He spoke very softly, lest he be overheard. The precaution might have been a useless one, but if the robot did intercept his remarks it gave no sign of it.

Fortunately, before Hilvar could press the inquiry any further, the polyp emerged once more from the lake. In the last few minutes it had become a good deal smaller and its movements were more disorganised. Even as Alvin watched, a segment of its complex, translucent body broke away from the main bulk and then disintegrated into multitudes of smaller sections, which swiftly disappeared. The creature was beginning to break up before their eyes.

Its voice, when it spoke again, was very erratic and hard to understand.

"Next cycle starting," it jerked out in a kind of fluctuating whisper. "Did not expect it so soon—only a few minutes left—stimulation too great—cannot hold together much longer."

Alvin and Hilvar stared at the creature in horrified fascination. Even though the process they were watching was a natural one, it was not pleasant to watch an intelligent creature apparently in its death-throes. They also felt an obscure sense of guilt; it was irrational to have the feeling, since it was of no great importance *when* the polyp began another cycle, but they realised that the unusual effort and excitement caused by their presence was responsible for this premature metamorphosis.

Alvin realised that he would have to act quickly, or his opportunity would be gone—perhaps only for a few years, perhaps for centuries.

"What have you decided?" he said eagerly. "Is the robot coming with us?"

There was an agonising pause while the polyp tried to force its dissolving body to obey its will. The speech-diaphragm fluttered, but no audible sound came from it. Then, as if in a despairing gesture of farewell, it waved its delicate palps feebly and let them fall back into the water, where they promptly broke adrift and went off floating out into the lake. In a matter of minutes, the transformation was over. Nothing of the creature larger than an inch across remained. The water was full of tiny, greenish specks which seemed to have a life and mobility of their own, and which rapidly disappeared into the vastness of the lake.

The ripples on the surface had now altogether died away, and Alvin knew that the steady pulse-beat that had sounded in the depths would now be stilled. The lake was dead again—or so it seemed. But that was an illusion; one day the unknown forces that had never failed to do their duty in the past would exert themselves again, and the polyp would be reborn. It was a strange and wonderful phenomenon, yet was it so much stranger than the organisation of the human body, itself a vast colony of separate, living cells?

Alvin wasted little effort on such speculations. He was oppressed by his sense of failure, even though he had never clearly conceived the goal he was aiming for. A dazzling opportunity had been missed, and might never again return. He stared sadly out across the lake, and it was some time before his mind registered the message which Hilvar was speaking quietly in his ear.

"Alvin," his friend said softly. "I think you have won your point."

He spun swiftly on his heels. The robot, which until now had been floating aloofly in the distance, never approaching within twenty feet of them, had moved up in silence and was now poised a yard above his head. Its unmoving eyes, with their wide angle of vision, gave no indication of its direction of interest. Probably it saw the entire hemisphere in front of it with equal clarity, but Alvin had little doubt that its attention was now focused upon him.

It was waiting for his next move. To some extent, at least, it was now under his control. It might follow him to Lys, perhaps even to Diaspar— unless it changed its mind. Until then he was its probationary master.

CHAPTER XIV

THE JOURNEY BACK to Airlee lasted almost three days—partly because Alvin, for his own reasons, was in no hurry to return. The physical exploration of Lys had now taken second place to a more important and exciting project; he was slowly making contact with the strange, obsessed intelligence which had now become his companion.

He suspected that the robot was trying to use him for its own purposes, which would be no more than poetic justice. What its motives were he could never be quite certain, since it still stubbornly refused to speak to him. For some reason of his own—perhaps fear that it might reveal too many of his secrets—the Master must have placed very efficient blocks upon its speech circuits, and Alvin's attempts to clear them were completely unsuccessful. Even indirect questioning of the "If you say nothing I shall assume you mean 'Yes' " type failed; the robot was much too intelligent to be taken in by such simple tricks.

In other respects, however, it was more co-operative. It would obey orders which did not require it to speak or reveal information. After a while Alvin found that he could control it, as he could direct the robots in Diaspar, by thought alone. This was a great step forward, and a little later the creature—it was hard to think of it as a mere machine—relaxed its guard still further and allowed him to see through its eyes. It did not object, it seemed, to such passive forms of communication, but it blocked all attempts at closer intimacy.

Hilvar's existence it ignored completely; it would obey none of his commands, and its mind was closed to all his probing. At first this was something of a disappointment to Alvin, who had hoped that Hilvar's greater mental powers would enable him to force open this treasure-chest of hidden memories. It was not until later that he realised the advantage of possessing a servant who would obey no one else in all the world.

The member of the expedition who strongly objected to the robot was Krif. Perhaps he imagined that he now had a rival, or perhaps he disapproved, on general principles, of anything that flew without wings. When no one was looking, he made several direct assaults on the robot, which had infuriated him still further by taking not the slightest notice of his attacks. Eventually Hilvar had been able to calm him down, and on the homeward journey in the ground-car he seemed to have resigned himself to the situation. Robot and insect escorted the vehicle as it glided silently through forest and field—each keeping to the side of its respective master and pretending that its rival was not there.

Seranis was already waiting for them as the car floated into Airlee. It was impossible, Alvin thought, to surprise these people. Their interlinked minds

kept them in touch with everything that was happening in their land. He wondered how they had reacted to his adventures in Shalmirane, which presumably everyone in Lys now knew about.

Seranis seemed to be worried and more uncertain than he had ever seen
her before, and Alvin remembered the choice that now lay before him. In the
excitement of the last few days he had almost forgotten it; he did not like
to spend energy worrying about problems that still lay in the future. But the
future was now upon him; he must decide in which of these two worlds he
wished to live.

The voice of Seranis was troubled when she began to speak, and Alvin
had the sudden impression that something had gone awry with the plans that
Lys had been making for him. What had been happening during his absence?
Had emissaries gone into Diaspar to tamper with Khedron's mind—and had
they failed in their duty?

"Alvin," began Seranis, "there are many things I did not tell you before,
but which you must now learn if you are to understand our actions.

"You know one of the reasons for the isolation of our two races. The fear
of the Invaders, that dark shadow in the depths of every human mind, turned
your people against the world and made them lose themselves in their own
dreams. Here in Lys that fear has never been so great, though we bore the
burden of the final attack. We had a better reason for our actions, and what
we did, we did with open eyes.

"Long ago, Alvin, men sought immortality and at last achieved it. They
forgot that a world which had banished death must also banish birth. The
power to extend life indefinitely might bring contentment to the individual, but
brought stagnation to the race. Ages ago we sacrificed our immortality, but
Diaspar still follows the false dream. That is why our ways parted—*and why
they must never meet again.*"

Although the words had been more than half-expected, the blow seemed
none the less for its anticipation. Yet Alvin refused to admit the failure of all
his plans—half-formed though they were—and only part of his brain was
listening to Seranis now. He understood and noted all her words, but the
conscious portion of his mind was retracing the road to Diaspar, trying to
imagine every obstacle that could be placed in his way.

Seranis was clearly unhappy. Her voice was almost pleading as it spoke,
and Alvin knew that she was talking not only to him but to her son. She must
be aware of the understanding and affection that had grown up between them
during the days they had spent together. Hilvar was watching his mother
intently as she spoke, and it seemed to Alvin that his gaze held not merely
concern but also more than a trace of censure.

"We do not wish to make you do anything against your will, but you must
surely realise what it would mean if our people met again. Between our
culture and yours is a gulf as great as any that ever separated Earth from its
ancient colonies. Think of this one fact, Alvin. You and Hilvar are now nearly
of the same age—*but both he and I will have been dead for centuries when
you are still a youth.* And this is only your first in an infinite series of lives."

The room was very quiet, so quiet that Alvin could hear the strange, plaintive cries of unknown beasts in the fields beyond the village. Presently he said, almost in a whisper:

"What do you want me to do?"

"We hoped that we could give you the choice of staying here or returning to Diaspar, but now that is impossible. To much has happened for us to leave the decision in your hands. Even in the short time you have been here, your influence has been highly disturbing. No, I am not reproving you; I am sure you intended no harm. But it would have been best to leave the creatures you met in Shalmirane to their own destiny.

"And as for Diaspar——" Seranis gave a gesture of annoyance. "Too many people know where you have gone; we did not act in time. What is most serious, the man who helped you discover Lys has vanished; neither your Council nor our agents can discover him, so he remains a potential danger to our security. Perhaps you are surprised that I am telling you all this, but it is quite safe for me to do so. I am afraid we have only one choice before us; we must send you back to Diaspar with a false set of memories. Those memories have been constructed with great care, and when you return home you will know nothing of us. You will believe that you have had rather dull and dangerous adventures in gloomy underground caverns, where the roofs continually collapsed behind you and you kept alive only through eating unappetising weeds and drinking from occasional springs. For the rest of your life you will believe this to be the truth, and everyone in Diaspar will accept your story. There will be no mystery, then, to lure any future explorers; they will think they know all there is to be known about Lys."

Seranis paused, and looked at Alvin with anxious eyes. "We are very sorry that this is necessary, and ask your forgiveness while you still remember us. You may not accept our verdict, but we know many facts that are hidden from you. At least you will have no regrets, for you will believe that you have discovered all that there is to be found."

Alvin wondered if that was true. He was not sure that he would ever settle down to the routine of life in Diaspar, even when he had convinced himself that nothing worthwhile existed beyond its walls. What was more, he had no intention of putting the matter to the test.

"When do you wish me to undergo this—treatment?" Alvin asked.

"Immediately. We are ready now. Open your mind to me, as you did before, and you will know nothing until you find yourself back in Diaspar."

Alvin was silent for a while. Then he said quietly: "I would like to say good-bye to Hilvar."

Seranis nodded.

"I understand. I will leave you here for a while, and return when you are ready." She walked over to the stairs that led down to the interior of the house, and left them alone on the roof.

It was some time before Alvin spoke to his friend; he felt a great sadness, yet also an unbroken determination not to permit the wreck of all his hopes. He looked once more down upon the village where he had found a measure of happiness, and which he might never see again if those who were ranged behind Seranis had their way. The ground-car was still standing beneath one of the wide-branching trees, with the patient robot hanging in the air above it. A few children had gathered around to examine this strange newcomer, but none of the adults seemed in the least interested.

"Hilvar," said Alvin abruptly, "I'm very sorry about this."

"So am I," Hilvar answered, his voice unstable with emotion. "I had hoped that you could have remained here."

"Do you think that what Seranis wants to do is right?"

"Do not blame my mother. She is only doing as she is asked," replied Hilvar. Though he had not answered his question, Alvin had not the heart to ask it again. It was unfair to put such a strain on his friend's loyalty.

"Then tell me this," asked Alvin, "how could your people stop me if I tried to leave, with my memories untouched?"

"It would be easy. If you tried to escape, we would take control of your mind and force you to come back."

Alvin had expected as much, and was discouraged. He wished that he could confide in Hilvar, who was obviously upset by their impending separation, but he dared not risk the failure of his plans. Very carefully, checking every detail, he traced out the only road that could lead him back to Diaspar on the terms he wished.

There was one risk which he had to face, and against which he could do nothing to protect himself. If Seranis broke her promise and dipped into his mind, all his careful preparations might be in vain.

He held out his hand to Hilvar, who grasped it firmly but seemed unable to speak.

"Let's go downstairs to meet Seranis," said Alvin. "I'd like to see some of the people in the village before I go."

Hilvar followed him silently into the peaceful coolness of the house, and then out through the hallway and on to the ring of coloured grass that surrounded the building, Seranis was waiting for him there, looking calm and resolute. She knew that Alvin was trying to hide something from her, and thought again of the precautions she had taken. As a man may flex his muscles before some great effort, she ran through the compulsion patterns she might have to use.

"Are you ready, Alvin?" she asked.

"Quite ready," replied Alvin, and there was a tone in his voice that made her look at him sharply.

"Then it will be best if you make your mind a blank, as you did before. You will feel and know nothing after that, until you find yourself back in Diaspar."

Alvin turned to Hilvar and said in a quick whisper that Seranis could not hear:

"Good-bye, Hilvar. Don't worry—*I'll be back.*" Then he faced Seranis again.

"I don't resent what you are trying to do," he said. "No doubt you believe it is for the best, but I think you are wrong. Diaspar and Lys should not remain apart for ever; one day they may need each other desperately. So I am going home with all that I have learned—*and I do not think that you can stop me.*"

He waited no longer, and it was just as well. Seranis never moved, but instantly he felt his body slipping from his control. The power that had brushed aside his own will was even greater than he had expected, and he realised that many hidden minds must be aiding Seranis. Helplessly he began to walk back into the house, and for an awful moment he thought his plan had failed.

Then there came a flash of steel and crystal, and the metal arms closed swiftly around him. His body fought against them, as he had known that it must do, but his struggles were useless. The ground fell away beneath him and he caught a glimpse of Hilvar, frozen by surprise with a foolish smile upon his face.

The robot was carrying him a dozen feet above the ground, much faster than a man could run. It took Seranis only a moment to understand his ruse, and his struggles died away as she relaxed her control. But she was not defeated yet, and presently there happened that which Alvin had feared and done his best to counteract.

There were now two separate entities fighting inside his mind, and one of them was pleading with the robot, begging it to set him down. The real Alvin waited, breathlessly, resisting only a little against forces he knew he could not hope to fight. He had gambled; there was no way of telling beforehand if this uncertain ally would obey orders as complex as those that he had given it. Under no circumstances, he had told the robot, must it obey any further commands of his until he was safely inside Diaspar. Those were the orders. If they were obeyed, Alvin had placed his fate beyond the reach of human interference.

Never hesitating, the machine raced on along the path he had so carefully mapped out for it. A part of him was still pleading angrily to be released, but he knew now that he was safe. And presently Seranis understood that too, for the forces inside his brain ceased to war with one another. Once more he was at peace, as ages ago an earlier wanderer had been when, lashed to the mast of his ship, he had heard the song of the Sirens die away across the wine-dark sea.

CHAPTER XV

ALVIN DID NOT relax until the chamber of the Moving Ways was around him once more. There had still been the danger that the people of Lys might be able to stop or even to reverse the vehicle in which he was travelling, and bring him back helplessly to his starting-point. But his return was an uneventful repetition of the outward trip; forty minutes after he had left Lys he was in the Tomb of Yarlan Zey.

The servants of the Council were waiting for him, dressed in the formal black robes which they had not worn for centuries. Alvin felt no surprise, and little alarm, at the presence of this reception committee. He had now overcome so many obstacles that one more made little difference. He had learned a great deal since leaving Diaspar, and with that knowledge had come a confidence verging upon arrogance. Moreover, he now had a powerful, if erratic, ally. The best minds of Lys had been unable to interfere with his plans; somehow, he believed that Diaspar could do no better.

There were rational grounds for this belief, but it was based partly upon something beyond reason—a faith in his destiny which had slowly been growing in Alvin's mind. The mystery of his origin, his success in doing what no earlier man had ever done, the way in which new vistas had opened up before him— all these things added to his self-confidence. Faith in one's own destiny was among the most valuable of the gifts which the gods could bestow upon a man, but Alvin did not know how many it had led to utter disaster.

"Alvin," said the leader of the city's proctors, "we have orders to accompany you wherever you go, until the Council has heard your case and rendered its verdict."

"With what offence am I charged?" asked Alvin. He was still exhilarated by the excitement and elation of his escape from Lys, and could not yet take this new development very seriously. Presumably Khedron had talked; he felt a brief annoyance at the Jester for betraying his secret.

"No charge has been made," came the reply. "If necessary, one will be framed after you have been heard."

"And when will that be?"

"Very soon, I imagine." The proctor was obviously ill at ease, and was not sure how to handle his unwelcome assignment. At one moment he would treat Alvin as a fellow-citizen, and then he would remember his duties as a custodian, and would adopt an attitude of exaggerated aloofness.

"This robot," he said abruptly, pointing to Alvin's companion, "where did it come from? Is it one of ours?"

"No," replied Alvin. "I found it in Lys, the country I have been to. I have brought it here to meet the Central Computer."

This calm statement produced a considerable commotion. The fact that there was something outside Diaspar was hard enough to accept, but that Alvin should have brought back one of its inhabitants and proposed to introduce it to the brain of the city was even worse. The proctors looked at each other with such helpless alarm that Alvin could hardly refrain from laughing at them.

As they walked back through the Park, his escort keeping discreetly at the rear and talking among itself in agitated whispers, Alvin considered his next move. The first thing he must do was to discover exactly what had happened during his absence. Khedron, Seranis had told him, had vanished. There were countless places where a man could hide in Diaspar, and since the Jester's knowledge of the city was unsurpassed it was not likely that he would be found until he chose to reappear. Perhaps, thought Alvin, he could leave a message where Khedron would be bound to see it, and arrange a rendezvous. However, the presence of his guard might make that impossible.

He had to admit that the surveillance was very discreet. By the time he had reached his apartment, he had almost forgotten the existence of the proctors.

He imagined that they would not interfere with his movements unless he attempted to leave Diaspar, and for the time being he had no intention of doing that. Indeed, he was fairly certain that it would be impossible to return to Lys by his original route. By this time, surely, the underground carrier system would have been put out of action by Seranis and her colleagues.

The proctors did not follow him into his room; they knew that there was only the one exit, and stationed themselves outside that. Having had no instructions regarding the robot, they let it accompany Alvin. It was not a machine which they had any desire to interfere with, since its alien construction was obvious. From its behaviour they could not tell whether it was a passive servant of Alvin's, or whether it was operating under its own volition. In view of this uncertainty, they were quite content to leave it entirely alone.

Once the wall had sealed itself behind him, Alvin materialised his favourite divan and threw himself down upon it. Luxuriating in his familiar surroundings, he called out of the memory units his last efforts in painting and sculpture, and examined them with a critical eye. If they had failed to satisfy him before, they were doubly displeasing now, and he could take no further pride in them. The person who had created them no longer existed; into the few days he had been away from Diaspar, it seemed to Alvin that he had crowded the experience of a lifetime.

He cancelled all these products of his adolescence, erasing them for ever and not merely returning them to the memory banks. The room was empty again, apart from the couch on which he was reclining and the robot that still watched with wide, unfathomable eyes. What did the robot think of Diaspar? wondered Alvin. Then he remembered that it was no stranger here, for it had known the city in the last days of its contact with the stars.

Not until he felt thoroughly at home once more did Alvin begin to call his friends. He began with Eriston and Etania, though out of a sense of duty rather than any real desire to see and speak to them again. He was not sorry when their communicators informed him that they were unavailable, and left them both a brief message announcing his return. This was quite unnecessary, since by now the whole city would know that he was back. However, he hoped that they would appreciate his thoughtfulness; he was beginning to learn consideration, though he had not yet realised that, like most virtues, it had little merit unless it was spontaneous and unselfconscious.

Then, acting on a sudden impulse, he called the number that Khedron had given him so long ago in the Tower of Loranne. He did not, of course, expect an answer, but there was always the possibility that Khedron had left a message. His guess was correct: but the message itself was shatteringly unexpected.

The wall dissolved, and Khedron was standing before him. The Jester looked tired and nervous, no longer the confident, slightly cynical person who had set Alvin on the path that led to Lys. There was a haunted look in his eyes, and he spoke as though he had very little time.

"Alvin," he began, "this is a recording. Only you can receive it, but you can make what use of it you wish. It will not matter to me.

"When I got back to the Tomb of Yarlan Zey, I found that Alystra had been following us. She must have told the Council that you had left Diaspar, and that I had helped you. Very soon the proctors were looking for me, and I decided to go into hiding. I am used to that—I have done it before when some of my jests failed to be appreciated." (There, thought Alvin, was a flash of the old Khedron.) "They could not have found me in a thousand years—but someone else nearly did. There are strangers in Diaspar, Alvin; they could only have come from Lys, and they are looking for me. I do not know what this means, and I do not like it. The fact that they nearly caught me, though they are in a city that must be strange to them, suggests that they possess telepathic powers. I could fight the Council, but this is an unknown peril which I do not care to face.

"I am therefore anticipating a step which I think the Council might well force upon me since it has been threatened before. I am going where no one can follow, and where I shall escape whatever changes are now about to happen to Diaspar. Perhaps I am foolish to do this; that is something which only time can prove. I shall know the answer one day.

"By now you will have guessed that I have gone back into the Hall of Creation, into the safety of the Memory Banks. Whatever happens, I put my trust in the Central Computer and the forces it controls for the benefit of Diaspar. If anything tampers with the Central Computer, we are all lost. If not, I have nothing to fear.

"To me, only a moment will seem to pass before I walk forth into Diaspar again, fifty or a hundred thousand years from now. I wonder what sort of city I shall find? It will be strange if you are there; some day, I suppose, we will meet again. I cannot say whether I look forward to that meeting, or fear it.

"I have never understood you, Alvin, though there was a time when I was vain enough to think I did. Only the Central Computer knows the truth, as it knows the truth about those other Uniques who have appeared from time to time down the ages and then were seen no more. Have you discovered what happened to them?

"One reason, I suppose, why I am escaping into the future is because I am impatient. I want to see the results of what you have started, but I am anxious to miss the intermediate stages—which I suspect may be unpleasant. It will be interesting to see, in that world which will be around me in only a few minutes of apparent time from now, whether you are remembered as a creator or as a destroyer—or whether you are remembered at all.

"Good-bye, Alvin. I had thought of giving you some advice, but I do not suppose you would take it. You will go your own way, as you always have, and your friends will be tools to use or discard as occasion suits.

"That is all. I can think of nothing more to say."

For a moment Khedron—the Khedron who no longer existed save as a pattern of electric charges in the memory cells of the city—looked at Alvin with resignation and, it seemed, with sadness. Then the screen was blank again.

Alvin remained motionless for a long time after the image of Khedron had faded. He was searching his soul as he had seldom done before in all his life, for he could not deny the truth of much that Khedron had said. When had he paused, in all his schemes and adventures, to consider the effect of what he was doing upon any of his friends? He had brought anxiety to them, and might soon bring worse—all because of his insatiable curiosity and the urge to discover what should not be known.

He had never been fond of Khedron; the Jester's astringent personality prevented any close relationship, even if Alvin had desired it. Yet now, as he thought of Khedron's parting words, he was shaken with remorse. Because of his actions, the Jester had fled from this age into the unknown future.

But surely, thought Alvin, he had no need to blame himself for that. It proved only what he had already known—that Khedron was a coward. Perhaps he was no more of a coward than anyone else in Diaspar; he had the additional misfortune of possessing a powerful imagination. Alvin could accept some responsibility for his fate, but by no means all.

Whom else in Diaspar had he harmed or distressed? He thought of Jeserac, his tutor, who had been patient with what must have been his most difficult pupil. He remembered all the little kindnesses that his parents had shown him over the years; now that he looked back upon it, there were more than he had imagined.

And he thought of Alystra. She had loved him, and he had taken that love or ignored it as he chose. Yet what else was he to have done? Would she have been any happier had he spurned her completely?

He understood now why he had never loved Alystra, nor any of the women he had known in Diaspar. That was another lesson that Lys had taught him. Diaspar had forgotten many things, and among them was the true meaning of love. In Airlee he had watched the mothers dandling their children on their knees, and had himself felt that protective tenderness for all small and helpless creatures that is love's unselfish twin. Yet now there was no woman in Diaspar who knew or cared for what had once been the final aim of love.

There were no real emotions, no deep passions, in the immortal city. Perhaps such things only thrived because of their very intransience, because they could not last for ever and lay always under the shadow which Diaspar had banished.

That was the moment, if such a moment ever existed, when Alvin realised what his destiny must be. Until now he had been the unconscious agent of his own impulses. If he could have known so archaic an analogy, he might have compared himself to a rider on a runaway horse. It had taken him to many strange places, and might do so again, but in its wild galloping it had shown him its powers and taught him where he really wished to go.

Alvin's reverie was rudely interrupted by the chimes of the wall-screen. The timbre of the sound told him at once that this was no incoming call, but that someone had arrived to see him. He gave the admission signal, and a moment later was facing Jeserac.

His tutor looked grave, but not unfriendly.

"I have been asked to take you to the Council, Alvin," he said. "It is waiting to hear you." Then Jeserac saw the robot, and examined it curiously. "So this is the companion you have brought back from your travels. I think it had better come with us."

This suited Alvin very well. The robot had already extricated him from one dangerous situation, and he might have to call upon it again. He wondered what the machine had thought about the adventures and vicissitudes in which he had involved it, and wished for the thousandth time that he could understand what was going on inside its closely-shuttered mind. Alvin had the impression that for the moment it had decided to watch, analyse, and draw its own conclusions, doing nothing of its own volition until it had judged the time was ripe. Then, perhaps quite suddenly, it might decide to act; and what it chose to do might not suit Alvin's plans. The only ally he possessed was bound to him by the most tenuous ties of self-interest and might desert him at any moment.

Alystra was waiting for them on the ramp that led out into the street. Even if Alvin had wished to blame her for whatever part she had played in revealing his secret, he did not have the heart to do so. Her distress was too obvious, and her eyes brimmed with tears as she ran up to greet him.

"Ah, Alvin!" she cried. "What are they going to do with you?"

Alvin took her hands in his with a tenderness that surprised them both.

"Don't worry, Alystra," he said. "Everything is going to be all right. After all, at the very worst the Council can only send me back to the Memory Banks —and somehow I don't think that will happen."

Her beauty and her unhappiness were so appealing that, even now, Alvin felt his body responding to her presence after its old fashion. But it was the lure of the body alone; he did not disdain it, but it was no longer enough. Gently he disengaged his hands and turned to follow Jeserac towards the Council Chamber.

Alystra's heart was lonely, but no longer bitter, as she watched him go. She knew now that she had not lost him, for he had never belonged to her. And with the acceptance of that knowledge, she had begun to put herself beyond the power of vain regrets.

Alvin scarcely noticed the curious or horrified glance of his fellow-citizens as he and his retinue made their way through the familiar streets. He was marshalling the arguments he might have to use, and arranging his story in the form most favourable to himself. From time to time he assured himself that he was not in the least alarmed, and that he was still master of the situation.

They waited only a few minutes in the anteroom, but it was long enough for Alvin to wonder why, if he was unafraid, his legs felt so curiously weak. The only time he had known this sensation before was when he had forced himself up the last slopes of that distant hill in Lys, where Hilvar had shown him the waterfall from whose summit they had seen the explosion of light which had drawn them to Shalmirane. He wondered what Hilvar was doing now, and if they would ever meet again. It was suddenly very important to him that they should.

The great doors dilated, and he followed Jeserac into the Council Chamber. The twenty members were already seated around their crescent-shaped table, and Alvin felt flattered as he noticed that there were no empty places. This must be the first time for many centuries that the entire Council had been gathered together without a single abstention. Its rare meetings were usually a complete formality, all ordinary business being dealt with by a few visiphone calls and, if necessary, an interview between the President and the Central Computer.

Alvin knew by sight most of the members of the Council, and felt reassured by the presence of so many familiar faces. Like Jeserac, they did not seem unfriendly—merely anxious and puzzled. They were, after all, reasonable men. They might be annoyed that someone had proved them wrong, but Alvin did not believe that they would bear him any resentment. Once this would have been a very rash assumption, but human nature had improved in some respects.

They would give him a fair hearing, but what they thought was not all-important. His judge now would not be the Council. It would be the Central Computer.

CHAPTER XVI

THERE WERE NO formalities. The President declared the meeting open, and then turned to Alvin.

"Alvin," he said, kindly enough, "we would like you to tell us what happened to you since you disappeared, ten days ago."

The use of the word "disappeared", thought Alvin, was highly significant. Even now, the Council was reluctant to admit that he had really gone outside Diaspar. He wondered if they knew that there had been strangers in the city, and rather doubted it. In that event, they would have shown considerably more alarm.

He told his story clearly and without any dramatics; it was strange and unbelievable enough to their ears, and needed no embellishment. Only at one place did he depart from strict accuracy, for he said nothing about the manner of his escape from Lys. It seemed more than likely that he might want to use the same method again.

It was fascinating to watch the way in which the attitude of the Council members altered during the course of his narrative. At first they were sceptical, refusing to accept the denial of all that they had believed, the violation of their deepest prejudices. When Alvin told them of his passionate desire to explore the world beyond the city, and his irrational conviction that such a world did exist, they stared at him as if he was some strange and incomprehensible animal. To their minds, indeed, he was. But finally they were compelled to admit that he had been right, and that they had been mistaken. As Alvin's story unfolded, any doubts they may have had slowly dissolved. They might not like what he had told them, but they could no longer deny its truth. If they felt tempted to do so, they had only to look at Alvin's silent companion.

There was only one aspect of his tale that roused their indignation—and then it was not directed towards him. A buzz of annoyance went around the chamber as Alvin explained the anxiety of Lys to avoid contamination with Diaspar, and the steps that Seranis had taken to prevent such a catastrophe. The city was proud of its culture, and with good reason. That anyone should regard them as inferiors was more than the Council members could tolerate.

Alvin was very careful not to give offence in anything he said; he wanted, as far as possible, to win the Council to his side. Throughout, he tried to give the impression that he had seen nothing wrong in what he had done, and that he expected praise rather than censure for his discoveries. It was the best policy he could have adopted, for it disarmed most of his would-be critics in advance. It also had the effect—though he had not intended this—of transferring any blame to the vanished K_dron. Alvin himself, it was clear to his listeners, was too young to see any danger in what he was doing. The Jester, however, should certainly have known better and had acted in a thoroughly irresponsible fashion. They did not yet know how fully Khedron himself had agreed with them.

Jeserac himself, as Alvin's tutor, was also deserving of some censure, and from time to time several of the councillors gave him thoughtful glances. He did not seem to mind, though he was perfectly well aware of what they were thinking. There was a certain honour in having instructed the most original mind that had come into Diaspar since the Dawn Ages, and nothing could rob Jeserac of that.

Not until Alvin had finished the factual account of his adventures did he attempt a little persuasion. Somehow, he would have to convince these men of the truths that he had learned in Lys, but how could he make them really understand something that they had never seen and could hardly imagine?

"It seems a great tragedy," he said, "that the two surviving branches of the human race should have become separated for such an enormous period of time. One day, perhaps, we may know how it happened, but it is more important now to repair the break—to prevent it happening again. When I was in Lys I protested against their view that they were superior to us; they may have much to teach us, but we also have much to teach them. If we both believe that we have nothing to learn from the other, is it not obvious that we will *both* be wrong?"

He looked expectantly along the line of faces, and was encouraged to go on.

"Our ancestors," he continued, "built an empire which reached to the stars. Men came and went at will among all those worlds—and now their descendants are afraid to stir beyond the walls of their city. *Shall I tell you why?*" He paused; there was no movement at all in the great, bare room.

"It is because we are afraid—afraid of something that happened at the beginning of history. I was told the truth in Lys, though I guessed it long ago. Must we always hide like cowards in Diaspar, pretending that nothing else exists— because a billion years ago the Invaders drove us back to Earth?"

He had put his finger on their secret fear—the fear which he had never shared and whose power he could therefore never fully understand. Now let them do what they pleased; he had spoken the truth as he saw it.

The President looked at him gravely.

"Have you anything more to say," he asked, "before we consider what is to be done?"

"Only one thing. I would like to take this robot to the Central Computer."

"But why? You know that the Computer is already aware of everything that has happened in this room."

"I still wish to go," replied Alvin politely but stubbornly. "I ask permission both of the Council and the Computer."

Before the President could reply, a clear, calm voice sounded through the chamber. Alvin had never heard it before in his life, but he knew what it was that spoke. The information machines, which were no more than outlying fragments of this great intelligence, could speak to men—but they did not possess this unmistakable accent of wisdom and authority.

"Let him come to me," said the Central Computer.

Alvin looked at the President. It was to his credit that he did not attempt to exploit his victory. He merely asked, "Have I your permission to leave?"

The President looked around the Council Chamber, saw no disagreement there, and replied a little helplessly:

"Very well. The proctors will accompany you, and will bring you back here when we have finished our discussion."

Alvin gave a slight bow of thanks, the great doors expanded before him, and he walked slowly out of the Chamber. Jeserac had accompanied him, and when the doors had closed once more, he turned to face his tutor.

"What do you think the Council will do now?" he asked anxiously. Jeserac smiled.

"Impatient as ever, aren't you?" he said. "I do not know what my guess is worth, but I imagine that they will decide to seal the Tomb of Yarlan Zey so that no one can ever again make your journey. Then Diaspar can continue as before, undisturbed by the outside world."

"That is what I am afraid of," said Alvin bitterly.

"And you still hope to prevent it?"

Alvin did not at once reply; he knew that Jeresac had read his intentions, but at least his tutor could not foresee his plans, for he had none. He had come to the stage when he could only improvise and meet each new situation as it arose.

"Do you blame me?" he said presently, and Jeserac was surprised by the new note in his voice. It was a hint of humility, the barest suggestion that for the first time Alvin sought the approval of his fellow-men. Jeserac was touched by it, but he was too wise to take it very seriously. Alvin was under a considerable strain, and it would be unsafe to assume that any improvement in his character was permanent.

"That is a very hard question to answer," said Jeserac slowly. "I am tempted to say that all knowledge is valuable, and it cannot be denied that you have added much to our knowledge. But you have also added to our dangers, and in the long run which will be more important? How often have you stopped to consider that?"

For a moment master and pupil regarded each other pensively, each perhaps seeing the other's point of view more clearly than ever before in his life. Then, with one impulse, they turned together down the long passage from the Council Chamber, with their escort still following patiently in the rear.

This world, Alvin knew, had not been made for man. Under the glare of the fierce blue lights—so dazzling that they pained the eyes—the long, broad corridors seemed to stretch to infinity. Down these great passageways the robots of Diaspar must come and go throughout their endless lives, yet not once in centuries did they echo to the sound of human feet.

Here was the underground city, the city of machines without which Diaspar could not exist. A few hundred yards ahead, the corridor would open into a circular chamber more than a mile across, its roof supported by great columns that must also bear the unimaginable weight of Power Centre. Here, according to the maps, the Central Computer brooded eternally over the fate of Diaspar.

The chamber was there, and it was even vaster than Alvin had dared to imagine—but where was the Computer? Somehow he had expected to meet a single huge machine, naïve though he knew that this conception was. The tremendous but meaningless panorama beneath him made him pause in wonder and uncertainty.

The corridor along which they had come ended high in the wall of the chamber—surely the largest cavity ever built by man—and on either side long ramps swept down to the distant floor. Covering the whole of that brilliantly lit expanse were hundreds of great white structures, so unexpected that for a moment Alvin thought he must be looking down upon a subterranean city. The impression was startlingly vivid, and it was one that he never wholly lost. Nowhere at all was the sight he had expected—the familiar gleam of metal which since the beginning of time Man had learned to associate with his servants.

Here was the end of an evolution almost as long as Man's. Its beginnings were lost in the mists of the Dawn Ages, when humanity had first learned the use of power and sent its noisy engines clanking about the world. Steam, water, wind—all had been harnessed for a little while and then abandoned. For centuries the energy of matter had run the world until it too had been superseded, and with each change the old machines were forgotten and the new ones took their place. Very slowly, over thousands of years, the ideal of the perfect machine was approached—that ideal which had once been a dream, then a distant prospect, and at last reality:

No machine may contain any moving parts.

Here was the ultimate expression of that ideal. Its achievement had taken Man perhaps a hundred million years, and in the moment of his triumph he had turned his back upon the machine for ever. It had reached finality, and thenceforth could sustain itself eternally while serving him.

Alvin no longer asked himself which of these silent white presences was the Central Computer. He knew that it comprised them all—and that it extended far beyond this chamber, including within its being all the countless other machines in Diaspar, whether they were mobile or motionless. As his own brain was the sum of many billion separate cells, arrayed throughout a volume of space a few inches across, so the physical elements of the Central Computer were scattered throughout the length and breadth of Diaspar. This chamber might hold no more than the switching system whereby all these dispersed units kept in touch with one another.

Uncertain where to go next, Alvin stared down the great sweeping ramps and across the silent arena. The Central Computer must know that he was here, as it knew everything that was happening in Diaspar. He could only wait for its instructions.

The now-familiar yet still awe-inspiring voice was so quiet and so close to him that he did not believe that his escort could also hear it. "Go down the left-hand ramp," it said. "I will direct you from there."

He walked slowly down the slope, the robot floating above him. Neither Jeserac nor the proctors followed; he wondered if they had received orders to remain here, or whether they had decided that they could supervise him just as well from their vantage point without the bother of making this long descent. Or perhaps they had come as close to the central shrine of Diaspar as they cared to approach. . . .

At the foot of the ramp, the quiet voice redirected Alvin, and he walked between an avenue of sleeping titan shapes. Three times the voice spoke to him again, until presently he knew that he had reached his goal.

The machine before which he was standing was smaller than most of its companions, but he felt dwarfed as he stood beneath it. The five tiers with their sweeping horizontal lines gave the impression of some crouching beast, and looking from it to his own robot Alvin found it hard to believe that both were products of the same evolution, and both described by the same word.

About three feet from the ground a wide transport panel ran the whole length of the structure. Alvin pressed his forehead against the smooth, curiously warm material and peered into the machine. At first he saw nothing; then, by shielding his eyes, he could distinguish thousands of faint points of light hanging in nothingness. They were ranged one beyond the other in a three-dimensional lattice, as strange and as meaningless to him as the stars must have been to ancient man. Though he watched for many minutes, forgetful of the passage of time, the coloured lights never moved from their places and their brilliance never changed.

If he could look into his own brain, Alvin realised, it would mean as little to him. The machine seemed inert and motionless because he could not see its thoughts.

For the first time, he began to have some dim understanding of the powers and forces which sustained the city. All his life he had accepted without question the miracle of the synthesisers, which age after age provided in an unending stream all the needs of Diaspar. Thousands of times he had watched that act of creation, seldom remembering that somewhere must exist the prototype of that which he had seen come into the world.

As a human mind may dwell for a little while upon a single thought, so the infinitely greater brains which were but a portion of the Central Computer could grasp and hold for ever the most intricate ideas. The patterns of all created things were frozen in these eternal minds, needing only the touch of a human will to make them reality.

The world had gone very far since, hour upon hour, the first cavemen had patiently chipped their arrowheads and knives from the stubborn stone. . . .

Alvin waited, not caring to speak until he had received some further sign of recognition. He wondered how the Central Computer was aware of his presence, and could see him and hear his voice. Nowhere were there any signs of sense organs—none of the grilles or screens or emotionless crystal eyes through which robots normally had knowledge of the world around them.

"State your problem," said the quiet voice in his ear. It seemed strange that this overwhelming expanse of machinery should sum up its thoughts so softly. Then Alvin realised that he was flattering himself; perhaps not even a millionth part of the Central Computer's brain was dealing with him. He was just one of the innumerable incidents that came to its simultaneous attention as it watched over Diaspar.

It was hard to talk to a presence who filled the whole of the space around you. Alvin's words seemed to die in the empty air as soon as he had uttered them.

"What am I?" he asked.

If he had put that question to one of the information machines in the city, he knew what the reply would have been. Indeed, he had often done so, and they had always answered, "You are a man." But now he was dealing with an intelligence of an altogether different order, and there was no need for painstaking semantic accuracy. The Central Computer would know what he meant, but that did not mean that it would answer him.

Indeed, the reply was exactly what Alvin had feared.

"I cannot answer that question. To do so would be to reveal the purpose of my builders, and hence to nullify it."

"Then my role was planned when the city was laid down?"

"That can be said of all men."

This reply made Alvin pause. It was true enough; the human inhabitants of Diaspar had been designed as carefully as its machines. The fact that he was a Unique gave Alvin rarity, but there was no necessary virtue in that.

He knew that he could learn nothing further here regarding the mystery of his origin. It was useless to try and trick this vast intelligence, or to hope that it would disclose information it had been ordered to conceal. Alvin was not unduly disappointed; he felt that he had already begun to glimpse the truth, and in any case this was not the main purpose of his visit.

He looked at the robot he had brought from Lys, and wondered how to make his next step. It might react violently if it knew what he was planning, so it was essential that it should not overhear what he intended to say to the Central Computer.

"Can you arrange a zone of silence?" he asked.

Instantly, he sensed the unmistakable "dead" feeling, the total blanketing of all sounds, which descended when one was inside such a zone. The voice of the

Computer, now curiously flat and sinister, spoke to him: "No one can hear us now. Say what you wish."

Alvin glanced at the robot; it had not moved from its position. Perhaps it suspected nothing, and he had been quite wrong in ever imagining that it had plans of its own. It might have followed him into Diaspar like a faithful, trusting servant, in which case what he was planning now seemed a particularly churlish trick.

"You must have heard how I met this robot," Alvin began. "It must possess priceless knowledge about the past, going back to the days before the city as we know it existed. It may even be able to tell us about other worlds than Earth, since it followed the Master on his travels. Unfortunately, its speech circuits are blocked. I do not know how effective that block is, but I am asking you to clear it."

His voice sounded dead and hollow as the zone of silence absorbed every word before it could form an echo. He waited, within that invisible and unreverberant void, for his request to be obeyed or rejected.

"Your order involves two problems," replied the Computer. "One is moral, one technical. This robot was designed to obey the orders of a certain man. What right have I to override them, even if I can?"

It was a question which Alvin had anticipated, and for which he had prepared several answers.

"We do not know what exact form the Master's prohibition took," he replied. "If you can talk to the robot, you may be able to persuade it that the circumstances in which the block was imposed have now changed."

It was, of course, the obvious approach. Alvin had attempted it himself, without success, but he hoped that the Central Computer, with its infinitely greater mental resources, might accomplish what he had failed to do.

"That depends entirely upon the nature of the block," came the reply. "It is possible to set up a block which, if tampered with, will cause the contents of the memory cells to be erased. However, I think it unlikely that the Master possessed sufficient skill to do that; it requires somewhat specialised techniques. I will ask your machine if an erasing circuit has been set up in its memory units."

"But suppose," said Alvin in sudden alarm, "it causes erasure of memory merely to *ask* if an erasing circuit exists?"

"There is a standard procedure for such cases, which I shall follow. I shall set up secondary instructions, telling the machine to ignore my question if such a situation exists. It is then simple to ensure that it will become involved in a logical paradox, so that whether it answers me or whether it says nothing it will be forced to disobey its instructions. In such an event all robots act in the same manner, for their own protection. They clear their input circuits and act as if no question has been asked."

Alvin felt rather sorry that he had raised the point, and after a moment's mental struggle decided that he too would adopt the same tactics and pretend that he had never asked the question. At least he was reassured on one point— the Central Computer was fully prepared to deal with any booby-traps that might exist in the robot's memory units. Alvin had no wish to see the machine reduced to a pile of junk; rather than that, he would willingly return it to Shalmirane with its secrets still intact.

He waited with what patience he could while the silent, impalpable meeting of intellects took place. Here was an encounter between two minds, both of them created by human genius in the long-lost golden age of its greatest achievement. And now both were beyond the full understanding of any living man.

Many minutes later, the hollow, anechoic voice of the Central Computer spoke again.

"I have established partial contact," it said. "At least I know the nature of the block, and I think I know why it was imposed. There is only one way in which it can be broken. Not until the Great Ones come to Earth will this robot speak again."

"But that is nonsense!" protested Alvin. "The Master's other disciple believed in them, too, and tried to explain what they were like to us. Most of the time it was talking gibberish. The Great Ones never existed, and never will exist."

It seemed a complete impasse, and Alvin felt a sense of bitter, helpless disappointment. He was barred from the truth by the wishes of a man who had been insane, and who had died a thousand million years ago.

"You may be correct," said the Central Computer, "in saying that the Great Ones never existed. But that does not mean that they never will exist."

There was another long silence while Alvin considered the meaning of this remark, and while the minds of the two robots made their delicate contact again. And then, without any warning, he was in Shalmirane.

CHAPTER XVII

I T W A S J U S T as he had last seen it, the great ebony bowl drinking the sunlight and reflecting none back to the eye. He stood among the ruins of the fortress, looking out across the lake whose motionless waters showed that the giant polyp was now a dispersed cloud of animalcules and no longer an organised, sentient being.

The robot was still beside him, but of Hilvar there was no sign. He had no time to wonder what that meant, or to worry about his friend's absence, for almost at once there occurred something so fantastic that all other thoughts were banished from his mind.

The sky began to crack in two. A thin wedge of darkness reached from horizon to zenith, and slowly widened as if night and chaos were breaking in upon the universe. Inexorably, the wedge expanded until it embraced a quarter of the sky. For all his knowledge of the real facts of astronomy, Alvin could not fight against the overwhelming impression that he and his world lay beneath a great blue dome—and that *something* was now breaking through that dome from outside.

The wedge of night had ceased to grow. The powers that had made it were peering down into the toy universe they had discovered, perhaps conferring among themselves as to whether it was worth their attention. Underneath that cosmic scrutiny, Alvin felt no alarm, no terror. He knew that he was face to face with power and wisdom, before which a man might feel awe but never fear.

And now they had decided—they would waste some fragments of eternity upon Earth and its peoples. They were coming through the window they had broken in the sky.

Like sparks from some celestial forge, they drifted down to Earth. Thicker and thicker they came, until a waterfall of fire was streaming down from heaven and splashing in pools of liquid light as it reached the ground. Alvin did not need the words that sounded in his ears like a benediction:

"The Great Ones have come."

The fire reached him, and it did not burn. It was everywhere, filling the great bowl of Shalmirane with its golden glow. As he watched in wonder, Alvin saw that it was not a featureless flood of light, but that it had form and structure. It began to resolve itself into distinct shapes, to gather into separate fiery whirlpools. The whirlpools spun more and more swiftly on their axes, their centres rising to form columns within which Alvin could glimpse mysterious evanescent shapes. From these glowing totem poles came a faint musical note, infinitely distant and hauntingly sweet.

"The Great Ones have come."

This time there was a reply. As Alvin heard the words: "The servants of the Master greet you. We have been waiting for your coming," he knew that the barriers were down. And in that moment, Shalmirane and its strange visitors were gone, and he was standing once more before the Central Computer in the depths of Diaspar.

It had all been illusion, no more real than the fantasy world of the Sagas in which he had spent so many of the hours of his youth. But how had it been created; whence had come the strange images he had seen?

"It was an unusual problem," said the quiet voice of the Central Computer. "I knew that the robot must have some visual conception of the Great Ones in its mind. If I could convince it that the sense impressions it received coincided with that image, the rest would be simple."

"And how did you do that?"

"Basically, by asking the robot what the Great Ones were like, and then seizing the pattern formed in its thoughts. The pattern was very incomplete, and I had to improvise a good deal. Once or twice the picture I created began to depart badly from the robot's conception, but when that happened I could sense the machine's growing perplexity and modify the image before it became suspicious. You will appreciate that I could employ hundreds of circuits where it could employ only one, and switch from one image to the other so quickly that the change could not be perceived. It was a kind of conjuring trick; I was able to saturate the robot's sensory circuits and also to overwhelm its critical faculties. What you saw was only the final, corrected image—the one which best fitted the Master's revelation. It was crude, but it sufficed. The robot was convinced of its genuineness long enough for the block to be lifted, and in that moment I was able to make complete contact with its mind. It is no longer insane; it will answer any questions you wish."

Alvin was still in a daze; the afterglow of that spurious apocalypse still burned in his mind, and he did not pretend fully to understand the Central Computer's explanation. No matter; a miracle of therapy had been accomplished, and the doors of knowledge had been flung open for him to enter.

Then he remembered the warning that the Central Computer had given him, and asked anxiously: "What about the moral objections you had to overriding the Master's orders?"

"I have discovered why they were imposed. When you examine his life story in detail, as you can now do, you will see that he claimed to have produced many miracles. His disciples believed him, and their conviction added to his power. But, of course, all those miracles had some simple explanation—when indeed they occurred at all. I find it surprising that otherwise intelligent men should have let themselves be deceived in such a manner."

"So the Master was a fraud?"

"No; it is not as simple as that. If he had been a mere impostor, he would never have achieved such success, and his movement would not have lasted so long. He was a good man, and much of what he taught was true and wise. In the end, he believed in his own miracles, but he knew that there was one witness who could refute them. The robot knew all his secrets; it was his mouthpiece and his colleague, yet if it was ever questioned too closely it could destroy the foundations of his power. So he ordered it never to reveal its memories until the last day of the universe, when the Great Ones would come. It is hard to believe that such a mixture of deception and sincerity could exist in the same man, but such was the case."

Alvin wondered what the robot felt about this escape from its ancient bondage. It was, surely, a sufficiently complex machine to understand such emotions as resentment. It might be angry with the Master for having enslaved it—and equally angry with Alvin and the Central Computer for having tricked it back into sanity.

The zone of silence had been lifted; there was no further need for secrecy. The moment for which Alvin had been waiting had come at last. He turned to the robot, and asked it the question that had haunted him ever since he had heard the story of the Master's saga.

And the robot replied.

Jeserac and the proctors were still waiting patiently when he rejoined them. At the top of the ramp, before they entered the corridor, Alvin looked back across the cave, and the illusion was stronger than ever. Lying beneath him was a dead city of strange white buildings, a city bleached by a fierce light not meant for human eyes. Dead it might be, for it had never lived, but it pulsed with energies more potent than any that had ever quickened organic matter. While the world endured these silent machines would still be here, never turning their minds from the thoughts that men of genius had given them long ago.

Though Jeserac tried to question Alvin on the way back to the Council Chamber, he learned nothing of his talk with the Central Computer. This was not merely discretion on Alvin's part; he was still too much lost in the wonder of what he had seen, too intoxicated with success, for any coherent conversation. Jeserac had to muster what patience he could, and hope that presently Alvin would emerge from his trance.

The streets of Diaspar were bathed with a light that seemed pale and wan after the glare of the machine city. But Alvin scarcely saw them; he had no regard for the familiar beauty of the great towers drifting past him, or the curious glances of his fellow-citizens. It was strange, he thought, how everything that had happened to him led up to this moment. Since he had met Khedron, events seemed to have moved automatically towards a predetermined goal. The Monitors—Lys—Shalmirane—at every stage he might have turned aside with unseeing eyes, but something had led him on. Was he the maker of his own destiny, or was he especially favoured by Fate? Perhaps it was merely a matter of probabilities, of the operation of the laws of chance. Any man might have found the path his footsteps had traced, and countless times in the past ages others must have gone almost as far. Those earlier Uniques, for example . . . what had happened to them? Perhaps he was merely the first to be lucky.

All the way back through the streets, Alvin was establishing closer and closer *rapport* with the machine he had released from its age-long thraldom. It had always been able to receive his thoughts, but previously he had never known whether it would obey any orders he gave it. Now that uncertainty was gone; he could talk to it as he would to another human being, though since he was not alone he directed it not to use verbal speech but such simple thought images as he could understand. He sometimes resented the fact that robots could talk freely to one another on the telepathic level, whereas many could not—except in Lys. Here was another power that Diaspar had lost or deliberately set aside.

He continued the silent but somewhat one-sided conversation while they were waiting in the anteroom of the Council Chamber. It was impossible not to compare his present situation with that in Lys, when Seranis and her colleagues had tried to bend him to their wills. He hoped that there would be no need for further conflict, but if one should arise he was now far better prepared for it.

His first glance at the faces of the Council members told Alvin what their decision had been. He was neither surprised nor particularly disappointed, and he showed none of the emotion the Councillors might have expected as he listened to the President's summing-up.

"Alvin," began the President, "we have considered with great care the situation which your discovery has brought about, and we have reached this unanimous decision. Because no one wishes any change in our way of life, and because only once in many millions of years is anyone born who is capable of leaving Diaspar even if the means exists, the tunnel system to Lys is unnecessary, and may well be a danger. The entrance to the Chamber of the Moving Ways has therefore been sealed.

"Moreover, since it is possible that there may be other ways of leaving the city, a search will be made of the Monitor memory units. That search has already begun.

"We have considered what action, if any, need be taken with regard to you. In view of your youth, and the peculiar circumstances of your origin, it is felt that you cannot be censured for what you have done. Indeed, by disclosing a potential danger to our way of life, you have done the city a service, and we record our appreciation of that fact."

There was a murmur of applause, and expressions of satisfaction spread across the faces of the Councillors. A difficult situation had been speedily dealt with, they had avoided the necessity of reprimanding Alvin, and now they could go their ways again feeling that they, the chief citizens of Diaspar, had done their duty. With reasonably good fortune, it might be centuries before the need arose again.

The President looked expectantly at Alvin; perhaps he hoped that Alvin would reciprocate and express his appreciation of the Council for letting him off so lightly. He was disappointed.

"May I ask one question?" said Alvin politely.

"Of course."

"The Central Computer, I take it, approved of your action?"

In the ordinary way, this would have been an impertinent question to ask. The Council was not supposed to justify its decisions, or explain how it had arrived at them. But Alvin himself had been taken into the confidence of the Central Computer, for some strange reason of its own. He was in a privileged position.

The question clearly caused some embarrassment, and the reply came rather reluctantly.

"Naturally we consulted with the Central Computer. It told us to use our own judgement."

Alvin had expected as much. The Central Computer would have been conferring with the Council at the same moment as it was talking to him—at the same moment, in fact, as it was attending to a million other tasks in Diaspar. It knew, as did Alvin, that any decision the Council now made was of no importance. The future had passed utterly beyond its control at the very moment when, in happy ignorance, it had decided that the crisis had been safely dealt with.

Alvin felt no sense of superiority, none of the sweet anticipation of impending triumph, as he looked at these foolish old men who thought themselves the rulers of Diaspar. He had seen the real ruler of the city, and had spoken to it in the grave silence of its brilliant, buried world. That was an encounter which had burned most of the arrogance out of his soul, but enough was left for a final venture that would surpass all that had gone before.

As he took leave of the Council, he wondered if they were surprised at his quiet acquiescence, his lack of indignation at the closing of the path to Lys. The proctors did not accompany him; he was no longer under observation, at least in so open a manner. Only Jeserac followed him out of the Council Chamber and into the coloured, crowded streets.

"Well, Alvin," he said. "You were on your best behaviour, but you cannot deceive me. What are you planning?"

Alvin smiled.

"I knew that you would suspect something; if you will come with me, I will show you why the subway to Lys is no longer important. And there is another experiment I want to try; it will not harm you, but you may not like it."

"Very well. I am still supposed to be your tutor, but it seems that the roles are now reversed. Where are you taking me?"

"We are going to the Tower of Loranne, and I am going to show you the world outside Diaspar."

Jerserac paled, but he stood his ground. Then, as if not trusting himself with words, he gave a stiff little nod and followed Alvin out on to the smoothly gliding surface of the moving way.

Jeserac showed no fear as they walked along the tunnel through which that cold wind blew for ever into Diaspar. The tunnel had changed now; the stone grille which had blocked access to the outer world had gone. It served no structural purpose, and the Central Computer had removed it without comment at Alvin's request. Later, it might instruct the Monitors to remember the grille again, and bring it back into existence. But for the moment the tunnel gaped unfenced and unguarded in the sheer outer wall of the city.

Not until Jeserac had almost reached the end of the airshaft did he realise that the outer world was now upon him. He looked at the widening circle of sky, and his steps became more and more uncertain until they finally slowed to a halt. Alvin remembered how Alystra had turned and fled from this same spot, and he wondered if he could induce Jeserac to go any further.

"I am only asking you to *look*," he begged, "not to leave the city. Surely you can manage to do that!"

In Airlee, during his brief stay, Alvin had seen a mother teaching her child to walk. He was irresistibly reminded of this as he coaxed Jeserac along the corridor, making encouraging remarks as his tutor advanced foot by reluctant foot. Jeserac, unlike Khedron, was no coward. He was prepared to fight against his compulsion, but it was a desperate struggle. Alvin was almost as exhausted as the older man by the time he had succeeded in getting Jeserac to a point where he could see the whole, uninterrupted sweep of the desert.

Once there, the interest and strange beauty of the scene, so alien to all that Jeserac had ever known in this or any previous existence, seemed to overcome his fears. He was clearly fascinated by the immense vista of the rolling sand-dunes and the far-off, ancient hills. It was late afternoon, and in a little while all this land would be visited by the night that never came to Diaspar.

"I asked you to come here," said Alvin, speaking quickly as if he could hardly control his impatience, "because I realise that you have earned more right than anyone to see where my travels have led me. I wanted you to see the desert, and

I also want you to be a witness, so that the Council will know what I have done.

"As I told the Council, I brought this robot from Lys in the hope that the Central Computer would be able to break the block that had been imposed on its memories by the man known as the Master. By a trick which I still don't fully understand, the Computer did that. Now I have access to all the memories in this machine, as well as to the special skills that had been designed into it. I'm going to use one of those skills now. Watch."

On a soundless order which Jeserac could only guess, the robot floated out of the tunnel entrance, picked up speed, and within seconds was no more than a distant metallic gleam in the sunlight. It was flying low over the desert, across the sand-dunes that lay criss-crossed like frozen waves. Jeserac had the unmistakable impression that it was searching—though for what, he could not imagine.

Then, abruptly, the glittering speck soared away from the desert and came to rest a thousand feet above the ground. At the same moment, Alvin gave an explosive sigh of satisfaction and relief. He glanced quickly at Jeserac, as if to say: "This is it!"

At first, not knowing what to expect, Jeserac could see no change. Then, scarcely believing his eyes, he saw that a cloud of dust was slowly rising from the desert.

Nothing is more terrible than movement where no movement should ever be again, but Jeserac was beyond surprise or fear as the sand-dunes began to slide apart. Beneath the desert something was stirring like a giant awakening from its sleep, and presently there came to Jeserac's ears the rumble of falling earth and the shriek of rock split asunder by irresistible force. Then, suddenly, a great geyser of sand erupted hundreds of feet into the air and the ground was hidden from sight.

Slowly the dust began to settle back into a jagged wound torn across the face of the desert. But Jeserac and Alvin still kept their eyes fixed steadfastly upon the open sky, which a little while ago had held only the waiting robot. Now at last Jeserac knew why Alvin had seemed so indifferent to the decision of the Council, why he had shown no emotion when he was told that the subway to Lys had been closed.

The covering of earth and rock could blur but could not conceal the proud lines of the ship still ascending from the riven desert. As Jeserac watched, it slowly turned towards them until it had foreshortened to a circle. Then, very leisurely, the circle started to expand.

Alvin began to speak, rather quickly, as if the time were short.

"This robot was designed to be the Master's companion and servant—and, above all, the pilot of his ship. Before he came to Lys, he landed at the Port of Diaspar, which now lies out there beneath those sands. Even in his day, it must have been largely deserted; I think that the Master's ship was one of the last ever to reach Earth. He lived for a while in Diaspar before he went to Shalmirane; the way must still have been open in those days. But he never needed the ship again, and all these ages it had been waiting out there beneath the sands. Like Diaspar itself, like this robot—like everything which the builders of the past considered really important—it was preserved by its own eternity circuits. As long as it had a source of power, it could never wear out or be destroyed; the image carried in its memory cells would never fade, and that image controlled its physical structure."

The ship was now very close, as the controlling robot guided it towards the tower. Jeserac could see that it was about a hundred feet long, and sharply pointed at both ends. There appeared to be no windows or other openings, though the thick layer of earth made it impossible to be certain of this.

Suddenly they were spattered with dirt as a section of the hull opened outwards, and Jeserac caught a glimpse of a small, bare room with a second door at its far end. The ship was hanging only a foot away from the mouth of the airvent, which it had approached very cautiously like a sensitive, living thing.

"Good-bye, Jeserac," said Alvin. "I cannot go back into Diaspar to say farewell to my friends: please do that for me. Tell Eriston and Etania that I hope to return soon; if I do not, I am grateful for all that they did. And I am grateful to you, even though you may not approve of the way I have applied your lessons.

"And as for the Council—tell it that a road that has once been opened cannot be closed again merely by passing a resolution."

The ship was now only a dark stain against the sky, and all of a sudden Jeserac lost it altogether. He never saw its going, but presently there echoed down from the heavens the most awe-inspiring of all the sounds that Man had ever made—the long-drawn thunder of air falling, mile after mile, into a tunnel of vacuum drilled suddenly across the sky.

Even when the last echoes had died away into the desert, Jeserac never moved. He was thinking of the boy who had gone—for to Jeserac, Alvin would always be a child, the only one to come into Diaspar since the cycle of birth and death had been broken, so long ago. Alvin would never grow up; to him the whole universe was a plaything, a puzzle to be unravelled for his own amusement. In his play he had now found the ultimate, deadly toy which might wreck what was left of human civilisation—but whatever the outcome, to him it would still be a game.

The sun was now low on the horizon, and a chill wind was blowing from the desert. But Jeserac still waited, conquering his fears; and presently for the first time in his life he saw the stars.

CHAPTER XVIII

Even in Diaspar, Alvin had seldom seen such luxury as that which lay before him when the inner door of the airlock slid aside. Whatever else he had been, at least the Master was no ascetic. Not until some time later did it occur to Alvin that all this comfort might be no vain extravagance; this little world must have been the Master's home on many long journeys among the stars.

There were no visible controls of any kind, but the large, oval screen which completely covered the far wall showed that this was no ordinary room. Ranged in a half circle before it were three low couches; the rest of the cabin was occupied by two small tables and a number of padded chairs—some of them obviously not designed for human occupants.

When he had made himself comfortable in front of the screen, Alvin looked around for the robot. To his surprise, it had disappeared; then he located it, neatly stowed away in a recess beneath the curved ceiling. It had brought the Master across space to Earth and then, as his servant, followed him into Lys. Now it was ready, as if the intervening aeons had never been, to carry out its old duties once again.

Alvin threw it an experimental command, and the great screen shivered into life. Before him was the Tower of Loranne, curiously foreshortened and apparently lying on its side. Further trials gave him views of the sky, of the city, and of great expanses of desert. The definition was brilliantly, almost unnaturally, clear, although there seemed to be no actual magnification. Alvin experimented for a little while until he could obtain any view he wished; then he was ready to start.

"Take me to Lys"—the command was a simple one, but how could the ship obey it when he himself had no idea of the direction? Alvin had not considered this, and when it did occur to him the machine was already moving across the desert at a tremendous speed. He shrugged his shoulders, accepting thankfully the fact that he now had servants wiser than himself.

It was difficult to judge the scale of the picture racing up the screen, but many miles must be passing every minute. Not far from the city the colour of the ground had changed abruptly to a dull grey, and Alvin knew that he was now passing over the bed of one of the lost oceans. Once Diaspar must have been very near the sea, though there had never been any hint of this even in the most ancient records. Old though the city was, the oceans must have passed away long before its building.

Hundreds of miles later, the ground rose sharply and the desert returned. Once Alvin halted his ship above a curious pattern of intersecting lines, showing faintly through the blanket of sand. For a moment it puzzled him; then he realised that he was looking down upon the ruins of some forgotten city. He did not stay for long; it was heart-breaking to think that billions of men had left no other trace of their existence save these furrows in the sand.

The smooth curve of the horizon was breaking up at last, crinkling into mountains that were beneath him almost as soon as they were glimpsed. The machine was slowing now, slowing and falling to earth in a great arc a hundred miles in length. And then below him was Lys, its forests and endless rivers forming a scene of such incomparable beauty that for a while he could go no further. To the east, the land was shadowed and the great lakes floated upon it like pools of darker night. But towards the sunset, the waters danced and sparkled with light, throwing back towards him such colours as he had never imagined.

It was not difficult to locate Airlee—which was fortunate, for the robot could guide him no further. Alvin had expected this, and felt a little glad to have discovered some limits to its powers. It was unlikely that it would ever have heard of Airlee, so the position of the village would never have been stored in its memory cells.

After a little experimenting, Alvin brought his ship to rest on the hillside which had given him his first glimpse of Lys. It was quite easy to control the machine; he had only to indicate his general desires and the robot attended to the details. It would, he imagined, ignore dangerous or impossible orders, though he had no intention of giving any if he could avoid it. Alvin was fairly certain that no one could have seen his arrival. He thought this rather important, for he had no desire to engage in mental combat with Seranis again. His plans were still somewhat vague, but he was running no risks until he had established friendly relations. The robot could act as his ambassador, while he remained safely in the ship.

He met no one on the road to Airlee. It was strange to sit in the spaceship while his field of vision moved effortlessly along the familiar path, and the whispering of the forest sounded in his ears. As yet he was unable to identify himself fully with the robot, and the strain of controlling it was still considerable.

It was nearly dark when he reached Airlee, and the little houses were floating in pools of light. Alvin kept to the shadows and had almost reached Seranis' home before he was discovered. Suddenly there was an angry, high-pitched buzzing and his view was blocked by a flurry of wings. He recoiled involuntarily before the onslaught; then he realised what had happened. Krif was once again expressing his resentment of anything that flew without wings.

Not wishing to hurt the beautiful but stupid creature, Alvin brought the robot to a halt and endured as best he could the blows that seemed to be raining upon him. Though he was sitting in comfort a mile away, he could not avoid flinching and was glad when Hilvar came out to investigate.

At his master's approach Krif departed, still buzzing balefully. In the silence that followed, Hilvar stood looking at the robot for a while. Then he smiled.

"Hello, Alvin," he said. "I'm glad you've come back. Or are you still in Diaspar?"

Not for the first time, Alvin felt an envious admiration for the speed and precision of Hilvar's mind.

"No," he said, wondering as he did so how clearly the robot echoed his voice. "I'm in Airlee, not very far away. But I'm staying here for the present."

Hilvar laughed.

"I think that's just as well. Seranis has forgiven you, but as for the Assembly —well, that is another matter. There is a conference going on here at the moment—the first we have ever had in Airlee."

"Do you mean," asked Alvin, "that your councillors have actually come here? With your telepathic powers, I should have thought that meetings weren't necessary."

"They are rare, but there are times when they are felt desirable. I don't know the exact nature of the crisis, but three senators are already here and the rest are expected soon."

Alvin could not help smiling at the way in which events in Diaspar had been mirrored here. Wherever he went, he now seemed to be leaving a trail of consternation and alarm behind him.

"I think it would be a good idea," he said, "if I could talk to this assembly of yours—as long as I can do so in safety."

"It would be safe for you to come here yourself," said Hilvar, "if the assembly promises not to try and take over your mind again. Otherwise, I should stay where you are. I'll lead your robot to the senators—they'll be rather upset to see it."

Alvin felt again that keen but treacherous sense of enjoyment and exhilaration as he followed Hilvar into the house. He was meeting the rulers of Lys on more equal terms now; though he felt no rancour against them, it was very pleasant to know that he was now master of the situation, and in command of powers which even yet he had not fully turned to account.

The door of the conference room was locked, and it was some time before Hilvar could attract attention. The minds of the senators, it seemed, were so completely engaged that it was difficult to break into their deliberations. Then the walls slid reluctantly aside, and Alvin moved his robot swiftly forward into the chamber.

The three senators froze in their seats as he floated towards them, but only the slightest flicker of surprise crossed Seranis' face. Perhaps Hilvar had already sent her a warning, or perhaps she had expected that, sooner or later, Alvin would return.

"Good evening," he said politely, as if this vicarious entry were the most natural thing in the world. "I've decided to come back."

Their surprise certainly exceeded his expectations. One of the senators, a young man with greying hair, was the first to recover.

"How did you get here?" he gasped.

The reason for his astonishment was obvious. Just as Diaspar had done, so Lys must also have put the subway out of action.

"Why, I came here just as I did last time," said Alvin, unable to resist amusing himself at their expense.

Two of the senators looked fixedly at the third, who spread his hands in a gesture of baffled resignation. Then the young man who had addressed him before spoke again.

"Didn't you have any—difficulty?" he asked.

"None at all," said Alvin, determined to increase their confusion. He saw that he had succeeded.

"I've come back," he continued, "under my own free will, and because I have some important news for you. However, in view of our previous disagreement I'm remaining out of sight for the moment. If I appear personally, will you promise not to try and restrict my movements again?"

No one said anything for a while, and Alvin wondered what thoughts were being silently exchanged. Then Seranis spoke for them all.

"We won't attempt to control you again—though I don't think we were successful before."

"Very well," replied Alvin, "I will come to Airlee as quickly as I can."

He waited until the robot had returned; then, very carefully, he gave the machine its instructions and made it repeat them back to him. Seranis, he was quite sure, would not break her word; nevertheless he preferred to safeguard his line of retreat.

The airlock closed silently behind him as he left the ship. A moment later there was a whispering "hiss . . ." like a long-drawn gasp of surprise, as the air made way for the rising ship. For an instant a dark shadow blotted out the stars; then the ship was gone.

Not until it had vanished did Alvin realise that he had made a slight but annoying miscalculation of the kind that could bring the best-laid plans to disaster. He had forgotten that the robot's senses were more acute than his own, and the night was far darker than he had expected. More than once he lost the path completely, and several times he barely avoided colliding with trees. It was almost pitch-black in the forest, and once something quite large came towards him through the undergrowth. There was the faintest crackling of twigs, and two emerald eyes were looking steadfastly at him from the level of his waist. He called softly, and an incredibly long tongue rasped across his hand. A moment later a powerful body rubbed affectionately against him and departed without a sound. He had no idea what it could be.

Presently the lights of the village were shining through the trees ahead, but he no longer needed their guidance for the path beneath his feet had now become a river of dim blue fire. The moss upon which he was walking was luminous, and his footprints left dark patches which slowly disappeared behind him. It was a beautiful and entrancing sight, and when Alvin stooped to pluck some of the strange moss it glowed for minutes in his cupped hands before its radiance died.

Hilvar met him for the second time outside the house, and for the second time introduced him to Seranis and the senators. They greeted him with a kind of wary and reluctant respect; if they wondered where the robot had gone, they made no comment.

"I'm very sorry," Alvin began, "that I had to leave your country in such an undignified fashion. It may interest you to know that it was nearly as difficult to escape from Diaspar. . . ." He let that remark sink in, then added quickly, "I have told my people all about Lys, and I did my best to give a favourable impression. But Diaspar will have nothing to do with you. In spite of all I could say, it wishes to avoid contamination with an inferior culture."

It was most satisfying to watch the senators' reactions, and even the urbane Seranis coloured slightly at his words. If he could make Lys and Diaspar sufficiently annoyed with each other, thought Alvin, his problem would be more than half solved. Each would be so anxious to prove the superiority of its way of life that the barriers between them would soon go down.

"Why have you come back to Lys?" asked Seranis.

"Because I want to convince you, as well as Diaspar, that you have made a mistake." He did not add his other reason—that in Lys was the only friend of whom he could be certain and whose help he now needed.

The senators were still silent, waiting for him to continue, and he knew that looking through their eyes and listening through their ears were many other unseen intelligences. He was the representative of Diaspar, and the whole of Lys was judging him by what he might say. It was a great responsibility, and he felt humbled before it. He marshalled his thoughts, and then began to speak.

His theme was Diaspar. He painted the city as he had last seen it, dreaming on the breast of the desert, its towers glowing like captive rainbows against the sky. From the treasure-house of memory he recalled the songs that the poets of old had written in praise of Diaspar, and he spoke of the countless men who had spent their lives to increase its beauty. No one, he told them, could ever exhaust the city's treasures, however long they lived; always there would be something new. For a while he described some of the wonders which the men of Diaspar had wrought; he tried to make them catch a glimpse at least of the loveliness which the artists of the past had created for men's eternal admiration. And he wondered a little wistfully if it were indeed true that the music of Diaspar was the last sound that Earth had ever broadcasted to the stars.

They heard him to the end without interruption or questioning. When he had finished it was very late, and Alvin felt more tired than he could ever before remember. The strain and excitement of the long day had told on him at last, and quite suddenly he was asleep.

When he awoke, he was in an unfamiliar room and it was some moments before he remembered that he was no longer in Diaspar. As consciousness returned, so the light grew around him, until presently he was bathed in the soft, cool radiance of the morning sun, streaming through the now transparent walls. He lay in drowsy half-awareness, recalling the events of the previous day, and wondering what forces he had now set in motion.

With a soft, musical sound, one of the walls began to pleat itself up in a manner so complicated that it eluded the eye. Hilvar stepped through the opening that had been formed, and looked at Alvin with an expression half of amusement, half of serious concern.

"Now that you're awake, Alvin," he said, "perhaps you'll at least tell me what your next move is, and how you managed to return here. The senators are just leaving to look at the subway; they can't understand how you managed to come back through it. Did you?"

Alvin jumped out of bed and stretched himself mightily.

"Perhaps we'd better overtake them," he said. "I don't want to make them waste their time. As for the question you asked me—in a little while I'll show you the answer to that."

They had almost reached the lake before they overtook the three senators, and both parties exchanged slightly self-conscious greetings. The Committee of Investigation could see that Alvin knew where it was going, and the unexpected encounter had clearly put it somewhat at a loss.

"I'm afraid I misled you last night," said Alvin cheerfully. "I didn't come to Lys by the old route, so your attempt to close it was quite unnecessary. As a matter of fact, the Council of Diaspar also closed it at their end, with equal lack of success."

The senators' faces were a study in perplexity as one solution after another chased through their brains.

"Then how *did* you get there?" said the leader. There was a sudden, dawning comprehension in his eyes, and Alvin could tell that he had begun to guess the truth. He wondered if he had intercepted the command his mind had just sent winging across the mountains. But he said nothing, and merely pointed in silence to the northern sky.

Too swiftly for the eye to follow, a needle of silver light arced across the mountains, leaving a mile-long trail of incandescence. Twenty thousand feet above Lys, it stopped. There was no deceleration, no slow braking of its colossal speed. It came to a halt instantly, so that the eye that had been following it moved on across a quarter of the heavens before the brain could arrest its motion. Down from the skies crashed a mighty peal of thunder, the sound of air battered and smashed by the violence of the ship's passage. A little later the ship itself, gleaming splendidly in the sunlight, came to rest upon the hillside a hundred yards away.

It was difficult to say who was the most surprised, but Alvin was the first to recover. As they walked—very nearly running—towards the spaceship, he wondered if it normally travelled in this meteoric fashion. The thought was disconcerting, although there had been no sensation of movement on his first voyage. Considerably more puzzling, however, was the fact that a day ago this resplendent creature had been hidden beneath a thick layer of iron-hard rock— the coating it had still retained when it had torn itself loose from the desert. Not until Alvin had reached the ship, and burnt his fingers by incautiously resting them on the hull, did he understand what had happened. Near the stern there were still traces of earth, but it had been fused into lava. All the rest had been swept away, leaving uncovered the stubborn shell which neither time nor any natural force could ever touch.

With Hilvar by his side, Alvin stood in the open door and looked back at the silent senators. He wondered what they were thinking—what, indeed, the whole of Lys was thinking. From their expressions, it almost seemed as if they were beyond thought. . . .

"I am going to Shalmirane," said Alvin, "and I will be back in Airlee within an hour or so. But that is only a beginning, and while I am away, there is a thought I would leave with you.

"This is no ordinary flyer of the kind in which men travelled over the Earth. It is a spaceship, one of the fastest ever built. If you want to know where I found it, you will find the answer in Diaspar. But you will have to go there, for Diaspar will never come to you."

He turned to Hilvar, and gestured to the door. Hilvar hesitated for a moment only, looking back once at the familiar scenes around him. Then he stepped forward into the airlock.

The senators watched until the ship, now moving quite slowly—for it had only a little way to go—had disappeared into the south. Then the grey-haired young man who led the group shrugged his shoulders philosophically and turned to one of his colleagues.

"You've always opposed us for wanting change," he said, "and so far you have won. But I don't think the future lies with either of our groups now. Lys and Diaspar have both come to the end of an era, and we must make the best of it."

"I am afraid you are right," came the gloomy reply. "This is a crisis, and Alvin knew what he was saying when he told us to go to Diaspar. They know about us now, so there is no further purpose in concealment. I think we had better get in touch with our cousins—we may find them more anxious to co-operate now."

"But the subway is closed at both ends!"

"We can open ours; it will not be long before Diaspar does the same."

The minds of the senators, those in Airlee and those scattered over the whole width of Lys, considered the proposal and disliked it heartily. But they saw no alternative.

Sooner than he had any right to expect, the seed that Alvin had planted was beginning to flower.

The mountains were still swimming in shadow when they reached Shalmirane. From their height the great bowl of the fortress looked very small; it seemed impossible that the fate of Earth had once depended on that tiny ebon circle.

When Alvin brought the ship to rest among the ruins by the lakeside, the desolation crowded in upon him, chilling his soul. He opened the airlock, and the stillness of the place crept into the ship. Hilvar, who had scarcely spoken during the entire flight, asked quietly: "Why have you come here again?"

Alvin did not answer until they had almost reached the edge of the lake. Then he said: "I wanted to show you what this ship was like. And I also hoped that the polyp might be in existence once more; I feel I owe it a debt, and I want to tell it what I've discovered."

"In that case," replied Hilvar, "you will have to wait. You have come back much too soon."

Alvin had expected that; it had been a remote chance and he was not disappointed that it had failed. The waters of the lake were perfectly still, no longer beating with that steady rhythm that had so puzzled them on their first visit. He knelt down at the water's edge and peered into the cold, dark depths.

Tiny translucent bells, trailing almost invisible tentacles, were drifting to and fro beneath the surface. Alvin plunged in his hand and scooped one up. He dropped it at once, with a slight exclamation of annoyance. It had stung him.

Some day—perhaps years, perhaps centuries in the future—these mindless jellies would reassemble and the great polyp would be reborn as its memories linked together and its consciousness flashed into existence once again. Alvin wondered how it would receive the discoveries he had made; it might not be pleased to learn the truth about the Master. Indeed, it might refuse to admit that all its ages of patient waiting had been in vain.

Yet had they? Deluded though these creatures might have been, their long vigil had at last brought its reward. As if by a miracle, they had saved from the past knowledge that else might have been lost for ever. Now they could rest at last, and their creed could go the way of a million other faiths that had once thought themselves eternal.

CHAPTER XIX

HILVAR AND ALVIN walked in reflective silence back to the waiting ship, and presently the fortress was once more a dark shadow among the hills. It dwindled swiftly until it became a black and lidless eye, staring up for ever into space, and soon they lost it in the great panorama of Lys.

Alvin did nothing to check the machine; still they rose until the whole of Lys lay spread beneath them, a green island in an ochre sea. Never before had Alvin been so high; when finally they came to rest the whole crescent of the Earth was visible below. Lys was very small now, only an emerald stain against the rusty desert—but far around the curve of the globe something was glittering like a many-coloured jewel. And so for the first time, Hilvar saw the city of Diaspar.

They sat for a long while watching the Earth turn beneath them. Of all Man's ancient powers, this surely was the one he could least afford to lose. Alvin wished he could show the world as he saw it now to the rulers of Lys and Diaspar.

"Hilvar," he said, "do you think that what I'm doing is right?"

The question surprised Hilvar, who did not suspect the sudden doubts that sometimes overwhelmed his friend, and still knew nothing of Alvin's meeting with the Central Computer and the impact which that had had upon his mind. It was not an easy question to answer dispassionately; like Khedron, though with less cause, Hilvar felt that his own character was becoming submerged.

He was being sucked helplessly into the vortex which Alvin left behind him on his way through life.

"I believe you are right," Hilvar answered slowly. "Our two peoples have been separated for long enough." That, he thought, was true, though he knew that his own feeling must bias his reply. But Alvin was still worried.

"There's one problem that bothers me," he continued in a troubled voice, "and that's the difference in our life-spans." He said no more, but each knew what the other was thinking.

"I've been worried about that as well," Hilvar admitted, "but I think the problem will solve itself in time when our people get to know each other again. We can't *both* be right—our lives may be too short, and yours are certainly far too long. Eventually there will be a compromise."

Alvin wondered. That way, it was true, lay the only hope, but the ages of transition would be hard indeed. He remembered again those bitter words of Seranis: "*Both he and I will have been dead for centuries while you are still a young man.*" Very well; he would accept the conditions. Even in Diaspar all friendships lay under the same shadow; whether it was a hundred or a million years away made little difference at the end.

Alvin knew, with a certainty that passed all logic, that the welfare of the race demanded the mingling of these two cultures; in such a case individual happiness was unimportant. For a moment Alvin saw humanity as something more than the living background of his own life, and he accepted without flinching the unhappiness his choice must one day bring.

Beneath them the world continued on its endless turning. Sensing his friend's mood, Hilvar said nothing, until presently Alvin broke the silence.

"When I first left Diaspar," he said, "I did not know what I hoped to find. Lys would have satisfied me once—more than satisfied me—yet now everything on Earth seems so small and unimportant. Each discovery I've made has raised bigger questions, and opened up wider horizons. I wonder where it will end. . . ."

Hilvar had never seen Alvin in so thoughtful a mood, and did not wish to interrupt his soliloquy. He had learned a great deal about his friend in the last few minutes.

"The robot told me," Alvin continued, "that this ship can reach the Seven Suns in less than a day. Do you think I should go?"

"Do you think I could stop you?" Hilvar replied quietly.

Alvin smiled.

"That's no answer," he said. "Who knows what lies out there in space? The Invaders may have left the Universe, but there may be other intelligences unfriendly to Man."

"Why should there be?" Hilvar asked. "That's one of the questions our philosophers have been debating for ages. A truly intelligent race is not likely to be unfriendly."

"But the Invaders——?"

"They are an enigma, I admit. If they were really vicious, they must have destroyed themselves by now. And even if they have not——" Hilvar pointed to the unending deserts below. "Once we had an Empire. What have we now that they would covet?"

Alvin was a little surprised that anyone else shared this point of view, so closely allied to his own.

"Do all your people think this way?" he asked.

"Only a minority. The average person doesn't worry about it, but would probably say that if the Invaders really wanted to destroy Earth, they'd have done it ages ago. I don't suppose anyone is actually afraid of them."

"Things are very different in Diaspar," said Alvin. "My people are great cowards. They are terrified of leaving their city, and I don't know what will happen when they hear that I've located a spaceship. Jeserac will have told the Council by now, and I would like to know what it is doing."

"I can tell you that. It is preparing to receive its first delegation from Lys. Seranis has just told me."

Alvin looked again at the screen. He could span the distance between Lys and Diaspar in a single glance; though one of his aims had been achieved, that seemed a small matter now. Yet he was very glad; now, surely, the long ages of sterile isolation would be ending.

The knowledge that he had succeeded in what had once been his main mission cleared away the last doubts from Alvin's mind. He had fulfilled his purpose here on Earth, more swiftly and more thoroughly than he had dared to hope. The way lay clear ahead for what might be his last, and would certainly be his greatest, adventure.

"Will you come with me, Hilvar?" he said, all too conscious of what he was asking.

Hilvar looked at him steadfastly.

"There was no need to ask that, Alvin," he said. "I told Seranis and all my friends that I was leaving with you—a good hour ago."

They were very high when Alvin gave the robot its final instructions. The ship had come to rest and the Earth was perhaps a thousand miles below, nearly filling the sky. It looked very uninviting; Alvin wondered how many ships in the past had hovered here for a little while and then continued on their way.

There was an appreciable pause, as if the robot was checking controls and circuits that had not been used for geological ages. Then came a very faint sound, the first that Alvin had ever heard from a machine. It was a tiny humming, which soared swiftly octave by octave until it was lost at the edge of hearing. There was no sense of change or motion, but suddenly he noticed that the stars were drifting across the screen. The Earth reappeared, and rolled past —then appeared again, in a slightly different position. The ship was "hunting", swinging in space like a compass needle seeking the north. For minutes the skies turned and twisted around them, until at last the ship came to rest, a giant projectile aimed at the stars.

Centred in the screen the great ring of the Seven Suns lay in its rainbow-hued beauty. A little of Earth was still visible as a dark crescent edged with the gold and crimson of the sunset. Something was happening now, Alvin knew, beyond all his experience. He waited, gripping his seat, while the seconds drifted by and the Seven Suns glittered on the screen.

There was no sound, only a sudden wrench that seemed to blur the vision— but Earth had vanished as if a giant hand had whipped it away. They were alone in space, alone with the stars and a strangely shrunken sun. Earth was gone as though it had never been.

Again came that wrench, and with it now the faintest murmur of sound, as if for the first time the generators were exerting some appreciable fraction of their power. Yet for a moment it seemed that nothing had happened; then Alvin realised that the sun itself was gone and that the stars were creeping slowly past the ship. He looked back for an instant and saw—nothing. All the heavens behind had vanished utterly, obliterated by a hemisphere of night. Even as he watched, he could see the stars plunge into it, to disappear like sparks falling upon water. The ship was travelling far faster than light, and Alvin knew that the familiar space of Earth and Sun held him no more.

When that sudden, vertiginous wrench came for the third time, his heart almost stopped beating. The strange blurring of vision was unmistakable now; for a moment, his surroundings seemed distorted out of recognition. The mean- ing of that distortion came to him in a flash of insight he could not explain. *It was real, and no delusion of his eyes.* Somehow he was catching, as he passed through the thin film of the Present, a glimpse of the changes that were occurring in the space around him.

At the same instant the murmur of the generators rose to a roar that shook the ship—a sound doubly impressive for it was the first cry of protest that Alvin had ever heard from a machine. Then it was all over, and the sudden silence seemed to ring in his ears. The great generators had done their work; they would not be needed again until the end of the voyage. The stars ahead flared blue-white and vanished into the ultraviolet. Yet by some magic of Science or Nature the Seven Suns were still visible, though now their positions and colours were subtly changed. The ship was hurtling towards them along a tunnel of darkness, beyond the boundaries of space and time, at a velocity too enormous for the mind to contemplate.

It was hard to believe that they had now been flung out of the Solar System at a speed which unless it were checked would soon take them through the heart of the Galaxy and into the greater emptiness beyond. Neither Alvin nor Hilvar could conceive the real immensity of their journey; the great sagas of exploration had completely changed Man's outlook towards the universe and even now, millions of centuries later, the ancient traditions had not wholly died. There had once been a ship, legend whispered, that had circumnavigated the Cosmos between the rising and the setting of the sun. The billions of miles between the stars meant nothing before such speeds. To Alvin this voyage was very little greater, and perhaps less dangerous, than his first journey to Lys.

It was Hilvar who voiced both their thoughts as the Seven Suns slowly brightened ahead.

"Alvin," he remarked, "that formation can't possibly be natural."

The other nodded.

"I've thought that for many years, but it still seems fantastic."

"The system may not have been built by Man," agreed Hilvar, "but intelligence must have created it. Nature could never have formed that perfect circle of stars, all equally brilliant. And there's nothing else in the visible universe like the Central Sun."

"Why should such a thing have been made, then?"

"Oh, I can think of many reasons. Perhaps it's a signal, so that any strange ship entering our universe will know where to look for life. Perhaps it marks the centre of galactic administration. Or perhaps—and somehow I feel that this is the real explanation—it's simply the greatest of all works of art. But it's foolish to speculate now. In a few hours we shall know the truth."

"*We shall know the truth.*" Perhaps, thought Alvin—but how much of it shall we ever know? It seemed strange that now, while he was leaving Diaspar, and indeed Earth itself, at a speed beyond all comprehension, his mind should turn once more to the mystery of his origin. Yet perhaps it was not so surprising; he had learned many things since he had first arrived in Lys, but until now he had had not a single moment for quiet reflection.

There was nothing he could do now but sit and wait; his immediate future was controlled by the wonderful machine—surely one of the supreme engineering achievements of all time—that was now carrying him into the heart of the universe. Now was the moment for thought and reflection, whether he wished it or not. But first he would tell Hilvar all that had happened to him since their hasty parting only two days before.

Hilvar absorbed the tale without comment and without asking for an explanation he seemed to understand at once everything that Alvin described, and showed no signs of surprise even when he heard of the meeting with the Central Computer and the operation it had performed upon the robot's mind. It was not that he was incapable of wonder, but that the history of the past was full of marvels that could match anything in Alvin's story.

"It's obvious," he said, when Alvin had finished talking, "that the Central Computer must have received special instructions regarding you when it was built. By now, you must have guessed why."

"I think so. Khedron gave me part of the answer when he explained how the men who designed Diaspar had taken steps to prevent it becoming decadent."

"Do you think you—and the other Uniques before you—are part of the social mechanism which prevents complete stagnation? So that whereas the Jesters are short-term correcting factors, you and your kind are long-term ones?"

Hilvar had expressed the idea better than Alvin could, yet this was not exactly what he had in mind.

"I believe the truth is more complicated than that. It almost looks as if there was a conflict of opinion when the city was built, between those who wanted to shut it off completely from the outside world, and those who wanted to maintain some contacts. The first faction won, but the others did not admit defeat. I think Yarlan Zey must have been one of their leaders, but he was not powerful enough to act openly. He did his best, by leaving the subway in existence and by ensuring that at long intervals someone would come out of the Hall of Creation who did not share the fears of all his fellow-men. In fact, I wonder——" Alvin paused, and his eyes veiled with thought so that for a moment he seemed oblivious of his surroundings.

"What are you thinking now?" asked Hilvar.

"It's just occurred to me—perhaps *I* am Yarlan Zey. It's perfectly possible. He may have fed his personality into the Memory Banks, relying on it to break the mould of Diaspar before it was too firmly established. One day I must discover what happened to those earlier Uniques; that may help to fill in the gaps in the picture."

"And Yarlan Zey—or whoever it was—also instructed the Central Computer to give special assistance to the Uniques, whenever they were created," mused Hilvar, following up this line of logic.

"That's right. The ironic thing is that I could have got all the information I needed direct from the Central Computer without any assistance from poor Khedron. It would have told me more than it ever told him. But there's no doubt that he saved me a good deal of time, and taught me much that I could never have learned by myself."

"I think your theory covers all the known facts," said Hilvar cautiously. "Unfortunately, it still leaves wide open the biggest problem of all—the original purpose of Diaspar. Why did your people try to pretend that the outer world didn't exist? *That's* a question I'd like to see answered."

"It's a question I intend to answer," replied Alvin. "But I don't know when —or how."

So they argued and dreamed, while hour by hour the Seven Suns drifted apart until they had filled that strange tunnel of night in which the ship was riding. Then, one by one, the six outer stars vanished at the brink of darkness and at last only the Central Sun was left. Though it could no longer be fully in their space, it still shone with the pearly light that marked it out from all other stars. Minute by minute its brilliance increased, until presently it was no longer a point but a tiny disc. And now the disc was beginning to expand before them——

There was the briefest of warnings; for a moment, a deep, bell-like note vibrated through the room. Alvin clenched the arms of his chair, though it was a futile enough gesture.

Once again the great generators exploded into life, and with an abruptness that was almost blinding, the stars reappeared. The ship had dropped back into space, back into the universe of suns and planets, the natural world where nothing could move more swiftly than light.

They were already within the system of the Seven Suns, for the great ring of coloured globes now dominated the sky. And what a sky it was! All the stars they had known, all the familiar constellations, had gone. The Milky Way was no longer a faint band of mist far to one side of the heavens; they were now at the centre of creation, and its great circle divided the universe in twain.

The ship was still moving very swiftly towards the Central Sun, and the six remaining stars of the system were coloured beacons ranged around the sky. Not far from the nearest of them were the tiny sparks of circling planets, worlds that must have been an enormous size to be visible over such a distance.

The cause of the Central Sun's nacreous light was now clearly visible. The great star was shrouded in an envelope of gas which softened its radiation and gave it its characteristic colour. The surrounding nebula could only be seen indirectly, and it was twisted into strange shapes that eluded the eye. But it was there, and the longer one stared the more extensive it seemed to be.

"Well, Alvin," said Hilvar, "we have a good many worlds to take our choice from. Or do you hope to explore them all?"

"It's lucky that won't be necessary," admitted Alvin. "If we can make contact anywhere, we'll get the information we need. The logical thing would be to head for the largest planet of the Central Sun."

"Unless it's too large. Some planets, I've heard, were so big that human life could not exist on them—men would be crushed under their own weight."

"I doubt if that will be true here, since I'm sure this system is entirely artificial. In any case, we'll be able to see from space whether there are any cities and buildings."

Hilvar pointed to the robot.

"Our problem has been solved for us. Don't forget our guide has been here before. He is taking us home—and I wonder what he thinks about it?"

That was something that Alvin had also wondered. But was it accurate— did it make any sense at all—to imagine that the robot felt anything resembling human emotions now that it was returning to the ancient home of the Master, after so many aeons?

In all his dealings with it, since the Central Computer had released the blocks which made it mute, the robot had never shown any sign of feelings or emotion. It had answered his questions and obeyed his commands, but its real personality had proved utterly inaccessible to him. That it had a personality Alvin was sure; otherwise he would not have felt that obscure sense of guilt which afflicted him when he recalled the trick he had played upon it—and upon its now dormant companion.

It still believed in everything that the Master had taught it; though it had seen him fake his miracles and tell lies to his followers, these inconvenient facts did not affect its loyalty. It was able, like many humans before it, to reconcile two conflicting sets of data.

Now it was following its immemorial memories back to their origin. Almost lost in the glare of the Central Sun was a pale spark of light, with around it the fainter gleams of yet smaller worlds. Their enormous journey was coming to its end; in a little while they would know if it had been in vain.

THE PLANET THEY were approaching was now only a few million miles away, a beautiful sphere of multicoloured light. There could be no darkness anywhere upon its surface, for as it turned beneath the Central Sun, the other stars would march one by one across its skies. Alvin now saw very clearly the meaning of the Master's dying words: "It is lovely to watch the coloured shadows on the planets of eternal light."

Now they were so close that they could see continents and oceans and a faint haze of atmosphere. Yet there was something puzzling about its markings, and presently they realised that the divisions between land and water were curiously regular. This planet's continents were not as Nature had left them—but how small a task the shaping of a world must have been to those who built its suns!

"Those aren't oceans at all!" Hilvar exclaimed suddenly "Look—you can see markings in them!"

Not until the planet was nearer could Alvin see clearly what his friend meant. Then he noticed faint bands and lines along the continental borders, well inside what he had taken to be the limits of the sea. The sight filled him with a sudden doubt, for he knew too well the meaning of those lines. He had seen them once before in the desert beyond Diaspar, and they told him that his journey had been in vain.

"This planet is as dry as Earth," he said dully. "Its water has all gone—those markings are the salt-beds where the seas have evaporated."

"They would never have let that happen," replied Hilvar. "I think that, after all, we are too late."

His disappointment was so bitter that Alvin did not trust himself to speak again but stared silently at the great world ahead. With impressive slowness the planet turned beneath the ship, and its surface rose majestically to meet them. Now they could see buildings—minute white incrustations everywhere save on the ocean beds themselves.

Once this world had been the centre of the Universe. Now it was still, the air was empty and on the ground were none of the scurrying dots that spoke of life. Yet the ship was still sliding purposefully over the frozen sea of stone—a sea which here and there had gathered itself into great waves that challenged the sky.

Presently the ship came to rest, as if the robot had at last traced its memories to their source. Below them was a column of snow-white stone springing from the centre of an immense marble amphitheatre. Alvin waited for a little while; then, as the machine remained motionless, he directed it to land at the foot of the pillar.

Even until now, Alvin had half hoped to find life on this planet. That hope vanished instantly as he left the airlock. Never before in his life, even in the desolation of Shalmirane, had he been in utter silence. On Earth there was always the murmur of voices, the stir of living creatures, or the sighing of the wind. Here were none of these, nor ever would be again.

"Why did you bring us to this spot?" asked Alvin. He felt little interest in the answer, but the momentum of his quest still carried him on even when he had lost all heart to pursue it further.

"The Master left from here," replied the robot.

"I thought that would be the explanation," said Hilvar. "Don't you see the irony of all this? He fled from this world in disgrace—now look at the memorial they built for him!"

The great column of stone was perhaps a hundred times the height of a man, and was set in a circle of metal slightly raised above the level of the plain. It was featureless, and bore no inscription. For how many thousands or millions of years wondered Alvin, had the Master's disciples gathered here to do him honour? And had they ever known that he died in exile on distant Earth?

It made no difference now. The Master and his disciples alike were buried in oblivion.

"Come outside," urged Hilvar, trying to jolt Alvin out of his mood of depression. "We have travelled half-way across the universe to see this place. At least you can make the effort to step out of doors."

Despite himself, Alvin smiled and followed Hilvar through the airlock. Once outside, his spirits began to revive a little. Even if this world was dead, it must contain much of interest, much that would help him to solve some of the mysteries of the past.

The air was musty, but breathable. Despite the many suns in the sky, the temperature was low. Only the white disc of the Central Sun provided any real heat, and that seemed to have lost its strength in its passage through the nebulous haze around the star. The other suns gave quotas of colour, but no warmth.

It took only a few minutes to make sure that the obelisk could tell them nothing. The stubborn material of which it was made showed definite signs of age; its edges were rounded, and the metal on which it was standing had been worn away by the feet of generations of disciples and visitors. It was strange to think that they might be the last of many billions of human beings ever to stand upon this spot.

Hilvar was about to suggest that they should return to the ship and fly across to the nearest of the surrounding buildings when Alvin noticed a long, narrow crack in the marble floor of the amphitheatre. They walked along it for a considerable distance, the crack widening all the time until presently it was too broad for a man's legs to straddle.

A moment later they stood beside its origin. The surface of the arena had been crushed and splintered into an enormous shallow depression, more than a mile long. No intelligence, no imagination was needed to picture its cause. Ages ago—though certainly long after this world had been deserted—an immense cylindrical shape had rested here, then lifted once more into space and left the planet to its memories.

Who had they been? Where had they come from? Alvin could only stare and wonder. He would never know if he had missed these earlier visitors by a thousand or a million years.

They walked in silence back to their own ship (how tiny that would have looked beside the monster which once had rested here!) and flew slowly across the arena until they came to the most impressive of the buildings flanking it. As they landed in front of the ornate entrance, Hilvar pointed out something that Alvin had noticed at the same moment.

"These buildings don't look safe. See all that fallen stone over there—it's a miracle they're still standing. If there were any storms on this planet, they would have been flattened ages ago. I don't think it would be wise to go inside any of them."

"I'm not going to; I'll send the robot—it can travel faster than we can, and it won't make any disturbance which might bring the roof crashing down on top of it." Hilvar approved of this precaution, but he also insisted on one which Alvin had overlooked. Before the robot left on its reconnaissance, Alvin made it pass on a set of instructions to the almost equally intelligent brain of the ship, so that whatever happened to their pilot they could at least return safely to Earth.

It took little time to convince both of them that this world had nothing to offer. Together they watched miles of empty, dust-carpeted corridors and passageways drift across the screen as the robot explored these empty labyrinths. All buildings designed by intelligent beings, whatever form their bodies may take, must comply with certain basic laws, and after a while even the most alien forms of architecture or design fail to evoke surprise, and the mind becomes hypnotised by sheer repetition, incapable of absorbing any more impressions. These buildings, it seemed, had been purely residential, and the beings who had lived in them had been approximately human in size. They might well have been men; it was true that there were a surprising number of rooms and enclosures that could be entered only by flying creatures, but that did not mean that the builders of this city were winged. They could have used the personal anti-gravity devices that had once been in common use but of which there was now no trace in Diaspar.

"Alvin," said Hilvar at last, "we could spend a million years exploring these buildings. It's obvious that they've not merely been abandoned—they were carefully stripped of everything valuable that they possessed. We are wasting our time."

"Then what do you suggest?" asked Alvin.

"We should look at two or three other areas of this planet and see if they are the same—as I expect they are. Then we should make an equally quick survey of the other planets, and only land if they seem fundamentally different or we notice something unusual. That's all we can hope to do unless we are going to stay here for the rest of our lives."

It was true enough; they were trying to contact intelligence not to carry out archaeological research. The former task could be achieved in a few days, if it could be achieved at all. The latter would take centuries of labour by armies of men and robots.

They left the planet two hours later, and were thankful to go. Even when it had been bustling with life, Alvin decided, this world of endless buildings would have been very depressing. There were no signs of any parks, any open spaces where there could have been vegetation. It had been an utterly sterile world, and it was hard to imagine the psychology of the beings who had lived there. If the next planet was identical with this, Alvin decided, he would probably abandon the search there and then.

It was not; indeed, a greater contrast would have been impossible to imagine. This planet was near the sun, and even from space it looked hot. It was partly covered with low clouds, indicating that water was plentiful, but there were no signs of any oceans. Nor was there any sign of intelligence; they circled the planet twice without glimpsing a single artefact of any kind. The entire globe, from poles down to the equator, was clothed with a blanket of virulent green.

"I think we should be very careful here," said Hilvar. "This world is alive —and I don't like the colour of that vegetation. It would be best to stay in the ship, and not to open the airlock at all."

"Not even to send out the robot?"

"No, not even that. You have forgotten what disease is, and though my people know how to deal with it, we are a long way from home and there may be dangers here which we cannot see. I think this is a world that has run amok. Once it may have been all one great garden or park, but when it was abandoned Nature took over again. It could never have been like this while the system was inhabited."

Alvin did not doubt that Hilvar was right. There was something evil, something hostile to all the order and regularity on which both Lys and Diaspar were based, in the biological anarchy below. Here a ceaseless battle had raged for a billion years; it would be well to be wary of the survivors.

They came cautiously down over a great level plain, so uniform that its flatness posed an immediate problem. The plain was bordered by higher ground, completely covered with trees whose height could only be guessed—they were so tightly packed, and so enmeshed with undergrowth, that their trunks were virtually buried. There were many winged creatures flying among their upper branches, though they moved so swiftly that it was impossible to tell whether they were animals or insects—or neither.

Here and there a forest giant had managed to climb a few scores of feet above its battling neighbours, who had formed a brief alliance to tear it down and destroy the advantage it had won. Despite the fact that this was a silent war, fought too slowly for the eye to see, the impression of merciless, implacable conflict was overwhelming.

The plain, by comparison, appeared placid and uneventful. It was flat, to within a few inches, right out to the horizon, and seemed to be covered with a thin, wiry grass. Though they descended to within fifty feet of it, there was no sign of any animal life, which Hilvar found somewhat surprising. Perhaps, he decided, it had been scared underground by their approach.

They hovered just above the plain while Alvin tried to convince Hilvar that it would be safe to open the airlock, and Hilvar patiently explained such conceptions as bacteria, fungi, viruses, and microbes—ideas which Alvin found hard to visualise, and harder still to apply to himself. The argument had been in progress for some minutes before they noticed a peculiar fact. The vision screen, which a moment ago had been showing the forest ahead of them, had now become blank.

"Did you turn that off?" said Hilvar, his mind, as usual, just one jump ahead of Alvin's.

"No," replied Alvin, a cold shiver running down his spine as he thought of the only explanation. "Did *you* turn it off?" he asked the robot.

"No," came the reply, echoing his own.

With a sigh of relief, Alvin dismissed the idea that the robot might have started to act of its own volition—that he might have a mechanical mutiny on his hands.

"Then why is the screen blank?" he asked.

"The image receptors have been covered."

"I don't understand," said Alvin, forgetting for a moment that the robot would only act on definite orders or questions. He recovered himself quickly and asked:

"What's covered the receptors?"

"I do not know."

The literal-mindedness of robots could sometimes be as exasperating as the discursiveness of humans. Before Alvin could continue the interrogation, Hilvar interrupted.

"Tell it to lift the ship," he said, and there was a note of urgency in his voice.

Alvin repeated the command. There was no sense of motion; there never was. Then, slowly, the image reformed on the vision screen, though for a moment it was blurred and distorted. But it showed enough to end the argument about landing.

The level plain was level no longer. A great bulge had formed immediately below them—a bulge which was ripped open at the top where the ship had torn free. Huge pseudo-pods were waving sluggishly across the gap, as if trying to recapture the prey that had just escaped from their clutches. As he stared in horrified fascination, Alvin caught a glimpse of a pulsing scarlet orifice, fringed with whip-like tentacles which were beating in unison, driving anything that came into their reach down into the gaping maw.

Foiled of its intended victim, the creature sank slowly into the ground—and it was then that Alvin realised that the plain below was merely the thin scum on the surface of a stagnant sea.

"What was that—*thing*?" he gasped.

"I'd have to go down and study it before I could tell you that," Hilvar replied matter-of-factly. "It may have been some form of primitive animal

—perhaps even a relative of our friend in Shalmirane. Certainly it was not intelligent, or it would have known better than to try and eat a spaceship."

Alvin felt shaken, though he knew that they had been in no possible danger. He wondered what else lived down there beneath that innocent sward, which seemed positively to invite him to come out and run upon its springy surface.

"I could spend a lot of time here," said Hilvar, obviously fascinated by what he had just seen. "Evolution must have produced some very interesting results under these conditions. Not only evolution, but *devolution* as well, as higher forms of life regressed when the planet was deserted. By now equilibrium must have been reached and—you're not leaving already?" His voice sounded quite plaintive as the landscape receded below them.

"I am," said Alvin. "I've seen a world with no life, and a world with too much, and I don't know which I dislike more."

Five thousand feet above the plain, the planet gave them one final surprise. They encountered a flotilla of huge, flabby balloons drifting down the wind. From each semi-transparent envelope, clusters of tendrils dangled to form what was virtually an inverted forest. Some plants, it seemed, in the effort to escape from the ferocious conflict on the surface had learned to conquer the air. By a miracle of adaptation, they had managed to prepare hydrogen and store it in bladders, so that they could lift themselves into the comparative peace of the lower atmosphere.

Yet it was not certain that even here they had found security. Their downward-hanging stems and leaves were infested with an entire fauna of spidery animals, which must spend their lives floating far above the surface of the globe, continuing the universal battle for existence on their lonely aerial islands. Presumably they must from time to time have some contact with the ground; Alvin saw one of the great balloons suddenly collapse and fall out of the sky, its broken envelope acting as a crude parachute. He wondered if this was an accident, or part of the life-cycle of these strange entities.

Hilvar slept while they waited for the next planet to approach. For some reason which the robot could not explain to them, the ship travelled slowly—at least by comparison with its universe-spanning haste—now that it was within a solar system. It took almost two hours to reach the world that Alvin had chosen for his third stop, and he was a little surprised that any mere interplanetary journey should last so long.

He woke Hilvar as they dropped down into the atmosphere.

"What do you make of *that*?" he asked, pointing to the vision screen.

Below them was a bleak landscape of blacks and greys, showing no sign of vegetation or any other direct evidence of life. But there was indirect evidence; the low hills and shallow valleys were dotted with perfectly-formed hemispheres, some of them arranged in complex, symmetrical patterns.

They had learned caution on the last planet, and after carefully considering all the possibilities remained poised high in the atmosphere while they sent the robot down to investigate. Through its eyes, they saw one of the hemispheres approach until the robot was floating only a few feet away from the completely smooth, featureless surface.

There was no sign of any entrance, nor any hint of the purpose which the structure served. It was quite large—over a hundred feet high; some of the other hemispheres were larger still. If it was a building, there appeared to be no way in or out.

After some hesitation, Alvin ordered the robot to move forward and touch the dome. To his utter astonishment, it refused to obey him. This indeed was mutiny—or so at first it seemed.

"Why don't you do as I tell you?" asked Alvin, when he had recovered from his astonishment.

"It is forbidden," came the reply.

"Forbidden by whom?"

"I do not know."

"Then how—no, cancel that. Was the order built into you?"

"No."

That seemed to eliminate one possibility. The builders of these domes might well have been the race who made the robot, and might have included this taboo in the machine's original instructions.

"When did you receive the order?" asked Alvin.

"I received it when I landed."

Alvin turned to Hilvar, the light of a new hope burning in his eyes.

"There's intelligence here! Can you sense it?"

"No," Hilvar replied. "The place seems as dead to me as the first world we visited."

"I'm going outside to join the robot. Whatever spoke to it may speak to me."

Hilvar did not argue the point, though he looked none too happy. They brought the ship to earth a hundred feet away from the dome, not far from the waiting robot, and opened the airlock.

Alvin knew that the lock could not be opened unless the ship's brain had already satisfied that the atmosphere was breathable. For a moment he thought it had made a mistake—the air was so thin and gave such little sustenance to his lungs. Then, by inhaling deeply, he found that he could grasp enough oxygen to survive, though he felt that a few minutes here would be all that he could endure.

Panting hard, they walked up to the robot and to the curving wall of the enigmatic dome. They took one more step—then stopped in unison as if hit by the same sudden blow. In their minds, like the tolling of a mighty gong, had boomed a single message:

Danger. Come no closer.

That was all. It was a message not in words, but in pure thought. Alvin was certain that any creature, whatever its level of intelligence, would receive the same warning, in the same utterly unmistakable fashion—deep within its mind.

It was a warning, not a threat. Somehow they knew that it was not directed *against* them; it was for their own protection. Here, it seemed to say, is something intrinsically dangerous, and we, its makers, are anxious that no one shall be hurt through blundering ignorantly into it.

Alvin and Hilvar stepped back several paces, and looked at each other, each waiting for his friend to say what was in his mind. Hilvar was the first to sum up the position.

"I was right, Alvin," he said. "There is no intelligence here. That warning is automatic—triggered by our presence when we get too close."

Alvin nodded in agreement.

"I wonder what they were trying to protect," he said. "There could be buildings—anything—under these domes."

"There's no way we can find out, if all the domes warn us off. It's interesting—the difference between the three planets we've visited. They took everything away from the first—they abandoned the second without bothering about it—but they went to a lot of trouble here. Perhaps they expected to come back some day, and wanted everything to be ready for them when they returned."

"But they never did—and that was a long time ago."

"They may have changed their minds."

It was curious, Alvin thought, how both he and Hilvar had unconsciously started using the word "they". Whoever or whatever "they" had been, their presence had been strong on the first planet—and was even stronger here. This was a world that had been carefully wrapped up, and put away until it might be needed again. . . .

"Let's go back to the ship," panted Alvin, "I can't breathe properly here."

As soon as the airlock had closed behind them, and they were at ease once more, they discussed their next move. To make a thorough investigation, they should sample a large number of domes, in the hope that they might find one that had no warning and which could be entered. If that failed—but Alvin would not face that possibility until he had to.

He faced it less than an hour later, and in a far more dramatic form than he would have dreamed. They had sent the robot down to a half a dozen domes, always with the same result, when they came across a scene which was badly out of place on this tidy, neatly packaged world.

Below them was a broad valley, sparsely sprinkled with the tantalising, impenetrable domes. At its centre was the unmistakable scar of a great explosion—an explosion which had thrown debris for miles in all directions and burned a shallow crater in the ground.

And beside the crater was the wreckage of a spaceship.

CHAPTER XXI

THEY LANDED CLOSE to the scene of this ancient tragedy, and walked slowly, conserving their breath, towards the immense, broken hull towering above them. Only a short section—either the prow or the stern—of the ship remained; presumably the rest had been destroyed in the explosion. As they approached the wreck, a thought slowly dawned in Alvin's mind, becoming stronger and stronger until it attained the status of certainty.

"Hilvar," he said, finding it hard to talk and walk at the same time, "I believe this is the ship that landed on the first planet we visited."

Hilvar nodded, preferring not to waste air. The same idea had already occurred to him. It was a good object lesson, he thought, for incautious visitors. He hoped it would not be lost on Alvin.

They reached the hull, and stared up into the exposed interior of the ship. It was like looking into a huge building that had been roughly sliced in two; floors and walls and ceilings, broken at the point of the explosion, gave a distorted chart of the ship's cross-section. What strange beings, wondered Alvin, still lay where they had died in the wreckage of their vessel?

"I don't understand this," said Hilvar suddenly. "This portion of the ship is badly damaged, but it's fairly intact. Where's the rest of it? Did it break in two out in space, and this part crash here?"

Not until they had sent the robot exploring again, and had themselves examined the area around the wreckage, did they learn the answer. There was no shadow of doubt; any reservations they might have had were banished when Alvin found the line of low moulds, each ten feet long, on the little hill beside the ship.

"So they landed here," mused Hilvar, "and ignored the warning. They were inquisitive, just as you are. They tried to open that dome."

He pointed to the other side of the crater, to the smooth, still unmarked shell within which the departed rulers of this world had sealed their treasures. But it was no longer a dome: it was now an almost complete sphere, for the ground in which it had been set had been blasted away.

"They wrecked their ship, and many of them were killed. Yet despite that, they managed to make repairs and leave again, cutting off this section and stripping out everything of value. What a task that must have been!"

Alvin scarcely heard him. He was looking at the curious marker that had first drawn him to this spot—the slim shaft ringed by a horizontal circle a third of the way down from its tip. Alien and unfamiliar though it was, he could respond to the mute message it had carried down the ages.

Underneath those stones, if he cared to disturb them, was the answer to one question at least. It could remain unanswered; whatever these creatures might have been, they had earned their right to rest.

Hilvar scarcely heard the words Alvin whispered as they walked slowly back to the ship.

"I hope they got home," he said.

"And where now?" asked Hilvar, when they were once more out in space. Alvin stared thoughtfully at the screen before replying.

"Do you think I should go back?" he said.

"It would be the sensible thing to do. Our luck may not hold out much longer, and who knows what other surprises these planets may have waiting for us?"

It was the voice of sanity and caution, and Alvin was now prepared to give it greater heed than he would have done a few days before. But he had come a long way, and waited all his life, for this moment; he would not turn back while there was still so much to see.

"We'll stay in the ship from now on," he said, "and we won't touch surface anywhere. That should be safe enough, surely."

Hilvar shrugged his shoulders, as if refusing to accept any responsibility for what might happen next. Now that Alvin was showing a certain amount of caution, he thought it unwise to admit that he was equally anxious to continue their exploring, though he had long ago abandoned all hope of meeting intelligent life upon any of these planets.

A double world lay ahead of them, a great planet with a smaller satellite beside it. The primary might have been the twin of the second world they had visited; it was clothed in that same blanket of livid green. There would be no point in landing there; this was a story they already knew.

Alvin brought the ship low over the surface of the satellite; he needed no warning from the complex mechanisms which protected him to know that there was no atmosphere here. All shadows had a sharp, clean edge, and there were no gradations between night and day. It was the first world on which he had seen something approaching night, for only one of the more distant suns was above the horizon in the area where they made first contact. The landscape was bathed in a dull red light, as though it had been dipped in blood.

For many miles they flew low above the mountains that were still as jagged and sharp as in the distant ages of their birth. This was a world that had never known change or decay, had never been scoured by winds and rains. No eternity circuits were needed here to preserve objects in their pristine freshness.

But if there was no air, then there could have been no life—or could there have been?

"Of course," said Hilvar, when Alvin put the question to him. "There's nothing biologically absurd in the idea. Life can't originate in airless space—but it can evolve forms that will survive in it. It must have happened millions of times, whenever an inhabited planet lost its atmosphere."

"But would you expect *intelligent* life forms to exist in a vacuum? Wouldn't they have protected themselves against the loss of their air?"

"Probably, if it occurred *after* they achieved enough intelligence to stop it happening. But if the atmosphere went while they were still in the primitive state, they would have to adapt or perish. After they had adapted, they might then develop a very high intelligence. In fact, they probably would—the incentive would be so great."

The argument, decided Alvin, was a purely theoretical one, as far as this planet was concerned. Nowhere was there any sign that it had ever borne life, intelligent or otherwise. But in that case, what was the purpose of this world? The entire multiple system of the Seven Suns, he was now certain was artificial, and this world must be part of its grand design.

It could, conceivably, be intended purely for ornament—to provide a moon in the sky of its giant companion. Even in that case, however, it seemed likely that it would be put to *some* use.

"Look," said Hilvar, pointing to the screen. "Over there, on the right."

Alvin changed the ship's course, and the landscape tilted around them. The red-lit rocks blurred with the speed of their motion; then the image stabilised, and sweeping below was the unmistakable evidence of life.

Unmistakable—yet also baffling. It took the form of a wide-spaced row of slender columns, each a hundred feet from its neighbour and twice as high. They stretched into the distance, dwindling in hypnotic perspective, until the far horizon swallowed them up.

Alvin swung the ship to the right, and began to race along the line of columns, wondering as he did so what purpose they could ever have served. They were absolutely uniform, marching in an unbroken file over hills and down into valleys. There was no sign that they had ever supported anything; they were smooth and featureless, tapering very slightly towards the top.

Quite abruptly, the line changed its course, turning sharply through a right-angle. Alvin overshot by several miles before he reacted and was able to swing the ship round in the new direction.

The columns continued with the same unbroken stride across the landscape, their spacing perfectly regular. Then, fifty miles from the last change of course, they turned abruptly through another right-angle. At this rate, thought Alvin, we will soon be back where we started.

The endless sequence of columns had so mesmerised them that when it was broken they were miles past the discontinuity before Hilvar cried out and made Alvin—who had noticed nothing—turn the ship back. They descended slowly, and as they circled above what Hilvar had found, a fantastic suspicion began to dawn in their minds—though at first neither dared mention it to the other.

Two of the columns had been broken off near their bases, and lay stretched out upon the rocks where they had fallen. Nor was that all; the two columns adjoining the gap had been bent outwards by some irresistible force.

There was no escape from the awesome conclusion. Now Alvin knew what they had been flying over; it was something he had seen often enough in Lys, but until this moment the shocking change of scale had prevented recognition.

"Hilvar," he said, still hardly daring to put his thoughts into words, "do you know what this is?"

"It seems hard to believe, but we've been flying round the edge of a corral. This thing is a fence—a fence that hasn't been strong enough."

"People who keep pets," said Alvin, with the nervous laugh men sometimes use to conceal their awe, "should make sure they know how to keep them under control."

Hilvar did not react to his forced levity; he was staring at the broken barricade, his brow furrowed with thought.

"I don't understand it," he said at last. "Where could it have got food on a planet like this? And why did it break out of its pen? I'd give a lot to know what kind of animal it was."

"Perhaps it was left here, and broke out because it was hungry," Alvin surmised. "Or something may have made it annoyed."

"Let's go lower," said Hilvar. "I want to have a look at the ground."

They descended until the ship was almost touching the barren rock, and it was then that they noticed that the plain was pitted wih innumerable small holes, no more than an inch or two wide. Outside the stockade, however, the ground was free from these mysterious pockmarks; they stopped abruptly at the line of the fence.

"You are right," said Hilvar. "It was hungry. But it wasn't an animal: it would be more accurate to call it a plant. It had exhausted the soil inside its pen, and had to find fresh food elsewhere. It probably moved quite slowly; perhaps it took years to break down those posts."

Alvin's imagination swiftly filled in the details he could never know with certainty. He did not doubt that Hilvar's analysis was basically correct, and that some botanical monster, perhaps moving too slowly for the eye to see, had fought a sluggish but relentless battle against the barriers that hemmed it in.

It might still be alive, even after all these ages, roving at will over the face of the planet. To look for it, however, would be a hopeless task, since it would mean quartering the surface of an entire globe. They made a desultory search in a few square miles around the gap, and located one great circular patch of pockmarks, almost five hundred feet across, where the creature had obviously stopped to feed—if one could apply that word to an organism that somehow drew its nourishment from solid rock.

As they lifted once more into space, Alvin felt a strange weariness come over him. He had seen so much, yet learned so little. There were many wonders on all these planets, but what he sought had fled them long ago. It would be useless, he knew, to visit the other worlds of the Seven Suns. Even if there was still intelligence in the Universe, where could he seek it now? He looked at the stars scattered like dust across the vision screen, and knew that what was left of Time was not enough to explore them all.

A feeling of loneliness and oppression such as he had never before experienced seemed to overwhelm him. He could understand now the fear of Diaspar for the great spaces of the Universe, the terror that had made his people gather in the little microcosm of their city. It was hard to believe that, after all, they had been right.

He turned to Hilvar for support. But Hilvar was standing, fists tightly clenched and with a glazed look in his eyes. His head was tilted on one side; he seemed to be listening, straining every sense into the emptiness around them.

"What is it?" said Alvin urgently. He had to repeat the question before Hilvar showed any sign of hearing it. He was still staring into nothingness when he finally replied.

"There's something coming," he said slowly. "Something that I don't understand."

It seemed to Alvin that the cabin had suddenly become very cold, and the racial nightmare of the Invaders reared up to confront him in all its terror. With an effort of will that sapped his strength, he forced his mind away from panic.

"Is it friendly?" he asked. "Shall I run for Earth?"

Hilvar did not answer the first question—only the second. His voice was very faint, but showed no sign of alarm or fear. It held rather a vast astonishment and curiosity, as if he had encountered something so surprising that he could not be bothered to deal with Alvin's anxious query.

"You're too late," he said. "It's already here."

The Galaxy had turned many times on its axis since consciousness first came to Vanamonde. He could recall little of those first aeons and the creatures who had tended him then—but he could remember still his desolation when they had gone and left him alone among the stars. Down the ages since, he had wandered from sun to sun, slowly evolving and increasing his powers. Once he had dreamed of finding again those who had attended his birth, and though the dream had faded now, it had never wholly died.

On countless worlds he had found the wreckage that life had left behind, but intelligence he had discovered only once—and from the Black Sun he had fled in terror. Yet the Universe was very large, and the search had scarcely begun.

Far away though it was in space and time, the great burst of power from the heart of the Galaxy beckoned to Vanamonde across the light-years. It was utterly unlike the radiation of the stars, and it had appeared in his field of consciousness as suddenly as a meteor trail across a cloudless sky. He moved through space and time towards it, to the latest moment of its existence, sloughing from him in the way he knew the dead, unchanging pattern of the past.

The long metal shape, with its infinite complexities of structure, he could not understand, for it was as strange to him as almost all the things of the physical world. Around it still clung the aura of power that had drawn him across the Universe, but that was of no interest to him now. Carefully, with the delicate nervousness of a wild beast half poised for flight, he reached out towards the two minds he had discovered.

And then he knew that his long search was ended.

Alvin grasped Hilvar by the shoulders and shook him violently, trying to drag him back to a great awareness of reality.

"Tell me what's happening!" he begged. "What do you want me to do?"

The remote, abstracted look faded from Hilvar's eyes.

"I still don't understand," he said, "but there's no need to be frightened —I'm sure of that. Whatever it is, it won't harm us. It seems simply— interested."

Alvin was about to reply when he was suddenly overwhelmed by a sensation unlike any he had ever known before. A warm, tingling glow seemed to spread through his body; it lasted only a few seconds, but when it was gone he was no longer merely Alvin. Something was sharing his brain, overlapping it as one circle may partly cover another. He was conscious, also, of Hilvar's mind close at hand, equally entangled in whatever creature had descended upon them. The sensation was strange rather than unpleasant, and it gave Alvin his first glimpse of true telepathy—the power which in his people had so degenerated that it could now be used only to control machines.

Alvin had rebelled at once when Seranis had tried to dominate his mind, he did not struggle against this intrusion. It would have been useless, and he knew that this creature, whatever it might be, was not unfriendly. He let himself relax, accepting without resistance the fact that an infinitely greater intelligence than his own was exploring his mind. But in that belief he was not wholly right.

One of these minds, Vanamonde saw at once, was more sympathetic and accessible than the other. He could tell that both were filled with wonder at his presence, and that surprised him greatly. It was hard to believe that they could have forgotten; forgetfulness, like mortality, was beyond the comprehension of Vanamonde.

Communication was very difficult; many of the thought-images of their minds were so strange that he could hardly recognise them. He was puzzled and a little frightened by the recurrent fear-pattern of the Invaders; it reminded him of his own emotions when the Black Sun first came into his field of knowledge.

But they knew nothing of the Black Sun, and now their own questions were beginning to form in his mind.

"*What are you?*"

He gave the only reply he could.

"I am Vanamonde."

There came a pause (how long the pattern of their thoughts took to form!) and then the question was repeated. They had not understood; that was strange, for surely their kind had given him his name for it to be among the memories of his birth. Those memories were very few, and they began strangely at a single point in time, but they were crystal-clear.

Again their tiny thoughts struggled up into his consciousness.

"Where are the people who built the Seven Suns? What happened to them?"

He did not know; they could scarcely believe him, and their disappointment came sharp and clear across the abyss separating their minds from his. But they were patient and he was glad to help them, for their quest was the same as his and they gave him the first companionship he had ever known.

As long as he lived, Alvin did not believe he would ever again undergo so strange an experience as this soundless conversation. It was hard to believe that he could be little more than a spectator, for he did not care to admit, even to himself, that Hilvar's mind was in some ways so much more capable than his own. He could only wait and wonder, half dazed by the torrent of thought just beyond the limits of his understanding

Presently Hilvar, rather pale and strained, broke off the contact and turned to his friend.

"Alvin," he said, his voice very tired. "There's something strange here. I don't understand it at all."

The news did a little to restore Alvin's self-esteem, and his face must have shown his feelings for Hilvar gave a sudden, sympathetic smile.

"I can't discover what this—Vanamonde—is," he continued. "It's a creature of tremendous knowledge, but it seems to have very little intelligence. Of course," he added, "it's mind may be of such a different order that we can't understand it—yet somehow I don't believe that is the right explanation."

"Well, what *have* you learned?" asked Alvin with some impatience. "Does it know anything about the Seven Suns?"

Hilvar's mind still seemed very far away.

"They were built by many races, including our own," he said absently. "It can give me facts like that, but it doesn't seem to understand their meaning. I believe it's conscious of the Past, without being able to interpret it. Everything that's happened seems jumbled together in its mind."

He paused thoughtfully for a moment; then his face lightened.

"There's only one thing to do; somehow or other, we must get Vanamonde to Earth so that our philosophers can study him."

"Would that be safe?" asked Alvin.

"Yes," answered Hilvar, thinking how uncharacteristic his friend's remark was. "Vanamonde is friendly. More than that, in fact, he seems almost affectionate."

And quite suddenly the thought that all the while had been hovering at the edge of Alvin's consciousness came clearly into view. He remembered Krif and all the animals that were constantly escaping, to the annoyance or alarm of Hilvar's friends. And he recalled—how long ago that seemed!—the zoological purpose behind their expedition to Shalmirane.

Hilvar had found a new pet.

CHAPTER XXII

Hᴏᴡ ᴄᴏᴍᴘʟᴇᴛᴇʟʏ ᴜɴᴛʜɪɴᴋᴀʙʟᴇ, Jeserac, mused, this conference would have seemed only a few short days ago. The six visitors from Lys sat facing the Council, along a table placed across the open end of the horseshoe. It was ironic to remember that not long ago Alvin had stood at that same spot and heard the council rule that Diaspar must be closed again from the world. Now the world had broken in upon it with a vengeance—and not only the world, but the universe.

The Council itself had already changed. No less than five of its members were missing. They had been unable to face the responsibilities and problems now confronting them, and had followed the path that Khedron had already taken. It was, thought Jeserac, proof that Diaspar had failed if so many of its citizens were unable to face their first real challenge in millions of years. Many thousands of them had already fled into the brief oblivion of the memory banks, hoping that when they awoke the crisis would be past and Diaspar would be its familiar self again. They would be disappointed.

Jeserac had been co-opted to fill one of the vacant places on the Council. Though he was under something of a cloud, owing to his position as Alvin's tutor, his presence was so obviously essential that no one had suggested excluding him. He sat at one end of the horseshoe-shaped table—a position which gave him several advantages. Not only could he study the profiles of the visitors, but he could also see the faces of his fellow-councillors—and their expressions were sufficiently instructive.

There was no doubt that Alvin had been right, and the Council was slowly realising the unpalatable truth. The delegates from Lys could think far more swiftly than the finest minds in Diaspar. Nor was that their only advantage, for they also showed an extraordinary degree of co-ordination which Jeserac guessed must be due to their telepathic powers. He wondered if they were reading the Councillors' thoughts, but decided that they would not have broken the solemn assurance without which this meeting would have been impossible.

Jeserac did not think that much progress had been made; for that matter, he did not see how it could be. The Council, which had barely accepted the existence of Lys, still seemed incapable of realising what had happened. But it was clearly frightened—and so, he guessed, were the visitors, though they managed to conceal the fact better.

Jeserac himself was not as terrified as he had expected; his fears were still there, but he had faced them at last. Something of Alvin's own recklessness— or was it courage?—had begun to change his outlook and give him new horizons. He did not believe he would ever be able to set foot beyond the walls of Diaspar, but now he understood the impulse that had driven Alvin to do so.

The President's question caught him unawares, but he recovered himself quickly.

"I think," he said, "that it was sheer chance that this situation never arose before. We know that there were fourteen earlier Uniques, and there must have been some definite plan behind their creation. That plan, I believe, was to ensure that Lys and Diaspar would not remain apart for ever. Alvin has seen to that, but he has also done something which I do not imagine was ever in the original scheme. Could the Central Computer confirm that?"

The impersonal voice replied at once.

"The Councillor knows that I cannot comment on the instructions given to me by my designers."

Jeserac accepted the mild reproof.

"Whatever the cause, we cannot dispute the facts. Alvin has gone out into space. When he returns, you may prevent him leaving again—though I doubt if you will succeed, for he may have learnt a great deal by then. And if what you fear has happened, there is nothing any of us can do about it. Earth is utterly helpless—as she has been for millions of centuries."

Jeserac paused and glanced along the tables. His words had pleased no one, nor had he expected them to do so.

"Yet I don't see why we should be alarmed. Earth is in no greater danger now than she has always been. Why should two men in a single small ship bring the wrath of the Invaders down upon us again? If we'll be honest with ourselves, we must admit that the Invaders could have destroyed our world ages ago."

There was a disapproving silence. This was heresy—and once Jeserac himself would have condemned it as such.

The President interrupted, frowning heavily.

"Is there not a legend that the Invaders spared Earth itself only on condition that Man never went into space again? And have we not now broken those conditions?"

"A legend, yes," said Jeserac. "We accept many things without question, and this is one of them. However, there is no proof of it. I find it hard to believe that anything of such importance would not be recorded in the memories of the Central Computer, yet it knows nothing of this pact. I have asked it, though only through the information machines. The council may care to ask the question directly."

Jeserac saw no reason why he should risk a second admonishment by trespassing on forbidden territory, and waited for the President's reply.

It never came, for in that moment the visitors from Lys suddenly started in their seats, while their faces froze in simultaneous expressions of incredulity and alarm. They seemed to be listening while some faraway voice poured its message into their ears.

The Councillors waited, their own apprehension growing minute by minute as the soundless conversation proceeded. Then the leader of the delegation shook himself free from his trance, and turned apologetically to the President.

"We have just had some very strange and disturbing news from Lys," he said.

"Has Alvin returned to Earth?" asked the President.

"No—not Alvin. Something else."

As he brought his faithful ship down in the glade of Airlee, Alvin wondered if ever in human history any ship had brought such a cargo to Earth—if, indeed, Vanamonde was located in the physical space of the machine. There had been no sign of him on the voyage; Hilvar believed, and his knowledge was more direct, that only Vanamonde's sphere of attention could be said to have any position in space. Vanamonde himself was not located anywhere— perhaps not even *anywhen*.

Seranis and five senators were waiting for them as they emerged from the ship. One of the senators Alvin had already met on his last visit; the other two from that previous meeting, were, he gathered, now in Diaspar. He wondered how the delegation was faring, and how the city had reacted to the presence of the first intruders from outside in so many millions of years.

"It seems, Alvin," said Seranis dryly, after she had greeted her son, "that you have a genius for discovering remarkable entities. Still, I think it will be some time before you can surpass your present achievement."

For once, it was Alvin's turn to be surprised.

"Then Vanamonde's arrived?"

"Yes, hours ago. Somehow he managed to trace the path your ship made on its outward journey—a staggering feat in itself, and one which raises interesting philosophical problems. There is some evidence that he reached Lys at the moment you discovered him, so that he is capable of infinite speeds. And that is not all. In the last few hours he has taught us more of history than we thought existed."

Alvin looked at her in amazement. Then he understood; it was not hard to imagine what the impact of Vanamonde must have been upon this people, with their keen perceptions and their wonderfully interlocking minds. They had reacted with surprising speed, and he had a sudden incongruous picture of Vanamonde, perhaps a little frightened, surrounded by the eager intellects of Lys.

"Have you discovered what he is?" Alvin asked.

"Yes. That was simple, though we still don't know his origin. He's a pure mentality and his knowledge seems to be unlimited. But he's childish, and I mean that quite literally."

"Of course!" cried Hilvar. "I should have guessed!"

Alvin looked puzzled, and Seranis took pity on him.

"I mean that although Vanamonde has a colossal, perhaps an infinite mind, he's immature and undeveloped. His actual intelligence is less than that of a human being"—she smiled a little wryly—"though his thought processes are much faster and he learns very quickly. He also has some powers we do not yet understand. The whole of the past seems open to his mind, in a way that's difficult to describe. He may have used that ability to follow your path back to Earth."

Alvin stood in silence, for once somewhat overcome. He realised how right

Hilvar had been to bring Vanamonde to Lys. And he knew how lucky he had been ever to outwit Seranis; that was not something he would do twice in a lifetime.

"Do you mean," he asked, "that Vanamonde has only just been born?"

"By his standards, yes. His actual age is very great, though apparently less than Man's. The extraordinary thing is that he insists that *we* created him, and there's no doubt that his origin is bound up with all the great mysteries of the past."

"What's happening to Vanamonde now?" asked Hilvar in a slightly possessive voice.

"The historians of Grevarn are questioning him. They are trying to map out the main outlines of the past, but the work will take years. Vanamonde can describe the past in perfect detail, but he doesn't understand what he sees; it's very difficult to work with him."

Alvin wondered how Seranis knew all this; then he realised that probably every waking mind in Lys was watching the progress of the great research. He felt a sense of pride in the knowledge that he had now made as great a mark on Lys as on Diaspar, yet with that pride was mingled frustration. Here was something which he could never fully share nor understand: the direct contact even between human minds was as great a mystery to him as music must be to a deaf man, or colour to a blind one. Yet the people of Lys were now exchanging thoughts with this unimaginably alien being, whom he had led to Earth but whom he could never detect with any sense that he possessed.

There was no place for him here; when the inquiry was finished, he would be told the answers. He had opened the gates of infinity, and now felt awe— even fear—for all that he had done. For his own peace of mind, he must return to the tiny, familiar world of Diaspar, seeking its shelter while he came to grips with his dreams and his ambition. There was irony here; the one who had spurned the city to venture out among the stars was coming home as a frightened child runs back to its mother.

CHAPTER XXIII

DIASPAR WAS NONE too pleased to see Alvin again. The city was still in a ferment, like a giant beehive that had been violently stirred with a stick. It was still reluctant to face reality, but those who refused to admit the existence of Lys and the outside world no longer had a place to hide. The memory banks had ceased to accept them; those who tried to cling to their dreams, and to seek refuge in the future, now walked in vain into the Hall of Creation. The dissolving, heatless flame refused to greet them; they no longer awoke, their minds washed clean, a hundred thousand years further down the river of time. No appeal to the Central Computer was of any avail, nor would it explain the reason for its actions. The intended refugees had to turn sadly back into the city, to face the problems of their age.

Alvin had landed at the periphery of the Park, not far from Council Hall. Until the last moment, he was not certain that he could bring the ship into the city, through whatever screens fenced its sky from the outer world. The firmament of Diaspar, like all else about it, was artificial, or at least partly so. Night, with its starry reminder of all that Man had lost, was never allowed to intrude upon the city; it was protected also from the storms that sometimes raged across the desert and filled the sky with moving walls of sand.

The invisible guardians let Alvin pass, and as Diaspar lay spread out beneath him, he knew that he had come home. However much the universe and its mysteries might call him, this was where he was born and where he belonged. It would never satisfy him, yet always he would return. He had gone half-way across the Galaxy to learn this simple truth.

The crowds had gathered even before the ship landed, and Alvin wondered how his fellow-citizens would receive him now that he had returned. He could read their faces easily enough, as he watched them through the viewing screen before he opened the airlock. The dominant emotion seemed to be curiosity—in itself something new in Diaspar. Mingled with that was apprehension, while here and there were unmistakable signs of fear. No one, Alvin thought a little wistfully, seemed glad to see him back. . . .

The Council, on the other hand, positively welcomed him—though not out of pure friendship. Though he had caused this crisis, he alone could give the facts on which future policy must be based. He was listened to with deep attention as he described his flight to the Seven Suns and his meeting with Vanamonde. Then he answered innumerable questions, with a patience which probably surprised his interrogators. Uppermost in their minds, he quickly discovered, was the fear of the Invaders, though they never mentioned the name and were clearly unhappy when he broached the subject directly.

"If the Invaders are still in this Universe," Alvin told the Council, "then surely I should have met them at its very centre. But there is no intelligent life among the Seven Suns; we had already guessed that before Vanamonde confirmed it. I believe that the Invaders departed ages ago; certainly Vanamonde, who appears to be at least as old as Diaspar, knows nothing of them."

"I have a suggestion," said one of the Councillors suddenly. "Vanamonde may be a descendant of the Invaders, in some way beyond our present understanding. He has forgotten his origin, but that does not mean that one day he may not be dangerous again."

Hilvar, who was present merely as a spectator, did not wait for permission to speak. It was the first time that Alvin had ever seen him angry.

"Vanamonde has looked into my mind," he said, "and I have glimpsed something of his. My people have already learned much about him, though they have not yet discovered what he is. But one thing is certain—he is friendly, and was glad to find us. We have nothing to fear from him."

There was a brief silence after this outburst, and Hilvar relaxed with a somewhat embarrassed expression. It was noticeable that the tension in the Council Chamber lessened from then on, as if a cloud had lifted from the spirits of those present. Certainly the President made no attempt, as he was supposed to do, to censure Hilvar for his interruption.

It was clear to Alvin, as he listened to the debate, that three schools of thought were represented on the Council. The conservatives, who were in a minority, still hoped that the clock could be turned back and that the old order could somehow be restored. Against all reason, they clung to the hope that Diaspar and Lys could be persuaded to forget each other again.

The progressives were an equally small minority; the fact that there were any on the Council at all pleased and surprised Alvin. They did not exactly welcome this invasion of the outer world, but they were determined to make the best of it. Some of them went so far as to suggest that there might be a way of breaking through the psychological barriers which for so long had sealed Diaspar even more effectively than the physical ones.

Most of the Council, accurately reflecting the mood of the city, had adopted an attitude of watchful caution, while they waited for the pattern of the future to emerge. They realised that they could make no general plans, nor try to carry out any definite policy, until the storm had passed.

Jeserac joined Alvin and Hilvar when the session was over. He seemed to have changed since they had last met—and last parted—in the Tower of Loranne, with the desert spread out beneath them. The change was not one that Alvin had expected, though it was one that he was to encounter more and more often in the days to come.

Jeserac seemed younger, as if the fires of life had found fresh fuel and were burning more brightly in his veins. Despite his age, he was one of those who could accept the challenge that Alvin had thrown to Diaspar.

"I have some news for you, Alvin," he said. "I think you know Senator Gerane."

Alvin was puzzled for a moment; then he remembered.

"Of course—he was one of the first men I met in Lys. Isn't he a member of their delegation?"

"Yes; we have grown to know each other quite well. He is a brilliant man, and understands more about the human mind than I would have believed possible—though he tells me that by the standards of Lys he is only a beginner. While he is here, he is starting a project which will be very close to your heart. He is hoping to analyse the compulsion which keeps us in the city, and he believes that once he has discovered how it was imposed, he will be able to remove it. About twenty of us are already co-operating with him."

"And you are one of them?"

"Yes," replied Jeserac, showing the nearest approach to bashfulness that Alvin had even seen or ever would see. "It is not easy, and certainly not pleasant—but it is stimulating."

"How does Gerane work?"

"He is operating through the Sagas. He has had a whole series of them constructed, and studies our reactions when we are experiencing them. I never thought at my age, that I should go back to my childhood recreations again!"

"What are the Sagas?" asked Hilvar.

"Imaginary dream-worlds," explained Alvin. "At least, most of them are imaginary, though some are probably based on historical facts. There are millions of them recorded in the memory cells of the city; you can take your choice of any kind of adventure or experience you wish, and it will seem utterly real to you while the impulses are being fed into your mind." He turned to Jeserac.

"What kind of Sagas does Gerane take you into?"

"Most of them are concerned, as you might expect with leaving Diaspar. Some have taken us back to our very earliest lives, to as near to the founding of the city as we can get. Gerane believes that the closer he can get to the origin of this compulsion, the more easily he will be able to undermine it."

Alvin felt very encouraged by this news. His work would be merely half accomplished if he had opened the gates of Diaspar—only to find that no one would pass through them.

"Do you *really* want to be able to leave Diaspar?" asked Hilvar shrewdly.

"No," replied Jeserac, without hesitation. "I am terrified of the idea. But I realise that we were completely wrong in thinking that Diaspar was all the world that mattered, and logic tells me that something has to be done to rectify the mistake. Emotionally, I am still quite incapable of leaving the city; perhaps I always shall be. Gerane thinks he can get some of us to go to Lys, and I am willing to help him with the experiment—even though half the time I hope that it will fail."

Alvin looked at his old tutor with a new respect. He no longer discounted the power of suggestion, nor underestimated the forces which could compel a man to act in defiance of logic. He could not help comparing Jeserac's calm courage with Khedron's panic flight into the future—though with his new understanding of human nature he no longer cared to condemn the Jester for what he had done.

Gerane, he was certain, would accomplish what he had set out to do. Jeserac might be too old to break the pattern of a lifetime, however willing he might be to start afresh. That did not matter, for others would succeed, with the skilled guidance of the psychologists of Lys. And once a few had escaped from their billion-year-old mould, it would only be a question of time before the remainder could follow.

He wondered what would happen to Diaspar—and to Lys—when the barriers were fully down. Somehow, the best elements of both must be saved, and welded into a new and healthier culture. It was a terrifying task, and would need all the wisdom and all the patience that each could bring to bear.

Some of the difficulties of the forthcoming adjustments had already been encountered. The visitors from Lys had, politely enough, refused to live in the homes provided for them in the city. They had set up their own temporary accommodation in the Park, among surroundings which reminded them of Lys. Hilvar was the only exception; though he disliked living in a house with indeterminate walls and ephemeral furniture, he bravely accepted Alvin's hospitality, reassured by the promise that they would not stay here for long.

Hilvar had never felt lonely in his life, but he knew loneliness in Diaspar. The city was more strange to him than Lys had been to Alvin, and he was oppressed and overwhelmed by its infinite complexity and by the myriads of strangers who seemed to crowd every inch of space around him. He knew, if only in a tenuous manner, everyone in Lys, whether he had met them or not. In a thousand lifetimes he could never know everyone in Diaspar, and though he realised that this was an irrational feeling, it left him vaguely depressed. Only his loyalty to Alvin held him here in a world which had nothing in common with his own.

He had often tried to analyse his feelings towards Alvin. His friendship sprang, he knew, from the same source that inspired his sympathy for all small and struggling creatures. This would have astonished those who thought of Alvin as wilful, subborn, and self-centred, needing no affection from anyone and incapable of returning it even if it was offered.

Hilvar knew better than this; he had sensed it instinctively from the first. Alvin was an explorer, and all explorers are seeking something they have lost. It is seldom that they find it, and more seldom still that the attainment brings them greater happiness than the quest.

What Alvin was seeking, Hilvar did not know. He was driven by forces that had been set in motion ages before, by the men of genius who planned Diaspar with such perverse skill—or by the men of even greater genius who had opposed them. Like every human being, Alvin was in some measure a machine, his actions predetermined by his inheritance. That did not alter his need for understanding and sympathy, nor did it render him immune to loneliness or frustration. To his own people, he was so unaccountable a creature that they sometimes forgot that he still shared their emotions. It needed a stranger from a totally different environment to see him as another human being.

Within a few days of arriving in Diaspar, Hilvar had met more people than ever before in his entire life. Met them—and had grown to know practically none. Because they were so crowded together, the inhabitants of the city maintained a reserve that was hard to penetrate. The only privacy they knew was that of the mind, and they still clung to this even as they made their way through the endless social activities of Diaspar. Hilvar felt sorry for them, though he knew that they felt no need for his sympathy. They did not realise what they were missing—they could not understand the warm sense of community, the feeling of *belonging*, which linked everyone together in the telepathic society of Lys. Indeed, though they were polite enough to try to conceal it, it was obvious that most of the people he spoke to looked upon him pityingly as leading an incredibly dull and drab existence.

Eriston and Etania, Alvin's guardians, Hilvar quickly dismissed as kindly but totally baffled nonentities. He found it very confusing to hear Alvin refer to them as his father and mother—words which in Lys still retained their ancient biological meaning. It required a continual effort of imagination to remember that the laws of life and death had been repealed by the makers of

Diaspar, and there were times when it seemed to Hilvar that despite all the activity around him, the city was half empty because it had no children.

He wondered what would happen to Diaspar now that its long isolation was over. The best thing the city could do, he decided, was to destroy the memory banks which had held it entranced for so many ages. Miraculous though they were—perhaps the supreme triumph of the science that had produced them—they were the creations of a sick culture, a culture that had been afraid of many things. Some of those fears had been based on reality, but others, it now seemed, lay in the imagination. Hilvar knew a little of the pattern that was beginning to emerge from the exploration of Vanamonde's mind. In a few days, Diaspar would know it too—and would discover how much of its past had been a myth.

Yet if the memory banks were destroyed, within a thousand years the city would be dead, since its people had lost the power to reproduce themselves. That was the dilemma that had to be faced, but already Hilvar had glimpsed one possible solution. There was always an answer to any technical problem, and his people were masters of the biological sciences. What had been done could be undone, if Diaspar so wished.

First, however, the city would have to learn what it had lost. Its education would take many years—perhaps many centuries. But it was beginning; very soon the impact of the first lesson would shake Diaspar as profoundly as had contact with Lys itself.

It would shake Lys too. For all the difference between the two cultures, they had sprung from the same roots—and they had shared the same illusions. They would both be healthier when they looked once more, with a calm and steadfast gaze into the past which they had lost.

CHAPTER XXIV

THE AMPHITHEATRE HAD been designed to hold the entire waking population of Diaspar, and scarcely one of its ten million places was empty. As he looked down the great curving sweep from his vantage point high up the slope, Alvin was irresistibly reminded of Shalmirane. The two craters were of the same shape, and almost the same size. If one packed the crater of Shalmirane with humanity, it would look very much like this.

There was, however, one fundamental difference between the two. The great bowl of Shalmirane existed; this amphitheatre did not. Nor had it ever done so; it was merely a phantom, a pattern of electronic charges, slumbering in the memory of the Central Computer until the need came to call it forth. Alvin knew that in reality he was still in his room, and that all the myriads of people who appeared to surround him were equally in their own homes. As long as he made no attempt to move from this spot, the illusion was perfect. He could believe that Diaspar had been abolished and that all its citizens had been assembled here in this enormous concavity.

Not once in a thousand years did the life of the city stop so that all its people could meet in Grand Assembly. In Lys also, Alvin knew, the equivalent of this gathering was taking place. There it would be a meeting of minds, but perhaps associated with it would be an apparent meeting of bodies, as imaginary yet as seemingly real as this.

He could recognise most of the faces around him, out to the limits of unaided vision. More than a mile away, and a thousand feet below, was the little circular stage upon which the attention of the entire world was now fixed. It was hard to believe that he could see anything from such a distance, but Alvin knew that when the address began he would hear and observe everything that happened as clearly as anyone else in Diaspar.

The stage was filled with mist; the mist became Callitrax, leader of the group whose task it had been to reconstruct the past from the information which Vanamonde had brought to Earth. It had been a stupendous, almost an impossible undertaking, and not merely because of the spans of time involved. Only once, with the mental help of Hilvar, had Alvin been given a brief glimpse into the mind of the strange being they had discovered—or who had discovered them. To Alvin, the thoughts of Vanamonde were as meaningless as a thousand voices shouting together in some vast, echoing cave. Yet the men of Lys could disentangle them, could record them to be analysed at leisure. Already, so it was rumoured—though Hilvar would neither deny nor confirm this—what they had discovered was so strange that it bore scarcely any resemblance to the history which all the human race had accepted for a billion years.

Callitrax began to speak. To Alvin, as to everyone else in Diaspar, the clear, precise voice seemed to come from a point only a few inches away. Then, in a manner that was hard to define, just as the geometry of a dream defies logic yet rouses no surprise in the mind of the dreamer, Alvin was standing beside Callitrax while at the same time he retained his position high up on the slope of the amphitheatre. The paradox did not puzzle him; he simply accepted it without question, like all the other masteries over time and space which science had given him.

Very briefly, Callitrax ran through the accepted history of the race. He spoke of the unknown peoples of the Dawn Civilisations, who had left behind them nothing but a handful of great names and the fading legends of the Empire. Even at the beginning, so the story went, Man had desired the stars—and had at last attained them. For millions of years he had expanded across the Galaxy, gathering system after system beneath his sway. Then, out of the darkness beyond the rim of the Universe, the Invaders had struck and wrenched from him all that he had won.

The retreat to the Solar System had been bitter and must have lasted many ages. Earth itself was barely saved by the fabulous battles that raged round

Shalmirane. When all was over, Man was left with only his memories and the world on which he had been born.

Since then, all else had been long-drawn anticlimax. As an ultimate irony, the race that had hoped to rule the Universe had abandoned most of its own tiny world, and had split into the two isolated cultures of Lys and Diaspar—oases of life in a desert that sundered them as effectively as the gulfs between the stars.

Callitrax paused; to Alvin, as to everyone in the great assembly, it seemed that the historian was looking directly at him with eyes that had witnessed things which even now they could not wholly credit.

"So much," said Callitrax, "for the tales we have believed since our records began. I must tell you now that they are false—false in every detail—*so false that even now we have not fully reconciled them with the truth.*"

He waited for the full meaning of his words to strike home. Then, speaking slowly and carefully, he gave to both Lys and Diaspar the knowledge that had been won from the mind of Vanamonde.

It was not even true that Man had reached the stars. The whole of his little empire was bounded by the orbits of Pluto and Persephone, for interstellar space proved a barrier beyond his power to cross. His entire civilisation was huddled round the sun, and was still very young when the stars reached him.

The impact must have been shattering. Despite his failures, Man had never doubted that one day he would conquer the deeps of space. He believed too that if the Universe held his equals, it did not hold his superiors. Now he knew that both beliefs were wrong, and that out among the stars were minds far greater than his own. For many centuries, first in the ships of other races and later in machines built with borrowed knowledge, Man had explored the Galaxy. Everywhere he found cultures he could understand but could not match, and here and there he encountered minds which would soon have passed altogether beyond his comprehension.

The shock was tremendous, but it proved the making of the race. Sadder and infinitely wiser, Man had returned to the Solar System to brood upon the knowledge he had gained. He would accept the challenge, and slowly he evolved a plan which gave hope for the future.

Once the physical sciences had been Man's greatest interest. Now he turned even more fiercely to genetics and the study of the mind. Whatever the cost, he would drive himself to the limits of his evolution.

The great experiment had consumed the entire energies of the race for millions of years. All that striving, all that sacrifice and toil, became only a handful of words in Callitrax's narrative. It had brought Man his greatest victories. He had banished disease; he could live for ever if he wished, and in mastering telepathy he had bent the most subtle of all powers to his will.

He was ready to go out again, relying upon his own resources, into the great spaces of the Galaxy. He would meet as an equal the races of the worlds from which he had once turned aside. And he would play his full part in the story of the Universe.

These things he did. From this age, perhaps the most spacious of all history, came the legends of the Empire. It had been an Empire of many races, but this had been forgotten in the drama, too tremendous for tragedy, in which it had come to its end.

The Empire had lasted for at least a million years. It must have known crises, perhaps even wars, but all these were lost in the sweep of great races moving together towards maturity.

"We can be proud," continued Callitrax, "of the part our ancestors played in this story. Even when they had reached their cultural plateau, they lost none of their initiative. We deal now with conjecture rather than proven fact, but it seems certain that the experiments which were at once the Empire's downfall and its crowning glory were inspired and directed by Man.

"The philosophy underlying these experiments appears to have been this. Contact with other species had shown Man how profoundly a race's world-picture depended upon its physical body and the sense organs with which it was equipped. It was argued that a true picture of the Universe could be obtained, if at all, only by a mind which was free from such physical limitations—a pure mentality, in fact. This was a conception common among many of Earth's ancient religious faiths, and it seems strange that an idea which had no rational origin should finally become one of the greatest goals of science.

"No disembodied intelligence had ever been encountered in the natural universe; the Empire set out to create one. We have forgotten, with so much else, the skills and knowledge which made this possible. The scientists of the Empire had mastered all the forces of Nature, all the secrets of time and space. As our minds are the by-product of an immensely intricate arrangement of brain cells, linked together by the network of the nervous system, so they strove to create a brain whose components were not material, but patterns embossed upon space itself. Such a brain, if one can call it that, would use electrical or yet higher forces for its operation, and would be completely free from the tyranny of matter. It could function with far greater speed than any organic intelligence; it could endure as long as there was an erg of free energy left in the Universe, and no limit could be seen for its powers. Once created, it would develop potentialities which even its makers could not foresee.

"Largely as a result of the experience gained in his own regeneration, Man suggested that the creation of such beings should be attempted. It was the greatest challenge ever thrown out to intelligence in the Universe, and after centuries of debate it was accepted. All the races of the Galaxy joined together in its fulfilment.

"More than a million years were to separate the dream from the reality. Civilisations were to rise and fall, again and yet again the age-long toil of worlds was to be lost, but the goal was never forgotten. One day we may know the full story of this, the greatest sustained effort in all history. Today we only know that its ending was a disaster that almost wrecked the Galaxy.

"Into this period Vanamonde's mind refuses to go. There is a narrow region of time which is blocked to him but only, we believe, by his own fears. At its beginning we can see the Empire at the summit of its glory, taut with the expectation of coming success. At its end, only a few thousand years later, the Empire is shattered and the stars themselves are dimmed as though drained of their power. Over the Galaxy hangs a pall of fear, a fear with which is linked the name 'The Mad Mind'.

"What must have happened in that short period is not hard to guess. The pure mentality had been created, but it was either insane or, as seems more likely from other sources, was implacably hostile to matter. For centuries it ravaged the Universe until brought under control by forces of which we cannot guess. Whatever weapon the Empire used in its extremity squandered the resources of the stars; from the memories of that conflict spring some, though not all, of the legends of the Invaders. But of this I shall presently say more.

"The Mad Mind could not be destroyed, for it was immortal. It was driven to the edge of the Galaxy and there imprisoned in a way we do not understand. Its prison was a strange artificial star known as the Black Sun, and there it remains to this day. When the Black Sun dies, it will be free again. How far in the future that day lies there is no way of telling."

Callitrax became silent, as if lost in his own thoughts, utterly unconscious of the fact that the eyes of all the world were upon him. In the long silence, Alvin glanced over the packed multitude around him, seeking to read their minds as they faced this revelation—and this unknown threat which must now replace the myth of the Invaders. For the most part, the faces of his fellow-citizens were frozen in disbelief; they were still struggling to reject their false past, and could not yet accept the yet stranger reality that had superseded it.

Callitrax began to speak again in a quiet, more subdued voice as he described the last days of the Empire. This was the age, Alvin realised as the picture unfolded before him, in which he would have liked to have lived. There had been adventure then, and a superb and dauntless courage—the courage that could snatch victory from the teeth of disaster.

"Though the Galaxy had been laid waste by the Mad Mind, the resources of the Empire were still enormous, and its spirit was unbroken. With a courage at which we can only marvel, the great experiment was resumed and a search made for the flaw that had caused the catastrophe. There were now, of course, many who opposed the work and predicted further disasters, but they were overruled. The project went ahead and, with the knowledge so bitterly gained, this time it succeeded.

"The new race that was born had a potential intellect that could not even be measured. But it was completely infantile; we do not know if this was expected by its creators, but it seems likely that they knew it to be inevitable. Millions of years would be needed before it reached maturity, and nothing could be done to hasten the process. Vanamonde was the first of these minds; there must be others elsewhere in the Galaxy, but we believe that only a very few were created, for Vanamonde has never encountered any of his fellows.

"The creation of the pure mentalities was the greatest achievement of Galactic civilisation; in it Man played a major and perhaps a dominant part. I have made no reference to Earth itself, for its history is merely a tiny thread in an enormous tapestry. Since it had always been drained of its most adventurous spirits, our planet had inevitably become highly conservative, and in the end it opposed the scientists who created Vanamonde. Certainly it played no part at all in the final act.

"The work of the Empire was now finished; the men of that age looked round at the stars they had ravaged in their desperate peril, and they made their decision. They would leave the Universe to Vanamonde.

"There is a mystery here—a mystery we may never solve, for Vanamonde cannot help us. All we know is that the Empire made contact with—something —very strange and very great, far away around the curve of the Cosmos, at the other extremity of space itself. What it was we can only guess, but its call must have been of immense urgency, and immense promise. Within a very short period of time our ancestors and their fellow-races had gone upon a journey which we cannot follow. Vanamonde's thoughts seem to be bounded by the confines of the Galaxy, but through his mind we have watched the beginnings of this great and mysterious adventure. Here is the image that we have reconstructed; now you are going to look more than a billion years into the past——"

A pale wraith of its former glory, the slowly turning wheel of the Galaxy hung in nothingness. Throughout its length were the great empty rents which the Mad Mind had torn—wounds that in ages to come the drifting stars would fill. But they would never replace the splendour that had gone.

Man was about to leave his Universe, as long ago he had left his world. And not only Man, but the thousand other races that had worked with him to make the Empire. They were gathered together, here at the edge of the Galaxy, with its whole thickness between them and the goal they would not reach for ages.

They had assembled a fleet before which imagination quailed. Its flagships were suns, its smallest vessels, planets. An entire globular cluster, with all its solar systems and all their teeming worlds, was about to be launched across infinity.

The long line of fire smashed through the heart of the Universe, leaping from star to star. In a moment of time a thousand suns had died, feeding their energies to the monstrous shape that had torn along the axis of the Galaxy, and was now receding into the abyss. . . .

"So the Empire left our Universe, to meet its destiny elsewhere. When its heirs, the pure mentalities, have reached their full stature, it may return again. But that day must still lie far ahead.

"This, in its briefest and most superficial outlines, is the story of Galactic civilisation. Our own history, which to us seems so important, is no more than a belated and trivial epilogue, though one so complex that we have not been able to unravel its details. It seems that many of the older, less adventurous races refused to leave their homes; our direct ancestors were among them. Most of these races fell into decadence and are now extinct, though some may still survive. Our own world barely escaped the same fate. During the Transition Centuries—which actually lasted for millions of years—

the knowledge of the past was lost or else deliberately destroyed. The latter, hard though it is to believe, seems more probable. For ages, Man sank into a superstitious yet still scientific barbarism during which he distorted history to remove his sense of impotence and failure. The legends of the Invader are completely false, although the desperate struggle against the Mad Mind undoubtedly contributed something to them. Nothing drove our ancestors back to Earth except the sickness in their souls.

"When we made this discovery, one problem in particular puzzled us in Lys. The Battle of Shalmirane never occurred—yet Shalmirane existed, and exists to this day. What is more, it was one of the greatest weapons of destruction ever built.

"It took us some time to resolve this puzzle, but the answer, once it was found, was very simple. Long ago our Earth had a single giant satellite, the Moon. When, in the tug of war between the tides and gravity, the Moon at last began to fall, it became necessary to destroy it. Shalmirane was built for that purpose, and round its use were woven the legends you all know."

Callitrax smiled a little ruefully at his immense audience.

"There are many such legends, partly true and partly false, and other paradoxes in our past which have not yet been resolved. That problem, though, is one for the psychologist rather than the historian. Even the records of the Central Computer cannot be wholly trusted, and bear clear evidence of tampering in the very remote past.

"On Earth, only Diaspar and Lys survived the period of decadence— Diaspar thanks to the perfection of its machines, Lys owing to its partial isolation and the unusual intellectual powers of its people. But both cultures, even when they had struggled back to their former level, were distorted by the fears and myths they had inherited.

"These fears need haunt us no longer. It is not my duty as an historian to predict the future, only to observe and interpret the past. But its lesson is clear enough; we have lived too long out of contact with reality, and now the time has come to rebuild our lives."

CHAPTER XXV

JESERAC WALKED IN silent wonder through the streets of a Diaspar he had never seen. So different was it, indeed, from the city in which he had passed all his lives that he would never have recognised it. Yet he knew that it was Diaspar, though *how* he knew, he did not pause to ask.

The streets were narrow, the buildings lower—and the Park was gone. Or rather, it did not yet exist. This was the Diaspar before the change, the Diaspar that had been open to the world and to the universe. The sky above the city was pale blue and flecked with ravelled wisps of clouds, slowly twisting and turning in the winds that blew across the face of this younger Earth.

Passing through and beyond the clouds were more substantial voyagers of the sky. Miles above the city, lacing the heavens with their silent tracery, the ships that linked Diaspar with the outer world came and went upon their business. Jeserac stared for a long time at the mystery and wonder of the open sky, and for a moment fear brushed against his soul. He felt naked and unprotected, conscious that this peaceful blue dome above his head was no more than the thinnest of shells—that beyond it lay Space, with all its mystery and menace.

The fear was not strong enough to paralyse his will. In part of his mind, Jeserac knew that this whole experience was a dream, and a dream could not harm him, until he woke once more in the city that he knew.

He was walking into the heart of Diaspar, towards the point where in his own age stood the Tomb of Yarlan Zey. There was no tomb here, in this ancient city—only a low, circular building with many arched doorways leading into it. By one of those doorways a man was waiting for him.

Jeserac should have been overcome with astonishment, but nothing could surprise him now. Somehow it seemed right and natural that he should now be face to face with the man who had built Diaspar.

"You recognise me, I imagine," said Yarlan Zey.

"Of course; I have seen your statue a thousand times. You are Yarlan Zey, and this is Diaspar as it was a billion years ago. I know I am dreaming, and that neither of us is really here."

"Then you need not be alarmed at anything that happens. So follow me, and remember that nothing can harm you, since whenever you wish you can wake up in Diaspar—in your own age."

Obediently, Jeserac followed Yarlan Zey into the building, his mind a receptive, uncritical sponge. Some memory, or echo of a memory, warned him of what was going to happen next, and he knew that once he would have shrunk from it in horror. Now, however, he felt no fear. Not only did he feel protected by the knowledge that this experience was not real, but the presence of Yarlan Zey seemed a talisman against any dangers that might confront him.

There were few people drifting down the glide-ways that led into the depths of the building, and they had no other company when presently they stood in silence beside the long, streamlined cylinder which, Jeserac knew, could carry him out of the city on a journey that would once have shattered his mind. When his guide pointed to the open door, he paused for no more than a moment on the threshold, and then was through.

"You see?" said Yarlan Zey with a smile. "Now relax, and remember that you are safe—that nothing can touch you."

Jeserac believed him. He felt only the faintest tremor of apprehension as the tunnel entrance slid silently towards him, and the machine in which he was travelling began to gain speed as it hurtled through the depths of the earth.

Whatever fears he might have had were forgotten in his eagerness to talk with this almost mythical figure from the past.

"Does it not seem strange to you," began Yarlan Zey, "that though the skies are open to us, we have tried to bury ourselves in the Earth? It is the beginning of the sickness whose ending you have seen in your age. Humanity is trying to hide; it is frightened of what lies out there in space, and soon it will have closed all the doors that lead into the Universe."

"But I saw spaceships in the sky above Diaspar," said Jeserac.

"You will not see them much longer. We have lost contact with the stars, and soon even the planets will be deserted. It took us millions of years to make the outward journey—but only centuries to come home again. And in a little while we will have abandoned almost all of Earth itself."

"Why did you do it?" asked Jeserac. He knew the answer, yet somehow felt impelled to ask the question.

"We needed a shelter to protect us from two fears—fear of Death, and fear of Space. We were a sick people and wanted no further part in the Universe— so we pretended that it did not exist. We had seen chaos raging through the stars, and yearned for peace and stability. Therefore Diaspar had to be closed, so that nothing new could ever enter it.

"We designed the city that you know, and invented a false past to conceal our cowardice. Oh, we were not the first to do that—but we were the first to do it so thoroughly. And we re-designed the human spirit, robbing it of ambition and the fiercer passions, so that it would be contented with the world it now possessed.

"It took a thousand years to build the city and all its machines. As each of us completed his task, his mind was washed clean of its memories, the carefully planned pattern of false ones was implanted, and his identity was stored in the city's circuits until the time came to call it forth again.

"So at last there came a day when there was not a single man alive in Diaspar; there was only the Central Computer, obeying the orders which we had fed into it, and controlling the memory banks in which we were sleeping. There was no one who had any contact with the past—and so at this point, history began.

"Then, one by one, in a predetermined sequence, we were called out of the memory circuits and given flesh again. Like a machine that had just been built and was now set operating for the first time, Diaspar began to carry out the duties for which it had been designed.

"Yet some of us had had doubts even from the beginning. Eternity was a long time; we recognised the risks involved in leaving no outlet, and trying to seal ourselves completely from the Universe. We could not defy the wishes of our culture, so we worked in secret, making the modifications we thought necessary.

"The Uniques were our invention. They would appear at long intervals and would, if circumstances allowed them, discover if there was anything beyond Diaspar that was worth the effort of contacting. We never imagined that it would take so long for one of them to succeed—nor did we imagine that his success would be so great."

Despite that suspension of the critical faculties which is the very essence of a dream, Jeserac wondered fleetingly how Yarlan Zey could speak with such knowledge of things that had happened a billion years after his time. It was very confusing ... he did not know where in time or space he was.

The journey was coming to an end; the walls of the tunnel no longer flashed past him at such breakneck speed. Yarlan Zey began to speak with an urgency, and an authority, which he had not shown before.

"The past is over; we did our work, for better or for ill, and that is finished with. When you were created, Jeserac, you were given that fear of the outer world, and that compulsion to stay within the city, that you share with everyone else in Diaspar. You know now that fear was groundless, that it was artificially imposed on you. I, Yarlan Zey, who gave it to you, now release you from its bondage. Do you understand?"

With those last words, the voice of Yarlan Zey became louder and louder, until it seemed to reverberate through all of space. The subterranean carrier in which he was speeding blurred and trembled around Jeserac as if his dream was coming to an end. Yet as the vision faded, he could still hear that imperious voice thundering into his brain:

"You are no longer afraid, Jeserac. *You are no longer afraid.*"

He struggled up towards wakefulness, as a diver climbs from the ocean depths back to the surface of the sea. Yarlan Zey had vanished, but there was a strange interregnum when voices which he knew but could not recognise talked to him encouragingly, and he felt himself supported by friendly hands. Then like a swift dawn reality came flooding back.

He opened his eyes, and saw Alvin and Hilvar and Gerane standing anxiously beside him. But he paid no heed to them; his mind was too filled with the wonder that now lay spread before him—the panorama of forests and rivers, and the blue vault of the open sky.

He was in Lys; and he was not afraid.

No one disturbed him as the timeless moment imprinted itself for ever on his mind. At last, when he had satisfied himself that this indeed was real, he turned to his companions.

"Thank you, Gerane," he said. "I never believed you would succeed."

The psychologist, looking very pleased with himself, was making delicate adjustments to a small machine that hung in the air beside him.

"You gave us some anxious moments," he admitted. "Once or twice you started to ask questions that couldn't be answered logically, and I was afraid I would have to break the sequence."

"Suppose Yarlan Zey had not convinced me—what would you have done then?"

"We would have kept you unconscious, and taken you back to Diaspar where you could have woken up naturally, without ever knowing that you'd been to Lys."

"And that image of Yarlan Zey you fed into my mind—how much of what he said was the truth?"

"Most of it, I believe. I was much more anxious that my little Saga should be convincing rather than historically accurate, but Callitrax has examined it and can find no errors. It is certainly consistent with all that we know about Yarlan Zey and the origins of Diaspar."

"So now we can really open the city," said Alvin. "It may take a long time, but eventually we'll be able to neutralise this fear so that everyone who wishes can leave Diaspar."

"It will take a long time," replied Gerane drily. "And don't forget that Lys is hardly large enough to hold several hundred million extra people, if all your people decide to come here. I don't think that's likely, but it's possible."

"That problem will solve itself," answered Alvin. "Lys may be tiny, but the world is wide. Why should we let the desert keep it all?"

"So you are still dreaming, Alvin," said Jeserac with a smile. "I was wondering what there was left for you to do."

Alvin did not answer; that was a question which had become more and more insistent in his own mind during the past few weeks. He remained lost in thought, falling behind the others, as they walked down the hill towards Airlee. Would the centuries that lay ahead of him be one long anticlimax?

The answer lay in his own hands. He had discharged his destiny; now, perhaps, he could begin to live.

CHAPTER XXVI

THERE IS A special sadness in achievement, in the knowledge that a long-desired goal has been attained at last, and that life must now be shaped towards new ends. Alvin knew that sadness as he wandered alone through the forests and fields of Lys. Not even Hilvar accompanied him, for there are times when a man must be apart even from his closest friends.

He did not wander aimlessly, though he never knew which village would be his next port of call. He was seeking no particular place, but a mood, an influence—indeed, a way of life. Diaspar had no need of him now; the ferments he had introduced into the city were working swiftly, and nothing he could do would accelerate or retard the changes that were happening there.

This peaceful land would also change. Often he wondered if he had done wrong, in the ruthless drive to satisfy his own curiosity, by opening up the ancient way between the two cultures. Yet surely it was better that Lys should know the truth—that it also, like Diaspar, had been partly founded upon fears and falsehoods.

Sometimes he wondered what shape the new society would take. He believed that Diaspar must escape from the prison of the memory banks, and restore again the cycle of life and death. Hilvar, he knew, was sure that this could be done, though his proposals were too technical for Alvin to follow. Perhaps the time would come again when love in Diaspar was no longer completely barren.

Was *this*, Alvin wondered, what he had always lacked in Diaspar—what he had really been seeking? He knew now that when power and ambition and curiosity were satisfied, there still were left the longings of the heart. No one had really lived until they had achieved that synthesis of love and desire which he had never dreamed existed until he came to Lys.

He had walked upon the planets of the Seven Suns—the first man to do so in a billion years. Yet that meant little to him now; sometimes he thought he would give all his achievements if he could hear the cry of a new-born child, and know that it was his own.

In Lys, he might one day find what he wanted; there was a warmth and understanding about its people, which, he now realised, was lacking in Diaspar. But before he could rest, before he could find peace, there was one decision yet to be made.

Into his hands had come power; that power he still possessed. It was a responsibility he had once sought and accepted with eagerness, but now he knew that he could have no peace while it was still his. Yet to throw it away would be the betrayal of a trust. . . .

He was in a village of tiny canals, at the edge of a wide lake, when he made his decision. The coloured houses, which seemed to float at anchor upon the gentle waves, formed a scene of almost unreal beauty. There was life and warmth and comfort here—everything he had missed among the desolate grandeur of the Seven Suns.

One day humanity would once more be ready for space. What new chapter Man would write among the stars, Alvin did not know. That would be no concern of his; his future lay here on Earth.

But he would make one more flight before he turned his back upon the stars.

When Alvin checked the upward rush of the ascending ship, the city was too distant to be recognised as the work of man, and the curve of the planet was already visible. Presently they could see the line of twilight, thousands of miles away on its unending march across the desert. Above and around were the stars, still brilliant for all the glory they had lost.

Hilvar and Jeserac were silent, guessing but not knowing with certainty why Alvin was making this flight, and why he had asked them to come with him. Neither felt like speech, as the desolate panorama unfolded below them. Its emptiness oppressed them both, and Jeserac felt a sudden contemptuous anger for the men of the past who had let the Earth's beauty die through their own neglect.

He hoped that Alvin was right in dreaming that all this could be changed. The power and the knowledge still existed—it needed only the will to turn back the centuries and make the oceans roll again. The water was still there, deep down in the hidden places of the Earth; or if necessary, transmutation plants could be built to make it.

There was so much to do in the years that lay ahead. Jeserac knew that he stood between two ages; around him he could feel the pulse of mankind begin-ning to quicken again. There were great problems to be faced—but Diaspar would face them. The recharting of the past would take centuries, but when it was finished Man would have recovered almost all that he had lost.

Yet could he regain it all? Jeserac wondered. It was hard to believe that the Galaxy would be reconquered, and even if that were achieved, what purpose would it serve?

Alvin broke into his reverie, and Jeserac turned from the screen.

"I wanted you to see this," said Alvin quietly. "You may never have another chance."

"You're not leaving Earth?"

"No; I want nothing more of space. Even if any other civilisations still survive in this Galaxy, I doubt if they will be worth the effort of finding. There is so much to do here; I know now that this is my home, and I am not going to leave it again."

He looked down at the great deserts, but his eyes saw instead the waters that would be sweeping over them a thousand years from now. Man had rediscovered his world, and he would make it beautiful while he remained upon it. And after that——

"We aren't ready to go out to the stars, and it will be a long time before we can face their challenge again. I have been wondering what I should do with this ship; if it stays here on Earth, I shall always be tempted to use it, and will never have any peace of mind. Yet I cannot waste it; I feel that it has been given into my trust, and I must use it for the benefit of the world.

"So this is what I have decided to do. I'm going to send it out of the Galaxy, with the robot in control, to discover what happened to our ancestors—and, if possible, *what* it was they left our universe to find. It must have been something wonderful for them to have abandoned so much to go in search of it.

"The robot will never tire, however long the journey takes. One day our cousins will receive my message, and they'll know that we are waiting for them here on Earth. They will return, and I hope that by then we will be worthy of them, however great they have become."

Alvin fell silent, staring into a future he had shaped but which he might never see. While Man was rebuilding his world, his ship would be crossing the dark-ness between the Galaxies, and in thousands of years to come it would return. Perhaps he would still be here to meet it, but if not, he was well content.

"I think you are wise," said Jeserac. Then, for the last time, the echo of an ancient fear rose up to plague him. "But suppose," he added, "the ship makes contact with something we do not wish to meet. . . ." His voice faded away as he recognised the source of his anxiety and he gave a wry, self-deprecatory smile that banished the last ghost of the Invaders.

"You forget," said Alvin, taking him more seriously than he expected, "that we will soon have Vanamonde to help us. We don't know what powers he pos-sesses, but everyone in Lys seems to think they are potentially unlimited. Isn't that so, Hilvar?"

Hilvar did not reply at once. It was true that Vanamonde was the other great enigma, the question-mark that would always lie across the future of humanity while it remained on Earth. Already, it seemed certain, Vanamonde's evolution towards self-consciousness had been accelerated by his contact with the philosophers of Lys. They had great hopes of future co-operation with the child-like supermind, believing that they could foreshorten the aeons which its natural development would require.

"I am not sure," confessed Hilvar. "Somehow, I don't think that we should expect too much from Vanamonde. We can help him now, but we will be only a brief incident in his total life-span. I don't think that his ultimate destiny has anything to do with ours."

Alvin looked at him in surprise.

"Why do you feel that?" he asked.

"I can't explain it," said Hilvar. "It's just an intuition." He could have added more, but he kept his silence. These matters were not capable of communication, and though Alvin would not laugh at his dream, he did not care to discuss it even with his friend.

It was more than a dream, he was sure of that, and it would haunt him for ever. Somehow it had leaked into his mind during that indescribable and unsharable contact he had had with Vanamonde. Did Vanamonde himself know what his lonely destiny must be?

One day the energies of the Black Sun would fail and it would release its prisoner. And then, at the end of the Universe, as Time itself was faltering to a stop, Vanamonde and the Mad Mind must meet each other among the corpses of the stars.

That conflict might ring down the curtain on Creation itself. Yet it was a conflict which had nothing to do with Man, and whose outcome he would never know. . . .

"Look!" said Alvin suddenly. "This is what I wanted to show you. Do you understand what it means?"

The ship was now above the Pole, and the planet beneath them was a perfect hemisphere. Looking down upon the belt of twilight, Jeserac and Hilvar could see at one instant both sunrise and sunset on opposite sides of the world. The symbolism was so perfect, and so striking, that they were to remember this moment all their lives.

In this universe the night was falling; the shadows were lengthening towards an east that would not know another dawn. But elsewhere the stars were still young and the light of morning lingered; and along the path he once had followed, Man would one day go again.

London, September 1954—
S.S. Himalaya—
Sydney, March 1955

THE DEEP RANGE

FOR MIKE

who led me to the sea

AUTHOR'S NOTE

In this novel I have made certain assumptions about the maximum
size of various marine animals which may be challenged by some
biologists. I do not think, however, that they will meet much
criticism from underwater explorers, who have often encountered
fish *several times* the size of the largest recorded specimens.

For an account of Heron Island as it is today, sixty-five years
before the opening of this story, I refer the reader to *The Coast of
Coral*, and I hope that the University of Queensland will appreciate
my slight extrapolation of its existing facilities.

PART ONE

The Apprentice

CHAPTER I

THERE WAS A killer loose on the range. The South Pacific air patrol had seen the great corpse staining the sea crimson as it wallowed in the waves. Within seconds, the intricate warning system had been alerted; from San Francisco to Brisbane, men were moving counters and drawing range circles on the charts. And Don Burley, still rubbing the sleep from his eyes, was hunched over the control board of Scoutsub 5 as it dropped down to the twenty-fathom line.

He was glad that the alert was in his area; it was the first real excitement for months. Even as he watched the instruments on which his life depended, his mind was ranging far ahead. What could have happened? The brief message had given no details; it had merely reported a freshly killed right whale lying on the surface about ten miles behind the main herd, which was still proceeding north in panic-stricken flight. The obvious assumption was that, somehow, a pack of killer whales had managed to penetrate the barriers protecting the range. If that was so, Don and all his fellow wardens were in for a busy time.

The pattern of green lights on the telltale board was a glowing symbol of security. As long as that pattern was unchanged, as long as none of those emerald stars winked to red, all was well with Don and his tiny craft. Air—fuel—power—this was the triumvirate that ruled his life. If any one of these failed, he would be sinking in a steel coffin down toward the pelagic ooze, as Johnnie Tyndall had done the season before last. But there was no reason why they should fail, and the accidents one foresaw, Don told himself reassuringly, were never those that happened.

He leaned across the tiny control board and spoke into the mike. Sub 5 was still close enough to the mother ship for radio to work, but before long he'd have to switch to the ultrasonics.

"Setting course 255, speed 50 knots, depth 20 fathoms, full sonar coverage. Estimated time to target area 40 minutes. Will report at ten-minute intervals until contact is made. That is all. Out."

The acknowledgment from the *Rorqual* was barely audible, and Don switched off the set. It was time to look around.

He dimmed the cabin lights so that he could see the scanner screen more clearly, pulled the Polaroid glasses down over his eyes, and peered into the depths. It took a few seconds for the two images to fuse together in his mind; then the 3-D display sprang into stereoscopic life.

This was the moment when Don felt like a god, able to hold within his hands a circle of the Pacific twenty miles across, and to see clear down to the still largely unexplored depths two thousand fathoms below. The slowly rotating beam of inaudible sound was searching the world in which he floated, seeking out friend and foe in the eternal darkness where light could never penetrate. The pattern of soundless shrieks, too shrill even for the hearing of the bats who had invented sonar millions of years before man, pulsed out into the watery night; the faint echoes came tingling back, were captured and amplified, and became floating, blue-green flecks on the screen.

Through long practice, Don could read their message with effortless ease. Five hundred feet below, stretching out to the limits of his submerged horizon, was the Scattering Layer—the blanket of life that covered half the world. The sunken meadow of the sea, it rose and fell with the passage of the sun, hovering always at the edge of darkness. During the night it had floated nearly to the surface, but the dawn was now driving it back into the depths.

It was no obstacle to his sonar. Don could see clear through its tenuous substance to the ooze of the Pacific floor, over which he was driving high as a cloud above the land, but the ultimate depths were no concern of his; the flocks he guarded, and the enemies who ravaged them, belonged to the upper levels of the sea.

Don flicked the switch of the depth selector, and his sonar beam concentrated itself into the horizontal plane. The glimmering echoes from the abyss vanished, and he could see more clearly what lay around him here in the ocean's stratospheric heights. That glowing cloud two miles ahead was an unusually large school of fish; he wondered if Base knew about it, and made an entry in his log. There were some larger blips at the edge of the school—the carnivores pursuing the cattle, ensuring that the endlessly turning wheel of life and death would never lose momentum. But this conflict was no affair of Don's; he was after bigger game.

Sub 5 drove on towards the west, a steel needle swifter and more deadly than any other creature that roamed the seas. The tiny cabin, now lit only by the flicker of lights from the instrument board, pulsed with power as the spinning turbines thrust the water aside. Don glanced at the chart and noted that he was already halfway to the target area. He wondered if he should surface to have a look at the dead whale; from its injuries he might be able to learn something about its assailants. But that would mean further delay, and in a case like this time was vital.

The long-range receiver bleeped plaintively, and Don switched over to Transcribe. He had never learned to read code by ear, as some people could do, but the ribbon of paper emerging from the message slot saved him the trouble.

AIR PATROL REPORTS SCHOOL 50-100 WHALES HEADING 90 DEGREES GRID REF X186593 Y432011 STOP MOVING AT SPEED AFTER CHANGE OF COURSE STOP NO SIGN OF ORCAS BUT PRESUME THEY ARE IN VICINITY STOP RORQUAL

Don considered this last piece of deduction highly unlikely. If the orcas—the dreaded killer whales—had indeed been responsible, they would surely have been spotted by now as they surfaced to breathe. Moreover, they would never have let the patrolling plane scare them away from their victim, but would have remained feasting on it until they had gorged themselves.

One thing was in his favour; the frightened herd was now heading almost directly towards him. Don started to set the co-ordinates on the plotting grid, then saw that it was no longer necessary. At the extreme edge of his screen, a flotilla of faint stars had appeared. He altered course slightly, and drove head on to the approaching school.

Part of the message was certainly correct; the whales were moving at unusually high speed. At the rate they were travelling, he would be among them in five minutes. He cut the motors and felt the backward tug of the water bringing him swiftly to rest.

Don Burley, a knight in armour, sat in his tiny, dim-lit room a hundred feet below the bright Pacific waves, testing his weapons for the conflict that lay ahead. In these moments of poised suspense, before action began, he often pictured himself thus, though he would have admitted it to no one in the world. He felt, too, a kinship with all shepherds who had guarded their flocks back to the dawn of time. Not only was he Sir Lancelot, he was also David, among ancient Palestinian hills, alert for the mountain lions that would prey upon his father's sheep.

Yet far nearer in time, and far closer in spirit, were the men who had marshalled the great herds of cattle on the American plains, scarcely three lifetimes ago. They would have understood his work, though his implements would have been magic to them. The pattern was the same; only the scale of things had altered. It made no fundamental difference that the beasts Don herded weighed a hundred tons and browsed on the endless savannahs of the sea.

The school was now less than two miles away, and Don checked his scanner's steady circling to concentrate on the sector ahead. The picture on the screen altered to a fan-shaped wedge as the sonar beam started to flick from side to side; now he could count every whale in the school, and could even make a good estimate of its size. With a practised eye, he began to look for stragglers.

Don could never have explained what drew him at once towards those four echoes at the southern fringe of the school. It was true that they were a little apart from the rest, but others had fallen as far behind. There is some sixth sense that a man acquires when he has stared long enough into a sonar screen—some hunch which enables him to extract more from the moving flecks than he has any right to do. Without conscious thought, Don reached for the controls and started the turbines whirling once more.

The main body of the whale pack was now sweeping past him to the east. He had no fear of a collision; the great animals, even in their panic, could sense his presence as easily as he could detect theirs, and by similar means. He wondered if he should switch on his beacon. They might recognise its sound pattern, and it would reassure them. But the still unknown enemy might recognise it too, and would be warned.

The four echoes that had attracted his attention were almost at the centre of the screen. He closed for an interception, and hunched low over the sonar display as if to drag from it by sheer willpower every scrap of information the scanner could give. There were two large echoes, some distance apart, and one was accompanied by a pair of smaller satellites. Don wondered if he was already too late; in his mind's eye he could picture the death struggle taking place in the water less than a mile ahead. Those two fainter blips would be the enemy, worrying a whale while its mate stood by in helpless terror, with no weapons of defence except its mighty flukes.

Now he was almost close enough for vision. The TV camera in Sub 5's prow strained through the gloom, but at first could show nothing but the fog of plankton. Then a vast, shadowy shape appeared in the centre of the screen, with two smaller companions below it. Don was seeing, with the greater precision but hopelessly limited range of light, what the sonar scanners had already told him.

Almost at once he saw his incredible mistake: the two satellites were calves. It was the first time he had ever met a whale with twins, although multiple births were not uncommon. In normal circumstances, the sight would have fascinated him, but now it meant that he had jumped to the wrong conclusion and had lost precious minutes. He must begin the search again.

As a routine check, he swung the camera towards the fourth blip on the sonar screen—the echo he had assumed, from its size, to be another adult whale. It is strange how a preconceived idea can affect a man's understanding of what he sees; seconds passed before Don could interpret the picture before his eyes—before he knew that, after all, he had come to the right place.

"Jesus!" he said softly. "I didn't know they grew that big." It was a shark, the largest he had ever seen. Its details were still obscured, but there was only one genus it could belong to. The whale shark and the basking shark might be of comparable size, but they were harmless herbivores. This was the king of all selachians, *Carcharodon*—the Great White Shark. Don tried to recall the figures for the largest known specimen. In 1990, or thereabouts, a fifty-footer had been killed off New Zealand, but this one was half as big again.

These thoughts flashed through his mind in an instant, and in that same moment he saw that the great beast was already manoeuvring for the kill. It was heading for one of the calves, and ignoring the frantic mother. Whether this was cowardice or common sense there was no way of telling; perhaps such distinctions were meaningless to the shark's tiny and utterly alien mind.

There was only one thing to do. It might spoil his chance of a quick kill, but the calf's life was more important. He punched the button of the siren, and a brief, mechanical scream erupted into the water around him.

Shark and whales were equally terrified by the deafening shriek. The shark jerked round in an impossibly tight curve, and Don was nearly jolted out of his seat as the autopilot snapped the sub on to a new course. Twisting and turning with an agility equal to that of any other sea creature of its size, Sub 5 began to close in upon the shark, its electronic brain automatically following the sonar echo and thus leaving Don free to concentrate on his armament. He needed that freedom; the next operation was going to be difficult unless he could hold a steady course for at least fifteen seconds. At a pinch he could use his tiny rocket torps to make a kill; had he been alone and faced with a pack of orcas, he would certainly have done so. But that was messy and brutal, and there was a neater way. He had always preferred the technique of the rapier to that of the hand grenade.

Now he was only fifty feet away, and closing rapidly. There might never be a better chance. He punched the launching stud.

From beneath the belly of the sub, something that looked like a sting ray hurtled forward. Don had checked the speed of his own craft; there was no need to come any closer now. The tiny, arrow-shaped hydrofoil, only a couple of feet across, could move far faster than his vessel and would close the gap in seconds. As it raced forward, it spun out the thin line of the control wire, like some underwater spider laying its thread. Along that wire passed the energy that powered the sting, and the signals that steered the missile to its goal. It responded so instantly to his orders that Don felt he was controlling some sensitive, high-spirited steed.

The shark saw the danger less than a second before impact. The resemblance of the sting to an ordinary ray confused it, as the designers had intended. Before the tiny brain could realise that no ray behaved like this, the missile had struck. The steel hypodermic, rammed forward by an exploding cartridge, drove through the shark's horny skin, and the great fish erupted in a frenzy of terror. Don backed rapidly away, for a blow from that tail would rattle him around like a pea in a can and might even damage the sub. There was nothing more for him to do, except to wait while the poison did its work.

The doomed killer was trying to arch its body so that it could snap at the poisoned dart. Don had now reeled the sting back into its slot amidships, pleased that he had been able to retrieve the missile undamaged. He watched with awe and a dispassionate pity as the great beast succumbed to its paralysis.

Its struggles were weakening. It was now swimming aimlessly back and forth, and once Don had to sidestep smartly to avoid a collision. As it lost control of buoyancy, the dying shark drifted up to the surface. Don did not bother to follow; that could wait until he had attended to more important business.

He found the cow and her two calves less than a mile away, and inspected them carefully. They were uninjured, so there was no need to call the vet in his highly specialised two-man sub which could handle any cetological crisis from a stomach-ache to a Caesarean.

The whales were no longer in the least alarmed, and a check on the sonar had shown that the entire school had ceased its panicky flight. He wondered if they already knew what had happened; much had been learned about their methods of communication, but much more was still a mystery.

"I hope you appreciate what I've done for you, old lady," he muttered. Then, reflecting that fifty tons of mother love was a slightly awe-inspiring sight, he blew his tanks and surfaced.

It was calm, so he opened the hatch and popped his head out of the tiny conning tower. The water was only inches below his chin, and from time to time a wave made a determined effort to swamp him. There was little danger of this happening, for he fitted the hatch so closely that he was quite an effective plug.

Fifty feet away, a long grey mound, like an overturned boat, was rolling on the surface. Don looked at it thoughtfully, wondering how much compressed air he'd better squirt into the corpse to prevent it sinking before one of the tenders could reach the spot. In a few minutes he would radio his report, but for the moment it was pleasant to drink the fresh Pacific breeze, to feel the open sky above his head, and to watch the sun begin its long climb towards noon.

Don Burley was the happy warrior, resting after the one battle that man would always have to fight. He was holding at bay the spectre of famine which had confronted all earlier ages, but which would never threaten the world again while the great plankton farms harvested their millions of tons of protein, and the whale herds obeyed their new masters. Man had come back to the sea, his ancient home, after aeons of exile; until the oceans froze, he would never be hungry again. . . .

Yet that, Don knew, was the least of his satisfactions. Even if what he was doing had been of no practical value, he would still have wished to do it. Nothing else that life could offer matched the contentment and the calm sense of power that filled him when he set out on a mission such as this. Power? Yes, that was the right word. But it was not a power that would ever be abused; he felt too great a kinship with all the creatures who shared the seas with him—even those it was his duty to destroy.

To all appearances, Don was completely relaxed, yet had any one of the many dials and lights filling his field of view called for attention he would have been instantly alert. His mind was already back on the *Rorqual*, and he found it increasingly hard to keep his thoughts away from his overdue breakfast. In order to make the time pass more swiftly, he started mentally composing his report. Quite a few people, he knew, were going to be surprised by it. The engineers who maintained the invisible fences of sound and electricity which now divided the mighty Pacific into manageable portions would have to start looking for the break; the marine biologists who were so confident that sharks never attacked whales would have to think up excuses. Both enterprises, Don was quite sure, would be successfully carried out, and then everything would be under control again, until the sea contrived its next crisis.

But the crisis to which Don was now unwittingly returning was a man-made one, organised without any malice towards him at the highest official levels. It had begun with a suggestion in the Space Department, duly referred up to the World Secretariat. It had risen still higher until it reached the World Assembly itself, where it had come to the approving ears of the senators directly interested. Thus converted from a suggestion to an order, it had filtered down through the Secretariat to the World Food Organisation, thence to the Marine Division, and finally to the Bureau of Whales. The whole process had taken the incredibly short time of four weeks.

Don, of course, knew nothing of this. As far as he was concerned, the complicated workings of global bureaucracy resolved themselves into the greeting his skipper gave him when he walked into the *Rorqual*'s mess for his belated breakfast.

"What kind of a job?" asked Don suspiciously. He remembered an unfortunate occasion when he had acted as a guide to a permanent undersecretary who had seemed to be a bit of a fool, and whom he had treated accordingly. It had later turned out that the P.U.—as might have been guessed from his position—was a very shrewd character indeed and knew exactly what Don was doing.

"They didn't tell me," said the skipper. "I'm not quite sure they know themselves. Give my love to Queensland, and keep away from the casinos on the Gold Coast."

"Much choice I have, on *my* pay," snorted Don. "Last time I went to Surfer's Paradise, I was lucky to get away with my shirt."

"But you brought back a couple of thousand on your first visit."

"Beginner's luck—it never happened again. I've lost it all since then, so I'll stop while I still break even. No more gambling for me."

"Is that a bet? Would you put five bucks on it?"

"Sure."

"Then pay over—you've already lost by accepting."

A spoonful of processed plankton hovered momentarily in mid-air while Don sought for a way out of the trap.

"Just try and get me to pay," he retorted. "You've got no witnesses, and I'm no gentleman." He hastily swallowed the last of his coffee, then pushed aside his chair and rose to go.

"Better start packing, I suppose. So long, Skipper—see you later."

The Captain of the *Rorqual* watched his first warden sweep out of the room like a small hurricane. For a moment the sound of Don's passage echoed back along the ship's corridors; then comparative silence descended again.

The skipper started to head back to the bridge. "Look out, Brisbane," he muttered to himself; then he began to rearrange the watches and to compose a masterly memorandum to HQ asking how he was expected to run a ship when thirty per cent of her crew were permanently absent on leave or special duty. By the time he reached the bridge, the only thing that had stopped him from resigning was the fact that, try as he might, he couldn't think of a better job.

CHAPTER 11

THOUGH HE HAD been kept waiting only a few minutes, Walter Franklin was already prowling impatiently around the reception room. Swiftly he examined and dismissed the deep-sea photographs hanging on the walls; then he sat for a moment on the edge of the table, leafing through the pile of magazines, reviews, and reports which always accumulated in such places. The popular magazines he had already seen—for the last few weeks he had had little else to do but read—and few of the others looked interesting. Somebody, he supposed, had to go through these lavishly electro-printed food-production reports as part of their job; he wondered how they avoided being hypnotised by the endless columns of statistics. *Neptune*, the house organ of the Marine Division, seemed a little more promising, but as most of the personalities discussed in its columns were unknown to him he soon became bored with it. Even its fairly lowbrow articles were largely over his head, assuming a knowledge of technical terms he did not possess.

The receptionist was watching him—certainly noticing his impatience, perhaps analysing the nervousness and insecurity that lay behind it. With a distinct effort, Franklin forced himself to sit down and to concentrate on yesterday's issue of the Brisbane *Courier*. He had almost become interested in an editorial requiem on Australian cricket, inspired by the recent Test results, when the young lady who guarded the director's office smiled sweetly at him and said: "Would you please go in now, Mr. Franklin?"

He had expected to find the director alone, or perhaps accompanied by a secretary. The husky young man sitting in the other visitor's chair seemed out of place in this orderly office, and was staring at him with more curiosity than friendliness. Franklin stiffened at once; they had been discussing him, he knew, and automatically he went on the defensive.

Director Cary, who knew almost as much about human beings as he did about marine mammals, sensed the strain immediately and did his best to dispel it.

"Ah, there you are, Franklin," he said with slightly excessive heartiness. "I hope you've been enjoying your stay here. Have my people been taking care of you?"

Franklin was spared the trouble of answering this question, for the director gave him no time to reply.

"I want you to meet Don Burley," he continued. "Don's First Warden on the *Rorqual*, and one of the best we've got. He's been assigned to look after you. Don, meet Walter Franklin."

They shook hands warily, weighing each other. Then Don's face broke into a reluctant smile. It was the smile of a man who had been given a job he didn't care for but who had decided to make the best of it.

"Pleased to meet you, Franklin," he said. "Welcome to the Mermaid Patrol."

Franklin tried to smile at the hoary joke, but his effort was not very successful. He knew that he should be friendly, and that these people were doing their best to help him. Yet the knowledge was that of the mind, not the heart; he could not relax and let himself meet them halfway. The fear of being pitied and the nagging suspicion that they had been talking about him behind his back, despite all the assurances he had been given, paralysed his will for friendliness.

Don Burley sensed nothing of this. He only knew that the director's office was not the right place to get acquainted with a new colleague, and before Franklin was fully aware of what had happened he was out of the building, buffeting his way through the shirt-sleeved crowds in George Street, and being steered into a minute bar opposite the new post office.

The noise of the city subsided, though through the tinted glass walls Franklin could see the shadowy shapes of the pedestrians moving to and fro. It was pleasantly cool here after the torrid streets; whether or not Brisbane should be air-conditioned—and if so, who should have the resulting multimillion-dollar contract—was still being argued by the local politicians, and meanwhile the citizens sweltered every summer.

Don Burley waited until Franklin had drunk his first beer and called for replacements. There was a mystery about his new pupil, and as soon as possible he intended to solve it. Someone very high up in the division—perhaps even in the World Secretariat itself—must have organised this. A first warden was not called away from his duties to wet-nurse someone who was obviously too old to go through the normal training channels. At a guess he would say that Franklin was the wrong side of thirty; he had never heard of anyone that age getting this sort of special treatment before.

One thing was obvious about Franklin at once, and that only added to the mystery. He was a spaceman; you could tell them a mile away. That should make a good opening gambit. Then he remembered that the director had warned him, "Don't ask Franklin too many questions. I don't know what his background is, but we've been specifically told not to talk about it with him."

That might make sense, mused Don. Perhaps he was a space pilot who had been grounded after some inexcusable lapse, such as absent-mindedly arriving at Venus when he should have gone to Mars

"Is this the first time," Don began cautiously, "that you've been to Australia?" It was not a very fortunate opening, and the conversation might have died there and then when Franklin replied: "I was born here."

Don, however, was not the sort of person who was easily abashed. He merely laughed and said, half-apologetically, "Nobody ever tells me anything, so I usually find out the hard way. I was born on the other side of the world—over in Ireland—but since I've been attached to the Pacific branch of the bureau I've more or less adopted Australia as a second home. Not that I spend much time ashore! On this job you're at sea eighty per cent of the time. A lot of people don't like that, you know."

"It would suit me," said Franklin, but left the remark hanging in the air. Burley began to feel exasperated—it was such hard work getting anything out of this fellow. The prospect of working with him for the next few weeks began to look very uninviting, and Don wondered what he had done to deserve such a fate. However, he struggled on manfully.

"The superintendent tells me that you've a good scientific and engineering background, so I can assume that you'll know most of the things that our people spend the first year learning. Have they filled you in on the administrative background?"

"They've given me a lot of facts and figures under hypnosis, so I could lecture you for a couple of hours on the Marine Division—its history, organisation, and current projects, with particular reference to the Bureau of Whales. But it doesn't *mean* anything to me at present."

Now we seem to be getting somewhere, Don told himself. The fellow can talk after all. A couple more beers, and he might even be human.

"That's the trouble with hypnotic training," agreed Don. "They can pump the information into you until it comes out of your ears, but you're never quite sure how much you really know. And they can't teach you manual skills, or train you to have the right reactions in emergencies. There's only one way of learning anything properly—and that's by actually doing the job."

He paused, momentarily distracted by a shapely silhouette parading on the other side of the translucent wall. Franklin noticed the direction of his gaze, and his features relaxed into a slight smile. For the first time the tension lifted, and Don began to feel that there was some hope of establishing contact with the enigma who was now his responsibility.

With a beery forefinger, Don started to trace maps on the plastic table top. "This is the setup," he began. "Our main training centre for shallow-water operations is here in the Capricorn Group, about four hundred miles north of Brisbane and forty miles out from the coast. The South Pacific fence starts here, and runs on east to New Caledonia and Fiji. When the whales migrate north from the polar feeding grounds to have their calves in the tropics, they're compelled to pass through the gaps we've left here. The most important of these gates, from our point of view, is the one right here off the Queensland coast, at the southern entrance to the Great Barrier Reef. The reef provides a kind of natural channel, averaging about fifty miles wide, almost up to the equator. Once we've herded the whales into it, we can keep them pretty well under control. It didn't take much doing; many of them used to come this way long before we appeared on the scene. By now the rest have been so well conditioned that even if we switched off the fence it would probably make no difference to their migratory pattern."

"By the way," interjected Franklin, "is the fence purely electrical?"

"Oh no. Electric fields control fish pretty well but don't work satisfactorily on mammals like whales. The fence is largely ultrasonic—a curtain of sound from a chain of generators half a mile below the surface. We can get fine control at the gates by broadcasting specific orders; you can set a whole herd stampeding in any direction you wish by playing back a recording of a whale in distress. But it's not very often we have to do anything drastic like that; as I said, nowadays they're too well trained."

"I can appreciate that," said Franklin. "In fact, I heard somewhere that the fence was more for keeping other animals out than for keeping the whales in."

"That's partly true, though we'd still need some kind of control for rounding up our herds at census or slaughtering. Even so, the fence isn't perfect. There are weak spots where generator fields overlap, and sometimes we have to switch off sections to allow normal fish migration. Then, the really big sharks, or the killer whales, can get through and play hell. The killers are our worst problem; they attack the whales when they are feeding in the Antarctic, and often the herds suffer ten per cent losses. No one will be happy until the killers are wiped out, but no one can think of an economical way of doing it. We can't patrol the entire ice pack with subs, though when I've seen what a killer can do to a whale I've often wished we could."

There was real feeling—almost passion—in Burley's voice, and Franklin looked at the warden with surprise. The "whale-boys", as they had been inevitably christened by a nostalgically minded public in search of heroes, were not supposed to be much inclined either to thought or emotions. Though Franklin knew perfectly well that the tough, uncomplicated characters who stalked tight lipped through the pages of contemporary submarine sagas had very little connection with reality, it was hard to escape from the popular clichés. Don Burley, it was true, was far from tight lipped, but in most other respects he seemed to fit the standard specification very well.

Franklin wondered how he was going to get on with his new mentor—indeed, with his new job. He still felt no enthusiasm for it; whether that would come, only time would show. It was obviously full of interesting and even fascinating problems and possibilities, and if it would occupy his mind and give him scope for his talents, that was as much as he could hope for. The long nightmare of the last year had destroyed, with so much else, his zest for life—the capacity he had once possessed for throwing himself heart and soul into some project.

It was difficult to believe that he could ever recapture the enthusiasm that had once taken him so far along paths he could never tread again. As he glanced at Don, who was still talking with the fluent lucidity of a man who knows and loves his job, Franklin felt a sudden and disturbing sense of guilt. Was it fair to Burley to take him away from his work and to turn him, whether he knew it or not, into a cross between a nursemaid and kindergarten teacher? Had Franklin realised that very similar thoughts had already crossed Burley's mind, his sympathy would have been quenched at once.

"Time we caught the shuttle to the airport," said Don, looking at his watch and hastily draining his beer. "The morning flight leaves in thirty minutes. I hope all your stuff's already been sent on."

"The hotel said they'd take care of it."

"Well, we can check at the airport. Let's go."

Half an hour later Franklin had a chance to relax again. It was typical of Burley, he soon discovered, to take things easily until the last possible moment and then to explode in a burst of activity. This burst carried them from the quiet bar to the even more efficiently silenced plane. As they took their seats, there was a brief incident that was to puzzle Don a good deal in the weeks that lay ahead.

"You take the window seat," he said. "I've flown this way dozens of times."

He took Franklin's refusal as ordinary politeness, and started to insist. Not until Franklin had turned down the offer several times, with increasing determination and even signs of annoyance, did Burley realise that his companion's behaviour had nothing to do with common courtesy. It seemed incredible, but Don could have sworn that the other was scared stiff. What sort of man, he wondered blankly, would be terrified of taking a window seat in an ordinary aircraft? All his gloomy premonitions about his new assignment, which had been partly dispelled during their earlier conversation, came crowding back with renewed vigour.

The city and the sunburned coast dropped below as the lifting jets carried them effortlessly up into the sky. Franklin was reading the paper with a fierce concentration that did not deceive Burley for a moment. He decided to wait for a while, and apply some more tests later in the flight.

The Glasshouse Mountains—these strangely shaped fangs jutting from the eroded plain—swept swiftly beneath. Then came the little coastal towns, through which the wealth of the immense farm lands of the interior had once passed to the world in the days before agriculture went to sea. And then—only minutes, it seemed, after take-off—the first islands of the Great Barrier Reef appeared like deeper shadows in the blue horizon mists.

The sun was shining almost straight into his eyes, but Don's memory could fill in the details which were lost in the glare from the burning waters. He could see the low, green islands surrounded by their narrow borders of sand and their immensely greater fringes of barely submerged coral. Against each island's private reef the waves of the Pacific would be marching forever, so that for a thousand miles into the north snowy crescents of foam would break the surface of the sea.

A century ago—fifty years, even—scarcely a dozen of these hundreds of islands had been inhabited. Now, with the aid of universal air transport, together with cheap power and water-purification plants, both the state and the private citizen had invaded the ancient solitude of the reef. A few fortunate individuals, by means that had never been made perfectly clear, had managed to acquire some of the smaller islands as their personal property. The entertainment and vacation industry had taken over others, and had not always improved on Nature's handiwork. But the greatest landowner in the reef was undoubtedly the World Food Organisation, with its complicated hierarchy of fisheries, marine farms, and research departments, the full extent of which, it was widely believed, no merely human brain could ever comprehend.

"We're nearly there," said Burley. "That's Lady Musgrave Island we've just passed—main generators for the western end of the fence. Capricorn Group under us now—Masterhead, One Tree, North-West, Wilson—and Heron in the middle, with all those buildings on it. The big tower is Administration—the aquarium's by that pool—and look, you can see a couple of subs tied up at that long jetty leading out to the edge of the reef."

As he spoke, Don watched Franklin out of the corner of his eye. The other had leaned towards the window as if following his companion's running commentary, yet Burley could swear that he was not looking at the panorama of reefs and islands spread out below. His face was tense and strained; there was an indrawn, hooded expression in his eyes as if he was forcing himself to see nothing.

With a mingling of pity and contempt, Don understood the symptoms if not their cause. Franklin was terrified of heights; so much, then, for the theory that he was a spaceman. Then what was he? Whatever the answer, he hardly seemed the sort of person with whom one would wish to share the cramped quarters of a two-man training sub. . . .

The plane's shock absorbers touched down on the rectangle of scorched and flattened coral that was the Heron Island landing platform. As he stepped out into the sunlight, blinking in the sudden glare, Franklin seemed to make an

abrupt recovery. Don had seen seasick passengers undergo equally swift transformations on their return to dry land. If Franklin is no better as a sailor than
an airman, he thought, this crazy assignment won't last more than a couple of
days and I'll be able to get back to work. Not that Don was in a great rush to
return immediately; Heron Island was a pleasant place where you could enjoy
yourself if you knew how to deal with the red tape that always entangled
headquarters establishments.

A light truck whisked them and their belongings along a road beneath an
avenue of Pisonia trees whose heavily leafed branches blocked all direct sunlight. The road was less than a quarter of a mile long, but it spanned the little
island from the jetties and maintenance plants on the west to the administration
buildings on the east. The two halves of the island were partly insulated from
each other by a narrow belt of jungle which had been carefully preserved in its
virgin state and which, Don remembered sentimentally, was full of interesting
tracks and secluded clearings.

Administration was expecting Mr. Franklin, and had made all the necessary
arrangements for him. He had been placed in a kind of privileged limbo, one
stage below the permanent staff like Burley, but several stages above the
ordinary trainees under instruction. Surprisingly, he had a room of his own—
something that even senior members of the bureau could not always expect
when they visited the island. This was a great relief to Don, who had been
afraid he might have to share quarters with his mysterious charge. Quite apart
from any other factors, that would have interfered badly with certain romantic
plans of his own.

He saw Franklin to his small but attractive room on the second floor of the
training wing, looking out across the miles of coral which stretched eastward
all the way to the horizon. In the courtyard below, a group of trainees, relaxing
between classes, was chatting with a second warden instructor whom Don
recognised from earlier visits but could not name. It was a pleasant feeling,
he mused, going back to school when you already knew all the answers.

"You should be comfortable here," he said to Franklin, who was busy
unpacking his baggage. "Quite a view, isn't it?"

Such poetic ecstasies were normally foreign to Don's nature, but he could not
resist the temptation of seeing how Franklin would react to the leagues of
coral-dappled ocean that lay before him. Rather to his disappointment, the
reaction was quite conventional; presumably Franklin was not worried by a
mere thirty feet of height. He looked out of the window, taking his time and
obviously admiring the vista of blues and greens which led the eye out into the
endless waters of the Pacific.

Serve you right, Don told himself—it's not fair to tease the poor devil.
Whatever he's got, it can't be fun to live with.

"I'll leave you to get settled in," said Don, backing out through the door.
"Lunch will be coming up in half an hour over at the mess—that building we
passed on the way in. See you there."

Franklin nodded absently as he sorted through his belongings and piled
shirts and underclothes on the bed. He wanted to be left alone while he adjusted

himself to the new life which, with no particular enthusiasm, he had now accepted as his own.

Burley had been gone for less than ten minutes when there was a knock on the door and a quiet voice said, "Can I come in?"

"Who's there?" asked Franklin, as he tidied up the debris and made his room look presentable.

"Dr. Myers."

The name meant nothing to Franklin, but his face twisted into a wry smile as he thought how appropriate it was that his very first visitor should be a doctor. What kind of a doctor, he thought he could guess.

Myers was a stocky, pleasantly ugly man in his early forties, with a disconcertingly direct gaze which seemed somewhat at variance with his friendly affable manner.

"Sorry to butt in on you when you've only just arrived," he said apologetically. "I had to do it now because I'm flying out to New Caledonia this afternoon and won't be back for a week. Professor Stevens asked me to look you up and give you his best wishes. If there's anything you want, just ring my office and we'll try to fix it for you."

Franklin admired the skilful way in which Myers had avoided all the obvious dangers. He did *not* say—true though it undoubtedly was—"I've discussed your case with Professor Stevens". Nor did he offer direct help; he managed to convey the assumption that Franklin wouldn't need it and was now quite capable of looking after himself.

"I appreciate that," said Franklin sincerely. He felt he was going to like Dr. Myers, and made up his mind not to resent the surveillance he would undoubtedly be getting. "Tell me," he added, "just what do the people here know about me?"

"Nothing at all, except that you are to be helped to qualify as a warden as quickly as possible. This isn't the first time this sort of thing has happened, you know—there have been high-pressure conversion courses before. Still, it's inevitable that there will be a good deal of curiosity about you; that may be your biggest problem."

"Burley is dying of curiosity already."

"Mind if I give you some advice?"

"Of course not—go ahead."

"You'll be working with Don continually. It's only fair to him, as well as to yourself, to confide in him when you feel you can do so. I'm sure you'll find him quite understanding. Or if you prefer, I'll do the explaining."

Franklin shook his head, not trusting himself to speak. It was not a matter of logic, for he knew that Myers was talking sense. Sooner or later it would all have to come out, and he might be making matters worse by postponing the inevitable. Yet his hold upon sanity and self-respect was still so precarious that he could not face the prospect of working with men who knew his secret, however sympathetic they might be.

"Very well. The choice is yours and we'll respect it. Good luck—and let's hope all our contacts will be purely social."

Long after Myers had gone, Franklin sat on the edge of the bed, staring out across the sea which would be his new domain. He would need the luck that the other had wished him, yet he was beginning to feel a renewed interest in life. It was not merely that people were anxious to help him; he had received more than enough help in the last few months. At last he was beginning to see how he could help himself, and so discover a purpose for his existence.

Presently he jolted himself out of his daydream and looked at his watch. He was already ten minutes late for lunch, and that was a bad start for his new life. He thought of Don Burley waiting impatiently in the mess and wondering what had happened to him.

"Coming, teacher," he said, as he put on his jacket and started out of the room. It was the first time he had made a joke with himself for longer than he could remember.

CHAPTER III

WHEN FRANKLIN FIRST saw Indra Langenburg she was covered with blood up to her elbows and was busily hacking away at the entrails of a ten-foot tiger shark she had just disembowelled. The huge beast was lying, its pale belly upturned to the sun, on the sandy beach where Franklin took his morning promenade. A thick chain still led to the hook in its mouth; it had obviously been caught during the night and then left behind by the falling tide.

Franklin stood for a moment looking at the unusual combination of attractive girl and dead monster, then said thoughtfully: "You know, this is not the sort of thing I like to see before breakfast. Exactly what are you doing?"

A brown, oval face with very serious eyes looked up at him. The foot-long, razor-sharp knife that was creating such havoc continued to slice expertly through gristle and guts.

"I'm writing a thesis," said a voice as serious as the eyes, "on the vitamin content of shark liver. It means catching a lot of sharks; this is my third this week. Would you like some teeth? I've got plenty, and they make nice souvenirs."

She walked to the head of the beast and inserted her knife in its gaping jaws, which had been propped apart by a block of wood. A quick jerk of her wrist, and an endless necklace of deadly ivory triangles, like a band saw made of bone, started to emerge from the shark's mouth.

"No thanks," said Franklin hastily, hoping she would not be offended. "Please don't let me interrupt your work."

He guessed that she was barely twenty, and was not surprised at meeting an unfamiliar girl on the little island, because the scientists at the Research Station did not have much contact with the administrative and training staff.

"You're new here, aren't you?" said the bloodstained biologist, sloshing a huge lump of liver into a bucket with every sign of satisfaction. "I didn't see you at the last HQ dance."

Franklin felt quite cheered by the inquiry. It was so pleasant to meet someone who knew nothing about him, and had not been speculating about his presence here. He felt he could talk freely and without restraint for the first time since landing on Heron Island.

"Yes—I've just come for a special training course. How long have you been here?"

He was making pointless conversation just for the pleasure of the company, and doubtless she knew it.

"Oh, about a month," she said carelessly. There was another slimy, squelching noise from the bucket, which was now nearly full. "I'm on leave here from the University of Miami."

"You're American, then?" Franklin asked. The girl answered solemnly: "No; my ancestors were Dutch, Burmese, and Scottish in about equal proportions. Just to make things a little complicated, I was born in Japan."

Franklin wondered if she was making fun of him, but there was no trace of guile in her expression. She seemed a really nice kid, he thought, but he couldn't stay here talking all day. He had only forty minutes for breakfast, and his morning class in submarine navigation started at nine.

He thought no more of the encounter, for he was continually meeting new faces as his circles of acquaintances steadily expanded. The high-pressure course he was taking gave him no time for much social life, and for that he was grateful. His mind was fully occupied once more; it had taken up the load with a smoothness that both surprised and gratified him. Perhaps those who had sent him here knew what they were doing better than he sometimes supposed.

All the empirical knowledge—the statistics, the factual data, the ins and outs of administration—had been more or less painlessly pumped into Franklin while he was under mild hypnosis. Prolonged question periods, where he was quizzed by a tape recorder that later filled in the right answers, then confirmed that the information had really taken and had not, as sometimes happened, shot straight through the mind leaving no permanent impression.

Don Burley had nothing to do with this side of Franklin's training, but, rather to his disgust, had no chance of relaxing when Franklin was being looked after elsewhere. The chief instructor had gleefully seized this opportunity of getting Don back into his clutches, and had "suggested", with great tact and charm, that when his other duties permitted Don might like to lecture to the three courses now under training on the island. Outranked and outmanoeuvred, Don had no alternative but to acquiesce with as good grace as possible. This assignment, it seemed, was not going to be the holiday he had hoped.

In one respect, however, his worst fears had not materialised. Franklin was not at all hard to get on with, as long as one kept completely away from personalities. He was very intelligent and had clearly had a technical training that in some ways was much better than Don's own. It was seldom necessary to explain anything to him more than once and long before they had reached the stage of trying him out on the synthetic trainers, Don could see that his pupil had the makings of a good pilot. He was skilful with his hands, reacted quickly and accurately, and had that indefinable poise which distinguishes the first-rate pilot from the merely competent one.

Yet Don knew that knowledge and skill were not in themselves sufficient. Something else was also needed, and there was no way yet of telling if Franklin possessed it. Not until Don had watched his reactions as he sank down into the depths of the sea would he know whether all this effort was to be of any use.

There was so much that Franklin had to learn that it seemed impossible that anyone could absorb it all in two months, as the programme insisted. Don himself had taken the normal six months, and he somewhat resented the assumption that anyone else could do it in a third of the time, even with the special coaching he was giving. Why, the mechanical side of the job alone— the layout and design of the various classes of subs—took at least two months to learn, even with the best of instructional aids. Yet at the same time he had to teach Franklin the principles of seamanship and underwater navigation, basic oceanography, submarine signalling and communication, and a substantial amount of ichthyology, marine psychology, and, of course, cetology. So far Franklin had never even seen a whale, dead or alive, and that first encounter was something that Don looked forward to witnessing. At such a moment one could learn all that one needed to know about a man's fitness for this job.

They had done two weeks' hard work together before Don first took Franklin under water. By this time they had established a curious relationship which was at once friendly and remote. Though they had long since ceased to call each other by their surnames, "Don" and "Walt" was as far as their intimacy went. Burley still knew absolutely nothing about Franklin's past, though he had evolved a good many theories. The one which he most favoured was that his pupil was an extremely talented criminal being rehabilitated, after total therapy. He wondered if Franklin was a murderer, which was a stimulating thought, and half hoped that this exciting hypothesis was true.

Franklin no longer showed any of the obvious peculiarities he had revealed on their first meeting, though he was undoubtedly more nervous and highly strung than the average. Since this was the case with many of the best wardens, it did not worry Don. Even his curiosity about Franklin's past had somewhat lessened, for he was far too busy to bother about it. He had learned to be patient when there was no alternative, and he did not doubt that sooner or later he would discover the whole story. Once or twice, he was almost certain, Franklin had been on the verge of some revelation, but then had drawn back. Each time Don had pretended that nothing had happened, and they had resumed their old impersonal relationship.

It was a clear morning, with only a slow swell moving across the face of the sea, as they walked along the narrow jetty that stretched from the western end of the island out to the edge of the reef. The tide was in, but though the reef flat was completely submerged the great plateau of coral was nowhere more than five or six feet below the surface, and its every detail was clearly visible through the crystal water. Neither Franklin nor Burley spared more than a few glances for the natural aquarium above which they were walking. It was too familiar to them both, and they knew that the real beauty and wonder of the reef lay in the deeper waters further out to sea.

Two hundred yards out from the island, the coral landscape suddenly dropped off into the depths, but the jetty continued upon taller stilts until it ended in a small group of sheds and offices. A valiant, and fairly successful, attempt had been made to avoid the grime and chaos usually inseparable from dockyards and piers; even the cranes had been designed so that they would not offend the eye. One of the terms under which the Queensland government had reluctantly leased the Capricorn Group to the World Food Organisation was that the beauty of the islands would not be jeopardised. On the whole, this part of the agreement had been well kept.

"I've ordered two torpedoes from the garage," said Burley as they walked down the flight of stairs at the end of the jetty and passed through the double doors of a large airlock. Franklin's ears gave the disconcerting internal "click" as they adjusted themselves to the increased pressure; he guessed that he was now about twenty feet below the water line. Around him was a brightly lighted chamber crammed with various types of underwater equipment, from simple lungs to elaborate propulsion devices. The two torpedoes that Don had requisitioned were lying in their cradles on a sloping ramp leading down into the still water at the far end of the chamber. They were painted the bright yellow reserved for training equipment, and Don looked at them with some distaste.

"It's a couple of years since I used one of these things," he said to Franklin. "You'll probably be better at it than I am. When I get myself wet, I like to be under my own power."

They stripped to swim trunks and pull-overs, then fastened on the harness of their breathing equipment. Don picked up one of the small but surprisingly heavy plastic cylinders and handed it to Franklin.

"These are the high-pressure jobs that I told you about," he said. "They're pumped to a thousand atmospheres, so the air in them is denser than water. Hence these buoyancy tanks at either end to keep them in neutral. The automatic adjustment is pretty good; as you use up your air the tanks slowly flood so that the cylinders stays just about weightless. Otherwise you'd come up to the surface like a cork whether you wanted to or not."

He looked at the pressure gauges on the tanks and gave a satisfied nod.

"They're nearly half charged," he said. "That's far more than we need. You can stay down for a day on one of these tanks when it's really pumped up, and we won't be gone more than an hour."

They adjusted the new, full-face masks that had already been checked for leaks and comfortable fitting. These would be as much their personal property as their toothbrushes while they were on the station, for no two people's faces were exactly the same shape and even the slightest leak could be disastrous.

When they had checked the air supply and the short-range underwater radio sets, they lay almost flat along the slim torpedoes, heads down behind the low, transparent shields which would protect them from the rush of water sweeping past at speeds of up to thirty knots. Franklin settled his feet comfortably in the stirrups, feeling for the throttle and jet reversal controls with his toes. The little joystick which allowed him to "fly" the torpedo like a plane was just in front of his face, in the centre of the instrument board. Apart from a few switches, the compass, and the meters giving speed, depth, and battery charge, there were no other controls.

Don gave Franklin his final instructions, ending with the words: "Keep about twenty feet away on my right, so that I can see you all the time. *If* anything goes wrong and you do have to dump the torp, for heaven's sake remember to cut the motor. We don't want it charging all over the reef. All set?"

"Yes—I'm ready," Franklin answered into his little microphone.

"Right—here we go."

The torpedoes slid easily down the ramps, and the water rose above their heads. This was no new experience to Franklin; like most other people in the world, he had occasionally tried his hand at underwater swimming and had sometimes used a lung just to see what it was like. He felt nothing but a pleasant sense of anticipation as the little turbine started to whir beneath him and the walls of the submerged chamber slid slowly past.

The light strengthened around them as they emerged into the open and pulled away from the piles of the jetty. Visibility was not very good—thirty feet at the most—but it would improve as they came to deeper water. Don swung his torpedo at right angles to the edge of the reef and headed out to sea at a leisurely five knots.

"The biggest danger with these toys," said Don's voice from the tiny loud-speaker by Franklin's ear, "is going too fast and running into something. It takes a lot of experience to judge underwater visibility. See what I mean?"

He banked steeply to avoid a towering mass of coral which had suddenly appeared ahead of them. If the demonstration had been planned, thought Franklin, Don had timed it beautifully. As the living mountain swept past, not more than ten feet away, he caught a glimpse of a myriad brilliantly coloured fish staring at him with apparent unconcern. By this time, he assumed, they must be so used to torpedoes and subs that they were quite unexcited by them. And since this entire area was rigidly protected, they had no reason to fear man.

A few minutes at cruising speed brought them out into the open water of the channel between the island and the adjacent reefs. Now they had room to manoeuvre, and Franklin followed his mentor in a series of rolls and loops and great submarine switchbacks that soon had him hopelessly lost. Sometimes they shot down to the sea bed, a hundred feet below, then broke surface like flying fish to check their position. All the time Don kept up a running commentary, interspersed with questions designed to see how Franklin was reacting to the ride.

It was one of the most exhilarating experiences he had ever known. The water was much clearer out here in the channel, and one could see for almost a hundred feet. Once they ran into a great school of bonitos, which formed an inquisitive escort until Don put on speed and left them behind. They saw no sharks, as Franklin had half expected, and he commented to Don on their absence.

"You won't see many while you're riding a torp," the other replied. "The noise of the jet scares them. If you want to meet the local sharks, you'll have to go swimming in the old-fashioned way—or cut your motor and wait until they come to look at you."

A dark mass was looming indistinctly from the sea bed, and they reduced speed to a gentle drift as they approached a little range of coral hills, twenty or thirty feet high.

"An old friend of mine lives around here," said Don. "I wonder if he's home? It's been about four years since I saw him last, but that won't seem much to him. He's been around for a couple of centuries."

They were now skirting the edge of a huge green-clad mushroom of coral, and Franklin peered into the shadows beneath it. There were a few large boulders there, and a pair of elegant angelfish which almost disappeared when they turned edge on to him. But he could see nothing else to justify Burley's interest.

It was very unsettling when one of the boulders began to move, fortunately not in his direction. The biggest fish he had ever seen—it was almost as long as the torpedo, and very much fatter—was staring at him with great bulbous eyes. Suddenly it opened its mouth in a menacing yawn, and Franklin felt like Jonah at the big moment of his career. He had a glimpse of huge, blubbery lips enclosing surprisingly tiny teeth; then the great jaws snapped shut again and he could almost feel the rush of displaced water.

Don seemed delighted at the encounter, which had obviously brought back memories of his own days as a trainee here.

"Well, it's nice to see old Slobberchops again! Isn't he a beauty? Seven hundred and fifty pounds if he's an ounce. We've been able to identify him on photos taken as far back as eighty years ago, and he wasn't much smaller then. It's a wonder he escaped the spear fishers before this area was made a reservation."

"I should think," said Franklin, "that it was a wonder the spear fishers escaped him."

"Oh, he's not really dangerous. Groupers only swallow things they can get down whole—those silly little teeth aren't much good for biting. And a full-sized man would be a trifle too much for him. Give him another century for that."

They left the giant grouper still patrolling the entrance to its cave, and continued on along the edge of the reef. For the next ten minutes they saw nothing of interest except a large ray, which was lying on the bottom and took off with an agitated flapping of its wings as soon as they approached. As it flew away into the distance, it seemed an uncannily accurate replica of the big delta-winged aircraft which had ruled the air for a short while, sixty or seventy years ago. It was strange, thought Franklin, how Nature had anticipated so many of man's inventions—for example, the precise shape of the vehicle on which he was riding, and even the jet principle by which it was propelled.

"I'm going to circle right around the reef," said Don. "It will take us about forty minutes to get home. Are you feeling O.K.?"

"I'm fine."

"No ear trouble?"

"My left ear bothered me a bit at first, but it seems to have popped now."

"Right—let's go. Follow just above and behind me, so I can see you in my rearview mirror. I was always afraid of running into you when you were on my right."

In the new formation, they sped on towards the east at a steady ten knots, following the irregular line of the reef. Don was well satisfied with the trip; Franklin had seemed perfectly at home under water—though one could never be sure of this until one had seen how he faced an emergency. That would be part of the next lesson; Franklin did not know it yet, but an emergency had been arranged.

CHAPTER IV

I T   W A S   H A R D to distinguish one day from another on the island. The weather had settled in for a period of prolonged calm, and the sun rose and set in a cloudless sky. But there was no danger of monotony, for there was far too much to learn and do.

Slowly, as his mind absorbed new knowledge and skills, Franklin was escaping from whatever nightmare must have engulfed him in the past. He was, Don sometimes thought, like an overtightened spring that was now unwinding. It was true that he still showed occasional signs of nervousness and impatience when there was no obvious cause for them, and once or twice there had been flare-ups that had caused brief interruptions in the training programme. One of these had been partly Don's fault, and the memory of it still left him annoyed with himself.

He had not been too bright that morning, owing to a late night with the boys who had just completed their course and were now full-fledged third wardens (probationary), very proud of the silver dolphins on their tunics. It would not be true to say that he had a hangover, but all his mental processes were extremely sluggish, and as bad luck would have it they were dealing with a subtle point in underwater acoustics. Even at the best of times, Don would have passed it by somewhat hastily, with a lame: "I've never been into the math, but it seems that if you take the compressibility and temperature curves this is what happens. . . ."

This worked on most pupils, but it failed to work on Franklin, who had an annoying fondness for going into unnecessary details. He began to draw curves and to differentiate equations while Don, anxious to conceal his ignorance, fumed in the background. It was soon obvious that Franklin had bitten off more than he could chew, and he appealed to his tutor for assistance. Don, both stupid and stubborn that morning, would not admit frankly that he didn't know, with the result that he gave the impression of refusing to co-operate. In no time at all, Franklin lost his temper and walked out in a huff, leaving Don to wander to the dispensary. He was not pleased to find that the entire stock of "morning-after" pills had already been consumed by the departing class.

Fortunately, such incidents were rare, for the two men had grown to respect each other's abilities and to make those allowances that are essential in every partnership. With the rest of the staff, and with the trainees, however, Franklin was not popular. This was partly because he avoided close contacts, which in the little world of the island gave him a reputation for being standoffish. The trainees also resented his special privileges—particularly the fact that he had a room of his own. And the staff, while grumbling mildly at the extra work he involved, were also annoyed because they could discover so little about him. Don had several times found himself, rather to his surprise, defending Franklin against the criticisms of his colleagues.

"He's not a bad chap when you get to know him," he had said. "If he doesn't want to talk about his past, that's his affair. The fact that a lot of people way up in the administration must be backing him is good enough for me. Besides, when I've finished with him he'll be a better warden than half the people in this room."

There were snorts of disbelief at this statement, and someone asked:

"Have you tried any tricks on him yet?"

"No, but I'm going to soon. I've thought up a nice one. Will let you know how he makes out."

"Five to one he panics."

"I'll take that. Start saving up your money."

Franklin knew nothing of his financial responsibilities when he and Don left the garage on their second torpedo ride, nor had he reason to suspect the entertainment that had been planned for him. This time they headed south as soon as they had cleared the jetty, cruising about thirty feet below the surface. In a few minutes they had passed the narrow channel blasted through the reef so that small ships could get in to the Research Station, and they circled once round the observation chamber from which the scientists could watch the inhabitants of the sea bed in comfort. There was no one inside at the moment to look out at them though the thick plate-glass windows; quite unexpectedly, Franklin found himself wondering what the little shark fancier was doing today.

"We'll head over to the Wistari Reef," said Don. "I want to give you some practice in navigation."

Don's torpedo swung round to the west as he set a new course, out into the deeper water. Visibility was not good today—less than thirty feet—and it was difficult to keep him in sight. Presently he halted and began to orbit slowly as he gave Franklin his instructions.

"I want you to hold course 250 for one minute at twenty knots, then 010 for the same time and speed. I'll meet you there. Got it?"

Franklin repeated the instructions and they checked the synchronisation of their watches. It was rather obvious what Don was doing; he had given his pupil two sides of an equilateral triangle to follow, and would doubtless proceed slowly along the third to make the appointment.

Carefully setting his course, Franklin pressed down the throttle and felt the surge of power as the torpedo leaped forward into the blue haze. The steady rush of water against his partly exposed legs was almost the only sensation of speed; without the shield, he would have been swept away in a moment. From time to time he caught a glimpse of the sea bed—drab and featureless here in the channel between the great reefs—and once he overtook a school of surprised batfish which scattered in dismay at his approach.

For the first time, Franklin suddenly realised, he was alone beneath the sea, totally surrounded by the element which would be his new domain. It supported and protected him—yet it would kill him in two or three minutes at the most if he made a mistake or if his equipment failed. That knowledge did not disturb him; it had little weight against the increasing confidence and sense of mastery he was acquiring day by day. He now knew and understood the challenge of the sea, and it was a challenge he wished to meet. With a lifting of the heart, he realised that he once more had a goal in life.

The first minute was up, and he reduced speed to four knots with the reverse jet. He had now covered a third of a mile and it was time to start on the second leg of the triangle, to make his rendezvous with Don.

The moment he swung the little joystick to starboard, he knew that something was wrong. The torpedo was wallowing like a pig, completely out of control. He cut speed to zero, and with all dynamic forces gone the vessel began to sink very slowly to the bottom.

Franklin lay motionless along the back of his recalcitrant steed, trying to analyse the situation. He was not so much alarmed as annoyed that his navigational exercise had been spoiled. It was no good calling Don, who would now be out of range—these little radio sets could not establish contact through more than a couple of hundred yards of water. What was the best thing to do?

Swiftly, his mind outlined alternative plans of action, and dismissed most of them at once. There was nothing he could do to repair the torp, for all the controls were sealed and, in any event, he had no tools. Since both rudder and elevator were out of action, the trouble was quite fundamental, and Franklin was unable to see how such a simultaneous breakdown could have happened.

He was now about fifty feet down, and gaining speed as he dropped to the bottom. The flat, sandy sea bed was just coming into sight, and for a moment Franklin had to fight the automatic impulse to press the button which would blow the torpedo's tanks and take him up to the surface. That would be the worst thing to do, natural though it was to seek air and sun when anything went wrong under water. Once on the bottom, he could take his time to think matters out, whereas if he surfaced the current might sweep him miles away. It was true that the station would soon pick up his radio calls once he was above water— but he wanted to extricate himself from this predicament without any outside help.

The torp grounded, throwing up a cloud of sand which soon drifted away in the slight current. A small grouper appeared from nowhere, staring at the intruder with its characteristic pop-eyed expression. Franklin had no time to bother with spectators, but climbed carefully off his vehicle and pulled himself to the stern. Without flippers, he had little mobility under water, but fortunately there were sufficient handholds for him to move along the torpedo without difficulty.

As Franklin had feared—but was still unable to explain—the rudder and elevator were flopping around uselessly. There was no resistance when he moved the little vanes by hand, and he wondered if there was any way in which he could fix external control lines and steer the torpedo manually. He had some nylon line, and a knife, in the pouch on his harness, but there seemed no practical way in which he could fasten the line to the smooth, streamlined vanes.

It looked as if he would have to walk home. That should not be too difficult —he could set the motor running at low speed and let the torp pull him along the bottom while he aimed it in the right direction by brute force. It would be clumsy, but seemed possible in theory, and he could think of nothing better.

He glanced at his watch; it had been only a couple of minutes since he had tried to turn at the leg of the triangle, so he was no more than a minute late at his destination. Don would not be anxious yet, but before long he would start searching for his lost pupil. Perhaps the best thing to do would be to stay right here until Don turned up, as he would be bound to do sooner or later. . . .

It was at this moment that suspicion dawned in Franklin's mind, and almost instantly became a full-fledged conviction. He recalled certain rumours he had heard, and remembered that Don's behaviour before they set out had been— well, slightly skittish was the only expression for it, as if he had been cherishing some secret joke.

So that was it. The torpedo had been sabotaged. Probably at this very moment Don was hovering out there at the limits of visibility, waiting to see what he would do and ready to step in if he ran into real trouble. Franklin glanced quickly around his hemisphere of vision, to see if the other torp was lurking in the mist, but was not surprised that there was no sign of it. Burley would be too clever to be caught so easily. This, thought Franklin, changed the situation completely. He not only had to extricate himself from his dilemma, but, if possible, he had to get his own back on Don as well.

He walked back to the control position, and switched on the motor. A slight pressure on the throttle, and the torp began to stir restlessly while a flurry of sand was gouged out of the sea bed by the jet. A little experimenting showed that it was possible to "walk" the machine, though it required continual adjustments of trim to stop it from climbing up to the surface or burying itself in the sand. It was, thought Franklin, going to take him a long time to get home this way, but he could do it if there was no alternative.

He had walked no more than a dozen paces, and had acquired quite a retinue of astonished fish, when another idea struck him. It seemed too good to be true, but it would do no harm to try. Climbing on to the torpedo and lying in the normal prone position, he adjusted the trim as carefully as he could by moving his weight back and forth. Then he tilted the nose towards the surface, pushed his hands out into the slipstream on either side, and started the motor at quarter speed.

It was hard on his wrists, and his responses had to be almost instantaneous to check the weaving and bucking of the torpedo. But with a little experimenting, he found he could use his hands for steering, though it was as difficult as riding a bicycle with one's arms crossed. At five knots, the area of his flattened palms was just sufficient to give control over the vehicle.

He wondered if anyone had ever ridden a torp this way before, and felt rather pleased with himself. Experimentally, he pushed the speed up to eight knots, but the pressure on his wrists and forearms was too great and he had to throttle back before he lost control.

There was no reason, Franklin told himself, why he should not now make his original redenzvous, just in case Don was waiting there for him. He would be about five minutes late, but at least it would prove that he could carry out his assignment in the face of obstacles which he was not quite sure were entirely man-made.

Don was nowhere in sight when he arrived, and Franklin guessed what had happened. His unexpected mobility had taken Burley by surprise, and the warden had lost him in the submarine haze. Well, he could keep on looking. Franklin made one radio call as a matter of principle, but there was no reply from his tutor. "I'm going home!" he shouted to the watery world around him; still there was silence. Don was probably a good quarter of a mile away, conducting an increasingly more anxious search for his lost pupil.

There was no point in remaining below the surface and adding to the difficulties of navigation and control. Franklin took his vehicle up to the top and found that he was less than a thousand yards from the Maintenance Section jetty. By keeping the torp tail heavy and nose up he was able to scorch along on the surface like a speedboat without the slightest trouble, and he was home in five minutes.

As soon as the torpedo had come out of the anticorrosion sprays which were used on all equipment after salt-water dives, Franklin got to work on it. When he pulled off the panel of the control compartment, he discovered that his was a very special model indeed. Without a circuit diagram, it was not possible to tell exactly what the radio-operated relay unit he had located could do, but he did not doubt that it had an interesting repertory. It could certainly cut off the motor, blow or flood the buoyancy tanks, and reverse the rudder and elevator controls. Franklin suspected that compass and depth gauge could also be sabotaged if required. Someone had obviously spent a great deal of loving care making this torpedo a suitable steed for overconfident pupils. . . .

He replaced the panel and reported his safe return to the officer on duty. "Visibility's very poor," he said, truthfully enough. "Don and I lost each other out there, so I thought I'd better come in. I guess he'll be along later."

There was considerable surprise in the mess when Franklin turned up without his instructor and settled quietly down in a corner to read a magazine. Forty

minutes later, a great slamming of doors announced Don's arrival. The
warden's face was a study in relief and perplexity as he looked around the room
and located his missing pupil, who stared back at him with his most innocent
expression and said: "What kept you?"

Burley turned to his colleagues and held out his hand.

"Pay up, boys," he ordered.

It had taken him long enough to make up his mind, but he realised that he
was beginning to like Franklin.

CHAPTER V

THE TWO MEN leaning on the rails around the main pool of the
aquarium did not, thought Indra as she walked up the road to the lab, look
like the usual run of visiting scientists. It was not until she had come closer
and was able to get a good look at them that she realised who they were. The
big fellow was First Warden Burley, so the other must be the famous
mystery man he was taking through a high-pressure course. She had
heard his name but couldn't remember it, not being particularly interested in the
activities of the training school. As a pure scienitist, she tended to look down on
the highly practical work of the Bureau of Whales—though had anyone accused
her outright of such intellectual snobbery she would have denied it with
indignation.

She had almost reached them before she realised that she had already met
the smaller man. For his part, Franklin was looking at her with a slightly
baffled, "Haven't we seen each other before?" expression.

"Hello," she said, coming to a standstill beside them. "Remember me? I'm
the girl who collects sharks."

Franklin smiled and answered: "Of course I remember: it still turns my
stomach sometimes. I hope you found plenty of vitamins."

Yet strangely enough, the puzzled expression—so typical of a man straining
after memories that will not come—still lingered in his eyes. It made him look
lost and more than a little worried, and Indra found herself reacting with a
sympathy which was disconcerting. She had already had several narrow escapes
from emotional entanglements on the island, and she reminded herself firmly
of her resolution: "Not until *after* I've got my master's degree . . ."

"So you know each other," said Don plaintively. "You might introduce me."
Don, Indra decided, was perfectly safe. He would start to flirt with her at once,
like any warden worthy of his calling. She did not mind that in the least;
though big leonine blonds were not precisely her type, it was always flattering
to feel that one was causing a stir, and she knew that there was no risk of any

serious attachment here. With Franklin, however, she felt much less sure of herself.

They chattered pleasantly enough, with a few bantering undertones, while they stood watching the big fish and porpoises circling slowly in the oval pool. The lab's main tank was really an artificial lagoon, filled and emptied twice a day by the tides, with a little assistance from a pumping plant. Wire-mesh barriers divided it into various sections through which mutually incompatible exhibits stared hungrily at each other; a small tiger shark, with the inevitable sucker fish glued to its back, kept patrolling its underwater cage, unable to take its eyes off the succulent pompano parading just outside. In some enclosures, however, surprising partnerships had developed. Brilliantly coloured crayfish, looking like overgrown shrimps that had been sprayed with paint guns, crawled a few inches away from the incessantly gaping jaws of a huge and hideous moray eel. A school of fingerlings, like sardines that had escaped from their tin, cruised past the nose of a quarter-ton grouper that could have swallowed them all at one gulp.

It was a peaceful little world, so different from the battlefield of the reef. But if the lab staff ever failed to make the normal feeding arrangements, this harmony would quickly vanish and in a few hours the population of the pool would start a catastrophic decline.

Don did most of the talking; he appeared to have quite forgotten that he had brought Franklin here to see some of the whale-recognition films in the lab's extensive library. He was clearly trying to impress Indra, and quite unaware of the fact that she saw through him completely. Franklin, on the other hand, obviously saw both sides of the game and was mildly entertained by it. Once, Indra caught his eyes, when Don was holding forth about the life and hard times of the average warden, and they exchanged the smiles of two people who share the same amusing secret. And at that moment Indra decided that, after all, her degree might not be the most important thing in the world. She was still determined not to get herself involved—but she had to learn more about Franklin. What was his first name? Walter. It was not one of her favourites, but it would do.

In his calm confidence that he was laying waste another susceptible female heart, Don was completely unaware of the undercurrents of emotion that were sweeping around him yet leaving him utterly untouched. When he suddenly realised that they were twenty minutes late for their appointment in the projection room, he pretended to blame Franklin, who accepted the reproof in a good-natured but slightly absent-minded manner. For the rest of the morning, indeed, Franklin was rather far away from his studies; but Don noticed nothing at all.

The first part of the course was now virtually completed; Franklin had learned the basic mechanics of the warden's profession and now needed the experience that only time would give. In almost every respect, he had exceeded Burley's hopes, partly because of his original scientific training, partly because of his innate intelligence. Yet there was more to it even than this; Franklin had a drive and determination that was sometimes frightening. It was as if success in this course was a matter of life and death to him. True, he had been slow in starting; for the first few days he had been listless and seemingly almost uninterested in his new career. Then he had come to life, as he awoke to the wonder and challenge—the endless opportunity—of the element he was attempting to master. Though Don was not much given to such fancies, it seemed to him that Franklin was like a man awakening from a long and troubled sleep.

The real test had been when they had first gone under water with the torpedoes. Franklin might never use a torp again—except for amusement—during his entire career; they were purely shallow-water units designed for very short-range work, and as a warden, Franklin would spend all his operational time snug and dry behind the protective walls of a sub. But unless a man was at ease and confident—though not overconfident—when he was actually immersed in water, the service had no use for him, however qualified he might be in other respects.

Franklin had also passed, with a satisfactory safety margin, the decompression, CO_2, and nitrogen narcosis tests. Burley had put him in the station's "torture chamber", where the doctors slowly increased the air pressure and took him down on a simulated dive. He had been perfectly normal down to 150 feet; thereafter his mental reactions became sluggish and he failed to do simple sums correctly when they were given to him over the intercom. At 300 feet he appeared to be mildly drunk and started cracking jokes which reduced him to tears of helpless laughter but which were quite unfunny to those outside —and embarrassingly so to Franklin himself when they played them back to him later. Three hundred and fifty feet down he still appeared to be conscious but refused to react to Don's voice, even when it started shouting outrageous insults. And at 400 feet he passed out completely, and they brought him slowly back to normal.

Though he would never have occasion to use them, he was also tested with the special breathing mixtures which enable a man to remain conscious and active at far greater depths. When he did any deep dives, he would not be wearing underwater breathing gear but would be sitting comfortably inside a sub breathing normal air at normal pressure. But a warden had to be a Jack of all underwater trades, and never knew what equipment he might have to use in an emergency.

Burley was no longer scared—as he had once been—at the thought of sharing a two-man training sub with Franklin. Despite the other's underlying reticence and the mystery which still surrounded him, they were partners now and knew how to work together. They had not yet become friends, but had reached a state which might be defined as one of tolerant respect.

On their first sub run, they kept to the shallow waters between the Great Barrier Reef and the mainland, while Franklin familiarised himself with the controls, and above all with the navigational instruments. If you could run a sub here, said Don, in this labyrinth of reefs and islands, you could run it anywhere. Apart from trying to charge Masthead Island at sixty knots, Franklin performed quite creditably. His fingers began to move over the complex control board with a careful precision which, Don knew, would soon develop into automatic skill. His scanning of the many meters and display screens would soon be unconscious, so that he would not even be aware that he saw them—until something called for his attention.

Don gave Franklin increasingly more complicated tasks to perform, such as tracing out improbable courses by dead reckoning and then checking his position on the sonar grid to see where he had actually arrived. It was not until he was quite sure that Franklin was proficient in handling a sub that they finally went out into deep water over the edge of the continental shelf.

Navigating a Scoutsub was merely the beginning; one had to learn to see and feel with its senses, to interpret all the patterns of information displayed on the control board by the many instruments which were continually probing the underwater world. The sonic senses were, perhaps, the most important. In utter darkness, or in completely turbid water, they could detect all obstacles out to a range of ten miles, with great accuracy and in considerable detail. They could show the contours of the ocean bed, or with equal ease could detect any fish more than two or three feet long that came within half a mile. Whales and the larger marine animals they could spot right out to the extreme limit of range, fixing them with pinpoint accuracy.

Visible light had a more limited role. Sometimes, in deep ocean waters far from the eternal rain of silt which sloughs down from the edge of the continents, it was possible to see as much as two hundred feet—but that was rare. In shallow coastal waters, the television eye could seldom peer more than fifty feet, but within its range it gave a definition unmatched by the sub's other senses.

Yet the subs had not only to see and feel; they also had to act. Franklin must learn to use the whole armoury of tools and weapons: borers to collect specimens of the sea bed, meters to check the efficiency of the fences, sampling devices, branders for painlessly marking uncooperative whales, electric probes to discourage marine beasts that became too inquisitive—and, most seldom used of all, the tiny torpedoes and poisoned darts that could slay in seconds the mightiest creatures of the seas.

In daily cruises far out into the Pacific, Franklin learned to use these tools of his new trade. Sometimes they went through the fence, and it seemed to Franklin that he could feel its eternal high-pitched shrieking in his very bones. Halfway around the world it now extended, its narrow fans of radiation reaching up to the surface from the deeply submerged generators.

What, wondered Franklin, would earlier ages have thought of this? In some ways it seemed the greatest and most daring of all man's presumptions. The sea, which had worked its will with man since the beginning of time, had been humbled at last. Not even the conquest of space had been a greater victory than this.

And yet—it was a victory that would never be final. The sea would always be waiting, and every year it would claim its victims. There was a roll of honour that Franklin had glimpsed briefly during his visit to the head office. Already it bore many names, and there was room for many more.

Slowly, Franklin was coming to terms with the sea, as must all men who have dealings with it. Though he had had little time for non-essential reading, he had dipped into *Moby Dick*, which had been half-jokingly, half-seriously called the bible of the Bureau of Whales. Much of it had seemed to him tedious, and so far removed from the world in which he was living that it had no relevance. Yet occasionally Melville's archaic, sonorous prose touched some chord in his own mind, and gave him a closer understanding of the ocean which he, too, must learn to hate and love.

Don Burley, however, had no use at all for *Moby Dick* and frequently made fun of those who were always quoting it.

"We could show Melville a thing or two!" he had once remarked to Franklin, in a very condescending tone.

"Of course we could," Franklin had answered. "But would you have the guts to stick a spear into a sperm whale from an open boat?"

Don did not reply. He was honest enough to admit that he did not know the answer.

Yet there was one question he was now close to answering. As he watched Franklin learn his new skills, with a swiftness which could undoubtedly make him a first warden in no more than four or five years, he knew with complete certainty what his pupil's last profession had been. If he chose to keep it a secret, that was his own affair. Don felt a little aggrieved by such lack of trust; but sooner or later, he told himself, Franklin would confide in him.

Yet it was not Don who was the first to learn the truth. By the sheerest of accidents, it was Indra.

CHAPTER VI

THEY NOW MET at least once a day in the mess, though Franklin had not yet made the irrevocable, almost unprecedented, step of moving from his table to the one at which the research staff dined. That would be a flamboyant declaration which would set every tongue on the island wagging happily, and in any case it would not be justified by the circumstances. As far as Indra and Franklin were concerned, the much-abused phrase "we're just friends" was still perfectly true.

Yet it was also true that they had grown very fond of each other, and that almost everyone except Don was aware of it. Several of Indra's colleagues had said to her approvingly, "You're thawing out the iceberg," and the compliment had flattered her. The few people who knew Franklin well enough to banter with him had made warning references to Don, pointing out that first wardens had reputations to maintain. Franklin's reaction had been a somewhat forced grin, concealing feelings which he could not fully analyse himself.

Loneliness, the need to escape from memories, a safety valve to guard him against the pressure under which he was working—these factors were at least as important as the normal feelings of any man for a girl as attractive as Indra. Whether this companionship would develop into anything more serious, he did not know. He was not even sure if he wished it to do so.

Nor, for her part, was Indra, though her old resolve was weakening. Sometimes she indulged in reveries wherein her career took very much of a second place. One day, of course, she was going to marry, and the man she would choose would be very much like Franklin. But that it might *be* Franklin was a thought from which she still shied away.

One of the problems of romance on Heron Island was that there were far too many people in too small a space. Even the fragment that was left of the original forest did not provide enough seclusion. At night, if one wandered through its paths and byways, carrying a flashlight to avoid the low-hanging branches, one had to be very tactful with the beam. One was liable to find that favourite spots had already been requisitioned, which would be extremely frustrating if there was nowhere else to go.

The fortunate scientists at the Research Station, however, had an invaluable escape route. All the large surface craft and all the underwater vessels belonged to Administration, though they were made available to the lab for official business. But by some historical accident, the lab had a tiny private fleet consisting of one launch and two catamarans. No one was quite sure who owned the latter, and it was noticeable that they were always at sea when the auditors arrived for the annual inventory.

The little cats did a great deal of work for the lab, since they drew only six inches of water and could operate safely over the reef except at low tide. With a stiff wind behind them, they could do twenty knots with ease, and races between the two craft were frequently arranged. When they were not being used for other business, the scientists would sail them to the neighbouring reefs and islands to impress their friends—usually of the opposite sex—with their prowess as seamen.

It was a little surprising that ships and occupants had always come back safely from these expeditions. The only casualties had been to morale; one first warden of many years seniority had had to be carried off the boat after a pleasure trip, and had sworn that nothing would ever induce him to travel on the *surface* of the sea again.

When Indra suggested to Franklin that he might like to sail to Masthead Island, he accepted at once. Then he said cautiously: "Who'll run the boat?"

Indra looked hurt.

"I will, of course," she answered. "I've done it dozens of times." She seemed to be half-expecting him to doubt her competence, but Franklin knew better than to do so. Indra, he had already discovered, was a very level-headed girl— perhaps too level-headed. If she said she could do a job, that was that.

There was still, however, one other point to be settled. The cats could take four people; who would the other two be?

Neither Indra nor Franklin actually voiced the final decision. It hovered in the air while they discussed various possible companions, starting with Don and working down the list of Indra's friends at the lab. Presently the conversation died out into one of those portentous pauses which can sometimes occur even in a roomful of chattering people.

In the sudden silence, each realised that the other was thinking the same thought, and that a new phase had begun in their relationship. They would take no one with them to Masthead; for the first time, they would have the solitude that had never been possible here. That this could lead only to one logical conclusion they refused to admit, even to themselves, the human mind having a remarkable capacity for self-deceit.

It was well into the afternoon before they were able to make all their arrangements and escape. Franklin felt very guilty about Don, and wondered what his reactions would be when he found out what had happened. He would probably be mortified, but he was not the sort to hold a grudge and he would take it like a man.

Indra had thought of everything. Food, drinks, sunburn lotion, towels—she had overlooked nothing that such an expedition might need. Franklin was impressed by her thoroughness, and was amused to find himself thinking that so competent a woman would be very useful to have around the house. Then he reminded himself hastily that women who were too efficient were seldom happy unless they ran their husbands' lives as well as their own.

There was a steady wind blowing from the mainland, and the cat bounded across the waves like a living creature. Franklin had never before been in a sailing boat, and he found the experience an exhilarating one. He lay back on the worn but comfortable padding of the open cockpit, while Heron Island receded into the distance at an astonishing speed. It was restful to watch the twin, creamy wakes trace their passage across the sea, and to caress with the eye the straining, power-filled curves of the sails. With a mild and fleeting regret, Franklin wished that all man's machines could be as simple and efficient as this one. What a contrast there was between this vessel and the crowded complexities of the subs he was now learning to handle! The thought passed swiftly; there were some tasks which could not be achieved by simple means, and one must accept the fact without complaint.

On their left, they were now skirting the long line of rounded coral boulders which centuries of storms had cast up upon the edge of the Wistari Reef. The waves were breaking against the submerged ramparts with a relentless and persistent fury which had never impressed Franklin so much as now. He had seen them often enough before—but never from so close at hand, in so frail a craft.

The boiling margin of the reef fell astern; now they had merely to wait while the winds brought them to their goal. Even if the wind failed—which was most unlikely—they could still make the trip on the little auxiliary hydro-jet engine, though that would only be used as a last resort. It was a matter of principle to return with a full fuel tank.

Although they were now together and alone for almost the first time since they had met, neither Franklin nor Indra felt any need to talk. There seemed a silent communion between them which they did not wish to break with words, being content to share the peace and wonder of the open sea and the open sky. They were enclosed between two hemispheres of flawless blue, clamped together at the misty rim of the horizon, and nothing else of the world remained. Even time seemed to have faltered to a stop; Franklin felt he could lie here for ever, relaxing in the gentle motion of the boat as it skimmed effortlessly over the waves.

Presently a low, dark cloud began to solidify, then to reveal itself as a tree-clad island with its narrow sandy shore and inevitable fringing reef. Indra bestirred herself and began to take an active interest in navigation once more, while Franklin looked rather anxiously at the breakers which seemed to surround the island in one continuous band.

"How are we going to get in?" he asked.

"Round the lee side; it won't be rough there, and the tide should be high enough for us to go in across the reef. If it isn't, we can always anchor and wade ashore."

Franklin was not altogether happy about so casual an approach to what seemed a serious problem, and he could only hope that Indra really did know what she was doing. If she made a mistake, they might have an uncomfortable though not particularly dangerous swim ahead, followed after a long wait by an ignominious rescue when someone came from the lab to look for them.

Either it was easier than it appeared to an anxious novice, or else Indra's seamanship was of a high order. They circled halfway round the island, until they came to a spot where the breakers subsided into a few choppy waves. Then Indra turned the prow of the cat towards the land, and headed straight for shore.

There were no sounds of grinding coral or splintering plastic. Like a bird, the catamaran flew in across the narrow edge of the reef, now clearly visible just below the broken and unsettled water. It skimmed past this danger zone, and then was over the peaceful surface of the lagoon, seeming to gain speed as it approached the beach. Seconds before impact, Indra furled the mainsail. With a soft thud, the vessel hit the sand and coasted up the gentle slope, coming to rest with more than half its length above the water line.

"Here we are," said Indra. "One uninhabited coral island, in full working order." She seemed more relaxed and lighthearted than Franklin had ever before seen her; he realised that she, too, had been working under pressure and was glad to escape from the daily routine for a few hours. Or was it the stimulating effect of his company that was turning her from a serious student into a vivacious girl? Whatever the explanation, he liked the change.

They climbed out of the boat and carried their gear up the beach into the shade of the coconut palms, which had been imported into these islands only during the last century to challenge the predominance of the Pisonia and the stilt-rooted pandanus. It seemed that someone else had also been here recently, for curious tracks apparently made by narrow-gauge caterpillar treads marched up out of the water and vanished inland. They would have been quite baffling to anyone who did not know that the big turtles had been coming ashore to lay their eggs.

As soon as the cat had been made secure, Franklin and Indra began a tour of exploration. It was true that one coral island was almost exactly the same as another; the same pattern was repeated endlessly over and over again, with few variations. Yet even when one was aware of that, and had landed on dozens of islands, every new one presented a fresh challenge which had to be accepted.

They began the circumnavigation of their little world, walking along the narrow belt of sand between the forest and the sea. Sometimes, when they came to a clearing, they made short forays inland, deliberately trying to lose themselves in the tangle of trees so that they could pretend that they were in the heart of Africa and not, at the very most, a hundred yards from the sea.

Once they stopped to dig with their hands at the spot where one of the turtle tracks terminated on a flat-ended sand dune. They gave up when they were two feet down and there was still no sign of the leathery, flexible eggs. The mother turtle, they solemnly decided, must have been making false trails to deceive her enemies. For the next ten minutes, they elaborated this fantasy into a startling thesis on reptile intelligence, which, far from gaining Indra new qualifications, would undoubtedly have cost her the degree she already possessed.

Inevitably the time came when, having helped each other over a patch of rough coral, their hands failed to separate even though the path was smooth once more. Neither speaking, yet each more conscious of the other's presence than they had ever been before, they walked on in the silence of shared contentment.

At a leisurely stroll, pausing whenever they felt like it to examine some curiosity of the plant or animal world, it took them almost two hours to circumnavigate the little island. By the time they had reached the cat they were very hungry, and Franklin began to unpack the food hamper with unconcealed eagerness while Indra started working on the stove.

"Now I'm going to brew you a billy of genuine Australian tea," she said.

Franklin gave her that twisted, whimsical smile which she found so attractive.

"It will hardly be a novelty to me," he said. "After all, I was born here."

She stared at him in astonishment which gradually turned to exasperation. "Well, you might have told me!" she said. "In fact, I really think——" Then she stopped, as if by a deliberate effort of will, leaving the uncompleted sentence hanging in mid-air. Franklin had no difficulty in finishing it. She had intended to say, "It's high time you told me something about yourself, and abandoned all this silly reticence."

The truth of the unspoken accusation made him flush, and for a moment some of his carefree happiness—the first he had known for so many months—drained away. Then a thought struck him which he had never faced before, since to do so might have jeopardised his friendship with Indra. She was a scientist and a woman, and therefore doubly inquisitive. Why was it that she had never asked him any questions about his past life? There could only be one explanation. Dr. Myers, who was unobtrusively watching over him despite the jovial pretence that he was doing nothing of the sort, must have spoken to her.

A little more of his contentment ebbed as he realised that Indra must feel sorry for him and must wonder, like everyone else, exactly what had happened to him. He would not, he told himself bitterly, accept a love that was founded on pity.

Indra seemed unaware of his sudden brooding silence and the conflict that now disturbed his mind. She was busy filling the little stove by a somewhat primitive method that involved siphoning fuel out of the hydrojet's tank, and Franklin was so amused by her repeated failures that he forgot his momentary annoyance. When at last she had managed to light the stove, they lay back under the palms, munching sandwiches and waiting for the water to boil. The sun was already far down the sky, and Franklin realised that they would probably not get back to Heron Island until well after nightfall. However, it would not be dark, for the moon was nearing full, so even without the aid of the local beacons the homeward journey would present no difficulties.

The billy-brewed tea was excellent, though doubtless far too anaemic for any old-time swagman. It washed down the remainder of their food very efficiently, and as they relaxed with sighs of satisfaction their hands once again found each other. Now, thought Franklin, I should be perfectly content. But he knew that he was not; something that he could not define was worrying him.

His unease had grown steadily stronger during the last few minutes, but he had tried to ignore it and force it down into his mind. He knew that it was utterly ridiculous and irrational to expect any danger here, on this empty and peaceful island. Yet little warning bells were ringing far down in the labyrinths of his brain, and he could not understand their signals.

Indra's casual question came as a welcome distraction. She was staring intently up into the western sky, obviously searching for something.

"Is it really true, Walter," she asked, "that if you know where to look for her you can see Venus in the daytime? She was so bright after sunset last night that I could almost believe it."

"It's perfectly true," Franklin answered. "In fact, it isn't even difficult. The big problem is to locate her in the first place; once you've done that, she's quite easy to see."

He propped himself up against a palm trunk, shaded his eyes from the glare of the descending sun, and began to search the western sky with little hope of discovering the elusive silver speck he knew to be shining there. He had noticed Venus dominating the evening sky during the last few weeks, but it was hard to judge how far she was from the sun when both were above the horizon at the same time.

Suddenly—unexpectedly—his eyes caught and held a solitary silver star hanging against the milky blue of the sky. "I've found her!" he exclaimed, raising his arm as a pointer. Indra squinted along it, but at first could see nothing.

"You've got spots before the eyes," she taunted.

"No—I'm not imagining things. Just keep on looking," Franklin answered, his eyes still focused on the dimensionless star which he knew he would lose if he turned away from it even for a second.

"But Venus can't be there," protested Indra. "That's much too far north."

In a single, sickening instant Franklin knew that she was right. If he had any doubt, he could see now that the star he was watching was moving swiftly across the sky, rising out of the west and so defying the laws which controlled all other heavenly bodies.

He was staring at the Space Station, the largest of all the satellites now circling Earth, as it raced along its thousand-mile-high orbit. He tried to turn his eyes away, to break the hypnotic spell of that man-made, unscintillating star. It was as if he was teetering on the edge of an abyss; the terror of those endless, trackless wastes between the worlds began to invade and dominate his mind, to threaten the very foundations of his sanity.

He would have won the struggle, no more than a little shaken, had it not been for a second accident of fate. With the explosive suddenness with which memory sometimes yields to persistent questioning, he knew what it was that had been worrying him for the last few minutes. It was the smell of the fuel that Indra had siphoned from the hydrojet—the unmistakable, slightly aromatic tang of synthene. And crowding hard upon that recognition was the memory of where he had last met that all-too-familiar odour.

Synthene—first developed as a rocket propellant—now obsolete like all other chemical fuels, except for low-powered applications like the propulsion of space suits.

Space suits.

It was too much; the double assault defeated him. Both sight and smell had turned traitor in the same instant. Within seconds, the patiently built dikes which now protected his mind went down before the rising tide of terror.

He could feel the Earth beneath him spinning dizzily through space. It seemed to be whirling faster and faster on its axis, trying to hurl him off like a stone from a sling by the sheer speed of its rotation. With a choking cry, he rolled over on his stomach, buried his face in the sand, and clung desperately to the rough trunk of the palm. It gave him no security; the endless fall began again. . . . Chief Engineer Franklin, second in command of the *Arcturus*, was in space once more, at the beginning of the nightmare he had hoped and prayed he need never retrace.

CHAPTER VII

I N T H E F I R S T shock of stunned surprise, Indra sat staring foolishly at Franklin as he grovelled in the sand and wept like a heartbroken child. Then compassion and common sense told her what to do; she moved swiftly to his side and threw her arms around his heaving shoulders.

"Walter!" she cried. "You're all right—there's nothing to be afraid of!"

The words seemed flat and foolish even as she uttered them, but they were the best she had to offer. Franklin did not seem to hear; he was still trembling uncontrollably, still clinging to the tree with desperate determination. It was pitiful to see a man reduced to such a state of abject fear, so robbed of all dignity and pride. As Indra crouched over him, she realised that between his sobs he was calling a name—and even at such a moment as this she could not depress a stab of jealousy. For it was the name of a woman; over and over again, in a voice so low as to be barely audible, Franklin would whisper "Irene!" and then be convulsed by a fresh paroxysm of weeping.

There was something here beyond Indra's slight knowledge of medicine. She hesitated for a moment, then hurried to the catamaran and broke open its little first-aid kit. It contained a vial of potent pain-killing capsules, prominently labelled ONLY ONE TO BE TAKEN AT ANY TIME, and with some difficulty she managed to force one of these into Franklin's mouth. Then she held him in her arms while his tremors slowly subsided and the violence of the attack ebbed away.

It is hard to draw any line between compassion and love. If such a division exists, Indra crossed it during this silent vigil. Franklin's loss of manhood had not disgusted her; she knew that something terrible indeed must have happened in his past to bring him to this state. Whatever it was, her own future would not be complete unless she could help him fight it.

Presently Franklin was quiet, though apparently still conscious. He did not resist when she rolled him over so that his face was no longer half-buried in the sand, and he relaxed his frenzied grip upon the tree. But his eyes were empty, and his mouth still moved silently though no words came from it.

"We're going home," whispered Indra, as if soothing a frightened child. "Come along—it's all right now."

She helped him to his feet, and he rose unresistingly. He even assisted her, in a mechanical way, to pack their equipment and to push the catamaran off the beach. He seemed nearly normal again, except that he would not speak and there was a sadness in his eyes that tore at Indra's heart.

They left the island under both sail and power, for Indra was determined to waste no time. Even now it had not occurred to her that she might be in any personal danger, so many miles from any help, with a man who might be mad. Her only concern was to get Franklin back to medical care as quickly as she could.

The light was failing fast; the sun had already touched the horizon and darkness was massing in the east. Beacons on the mainland and the surrounding islands began, one by one, to spring to life. And, more brilliant than any of them, there in the west was Venus, which had somehow caused all this trouble. . . .

Presently Franklin spoke, his words forced but perfectly rational.

"I'm very sorry about this, Indra," he said. "I'm afraid I spoiled your trip."

"Don't be silly," she answered. "It wasn't your fault. Just take it easy—don't talk unless you want to." He relapsed into silence, and spoke no more for the rest of the voyage. When Indra reached out to hold his hand again, he stiffened defensively in a way which said, without actually rejecting her, that he would prefer no such contact. She felt hurt, but obeyed his unspoken request. In any event, she was busy enough picking out the beacons as she made the tricky passage between the reefs.

She had not intended to be out as late as this, even though the rising moon was now flooding the sea with light. The wind had freshened, and all too close at hand the breakers along the Wistari Reef were appearing and vanishing in deadly lines of luminous, ghostly white. She kept one eye on them, and the other on the winking beacon that marked the end of the Heron jetty. Not until she could see the jetty itself and make out the details of the island was she able to relax and give her attention once more to Franklin.

He appeared almost normal again when they had berthed the catamaran and walked back to the lab. Indra could not see his expression, for there were no lights here on this part of the beach, and the palms shaded them from the moon. As far as she could tell, his voice was under full control when he bade her good-night.

"Thank you for everything, Indra. No one could have done more."

"Let me take you to Dr. Myers right away. You've got to see him."

"No—there's nothing he can do. I'm quite all right now—it won't happen again."

"I still think you should see him. I'll take you to your room and then go and call him."

Franklin shook his head violently.

"That's one thing I don't want you to do. Promise me you won't call him."

Sorely troubled, Indra debated with her conscience. The wisest thing to do, she was sure, was to make the promise—and then to break it. Yet if she did so, Franklin might never forgive her. In the end, she compromised.

"Will you go and see him yourself, if you won't let me take you?"

Franklin hesitated before answering. It seemed a shame that his parting words with this girl, whom he might have loved, should be a lie. But in the drugged calm that had come upon him now he knew what he must do.

"I'll call him in the morning—and thanks again." Then he broke away, with a fierce finality, before Indra could question him further.

She watched him disappear into the darkness, along the path that led to the training and administration section. Happiness and anxiety were contending for her soul—happiness because she had found love, anxiety because it was threatened by forces she did not understand. The anxiety resolved itself into a single nagging fear: Should she have insisted, even against his will, that Franklin see Dr. Myers at once?

She would have had no doubt of the answer could she have watched Franklin double back through the moonlit forest and make his way, like a man in a waking dream, to the dock from which had begun all his journeys down into the sea.

The rational part of his mind was now merely the passive tool of his emotions, and they were set upon a single goal. He had been hurt too badly for reason to control him now; like an injured animal, he could think of nothing but the abating of his pain. He was seeking the only place where for a little while he had found peace and contentment.

The jetty was deserted as he made the long, lonely walk out to the edge of the reef. Down in the submarine hangar, twenty feet below the water line, he made his final preparations with as much care as he had ever done on his many earlier trips. He felt a fleeting sense of guilt at robbing the bureau of some fairly valuable equipment and still more valuable training time; but it was not his fault that he had no other choice.

Very quietly, the torp slipped out beneath the submerged archway and set course for the open sea. It was the first time that Franklin had ever been out at night; only the fully enclosed subs operated after darkness, for night navigation involved dangers which it was foolhardy for unprotected men to face. That was the least of Franklin's worries as he set the course he remembered so well and headed out into the channel that would lead him to the sea.

Part of the pain, but none of the determination, lifted from his mind. This was where he belonged; this was where he had found happiness. This was where he would find oblivion.

He was in a world of midnight blue which the pale rays of the moon could do little to illumine. Around him strange shapes moved like phosphorescent ghosts, as the creatures of the reef were attracted or scattered by the sound of his passing. Below him, no more than shadows in a deeper darkness, he could see the coral hills and valleys he had grown to know so well. With a resignation beyond sadness, he bade them all adieu.

There was no point in lingering, now that his destiny was clear before him. He pushed the throttle full down, and the torpedo leaped forward like a horse that had been given the spur. The islands of the Great Barrier Reef were falling swiftly behind him, and he was heading out into the Pacific at a speed which no other creature of the sea could match.

Only once did he glance up at the world he had abandoned. The water was fantastically clear, and a hundred feet above his head he could see the silver track of the moon upon the sea, as few men could ever have witnessed it before. He could even see the hazy, dancing patch of light that was the moon itself, refracted through the water surface yet occasionally freezing, when the moving waves brought a moment of stability, into a perfect, flawless image.

And once a very large shark—the largest he had even seen—tried to pursue him. The great streamlined shadow, leaving its phosphorescent wake, appeared suddenly almost dead ahead of him, and he made no effort to avoid it. As it swept past he caught a glimpse of the inhuman, staring eye, the slatted gills, and the inevitable retinue of pilot fish and remora. When he glanced back the shark was following him—whether motivated by curiosity, sex, or hunger he neither knew nor cared. It remained in sight for almost a minute before his superior speed left it behind. He had never met a shark that had reacted in this way before; usually they were terrified of the turbine's warning scream. But the laws that ruled the reef during the day were not those that prevailed in the hours of darkness.

He raced on through the luminous night that covered half the world, crouching behind his curved shield for protection against the turbulent waters he was sundering in his haste to reach the open sea. Even now he was navigating with all his old skill and precision; he knew exactly where he was, exactly when he would reach his objective—and exactly how deep were the waters he was now entering. In a few minutes, the sea bed would start slanting sharply down and he must say his last farewell to the reef.

He tilted the nose of the torp imperceptibly towards the depths and at the same time cut his speed to a quarter. The mad, roaring rush of waters ceased; he was sliding gently down a long, invisible slope whose end he would never see.

Slowly the pale and filtered moonlight began to fade as the water thickened above him. Deliberately, he avoided looking at the illuminated depth gauge, avoided all thought of the fathoms that now lay overhead. He could feel the pressure on his body increasing minute by minute, but it was not in the least unpleasant. Indeed, he welcomed it; he gave himself, a willing sacrifice, gladly into the grasp of the great mother of life.

The darkness was now complete. He was alone, driving through a night stranger and more palpable than any to be found upon the land. From time to time he could see, at an unguessable distance below him, tiny explosions of light as the unknown creatures of the open sea went about their mysterious business. Sometimes an entire, ephemeral galaxy would thrust forth and within seconds die; perhaps that other galaxy, he told himself, was of no longer duration, of no greater importance, when seen against the background of eternity.

The dreamy sleep of nitrogen narcosis was now almost upon him; no other human being, using a compressed-air lung alone, could ever have been so deep and returned to tell the tale. He was breathing air at more than ten times normal pressure, and still the torpedo was boring down into the lightless depths. All responsibility, all regrets, all fears had been washed away from his mind by the blissful euphoria that had invaded every level of consciousness.

And yet, at the very end, there was one regret. He felt a mild and wistful sadness, that Indra must now begin again her search for the happiness he might have given her.

Thereafter there was only the sea, and a mindless machine creeping ever more slowly down to the hundred-fathom line and the Pacific wastes.

CHAPTER VIII

T H E R E   W E R E   F O U R people in the room, and not one of them was talking now. The chief instructor was biting his lip nervously, Don Burley sat looking stunned, and Indra was trying not to cry. Only Dr. Myers seemed fairly well under control, and was silently cursing the fantastic, the still inexplicable bad luck that had brought this situation upon them. He would have sworn that

Franklin was well on the road to recovery, well past any serious crisis. And now this!

"There's only one thing to do," said the chief instructor suddenly. "And that's to send out all our underwater craft on a general search."

Don Burley stirred himself, slowly and as if carrying a great weight upon his shoulders.

"It's twelve hours now. In that time he could have covered five hundred miles. And there are only six qualified pilots on the station."

"I know—it would be like looking for a needle in a haystack. But it's the only thing we can do."

"Sometimes a few minutes of thought can save a good many hours of random searching," said Myers. "After all a day, a little extra time will make no difference. With your permission, I'd like to have a private talk with Miss Langenburg."

"Of course—if she agrees."

Indra nodded dumbly. She was still blaming herself bitterly for what had happened—for not going to the doctor immediately when they had returned to the island. Her intuition had failed her then; now it told her that there was no possibility of any hope, and she could only pray that it was wrong again.

"Now, Indra," said Myers kindly when the others had left the room, "if we want to help Franklin we've got to keep our heads, and try to guess what he's done. So stop blaming yourself—this isn't your fault. I'm not sure if it's anyone's fault."

It might be mine, he added grimly to himself. But who could have guessed? We understand so little about astrophobia, even now . . . and heaven knows it's not in my line.

Indra managed a brave smile. Until yesterday, she had thought she was very grown-up and able to take care of herself in any situation. But yesterday was a very, very long time ago.

"Please tell me," she said, "what is the matter with Walter. I think it would help me to understand."

It was a sensible and reasonable request; even before Indra had made it, Myers had come to the same conclusion.

"Very well—but remember, this is confidential, for Walter's own sake. I'm only telling it to you because this is an emergency and you may be able to help him if you know the facts.

"Until a year ago, Walter was a highly qualified spaceman. In fact, he was chief engineer of a liner on the Martian run, which as you know is a very responsible position indeed, and that was certainly merely the beginning of his career.

"Well, there was some kind of emergency in mid-orbit, and the ion drive had to be shut off. Walter went outside in a space suit to fix it—nothing unusual about that, of course. Before he had finished the job, however, his suit failed. No—I don't meant it leaked. What happened was that the propulsion system jammed on, and he couldn't shut off the rockets that allowed him to move around in space.

"So there he was, millions of miles from anywhere, building up speed away from his ship. To make matters worse, he'd crashed against some part of the liner when he started, and that had snapped off his radio antenna. So he couldn't talk or receive messages—couldn't call for help or find out what his friends were doing for him. He was completely alone, and in a few minutes he couldn't even see the liner.

"Now, no one who has not been in a situation like that can possibly imagine what it's like. We can try, but we can't really picture being absolutely isolated, with stars all around us, not knowing if we'll ever be rescued. No vertigo that can ever be experienced on Earth can match it—not even seasickness at its worst, and that's bad enough.

"It was four hours before Walter was rescued. He was actually quite safe, and probably knew it—but that didn't make any difference. The ship's radar had tracked him, but until the drive was repaired it couldn't go after him. When they did get him aboard he was—well, let's say he was in a pretty bad way.

"It took the best psychologists on earth almost a year to straighten him out, and as we've seen, the job wasn't finished properly. And there was one factor that the psychologists could do nothing about."

Myers paused, wondering how Indra was taking all this, how it would affect her feelings towards Franklin. She seemed to have got over her initial shock; she was not, thank God, the hysterical type it was so difficult to do anything with.

"You see, Walter was married. He had a wife and family on Mars, and was very fond of them. His wife was a second-generation colonist, the children, of course, third-generation ones. They had spent all their lives under Martian gravity—had been conceived and born in it. And so they could never come to Earth, where they would be crushed under three times their normal weight.

"At the same time, Walter could never go back into space. We could patch up his mind so that he could function efficiently here on Earth, but that was the best we could do. He could never again face free fall, the knowledge that there was space all around him, all the way out to the stars. And so he was an exile on his own world, unable ever to see his family again.

"We did our best for him, and I still think it was a good best. This work here could use his skills, but there were also profound psychological reasons why we thought it might suit him, and would enable him to rebuild his life. I think you probably know those reasons as well as I do, Indra—if not better. You are a marine biologist and know the links we have with the sea. We have no such links with space, and so we shall never feel at home there—at least as long as we are men.

"I studied Franklin while he was here; he knew I was doing it, and didn't mind. All the while he was improving, getting to love the work. Don was very pleased with his progress—he was the best pupil he'd ever met. And when I heard—don't ask me how!—that he was going around with you, I was delighted. For he has to rebuild his life all along the line, you know. I hope you don't mind me putting it this way, but when I found he was spending his spare time with you, and even making time to do it, I knew he had stopped looking back.

"And now—this breakdown. I don't mind admitting that I'm completely in the dark. You say that you were looking up at the Space Station, but that doesn't seem enough cause. Walter had a rather bad fear of heights when he came here, but he'd largely got over that. Besides, he must have seen the station dozens of times in the morning or evening. There must have been some other factor we don't know."

Dr. Myers stopped his rapid delivery, then said gently, as if the thought had only just struck him: "Tell me, Indra—had you been making love?"

"No," she said without hesitation or embarrassment. "There was nothing like that."

It was a little hard to believe, but he knew it was the truth. He could detect —so clear and unmistakable!—the note of regret in her voice.

"I was wondering if he had any guilt feelings about his wife. Whether he knows it or not, you probably remind him of her, which is why he was attracted to you in the first place. Anyway, *that* line of reasoning isn't enough to explain what happened, so let's forget it.

"All we know is that there was an attack, and a very bad one. Giving him that sedative was the best thing you could have done in the circumstances. You're *quite* sure that he never gave any indication of what he intended to do when you got him back to Heron?"

"Quite sure. All he said was, 'Don't tell Dr. Myers.' He said there was nothing you could do."

That, thought Myers grimly, might well be true, and he did not like the sound of it. There was only one reason why a man might hide from the only person who could help him. That was because he had decided he was now beyond help.

"But he promised," Indra continued, "to see you in the morning."

Myers did not reply. By this time they both knew that that promise had been nothing more than a ruse.

Indra still clung desperately to one last hope.

"Surely," she said, her voice quivering as if she did not really believe her own words, "if he'd intended to do—something drastic—he'd have left a message for somebody."

Myers looked at her sadly, his mind now completely made up.

"His parents are dead," he replied. "He said good-bye to his wife long ago. What message was there for him to leave?"

Indra knew, with a sickening certainty, that he spoke the truth. She might well be the only person on Earth for whom Franklin felt any affection. And he had made his farewell with her. . . .

Reluctantly, Myers rose to his feet.

"There's nothing we can do," he said, "except to start a general search. There may be a chance that he's just blowing off steam at full throttle, and will creep in shamefaced some time this morning. It's happened before."

He patted Indra's bowed shoulders, then helped her out of the chair. "Don't be too upset, my dear. Everyone will do his best." But in his heart, he knew it was too late. It had been too late hours before, and they were going through

the motions of search and rescue because there were times when no one expected
logic to be obeyed.

They walked together to the assistant chief instructor's office, where the C.I.
and Burley were waiting for them. Dr. Myers threw open the door—and stood
paralysed on the threshold. For a moment he thought that he had two more
patients—or that he had gone insane himself. Don and the chief instructor, all
distinctions of rank forgotten, had their arms around each other's shoulders
and were shaking with hysterical laughter. There was no doubt of the hysteria;
it was that of relief. And there was equally no doubt about the laughter.

Dr. Myers stared at this improbable scene for perhaps five seconds, then
glanced swiftly around the room. At once he saw the message form lying on
the floor where one of his temporarily disordered colleagues had dropped it.
Without asking their permission, he rushed forward and picked it up.

He had to read it several times before it made any sense; then he, too, began
to laugh as he had not done for years.

CHAPTER IX

C APTAIN BERT DARRYL was looking forward to a quiet trip; if
there was any justice in this world, he was certainly due for one. Last time
there had been that awkward affair with the cops at Mackay; the time
before there had been that uncharted rock off Lizard Island; and before *that*,
by crikey, there'd been that trigger-happy young fool who had used a non-
detachable harpoon on a fifteen-foot tiger and had been towed all over the sea
bed.

As far as one could tell by appearances, his customers seemed a reasonable
lot this time. Of course, the Sports Agency always guaranteed their reliability
as well as their credit—but all the same it was surprising what he sometimes
got saddled with. Still, a man had to earn a living, and it cost a lot to keep this
old bucket waterproof.

By an odd coincidence, his customers always had the same names—Mr.
Jones, Mr. Robinson, Mr. Brown, Mr. Smith. Captain Bert thought it was a
crazy idea, but that was just another of the agency's little ways. It certainly
made life interesting, trying to figure out who they really were. Some of them
were so cautious that they wore rubber face masks the whole trip—yes, even
under their diving masks. They would be the important boys who were scared
of being recognised. Think of the scandal, for instance, if a supreme court
judge or chief secretary of the Space Department was found poaching on a
World Food reservation! Captain Bert thought of it, and chuckled.

The little five-berth sports cruiser was still forty miles off the outer edge of the reef, feeling her way in from the Pacific. Of course, it was risky operating so near the Capricorns, right in enemy territory as it were. But the biggest fish were here, just because they were the best protected. You had to take a chance if you wanted to keep your clients satisfied. . . .

Captain Bert had worked out his tactics carefully, as he always did. There were never any patrols out at night, and even if there were, his long-range sonar would spot them and he could run for it. So it would be perfectly safe creeping up during darkness, getting into position just before dawn, and pushing his eager beavers out of the air lock as soon as the sun came up. He would lie doggo on the bottom, keeping in touch through the radios. If they got out of range, they'd still have his low-powered sonar beacon to home on. And if they got too far away to pick up *that*, serve 'em jolly well right. He patted his jacket where the four blood chits reposed safely, absolving him of all responsibility if anything happened to Messrs. Smith, Jones, Robinson, or Brown. There were times when he wondered if it was really any use, considering these weren't their real names, but the agency told him not to worry. Captain Bert was not the worrying type, or he would have given up this job long ago.

As the moment, Messrs. S., J., R., and B. were lying on their respective couches, putting the final touches to the equipment they would not need until morning. Smith and Jones had brand-new guns that had obviously never been fired before, and their webbing was fitting with every conceivable underwater gadget. Captain Bert looked at them sardonically; they represented a type he knew very well. They were the boys who were so keen on their equipment that they never did any shooting, either with the guns or their cameras. They would wander happily around the reef, making such a noise that every fish within miles would know exactly what they were up to. Their beautiful guns, which could drill a thousand-pound shark at fifty feet, would probably never be fired. But they wouldn't really mind; they would enjoy themselves.

Now Robinson was a very different matter. His gun was slightly dented, and about five years old. It had seen service, and he obviously knew how to handle it. He was not one of those catalogue-obsessed sportsmen who had to buy the current year's model as soon as it came out, like a woman who couldn't bear to be behind the fashion. Mr. Robinson, Captain Bert decided, would be the one who would bring back the biggest catch.

As for Brown—Robinson's partner—he was the only one that Captain Bert hadn't been able to classify. A well-built, strong-featured man in the forties, he was the oldest of the hunters and his face was vaguely familiar. He was probably some official in the upper echelons of the state, who had felt the need to sow a few wild oats. Captain Bert, who was constitutionally unable to work for the World State or any other employer, could understand just how he felt.

There were more than a thousand feet of water below them, and the reef was still miles ahead. But one never took anything for granted in this business, and Captain Bert's eyes were seldom far from the dials and screens of the control board, even while he watched his little crew preparing for their morning's fun. The clear and tiny echo had barely appeared on the sonar scanner before he had fastened on to it.

"Big shark coming, boys," he announced jovially. There was a general rush to the screen.

"How do you know it's a shark?" someone asked.

"Pretty sure to be. Couldn't be a whale—they can't leave the channel inside the reef."

"Sure it's not a sub?" said one anxious voice.

"Naow. Look at the size of it. A sub would be ten times as bright on the screen. Don't be a nervous Nelly."

The questioner subsided, duly abashed. No one said anything for the next five minutes, as the distant echo closed in towards the centre of the screen.

"It'll pass within a quarter of a mile of us," said Mr. Smith. "What about changing course and seeing if we can make contact?"

"Not a hope. He'll run for it as soon as he picks up our motors. If we stopped still he might come and sniff us over. Anyway, what would be the use? You couldn't get at him. It's night and he's well below the depth where you could operate."

Their attention was momentarily distracted by a large school of fish—probably tuna, the captain said—which appeared on the southern sector of the screen. When that had gone past, the distinguished-looking Mr. Brown said thoughtfully: "Surely a shark would have changed course by now."

Captain Bert thought so too, and was beginning to be puzzled. "Think we'll have a look at it," he said. "Won't do any harm."

He altered course imperceptibly; the strange echo continued on its unvarying way. It was moving quite slowly, and there would be no difficulty in getting within visual distance without risk of collision. At the point of nearest approach, Captain Bert switched on the camera and the U.V. searchlight—and gulped.

"We're rumbled, boys. It's a cop."

There were four simultaneous gasps of dismay, then a chorus of "But you told us . . ." which the captain silenced with a few well-chosen words while he continued to study the screen.

"Something funny here," he said. "I was right first time. That's no sub—it's only a torp. So it can't detect us, anyway—they don't carry that kind of gear. But what the hell's it doing out here at night."

"Let's run for it!" pleaded several anxious voices.

"Shurrup!" shouted Captain Bert. "Let me think." He glanced at the depth indicator. "Crikey," he muttered, this time in a much more subdued voice. "We're a hundred fathoms down. Unless that lad's breathing some fancy mixture, he's had it."

He peered closely at the image on the TV screen; it was hard to be certain, but the figure strapped to the slowly moving torp seemed abnormally still. Yes —there was no doubt of it; he could tell from the attitude of the head. The pilot was certainly unconscious, probably dead.

"This is a bloody nuisance," announced the skipper, "but there's nothing else to do. We've got to fetch that guy in."

Someone started to protest, then thought better of it. Captain Bert was right, of course. The later consequences would have to be dealt with as they arose.

"But how are you going to do it?" asked Smith. "We can't go outside at this depth."

"It won't be easy," admitted the captain. "It's lucky he's moving so slowly. I think I can flip him over."

He nosed in towards the torp, making infinitely delicate adjustments with the controls. Suddenly there was a clange that made everybody jump except the skipper, who knew when it was coming and exactly how loud it would be.

He backed away, and breathed a sigh of relief.

"Made it first time!" he said smugly. The torp had rolled over on its back, with the helpless figure of its rider now dangling beneath it in his harness. But instead of heading down into the depths, it was now climbing towards the distant surface.

They followed it up to the two-hundred-foot mark while Captain Bert gave his detailed instructions. There was still a chance, he told his passengers, that the pilot might be alive. But if he reached the surface, he'd certainly be dead—compression sickness would get him as he dropped from ten atmospheres to one.

"So we've got to haul him in around the hundred-and-fifty-foot level—no higher—and then start staging him in the airlock. Well, who's going to do it? *I* can't leave the controls."

No one doubted that the captain was giving the single and sufficient reason, and that he would have gone outside without hesitation had there been anyone else aboard who could operate the sub. After a short pause, Smith said: "I've been three hundred feet down on normal air."

"So have I," interjected Jones. "Not at night, of course," he added thoughtfully.

They weren't exactly volunteering, but it would do. They listened to the skipper's instructions like men about to go over the top, then put on their equipment and went reluctantly into the airlock.

Fortunately, they were in good training and he was able to bring them up to the full pressure in a couple of minutes. "O.K., boys," he said. "I'm opening the door—here you go!"

It would have helped them could they have seen his searchlight, but it had been carefully filtered to remove all visible light. Their hand torches were feeble glow-worms by comparison, as he watched them moving across the still-ascending torp. Jones went first, while Smith played out the line from the airlock. Both vessels were moving faster than man could swim, and it was necessary to play Jones like a fish on a line so that as he trailed behind the sub he could work his way across to the torpedo. He was probably not enjoying it, thought the skipper, but he managed to reach the torp on the second try.

After that, the rest was straightforward. Jones cut out the torp's motor, and when the two vessels had come to a halt Smith went to help him. They unstrapped the pilot and carried him back to the sub; his face mask was unflooded, so there was still hope for him. It was not easy to manhandle his helpless body into the tiny airlock, and Smith had to stay outside, feeling horribly lonely, while his partner went ahead.

And thus it was that, thirty minutes later, Walter Franklin woke in a surprising but not totally unfamiliar environment. He was lying in a bunk aboard a small cruiser-class sub, and five men were standing around him. Oddest of all, four of the men had handkerchiefs tied over their faces so that he could only see their eyes. . . .

He looked at the fifth man—at his scarred and grizzled countenance and his rakish goatee. The dirty nautical cap was really quite superfluous; no one would have doubted that this was the skipper.

A raging headache made it hard for Franklin to think straight. He had to make several attempts before he could get out the words: "Where am I?"

"Never you mind, mate," replied the bearded character. "What *we* want to know is what the hell were you doing at a hundred fathoms with a standard compressed-air set. Crikey, he's fainted again!"

The second time Franklin revived, he felt a good deal better, and sufficiently interested in life to want to know what was going on around him. He supposed he should be grateful to these people, whoever they were, but at the moment he felt neither relief nor disappointment at having been rescued.

"What's all this for?" he said, pointing to the conspiratorial handkerchiefs. The skipper, who was now sitting at the controls, turned his head and answered laconically: "Haven't you worked out where you are yet?"

"No."

"Mean ter say you don't know who I am?"

"Sorry—I don't."

There was a grunt that might have signified disbelief or disappointment.

"Guess you must be one of the new boys. I'm Bert Darryl, and you're on board the *Sea Lion*. Those two gentlemen behind you risked their necks getting you in."

Franklin turned in the direction indicated, and looked at the blank triangles of linen.

"Thanks," he said, and then stopped, unable to think of any further comment. Now he knew where he was, and could guess what had happened.

So this was the famous—or notorious, depending on the point of view— Captain Darryl, whose advertisements you saw in all the sporting and marine journals. Captain Darryl, the organiser of thrilling underwater safaris; the intrepid and skilful hunter—and the equally intrepid and skilful poacher, whose immunity from prosecution had long been a source of cynical comment among the wardens. Captain Darryl—one of the few genuine adventurers of this regimented age, according to some. Captain Darryl, the big phony, according to others. . . .

Franklin now understood why the rest of the crew was masked. This was one of the captain's less legitimate enterprises, and Franklin had heard that on these occasions his customers were often from the very highest ranks of society. No one else could afford to pay his fees; it must cost a lot to run the *Sea Lion*, even though Captain Darryl was reputed never to pay cash for anything and to owe money at every port between Sydney and Darwin.

Franklin glanced at the anonymous figures around him, wondering who they might be and whether he knew any of them. Only a half-hearted effort had been made to hide the powerful big-game guns piled on the other bunk. Just where was the captain taking his customers, and what were they after? In the circumstances, he had better keep his eyes shut and learn as little as possible.

Captain Darryl had already come to the same conclusion.

"You realise, mate," he said over his shoulder as he carefully blocked Franklin's view of the course settings, "that your presence aboard is just a little bit embarrassing. Still, we couldn't let you drown, even though you deserved it for a silly stunt like that. The point is—what are we going to do with you now?"

"You could put me ashore on Heron. We can't be very far away." Franklin smiled as he spoke, to show how seriously he intended the suggestion to be taken. It was strange how cheerful and lighthearted he now felt; perhaps it was a merely physical reaction—and perhaps he was really glad at having been given a second chance, a new lease on life.

"What a hope!" snorted the captain. "These gentlemen have paid for their day's sport, and they don't want you boy scouts spoiling it."

"They can take off those handkerchiefs, anyway. They don't look very comfortable—and if I recognise someone, I won't give him away."

Rather reluctantly, the disguises were removed. As he had expected—and hoped—there was no one here whom he knew, either from photographs or direct contact.

"Only one thing for it," said the captain. "We'll have to dump you somewhere before we go into action." He scratched his head as he reviewed his marvellously detailed mental image of the Capricorn Group, then came to a decision. "Anyway, we're stuck with you for tonight, and I guess we'll have to sleep in shifts. If you'd like to make yourself useful, you can get to work in the galley."

"Aye, aye, sir," said Franklin.

The dawn was just breaking when he hit the sandy beach, staggered to his feet, and removed his flippers. ("They're my second-best pair, so mind you post them back to me," Captain Bert had said as he pushed him through the air lock.) Out there beyond the reef, the *Sea Lion* was departing on her dubious business, and the hunters were getting ready for their sortie. Though it was against his principles and his duties, Franklin could not help wishing them luck.

Captain Bert had promised to radio Brisbane in four hours' time, and the message would be passed on to Heron Island immediately. Presumably that four hours would give the captain and his clients the time they needed to make their assault and to get clear of W.F.O. waters.

Franklin walked up the beach, stripped off his wet equipment and clothes, and lay down to watch the sunrise he had never dreamed he would see. He had four hours to wait, to wrestle with his thoughts and to face life once more. But he did not need the time, for he had made the decision hours ago.

His life was no longer his to throw away if he chose; not when it had been given back to him, at the risk of their own, by men he had never met before and would never see again.

CHAPTER X

"You REALISE, OF course," said Myers, "that I'm only the station doctor, not a high-powered psychiatrist. So I'll have to send you back to Professor Stevens and his merry men."

"Is that really necessary?" asked Franklin.

"I don't think it is, but I can't accept the responsibility. If I was a gambler like Don, I'd take very long odds that you'll never play this trick again. But doctors can't afford to gamble, and anyway I think it would be a good idea to get you off Heron for a few days."

"I'll finish the course in a couple of weeks. Can't it wait until then?"

"Don't argue with doctors, Walt—you can't win. And if my arithmetic is correct, a month and a half is *not* a couple of weeks. The course can wait for a few days; I don't think Prof Stevens will keep you very long. He'll probably give you a good dressing-down and will send you straight back. Meanwhile, if you're interested in my views, I'd like to get 'em off my chest."

"Go ahead."

"First of all, we know *why* you had that attack when you did. Smell is the most evocative of all the senses, and now that you've told me that a spaceship airlock always smells of synthene the whole business makes sense. It was hard luck that you got a whiff of the stuff just when you were looking at the Space Station: the damn thing's nearly hypnotised me sometimes when I've watched it scuttling across the sky like some mad meteor.

"But that isn't the whole explanation, Walter. You had to be, let's say, emotionally sensitised to make you susceptible. Tell me—have you got a photograph of your wife here?"

Franklin seemed more puzzled than disturbed by the unexpected, indeed apparently incongruous, question.

"Yes," he said. "Why do you ask?"

"Never mind. May I have a look at it?"

After a good deal of searching, which Myers was quite sure was unnecessary, Franklin produced a leather wallet and handed it over. He did not look at Myers as the doctor studied the woman who was now parted from her husband by laws more inviolable than any that man could make.

She was small and dark, with lustrous brown eyes. A single glance told Myers all that he wanted to know, yet he continued to gaze at the photograph with an unanalysable mixture of compassion and curiosity. How, he wondered, was Franklin's wife meeting her problem? Was she, too, rebuilding her life on that far world to which she was forever bound by genetics and gravity? No, forever was not quite accurate. She could safely journey to the Moon, which had only the gravity of her native world. But there would be no purpose in doing so, for Franklin could never face even the trifling voyage from Earth to Moon.

With a sigh, Dr. Myers closed the wallet. Even in the most perfect of social systems, the most peaceful and contented of worlds, there would still be heartbreak and tragedy. And as man extended his powers over the universe, he would inevitably create new evils and new problems to plague him. Yet, apart from its details, there was nothing really novel about this case. All down the ages, men had been separated—often forever—from those they loved by the accident of geography or the malice of their fellows.

"Listen, Walt," said Myers as he handed back the wallet. "I know a few things about you that even Prof Stevens doesn't, so here's my contribution.

"Whether you realise it consciously or not, Indra is like your wife. That, of course, is why you were attracted to her in the first place. At the same time, that attraction has set up a conflict in your mind. You don't want to be unfaithful even to someone—please excuse me for speaking so bluntly—who might as well be dead as far as you are concerned. Well—do you agree with my analysis?"

Franklin took a long time to answer. Then he said at last: "I think there may be something in that. But what am I to do?"

"This may sound cynical, but there is an old saying which applies in this case. 'Co-operate with the inevitable.' Once you admit that certain aspects of your life are fixed and have to be accepted, you will stop fighting against them. It won't be a surrender; it will give you the energy you need for the battles that still have to be won."

"What does Indra really think about me?"

"The silly girl's in love with you, if that's what you want to know. So the least you can do is to make it up to her for all the trouble you've caused."

"Then do you think I should marry again?"

"The fact that you can ask that question is a good sign, but I can't answer it with a simple 'yes' or 'no'. We've done our best to rebuild your professional life; we can't give you so much help with your emotional one. Obviously, it's highly desirable for you to establish a firm and stable relationship to replace the one you have lost. As for Indra—well, she's a charming and intelligent girl, but no one can say how much of her present feelings are due to sympathy. So don't rush matters; let them take their time. You can't afford to make any mistakes.

"Well, that finishes the sermon—except for one item. Part of the trouble with you, Walter Franklin, is that you've always been too independent and self-reliant. You refused to admit that you had limitations, that you needed help from anyone else. So when you came up against something that was too big for you, you really went to pieces, and you've been hating yourself for it ever since.

"Now that's all over and done with; even if the old Walt Franklin was a bit of a stinker, we can make a better job of the Mark II. Don't you agree?"

Franklin gave a wry smile; he felt emotionally exhausted, yet at the same time most of the remaining shadows had lifted from his mind. Hard though it had been for him to accept help, he had surrendered at last and he felt better for it.

"Thanks for the treatment, Doc," he said. "I don't believe the specialists could do any better, and I'm quite sure now that this trip back to Prof Stevens isn't necessary."

"So am I—but you're going just the same. Now clear out and let me get on with my proper work of putting sticking plaster on coral cuts."

Franklin was halfway through the door when he paused with a sudden, anxious query.

"I almost forgot—Don particularly wants to take me out tomorrow in the sub. Will that be O.K.?"

"Oh, sure—Don's big enough to look after you. Just get back in time for the noon plane, that's all I ask."

As Franklin walked away from the office and two rooms grandly called "Medical Centre" he felt no resentment at having been ordered off the island. He had received far more tolerance and consideration than he had expected—perhaps more than he deserved. All the mild hostility that had been focused upon him by the less-privileged trainees had vanished at a stroke, but it would be best for him to escape for a few days from an atmosphere that had become embarrassingly sympathetic. In particular, he found it hard to talk without a sense of strain with Don and Indra.

He thought again of Dr. Myers' advice, and remembered the jolting leap his heart had given at the words "The silly girl's in love with you." Yet it would be unfair, he knew, to take advantage of the present emotional situation; they could only know what they meant to each other when they had both had time for careful and mature thought. Put that way, it seemed a little cold-blooded and calculating. If one was really in love, did one stop to weigh the pros and cons?

He knew the answer to that. As Myers had said, he could not afford any more mistakes. It was far better to take his time and be certain than to risk the happiness of two lives.

The sun had barely lifted above the miles of reef extending to the east when Don Burley hauled Franklin out of bed. Don's attitude towards him had undergone a change which it was not easy to define. He had been shocked and distressed by what had occurred and had tried, in his somewhat boisterous manner, to express sympathy and understanding. At the same time, his *amour-propre* had been hurt; he could not quite believe, even now, that Indra had never been seriously interested in him but only in Franklin, whom he had never thought of as a rival. It was not that he was jealous of Franklin; jealousy was an emotion beyond him. He was worried—as most men are occasionally throughout their lives—by his discovery that he did not understand women as well as he had believed.

Franklin had already packed, and his room looked bleak and bare. Even though he might be gone for only a few days, the accommodation was needed too badly for it to be left vacant just to suit his convenience. It served him right, he told himself philosophically.

Don was in a hurry, which was not unusual, but there was also a conspiratorial air about him, as if he had planned some big surprise for Franklin and was almost childishly anxious that everything should come off as intended. In any other circumstances, Franklin would have suspected some practical joke, but that could hardly be the explanation now.

By this time, the little training sub had become practically an extension of his own body, and he followed the courses Don gave him until he knew, by mental dead reckoning, that they were somewhere out in the thirty mile-wide channel between Wistari Reef and the mainland. For some reason of his own, which he refused to explain, Don had switched off the pilot's main sonar screen, so that Franklin was navigating blind. Don himself could see everything that was in the vicinity by looking at the repeater set at the rear of the cabin, and though Franklin was occasionally tempted to glance back at it he managed to resist the impulse. This was, after all, a legitimate part of his training; one day he might have to navigate a sub that had been blinded by a breakdown of its underwater senses.

"You can surface now," said Don at last. He was trying to be casual, but the undercurrent of excitement in his voice could not be concealed. Franklin blew the tanks, and even without looking at the depth gauge knew when he broke surface by the unmistakable rolling of the sub. It was not a comfortable sensation, and he hoped that they would not stay here for long.

Don gave one more glance at his private sonar screen, then gestured to the hatch overhead.

"Open up," he said. "Let's have a look at the scenery."

"We may ship some water," protested Franklin. "It feels pretty rough."

"With the two of us in that hatch, not much is going to leak past. Here—put on this cape. That'll keep the spray out of the works."

It seemed a crazy idea, but Don must have a good reason. Overhead, a tiny elliptical patch of sky appeared as the outer seal of the conning tower opened. Don scrambled up the ladder first; then Franklin followed, blinking his eyes against the wind-swept spray.

Yes, Don had known what he was doing. There was little wonder that he had been so anxious to make this trip before Franklin left the island. In his own way, Don was a good psychologist, and Franklin felt an inexpressible gratitude towards him. For this was one of the great moments of his life; he could think of only one other to match it: the moment when he had first seen Earth, in all its heart-stopping beauty, floating against the infinitely distant background of the stars. This scene, also, filled his soul with the same awe, the same sense of being in the presence of cosmic forces.

The whales were moving north, and he was among them. During the night, the leaders must have passed through the Queensland Gate, on the way to the warm seas in which their young could be safely born. A living armada was all around him, ploughing steadfastly through the waves with effortless power. The great dark bodies emerged streaming from the water, then sank with scarcely a ripple back into the sea. As Franklin watched, too fascinated to feel any sense of danger, one of the enormous beasts surfaced less than forty feet away. There was a roaring whistle of air as it emptied its lungs, and he caught a mercifully weakened breath of the fetid air. A ridiculously tiny eye stared at him—an eye that seemed lost in the monstrous, misshapen head. For a moment the two mammals—the biped who had abandoned the sea, the quadruped who had returned to it—regarded each other across the evolutionary gulf that separated them. What did a man look like to a whale? Franklin asked himself, and wondered if there was any way of finding the answer. Then the titanic bulk tilted down into the sea, the great flukes lifted themselves into the air, and the waters flowed back to fill the sudden void.

A distant clap of thunder made him look towards the mainland. Half a mile away, the giants were playing. As he watched, a shape so strange that it was hard to relate it to any of the films and pictures he had seen emerged from the waves with breath-taking slowness, and hung poised for a moment completely out of the water. As a ballet dancer seems at the climax of his leap to defy gravity, so for an instant the whale appeared to hang upon the horizon. Then, with that same unhurried grace, it tumbled back into the sea, and seconds later the crash of the impact came echoing over the waves.

The sheer slowness of that huge leap gave it a dreamlike quality, as if the sense of time had been distorted. Nothing else conveyed so clearly to Franklin the immense size of the beasts that now surrounded him like moving islands. Rather belatedly, he wondered what would happen if one of the whales surfaced beneath the sub, or decided to take too close an interest in it. . . .

"No need to worry," Don reassured him. "They know who we are. Sometimes they'll come and rub against us to remove parasites, and then it gets a bit uncomfortable. As for bumping into us accidentally—they can see where they're going a good deal better than we can."

As if to refute this statement, a streamlined mountain emerged dripping from the sea and showered water down upon them. The sub rocked crazily, and for a moment Franklin feared it was going to overturn; then it righted itself, and he realised that he could, quite literally, reach out and touch the barnacle-encrusted head now lying on the waves. The weirdly shaped mouth opened in a prodigious yawn, the hundreds of strips of whalebone fluttering like a Venetian blind in a breeze.

Had he been alone, Franklin would have been scared stiff, but Don seemed the complete master of the situation. He leaned out of the hatch and yelled in the direction of the whale's invisible ear: "Move over momma! We're not your baby!"

The great mouth with its hanging draperies of bone snapped shut, the beady little eye—strangely like a cow's and seemingly not much larger—looked at them with what might have been a hurt expression. Then the sub rocked once more, and the whale was gone.

"It's quite safe, you see," Don explained. "They're peaceful, good-natured beasts, except when they have their calves with them. Just like any other cattle."

"But would you get this close to any of the toothed whales—the sperm whale, for instance?"

"That depends. If it was an old rogue male—a real Moby Dick—I wouldn't care to try it. Same with killer whales; they might think I was good eating, though I could scare them off easily enough by turning on the hooter. I once got into a harem of about a dozen sperm whales, and the ladies didn't seem to mind, even though some of them had calves with them. Nor did the old man, oddly enough. I suppose he knew I wasn't a rival." He paused thoughtfully, then continued. "That was the only time I've actually seen whales mating. It was pretty awe-inspiring—gave me such an inferiority complex it put me off my stroke for a week."

"How many would you say there are in this school?" asked Franklin.

"Oh, about a hundred. The recorders at the gate will give the exact figure. So you can say there are at least five thousand tons of the best meat and oil swimming around us—a couple of million dollars, if it's worth a penny. Doesn't all that cash make you feel good?"

"No," said Franklin. "And I'm damn sure it doesn't make any difference to you. Now I know why you like this job, and there's no need to put on an act about it."

Don made no attempt to answer. They stood together in the cramped hatchway, not feeling the spray upon their faces, sharing the same thoughts and emotions, as the mightiest animals the world had ever seen drove purposefully past them to the north. It was then that Franklin knew, with a final certainty, that his life was firmly set upon its new course. Though much had been taken from him which he would never cease to regret, he had passed the stage of futile grief and solitary brooding. He had lost the freedom of space, but he had won the freedom of the seas.

That was enough for any man.

CHAPTER XI

ATTACHED IS THE medical report on Walter Franklin, who has now successfully completed his training and has qualified as third warden with the highest rating ever recorded. In view of certain complaints from senior members of Establishment and Personnel Branch that earlier reports were too technical for comprehension, I am giving this summary in language understandable even to administrative officers.

Despite a number of personality defects, W.F.'s capability rating places him in that small group from which future heads of technical departments must be drawn—a group so desperately small that, as I have frequently pointed out, the very existence of the state is threatened unless we can enlarge it. The accident which eliminated W.F. from the Space Service, in which he would have undoubtedly had a distinguished career, left him in full possession of all his talents and presented us with an opportunity which it would have been criminal to waste. Not only did it give us a chance of studying what has since become the classic textbook case of astrophobia, but it offered us a striking challenge in rehabilitation. The analogies between sea and space have often been pointed out, and a man used to one can readily adapt to the other. In this case, however, the differences between the two media were equally important; at the simplest level, the fact that the sea is a continuous and sustaining fluid, in which vision is always limited to no more than a few yards, gave W.F. the sense of security he had lost in space.

The fact that, towards the end of his training, he attempted suicide may at first appear to argue against the correctness of our treatment. This is not the case; the attempt was due to a combination of quite unforeseeable factors (Paragraphs 57–86 of attached report), and its outcome, as often happens, was an improvement in the stability of the subject. The method chosen for the attempt is also highly significant in itself and proves that we had made a correct choice of W.F.'s new vocation. The seriousness of the attempt may also be questioned; had W.F. been really determined to kill himself, he would have chosen a simpler and less fallible method of doing so.

Now that the subject has re-established—apparently successfully—his emotional life and has shown only trivial symptoms of disturbance, I am confident that we need expect no more trouble. Above all, it is important that we interfere with him as little as possible. His independence and originality of mind, though no longer as exaggerated as they were, are a fundamental part of his personality and will largely determine his future progress.

Only time will show whether all the skill and effort lavished on this case will be repaid in cents and dollars. Even if it is not, those engaged upon it have already received their reward in the rebuilding of a life, which will certainly be useful and may be invaluable.

Ian K. Stevens
Director, Division of Applied Psychiatry,
World Health Organisation

PART TWO

The Warden

CHAPTER XII

S ECOND W ARDEN W ALTER F RANKLIN was having his monthly shave when the emergency call came through. It had always seemed a little surprising to him that, after so many years of research, the biochemists had not yet found an inhibitor that would put one's bristles permanently out of action. Still, one should not be ungrateful; only a couple of generations ago, incredible though it seemed, men had been forced to shave themselves every day, using a variety of complicated, expensive, and sometimes lethal instruments.

Franklin did not stop to wipe the layer of cream from his face when he heard the shrill whining of the communicator alarm. He was out of the bathroom, through the kitchen, and into the hall before the sound had died away and the instrument had been able to get its second breath. As he punched the Receive button, the screen lighted up and he was looking into the familiar but now harassed face of the Headquarters operator.

"You're to report for duty at once, Mr. Franklin," she said breathlessly.

"What's the trouble?"

"It's Farms, sir. The fence is down somewhere and one of the herds has broken through. It's eating the spring crop, and we've got to get it out as quickly as we can."

"Oh, is that all?" said Franklin. "I'll be over at the dock in ten minutes."

It was an emergency all right, but not one about which he could feel very excited. Of course, Farms would be yelling its head off as its production quota was being whittled down by thousands of half-ton nibbles. But he was secretly on the side of the whales; if they'd managed to break into the great plankton prairies, then good luck to them.

"What's all the fuss about?" said Indra as she came out of the bedroom, her long, dark hair looking attractive even at this time of the morning as it hung in lustrous tresses over her shoulders. When Franklin told her, she appeared worried.

"It's a bigger emergency than you seem to think," she said. "Unless you act quickly, you may have some very sick whales on your hands. The spring overturn was only two weeks ago, and it's the biggest one we've ever had. So your greedy pets will be gorging themselves silly."

Franklin realised that she was perfectly right. The plankton farms were no affair of his, and formed a completely independent section of the Marine Division. But he knew a great deal about them, since they were an alternative and to some extent rival method of getting food from the sea. The plankton enthusiasts claimed, with a good deal of justice, that crop growing was more efficient than herding, since the whales themselves fed on the plankton and were therefore farther down the food chain. Why waste ten pounds of plankton, they argued, to produce one pound of whale, when you could harvest it directly?

The debate had been in progress for at least twenty years, and so far neither side could claim to have won. Sometimes the argument had been quite acrimonious and had echoed, on an infinitely larger and more sophisticated scale, the rivalry between homesteaders and cattle barons in the days when the American Midwest was being settled. But unfortunately for latter-day mythmakers, competing departments of the Marine Division of the World Food Organisation fought each other purely with official minutes and the efficient but unspectacular weapons of bureaucracy. There were no gun fighters prowling the range, and if the fence had gone do... it would be due to purely technical troubles, not midnight sabotage. . . .

In the sea as on the land, all life depends upon vegetation. And the amount of vegetation in turn depends upon the mineral content of the medium in which it grows—the nitrates, phosphates, and scores of other basic chemicals. In the ocean, there is always a tendency for these vital substances to accumulate in the depths, far below the regions where light penetrates and therefore plants can exist and grow. The upper few hundred feet of the sea is the primary source of its life; everything below that level preys, at second or third hand, on the food formed above.

Every spring, as the warmth of the new year seeps down into the ocean, the waters far below respond to the invisible sun. They expand and rise, lifting to the surface, in untold billions of tons, the salts and minerals they bear. Thus fertilised by food from below and sun from above, the floating plants multiply with explosive violence, and the creatures which browse upon them flourish accordingly. And so spring comes to the meadows of the sea.

This was the cycle that had repeated itself at least a billion times before man appeared on the scene. And now he had changed it. Not content with the upwelling of minerals produced by Nature, he had sunk his atomic generators at strategic spots far down into the sea, where the raw heat they produced would start immense, submerged fountains lifting their chemical treasure towards the fruitful sun. This artificial enhancement of the natural overturn had been one of the most unexpected, as well as the most rewarding, of all the many applications of nuclear energy. By this means alone, the output of food from the sea had been increased by almost ten per cent.

And now the whales were busily doing their best to restore the balance.

The roundup would have to be a combined sea and air operation. There were too few of the subs, and they were far too slow, to do the job unassisted. Three of them—including Franklin's one-man scout—were being flown to the scene of the breakthrough by a cargo plane which would drop them and then co-operate by spotting the movements of the whales from the air, if they had scattered over too large an area for the subs' sonar to pick them up. Two other planes would also try to scare the whales by dropping noise generators near them, but this technique had never worked well in the past and no one really expected much success from it now.

Within twenty minutes of the alarm, Franklin was watching the enormous food-processing plants of Pearl Harbor falling below as the jets of the freighter hauled him up into the sky. Even now, he was still not fond of flying and tried to avoid it when he could. But it no longer worried him, and he could look down on the world beneath without qualms.

A hundred miles east of Hawaii, the sea turned suddenly from blue to gold. The moving fields, rich with the year's first crop, covered the Pacific clear out to the horizon, and showed no sign of ending as the plane raced on towards the rising sun. Here and there the mile-long skimmers of the floating harvesters lay upon the surface like the enigmatic toys of some giant children, while beside them, smaller and more compact, were the pontoons and rafts of the concentration equipment. It was an impressive sight, even in these days of mammoth engineering achievements, but it did not move Franklin. He could not become excited over a billion tons of assorted diatoms and shrimps—not even though he knew that they fed a quarter of the human race.

"Just passing over the Hawaiian Corridor," said the pilot's voice from the speaker. "We should see the break in a minute."

"I can see it now," said one of the other wardens, leaning past Franklin and pointing out to sea. "There they are—having the time of their lives."

It was a spectacle which must be making the poor farmers tear their hair. Franklin suddenly remembered an old nursery rhyme he had not thought of for at least thirty years.

> *Little Boy Blue, come blow your horn,*
> *The sheep's in the meadow, the cow's in the corn.*

There was no doubt that the cows were in the corn, and Little Boy Blue was going to have a busy time getting them out. Far below, myriads of narrow swathes were being carved in the endless yellow sea, as the ravenous, slowly moving mountains ate their way into the rich plankton meadows. A blue line of exposed water marked the track of each whale as it meandered through what must be a cetacean heaven—a heaven from which it was Franklin's job to expel it as promptly as possible.

The three wardens, after a final radio briefing, left the cabin and went down to the hold, where the little subs were already hanging from the davits which would lower them into the sea. There would be no difficulty about this operation; what might not be so easy would be getting them back again, and if the sea became rough they might have to go home under their own power.

It seemed strange to be inside a submarine inside an aeroplane, but Franklin had little time for such thoughts as he went through the routine cockpit drill. Then the speaker on his control panel remarked: "Hovering at thirty feet; now opening cargo hatches. Stand by, Number One Sub." Franklin was number two; the great cargo craft was poised so steadily, and the hoists moved down so smoothly, that he never felt any impact as the sub dropped into its natural element. Then the three scouts were fanning out along the tracks that had been assigned to them, like mechanised sheep dogs rounding up a flock.

Almost at once, Franklin realised that this operation was not going to be as simple as it looked. The sub was driving through a thick soup that completely eliminated vision and even interfered seriously with sonar. What was still more serious, the hydrojet motors were labouring unhappily as their impellers chewed through the mush. He could not afford to get his propulsion system clogged; the best thing to do would be to dive below the plankton layer and not to surface until it was absolutely necessary.

Three hundred feet down, the water was merely murky and though vision was still impossible he could make good speed. He wondered if the greedily feasting whales above his head knew of his approach and realised that their idyll was coming to an end. On the sonar screen he could see their luminous echoes moving slowly across the ghostly mirror of the air-water surface which his sound beams could not penetrate. It was odd how similar the surface of the sea looked from below both to the naked eye and to the acoustical senses of the sonar.

The characteristically compact little echoes of the two other subs were moving out to the flanks of the scattered herd. Franklin glanced at the chronometer; in less than a minute, the drive was due to begin. He switched on the external microphones and listened to the voices of the sea.

How could anyone have ever thought that the sea was silent! Even man's limited hearing could detect many of its sounds—the clashing of chitinous claws, the moan of great boulders made restive by the ocean swell, the high-pitched squeak of porpoises, the unmistakable "flick" of the shark's tail as it suddenly accelerates on a new course. But these were merely the sounds in the audible spectrum; to listen to the full music of the sea one must go both below and above the range of human hearing. This was a simple enough task for the sub's frequency converters; if he wished, Franklin could tune in to any sounds from almost a million cycles a second down to vibrations as sluggish as the slow opening of an ancient, rusty door.

He set the receiver to the broadest band, and at once his mind began to interpret the multitudinous messages that came pouring into the little cabin from the watery world outside. The man-made noises he dismissed at once; the sounds of his own sub and the more distant whines of his companion vessels were largely eliminated by the special filters designed for that purpose. But he could just detect the distinctive whistles of the three sonar sets—his own almost blanketing the others—and beyond those the faint and far-off BEEP-BEEP-BEEP of the Hawaiian Corridor. The double fence which was supposed to channel the whales safely through the rich sea farm sent out its pulses at five-second intervals, and though the nearest portion of the fence was out of action the more distant parts of the sonic barrier could be clearly heard. The pulses were curiously distorted and drawn-out into a faint continuous echo as each new burst of sound was followed at once by the delayed waves from more and more remote regions of the fence. Franklin could hear each pulse running away into the distance, as sometimes a clap of thunder may be heard racing across the sky.

Against this background, the sounds of the natural world stood out sharp and clear. From all directions, with never a moment's silence, came the shrill shrieks and squealings of the whales as they talked to one another or merely gave vent to their high spirits and enjoyment. Franklin could distinguish between the voices of the males and the females, but he was not one of those experts who could identify individuals and even interpret what they were trying to express.

There is no more eerie sound in all the world than the screaming of a herd of whales, when one moves among it in the depths of the sea. Franklin had only to close his eyes and he could imagine that he was lost in some demon-haunted forest, while ghosts and goblins closed in upon him. Could Hector Berlioz have heard this banshee chorus, he would have known that Nature had already anticipated his "Dream of the Witches' Sabbath".

But weirdness lies only in unfamiliarity, and this sound was now part of Franklin's life. It no longer gave him nightmares, as it had sometimes done in his early days. Indeed, the main emotion that it now inspired in him was an affectionate amusement, together with a slight surprise that such enormous animals produced such falsetto screams.

Yet there was a memory that the sound of the sea sometimes evoked. It no longer had power to hurt him, though it could still fill his heart with a wistful sadness. He remembered all the times he had spent in the signals rooms of space ships or space stations, listening to the radio waves coming in as the monitors combed the spectrum in their automatic search. Sometimes there had been, like these same ghostly voices calling in the night, the sound of distant ships or beacons, or the torrents of high-speed code as the colonies talked with Mother Earth. And always one could hear a perpetual murmuring background to man's feeble transmitters, the endless susurration of the stars and galaxies themselves as they drenched the whole universe with radiation.

The chronometer hand came around to zero. It had not scythed away the first second before the sea erupted in a hellish cacophony of sound—a rising and falling ululation that made Franklin reach swiftly for the volume control. The sonic mines had been dropped, and he felt sorry for any whales who were unlucky enough to be near them. Almost at once the pattern of echoes on the screen began to change, as the terrified beasts started to flee in panic towards the west. Franklin watched closely, preparing to head off any part of the herd that looked like it would miss the gap in the fence and turn back into the farms.

The noise generators must have been improved, he decided, since the last time this trick had been tried—or else these whales were more amenable. Only a few stragglers tried to break away, and it was no more than ten minutes' work to round them up on the right path and scare them back with the subs' own sirens. Half an hour after the mines had been dropped the entire herd had been funnelled back through the invisible gap in the fence, and was milling around inside the narrow corridor. There was nothing for the subs to do but to stand by until the engineers had carried out their repairs and the curtain of sound was once more complete.

No one could claim that it was a famous victory. It was just another day's work, a minor battle in an endless campaign. Already the excitement of the chase had died away, and Franklin was wondering how long it would be before the freighter could hoist them out of the ocean and fly them back to Hawaii. This was, after all, supposed to be his day off, and he had promised to take Peter down to Waikiki and start teaching him how to swim.

Even when he is merely standing by, a good warden never lets his attention stray for long from his sonar screen. Every three minutes, without any conscious thought, Franklin switched to the long-range scan and tilted the transmitter down towards the sea bed, just to keep track of what was going on around him. He did not doubt that his colleagues were doing exactly the same, between wondering how long it would be before they were relieved. . . .

At the very limit of his range, ten miles away and almost two miles down, a faint echo had crawled on to the edge of the screen. Franklin looked at it with mild interest; then his brows knit in perplexity. It must be an unusually large object to be visible at such a distance—something quite as large as a whale. But no whale could be swimming at such a depth; though sperm whales had been encountered almost a mile down, this was beyond the limits at which they could operate, fabulous divers though they were. A deep-sea shark? Possibly, thought Franklin; it would do no harm to have a closer look at it.

He locked the scanner on to the distant echo and expanded the image as far as the screen magnification would allow. It was too far away to make out any detail, but he could see now that he was looking at a long, thin object—and that it was moving quite rapidly. He stared at it for a moment, then called his colleagues. Unnecessary chatter was discouraged on operations, but here was a minor mystery that intrigued him.

"Sub Two calling," he said. "I've a large echo bearing 185 degrees, range 9.7 miles, depth 1.8 miles. Looks like another sub. You know if anyone else is operating around here?"

"Sub One calling Sub Two," came the first reply. "That's outside my range. Could be a Research Department sub down there. How big would you say your echo is?"

"About a hundred feet long. Maybe more. It's doing over ten knots."

"Sub Three calling. There's no research vessel around here. The *Nautilus IV* is laid up for repairs, and the *Cousteau*'s in the Atlantic. Must be a fish you've got hold of."

"There aren't any fish this size. Have I permission to go after it? I think we ought to check up."

"Permission granted," answered Sub One. "We'll hold the gap here. Keep in touch."

Franklin swung the sub around to the south, and brought the little vessel up to maximum speed with a smooth rush of power. The echo he was chasing was already too deep for him to reach, but there was always the chance that it might come back to the surface. Even if it did not, he would be able to get a much clearer image when he had shortened his range.

He had travelled only two miles when he saw that the chase was hopeless. There could be no doubt; his quarry had detected either the vibrations of his motor or his sonar and was plunging at full speed straight down to the bottom. He managed to get within four miles, and then the signal was lost in the confused maze of echoes from the ocean bed. His last glimpse of it confirmed his earlier impression of great length and relative thinness, but he was still unable to make out any details of its structure.

"So it got away from you," said Sub One. "I thought it would."

"Then you know what it was?"

"No—nor does anyone else. And if you'll take my advice, you won't talk to any reporters about it. If you do, you'll never live it down."

Momentarily frozen with astonishment, Franklin stared at the little loud-speaker from which the words had just come. So they had not been pulling his leg, as he had always assumed. He remembered some of the tales he had heard in the bar at Heron Island and wherever wardens gathered together after duty. He had laughed at them then, but now he knew that the tales were true.

That nervous echo skittering hastily out of range had been nothing less than the Great Sea Serpent.

Indra, who was still doing part-time work at the Hawaii Aquarium when her household duties permitted, was not as impressed as her husband had expected. In fact, her first comment was somewhat deflating.

"Yes, but *which* sea serpent? You know there are at least three totally different types."

"I certainly didn't."

"Well, first of all there's a giant eel which has been seen on three or four occasions but never properly identified, though its larvae were caught back in the 1940s. It's know to grow up to sixty feet long, and that's enough of a sea serpent for most people. But the really spectacular one is the oarfish—*Regalecus glesne*. That's got a face like a horse, a crest of brilliant red quills like an Indian brave's headdress—and a snakelike body which may be seventy feet long. Since we know that these things exist, how do you expect us to be surprised at anything the sea can produce?"

"What about the third type you mentioned?"

"That's the one we haven't identified or even described. We just call it 'X' because people still laugh when you talk about sea serpents. The only thing that we know about it is that it undoubtedly exists, that it's extremely sly, and that it lives in deep water. One day we'll catch it, but when we do it will probably be through pure luck."

Franklin was very thoughtful for the rest of the evening. He did not like to admit that, despite all the instruments that man now used to probe the sea, despite his own continual patrolling of the depths, the ocean still held many secrets and would retain them for ages yet to come. And he knew that, though he might never see it again, he would be haunted all his life by the memory of that distant, tantalising echo as it descended swiftly into the abyss that was its home.

CHAPTER XIII

THERE ARE MANY misconceptions about the glamour of a warden's life. Franklin had never shared them, so he was neither surprised nor disappointed that so much of his time was spent on long, uneventful patrols far out at sea. Indeed, he welcomed them. They gave him time to think, yet not time to brood—and it was on these lonely missions in the living heart of the sea that his last fears were shed and his mental scars finally healed.

The warden's year was dominated by the pattern of whale migration, but that pattern was itself continually changing as new areas of the sea were fenced and fertilised. He might spend summer moving cautiously through the polar ice, and winter beating back and forth across the equator. Sometimes he would operate from shore stations, sometimes from mobile bases like the *Rorqual*, the *Pequod*, or the *Cachelot*. One season he might be wholly concerned with the great whalebone or baleen whales, who literally strained their food from the sea as they swam, mouth open, through the rich plankton soup. And another season he would have to deal with their very different cousins, the fierce, toothed cetaceans of whom the sperm whales were the most important representatives. These were no gentle herbivores, but pursued and fought their monstrous prey in the lightless deep half a mile from the last rays of the sun.

There would be weeks or even months when a warden would never see a whale. The bureau had many calls on its equipment and personnel, and whales were not its only business. Everyone who had dealings with the sea appeared to come, sooner or later, to the Bureau of Whales with an appeal for help. Sometimes the requests were tragic; several times a year subs were sent on usually fruitless searches for drowned sportsmen or explorers.

At the other extreme, there was a standing joke that a senator had once asked the Sydney office to locate his false teeth, lost when the Bondi surf worked its will upon him. It was said that he had received, with great promptness, the foot-wide jaws of a tiger shark, with an apologetic note saying that these were the only unwanted teeth that an extensive search had been able to find off Bondi Beach.

Some tasks that came the warden's way had a certain glamour, and were eagerly sought after when they arose. A very small and understaffed section of the Bureau of Fisheries was concerned with pearls, and during the slack season wardens were sometimes detached from their normal work and allowed to assist on the pearl beds.

Franklin had one such tour of duty in the Persian Gulf. It was straightforward work, not unlike gardening, and since it involved diving to depths never greater than two hundred feet simple compressed-air equipment was used and the diver employed a torpedo for moving around. The best areas for pearl cultivation had been carefully populated with selected stock, and the main problem was protecting the oysters from their natural enemies—particularly starfish and rays. When they had time to mature, they were collected and carried back to the surface for inspection—one of the few jobs that no one had ever been able to mechanise.

Any pearls discovered belonged, of course, to the Bureau of Fisheries. But it was noticeable that the wives of all the wardens posted to this duty very soon afterwards sported pearl necklaces or earrings—and Indra was no exception to this rule.

She had received her necklace the day she gave birth to Peter, and with the arrival of his son it seemed to Franklin that the old chapter of his life had finally closed. It was not true, of course; he could never forget—nor did he wish to— that Irene had given him Roy and Rupert, on a world which was now as remote to him as a planet of the furthest star. But the ache of that irrevocable parting had subsided at last, for no grief can endure forever.

He was glad—though he had once bitterly resented it— that it was impossible to talk to anyone on Mars, or indeed anywhere in space beyond the orbit of the Moon. The six-minute time lag for the round trip, even when the planet was at its nearest, made conversation out of the question, so he could never torture himself by feeling in the presence of Irene and the boys by calling them up on the visiphone. Every Christmas they exchanged recordings and talked over the events of the year; apart from occasional letters, that was the only personal contact they now had, and the only one that Franklin needed.

There was no way of telling how well Irene had adjusted to her virtual widowhood. The boys must have helped, but there were times when Franklin wished that she had married again, for their sakes as well as hers. Yet somehow he had never been able to suggest it, and she had never raised the subject, even when he had made this step himself.

Did she resent Indra? That again was hard to tell. Perhaps some jealousy was inevitable; Indra herself, during the occasional quarrels that punctuated their marriage, made it clear that she sometimes disliked the thought of being only the second woman in Franklin's life.

Such quarrels were rare, and after the birth of Peter they were rarer. A married couple forms a dynamically unstable system until the arrival of the first child converts it from a double to a triple group.

Franklin was as happy now as he had ever hoped to be. His family gave him the emotional security he needed; his work provided the interest and adventure which he had sought in space, only to lose again. There was more life and wonder in the sea than in all the endless empty leagues between the planets, and it was seldom now that his heart ached for the blue beauty of the crescent Earth, the swirling silver mist of the Milky Way, or the tense excitement of landfall on the moons of Mars at the end of a long voyage.

The sea had begun to shape his life and thought, as it must that of all men worthy to master it and learn its secrets. He felt a kinship with all the creatures that moved throughout its length and depth, even when they were enemies which it was his duty to destroy. But above all, he felt a sympathy and an almost mystical reverence, of which he was half ashamed, towards the great beasts whose destinies he ruled.

He believed that most wardens knew that feeling, though they were careful to avoid admitting it in their shoptalk. The nearest they came to it was when they accused each other of being "whale happy", a somewhat indefinable term which might be summed up as acting more like a whale than a man in a given situation. It was a form of identification without which no warden could be really good at his job, but there were times when it could become too extreme. The classic case—which everyone swore was perfectly true—was that of the senior warden who felt he was suffocating unless he brought his sub up to blow every ten minutes.

Being regarded—and regarding themselves—as the elite of the world's army of underwater experts, the wardens were always called upon when there was some unusual job that no one else cared to perform. Sometimes these jobs were so suicidal that it was necessary to explain to the would-be client that he must find another way out of his difficulties.

But occasionally there was no other way, and risks had to be taken. The bureau still remembered how Chief Warden Kircher, back in '22, had gone up the giant intake pipes through which the cooling water flowed into the fusion power plant supplying half the South American continent. One of the filter grilles had started to come loose, and could be fixed only by a man on the spot. With strong ropes tied around his body to prevent him from being sucked through the wire meshing, Kircher had descended into the roaring darkness. He had done the job and returned safely; but that was the last time he ever went under water.

So far, all Franklin's missions had been fairly conventional ones; he had had to face nothing as hair-raising as Kircher's exploit, and was not sure how he would react if such an occasion arose. Of course, he could always turn down any assignment that involved abnormal risks; his contract was quite specific on that point. But the "suicide clause", as it was sardonically called, was very much a dead letter. Any warden who invoked it, except under the most extreme circumstances, would incur no displeasure from his superiors, but he would thereafter find it very hard to live with his colleagues.

Franklin's first operation beyond the call of duty did not come his way for almost five years—five busy, crowded, yet in retrospect curiously uneventful, years. But when it came, it more than made up for the delay.

THE CHIEF ACCOUNTANT dropped his tables and charts on the desk, and peered triumphantly at his little audience over the rims of his antiquated spectacles.

"So you see, gentlemen," he said, "there's no doubt about it. In this area here"—he stabbed at the map again—"sperm whale casualties have been abnormally high. It's no longer a question of the usual random variations in the census numbers. During the migrations of the last five years, no less than nine plus or minus two whales have disappeared in this rather small area.

"Now, as you are all aware, the sperm whale has no natural enemies, except for the orcas that occasionally attack small females with calves. But we are quite sure that no killer packs have broken into this area for several years, and at least three adult males have disappeared. In our opinion, that left only one possibility.

"The sea bed here is slightly less than four thousand feet down, which means that a sperm whale can just reach it with a few minutes' time for hunting on the bottom before it has to return for air. Now, ever since it was discovered that Physeter feeds almost exclusively on squids, naturalists have wondered whether a squid can ever win when a whale attacks it. The general opinion was that it couldn't, because the whale is much larger and more powerful.

"But we must remember that even today no one knows how big the giant squid does grow; the Biology Section tells me that tentacles of *Bathyteutis Maximus* have been found up to eighty feet long. Moreover, a squid would only have to keep a whale held down for a matter of a few minutes at this depth, and the animal would drown before it could get back to the surface. So a couple of years ago we formulated the theory that in this area there lives at least one abnormally large squid. We—ahem—christened him Percy.

"Until last week, Percy was only a theory. Then, as you know, Whale S.87693 was found dead on the surface, badly mauled and with its body covered with the typical scars caused by squid claws and suckers. I would like you to look at this photograph."

He pulled a set of large glossy prints out of his briefcase and passed them around. Each showed a small portion of a whale's body which was mottled with white streaks and perfectly circular rings. A foot ruler lay incongruously in the middle of the picture to give an idea of the scale.

"Those, gentlemen, are sucker marks. They go up to six inches in diameter. I think we can say that Percy is no longer a theory. The question is: What do we do about him? He is costing us at least twenty thousand dollars a year. I should welcome any suggestions."

There was a brief silence while the little group of officials looked thoughtfully at the photographs. Then the director said: "I've asked Mr. Franklin to come along and give his opinion. What do you say, Walter? Can you deal with Percy?"

"If I can find him, yes. But the bottom's pretty rugged down there, and it might be a long search. I couldn't use a normal sub, of course—there'd be no safety margin at that depth, especially if Percy started putting on the squeeze. Incidentally, what size do you think he is?"

The chief accountant, usually so glib with figures, hesitated for an appreciable instant before replying.

"This isn't *my* estimate," he said apologetically, "but the biologists say he may be a hundred and fifty feet long."

There were some subdued whistles, but the director seemed unimpressed. Long ago he had learned the truth of the old cliché that there were bigger fish in the sea than ever came out of it. He knew also that, in a medium where gravity set no limit to size, a creature could continue to grow almost indefinitely as long as it could avoid death. And of all the inhabitants of the sea, the giant squid was perhaps the safest from attack. Even its one enemy, the sperm whale, could not reach it if it remained below the four-thousand-foot level.

"There are dozens of ways we can kill Percy if we can locate him," put in the chief biologist. "Explosives, poison, electrocution—any of them would do. But unless there's no alternative, I think we should avoid killing. He must be one of the biggest animals alive on this planet, and it would be a crime to murder him."

"*Please*, Dr. Roberts!" protested the director. "May I remind you that this bureau is only concerned with food production—not with research or the conservation of any animals except whales. And I do think that murder is rather a strong term to apply to an overgrown mollusk."

Dr. Roberts seemed quite unabashed by the mild reprimand.

"I agree, sir," he said cheerfully, "that production is our main job, and that we must always keep economic factors in mind. At the same time, we're continually co-operating with the Department of Scientific Research and this seems another case where we can work together to our mutual advantage. In fact, we might even make a profit in the long run."

"Go on," said the director, a slight twinkle in his eye. He wondered what ingenious plan the scientists who were supposed to be working for him had cooked up with their opposite numbers in Research.

"No giant squid has ever been captured alive, simply because we've never had the tools for the job. It would be an expensive operation, but if we are going to chase Percy anyway, the additional cost should not be very great. So I suggest that we try to bring him back alive."

No one bothered to ask how. If Dr. Roberts said it could be done, that meant he had already worked out a plan of campaign. The directors, as usual, bypassed the minor technical details involved in hauling up several tons of fighting squid from a depth of a mile, and went straight to the important point.

"Will Research pay for any of this? And what will you do with Percy when you've caught him?"

"Unofficially, Research will provide the additional equipment if we make the subs and pilots available. We'll also need that floating dock we borrowed from Maintenance last year; it's big enough to hold two whales, so it can certainly hold one squid. There'll be some additional expenditure here—extra aeration plant for the water, electrified mesh to stop Percy climbing out, and so on. In fact, I suggest that we use the dock as a lab while we're studying him."

"And after that?"

"Why, we sell him."

"The demand for hundred-and-fifty-foot squids as household pets would seem to be rather small."

Like an actor throwing away his best line, Dr. Roberts casually produced his trump card.

"If we can deliver Percy alive and in good condition, Marineland will pay fifty thousand dollars for him. That was Professor Milton's first informal offer when I spoke to him this morning. I've no doubt that we can get more than that; I've even been wondering if we could arrange things on a royalty basis. After all, a giant squid would be the biggest attraction Marineland ever had."

"Research was bad enough," grumbled the director. "Now it looks as if you're trying to get us involved in the entertainment business. Still, as far as I'm concerned it sounds fairly plausible. If Accounts can convince me that the project is not too expensive, and if no other snags turn up, we'll go ahead with it. That is, of course, if Mr. Franklin and his colleagues think it can be done. They're the people who'll have to do the work."

"If Dr. Roberts has any practical plan, I'll be glad to discuss it with him. It's certainly a very interesting project."

That, thought Franklin, was the understatement of the year. But he was not the sort of man who ever waxed too enthusiastic over any enterprise, having long ago decided that this always resulted in eventual disappointment. If "Operation Percy" came off, it would be the most exciting job he had ever had in his five years as a warden. But it was too good to be true; something would turn up to cancel the whole project.

It did not. Less than a month later, he was dropping down to the sea bed in a specially modified deep-water scout. Two hundred feet behind him, Don Burley was following in a second machine. It was the first time they had worked together since those far-off days on Heron Island, but when Franklin had been asked to choose his partner he had automatically thought of Don. This was the chance of a lifetime, and Don would never forgive him if he selected anyone else.

Franklin sometimes wondered if Don resented his own rapid rise in the service. Five years ago, Don had been a first warden; Franklin, a completely inexperienced trainee. Now they were both first wardens, and before long Franklin would probably be promoted again. He did not altogether welcome this, for, though he was ambitious enough, he knew that the higher he rose in the bureau the less time he would spend at sea. Perhaps Don knew what he was doing; it was very hard to picture him settling down in an office. . . .

"Better try your lights," said Don's voice from the speaker. "Doc Roberts wants me to get a photograph of you."

"Right," Franklin replied. "Here goes."

"My—you *do* look pretty! If I was another squid, I'm sure I'd find you irresistible. Swing broadside a minute. Thanks. Talk about a Christmas tree! It's the first time I've ever seen one making ten knots at six hundred fathoms."

Franklin grinned and switched off the illuminations. This idea of Dr. Roberts' was simple enough, but it remained to be seen if it would work. In the lightless abyss, many creatures carry constellations of luminous organs which they can switch on or off at will, and the giant squid, with its enormous eyes, is particularly sensitive to such lights. It uses them not only to lure its prey into its clutches, but also to attract its mates. If squids were as intelligent as they were supposed to be, thought Franklin, Percy would soon see through his disguise. It would be ironic however, if a deep-diving sperm whale was deceived and he had an unwanted fight on his hands.

The rocky bottom was now only five hundred feet below, every detail of it clearly traced on the short-range sonar scanner. It looked like an unpromising place for a search; there might be countless caves here in which Percy could hide beyond all hope of detection. On the other hand, the whales had detected him—to their cost. And anything that Physeter can do, Franklin, told himself, my sub can do just as well.

"We're in luck," said Don. "The water's as clear as I've ever seen it down here. As long as we don't stir up any mud, we'll be able to see a couple of hundred feet."

That was important; Franklin's luminous lures would be useless if the water was too turbid for them to be visible. He switched on the external TV camera, and quickly located the faint glow of Don's starboard light, two hundred feet away. Yes, this was extremely good luck; it should simplify their task enormously.

Franklin tuned in to the nearest beacon and fixed his position with the utmost accuracy. To make doubly sure, he got Don to do the same, and they split the difference between them. Then, cruising slowly on parallel courses, they began their careful search of the sea bed.

It was unusual to find bare rock at such a depth, for the ocean bed is normally covered with a layer of mud and sediment hundreds or even thousands of feet thick. There must, Franklin decided, be powerful currents scouring this area clear—but there was certainly no current now, as his drift meter assured him. It was probably seasonal, and associated with the ten-thousand-foot-deeper cleft of the Miller Canyon, only five miles away.

Every few seconds, Franklin switched on his pattern of coloured lights, then watched the screen eagerly to see if there was any response. Before long he had half a dozen fantastic deep-sea fish following him—nightmare creatures, two or three feet long, with enormous jaws and ridiculously attenuated feelers and tendrils trailing from their bodies. The lure of his lights apparently overcame their fear of his engine vibration, which was an encouraging sign. Though his speed quickly left them behind, they were continually replaced by new monsters, no two of which appeared to be exactly the same.

Franklin paid relatively little attention to the TV screen; the longer-range senses of the sonar, warning him of what lay in the thousand feet ahead of him, were more important. Not only had he to keep a look-out for his quarry, but he had to avoid rocks and hillocks which might suddenly rear up in the track of the sub. He was doing only ten knots, which was slow enough, but it required all his concentration. Sometimes he felt as if he was flying at treetop height over hilly country in a thick fog.

They travelled five uneventful miles, then made a hairpin turn and came back on a parallel course. If they were doing nothing else, thought Franklin, at least they were producing a survey of this area in more detail than it had ever been mapped before. Both he and Don were operating with their recorders on, so that the profile of the sea bed beneath them was being automatically mapped.

"Whoever said this was an exciting life?" said Don when they made their fourth turn. "I've not even seen a baby octopus. Maybe we're scaring the squids away."

"Roberts said they're not very sensitive to vibrations, so I don't think that's likely. And somehow I feel that Percy isn't the sort who's easily scared."

"*If* he exists," said Don sceptically.

"Don't forget those six-inch sucker marks. What do you think made them—mice?"

"Hey!" said Don. "Have a look at that echo on bearing 250, range 750 feet. Looks like a rock, but I thought it moved then."

Another false alarm, Franklin told himself. No—the echo did seem a bit fuzzy. By God, it *was* moving!

"Cut speed to half a knot," he ordered. "Drop back behind me—I'll creep up slowly and switch on my lights."

"It's a weird-looking echo. Keeps changing size all the time."

"That sounds like our boy. Here we go."

The sub was now moving across an endless, slightly tilted plain, still accompanied by its inquisitive retinue of finned dragons. On the TV screen all objects were lost in the haze at a distance of about a hundred and fifty feet; the full power of the ultraviolet projectors could probe the water no further than this. Franklin switched off his headlights and all external illumination, and continued his cautious approach using the sonar screen alone.

At five hundred feet the echo began to show its unmistakable structure; at four hundred feet there was no longer any doubt; at three hundred feet Franklin's escort fish suddenly fled at high speed as if aware that this was no healthy spot. At two hundred feet he turned on his visual lures, but he waited a few seconds before switching on the searchlights and TV.

A forest was walking across the sea bed—a forest of writhing, serpentine trunks. The great squid froze for a moment as if impaled by the searchlights; probably it could see them, though they were invisible to human eyes. Then it gathered up its tentacles with incredible swiftness, folding itself into a compact, streamlined mass—and shot straight towards the sub under the full power of its own jet propulsion.

It swerved at the last minute, and Franklin caught a glimpse of a huge and lidless eye that must have been at least a foot in diameter. A second later there was a violent blow on the hull, followed by a scraping sound as of great claws being dragged across metal. Franklin remembered the scars he had so often seen on the blubbery hides of sperm whales, and was glad of the thickness of steel that protected him. He could hear the wiring of his external illumination being ripped away; no matter—it had served its purpose.

It was impossible to tell what the squid was doing; from time to time the sub rocked violently, but Franklin made no effort to escape. Unless things got a little too rough, he proposed to stay here and take it.

"Can you see what he's doing?" he asked Don, rather plaintively.

"Yes—he's got his eight arms wrapped around you, and the two tentacles are waving hopefully at me. And he's going through the most beautiful colour changes you can imagine—I can't begin to describe them. I wish I knew whether he's really trying to eat you—or whether he's just being affectionate."

"Whichever it is, it's not very comfortable. Hurry up and take your photos so that I can get out of here."

"Right—give me another couple of minutes so I can get a movie sequence as well. Then I'll try to plant my harpoon."

It seemed a long two minutes, but at last Don had finished. Percy still showed none of the shyness which Dr. Roberts had rather confidently predicted, though by this time he could hardly have imagined that Franklin's sub was another squid.

Don planted his dart with neatness and precision in the thickest part of Percy's mantle, where it would lodge securely but would do no damage. At the sudden sting, the great mollusk abruptly released its grip, and Franklin took the opportunity for going full speed ahead. He felt the horny palps grating over the stern of the sub; then he was free and rising swiftly up towards the distant sky. He felt rather pleased that he had managed to escape without using any of the battery of weapons that had been provided for this very purpose.

Don followed him at once, and they circled five hundred feet above the sea bed—far beyond visual range. On the sonar screen the rocky bottom was a sharply defined plane, but now at its centre pulsed a tiny, brilliant star. The little beacon—less than six inches long and barely an inch wide—that had been anchored in Percy was already doing its job. It would continue to operate for more than a week before its batteries failed.

"We've tagged him!" cried Don gleefully. "Now he can't hide."

"As long as he doesn't get rid of that dart," said Franklin cautiously. "If he works it out, we'll have to start looking for him all over again."

"*I* aimed it," pointed out Don severely. "Bet you ten to one it stays put."

"If I've learned one thing in this game," said Franklin, "it's not to accept your bets." He brought the drive up to maximum cruising power, and pointed the sub's nose to the surface, still more than half a mile away. "Let's not keep Doc Roberts waiting—the poor man will be crazy with impatience. Besides, I want to see those pictures myself. It's the first time I've ever played a starring role with a giant squid."

And this, he reminded himself, was only the curtain raiser. The main feature had still to begin.

CHAPTER XV

"How nice it is," said Franklin, as he relaxed lazily in the contour-form chair on the porch, "to have a wife who's not scared stiff of the job I'm doing."

"There are times when I am," admitted Indra. "I don't like these deep-water operations. If anything goes wrong down there, you don't have a chance."

"You can drown just as easily in ten feet of water as ten thousand."

"That's silly, and you know it. Besides, no warden has ever been killed by drowning, as far as I've ever heard. The things that happen to them are never as nice and simple as that."

"I'm sorry I started this conversation," said Franklin ruefully, glancing around to see if Peter was safely out of earshot. "Anyway, you're not worried about Operation Percy, are you?"

"No, I don't think so. I'm as anxious as everybody else to see you catch him —and I'm still more interested to see if Dr. Roberts can keep him alive." She rose to her feet and walked over to the bookshelf recessed into the wall. Ploughing through the usual pile of papers and magazines that had accumulated there, she finally unearthed the volume for which she was looking.

"Listen to this," she continued, "and remember that it was written almost two hundred years ago." She began to read in her best lecture-room voice, while Franklin listened at first with mild reluctance, and then with complete absorption.

"In the distance, a great white mass lazily rose, and rising higher and higher, and disentangling itself from the azure, at last gleamed before our prow like a snow-slide, new slid from the hills. Thus glistening for a moment, as slowly it subsided, and sank. Then once more arose, and slightly gleamed. It seemed not a whale; and yet is this Moby Dick? thought Daggoo. Again the phantom went down, but on reappearing once more, like a stiletto-like cry that startled every man from his nod, the negro yelled out—'There! there again! there she breaches! Right ahead! The White Whale! The White Whale!'

"The four boats were soon on the water; Ahab's in advance, and all swiftly pulling towards their prey. Soon it went down, and while, with oars suspended, we were awaiting its appearance, lo! in the same spot where it sank, once more it slowly rose. Almost forgetting for the moment all thoughts of Moby Dick, we now gazed at the most wondrous phenomenon which the secret seas have hitherto revealed to mankind. A vast pulpy mass, furlongs in length and breadth, of a glancing cream-colour, lay floating on the water, innumerable long arms radiating from its centre, and curling and twisting like a nest of anacondas, as if blindly to catch at any hapless object within reach. No perceptible face or front did it have; no conceivable token of either sensation or instinct; but undulated there on the billows, an unearthly, formless, chance-like apparition of life.

"As with a low sucking sound it slowly disappeared again, Starbuck still gazing at the agitated waters where it had sunk, with a wild voice exclaimed— 'Almost rather had I seen Moby Dick and fought him, than to have seen thee, thou white ghost!'

" 'What was it, Sir?' said Flask.

" 'The great live squid, which, they say, few whale-ships ever beheld, and returned to their ports to tell of it.'

"But Ahab said nothing; turning his boat, he sailed back to the vessel; the rest as silently following."

Indra paused, closed the book, and waited for her husband's response. Franklin stirred himself in the too-comfortable couch and said thoughtfully: "I'd forgotten that bit—if I ever read as far. It rings true to life, but what was a squid doing on the surface?"

"It was probably dying. They sometimes surface at night, but never in the daytime, and Melville says this was on 'one transparent blue morning'."

"Anyway, what's a furlong? I'd like to know if Melville's squid was as big as Percy. The photos make him a hundred and thirty feet from his flukes to the tips of his feelers."

"So he beats the largest blue whale ever recorded."

"Yes, by a couple of feet. But of course he doesn't weigh a tenth as much."

Franklin heaved himself from his couch and went in search of a dictionary. Presently Indra heard indignant noises coming from the living room, and called out: "What's the matter?"

"It says here that a furlong is an obsolete measure of length equal to an eighth of a mile. Melville was talking through his hat."

"He's usually very accurate, at least as far as whales are concerned. But 'furlong' is obviously ridiculous—I'm surprised no one's spotted it before. He must have meant fathoms, or else the printer got it wrong."

Slightly mollified, Franklin put down the dictionary and came back to the porch. He was just in time to see Don Burley arrive, sweep Indra off her feet, plant a large but brotherly kiss on her forehead, and dump her back in her chair.

"Come along, Walt!" he said. "Got your things packed? I'll give you a lift to the airport."

"Where's Peter hiding?" said Franklin. "Peter! Come and say good-bye—Daddy's off to work."

A four-year-old bundle of uncontrollable energy came flying into the room, almost capsizing his father as he jumped into his arms.

"Daddy's going to bring me back a 'quid?" he asked.

"Hey—how did you know about all this?"

"It was on the news this morning, while you were still asleep," explained Indra. "They showed a few seconds of Don's film, too."

"I was afraid of that. Now we'll have to work with a crowd of cameramen and reporters looking over our shoulders. That means that something's sure to go wrong."

"They can't follow us down to the bottom, anyway," said Burley.

"I hope you're right—but don't forget we're not the only people with deep-sea subs."

"I don't know how you put up with him," Don protested to Indra. "Does he *always* look on the black side of things?"

"Not always," smiled Indra, as she unravelled Peter from his father. "He's cheerful at least twice a week."

Her smile faded as she watched the sleek sportster go whispering down the hill. She was very fond of Don, who was practically a member of the family, and there were times when she worried about him. It seemed a pity that he had never married and settled down; the nomadic, promiscuous life he led could hardly be very satisfying. Since they had known him, he had spent almost all his time on or under the sea, apart from hectic leaves when he had used their home as a base—at their invitation but often to their embarrassment when there were unexpected lady guests to entertain at breakfast.

Their own life, by many standards, had been nomadic enough, but at least they had always had a place they could call home. That apartment in Brisbane, where her brief but happy career as a lecturer at the University of Queensland had ended with the birth of Peter; that bungalow in Fiji, with the roof that had a mobile leak which the builders could never find; the married quarters at the South Georgia whaling station (she could still smell the mountains of offal, and see the gulls wheeling over the flensing yards); and finally, this house looking out across the sea to the other islands of Hawaii. Four homes in five years might seem excessive to many people, but for a warden's wife Indra knew she had done well.

She had few regrets for the career that had been temporarily interrupted. When Peter was old enough, she told herself, she would go back to her research; even now she read all the literature and kept in touch with current work. Only a few months ago the *Journal of Selachians* had published her letter "On the possible evolution of the Goblin Shark (*Scapanorhynchus owstoni*)", and she had since been involved in an enjoyable controversy with all five of the scientists qualified to discuss the subject.

Even if nothing came of these dreams, it was pleasant to have them and to know you might make the best of both worlds. So Indra Franklin, housewife and ichthyologist, told herself as she went back into the kitchen to prepare lunch for her ever-hungry son.

The floating dock had been modified in many ways that would have baffled its original designers. A thick steel mesh, supported on sturdy insulators, extended its entire length, and above this mesh was a canvas awning to cut out the sunlight which would injure Percy's sensitive eyes and skin. The only illumination inside the dock came from a battery of amber-tinted bulbs; at the moment, however, the great doors at either end of the huge concrete box were open, letting in both sunlight and water.

The two subs, barely awash, lay tied up beside the crowded catwalk as Dr. Roberts gave his final instructions.

"I'll try not to bother you too much when you're down there," he said, "but for heaven's sake tell me what's going on."

"We'll be too busy to give a running commentary," answered Don with a grin, "but we'll do our best. And if anything goes wrong, trust us to yell right away. All set, Walt?"

"O.K.," said Franklin, climbing down into the hatch. "See you in five hours, with Percy—I hope."

They wasted no time in diving to the sea bed; less than ten minutes later there was four thousand feet of water overhead, and the familiar rocky terrain was imaged on TV and sonar screen. But there was no sign of the pulsing star that should have indicated the presence of Percy.

"Hope the beacon hasn't packed up," said Franklin as he reported this news to the hopefully waiting scientists. "If it has, it may take us days to locate him again."

"Do you suppose he's left the area? I wouldn't blame him," added Don.

Dr. Roberts' voice, still confident and assured, came down to them from the distant world of sun and light almost a mile above.

"He's probably hiding in a cleft, or shielded by rock. I suggest you rise five hundred feet so that you're well clear of all the sea-bed irregularities, and start a high-speed search. That beacon has a range of more than a mile, so you'll pick him up pretty quickly."

An hour later even the doctor sounded less confident, and from the comments that leaked down to them over the sonar communicator it appeared that the reporters and TV networks were getting impatient.

"There's only one place he can be," said Roberts at last. "If he's there at all, and the beacon's still working, he must have gone down into the Miller Canyon."

"That's fifteen thousand feet deep," protested Don. "These subs are only cleared for twelve."

"I know—I know. But he won't have gone to the bottom. He's probably hunting somewhere down the slope. You'll see him easily if he's there."

"Right," replied Franklin, not very optimistically. "We'll go and have a look but if he's more than twelve thousand feet down, he'll have to stay there."

On the sonar screen, the canyon was clearly visible as a sudden gap in the luminous image of the sea bed. It came rapidly closer as the two subs raced towards it at forty knots—the fastest creatures, Franklin mused, anywhere beneath the surface of the sea. He had once flown low towards the Grand Canyon, and seen the land below suddenly whipped away as the enormous cavity gaped beneath him. And now, though he must rely for vision solely on the pattern of echoes brought back by his probing sound waves, he felt exactly that same sensation as he swept across the edge of this still mightier chasm in the ocean floor.

He had scarcely finished the thought when Don's voice, high-pitched with excitement, came yelling from the speaker.

"There he is! A thousand feet down!"

"No need to break my eardrums," grumbled Franklin. "I can see him."

The precipitous slope of the canyon wall was etched like an almost vertical line down the centre of the sonar screen. Creeping along the face of that wall was a tiny, twinkling star for which they had been searching. The patient beacon had betrayed Percy to his hunters.

They reported the situation to Dr. Roberts; Franklin could picture the jubilation and excitement up above, some hints of which trickled down through the open microphone. Presently Dr. Roberts, a little breathless, asked: "Do you think you can still carry out our plan?"

"I'll try," he answered. "It won't be easy with this cliff face right beside us, and I hope there aren't any caves Percy can crawl into. You ready, Don?"

"All set to follow you down."

"I think I can reach him without using the motors. Here we go."

Franklin flooded the nose tanks, and went down in a long, steep glide—a silent glide, he hoped. By this time, Percy would have learned caution and would probably run for it as soon as he knew that they were around.

The squid was cruising along the face of the canyon, and Franklin marvelled that it could find any food in such a forbidding and apparently lifeless spot. Every time it expelled a jet of water from the tube of its siphon it moved forward in a distinct jerk; it seemed unaware that it was no longer alone, since it had not changed course since Franklin had first observed it.

"Two hundred feet—I'm going to switch on my lights again," he told Don.

"He won't see you—visibility's only about eighty today."

"Yes, but I'm still closing in—he's spotted me! Here he comes!"

Franklin had not really expected that the trick would work a second time on an animal as intelligent as Percy. But almost at once he felt the sudden thud, followed by the rasping of horny claws as the great tentacles closed around the sub. Though he knew that he was perfectly safe, and that no animal could harm walls that had been built to withstand pressures of a thousand tons on every square foot, that grating, slithering sound was one calculated to give him nightmares.

Then, quite suddenly, there was silence. He heard Don exclaim, "Christ, that stuff acts quickly! He's out cold." Almost at once Dr. Roberts interjected anxiously: "Don't give him too much! And keep him moving so that he'll still breathe!"

Don was too busy to answer. Having carried out his role as decoy, Franklin could do nothing but watch as his partner manoeuvred dexterously around the great mollusk. The anaesthetic bomb had paralysed it completely; it was slowly sinking, its tentacles stretched limply upward. Pieces of fish, some of them over a foot across, were floating away from the cruel beak as the monster disgorged its last meal.

"Can you get underneath?" Don asked hurriedly. "He's sinking too fast for me."

Franklin threw on the drive and went around in a tight curve. There was a soft thump, as of a snowdrift falling from the roof, and he knew that five or ten tons of gelatinous body were now draped over the sub.

"Fine—hold him there—I'm getting into position."

Franklin was now blind, but the occasional clanks and whirs coming from the water outside told him what was happening. Presently Don said triumphantly: "All set! We're ready to go."

The weight lifted from the sub, and Franklin could see again. Percy had been neatly gaffed. A band of thick, elastic webbing had been fastened around his body at the narrowest part, just behind the flukes. From this harness a cable extended to Don's sub, invisible in the haze a hundred feet away. Percy was being towed through the water in his normal direction of motion—backward. Had he been conscious and actively resisting, he could have escaped easily enough, but in his present state the collar he was wearing enabled Don to handle him without difficulty. The fun would begin when he started to revive. . . .

Franklin gave a brief eyewitness description of the scene for the benefit of his patiently waiting colleagues a mile above. It was probably being broadcast, and he hoped that Indra and Peter were listening. Then he settled down to keep an eye on Percy as the long haul back to the surface began.

They could not move at more than two knots, lest the collar lose its none-too-secure grip on the great mass of jelly it was towing. In any event, the trip back to the surface had to take at least three hours, to give Percy a fair chance of adjusting to the pressure difference. Since an airbreathing—and therefore more vulnerable—animal like a sperm whale could endure almost the same pressure change in ten or twenty minutes, this caution was probably excessive. But Dr. Roberts was taking no chances with his unprecedented catch.

They had been climbing slowly for nearly an hour, and had reached the three-thousand-foot level, when Percy showed signs of life. The two long arms, terminating in their great sucker-covered palps, began to writhe purposefully; the monstrous eyes, into which Franklin had been staring half hypnotised from a distance of no more than five feet, began to light once more with intelligence. Quite unaware that he was speaking in a breathless whisper, he swiftly reported these symptoms to Dr. Roberts.

The doctor's first reaction was a hearty sigh of relief: "Good!" he said. "I was afraid we might have killed him. Can you see if he's breathing properly? Is the siphon contracting?"

Franklin dropped a few feet so that he could get a better view of the fleshy tube projecting from the squid's mantle. It was opening and closing in an unsteady rhythm which seemed to be getting stronger and more regular at every beat.

"Splendid!" said Dr. Roberts. "He's in fine shape. As soon as he starts to wriggle too hard, give him one of the small bombs. But leave it until the last possible moment."

Franklin wondered how that moment was to be decided. Percy was now beginning to glow a beautiful blue; even with the searchlights switched off he was clearly visible. Blue, he remembered Dr. Roberts saying, was a sign of excitement in squids. In that case, it was high time he did something.

"Better let go that bomb. I think he's getting lively," he told Don.

"Right—here it is."

A glass bubble floated across Franklin's screen and swiftly vanished from sight.

"The damn thing never broke!" he cried. "Let go another one!"

"O.K.—here's number two. I hope this works; I've only got five left."

But once again the narcotic bomb failed. This time Franklin never saw the sphere; he only knew that instead of relaxing into slumber once more Percy was becoming more active second by second. The eight short tentacles—short, that is, compared with the almost hundred-foot reach of the pair carrying the grasping palps—were now beginning to twine briskly together. He recalled Melville's phrase: "Like a nest of anacondas." No; somehow that did not seem to fit. It was more like a miser—a submarine Shylock—twisting his fingers together as he gloated over his wealth. In any event, it was a disconcerting sight when those fingers were a foot in diameter and were operating only two yards away. . . .

"You'll just have to keep on trying," he told Don. "Unless we stop him soon, he'll get away."

An instant later he breathed a sigh of relief as he saw broken shards of glass drifting by. They would have been quite invisible, surrounded as they were by water, had they not been fluorescing brilliantly under the light of his ultraviolet searchlight. But for the moment he was too relieved to wonder why he had been able to see something as proverbially elusive as a piece of broken glass in water; he only knew that Percy had suddenly relaxed again and no longer appeared to be working himself into a rage.

"What happened?" said Dr. Roberts plaintively from above.

"These confounded knockout drops of yours. Two of them didn't work. That leaves me with just four—and at the present rate of failure, I'll be lucky if even one goes off."

"I don't understand it. The mechanism worked perfectly every time we tested it in the lab."

"Did you test it at a hundred atmospheres pressure?"

"Er—no. It didn't seem necessary."

Don's "Huh!" seemed to say all that was needful about biologists who tried to dabble with engineering, and there was silence on all channels for the next few minutes of slow ascent. Then Dr. Roberts, sounding a little diffident, came back to the subject.

"Since we can't rely on the bombs," he said, "you'd better come up more quickly. He'll revive again in about thirty minutes."

"Right—I'll double speed. I only hope this collar doesn't slip off."

The next twenty minutes were perfectly uneventful; then everything started to happen at once.

"He's coming around again," said Franklin. "I think the higher speed has waked him up."

"I was afraid of that," Dr. Roberts answered. "Hold on as long as you can, and then let go a bomb. We can only pray that *one* of them will work."

A new voice suddenly cut into the circuit.

"Captain here. Lookout has just spotted some sperm whales about two miles away. They seem to be heading towards us; I suggest you have a look at them—we've got no horizontal search sonar on this ship."

Franklin switched quickly over to the long-range scanner and picked up the echoes at once.

"Nothing to worry about," he said. "If they come too close, we can scare them away." He glanced back at the TV screen and saw that Percy was now getting very restive.

"Let go your bomb," he told Don, "and keep your fingers crossed."

"I'm not betting on *this*," Don answered. "Anything happen?"

"No; another dud. Try again."

"That leaves three. Here goes."

"Sorry—I can see that one. It isn't cracked."

"Two left. Now there's only one."

"That's a dud too. What had we better do, Doc? Risk the last one? I'm afraid Percy will slip off in a minute."

"There's nothing else we can do," replied Dr. Roberts, his voice now clearly showing the strain. "Go ahead, Don."

Almost at once Franklin gave a cry of satisfaction.

"We've made it!" he shouted. "He's knocked cold again! How long do you think it will keep him under this time?"

"We can't rely on more than twenty minutes, so plan your ascent accordingly. We're right above you—and remember what I said about taking at least ten minutes over that last two hundred feet. I don't want any pressure damage after all the trouble we've been to."

"Just a minute," put in Don. "I've been looking at those whales. They've put on speed and they're coming straight towards us. I think they've detected Percy—or the beacon we put in him."

"So what?" said Franklin. "We can frighten them with—oh."

"Yes—I thought you'd forgotten that. These aren't patrol subs, Walt. No siren on them. And you can't scare sperm whales just by revving your engines."

That was true enough, though it would not have been fifty years ago, when the great beasts had been hunted almost to extinction. But a dozen generations had lived and died since then; now they recognised the subs as harmless, and certainly no obstacle to the meal they were anticipating. There was a real danger that the helpless Percy be eaten before he could be safely caged.

"I think we'll make it," said Franklin, as he anxiously calculated the speed of the approaching whales. This was a hazard that no one could have anticipated; it was typical of the way in which underwater operations developed unexpected snags and complications.

"I'm going straight up to the two-hundred-foot level," Don told him. "We'll wait there just as long as it's safe, and then run for the ship. What do you think of that, Doc?"

"It's the only thing to do. But remember that those whales can make fifteen knots if they have to."

"Yes, but they can't keep it up for long, even if they see their dinner slipping away. Here we go."

The subs increased their rate of ascent, while the water brightened around them and the enormous pressure slowly relaxed. At last they were back in the narrow zone where an unprotected man could safely dive. The mother ship was less than a hundred yards away, but this final stage in the climb back to the surface was the most critical of all. In this last two hundred feet, the pressure would drop swiftly from eight atmospheres to only one—as great a change in ratio as had occurred in the previous quarter of a mile. There were no enclosed air spaces in Percy which might cause him to explode if the ascent was too swift, but no one could be certain what other internal damage might occur.

"Whales only half a mile away," reported Franklin. "Who said they couldn't keep up that speed? They'll be here in two minutes."

"You'll have to hold them off somehow," said Dr. Roberts, a note of desperation in his voice.

"Any suggestions?" asked Franklin, a little sarcastically.

"Suppose you pretend to attack; that might make them break off."

This, Franklin told himself, was not his idea of fun. But there seemed no alternative; with a last glance at Percy, who was now beginning to stir again, he started off at half-speed to meet the advancing whales.

There were three echoes dead ahead of him—not very large ones, but he did not let that encourage him. Even if those were the relatively diminutive females, each one was as big as ten elephants and they were coming towards him at a combined speed of forty miles an hour. He was making all the noise he could, but so far it seemed to be having no effect.

Then he heard Don shouting: "Percy's waking up fast! I can feel him starting to move."

"Come straight in," ordered Dr. Roberts. "We've got the doors open."

"And get ready to close the back door as soon as I've slipped the cable. I'm going straight through—I don't want to share your swimming pool with Percy when he finds what's happened to him."

Franklin heard all this chattering with only half an ear. Those three approaching echoes were ominously close. Were they going to call his bluff? Sperm whales were among the most pugnacious animals in the sea, as different from their vegetarian cousins as wild buffaloes from a herd of prize Guernseys. It was a sperm whale that had rammed and sunk the *Essex* and thus inspired the closing chapter of *Moby Dick*; he had no desire to figure in a submarine sequel.

Yet he held stubbornly to his course, though now the racing echoes were less than fifteen seconds away. Then he saw that they were beginning to separate; even if they were not scared, the whales had become confused. Probably the noise of his motors had made them lose contact with their target. He cut his speed to zero, and the three whales began to circle him inquisitively, at a range of about a hundred feet. Sometimes he caught a shadowy glimpse of them on the TV screen. As he had thought, they were young females, and he felt a little sorry to have robbed them of what should have been their rightful food.

He had broken the momentum of their charge; now it was up to Don to finish his side of the mission. From the brief and occasionally lurid comments from the loudspeaker, it was obvious that this was no easy task. Percy was not yet fully conscious, but he knew that something was wrong and he was beginning to object.

The men on the floating dock had the best view of the final stages. Don surfaced about fifty yards away—and the sea behind him became covered with an undulating mass of jelly, twisting and rolling on the waves. At the greatest speed he dared to risk, Don headed for the open end of the dock. One of Percy's tentacles made a half-hearted grab at the entrance, as if in a somnambulistic effort to avoid captivity, but the speed at which he was being hurried through the water broke his grip. As soon as he was safely inside, the massive steel gates began to close like horizontally operating jaws, and Don jettisoned the towrope fastened around the squid's flukes. He wasted no time in leaving from the other exit, and the second set of lock gates started to close even before he was through. The caging of Percy had taken less than a quarter of a minute.

When Franklin surfaced, in company with three disappointed but not hostile sperm whales, it was some time before he could attract any attention. The entire personnel of the dock were busy staring, with awe, triumph, scientific curiosity, and even downright disbelief, at the monstrous captive now swiftly reviving in his great concrete tank. The water was being thoroughly aerated by the streams of bubbles from a score of pipes, and the last traces of the drugs that had paralysed him were being flushed out of Percy's system. Beneath the dim amber light that was now the sole illumination inside the dock, the giant squid began to investigate its prison.

First it swam slowly from end to end of the rectangular concrete box, exploring the sides with its tentacles. Then the two immense palps started to climb into the air, waving towards the breathless watchers gathered round the edge of the dock. They touched the electrified netting—and flicked away with a speed that almost eluded the eye. Twice again Percy repeated the experiment before he had convinced himself that there was no way out in this direction, all the while staring up at the puny spectators with a gaze that seemed to betoken an intelligence every wit as great as theirs.

By the time Don and Franklin came aboard, the squid appeared to have settled down in captivity, and was showing a mild interest in a number of fish that had been dropped into its tank. As the two wardens joined Dr. Roberts behind the wire meshing, they had their first clear and complete view of the monster they had hauled up from the ocean depths.

Their eyes ran along the hundred and more feet of flexible, sinewy strength, the countless claw-ringed suckers, the slowly pulsing jet, and the huge staring eyes of the most superbly equipped beast of prey the world had ever seen. Then Don summed up the thoughts that they were both feeling.

"He's all yours, Doc. I hope you know how to handle him."

Dr. Roberts smiled confidently enough. He was a very happy man, though a small worry was beginning to invade his mind. He had no doubt at all that he could handle Percy, and he was perfectly right. But he was not so sure that he could handle the director when the bills came in for the research equipment he was going to order—and for the mountains of fish that Percy was going to eat.

CHAPTER XVI

THE SECRETARY OF the Department of Scientific Research had listened to him attentively enough—and not merely with attention, Franklin told himself, but with a flattering interest. When he had finished the sales talk which had taken such long and careful preparation, he felt a sudden and unexpected emotional letdown. He knew that he had done his best; what happened now was largely out of his hands.

"There are a few points I would like to clear up," said the secretary. "The first is a rather obvious one. Why didn't you go to the Marine Division's own research department instead of coming all the way up to World Secretariat level and contacting D.S.R.?"

It was, Franklin admitted, a rather obvious point—and a somewhat delicate one. But he knew that it would be raised, and he had come prepared.

"Naturally, Mr. Farlan," he answered, "I did my best to get support in the division. There was a good deal of interest, especially after we'd captured that squid. But Operation Percy turned out to be much more expensive than anyone had calculated, and there were a lot of awkward questions about it. The whole affair ended with several of our scientists transferring to other divisions."

"I know," interjected the secretary with a smile. "We've got some of them."

"So any research that isn't of direct practical importance is now frowned on in the division, which is one reason why I came to you. And, frankly, it hasn't the authority to do the sort of thing I propose. The cost of running even two deep-sea subs is considerable, and would have to be approved at higher than divisional level."

"But if it was approved, you are confident that the staff could be made available?"

"Yes, at the right time of the year. Now that the fence is practically one hundred per cent reliable—there's been no major breakdown for three years— we wardens have a fairly slack time except at the annual roundups and slaughterings. That's why it seemed a good idea——"

"To utilise the wasted talents of the wardens?"

"Well, that's putting it a little bluntly. I don't want to give the idea that there is any inefficiency in the bureau."

"I wouldn't dream of suggesting such a thing," smiled the secretary. "The other point is a more personal one. Why are you so keen on this project? You have obviously spent a lot of time and trouble on it—and, if I may say so, risked the disapproval of your superiors by coming directly to me."

That question was not so easy to answer, even to someone you knew well, still less to a stranger. Would this man, who had risen so high in the service of the state, understand the fascination of a mysterious echo on a sonar screen, glimpsed only once, and that years ago? Yes, he would, for he was at least partly a scientist.

"As a chief warden," explained Franklin, "I probably won't be on sea duty much longer. I'm thirty-eight, and getting old for this kind of work. And I've an inquisitive type of mind; perhaps I should have been a scientist myself. This is a problem I'd like to see settled, though I know the odds against it are prety high."

"I can appreciate that. This chart of confirmed sightings covers about half the world's oceans."

"Yes, I know it looks hopeless, but with the new sonar sets we can scan a volume three times as great as we used to, and an echo that size is easy to pick up. It's only a matter of time before somebody detects it."

"And you want to be that somebody. Well, that's reasonable enough. When I got your original letter I had a talk with my marine biology people, and got about three different opinions—none of them very encouraging. Some of those who admit that these echoes have been seen say that they are probably ghosts due to faults in the sonar sets or returns from discontinuities of some kind in the water."

Franklin snorted. "Anyone who's seen them would know better than that. After all, we're familiar with all the ordinary sonar ghosts and false returns. We have to be."

"Yes, that's what I feel. Some more of my people think that the—let us say—conventional sea serpents have already been accounted for by squids, oarfish, and eels, and that what your patrols have been seeing is either one of these or else a large deep-sea shark."

Franklin shook his head. "I know what all those echoes look like. This is quite different."

"The third objection is a theoretical one. There simply isn't enough food in the extreme ocean depths to support any very large and active forms of life."

"No one can be sure of that. Only in the last century scientists were saying that there could be no life at all on the ocean bed. We know what nonsense *that* turned out to be."

"Well, you've made a good case. I'll see what can be done."

"Thank you very much, Mr. Farlan. Perhaps it would be best if no one in the bureau knew that I'd come to see you."

"We won't tell them, but they'll guess." The secretary rose to his feet, and Franklin assumed that the interview was over. He was wrong.

"Before you go, Mr. Franklin," said the secretary, "you might be able to clear up one little matter that's been worrying me for a good many years."

"What's that, sir?"

"I've never understood what a presumably well-trained warden would be doing in the middle of the night off the Great Barrier Reef, breathing compressed air five hundred feet down."

There was a long silence while the two men, their relationship suddenly altered, stared at each other across the room. Franklin searched his memory, but the other's face evoked no echoes; that was so long ago, and he had met so many people during the intervening years.

"Were you one of the men who pulled me in?" he asked. "If so, I've a lot to thank you for." He paused for a moment, then added, "You see, that wasn't an accident."

"I rather thought so; that explains everything. But before we change the subject, just what happened to Bert Darryl? I've never been able to find the true story."

"Oh, eventually he ran out of credit; he could never make the *Sea Lion* pay its way. The last time I ever saw him was in Melbourne; he was heartbroken because customs duties had been abolished and there was no way an honest smuggler could make a living. Finally he tried to collect the insurance on the *Sea Lion*; he had a convincing fire and had to abandon ship off Cairns. She went to the bottom, but the appraisers went after her, and started asking some very awkward questions when they found that all the valuable fittings had been removed before the fire. I don't know how the captain got out of that mess.

"That was about the end of the old rascal. He took to the bottle in earnest, and one night up in Darwin he decided to go for a swim off the jetty. But he'd forgotten that it was low tide—and in Darwin the tide drops thirty feet. So he broke his neck, and a lot of people besides his creditors were genuinely sorry."

"Poor old Bert. The world will be a dull place when there aren't any more people like him."

That was rather a heretical remark, thought Franklin, coming from the lips of so senior a member of the World Secretariat. But it pleased him greatly, and not merely because he agreed with it. He knew now that he had unexpectedly acquired an influential friend, and that the chances of his project going forward had been immeasurably improved.

He did not expect anything to happen in a hurry, so was not disappointed as the weeks passed in silence. In any event, he was kept busy; the slack season was still three months away, and meanwhile a whole series of minor but annoying crises crowded upon him.

And there was one that was neither minor nor anything, if indeed it could be called a crisis at all. Anne Franklin arrived wide-eyed and wide-mouthed into the world, and Indra began to have her first serious doubts of continuing her academic career.

Franklin, to his great disappointment, was not home when his daughter was born. He had been in charge of a small task force of six subs, carrying out an offensive sweep off the Pribilof Islands in an attempt to cut down the number of killer whales. It was not the first mission of its kind, but it was the most successful, thanks to the use of improved techniques. The characteristic calls of seals and the smaller whales had been recorded and played back into the sea, while the subs had waited silently for the killers to appear.

They had done so in hundreds, and the slaughter had been immense. By the time the little fleet returned to Base, more than a thousand orcas had been killed. It had been hard and sometimes dangerous work, and despite its importance Franklin had found this scientific butchery extremely depressing. He could not help admiring the beauty, speed, and ferocity of the hunters he was himself hunting, and towards the end of the mission he was almost glad when the rate of kill began to fall off. It seemed that the orcas were learning by bitter experience, and the bureau's statisticians would have to decide whether or not it would be economically worth while repeating the operation next season.

Franklin had barely had time to thaw out from this mission and to fondle Anne gingerly, without extracting any signs of recognition from her, when he was shot off to South Georgia. His problem there was to discover why the whales, who had previously swum into the slaughtering pens without any qualms, had suddenly become suspicious and shown a great reluctance to enter the electrified sluices. As it turned out, he did nothing at all to solve the mystery; while he was still looking for psychological factors, a bright young plant inspector discovered that some of the bloody waste from the processing plants was accidentally leaking back into the sea. It was not surprising that the whales, though their sense of smell was not as strongly developed as in other marine animals, had become alarmed as the moving barriers tried to guide them to the place where so many of their relatives had met their doom.

As a chief warden, already being groomed for higher things, Franklin was now a kind of mobile trouble shooter who might be sent anywhere in the world on the bureau's business. Apart from the effect on his home life, he welcomed this state of affairs. Once a man had learned the mechanics of a warden's trade, straightforward patrolling and herding had little future in it. People like Don Burley got all the excitement and pleasure they needed from it, but then Don was neither ambitious nor much of an intellectual heavy-weight. Franklin told himself this without any sense of superiority; it was a simple statement of fact which Don would be the first to admit.

He was in England, giving evidence as an expert witness before the Whaling Commission—the bureau's state-appointed watchdog—when he received a plaintive call from Dr. Lundquist, who had taken over when Dr. Roberts had left the Bureau of Whales to accept a much more lucrative appointment at the Marineland aquarium.

"I've just had three crates of gear delivered from the Department of Scientific Research. It's nothing we ever ordered, but your name is on it. What's it all about?"

Franklin thought quickly. It *would* arrive when he was away, and if the director came across it before he could prepare the ground there would be fireworks.

"It's too long a story to give now," Franklin answered. "I've got to go before the committee in ten minutes. Just push it out of the way somewhere until I get back—I'll explain everything then."

"I hope it's all right—it's most unusual."

"Nothing to worry about—see you the day after tomorrow. If Don Burley comes to Base, let him have a look at the stuff. But I'll fix all the paper work when I get back."

That, he told himself, would be the worst part of the whole job. Getting equipment that had never been officially requisitioned on to the bureau's inventory without too many questions was going to be at least as difficult as locating the Great Sea Serpent. . . .

He need not have worried. His new and influential ally, the secretary of the Department of Scientific Research, had already anticipated most of his problems. The equipment was to be on loan to the bureau, and was to be returned as soon as it had done its job. What was more, the director had been given the impression that the whole thing was a D.S.R. project; he might have his doubts, but Franklin was officially covered.

"Since you seem to know all about it, Walter," he said in the lab when the gear was finally unpacked, "you'd better explain what it's supposed to do."

"It's an automatic recorder, much more sophisticated than the ones we have at the gates for counting the whales as they go through. Essentially, it's a long-range sonar scanner that explores a volume of space fifteen miles in radius, clear down to the bottom of the sea. It rejects all fixed echoes, and will only record moving objects. And it can also be set to ignore all objects of less than any desired size. In other words, we can use it to count the number of whales more than, say, fifty feet long, and take no notice of the others. It does this once every six minutes—two hundred and forty times a day—so it will give a virtually continuous census of any desired region."

"Quite ingenious. I suppose D.S.R. wants us to moor the thing somewhere and service it?"

"Yes—and to collect the recordings every week. They should be very useful to us as well. Er—there are three of the things, by the way."

"Trust D.S.R. to do it in style! I wish we had as much money to throw around. Let me know how the things work—if they do."

It was as simple as that, and there had been no mention at all of sea serpents.

Nor was there any sign of them for more than two months. Every week, whatever patrol sub happened to be in the neighbourhood would bring back the records from the three instruments, moored half a mile below sea level at the spots Franklin had chosen after a careful study of all the known sightings. With an eagerness which slowly subsided to a stubborn determination, he examined the hundreds of feet of old-fashioned sixteen-millimetre film—still unsurpassed in its own field as a recording medium. He looked at thousands of echoes as he projected the film, condensing into minutes the comings and goings of giant sea creatures through many days and nights.

Usually the pictures were blank, for he had set the discriminator to reject all echoes from objects less than seventy feet in length. That, he calculated, should eliminate all but the very largest whales—and the quarry he was seeking. When the herds were on the move, however, the film would be dotted with echoes which would jump across the screen at fantastically exaggerated speeds as he projected the images. He was watching the life of the sea accelerated almost ten thousand times.

After two months of fruitless watching, he began to wonder if he had chosen the wrong places for all three recorders, and was making plans to move them. When the next rolls of film came back, he told himself, he would do just that, and he had already decided on the new locations.

But this time he found what he had been looking for. It was on the edge of the screen, and had been caught by only four sweeps of the scanner. Two days ago that unforgotten, curiously linear echo had appeared on the recorder; now he had evidence, but he still lacked proof.

He moved the other two recorders into the area, arranging the three instruments in a great triangle fifteen miles on a side, so that their fields overlapped. Then it was a question of waiting with what patience he could until another week had passed.

The wait was worth it; at the end of that time he had all the ammunition he needed for his campaign. The proof was there, clear and undeniable.

A very large animal, too long and thin to be any of the known creatures of the sea, lived at the astonishing depth of twenty thousand feet and came halfway to the surface twice a day, presumably to feed. From its intermittent appearance on the screens of the recorders, Franklin was able to get a fairly good idea of its habits and movements. Unless it suddenly left the area and he lost track of it, there should be no great difficulty in repeating the succcess of Operation Percy.

He should have remembered that in the sea nothing is ever twice the same.

CHAPTER XVII

"YOU KNOW DEAR," said Indra, "I'm rather glad this is going to be one of your last missions."

"If you think I'm getting too old——"

"Oh, it's not only that. When you're on headquarters duty we'll be able to start leading a normal social life. I'll be able to invite people to dinner without having to apologise because you've suddenly been called out to round up a sick whale. And it will be better for the children; I won't have to keep explaining to them who the strange man is they sometimes meet around the house."

"Well, it's not *that* bad, is it, Pete?" laughed Franklin, tousling his son's dark, unruly hair.

"When are you going to take me down in a sub, Daddy?" asked Peter, for approximately the hundredth time.

"One of these days, when you're big enough not to get in the way."

"But if you wait until I am big, I *will* get in the way."

"There's logic for you!" said Indra. "I told you my child was a genius."

"He may have got his hair from you," said Franklin, "but it doesn't follow that you're responsible for what lies beneath it." He turned to Don, who was making ridiculous noises for Anne's benefit. She seemed unable to decide whether to laugh or to burst into tears, but was obviously giving the problem her urgent attention. "When are you going to settle down to the joys of domesticity? You can't be an honorary uncle all your life."

For once, Don looked a little embarrassed.

"As a matter of fact," he said slowly, "I'm thinking about it. I've met someone at last who looks as if she might be willing."

"Congratulations! I thought you and Marie were seeing a lot of each other."

Don looked still more embarrassed.

"Well—ah—it isn't Marie. I was just trying to say good-bye to *her*."

"Oh," said Franklin, considerably deflated. "Who is it?"

"I don't think you know her. She's named June—June Curtis. She isn't in the bureau at all, which is an advantage in some ways. I've not quite made up my mind yet, but I'll probably ask her next week."

"There's only one thing to do," said Indra firmly. "As soon as you come back from this hunt, bring her around to dinner and I'll tell you what we think of her."

"And I'll tell her what we think of *you*," put in Franklin. "We can't be fairer than that, can we?"

He remembered Indra's words—"this is going to be one of your last missions"—as the little depth ship slanted swiftly down into the eternal night.

It was not strictly true, of course; even though he had now been promoted to a permanent shore position, he would still occasionally go to sea. But the opportunities would become fewer and fewer; this was his swan song as a warden, and he did not know whether to be sorry or glad.

For seven years he had roamed the oceans—one year of his life to each of the seas—and in that time he had grown to know the creatures of the deep as man could never have done in any earlier age. He had watched the sea in all its moods; he had coasted over mirror-flat waters, and had felt the surge of mighty waves lifting his vessel when it was a hundred feet below the storm-tossed surface. He had looked upon beauty and horror and birth and death in their multitudinous forms, as he moved through a liquid world so teeming with life that by comparison the land was an empty desert.

No man could ever exhaust the wonder of the sea, but Franklin knew that the time had come for him to take up new tasks. He looked at the sonar screen for the accompanying cigar of light which was Don's ship, and thought affectionately of their common characteristics and of the differences which now must take them further apart. Who would have imagined, he told himself, that they would become such good friends, that far-off day when they had met warily as instructor and pupil?

That had been only seven years ago, but already it was hard for him to remember the sort of person he had been in those days. He felt an abiding gratitude for the psychologists who had not only rebuilt his mind but had found him the work that could rebuild his life.

His thoughts completed the next, inevitable step. Memory tried to recreate Irene and the boys—good heavens, Rupert would be twelve years old now!— around whom his whole existence had once revolved, but who now were strangers drifting further and further apart year by year. The last photograph he had of them was already more than a year old; the last letter from Irene had been posted on Mars six months ago, and he reminded himself guiltily that he had not yet answered it.

All the grief had gone long ago; he felt no pain at being an exile in his own world, no ache to see once more the faces of friends he had known in the days when he counted all space his empire. There was only a wistful sadness, not even wholly unpleasant, and a mild regret for the inconstancy of sorrow.

Don's voice broke into his reverie, which had never taken his attention away from his crowded instrument panel.

"We're just passing my record, Walt. Ten thousand's the deepest I've ever been."

"And we're only halfway there. Still, what difference does it make if you've got the right ship? It just takes a bit longer to go down, and a bit longer to come up. These subs would still have a safety factor of five at the bottom of the Philippine Trench."

"That's true enough, but you can't convince me there's no psychological difference. Don't *you* feel two miles of water on your shoulders?"

It was most unlike Don to be so imaginative; usually it was Franklin who made such remarks and was promptly laughed at. If Don was getting moody, it would be best to give him some of his own medicine.

"Tell me when you've got to start bailing," said Franklin. "If the water gets up to your chin, we'll turn back."

He had to admit that the feeble joke helped his own morale. The knowledge that the pressure around him was rising steadily to five tons per square inch did have a definite effect on his mind—an effect he had never experienced in shallow-water operations where disaster could be just as instantaneous, just as total. He had complete confidence in his equipment and knew that curious feeling of depression which seemed to have taken most of the zest out of the project into which he had put so much effort.

Five thousand feet lower down, that zest returned with all its old vigour. They both saw the echo simultaneously, and for a moment were shouting at cross purposes until they remembered their signals discipline. When silence had been restored, Franklin gave his orders.

"Cut your motor to quarter speed," he said. "We know the beast's very sensitive and we don't want to scare it until the last minute."

"Can't we flood the bow tanks and glide down?"

"Take too long—he's still three thousand feet below. And cut your sonar to minimum power; I don't want him picking up our pulses."

The animal was moving in a curiously erratic path at a constant depth, sometimes making little darts to right or left as if in search of food. It was following the slopes of an unusually steep submarine mountain, which rose abruptly some four thousand feet from the sea bed. Not for the first time, Franklin thought what a pity it was that the world's most stupendous scenery was all sunk beyond sight in the ocean depths. Nothing on the land could compare with the hundred-mile-wide canyons of the North Atlantic, or the monstrous potholes that gave the Pacific the deepest soundings on earth.

They sank slowly below the summit of the submerged mountain—a mountain whose topmost peak was three miles below sea level. Only a little way beneath them now that mysteriously elongated echo seemed to be undulating through the water with a sinuous motion which reminded Franklin irresistibly of a snake. It would, he thought, be ironic if the Great Sea Serpent turned out to be exactly that. But that was impossible, for there were no water-breathing snakes.

Neither man spoke during the slow and cautious approach to their goal. They both realised that this was one of the great moments of their lives, and wished to savour it to the full. Until now, Don had been mildly sceptical, believing that whatever they found would be no more than some already-known species of animal. But as the echo on the screen expanded, so its strangeness grew. This was something wholly new.

The mountain was now looming above them; they were skirting the foot of a cliff more than two thousand feet high, and their quarry was less than half a mile ahead. Franklin felt his hand itching to throw on the ultraviolet searchlights which in an instant might solve the oldest mystery of the sea, and bring him enduring fame. How important to him was that? he asked himself, as the seconds ticked slowly by. That it was important, he did not attempt to hide from himself. In all his career, he might never have another opportunity like this. . . .

Suddenly, without the slightest warning, the sub trembled as if struck by a hammer. At the same moment Don cried out: "My God—what was that?"

"Some damn fool is letting off explosives," Franklin replied, rage and frustration completely banishing fear. "Wasn't everyone notified of our dive?"

"That's no explosion. I've felt it before—it's an earthquake."

No other word could so swiftly have conjured up once more all that terror of the ultimate depths which Franklin had felt brushing briefly against his mind during their descent. At once the immeasurable weight of the waters crushed down upon them like a physical burden; his sturdy craft seemed the frailest of cockleshells, already doomed by forces which all man's science could no longer hold at bay.

He knew that earthquakes were common in the deep Pacific, where the weights of rock and water were forever poised in precarious equilibrium. Once or twice on patrols he had felt distant shocks—but this time, he felt certain, he was near the epicentre.

"Make full speed for the surface," he ordered. "That may be just the beginning."

"But we only need another five minutes," Don protested. "Let's chance it, Walt."

Franklin was sorely tempted. That single shock might be the only one; the strain on the tortured strata miles below might have been relieved. He glanced at the echo they had been chasing; it was moving much faster now, as if it, too, had been frightened by this display of Nature's slumbering power.

"We'll risk it," Franklin decided. "But if there's another one we'll go straight up."

"Fair enough," answered Don. "I'll bet you ten to one——"

He never completed the sentence. This time the hammer blow was no more violent, but it was sustained. The entire ocean seemed to be in travail as the shock waves, travelling at almost a mile a second, were reflected back and forth between surface and sea bed. Franklin shouted the one word "Up!" and tilted the sub as steeply as he dared towards the distant sky.

But the sky was gone. The sharply defined plane which marked the water-air interface on the sonar screen had vanished, replaced by a meaningless jumble of hazy echoes. For a moment Franklin assumed that the set had been put out of action by the shocks; then his mind interpreted the incredible, the terrifying picture that was taking shape upon the screen.

"Don," he yelled, "run for the open sea—the mountain's falling!"

The billions of tons of rock that had been towering above them were sliding down into the deep. The whole face of the mountain had split away and was descending in a waterfall of stone, moving with a deceptive slowness and an utterly irresistible power. It was an avalanche in slow motion, but Franklin knew that within seconds the waters through which the sub was driving would be torn with falling debris.

He was moving at full speed, yet he seemed motionless. Even without the amplifiers, he could hear through the hull the rumble and roar of grinding rock. More than half the sonar image was now obliterated, either by solid fragments or by the immense clouds of mud and silt that were now beginning to fill the sea. He was becoming blind; there was nothing he could do but hold his course and pray.

With a muffled thud, something crashed against the hull and the sub groaned from end to end. For a moment Franklin thought he had lost control; then he managed to fight the vessel back to an even keel. No sooner had he done this than he realised he was in the grip of a powerful current, presumably due to water displaced by the collapsing mountain. He welcomed it, for it was sweeping him to the safety of the open sea, and for the first time he dared to hope.

Where was Don? It was impossible to see his echo in the shifting chaos of the sonar screen. Franklin switched his communication set to high power and started calling through the moving darkness. There was no reply; probably Don was too busy to answer, even if he had received the signal.

The pounding shock waves had ceased; with them had gone the worst of Franklin's fears. There was no danger now of the hull being cracked by pressure, and by this time, surely, he was clear of the slowly toppling mountain. The current that had been aiding his engines had now lost its strength, proving that he was far away from its source. On the sonar screen, the luminous haze that had blocked all vision was fading minute by minute as the silt and debris subsided.

Slowly the wrecked face of the mountain emerged from the mist of conflicting echoes. The pattern on the screen began to stabilise itself, and presently Franklin could see the great scar left by the avalanche. The sea bed itself was still hidden in a vast fog of mud; it might be hours before it would be visible again and the damage wrought by Nature's paroxysm could be ascertained.

Franklin watched and waited as the screen cleared. With each sweep of the scanner, the sparkle of interference faded; the water was still turbid, but no longer full of suspended matter. He could see for a mile—then two—then three.

And in all that space there was no sign of the sharp and brilliant echo that would mark Don's ship. Hope faded as his radius of vision grew and the screen remained empty. Again and again he called into the lonely silence, while grief and helplessness strove for the mastery of his soul.

He exploded the signal grenades that would alert all the hydrophones in the Pacific and send help racing to him by sea and air. But even as he began his slowly descending spiral search, he knew that it was in vain.

Don Burley had lost his last bet.

PART THREE

The Bureaucrat

CHAPTER XVIII

THE GREAT MERCATOR chart that covered the whole of one wall was a most unusual one. All the land areas were completely blank; as far as this map maker was concerned, the continents had never been explored. But the sea was crammed with detail, and scattered over its face were countless spots of coloured light, projected by some mechanism inside the wall. Those spots moved slowly from hour to hour, recording as they did so, for skilled eyes to read, the migration of all the main schools of whales that roamed the seas.

Franklin had seen the master chart scores of times during the last fourteen years—but never from this vantage point. For he was looking at it now from the director's chair.

"There's no need for me to warn you, Walter," said his ex-chief, "that you are taking over the bureau at a very tricky time. Sometime in the next five years we're going to have a showdown with the farms. Unless we can improve our efficiency, plankton-derived proteins will soon be substantially cheaper than any we can deliver.

"And that's only one of our problems. The staff position is getting more difficult every year—and this sort of thing isn't going to help."

He pushed a folder across to Franklin, who smiled wryly when he saw what it contained. The advertisement was familiar enough; it had appeared in all the major magazines during the past week, and must have cost the Space Department a small fortune.

An underwater scene of improbable clarity and colour was spread across two pages. Vast scaly monsters, more huge and hideous than any that had lived on Earth since the Jurassic period, were battling each other in the crystalline depths. Franklin knew, from the photographs he had seen, that they were very accurately painted, and he did not grudge the illustrator his artistic licence in the matter of underwater clarity.

The text was dignified and avoided sensationalism; the painting was sensational enough and needed no embellishment. The Space Department, he read, urgently needed young men as wardens and food production experts for the exploitation of the seas of Venus. The work, it was added, was probably the most exciting and rewarding to be found anywhere in the solar system; pay was good and the qualifications were not as high as those needed for space pilot or astrogator. After the short list of physical and educational requirements, the advertisement ended with the words which the Venus Commission had been plugging for the last six months, and which Franklin had grown heartily tired of seeing: HELP TO BUILD A SECOND EARTH.

"Meanwhile," said the ex-director, "our problem is to keep the first one going, when the bright youngsters who might be joining us are running away to Venus. And between you and me, I shouldn't be surprised if the Space Department has been after some of our men."

"They wouldn't do a thing like that!"

"Wouldn't they now? Anyway, there's a transfer application in from First Warden McRae; if you can't talk him out of it, try to find what made him want to leave."

Life was certainly going to be difficult, Franklin thought. Joe McRae was an old friend; could he impose on that friendship now that he was Joe's boss?

"Another of your little problems is going to be keeping the scientists under control. Lundquist is worse than Roberts ever was; he's got about six crazy schemes going, and at least Roberts only had one brainstorm at a time. He spends half his time over on Heron Island. It might be a good idea to fly over and have a look at him. That was something I never had a chance to get round to."

Franklin was still listening politely as his predecessor continued, with obvious relish, to point out the many disadvantages of his new post. Most of them he already knew, and his mind was now far away. He was thinking how pleasant it would be to begin his directorate with an official visit to Heron Island, which he had not seen for nearly five years, and which had so many memories of his first days in the bureau.

Dr. Lundquist was flattered by the new director's visit, being innocent enough to hope that it might lead to increased support for his activities. He would not have been so enthusiastic had he guessed that the opposite was more likely to be the case. No one could have been more sympathetic than Franklin to scientific research, but now that he had to approve the bills himself he found that his point of view was subtly altered. Whatever Lundquist was doing would have to be of direct value to the bureau. Otherwise it was out—unless the Department of Scientific Research could be talked into taking it over.

Lundquist was a small, intense little man whose rapid and somewhat jerky movements reminded Franklin of a sparrow. He was an enthusiast of a type seldom met these days, and he combined a sound scientific background with an unfettered imagination. How unfettered, Franklin was soon to discover.

Yet at first sight it seemed that most of the work going on at the lab was of a fairly routine nature. Franklin spent a dull half-hour while two young scientists explained the methods they were developing to keep whales free of the many parasites that plagued them, and then escaped by the skin of his teeth from a lecture on cetacean obstetrics. He listened with more interest to the latest work on artificial insemination, having in the past helped with some of the early—and often hilariously unsuccesful—experiments along this line. He sniffed cautiously at some synthetic ambergris, and agreed that it seemed just like the real thing. And he listened to the recorded heartbeat of a whale before and after the cardiac operation that had saved his life, and pretended that he could hear the difference.

Everything here was perfectly in order, and just as he had expected. Then Lunquist steered him out of the lab and down to the big pool, saying as he did so: "I think you'll find this more interesting. It's only in the experimental stage, of course, but it has possibilities."

The scientist looked at his watch and muttered to himself, "Two minutes to go; she's usually in sight by now." He glanced out beyond the reef, then said with satisfaction, "Ah—there she is!"

A long black mound was moving in towards the island, and a moment later Franklin saw the typical stubby spout of vapour which identified the humpback whale. Almost at once he saw a second, much smaller spout, and realised that he was watching a female and her calf. Without hesitation, both animals came in through the narrow channel that had been blasted through the coral years ago so that small boats could come up to the lab. They turned left into a large tidal pool that had been here on Franklin's last visit, and remained there waiting patiently like well-trained dogs.

Two lab technicians, wearing oilskins, were trundling something that looked like a fire extinguisher to the edge of the pool. Lundquist and Franklin hurried to join them, and it was soon obvious why the oilskins were necessary on this bright and cloudless day. Every time the whales spouted there was a miniature rainstorm, and Franklin was glad to borrow protection from the descending and nauseous spray.

Even a warden seldom saw a live whale at such close quarters, and under such ideal conditions. The mother was about fifty feet long, and, like all humpbacks, very massively built. She was no beauty, Franklin decided, and the large, irregular warts along the leading edges of her flippers did nothing to add to her appearance. The little calf was about twenty feet in length, and did not appear to be too happy in its confined quarters, for it was anxiously circling its stolid mother.

One of the scientists gave a curious, high-pitched shout, and at once the whale rolled over on her side, bringing half of her pleated belly out of the water. She did not seem to mind when a large rubber cup was placed over the now-exposed teat; indeed, she was obviously co-operating, for the meter on the collecting tank was recording an astonishing rate of flow.

"You know, of course," explained Lundquist, "that the cows eject their milk under pressure, so that the calves can feed when the teats are submerged without getting water in their mouths. But when the calves are *very* young, the mother rolls over like this so that the baby can feed above water. It makes things a lot simpler for us."

The obedient whale, without any instructions that Franklin could detect, had now circled round in her pen and was rolling over on the other side, so that her second teat could be milked. He looked at the meter; it now registered just under fifty gallons, and was still rising. The calf was obviously getting worried, or perhaps it had become excited by the milk that had accidentally spilled into the water. It made several attempts to bunt its mechanical rival out of the way, and had to be discouraged by a few sharp smacks.

Franklin was impressed, but not surprised. He knew that this was not the first time that whales had been milked, though he did not know that it could now be done with such neatness and dispatch. But where was it leading? Knowing Dr. Lundquist, he could guess.

"Now," said the scientist, obviously hoping that the demonstration had made its desired impact, "we can get at least five hundred pounds of milk a day from a cow without interfering with the calf's growth. And if we start breeding for milk as the farmers have done on land, we should be able to get a ton a day without any trouble. You think that's a lot? I regard it as quite a modest target. After all, prize cattle have given over a hundred pounds of milk a day— and a whale weighs a good deal more than twenty times as much as a cow!"

Franklin did his best to interrupt the statistics.

"That's all very well," he said. "I don't doubt your figures. And equally I don't doubt that you can process the milk to remove that oily taste—yes, I've tried it, thanks. But how the devil are you going to round up all the cows in a herd—especially a herd that migrates ten thousand miles a year?"

"Oh, we've worked all that out. It's partly a matter of training, and we've learned a lot getting Susan here to obey our underwater recordings. Have you ever been to a dairy farm and watched how the cows walk into the autolactor at milking time and walk out again—without a human being coming within miles of the place? And believe me, whales are a lot smarter and more easily trained than cows! I've sketched out the rough designs for a milk tanker that can deal with four whales at once, and could follow the herd as it migrates. In any case, now that we can control the plankton yield we can stop migration if we want to, and keep the whales in the tropics without them getting hungry. The whole thing's quite practical, I assure you."

Despite himself, Franklin was fascinated by the idea. It had been suggested, in some form or other, for many years, but Dr. Lundquist seemed to have been the first to do anything about it.

The mother whale and her still somewhat indignant calf had now set out to sea, and were soon spouting and diving noisily beyond the edge of the reef. As Franklin watched them go, he wondered if in a few years' time he would see hundreds of the great beasts lined up obediently as they swam to the mobile milking plants, each delivering a ton of what was known to be one of the richest foods on earth. But it might remain only a dream; there would be countless practical problems to be faced, and what had been achieved on the laboratory scale with a single animal might prove out of the question in the sea.

"What I'd like you to do," he said to Lundquist, "is to let me have a report showing what an—er—whale dairy would require in terms of equipment and personnel. Try to give costs wherever you can. And then estimate how much milk it could deliver, and what the processing plants would pay for that. Then we'll have something definite to work on. At the moment it's an interesting experiment, but no one can say if it has any practical application."

Lundquist seemed slightly disappointed at Franklin's lack of enthusiasm, but rapidly warmed up again as they walked away from the pool. If Franklin had thought that a little project like setting up a whale dairy had exhausted Lundquist's powers of extrapolation, he was going to learn better.

"The next proposal I want to talk about," began the scientist, "is still entirely in the planning stage. I know that one of our most serious problems is staff shortage, and I've been trying to think of ways in which we can improve efficiency by releasing men from routine jobs."

"Surely that process has gone about as far as it can, short of making everything completely automatic? Anyway, it's less than a year since the last team of efficiency experts went over us." (And, added Franklin to himself, the bureau isn't quite back to normal yet.)

"My approach to the problem," explained Lundquist, "is a little unconventional, and as an ex-warden yourself I think you'll be particularly interested in it. As you know, it normally takes two or even three subs to round up a large school of whales; if a single sub tries it, they'll scatter in all directions. Now this has often seemed to me a shocking waste of manpower and equipment, since all the thinking could be done by a single warden. He only needs his partners to make the right noises in the right places—something a machine could do just as well."

"If you're thinking of automatic slave subs," said Franklin, "it's been tried—and it didn't work. A warden can't handle two ships at once, let alone three."

"I know all about *that* experiment," answered Lundquist. "It could have been a success if they'd tackled it properly. But my idea is much more revolutionary. Tell me—does the name 'sheep dog' mean anything to you?"

Franklin wrinkled his brow. "I think so," he replied. "Weren't they dogs that the old-time shepherds used to protect their flocks, a few hundred years ago?"

"It happened until less than a hundred years ago. And 'protect' is an understatement with a vengeance. I've been looking at film records of sheep dogs in action, and no one who hadn't seen them would believe some of the things they could do. Those dogs were so intelligent and so well-trained that they could make a flock of sheep do anything the shepherd wanted, merely at a word of command from him. They could split a flock into sections, single out one solitary sheep from its fellows, or keep a flock motionless in one spot as long as their master ordered.

"Do you see what I am driving at? We've been training dogs for centuries, so such a performance doesn't seem miraculous to us. What I am suggesting is that we repeat the pattern in the sea. We know that a good many marine mammals—seals and porpoises, for instance—are at least as intelligent as dogs, but except in circuses and places like Marineland there's been no attempt to train them. You've seen the tricks our porpoises here can do, and you know how affectionate and friendly they are. When you've watched these old films of sheep-dog trials, you'll agree that anything a dog could do a hundred years ago we can teach a porpoise to do today."

"Just a minute," said Franklin, a little overwhelmed. "Let me get this straight. Are you proposing that every warden should have a couple of—er—hounds working with him when he rounds up a school of whales?"

"For certain operations, yes. Of course, the technique would have limitations;

no marine animal has the speed and range of a sub, and the hounds, as you've called them, couldn't always get to the places where they were needed. But I've done some studies and I think it would be possible to double the effectiveness of our wardens in this way, by eliminating the times when they had to work in pairs or trios."

"But," protested Franklin, "what notice would whales take of porpoises? They'd ignore them completely."

"Oh, I wasn't suggesting that we should use porpoises; that was merely an example. You're quite right—the whales wouldn't even notice them. We'll have to use an animal that's fairly large, at least as intelligent as the porpoise, and which whales will pay a great deal of attention to indeed. There's only one animal that fills the bill, and I'd like your authority to catch one and train it."

"Go on," said Franklin, with such a note of resignation in his voice that even Lundquist, who had little sense of humour, was forced to smile.

"What I want to do," he continued, "is to catch a couple of killer whales and train them to work with one of our wardens."

Franklin thought of the thirty-foot torpedoes of ravening power he had so often chased and slaughtered in the frozen polar seas. It was hard to picture one of these ferocious beasts tamed to man's bidding; then he remembered the chasm between the sheep dog and the wolf, and how that had long ago been bridged. Yes, it could be done again—if it was worthwhile.

When in doubt, ask for a report, one of his superiors had once told him. Well, he was going to bring back at least two from Heron Island, and they would both make very thought-provoking reading. But Lundquist's schemes, exciting though they were, belonged to the future; Franklin had to run the bureau as it was here and now. He would prefer to avoid drastic changes for a few years, until he had learned his way about. Besides, even if Lundquist's ideas could be proved practical, it would be a long, stiff battle selling them to the people who approved the funds. "I want to buy fifty milking machines for whales, please." Yes, Franklin could picture the reaction in certain conservative quarters. And as for training killer whales—why, they would think he had gone completely crazy.

He watched the island fall away as the plane lifted him towards home (strange, after all his travels, that he should be living again in the country of his birth). It was almost fifteen years since he had first made this journey with poor old Don; how glad Don would have been, could he have seen this final fruit of his careful training! And Professor Stevens, too—Franklin had always been a little scared of him, but now he could have looked him in the face, had he still been alive. With a twinge of remorse, he realised that he had never properly thanked the psychologist for all that he had done.

Fifteen years from a neurotic trainee to director of the bureau; that wasn't bad going. And what now, Walter? Franklin asked himself. He felt no need of any further achievement; perhaps his ambition was now satisfied. He would be quite content to guide the bureau into a placid and uneventful future.

It was lucky for his peace of mind that he had no idea how futile that hope was going to be.

CHAPTER XIX

THE PHOTOGRAPHER HAD finished, but the young man who had been Franklin's shadow for the last two days still seemed to have an unlimited supply of notebooks and questions. Was it worth all this trouble to have your undistinguished features—probably superimposed on a montage of whales—displayed upon every bookstand in the world? Franklin doubted it, but he had no choice in the matter. He remembered the saying: "Public servants have no private lives." Like all aphorisms, it was only half true. No one had ever heard of the last director of the bureau, and he might have led an equally inconspicuous existence if the Marine Division's Public Relations Department had not decreed otherwise.

"Quite a number of your people, Mr. Franklin," said the young man from *Earth Magazine*, "have told me about your interest in the so-called Great Sea Serpent, and the mission in which First Warden Burley was killed. Have there been any further developments in this field?"

Franklin sighed; he had been afraid that this would come up sooner or later, and he hoped that it wouldn't be overplayed in the resulting article. He walked over to his private file cabinet, and pulled out a thick folder of notes and photographs.

"Here are all the sightings, Bob," he said. "You might like to have a glance through them—I've kept the record up to date. One day I hope we'll have the answer; you can say it's still a hobby of mine, but it's one I've had no chance of doing anything about for the last eight years. It's up to the Department of Scientific Research now—not the Bureau of Whales. We've other jobs to do."

He could have added a good deal more, but decided against it. If Secretary Farlan had not been transferred from D.S.R. soon after the tragic failure of their mission, they might have had a second chance. But in the inquiries and recriminations that had followed the disaster, the opportunity had been lost, possibly for years. Perhaps in every man's life there must be some cherished failure, some unfinished business which outweighed many successes.

"Then there's only one other question I want to ask," continued the reporter. "What about the future of the bureau? Have you any interesting long-term plans you'd care to talk about?"

This was another tricky one. Franklin had learned long ago that men in his position must co-operate with the press, and in the last two days his busy interrogator had practically become one of the family. But there were some things that sounded a little too far-fetched, and he had contrived to keep Dr. Lundquist out of the way when Bob had flown over to Heron Island. True, he had seen the prototype milking machine and been duly impressed by it, but he had been told nothing about the two young killer whales being maintained, at great trouble and expense, in the enclosure off the eastern edge of the reef.

"Well, Bob," he began slowly, "by this time you probably know the statistics better than I do. We hope to increase the size of our herds by ten per cent over the next five years. If this milking scheme comes off—and it's still purely experimental—we'll start putting back on the sperm whales and will build up the humpbacks. At the moment we are providing twelve and a half per cent of the total food requirements of the human race, and that's quite a responsibility. I hope to see it fifteen per cent while I'm still in office."

"So that everyone in the world will have whale steak at least once a week, eh?"

"Put it that way if you like. But people are eating whale all day without knowing it—every time they use cooking fat or spread margarine on a piece of bread. We could double our output and we'd get no credit for it, since our products are almost always disguised in something else."

"The Art Department is going to put that right; when the story appears, we'll have a picture of the average household's groceries for a week, with a clock face on each item showing what percentage of it comes from whales."

"That'll be fine. Er—by the way—have you decided what you're going to call me?"

The reporter grinned.

"That's up to my editor," he answered. "But I'll tell him to avoid the word 'whaleboy' like the plague. It's too hackneyed, anyway."

"Well, I'll believe you when we see the article. Every journalist promises he won't call us that, but it seems they can never resist the temptation. Incidentally, when do you expect the story to appear?"

"Unless some news story crowds it off, in about four weeks. You'll get the proofs, of course, before that—probably by the end of next week."

Franklin saw him off through the outer office, half sorry to lose an entertaining companion who, even if he asked awkward questions, more than made up for it by the stories he could tell about most of the famous men on the planet. Now, he supposed, he belonged to that group himself, for at least a hundred million people would read the current "Men of *Earth*" series.

The story appeared, as promised, four weeks later. It was accurate, well written, and contained one mistake so trivial that Franklin himself had failed to notice it when he checked the proofs. The photographic coverage was excellent and contained an astonishing study of a baby whale suckling its mother—a shot obviously obtained at enormous risk and after months of patient stalking. The fact that it was actually taken in the pool at Heron Island without the photographer even getting his feet wet was an irrelevance not allowed to distract the reader.

Apart from the shocking pun beneath the cover picture ("Prince of Whales", indeed!), Franklin was delighted with it; so was everyone else in the bureau, the Marine Division, and even the World Food Organisation itself. No one could have guessed that within a few weeks it was to involve the Bureau of Whales in the greatest crisis of its entire history.

It was not lack of foresight; sometimes the future can be charted in advance, and plans made to meet it. But there are also times in human affairs when events that seem to have no possible connection—to be as remote as if they occurred on different planets—may react upon each other with shattering violence.

The Bureau of Whales was an organisation which had taken half a century to build up, and which now employed twenty thousand men and possessed equipment valued at over two billion dollars. It was a typical unit of the scientific world state, with all the power and prestige which that implied.

And now it was to be shaken to its foundations by the gentle words of a man who had lived half a thousand years before the birth of Christ.

Franklin was in London when the first hint of trouble came. It was not unusual for officers of the World Food Organisation to bypass his immediate superiors in the Marine Division and to contact him directly. What was unusual, however, was for the secretary of the W.F.O. himself to interfere with the everyday working of the bureau, causing Franklin to cancel all his engagements and to find himself, still a little dazed, flying halfway around the world to a small town in Ceylon of which he had never heard before and whose name he could not even pronounce.

Fortunately, it had been a hot summer in London and the extra ten degrees at Colombo was not unduly oppressive. Franklin was met at the airport by the local W.F.O. representative, looking very cool and comfortable in the sarong which had now been adopted by even the most conservative of westerners. He shook hands with the usual array of minor officials, was relieved to see that there were no reporters around who might tell him more about this mission than he knew himself, and swiftly transferred to the cross-country plane which would take him on the last hundred miles of his journey.

"Now," he said, when he had recovered his breath and the miles of neatly laid-out automatic tea plantations were flashing past beneath him, "you'd better start briefing me. Why is it so important to rush me to Anna—whatever you call the place?"

"Anuradhapura. Hasn't the secretary told you?"

"We had just five minutes at London Airport. So you might as well start from scratch."

"Well, this is something that has been building up for several years. We've warned Headquarters, but they've never taken us seriously. Now your interview in *Earth* has brought matters to a head; the Mahanayake Thero of Anuradhapura—he's the most influential man in the East, and you're going to hear a lot more about him—read it and promptly asked us to grant him facilities for a tour of the bureau. We can't refuse, of course, but we know perfectly well what he intends to do. He'll take a team of cameramen with him and will collect enough material to launch an all-out propaganda campaign against the bureau. Then, when it's had time to sink in, he'll demand a referendum. And if that goes against us, we *will* be in trouble."

The pieces of the jigsaw fell into place; the pattern was at last clear. For a moment Franklin felt annoyed that he had been diverted across the world to deal with so absurd a challenge. Then he realised that the men who had sent him here did not consider it absurd; they must know, better than he did, the strength of the forces that were being marshalled. It was never wise to underestimate the power of religion, even a religion as pacific and tolerant as Buddhism.

The position was one which, even a hundred years ago, would have seemed unthinkable, but the catastrophic political and social changes of the last century had all combined to give it a certain inevitability. With the failure or weakening of its three great rivals, Buddhism was now the only religion that still possessed any real power over the minds of men.

Christianity, which had never fully recovered from the shattering blow given it by Darwin and Freud, had finally unexpectedly succumbed before the archaeological discoveries of the late twentieth century. The Hindu religion, with its fantastic pantheon of gods and goddesses, had failed to survive in an age of scientific rationalism. And the Mohammedan faith, weakened by the same forces, had suffered additional loss of prestige when the rising Star of David had outshone the pale crescent of the Prophet.

These beliefs still survived, and would linger on for generations yet, but all their power was gone. Only the teachings of the Buddha had maintained and even increased their influence, as they filled the vacuum left by the other faiths. Being a philosophy and not a religion, and relying on no revelations vulnerable to the archaeologist's hammer, Buddhism had been largely unaffected by the shocks that had destroyed the other giants. It had been purged and purified by internal reformations, but its basic structure was unchanged.

One of the fundamentals of Buddhism, as Franklin knew well enough, was respect for all other living creatures. It was a law that few Buddhists had ever obeyed to the letter, excusing themselves with the sophistry that it was quite in order to eat the flesh of an animal that somone else had killed. In recent years, however, attempts had been made to enforce this rule more rigorously, and there had been endless debates between vegetarians and meat eaters covering the whole spectrum of crankiness. That these arguments could have any practical effect on the work of the World Food Organisation was something that Franklin had never seriously considered.

"Tell me," he asked, as the fertile hills rolled swiftly past beneath him, "what sort of man is this Thero you're taking me to see?"

"Thero is his title; you can translate it by archbishop if you like. His real name is Alexander Boyce, and he was born in Scotland sixty years ago."

"Scotland?"

"Yes—he was the first westerner ever to reach the top of the Buddhist hierarchy, and he had to overcome a lot of opposition to do it. A bhikku—er, monk —friend of mine once complained that the Maha Thero was a typical elder of the kirk, born a few hundred years too late—so he'd reformed Buddhism instead of the Church of Scotland."

"How did he get to Ceylon in the first place?"

"Believe it or not, he came out as a junior technician in a film company. He was about twenty then. The story is that he went to film the statue of the Dying

Buddha at the cave temple of Dambulla, and became converted. After that it took him twenty years to rise to the top, and he's been responsible for most of the reforms that have taken place since then. Religions get corrupt after a couple of thousand years and need a spring-cleaning. The Maha Thero did that job for Buddhism in Ceylon by getting rid of the Hindu gods that had crept into the temples."

"And now he's looking around for fresh worlds to conquer?"

"It rather seems like it. He pretends to have nothing to do with politics, but he's thrown out a couple of governments just by raising his finger, and he's got a huge following in the East. His 'Voice of Buddha' programmes are listened to by several hundred million people, and it's estimated that at least a billion are sympathetic towards him even if they won't go all the way with his views. So you'll understand why we are taking this seriously."

Now that he had penetrated the disguise of an unfamiliar name, Franklin remembered that the Venerable Alexander Boyce had been the subject of a cover story in *Earth Magazine* two or three years ago. So they had something in common; he wished now that he had read that article, but at the time it had been of no interest to him and he could not even recall the Thero's appearance.

"He's a deceptively quiet little man, very easy to get on with," was the reply to his question. "You'll find him reasonable and friendly, but once he's made up his mind he grinds through all opposition like a glacier. He's not a fanatic, if that's what you are thinking. If you can prove to him that any course of action is essential, he won't stand in the way even though he may not like what you're doing. He's not happy about our local drive for increased meat production, but he realises that everybody can't be a vegetarian. We compromised with him by not building our new slaughterhouse in either of the sacred cities, as we'd intended to do originally."

"Then why should he suddenly have taken an interest in the Bureau of Whales?"

"He's probably decided to make a stand somewhere. And besides—don't you think whales are in a different class from other animals?" The remark was made half apologetically, as if in the expectation of denial or even ridicule.

Franklin did not answer; it was a question he had been trying to decide for twenty years, and the scene now passing below absolved him from the necessity.

He was flying over what had once been the greatest city in the world—a city against which Rome and Athens in their prime had been no more than villages —a city unchallenged in size of population until the heydays of London and New York, two thousand years later. A ring of huge artificial lakes, some of them miles across, surrounded the ancient home of the Singhalese kings. Even from the air, the modern town of Anuradhapura showed startling contrasts of old and new. Dotted here and there among the colourful, gossamer buildings of the twenty-first century were the immense, bell-shaped domes of the great dagobas. The mightiest of all—the Abhayagiri Dagoba—was pointed out to Franklin as the plane flew low over it. The brickwork of the dome had long ago been overgrown with grass and even small trees, so that the great temple now appeared no more than a curiously symmetrical hill surmounted by a broken spire. It was a hill exceeded in size by one only of the pyramids that the Pharaohs had built beside the Nile.

By the time that Franklin had reached the local Food Production office, conferred with the superintendent, donated a few platitudes to a reporter who had somehow discovered his presence, and eaten a leisurely meal, he felt that he knew how to handle the situation. It was, after all, merely another public relations problem; there had been a very similar one about three weeks ago, when a sensational and quite inaccurate newspaper story about methods of whale slaughtering had brought a dozen Societies for the Prevention of Cruelty down upon his head. A fact-finding commission had disposed of the charges very quickly, and no permanent damage had been done to anybody except the reporter concerned.

He did not feel quite so confident, a few hours later, as he stood looking up at the soaring, gilded spire of the Ruanveliseya Dagoba. The immense white dome had been so skilfully restored that it seemed inconceivable that almost twenty-two centuries had passed since its foundations were laid. Completely surrounding the paved courtyard of the temple was a line of life-sized elephants, forming a wall more than a quarter of a mile long. Art and faith had united here to produce one of the world's masterpieces of architecture, and the sense of antiquity was overwhelming. How many of the creations of modern man, wondered Franklin, would be so perfectly preserved in the year 4000?

The great flagstones in the courtyard were burning hot, and he was glad that he had retained his stockings when he left his shoes at the gate. At the base of the dome, which rose like a shining mountain towards the cloudless blue sky, was a single-storied modern building whose clean lines and white plastic walls harmonised well with the work of architects who had died a hundred years before the beginning of the Christian era.

A saffron-robed bhikku led Franklin into the Thero's neat and comfortably air-conditioned office. It might have been that of any busy administrator, anywhere in the world, and the sense of strangeness, which had made him ill at ease ever since he had entered the courtyard of the temple, began to fade.

The Maha Thero rose to greet him; he was a small man, his head barely reaching the level of Franklin's shoulders. His gleaming, shaven scalp somehow depersonalised him, making it hard to judge what he was thinking and harder still to fit him into any familiar categories. At first sight, Franklin was not impressed; then he remembered how many small men had been movers and shakers of the world.

Even after forty years, the Mahanayake Thero had not lost the accent of his birth. At first it seemed incongruous, if not slightly comic, in these surroundings, but within a few minutes Franklin was completely unaware of it.

"It's very good of you to come all this way to see me, Mr. Franklin," said the Thero affably as he shook hands. "I must admit that I hardly expected my request to be dealt with quite so promptly. It hasn't inconvenienced you, I trust?"

"No," replied Franklin manfully. "In fact," he added with rather more truth, "this visit is a novel experience, and I'm grateful for the opportunity of making it."

"Excellent!" said the Thero, apparently with genuine pleasure. "I feel just the same way about my trip down to your South Georgia base, though I don't suppose I'll enjoy the weather there."

Franklin remembered his instructions—"Head him off if you possibly can, but don't try to put any fast ones across on him." Well, he had been given an opening here.

"That's one point I wanted to raise with you, Your Reverence," he answered, hoping he had chosen the correct honorific. "It's midwinter in South Georgia, and the base is virtually closed down until the late spring. It won't be operating again for about five months."

"How foolish of me—I should have remembered. But I've never been to the Antarctic and I've always wanted to; I suppose I was trying to give myself an excuse. Well—it will have to be one of the northern bases. Which do you suggest—Greenland or Iceland? Just tell me which is more convenient. We don't want to cause any trouble."

It was that last phrase which defeated Franklin before the battle had fairly begun. He knew now that he was dealing with an adversary who could be neither fooled nor deflected from his course. He would simply have to go along with the Thero, dragging his heels as hard as he could, and hoping for the best.

CHAPTER XX

THE WIDE BAY was dotted with feathery plumes of mist as the great herd milled around in uncertain circles, not alarmed by the voices that had called it to this spot between the mountains, but merely undecided as to their meaning. All their lives the whales had obeyed the orders that came, sometimes in the form of water-borne vibrations, sometimes in electric shocks, from the small creatures whom they recognised as masters. Those orders, they had come to learn, had never harmed them; often, indeed, they had led them to fertile pastures which they would never have found unaided, for they were in regions of the sea which all their experience and the memories of a million years told them should be barren. And sometimes the small masters had protected them from the killers, turning aside the ravening packs before they could tear their living victims into fragments.

They had no enemies and no fears. For generations now they had roamed the peaceful oceans of the world, growing fatter and sleeker and more contented than all their ancestors back to the beginning of time. In fifty years they had grown, on average, ten per cent longer and thirty per cent heavier, thanks to the careful stewardship of the masters. Even now the lord of all their race, the hundred-and-fifty-one-foot blue whale B.69322, universally known as Leviathan, was sporting in the Gulf Stream with his mate and newborn calf. Leviathan could never have reached his present size in any earlier age; though such matters were beyond proof, he was probably the largest animal that had ever existed in the entire history of Earth.

Order was emerging out of chaos as the directing fields started to guide the herd along invisible channels. Presently the electric barriers gave way to concrete ones; the whales were swimming along four parallel canals, too narrow for more than one to pass at a time. Automatic senses weighed and measured them, rejecting all those below a certain size and diverting them back into the sea—doubtless a little puzzled, and quite unaware how seriously their numbers had been depleted.

The whales that had passed the test swam on trustfully along the two remaining channels until presently they came to a large lagoon. Some tasks could not be left entirely to machines; there were human inspectors here to see that no mistakes had been made, to check the condition of the animals, and to log the numbers of the doomed beasts as they left the lagoon on their last, short swim into the killing pens.

"B.52111 coming up," said Franklin to the Thero as they stood together in the observation chamber. "Seventy-foot female, known to have had five calves —past the best age for breeding." Behind him, he knew the cameras were silently recording the scene as their ivory-skulled, saffron-robed operators handled them with a professional skill which had surprised him until he learned that they had all been trained in Hollywood.

The whale never had any warning; it probably never even felt the gentle touch of the flexible copper fingers as they brushed its body. One moment it was swimming quietly along the pen; a second later it was a lifeless hulk, continuing to move forward under its own momentum. The fifty-thousand-ampere current, passing through the heart like a stroke of lightning, had not even allowed time for a final convulsion.

At the end of the killing pen, the wide conveyor belt took the weight of the immense body and carried it up a short slope until it was completely clear of the water. Then it began to move slowly forward along an endless series of spinning rollers which seemed to stretch halfway to the horizon.

'This is the longest conveyor of its kind in the world," Franklin explained with justifiable pride. "It may have as many as ten whales—say a thousand tons—on it at one time. Although it involves us in considerable expense, and greatly restricts our choice of site, we always have the processing plant at least half a mile from the pens, so there is no danger of the whales being frightened by the smell of blood. I think you'll agree that not only is the slaughtering instantaneous but the animals show no alarm whatsoever right up to the end."

"Perfectly true," said the Thero. "It all seems very humane. Still, if the whales did get frightened it would be very difficult to handle them, wouldn't it? I wonder if you would go to all this trouble merely to spare their feelings?"

It was a shrewd question, and like a good many he had been asked in the last few days Franklin was not quite sure how to answer it.

"I suppose," he said slowly, "that would depend on whether we could get the money. It would be up to the World Assembly, in the final analysis. The finance committees would have to decide how kind we could afford to be. It's a theoretical question, anyway."

"Of course—but other questions aren't so theoretical," answered the Venerable Boyce, looking thoughtfully at the eighty tons of flesh and bone moving away into the distance. "Shall we get back to the car? I want to see what happens at the other end."

And I, thought Franklin grimly, will be very interested to see how you and your colleagues take it. Most visitors who went through the processing yards emerged rather pale and shaken, and quite a few had been known to faint. It was a standard joke in the bureau that this lesson in food production removed the appetites of all who watched it for several hours after the experience.

The stench hit them while they were still a hundred yards away. Out of the corner of his eye, Franklin could see that the young bhikku carrying the sound recorder was already showing signs of distress, but the Maha Thero seemed completely unaffected. He was still calm and dispassionate five minutes later as he stared down into the reeking inferno where the great carcasses were torn asunder into mountains of meat and bone and guts.

"Just think of it," said Franklin, "for almost two hundred years this job was done by men, often working on board a pitching deck in filthy weather. It's not pretty to watch even now, but can you imagine being down there hacking away with a knife nearly as big as yourself?"

"I think I could," answered the Thero, "but I'd prefer not to." He turned to his cameramen and gave some brief instructions, then watched intently as the next whale arrived on the conveyor belt.

The great body had already been scanned by photo-electric eyes and its dimensions fed in the computer controlling the operations. Even when one knew how it was done, it was uncanny to watch the precision with which the knives and saws moved out on their extensible arms, made their carefully planned pattern of cuts, and then retreated again. Huge grabs seized the foot-thick blanket of blubber and stripped it off as a man peels a banana, leaving the naked, bleeding carcass to move on along the conveyor to the first stage of its dismemberment.

The whale travelled as fast as a man could comfortably walk, and disintegrated before the eyes of the watchers as they kept pace with it. Slabs of meat as large as elephants were torn away and went sliding down side chutes; circular saws whirred through the scaffolding of ribs in a cloud of bone dust; the interlinked plastic bags of the intestines, stuffed with perhaps a ton of shrimps and plankton from the whale's last meal, were dragged away in noisome heaps.

It had taken less than two minutes to reduce a lord of the sea to a bloody shambles which no one but an expert could have recognised. Not even the bones were wasted; at the end of the conveyor belt, the disarticulated skeleton fell into a pit where it would be ground into fertiliser.

"This is the end of the line," said Franklin, "but as far as the processing side is concerned it's only the beginning. The oil has to be extracted from the blubber you saw peeled off in stage one; the meat has to be cut down into more manageable portions and sterilised—we use a high-intensity neutron source for that—and about ten other basic products have to be sorted out and packed for shipment. I'll be glad to show you around any part of the factory you'd like to see. It won't be quite so gruesome as the operations we've just been watching."

The Thero stood for a moment in thoughtful silence, studying the notes he had been making in his incredibly tiny handwriting. Then he looked back along the blood-stained quarter-mile of moving belt, towards the next whale arriving from the killing pen.

"There's one sequence I'm not sure we managed to film properly," he said, coming to a sudden decision. "If you don't mind, I'd like to go back to the beginning and start again."

Franklin caught the recorder as the young monk dropped it, "Never mind, son," he said reassuringly, "the first time is always the worst. When you've been here a few days, you'll be quite puzzled when newcomers complain of the stink."

That was hard to believe, but the permanent staff had assured him that it was perfectly true. He only hoped that the Venerable Boyce was not so thoroughgoing that he would have a chance of putting it to the proof.

"And now, Your Reverence," said Franklin, as the plane lifted above the snow-covered mountains and began the homeward flight to London and Ceylon, "do you mind if I ask how you intend to use all the material you've gathered?'

During the two days they had been together, priest and administrator had established a degree of friendship and mutual respect that Franklin, for his part, still found as surprising as it was pleasant. He considered—as who does not?—that he was good at summing men up, but there were depths in the Mahanayake Thero beyond his powers of analysis. It did not matter; he now knew instinctively that he was in the presence not only of power but also of— there was no escaping from that trite and jejune word—goodness. He had even begun to wonder, with a mounting awe that at any moment might deepen into certainty, if the man who was now his companion would go down into history as a saint.

"I have nothing to hide," said the Thero gently, "and as you know, deceit is contrary to the teachings of the Buddha. Our position is quite simple. We believe that all creatures have a right to life, and it therefore follows that what you are doing is wrong. Accordingly, we would like to see it stopped."

That was what Franklin had expected, but it was the first time he had obtained a definite statement. He felt a slight sense of disappointment; surely someone as intelligent as the Thero must realise that such a move was totally impracticable, since it would involve cutting off one-eighth of the total food supply of the world. And for that matter, why stop at whales? What about cows, sheep, pigs—all the animals that man kept in luxury and then slaughtered at his convenience?

"I know what you are thinking," said the Thero, before he could voice his objections. "We are fully aware of the problems involved, and realise that it will be necessary to move slowly. But a start must be made somewhere, and the Bureau of Whales gives us the most dramatic presentation of our case."

"Thank you," answered Franklin dryly. "But is that altogether fair? What you've seen here happens in every slaughterhouse on the planet. The fact that the scale of operations is different hardly alters the case."

"I quite agree. But we are practical men, not fanatics. We know perfectly well that alternative food sources will have to be found before the world's meat supplies can be cut off."

Franklin shook his head in vigorous disagreement.

"I'm sorry," he said, "but even if you could solve the supply problem, you're not going to turn the entire population of the planet into vegetarians—unless you are anxious to encourage emigration to Mars and Venus. I'd shoot myself if I thought I could never eat a lamb chop or a well-done steak again. So your plans are bound to fail on two counts: human psychology and the sheer facts of food production."

The Maha Thero looked a little hurt.

"My dear Director," he said, "surely you don't think we would overlook something as obvious as that? But let me finish putting our point of view before I explain how we propose to implement it. I'll be interested in studying your reactions, because you represent the maximum—ah—consumer resistance we are likely to meet."

"Very well," smiled Franklin. "See if you can convert me out of my job."

"Since the beginning of history," said the Thero, "man has assumed that the other animals exist only for his benefit. He has wiped out whole species, sometimes through sheer greed, sometimes because they destroyed his crops or interfered with his other activities. I won't deny that he often had justification, and frequently no alternative. But down the ages man has blackened his soul with his crimes against the animal kingdom—some of the very worst, incidentally, being in your particular profession, only sixty or seventy years ago. I've read of cases where harpooned whales died after hours of such frightful torment that not a scrap of their meat could be used—it was poisoned with the toxins produced by the animal's death agonies."

"Very exceptional," interjected Franklin. "And anyway we've put a stop to that."

"True, but it's all part of the debt we have to discharge."

"Svend Foyn wouldn't have agreed with you. When he invented the explosive harpoon, back in the 1870s, he made an entry in his diary thanking God for having done all the work."

"An interesting point of view," answered the Thero dryly. "I wish I'd had a chance of arguing it with him. You know, there is a simple test which divides the human race into two classes. If a man is walking along the street and sees a beetle crawling just where he is going to place his foot—well, he can break his stride and miss it or he can crush it into pulp. Which would *you* do, Mr. Franklin?"

"It would depend on the beetle. If I knew it was poisonous, or a pest, I'd kill it. Otherwise I'd let it go. That, surely, is what any reasonable man would do."

"Then we are not reasonable. We believe that killing is only justified to save the life of a higher creature—and it is surprising how seldom that situation arises. But let me get back to my argument; we seem to have lost our way.

"About a hundred years ago an Irish poet named Lord Dunsany wrote a play called *The Use of Man*, which you'll be seeing on one of our TV programmes before long. In it a man dreams that he's magically transported out of the solar system to appear before a tribunal of animals—and if he cannot find two to speak on his behalf, the human race is doomed. Only the dog will come forward to fawn over his master; all the others remember their old grievances and maintain that they would have been better off if man had never existed. The sentence of annihilation is about to be pronounced when another sponsor arrives in the nick of time, and humanity is saved. The only creature who has any use for man is—the mosquito.

"Now you may think that this is merely an amusing jest; so, I am sure, did Dunsany—who happened to be a keen hunter. But poets often speak hidden truth of which they themselves are unaware, and I believe that this almost forgotten play contains an allegory of profound importance to the human race.

"Within a century or so, Franklin, we will literally be going outside the solar system. Sooner or later we will meet types of intelligent life much higher than our own, yet in forms completely alien. And when that time comes, the treatment man receives from his superiors may well depend upon the way he has behaved towards other creatures of his own world."

The words were spoken so quietly, yet with such conviction, that they struck a sudden chill into Franklin's soul. For the first time he felt that there might be something in the other's point of view—something, that is, besides mere humanitarianism. (But could humanitarianism ever be "mere"?) He had never liked the final climax of his work, for he had long ago developed a great affection for his monstrous charges, but he had always regarded it as a regrettable necessity.

"I grant that your points are well made," he admitted, "but whether we like them or not, we have to accept the realities of life. I don't know who coined the phrase 'Nature red in tooth and claw', but that's the way she is. And if the world has to choose between food and ethics, I know which will win."

The Thero gave that secret, gentle smile which, consciously or otherwise, seemed to echo the benign gaze that so many generations of artists had made the hallmark of the Buddha.

"But that is just the point, my dear Franklin," he answered. "There is no longer any need for a choice. Ours is the first generation in the world's history that can break the ancient cycle, and eat what it pleases without spilling the blood of innocent creatures. I am sincerely grateful to you for helping to show me how."

"Me!" exploded Franklin.

"Exactly," said the Thero, the extent of his smile now far exceeding the canons of Buddhist art. "And now, if you will excuse me, I think I'll go to sleep."

CHAPTER XXI

"So this," grumbled Franklin, "is my reward for twenty years of devoted public service—to be regarded even by my own family as a blood-stained butcher."

"But all that was true, wasn't it?" said Anne, pointing to the TV screen, which a few seconds ago had been dripping with gore.

"Of course it was. But it was also very cleverly edited propaganda. I could make out just as good a case for our side."

"Are you sure of that?" asked Indra. "The division will certainly want you to, but it may not be easy."

Franklin snorted indignantly.

"Why, those statistics are all nonsense! The very idea of switching our entire herds to milking instead of slaughtering is just crazy. If we converted all our resources to whalemilk production we couldn't make up a quarter of the loss of fats and protein involved in closing down the processing plants."

"Now, Walter," said Indra placidly, "there's no need to break a blood vessel trying to keep calm. What's really upset you is the suggestion that the plankton farms should be extended to make up the deficit."

"Well, you're the biologist. Is it practical to turn that pea soup into prime ribs of beef or T-bone steaks?"

"It's obviously *possible*. It was a very clever move, having the chef of the Waldorf tasting both the genuine and the synthetic product, and being unable to tell the difference. There's no doubt you're going to have a lovely fight on your hands—the farm people will jump right in on the Thero's side of the fence, and the whole Marine Division will be split wide open."

"He probably planned that," said Franklin with reluctant admiration. "He's diabolically well-informed. I wish now I hadn't said so much about the possibilities of milk production during that interview—and they did overplay it a bit in the final article. I'm sure that's what started the whole business."

"That's another thing I was going to mention. Where did he get the figures on which he based his statistics? As far as I know, they have never been published anywhere outside the bureau."

"You're right," conceded Franklin. "I should have thought of that before.

First thing tomorrow morning I'm going out to Heron Island to have a little talk with Dr. Lundquist."

"Will you take me, Daddy?" pleaded Anne.

"Not this time, young lady. I wouldn't like an innocent daughter of mine to hear some of the things I may have to say."

"Dr. Lundquist is out in the lagoon, sir," said the chief lab assistant. "There's no way of contacting him until he decides to come up."

"Oh, isn't there? I could go down and tap him on the shoulder."

"I don't think that would be at all wise, sir. Attila and Genghis Khan aren't very fond of strangers."

"Good God—is he swimming with *them*!"

"Oh yes—they're quite fond of him, and they've got very friendly with the wardens who work with them. But anyone else might be eaten rather quickly."

Quite a lot seemed to be going on, thought Franklin, that he knew very little about. He decided to walk to the lagoon; unless it was extremely hot, or one had something to carry, it was never worth while to take a car for such short distances.

He had changed his mind by the time he reached the new eastern jetty. Either Heron Island was getting bigger or he was beginning to feel his years. He sat down on the keel of an upturned dinghy, and looked out to sea. The tide was in, but the sharp dividing line marking the edge of the reef was clearly visible, and in the fenced-off enclosure the spouts of two killer whales appeared as intermittent plumes of mist. There was a small boat out there, with somebody in it, but it was too far away for him to tell whether it was Dr. Lundquist or one of his assistants.

He waited for a few minutes, then telephoned for a boat to carry him out to the reef. In slightly more time than it would have taken him to swim there, he arrived at the enclosure and had his first good look at Attila and Genghis Khan.

The two killer whales were a little under thirty feet long, and as his boat approached them they simultaneously reared out of the water and stared at him with their huge, intelligent eyes. The unusual attitude, and the pure white of the bodies now presented to him, gave Franklin the uncanny impression that he was face to face not with animals but with beings who might be higher in the order of creation than himself. He knew that the truth was far otherwise, and reminded himself that he was looking at the most ruthless killer in the sea.

No, that was not quite correct. The *second* most ruthless killer in the sea. . . .

The whales dropped back into the water, apparently satisfied with their scrutiny. It was then that Franklin made out Lundquist, working about thirty feet down with a small torpedo loaded with instruments. Probably the commotion had disturbed him, because he came quickly to the surface and lay treading water, with his face mask pushed back, as he recognised his visitor.

"Good morning, Mr. Franklin. I wasn't expecting you today. What do you think of my pupils?"

"Very impressive. How well are they learning their lessons?"

"There's no doubt about it—they're brilliant. Even cleverer than porpoises, and surprisingly affectionate when they get to know you. I can teach them to do anything now. If I wanted to commit the perfect murder, I could tell them that you were a seal on an ice floe, and they'd have the boat over in two seconds."

"In that case, I'd prefer to continue our conversation back on land. Have you finished whatever you're doing?"

"It's never finished, but that doesn't matter. I'll ride the torp back—no need to lift all this gear into the boat."

The scientist swung his tiny metal fish around towards the island, and promptly set off at a speed which the dinghy could not hope to match. At once the two killers streaked after him, their huge dorsal fins leaving a creamy wake in the water. It seemed a dangerous game of tag to play, but before Franklin could discover what would happen when the killers caught the torpedo, Lundquist had crossed the shallow but clearly marked mesh around the enclosure, and the two whales broke their rush in a flurry of spray.

Franklin was very thoughtful on the way back to land. He had known Lundquist for years, but now he felt that this was the first time he had ever really seen him. There had never been any doubt concerning his originality—indeed, his brilliance—but he also appeared to possess unsuspected courage and initiative. None of which, Franklin determined grimly, would help him unless he had a satisfactory answer to certain questions.

Dressed in his everyday clothes, and back in the familiar laboratory surroundings, Lundquist was the man Franklin had always known. "Now, John," he began, "I suppose you've seen this television propaganda against the bureau?"

"Of course. But is it *against* us?"

"It's certainly against our main activity, but we won't argue that point. What I want to know is this: Have you been in touch with the Maha Thero?"

"Oh yes. He contacted me immediately after that article appeared in *Earth Magazine.*"

"And you passed on confidential information to him?"

Lundquist looked sincerely hurt.

"I resent that, Mr. Franklin. The only information I gave him was an advance proof of my paper on whalemilk production, which comes out in the *Cetological Review* next month. You approved it for publication yourself."

The accusations that Franklin was going to make collapsed around his ears, and he felt suddenly rather ashamed of himself.

"I'm sorry, John," he said. "I take that back. All this has made me a bit jumpy, and I just want to sort out the facts before HQ starts chasing me. But don't you think you should have told me about this inquiry?"

"Frankly, I don't see why. We get all sorts of queries every day, and I saw no reason to suppose that this was not just another routine one. Of course, I was pleased that somebody was taking a particular interest in my special project, and I gave them all the help I could."

"Very well," said Franklin resignedly. "Let's forget the post-mortem. But answer for me this question: As a scientist, do you really believe that we can afford to stop whale slaughtering and switch over to milk and synthetics?"

"Given ten years, we can do it if we have to. There's no technical objection that I can see. Of course I can't guarantee the figures on the plankton-farming side, but you can bet your life that the Thero had accurate sources of information there as well."

"But you realise what this will mean! If it starts with whales, sooner or later it will go right down the line through all the domestic animals."

"And why not? The prospect rather appeals to me. If science and religion can combine to take some of the cruelty out of Nature, isn't that a good thing?"

"You sound like a crypto-Buddhist—and I'm tired of pointing out that there's no cruelty in what we are doing. Meanwhile, if the Thero asks any more questions, kindly refer him to me."

"Very good, Mr. Franklin," Lundquist replied rather stiffly. There was an awkward pause, providentially broken by the arrival of a messenger.

"Headquarters wants to speak to you, Mr. Franklin. It's urgent."

"I bet it is," muttered Franklin. Then he caught sight of Lundquist's still somewhat hostile expression, and could not suppress a smile.

"If you can train orcas to be wardens, John," he said, "you'd better start looking around for a suitable mammal—preferably amphibious—to be the next director."

On a planet of instantaneous and universal communications, ideas spread from pole to pole more rapidly than they could once have done by word of mouth in a single village. The skilfully edited and presented programme which had spoiled the appetites of a mere twenty million people on its first appearance had a far larger audience on its second. Soon there were few other topics of conversation; one of the disadvantages of life in a peaceful and well-organised world state was that with the disappearance of wars and crises very little was left of what was once called "news". Indeed, the complaint had often been made that since the ending of national sovereignty, history had also been abolished. So the argument raged in club and kitchen, in World Assembly and lonely space freighter, with no competition from any other quarter.

The World Food Organisation maintained a dignified silence, but behind the scenes there was furious activity. Matters were not helped by the brisk lobbying of the farm group, which it had taken no great foresight on Indra's part to predict. Franklin was particularly annoyed by the efforts of the rival department to profit from his difficulties, and made several protests to the Director of Plankton Farms when the infighting became a little too rough. "Damn it all, Ted," he had snarled over the viewphone on one occasion, "you're just as big a butcher as I am. Every ton of raw plankton you process contains half a billion shrimps with as much right to life, liberty, and the pursuit of happiness as my whales. So don't try to stand in a white sheet. Sooner or later the Thero will work down to you—this is only the thin edge of the wedge."

"Maybe you're right, Walter," the culprit had admitted cheerfully enough, "but I think the farms will last out my time. It's not easy to make people sentimental over shrimps—they don't have cute little ten-ton babies to nurse."

That was perfectly true; it was very hard to draw the line between maudlin sentimentality and rational humanitarianism. Franklin remembered a recent cartoon showing the Thero raising his arms in protest while a shrieking cabbage was brutally dragged from the ground. The artist had taken no sides; he had merely summed up the viewpoint of those who considered that a great deal of fuss was being made about nothing. Perhaps this whole affair would blow over in a few weeks when people became bored and started arguing about something else—but he doubted it. That first television programme had shown that the Thero was an expert in moulding public opinion; he could be relied upon not to let his campaign lose momentum.

It took less than a month for the Thero to obtain the ten per cent vote needed under the constitution to set up a commission of inquiry. The fact that one-tenth of the human race was sufficiently interested in the matter to request that all the facts be laid before it did not mean that they agreed with the Thero; mere curiosity and the pleasure of seeing a department of the state fighting a defensive rear-guard action was quite enough to account for the vote. In itself, a commission of inquiry meant very little. What would matter would be the final referendum on the commission's report, and it would be months before that could be arranged.

One of the unexpected results of the twentieth century's electronic revolution was that for the first time in history it was possible to have a truly democratic government—in the sense that every citizen could express his views on matters of policy. What the Athenians, with indifferent success, had tried to do with a few thousand score of free men could now be achieved in a global society of five billion. Automatic sampling devices originally devised for the rating of television programmes had turned out to have a far wider significance, by making it a relatively simple and inexpensive matter to discover exactly what the public really thought on any subject.

Naturally, there had to be safeguards, and such a system would have been disastrous before the days of universal education—before, in fact, the beginning of the twenty-first century. Even now, it was possible for some emotionally laden issue to force a vote that was really against the best interests of the community, and no government could function unless it held the final right to decide matters of policy during its terms of office. Even if the world demanded some course of action by a ninety-nine per cent vote, the state could ignore the expressed will of the people—but it would have to account for its behaviour at the next election.

Franklin did not relish the privilege of being a key witness at the commission's hearings, but he knew that there was no way in which he could escape this ordeal. Much of his time was now spent in collecting data to refute the arguments of those who wished to put an end to whale slaughtering, and it proved to be a more difficult task than he had imagined. One could not present a neat, clear-cut case by saying that processed whale meat cost so much per pound by the time it reached the consumer's table whereas synthetic meats derived from plankton or algae would cost more. Nobody knew—there were far too many variables. The biggest unknown of all was the cost of running the proposed sea dairies, if it was decided to breed whales purely for milk and not for slaughter.

The data were insufficient. It would be honest to say so, but there was pressure on him to state outright that the suspension of whale slaughtering would never be a practical or economic possibility. His own loyalty to the bureau, not to mention the security of his present position, prompted him in the same direction.

But it was not merely a matter of economics; there were emotional factors which disturbed Franklin's judgment and made it impossible for him to make up his mind. The days he had spent with the Maha Thero, and his brief glimpse of a civilisation and a way of thought far older than his own, had affected him more deeply than he had realised. Like most men of his highly materialistic era, he was intoxicated with the scientific and sociological triumphs which had irradiated the opening decades of the twenty-first century. He prided himself on his sceptical rationalism, and his total freedom from superstition. The fundamental questions of philosophy had never bothered him greatly; he knew that they existed, but they seemed the concern of other people.

And now, whether he liked it or not, he had been challenged from a quarter so unexpected that he was almost defenceless. He had always considered himself a humane man, but now he had been reminded that humanity might not be enough. As he struggled with his thoughts, he became progressively more and more irritable with the world around him, and matters finally became so bad that Indra had to take action.

"Walter," she said firmly, when Anne had gone tearfully to bed after a row in which there was a good deal of blame on both sides, "it will save a lot of trouble if you face the facts and stop trying to fool yourself."

"What the devil do you mean?"

"You've been angry with everybody this last week—with just one exception. You've lost your temper with Lundquist—though that was partly my fault—with the press, with just about every other bureau in the division, with the children, and any moment you're going to lose it with me. But there's one person you're not angry with—and that's the Maha Thero, who's the cause of all the trouble."

"Why should I be? He's crazy, of course, but he's a saint—or as near it as I ever care to meet."

"I'm not arguing about that. I'm merely saying that you really agree with him, but you won't admit it."

Franklin started to explode. "That's utterly ridiculous!" he began. Then his indignation petered out. It *was* ridiculous; but it was also perfectly true.

He felt a great calm come upon him; he was no longer angry with the world and with himself. His childish resentment of the fact that *he* should be the man involved in a dilemma not of his making suddenly evaporated. There was no reason why he should be ashamed of the fact that he had grown to love the great beasts he guarded; if their slaughter could be avoided, he should welcome it, whatever the consequences to the bureau.

The parting smile of the Thero suddenly floated up into his memory. Had that extraordinary man foreseen that he would win him around to his point of view? If his gentle persuasiveness—which he had not hesitated to combine with the shock tactics of that bloodstained television programme—could work with Franklin himself, then the battle was already half over.

CHAPTER XXII

LIFE WAS A good deal simpler in the old days, thought Indra with a sigh. It was true that Peter and Anne were both at school or college most of the time, but somehow that had given her none of the additional leisure she had expected. There was so much entertaining and visiting to do, now that Walter had moved into the upper echelons of the state. Though perhaps that was exaggerating a little; the director of the Bureau of Whales was still a long way —at least six steps—down from the rarefied heights in which the president and his advisers dwelt.

But there were some things that cut right across official rank. No one could deny that there was a glamour about Walt's job and an interest in his activities that had made him known to a far wider circle than the other directors of the Marine Division, even before the *Earth Magazine* article or the present controversy over whale slaughtering. How many people could name the director of Plankton Farms or of Fresh-Water Food Production? Not one to every hundred that had heard of Walter. It was a fact that made her proud, even though at the same time it exposed Walter to a good deal of interdepartmental jealousy.

Now, however, it seemed likely to expose him to worse than that. So far, no one in the bureau, still less any of the higher officials of the Marine Division or the World Food Organisation imagined for one moment that Walter had any private doubts or that he was not wholeheartedly in support of the *status quo*.

Her attempts to read the current *Nature* were interrupted by the private-line viewphone. It had been installed, despite her bitter protests, the day that Walter had become director. The public service, it seemed, was not good enough; now the office could get hold of Walter whenever it liked, unless he took precautions to frustrate it.

"Oh, good morning, Mrs. Franklin," said the operator, who was now practically a friend of the family. "Is the director in?"

"I'm afraid not," said Indra with satisfaction. "He hasn't had a day off for about a month, and he's out sailing in the bay with Peter. If you want to catch him, you'll have to send a plane out; J.94's radio has broken down again."

"*Both* sets? That's odd. Still, it's not urgent. When he comes in, will you give him this memo?"

There was a barely audible click, and a sheet of paper drifted down into the extra large-sized memorandum basket. Indra read it, gave the operator an absent-minded farewell, and at once called Franklin on his perfectly serviceable radio.

The creak of the rigging, the soft rush of water past the smooth hull—even the occasional cry of a sea bird—these sounds came clearly from the speaker and transported her at once out into Moreton Bay.

"I thought you'd like to know, Walter," she said, "the Policy Board is having its special meeting next Wednesday, here in Brisbane. That gives you three days to decide what you're going to tell them."

There was a slight pause during which she could hear her husband moving about the boat; then Franklin answered: "Thanks, dear. I know what I've got to say—I just don't know how to say it. But there's something I've thought of that you can do to help. You know all the wardens' wives—suppose you call up as many as you can, and try to find what their husbands feel about this business. Can you do that without making it look too obvious? It's not so easy for me, nowadays, to find what the men in the field are thinking. They're too liable to tell me what they imagine I want to know."

There was a wistful note in Franklin's voice which Indra had been hearing more and more frequently these days, though she knew her husband well enough to be quite sure that he had no real regrets for having taken on his present responsibilities.

"That's a good idea," she said. "There are at least a dozen people I should have called up weeks ago, and this will give me an excuse. It probably means that we'll have to have another party though."

"I don't mind that, as long as I'm still director and can afford to pay for it. But if I revert to a warden's pay in a month or so, we'll have to cut out the entertaining."

"You don't really think——"

"Oh, it won't be as bad as that. But they may shift me to some nice safe job, though I can't imagine what use I am now outside the bureau. GET OUT OF THE WAY, YOU BLASTED FOOL—CAN'T YOU SEE WHERE YOU'RE GOING. Sorry, dear—too many week-end sailors around. We'll be back in ninety minutes, unless some idiot rams us. Pete says he wants honey for tea. Bye now."

Indra looked thoughtfully at the radio as the sounds of the distant boat ceased abruptly. She half wished that she had accompanied Walter and Pete on their cruise out into the bay, but she had faced the fact that her son now needed his father's company rather than hers. There were times when she grudged this, realising that in a few months they would both lose the boy whose mind and body they had formed, but who was now slipping from their grasp.

It was inevitable, of course; the ties that bound father and son together must now drive them apart. She doubted if Peter realised why he was so determined to get into space; after all, it was a common enough ambition among boys of his age. But he was one of the youngest ever to obtain a triplanetary scholarship, and it was easy to understand why. He was determined to conquer the element that had defeated his father.

But enough of this daydreaming, she told herself. She got out her file of visiphone numbers, and began to tick off the names of all the wardens' wives who would be at home.

The Policy Board normally met twice a year, and very seldom had much policy to discuss, since more of the bureau's work was satisfactorily taken care of by the committees dealing with finance, production, staff, and technical development. Franklin served on all of these, though only as an ordinary member, since the chairman was always someone from the Marine Division or the World Secretariat. He sometimes came back from the meetings depressed and discouraged; what was very unusual was for him to come back in a bad temper as well.

Indra knew that something had gone wrong the moment he entered the house. "Let me know the worst," she said resignedly as her exhausted husband flopped into the most comfortable chair in sight. "Do you have to find a new job?"

She was only half joking, and Franklin managed a wan smile. "It's not as bad as that," he answered, "but there's more in this business than I thought. Old Burrows had got it all worked out before he took the chair; someone in the Secretariat had briefed him pretty thoroughly. What it comes to is this: Unless it can be proved that food production from whale milk and synthetics will be *drastically* cheaper than the present method, whale slaughter will continue. Even a ten per cent saving isn't regarded as good enough to justify a switch-over. As Burrows put it, we're concerned with cost accounting, not abstruse philosophical principles like justice to animals.

"That's reasonable enough, I suppose, and certainly I wouldn't try to fight it. The trouble started during the break for coffee, when Burrows got me into a corner and asked me what the wardens thought about the whole business. So I told him that eighty per cent of them would like to see slaughtering stopped, even if it meant a rise in food costs. I don't know why he asked me this particular question, unless news of our little survey has leaked out.

"Anyway, it upset him a bit and I could see him trying to get around to something. Then he put it bluntly that I'd be a key witness when the inquiry started, and that the Marine Division wouldn't like me to plead the Thero's case in open court with a few million people watching. 'Suppose I'm asked for my personal opinion?' I said. 'No one's worked harder than me to increase the whale-meat and oil production, but as soon as it's possible I'd like to see the bureau become a purely conservation service.' He asked if this was my considered viewpoint and I told him it was.

"Then things got a bit personal, though still in a friendly sort of way, and we agreed that there was a distinct cleavage of opinion between the people who handled whales as whales and those who saw them only as statistics on food-production charts. After that Burrows went off and made some phone calls, and kept us all waiting around for half an hour while he talked to a few people up in the Secretariat. He finally came back with what were virtually my orders, though he was careful not to put it that way. It comes to this: I've got to be an obedient little ventriloquist's dummy at the inquiry."

"But suppose the other side asks you outright for your personal views?"

"Our counsel will try to head them off, and if he fails I'm not supposed to have any personal views."

"And what's the point of all this?"

"That's what I asked Burrows, and I finally managed to get it out of him. There are political issues involved. The Secretariat is afraid that the Maha Thero will get too powerful if he wins this case, so it's going to be fought whatever its merits."

"Now I understand," said Indra slowly. "Do you think that the Thero is after political power?"

"For its own sake—no. But he may be trying to gain influence to put across his religious ideas, and that's what the Secretariat's afraid of."

"And what are you going to do about it?"

"I don't know," Franklin answered. "I really don't know."

He was still undecided when the hearings began and the Maha Thero made his first personal appearance before a world-wide audience. He was not, Franklin could not help thinking as he looked at the small, yellow-robed figure with its gleaming skull, very impressive at first sight. Indeed, there was something almost comic about him—until he began to speak, and one knew without any doubt that one was in the presence both of power and conviction.

"I would like to make one thing perfectly clear," said the Maha Thero, addressing not only the chairman of the commission but also the unseen millions who were watching this first hearing. "It is not true that we are trying to enforce vegetarianism on the world, as some of our opponents have tried to maintain. The Buddha himself did not abstain from eating meat, when it was given to him; nor do we, for a guest should accept gratefully whatever his host offers.

"Our attitude is based on something deeper and more fundamental than food prejudices, which are usually only a matter of conditioning. What is more, we believe that most reasonable men, whether their religious beliefs are the same as ours or not, will eventually accept our point of view.

"It can be summed up very simply, though it is the result of twenty-six centuries of thought. We consider that it is wrong to inflict injury or death on any living creature, but we are not so foolish as to imagine that it can be avoided altogether. Thus we recognise, for example, the need to kill microbes and insect pests, much though we may regret the necessity.

"But as soon as such killing is no longer essential, it should cease. We believe that this point has now arrived as far as many of the higher animals are concerned. The production of all types of synthetic protein from purely vegetable sources is now an economic possibility—or it will be if the effort is made to achieve it. Within a generation, we can shed the burden of guilt which, however lightly or heavily it has weighed on individual consciences, must at some time or other have haunted all thinking men as they look at the world of life which shares their planet.

"Yet this is not an attitude which we seek to enforce on anyone against his will. Good actions lose any merit if they are imposed by force. We will be content to let the facts we will present speak for themselves, so that the world may make its own choice."

It was, thought Franklin, a simple, straightforward speech, quite devoid of any of the fanaticism which would have fatally prejudiced the case in this rational age. And yet the whole matter was one that went beyond reason; in a purely logical world, this controversy could never have arisen, for no one would have doubted man's right to use the animal kingdom as he felt fit. Logic, however, could be easily discredited here; it could be used too readily to make out a convincing case for cannibalism.

The Thero had not mentioned, anywhere in his argument, one point which had made a considerable impact on Franklin. He had not raised the possibility that man might someday come into contact with alien life forms that might judge him by his conduct towards the rest of the animal kingdom. Did he think that this was so far-fetched an idea that the general public would be unable to take it seriously, and would thus grow to regard his whole campaign as a joke? Or had he realised that it was an argument that might particularly appeal to an ex-astronaut? There was no way of guessing; in either event it proved that the Thero was a shrewd judge both of private and public reactions.

Franklin switched off the receiver; the scenes it was showing now were quite familiar to him, since he had helped the Thero to film them. The Marine Division, he thought wryly, would now be regretting the facilities it had offered His Reverence, but there was nothing else it could have done in the circumstances.

In two days he would be appearing to give his evidence; already he felt more like a criminal on trial than a witness. And in truth he was on trial—or, to be more accurate, his conscience was. It was strange to think that having once tried to kill himself, he now objected to killing other creatures. There was some connection here, but it was too complicated for him to unravel—and even if he did, it would not help him to solve his dilemma.

Yet the solution was on the way, and from a totally unexpected direction.

CHAPTER XXIII

FRANKLIN WAS BOARDING the plane that would take him to the hearings when the "Sub-Smash" signal came through. He stood in the doorway, reading the scarlet-tabbed message that had been rushed out to him, and at that moment all his other problems ceased to exist.

The SOS was from the Bureau of Mines, the largest of all the sections of the Marine Division. Its title was a slightly misleading one, for it did not run a single mine in the strict sense of the word. Twenty or thirty years ago there had indeed been mines on the ocean beds, but now the sea itself was an inexhaustible treasure chest. Almost every one of the natural elements could be extracted directly and economically from the millions of tons of dissolved matter in each cubic mile of sea water. With the perfection of selective ion-exchange filters, the nightmare of metal shortages had been banished forever.

The Bureau of Mines was also responsible for the hundreds of oil wells that now dotted the sea beds, pumping up the precious fluid that was the basic material for half the chemical plants on earth—and which earlier generations, with criminal shortsightedness, had actually burned for fuel. There were plenty of accidents that could befall the bureau's world-wide empire; only last year Franklin had lent it a whaling sub in an unsuccessful attempt to salvage a tank of gold concentrate. But this was far more serious, as he discovered after he had put through a few priority calls.

Thirty minutes later he was airborne, though not in the direction he had expected to be going. And it was almost an hour after he had taken off before all the orders had been given and he at last had a chance of calling Indra.

She was surprised at the unexpected call, but her surprise quickly turned to alarm. "Listen, dear," Franklin began, "I'm not going to Berne after all. Mines has had a serious accident and has appealed for our help. One of their subs is trapped on the bottom—it was drilling a well and hit a high-pressure gas pocket. The derrick was blown over and toppled on the sub so that it can't get away. There's a load of VIP's aboard, including a senator and the director of Mines. I don't know how we're going to pull them out, but we'll do our best. I'll call you again when I've got time."

"Will you have to go down yourself?" asked Indra anxiously.

"Probably. Now don't look so upset! I've been doing it for years!"

"I'm *not* upset," retorted Indra, and Franklin knew better than to contradict her. "Good-bye, darling," he continued, "give my love to Anne, and don't worry."

Indra watched the image fade. It had already vanished when she realised that Walter had not looked so happy for weeks. Perhaps that was not the right word to use when men's lives were at stake; it would be truer to say that he looked full of life and enthusiasm. She smiled, knowing full well the reason why.

Now Walter could get away from the problems of his office, and could lose himself again, if only for a while, in the clear-cut and elemental simplicities of the sea.

"There she is," said the pilot of the sub, pointing to the image forming at the edge of the sonar screen. "On hard rock eleven hundred feet down. In a couple of minutes we'll be able to make out the details."

"How's the water clarity—can we use TV?"

"I doubt it. That gas geyser is still spouting—there it is—that fuzzy echo. It's stirred up all the mud for miles around."

Franklin stared at the screen, comparing the image forming there with the plans and sketches on the desk. The smooth ovoid of the big shallow-water sub was partly obscured by the wreckage of the drills and derrick—a thousand or more tons of steel pinning it to the ocean bed. It was not surprising that, though it had blown its buoyancy tanks and turned its jets on to full power, the vessel had been unable to move more than a foot or two.

"It's a nice mess," said Franklin thoughtfully. "How long will it take for the big tugs to get here?"

"At least four days. *Hercules* can lift five thousand tons, but she's down at Singapore. And she's too big to be flown here; she'll have to come under her own steam. You're the only people with subs small enough to be airlifted."

That was true enough, thought Franklin, but it also meant that they were not big enough to do any heavy work. The only hope was that they could operate cutting torches and carve up the derrick until the trapped sub was able to escape.

Another of the bureau's scouts was already at work; someone, Franklin told himself, had earned a citation for the speed with which the torches had been fitted to a vessel not designed to carry them. He doubted if even the Space Department, for all its fabled efficiency, could have acted any more swiftly than this.

"Captain Jacobsen calling," said the loudspeaker. "Glad to have you with us, Mr. Franklin. Your boys are doing a good job, but it looks as if it will take time."

"How are things inside?"

"Not so bad. The only thing that worries me is the hull between bulkheads three and four. It took the impact there, and there's some distortion."

"Can you close off the section if a leak develops?"

"Not very well," said Jacobsen dryly. "It happens to be the middle of the control room. If we have to evacuate that, we'll be completely helpless."

"What about your passengers?"

"Er—they're fine," replied the captain, in a tone suggesting that he was giving some of them the benefit of a good deal of doubt. "Senator Chamberlain would like a word with you."

"Hello, Franklin," began the senator. "Didn't expect to meet you again under these circumstances. How long do you think it will take to get us out?"

The senator had a good memory, or else he had been well briefed. Franklin had met him on not more than three occasions—the last time in Canberra, at a session of the Committee for the Conservation of Natural Resources. As a witness, Franklin had been before the C.C.N.R. for about ten minutes, and he would not have expected its busy chairman to remember the fact.

"I can't make any promises, Senator," he answered cautiously. "It may take some time to clear away all this rubbish. But we'll manage all right—no need to worry about that."

As the sub drew closer, he was not so sure. The derrick was over two hundred feet long, and it would be a slow business nibbling it away in sections that the little scout-subs could handle.

For the next ten minutes there was a three-cornered conference between Franklin, Captain Jacobsen, and Chief Warden Barlow, skipper of the second scout-sub. At the end of that time they had agreed that the best plan was to continue to cut away the derrick; even taking the most pessimistic view, they should be able to finish the job at least two days before the *Hercules* could arrive. Unless, of course, there were any unexpected snags; the only possible danger seemed to be the one that Captain Jacobsen had mentioned. Like all large undersea vessels, his ship carried an air-purifying plant which would keep the atmosphere breathable for weeks, but if the hull failed in the region of the control room all the sub's essential services would be disrupted. The occupants might retreat behind the pressure bulkheads, but that would give them only a temporary reprieve, because the air would start to become foul immediately. Moreover, with part of the sub flooded, it would be extremely difficult even for the *Hercules* to lift her.

Before he joined Barlow in the attack on the derrick, Franklin called Base on the long-range transmitter and ordered all the additional equipment that might conceivably be needed. He asked for two more subs to be flown out at once, and started the workshops mass producing buoyancy tanks by the simple process of screwing air couplings on to old oil drums. If enough of these could be hitched to the derrick, it might be lifted without any help from the submarine salvage vessel.

There was one other piece of equipment which he hesitated for some time before ordering. Then he muttered to himself: "Better get too much than too little," and sent off the requisition, even though he knew that the Stores Department would probably think him crazy.

The work of cutting through the girders of the smashed derrick was tedious, but not difficult. The two subs worked together, one burning through the steel while the other pulled away the detached section as soon as it came loose. Soon Franklin became completely unconscious of time; all that existed was the short length of metal which he was dealing with at that particular moment. Messages and instructions continually came and went, but another part of his mind dealt with them. Hands and brain were functioning as two separate entities.

The water, which had been completely turbid when they arrived, was now clearing rapidly. The roaring geyser of gas that was bursting from the sea bed barely a hundred yards away must have sucked in fresh water to sweep away the mud it had originally disturbed. Whatever the explanation, it made the task of salvage very much simpler, since the subs' external eyes could function again.

Franklin was almost taken aback when the reinforcements arrived. It seemed impossible that he had been here for more than six hours; he felt neither tired nor hungry. The two subs brought with them, like a long procession of tin cans, the first batch of the buoyancy tanks he had ordered.

Now the plan of campaign was altered. One by one the oil drums were clipped to the derrick, air hoses were coupled to them, and the water inside them was blown out until they strained upward like captive balloons. Each had a lifting power of two or three tons; by the time a hundred had been attached, Franklin calculated, the trapped sub might be able to escape without any further help.

The remote handling equipment on the outside of the scoutsub, so seldom used in normal operations, now seemed an extension of his own arms. It had been at least four years since he had manipulated the ingenious metal fingers that enabled a man to work in places where his unprotected body could never go—and he remembered, from ten years earlier still, the first time he had attempted to tie a knot and the hopeless tangle he had made of it. That was one of the skills he had hardly ever used; who would have imagined that it would be vital now that he had left the sea and was no longer a warden?

They were starting to pump out the second batch of oil drums when Captain Jacobsen called.

"I'm afraid I've got bad news, Franklin," he said, his voice heavy with apprehension. "There's water coming in, and the leak's increasing. At the present rate, we'll have to abandon the control room in a couple of hours."

This was the news that Franklin had feared. It transformed a straight-forward salvage job into a race against time—a race hopelessly handicapped, since it would take at least a day to cut away the rest of the derrick.

"What's your internal air pressure?" he asked Captain Jacobsen.

"I've already pushed it up to five atmospheres. It's not safe to put it up any farther."

"Take it up to eight if you can. Even if half of you pass out, that won't matter as long as someone remains in control. And it may help to keep the leak from spreading, which is the important thing."

"I'll do that—but if most of us are unconscious, it won't be easy to evacuate the control room."

There were too many people listening for Franklin to make the obvious reply—that if the control room had to be abandoned it wouldn't matter anyway. Captain Jacobsen knew that as well as he did, but some of his passengers might not realise that such a move would end any chance of rescue.

The decision he had hoped he would not have to make was now upon him. This slow whittling away of the wreckage was not good enough; they would have to use explosives, cutting the fallen derrick at the centre, so that the lower, unsupported portion would drop back to the sea bed and its weight would no longer pin down the sub.

It had been the obvious thing to do, even from the beginning, but there were two objections: one was the risk of using explosives so near the sub's already weakened hull; the other was the problem of placing the charges in the correct spot. Of the derrick's four main girders, the two upper ones were easily accessible, but the lower pair could not be reached by the remote handling mechanisms of the scoutsubs. It was the sort of job that only an unencumbered diver could do, and in shallow water it would not have taken more than a few minutes.

Unfortunately, this was not shallow water; they were eleven hundred feet down—and at a pressure of over thirty atmospheres.

CHAPTER XXIV

"IT'S TOO GREAT a risk, Franklin. I won't allow it." It was not often, thought Franklin, that one had a chance of arguing with a senator. And if necessary he would not merely argue; he would defy.

"I know there's a danger, sir," he admitted, "but there's no alternative. It's a calculated risk—one life against twenty-three."

"But I thought it was suicide for an unprotected man to dive below a few hundred feet."

"It is if he's breathing compressed air. The nitrogen knocks him out first, and then oxygen poisoning gets him. But with the right mixture it's quite possible. With the gear I'm using, men have been down fifteen hundred feet."

"I don't want to contradict you, Mr. Franklin," said Captain Jacobsen quietly, "but I believe that only one man has reached fifteen hundred—and then under carefully controlled conditions. *And* he wasn't attempting to do any work."

"Nor am I; I just have to place those two charges."

"But the pressure!"

"Pressure never makes any difference, Senator, as long as it's balanced. There may be a hundred tons squeezing on my lungs—but I'll have a hundred tons inside and won't feel it."

"Forgive me mentioning this—but wouldn't it be better to send a younger man?"

"I won't delegate this job, and age makes no difference to diving ability. I'm in good health, and that's all that matters."

"Take her up," he said. "They'll argue all day if we stay here. I want to get into that rig before I change my mind."

He was wrestling with his thoughts all the way to the surface. Was he being a fool, taking risks which a man in his position, with a wife and family, ought never to face? Or was he still, after all these years, trying to prove that he was no coward, by deliberately meeting a danger from which he had once been rescued by a miracle?

Presently he was aware of other and perhaps less flattering motives. In a sense, he was trying to escape from responsibility. Whether his mission failed or succeeded, he would be a hero—and as such it would not be quite so easy for the Secretariat to push him around. It was an interesting problem; could one make up for lack of moral courage by proving physical bravery?

When the sub broke surface, he had not so much resolved these questions as dismissed them. There might be truth in every one of the charges he was making against himself; it did not matter. He knew in his heart that what he was doing was the right thing, the only thing. There was no other way in which the men almost a quarter of a mile below him could be saved, and against that fact all other considerations were meaningless.

The escaping oil from the well had made the sea so flat that the pilot of the cargo plane had made a landing, though his machine was not intended for amphibious operations. One of the scoutsubs was floating on the surface while her crew wrestled with the next batch of buoyancy tanks to be sunk. Men from the plane were helping them, working in collapsible boats that had been tossed into the water and automatically inflated.

Commander Henson, the Marine Division's master diver, was waiting in the plane with the equipment. There was another brief argument before the commander capitulated with good grace and, Franklin thought, a certain amount of relief. If anyone else was to attempt this mission, there was no doubt that Henson, with his unparalleled experience, was the obvious choice. Franklin even hesitated for a moment, wondering if by stubbornly insisting on going himself, he might not be reducing the chances of success. But he had been on the bottom and knew exactly what conditions were down there; it would waste precious time if Henson went down in the sub to make a reconnaissance.

Franklin swallowed his pH pills, took his injections, and climbed into the flexible rubber suit which would protect him from the near-zero temperature on the sea bed. He hated suits—they interfered with movement and upset one's buoyancy—but this was a case where he had no choice. The complex breathing unit, with its three cylinders—one the ominous red of compressed hydrogen—was strapped to his back, and he was lowered into the sea.

Commander Henson swam around him for five minutes while all the fittings were checked, the weight belt was adjusted, and the sonar transmitter tested. He was breathing easily enough on normal air, and would not switch over to the oxyhydrogen mixture until he had reached a depth of three hundred feet. The change-over was automatic, and the demand regulator also adjusted the oxygen flow so that the mixture ratio was correct at any depth. As correct as it could be, that is, for a region in which man was never intended to live. . . .

At last everything was ready. The explosive charges were securely attached to his belt, and he gripped the handrail around the tiny conning tower of the sub. "Take her down," he said to the pilot. "Fifty feet a minute, and keep your forward speed below two knots."

"Fifty feet a minute it is. If we pick up speed, I'll kill it with the reverse jets."

Almost at once, daylight faded to a gloomy and depressing green. The water here on the surface was almost opaque, owing to the debris thrown up by the oil well. Franklin could not even see the width of the conning tower; less than two feet from his eyes the metal rail blurred and faded into nothingness. He was not worried; if necessary, he could work by touch alone, but he knew that the water was much clearer on the bottom.

Only thirty feet down, he had to stop the descent for almost a minute while he cleared his ears. He blew and swallowed frantically before the comforting "click" inside his head told him that all was well; how humiliating it would have been, he thought, had he been forced back to the surface because of a blocked Eustachian tube! No one would have blamed him, of course; even a mild cold could completely incapacitate the best diver—but the anticlimax would have been hard to live down.

The light was fading swiftly as the sun's rays lost their battle with the turbid water. A hundred feet down, he seemed to be in a world of misty moonlight, a world completely lacking colour or warmth. His ears were giving him no trouble now, and he was breathing without effort, but he felt a subtle depression creeping over him. It was, he was sure, only an effect of the failing light—not a premonition of the thousand feet of descent that still lay ahead of him.

To occupy his mind, he called the pilot and asked for a progress report. Fifty drums had now been attached to the derrick, giving a total lift of well over a hundred tons. Six of the passengers in the trapped sub had become unconscious but appeared to be in no danger; the remaining seventeen were uncomfortable, but had adapted themselves to the increased pressure. The leak was getting no worse, but there were now three inches of water in the control room, and before long there would be danger of short circuits.

"Three hundred feet down," said Commander Henson's voice. "Check your hydrogen-flow meter—you should be starting the switch-over now."

Franklin glanced down at the compact little instrument panel. Yes, the automatic change-over was taking place. He could detect no difference in the air he was breathing, but in the next few hundred feet of descent most of the dangerous nitrogen would be flushed out. It seemed strange to replace it with hydrogen, a far more reactive—and even explosive—gas, but hydrogen produced no narcotic effects and was not trapped in the body tissues as readily as nitrogen.

It seemed to have grown no darker in the last hundred feet; his eyes had accustomed themselves to the low level of illumination, and the water was slightly clearer. He could now see for two or three yards along the smooth hull he was riding down into the depths where only a handful of unprotected men had ever ventured—and fewer still returned to tell the story.

Commander Henson called him again. "You should be on fifty per cent hydrogen now. Can you taste it?"

"Yes—a metallic sort of flavour. Not unpleasant, though."

"Talk as slowly as you can," said the commander. "It's hard to understand you—your voice sounds so high-pitched now. Are you feeling quite O.K.?"

"Yes," replied Franklin, glancing at his depth gauge. "Will you increase my rate of descent to a hundred feet a minute? We've no time to waste."

At once he felt the vessel sinking more swiftly beneath him as the ballast tanks were flooded, and for the first time he began to feel the pressure around him as something palpable. He was going down so quickly that there was a slight lag as the insulating layer of air in his suit adjusted to the pressure change; his arms and legs seemed to be gripped as if by a huge and gentle vice, which slowed his movements without actually restricting them.

The light had now nearly gone, and as if in anticipation of his order the pilot of the sub switched on his twin searchlights. There was nothing for them to illumine, here in this empty void midway between sea bed and sky, but it was assuring to see the double nimbus of scattered radiance floating in the water ahead of him. The violet filters had been removed, for his benefit, and now that his eyes had something distant to focus upon he no longer felt so oppressively shut in and confined.

Eight hundred feet down—more than three-quarters of the way to the bottom. "Better level off for three minutes," advised Commander Henson. "I'd like to keep you here for half an hour, but we'll have to make it up on the way back."

Franklin submitted to the delay with what grace he could. It seemed incredibly long; perhaps his time sense had been distorted, so that what was really a minute appeared like ten. He was going to ask Commander Henson if his watch had stopped when he suddenly remembered that he had a perfectly good one of his own. The fact that he had forgotten something so obvious was, he realised, rather a bad sign; it suggested that he was becoming stupid. However, if he was intelligent enough to know that he was becoming stupid things could not be too bad. ... Luckily the descent started again before he could get too involved in this line of argument.

And now he could hear, growing louder and louder each minute, the incessant roar of the great geyser of gas belching from the shaft which inquisitive and interfering man had drilled in the ocean bed. It shook the sea around him, already making it hard to hear the advice and comments of his helpers. There was a danger here as great as that of pressure itself; if the gas jet caught him, he might be tossed hundreds of feet upwards in a matter of seconds and would explode like a deep-sea fish dragged suddenly to the surface.

"We're nearly there," said the pilot, after they had been sinking for what seemed an age. "You should be able to see the derrick in a minute; I'll switch on the lower lights."

Franklin swung himself over the edge of the now slowly moving sub and peered down the misty columns of light. At first he could see nothing; then, at an indeterminate distance, he made out mysterious rectangles and circles. They baffled him for a moment before he realised that he was seeing the air-filled drums which were now straining to lift the shattered derrick.

Almost at once he was able to make out the framework of twisted girders below them, and presently a brilliant star—fantastically out of place in this dreary underworld—burst into life just outside the cone of his searchlights. He was watching one of the cutting torches at work, manipulated by the mechanical hands of a sub just beyond visual range.

With great care, his own vessel positioned him beside the derrick, and for the first time he realised how hopeless his task would have been had he been compelled to rely on touch to find his way around. He could see the two girders to which he had to attach his charge; they were hemmed in by a maze of smaller rods, beams, and cables through which he must somehow make his way.

Franklin released his hold on the sub which had towed him so effortlessly into the depths, and with slow, easy strokes swam towards the derrick. As he approached, he saw for the first time the looming mass of the trapped sub, and his heart sank as he thought of all the problems that must still be solved before it could be extricated. On a sudden impulse, he swam towards the helpless vessel and banged sharply on the hull with the pair of wire cutters from his little tool kit. The men inside knew that he was here, of course, but the signal would have an altogether disproportionate effect on their morale.

Then he started work. Trying to ignore the throbbing vibration which filled all the water around him and made it difficult to think, he began a careful survey of the metal maze into which he must swim.

It would not be difficult to reach the nearest girder and place the charge. There was an open space between three I beams, blocked only by a loop of cable which could be easily pushed out of the way (but he'd have to watch that it didn't tangle in his equipment when he swam past it). Then the girder would be dead ahead of him; what was more, there was room to turn around, so that he could avoid the unpleasant necessity of creeping out backward.

He checked again, and could see no snags. To make doubly sure, he talked it over with Commander Henson, who could see the situation almost as well on the TV screen of the sub. Then he swam slowly into the derrick, working his way along the metal framework with his gloved hands. He was quite surprised to find that, even at this depth, there was no shortage of the barnacles and other marine growths which always make it dangerous to touch any object which had been underwater for more than a few months.

The steel structure was vibrating like a giant tuning fork; he could feel the roaring power of the uncapped well both through the sea surrounding him and through the metal beneath his hands. He seemed to be imprisoned in an enormous, throbbing cage; the sheer noise, as well as the awful pressure, was beginning to make him dull and lethargic. It now needed a positive effort of will to take any action; he had to keep reminding himself that many lives besides his own depended upon what he was doing.

He reached the girder and slowly taped the flat package against the metal. It took a long time to do it to his satisfaction, but at last the explosive was in place and he felt sure that the vibration would not dislodge it. Then he looked around for his second objective—the girder forming the other edge of the derrick.

He had stirred up a good deal of dirt and could no longer see so clearly, but it seemed to Franklin that there was nothing to stop him crossing the interior of the derrick and completing the job. The alternative was to go back the way he had come, and then swim right around to the other side of the wreckage. In normal circumstances that would have been easy enough—but now every movement had to be considered with care, every expenditure of effort made grudgingly only after its need had been established beyond all doubt.

With infinite caution, he began to move through the throbbing mist. The glare of the searchlights, pouring down upon him, was so dazzling that it pained his eyes. It never occurred to him that he had only to speak into his microphone and the illumination would be reduced instantly to whatever level he wished. Instead, he tried to keep in whatever shadow he could find among the confused pile of wreckage through which he was moving.

He reached the girder, and crouched over it for a long time while he tried to remember what he was supposed to be doing here. It took Commander Henson's voice, shouting in his ears like some far-off echo, to call him back to reality. Very carefully and slowly he taped the precious slab into position; then he floated beside it, admiring his meaningless handiwork, while the annoying voice in his ear grew ever more insistent. He could stop it, he realised, by throwing away his face mask and the irritating little speaker it contained. For a moment he toyed with this idea, but discovered that he was not strong enough to undo the straps holding the mask in place. It was too bad; perhaps the voice would shut up if he did what it told him to.

Unfortunately, he had no idea which was the right way out of the maze in which he was now comfortably ensconced. The light and noise were very confusing; when he moved in any direction, he sooner or later banged into something and had to turn back. This annoyed but did not alarm him, for he was quite happy where he was.

But the voice would not give him any peace. It was no longer at all friendly and helpful; he dimly realised that it was being downright rude, and was ordering him about in a manner in which—though he could not remember why—people did not usually speak to him. He was being given careful and detailed instructions which were repeated over and over again, with increasing emphasis, until he sluggishly obeyed them. He was too tired to answer back, but he wept a little at the indignity to which he was being subjected. He had never been called such things in his life, and it was very seldom indeed that he had heard such shocking languge as was now coming through his speaker. Who on earth would yell at him this way? "Not that way, you goddammed fool, sir! To the left—LEFT! That's fine—now forward a bit more—don't stop there! Christ, he's gone to sleep again. WAKE UP—SNAP OUT OF IT OR I'LL KNOCK YOUR BLOODY BLOCK OFF! That's a good boy—you're nearly there—just another couple of feet . . ." and so on endlessly, and some of it with very much worse language than that.

Then, quite to his surprise, there was no longer twisted metal around him. He was swimming slowly in the open, but he was not swimming for long. Metal fingers closed upon him, none too gently, and he was lifted into the roaring night.

From far away he heard four short, muffled explosions, and something deep down in his mind told him that for two of these he was responsible. But he saw nothing of the swift drama a hundred feet below as the radio fuses detonated and the great derrick snapped in two. The section lying across the trapped submarine was still too heavy to be lifted clear by the buoyancy tanks, but now that it was free to move it teetered for a moment like a giant seesaw, then slipped aside and crashed on to the sea bed.

The big sub, all restraint removed, began to move upward with increasing speed; Franklin felt the wash of its close passage, but was too bemused to realise what it meant. He was still struggling back into hazy consciousness; around eight hundred feet, quite abruptly, he started to react to Henson's bullying ministrations, and, to the commander's vast relief, began to answer him back in kind. He cursed wildly for about a hundred feet, then became fully aware of his surroundings and ground to an embarrassed halt. Only then did he realise that his mission had been successful and that the men he had set out to rescue were already far above him on their way back to the surface.

Franklin could make no such speed. A decompression chamber was waiting for him at the three-hundred-foot level, and in its cramped confines he was to fly back to Brisbane and spend eighteen tedious hours before all the absorbed gas had escaped from his body. And by the time the doctors let him out of their clutches, it was far too late to suppress the tape recording that had circulated throughout the entire bureau. He was a hero to the whole world, but if he ever grew conceited he need only remind himself that all his staff had listened gleefully to every word of Commander Henson's fluently profane cajoling of their director.

CHAPTER XXV

PETER NEVER LOOKED back as he walked up the gangplank into the projectile from which, in little more than half an hour, he would have his first view of the receding Earth. Franklin could understand why his son kept his head averted; young men of eighteen do not cry in public. Nor, for that matter, he told himself fiercely, do middle-aged directors of important bureaux.

Anne had no such inhibitions; she was weeping steadily despite all that Indra could do to comfort her. Not until the doors of the spaceship had finally sealed and the thirty-minute warning siren had drowned all other noises did she subside into an intermittent sniffling.

The tide of spectators, of friends and relatives, of cameramen and Space Department officials, began to retreat before the moving barriers. Clasping hands with his wife and daughter, Franklin let himself be swept along with the flood of humanity. What hopes and fears, sorrows and joys surrounded him now! He tried to remember his emotions at his first take-off; it must have been one of the great moments of his life—yet all recollection of it had gone, obliterated by thirty years of later experience.

And now Peter was setting out on the road his father had travelled half a lifetime before. May you have better luck among the stars than I did, Franklin prayed. He wished he could be there at Port Lowell when Irene greeted the boy who might have been her son, and wondered how Roy and Rupert would receive their half-brother. He was sure that they would be glad to meet him;

Peter would not be as lonely on Mars as Ensign Walter Franklin had once been.

They waited in silence while the long minutes wore away. By this time, Peter would be so interested in the strange and exciting world that was to be his home for the next week that he would already have forgotten the pain of parting. He could not be blamed if his eyes were fixed on the new life which lay before him in all its unknown promise.

And what of his own life? Franklin asked himself. Now that he had launched his son into the future, could he say that he had been a success? It was a question he found very hard to answer honestly. So many things he had attempted had ended in failure or even in disaster. He knew now that he was unlikely to rise any farther in the service of the state; he might be a hero, but he had upset too many people when he became the surprised and somewhat reluctant ally of the Maha Thero. Certainly he had no hope of promotion—nor did he desire it —during the five or ten years which would be needed to complete the re-organisation of the Bureau of Whales. He had been told in as many words that since he was partly responsible for the situation—the mess, it was generally called—he could sort it out himself.

One thing he would never know. If fate had not brought him public admiration and the even more valuable—because less fickle—friendship of Senator Chamberlain, would he have had the courage of his new-found convictions? It had been easy, as the latest hero that the world had taken to its heart but would forget tomorrow, to stand up in the witness box and state his beliefs. His superiors could fume and fret, but there was nothing they could do but accept his defection with the best grace they could muster. There were times when he almost wished that the accident of fame had not come to his rescue. And had his evidence, after all, been decisive? He suspected that it had. The result of the referendum had been close, and the Maha Thero might not have carried the day without his help.

The three sharp blasts of the siren broke into his reverie. In that awe-inspiring silence which still seemed so uncanny to those who remembered the age of rockets, the great ship sloughed away its hundred thousand tons of weight and began the climb back to its natural element. Half a mile above the plain, its own gravity field took over completely, so that it was no longer concerned with terrestrial ideas of "up" or "down". It lifted its prow towards the zenith, and hung poised for a moment like a metal obelisk miraculously supported among the clouds. Then, in that same awful silence, it blurred itself into a line—and the sky was empty.

The tension broke. There were a few stifled sobs, but many more laughs and jokes, perhaps a little too high-pitched to be altogether convincing. Franklin put his arms around Anna and Indra, and began to shepherd them towards the exit.

To his son, he willingly bequeathed the shoreless seas of space. For himself, the oceans of this world were sufficient. Therein dwelt all his subjects, from the moving mountain of Leviathan to the newborn dolphin that had not yet learned to suckle under water.

He would guard them to the best of his knowledge and ability. Already he could see clearly the future role of the bureau, when its wardens would be in truth the protectors of all the creatures moving in the sea. All? No—that, of course, was absurd; nothing could change or even greatly alleviate the incessant cruelty and slaughter that raged through all the oceans of the world. But with the great mammals who were his kindred, man could make a start, imposing his truce upon the battlefield of Nature.

What might come of that in the ages ahead, no one could guess. Even Lundquist's daring and still unproved plan for taming the killer whales might no more than hint of what the next few decades would bring. They might even bring the answer to the mystery which haunted him still, and which he had so nearly solved when the submarine earthquake robbed him of his best friend.

A chapter—perhaps the best chapter—of his life was closing. The future would have many problems, but he did not believe that ever again would he have to face such challenges as he had met in the past. In a sense, his work was done, even though the details were merely beginning.

He looked once more at the empty sky, and the words that the Mahanayake Thero had spoken to him as they flew back from the Greenland station rose up out of memory like a ground swell on the sea. He would never forget that chilling thought: *"When that time comes, the treatment man receives from his superiors may well depend upon the way he has behaved towards the other creatures of his own world."*

Perhaps he was a fool to let such phantasms of a remote and unknowable future have any influence upon his thoughts and acts, but he had no regrets for what he had done. As he stared into the blue infinity that had swallowed his son, the stars seemed suddenly very close. "Give us another hundred years," he whispered, "and we'll face you with clean hands and hearts—whatever shape you be."

"Come along, dear," said Indra, her voice still a little unsteady. "You haven't much time. The office asked me to remind you—the Committee on Interdepartmental Standardisation meets in half an hour."

"I know," said Franklin, blowing his nose firmly and finally. "I wouldn't dream of keeping it waiting."

A FALL OF
MOONDUST

TO
LIZ AND MIKE

AUTHOR'S NOTE

A Fall of Moondust was written in 1960, several years before the Ranger, Lunik and Surveyor spacecraft gave us our first close-ups of lunar detail. It is now highly probable that—as indeed I was careful to point out in the opening chapter—there are no extensive areas of deep dust on the Moon.

Nevertheless, the great achievements in astronautics of the past few years have not ruled out the idea upon which this story is based. It will be a long, long time before we can be sure that there is nothing like the "Sea of Thirst" *anywhere* on the Moon's 15,000,000 square miles of territory—an area as great as the continent of Africa, still waiting to be explored and still, we can be quite certain, full of unexpected and perhaps dangerous surprises.

CHAPTER I

To be the skipper of the only boat on the Moon was a distinction that Pat Harris enjoyed. As the passengers filed aboard *Selene*, jockeying for window seats, he wondered what sort of trip it would be this time. In the rear-view mirror he could see Miss Wilkins, very smart in her blue Lunar Tourist Commission uniform, putting on her usual welcome act. He always tried to think of her as "Miss Wilkins", not Sue, when they were on duty together; it helped to keep his mind on business. But what she thought of him, he had never really discovered.

There were no familiar faces; this was a new bunch, eager for their first cruise. Most of the passengers were typical tourists—elderly people, visiting a world that had been the very symbol of inaccessibility when they were young. There were only four or five passengers on the low side of thirty, and they were probably technical personnel on vacation from one of the lunar bases. It was a fairly good working rule, Pat had discovered, that all the older people came from Earth, while the youngsters were residents of the Moon.

But to all of them the Sea of Thirst was a novelty. Beyond *Selene*'s observation windows its grey, dusty surface marched onwards unbroken until it reached the stars. Above it hung the waning crescent Earth, poised for ever in the sky from which it had not moved in a billion years. The brilliant, blue-green light of the mother world flooded this strange land with a cold radiance—and cold it was indeed, perhaps three hundred below zero on the exposed surface.

No one could have told, merely by looking at it, whether the Sea was liquid or solid. It was completely flat and featureless, quite free from the myriad cracks and fissures that scarred all the rest of this barren world. Not a single hillock, boulder or pebble broke its monotonous uniformity. No sea on Earth—no mill-pond, even—was ever as calm as this.

It was a sea of dust, not water, and therefore it was alien to all the experience of men—therefore, also, it fascinated and attracted them. Fine as talcum powder, drier in this vacuum than the parched sands of the Sahara, it flowed as easily and effortlessly as any liquid. A heavy object dropped into it would disappear instantly, without a splash, leaving no scar to mark its passage. Nothing could move upon its treacherous surface except the small, two man dust-skis—and *Selene* herself, an improbable combination of sledge and bus, not unlike the Sno-cats that had opened up the Antarctic a lifetime ago.

Selene's official designation was Dust-cruiser, Mark 1, though to the best of Pat's knowledge a Mark 2 did not exist even on the drawing-board. She was called "ship", "boat" or "moon-bus" according to taste; Pat preferred "boat", for it prevented confusion. When he used that word, no one would mistake him for the skipper of a space-ship—and space-ship captains were, of course, two a penny.

"Welcome aboard *Selene*," said Miss Wilkins, when everyone had settled down. "Captain Harris and I are pleased to have you with us. Our trip will last four hours, and our first objective will be Crater Lake, a hundred kilometres east of here in the Mountains of Inaccessibility——."

Pat scarcely heard the familiar introductions; he was busy with his count-down. *Selene* was virtually a grounded space-ship; she had to be, since she was travelling in a vacuum, and must protect her frail cargo from the hostile world beyond her walls. Though she never left the surface of the Moon, and was pro-pelled by electric motors instead of rockets, she carried all the basic equipment of a full-fledged ship of space—and all of it had to be checked before departure.

Oxygen—O.K. Power—O.K. Radio—O.K. ("Hello, Rainbow Base, *Selene* testing. Are you receiving my beacon?") Inertial navigator—zeroed. Airlock Safety—On. Cabin Leak detector—O.K. Internal lights—O.K. Gangway—disconnected. And so on for more than fifty items, every one of which would automatically call attention to itself in case of trouble. But Pat Harris, like all spacemen hankering after old age, never relied on autowarnings if he could carry out the check himself.

At last he was ready. The almost silent motors started to spin, but the blades were still feathered and *Selene* barely quivered at her moorings. Then he eased the port fan into fine pitch, and she began to curve slowly to the right. When she was clear of the embarkation building, he straightened her out and pushed the throttle forward.

She handled very well, when one considered the complete novelty of her design. There were no millenia of trial and error here, stretching back to the first Neolithic man who ever launched a log out into a stream. *Selene* was the very first of her line, created in the brains of a few engineers who had sat down at a table and asked themselves: "How do we build a vehicle that will skim over a sea of dust?"

Some of them, harking back to Ole Man River, had wanted to make her a stern-wheeler, but the more efficient submerged fans had carried the day. As they drilled through the dust, driving her before them, they produced a wake like that of a high-speed mole, but it vanished within seconds, leaving the Sea unmarked by any sign of the boat's passage.

Now the squat pressure-domes of Port Roris were dropping swiftly below the skyline. In less than ten minutes they had vanished from sight: *Selene* was utterly alone. She was at the centre of something for which the languages of mankind have no name.

As Pat switched off the motors and the boat coasted to rest, he waited for the silence to grow around him. It was always the same; it took a little while for the passengers to realise the strangeness of what lay outside. They had crossed space and seen stars all about them; they had looked up—or down—

at the dazzling face of Earth, but this was different. It was neither land nor sea, neither air nor space, but a little of each.

Before the silence grew oppressive—if he left it too long, someone would get scared—Pat rose to his feet and faced his passengers.

"Good evening, ladies and gentlemen," he began. "I hope Miss Wilkins has been making you comfortable. We've stopped here because this is a good place to introduce you to the Sea—to give you the feel of it, as it were."

He pointed to the windows, and the ghostly greyness that lay beyond.

"Just how far away," he asked quietly, "do you imagine our horizon is? Or to put it in another way, how big would a man appear to you, if he was standing out there where the stars seem to meet the ground?"

It was a question that no one could possibly answer, from the evidence of sight alone. Logic said "The Moon's a small world—the horizon *must* be very close." But the senses gave a wholly different verdict; this land, they reported, is absolutely flat, and stretches to infinity. It divides the Universe in twain; for ever and ever, it rolls onwards beneath the stars. . . .

The illusion remained, even when one knew its cause. The eye has no way of judging distances, when there is nothing for it to focus upon. Vision slipped and skidded helplessly on this featureless ocean of dust. There was not even— as there must always be on Earth—the softening haze of the atmosphere to give some hint of nearness or farness. The stars were unwinking needle points of light, clear down to that indeterminate horizon.

"Believe it or not," continued Pat, "you can see just three kilometres—or two miles, for those of you who haven't been able to go metric yet. I know it looks a couple of lightyears out to the horizon, but you could walk in twenty minutes, if you could walk on this stuff at all."

He moved back to his seat, and started the motors once more.

"Nothing much to see for the next sixty kilometres," he called over his shoulders, "so we'll get a move on."

Selene surged forward. For the first time there was a real sensation of speed. The boat's wake became longer and more disturbed as the spinning fans bit fiercely into the dust. Now the dust itself was being tossed up on either side in great ghostly plumes; from a distance, *Selene* would have looked like a snow-plough driving its way across a winter landscape, beneath a frosty moon. But those grey, slowly collapsing parabolas were not snow, and the lamp that lit their trajectory was the planet Earth.

The passengers relaxed, enjoying the smooth, almost silent ride. Every one of them had travelled hundreds of times faster than this, on the journey to the Moon—but in space one was never conscious of speed, and this swift glide across the dust was far more exciting. When Harris swung *Selene* into a tight turn, so that she orbited in a circle, the boat almost overtook the falling veils of powder her fans had hurled into the sky. It seemed altogether wrong that this impalpable dust should rise and fall in such clean-cut curves, utterly unaffected by air resistance. On Earth it would have drifted for hours—perhaps for days.

As soon as the boat had straightened out on a steady course and there was nothing to look at except the empty plain, the passengers began to read the literature thoughtfully provided for them. Each had been given a folder of photographs, maps, souvenirs ("This is to certify that Mr./Mrs./Miss . . . has sailed the Seas of the Moon, aboard Dust-cruiser *Selene*") and informative text. They had only to read this to discover all that they wanted to know about the Sea of Thirst, and perhaps a little more.

Most of the Moon, they read, was covered by a thin layer of dust, usually no more than a few millimetres deep. Some of this was debris from the stars—the remains of meteorites that had fallen upon the Moon's unprotected face for at least five billion years. Some had flaked from the lunar rocks as they expanded and contracted in the fierce temperature extremes between day and night. Whatever its source, it was so finely divided that it would flow like a liquid, even under this feeble gravity.

Over the ages, it had drifted down from the mountains into the lowlands, to form pools and lakes. The first explorers had expected this, and had usually been prepared for it. But the Sea of Thirst was a surprise; no one had anticipated finding a dust-bowl more than a hundred kilometres across.

As the lunar "seas" went, it was very small; indeed, the astronomers had never officially recognised its title, pointing out that it was only a small portion of the Sinus Roris—the Bay of Dew. And how, they protested, could part of a Bay be an entire Sea? But the name, invented by a copy-writer of the Lunar Tourist Commission, had stuck despite their objections. It was at least as appropriate as the names of the other so-called Seas—Sea of Clouds, Sea of Rains, Sea of Tranquillity. Not to mention Sea of Nectar. . . .

The brochure also contained some reassuring information, designed to quell the fears of the most nervous traveller, and to prove that the Tourist Commission had thought of everything. "All possible precautions have been taken for your safety," it stated. "*Selene* carries an oxygen reserve sufficient to last for more than a week, and all essential equipment is duplicated. An automatic radio beacon signals your position at regular intervals, and in the extremely improbable event of a complete power failure, a Dust-ski from Port Roris would tow you home with little delay. Above all, there is no need to worry about rough weather. No matter how bad a sailor you may be, you can't get sea-sick on the Moon. There are never any storms on the Sea of Thirst; it is always a flat calm."

Those last comforting words had been written in all good faith, for who could have imagined that they would soon be proved untrue?

As *Selene* raced silently through the earthlight night, the Moon went about its business. There was a great deal of business now, after the aeons of sleep. More had happened here in the last fifty years than in the five billions before that, and much was to happen soon.

In the first city that Man had ever built outside his native world, Chief Administrator Olsen was taking a stroll through the park. He was very proud of the park, as were all the twenty-five thousand inhabitants of Port Clavius. It was small, of course—though not as small as was implied by that miserable TV commentator who'd called it "a window-box with delusions of grandeur".

And certainly there were no parks, gardens, or anything else on Earth where you could find sunflowers ten metres high.

Far overhead, wispy cirrus clouds were sailing by—or so it seemed. They were, of course, only images projected on the inside of the dome, but the illusion was so perfect that it sometimes made the C.A. homesick. Homesick? He corrected himself; *this* was home.

Yet in his heart of hearts, he knew it was not true. To his children it would be, but not to him. He had been born in Stockholm, Earth; they had been born in Port Clavius. They were citizens of the Moon; he was tied to Earth with bonds that might weaken with the years, but would never break.

Less than a kilometre away, just outside the main dome, the head of the Lunar Tourist Commission inspected the latest returns, and permitted himself a mild feeling of satisfaction. The improvement over the last season had been maintained; not that there *were* seasons on the Moon, but it was noticeable that more tourists came when it was winter in Earth's northern hemisphere.

How could he keep it up? That was always the problem, for tourists wanted variety and you couldn't give them the same thing over and over again. The novel scenery, the low gravity, the view of Earth, the mysteries of Farside, the spectacular heavens, the pioneer settlements (where tourists were not always welcomed, anyway)—after you'd listed those, what else did the Moon have to offer? What a pity there were not native Selenites with quaint customs and quainter physiques at which visitors could click their cameras. Alas, the largest life-form ever discovered on the Moon needed a microscope to show it—and its ancestors had come here on Lunik 2, only a decade ahead of Man himself.

Commissioner Davis riffled mentally through the items that had arrived by the last telefax, wondering if there was anything here that would help him. There was, of course, the usual request from a TV company he'd never heard of, anxious to make yet another documentary on the Moon—if all expenses were paid. The answer to that one would be "No"; if he accepted all these kind offers, his department would soon be broke.

Then there was a chatty letter from his opposite number in the Greater New Orleans Tourist Commission, Inc., suggesting an exchange of personnel. It was hard to see how that would help the Moon, or New Orleans either, but it would cost nothing and might produce some goodwill. And—this was more interesting—there was a request from the water-ski-ing champion of Australia, asking if anyone had ever tried to ski on the Sea of Thirst.

Yes—there was definitely an idea here; he was surprised that someone had not tried it already. Perhaps they had, behind *Selene* or one of the small dust-skis. It was certainly worth a test; he was always on the look-out for new forms of lunar recreation, and the Sea of Thirst was one of his pet projects.

It was a project which, within a very few hours, was going to turn into a nightmare.

CHAPTER II

A H E A D O F *Selene*, the horizon was no longer a perfect, unbroken arc; a jagged line of mountains had risen above the edge of the Moon. As the cruiser raced towards them, they seemed to climb slowly up the sky, as if lifted upon some gigantic elevator.

"The Inaccessible Mountains," announced Miss Wilkins. "So-called because they're entirely surrounded by the Sea. You'll notice, too, that they're much steeper than most lunar mountains."

She did not labour this, as it was an unfortunate fact that the majority of lunar peaks were a severe disappointment. The huge craters which looked so impressive on photographs taken from Earth turned out upon close inspection to be gently rolling hills, their relief grossly exaggerated by the shadows they cast at dawn and sunset. There was not a single lunar crater whose ramparts soared as abruptly as the streets of San Francisco, and there were very few that could provide a serious obstacle to a determined cyclist. No one would have guessed this, however, from the publications of the Tourist Commission, which featured only the most spectacular cliffs and canyons, photographed from carefully chosen vantage points.

"They've never been thoroughly explored, even now," Miss Wilkins continued. "Last year we took a party of geologists there, and landed them on that promontory, but they were only able to go a few kilometres into the interior. So there may be *anything* up in those hills; we simply don't know."

Good for Sue, Pat told himself; she was a first-rate guide, and knew what to leave to the imagination, and what to explain in detail. She had an easy, relaxed tone, with no trace of that fatal sing-song that was the occupational disease of so many professional guides. And she had mastered her subject thoroughly; it was very rare for her to be asked a question that she could not answer. Altogether, she was a formidable young lady, and though she often figured in Pat's erotic reveries, he was secretly a little afraid of her.

The passengers stared with fascinated wonder at the approaching peaks. On the still-mysterious Moon, here was a deeper mystery. Rising like an island out of the strange sea that guarded them, the Inaccessible Mountains remained a challenge for the next generation of explorers. Despite their name, it was now easy enough to reach them—but with millions of square kilometres of less difficult territory still unexamined, they would have to wait their turn.

Selene was swinging into their shadows; before anyone had realised what was happening, the low-hanging Earth had been eclipsed. Its brilliant light still played upon the peaks far overhead, but down here all was utter darkness.

"I'll turn off the cabin lights," said the stewardess, "so you can get a better view."

As the dim red background illumination vanished, each traveller felt he was alone in the lunar night. Even the reflected radiance of earth on those high peaks was disappearing as the cruiser raced further into shadows. Within minutes, only the stars were left—cold, steady points of light in a blackness so complete that the mind rebelled against it.

It was hard to recognise the familiar constellations among this multitude of stars. The eye became entangled in patterns never seen from Earth, and lost itself in a glittering maze of clusters and nebulae. In all that resplendent panorama, there was only one unmistakable landmark—the dazzling beacon of Venus, far outshining all other heavenly bodies, heralding the approach of dawn.

It was several minutes before the travellers realised that not all the wonder lay in the sky. Behind the speeding cruiser stretched a long, phosphorescent wake, as if a magic finger had traced a line of light across the Moon's dark and dusty face. *Selene* was drawing a comet-tail behind her, as surely as any ship ploughing its way through the tropical oceans of Earth.

Yet there were no micro-organisms here, lighting this dead sea with their tiny lamps. Only countless grains of dust, sparkling one against the other as the static discharges caused by *Selene*'s swift passage neutralised themselves. Even when one knew the explanations, it was still beautiful to watch—to look back into the night and to see this luminous, electric ribbon continually renewed, continually dying away, as if the Milky Way itself were reflected in the lunar surface.

The shining wake was lost in the glare as Pat switched on the searchlight. Ominously close at hand, a great wall of rock was sliding past. At this point the face of the mountains rose almost sheer from the surrounding sea of dust; it towered overhead to unknown heights, for only where the racing oval of light fell upon it did it appear to flash suddenly into real existence.

Here were mountains against which the Himalayas, the Rockies, the Alps were new-born babies. On Earth, the forces of erosion began to tear at all mountains as soon as they were formed, so that after a few million years they were mere ghosts of their former selves. But the Moon knew neither wind nor rain; there was nothing here to wear away the rocks except the immeasurably slow flaking of the dust as their surface layers contracted in the chill of night. These mountains were as old as the world that had given them birth.

Pat was quite proud of his showmanship, and had planned the next act very carefully. It looked dangerous, but was perfectly safe, for *Selene* had been over this course a hundred times and the electronic memory of her guidance system knew the way better than any human pilot. Suddenly, he switched off the searchlight—and now the passengers could tell that while they had been dazzled by the glare on one side, the mountains had been stealthily closing in upon them from the other.

In almost total darkness, *Selene* was racing up a narrow canyon—and not even on a straight course, for from time to time she zigged and zagged to avoid invisible obstacles. Some of them, indeed, were not merely invisible but nonexistent; Pat had programmed this course, at slow speed and in the safety of daylight, for maximum impact on the nerves. The "Ahs!" and "Ohs!" from the darkened cabin behind him proved that he had done a good job.

Far above, a narrow ribbon of stars was all that could be seen of the outside world; it swung in crazy arcs from right to left and back again with each abrupt change of *Selene*'s course. The Night Ride, as Pat privately called it, lasted for about five minutes, but seemed very much longer. When he once again switched on the floods, so that the cruiser was moving in the centre of a great pool of light, there was a sigh of mingled relief and disappointment from the passengers. This was an experience none of them would forget in a hurry.

Now that vision had been restored, they could see that they were travelling up a steep-walled valley or gorge, the sides of which were slowly drawing apart. Presently the canyon had widened into a roughly oval amphitheatre about three kilometres across—the heart of an extinct volcano, breached aeons ago, in the days when even the Moon was young.

The crater was extremely small, by lunar standards, but it was unique. The ubiquitous dust had flooded into it, working its way up the valley age after age, so that now the tourists from Earth could ride in cushioned comfort into what had once been a cauldron filled with the fires of Hell. Those fires had died long before the dawn of terrestrial life, and would never wake again. But there were other forces that had not died, and were merely biding their time.

When *Selene* began a slow circuit of the steeply walled amphitheatre, more than one of her passengers remembered a cruise in some mountain lake at home. Here was the same sheltered stillness, the same sense of unknown depths beneath the boat. Earth had many Crater Lakes, but the Moon only one— though it had far more craters.

Taking his time, Pat made two complete circuits of the lake, while the floodlights played upon its enclosing walls. This was the best way to see it; during the daytime, when the sun blasted it with heat and light, it lost much of its magic. But now it belonged to the kingdom of fantasy, as if it had come from the haunted brain of Edgar Allan Poe. Ever and again one seemed to glimpse strange shapes moving at the edge of vision, beyond the narrow range of the lights. It was pure imagination of course; nothing moved in all this land except the shadows of the sun and earth. There could be no ghosts upon a world that had never known life.

It was time to turn back, to sail down the canyon into the open sea. Pat aimed the blunt prow of *Selene* towards the narrow rift in the mountains, and the high walls enfolded them again. On the outward journey he left the lights on, so that the passengers could see where they were going, besides, that trick of the Night Ride would not work so well a second time.

Far ahead, beyond the reach of *Selene*'s own illumination, a light was growing, spreading softly across the rocks and crags. Even in her last quarter, Earth still had the power of a dozen full moons, and now that they were emerging from the shadow of the mountains she was once more the mistress of the skies. Everyone of the twenty-two men and women aboard *Selene* looked up at that blue-green crescent, admiring its beauty, wondering at its brilliance. How strange, that the familiar fields and lakes and forests of Earth shone with such celestial glory when one looked at them from afar! Perhaps there was a lesson here; perhaps no man could appreciate his own world, until he had seen it from space.

And upon Earth, there must be many eyes turned towards the waxing Moon —more than ever before, now that the Moon meant so much to mankind. It was possible, but unlikely, that even now some of those eyes were peering through powerful telescopes at the faint spark of *Selene*'s floodlights as it crept through the lunar night. But it would mean nothing to them, when that spark flickered and died.

For a million years the bubble had been growing, like a vast abscess, below the root of the mountains. Throughout the entire history of Man, gas from the Moon's not-yet-wholly-dead interior had been forcing itself along lines of weakness, accumulating in cavities hundreds of metres below the surface. On nearby Earth, the Ice Ages had marched past, one by one, while the buried caverns grew and merged and at last coalesced. Now the abscess was about to burst.

Captain Harris had left the controls on Autopilot and was talking to the front row of passengers when the first tremor shook the boat. For a fraction of a second he wondered if a fan blade had hit some submerged obstacle; then, quite literally, the bottom fell out of his world.

It fell slowly, as all things must upon the Moon. Ahead of *Selene*, in a circle many acres in extent, the smooth plain puckered like a navel. The Sea was alive and moving, stirred by the forces that had woken it from its age-long sleep. The centre of the disturbance deepened into a funnel, as if a giant whirlpool was forming in the dust. Every stage of that nightmare transformation was pitilessly illuminated by the earthlight, until the crater was so deep that its far wall was completely lost in shadow, and it seemed as if *Selene* was racing into a curving crescent of utter blackness—an arc of annihilation.

The truth was almost as bad. By the time that Pat had reached the controls, the boat was sliding and skittering far down that impossible slope. Its own momentum, and the accelerating flow of the dust beneath it, was carrying it headlong into the depths. There was nothing he could do but attempt to keep on an even keel, and to hope that their speed would carry them up the far side of the crater before it collapsed upon them.

If the passengers screamed or cried out, Pat never heard them. He was conscious only of that dreadful, sickening slide, and of his own attempts to keep the cruiser from capsizing. Yet even as he fought with the controls, feeding power first to one fan, then to the other in an effort to straighten *Selene*'s course, a strange, nagging memory was teasing his mind. Somewhere, somehow, he had seen this happen before. . . .

That was ridiculous, of course, but the memory would not leave him. Not until he reached the bottom of the funnel and saw the endless slope of dust rolling down from the crater's star-fringed lip, did the veil of time lift for a moment.

He was a boy again, playing in the hot sand of a forgotten summer. He had found a tiny pit, perfectly smooth and symmetrical, and there was something lurking in its depths—something completely buried except for its waiting jaws. The boy had watched, wondering, already conscious of the fact that this was the stage for some microscopic drama. He had seen an ant, mindlessly intent upon its mission, stumble at the edge of the crater and topple down the slope.

It would have escaped easily enough—but when the first grain of sand had rolled to the bottom of the pit, the waiting ogre had reared out of its lair. With its forelegs it had hurled a fusillade of sand at the struggling insect, until the avalanche had overwhelmed it and brought it sliding down into the throat of the crater.

As *Selene* was sliding now. No ant-lion had dug this pit on the surface of the Moon, but Pat felt as helpless now as that doomed insect he had watched so many years ago. Like it, he was struggling to reach the safety of the rim, while the moving ground swept him back into the depths where death was waiting. A swift death for the ant, a protracted one for him and his companions.

The straining motors were making some headway, but not enough. The falling dust was gaining speed—and, what was worse, it was rising outside the walls of the cruiser. Now it had reached the lower edge of the windows; now it was creeping up the panes; and at last it had covered them completely. Harris cut the motors before they tore themselves to pieces, and as he did so the rising tide blotted out the last glimpse of the crescent Earth. In darkness and in silence, they were sinking into the Moon.

CHAPTER III

IN THE BANKED communications racks of Traffic Control, Earthside North, an electronic memory stirred uneasily. The time was one second past twenty-hundred hours G.M.T.; a pattern of pulses that should arrive automatically on every hour had failed to make its appearance.

With a swiftness beyond human thought, the handful of cells and microscopic relays looked for instructions. "WAIT FIVE SECONDS", said the coded orders. "IF NOTHING HAPPENS, CLOSE CIRCUIT 10011001."

The minute portion of the traffic computer as yet concerned with the problem waited patiently for this enormous period of time—long enough to make a hundred million twenty-figure additions, or to print most of the Library of Congress. Then it closed circuit 10011001.

High above the surface of the Moon, from an antenna which, curiously enough, was aimed directly at the face of the Earth, a radio pulse launched itself into space. In a sixth of a second it had flashed the fifty thousand kilometres to the relay satellite known as Lagrange II, directly in the line between

Moon and Earth. Another sixth of a second and the pulse had returned, much amplified, flooding Earthside North from Pole to Equator.

In terms of human speech, it carried a simple message. "HELLO, SELENE", the pulse said. "I AM NOT RECEIVING YOUR BEACON. PLEASE REPLY AT ONCE."

The computer waited for another five seconds. Then it sent out the pulse again, and yet again. Geological ages had passed in the world of electronics, but the machine was infinitely patient.

Once more, it consulted its instructions. Now they said: "CLOSE CIRCUIT 10101010". The computer obeyed. In Traffic Control, a green light flared suddenly to red, a buzzer started to saw the air with its alarm. For the first time, men as well as machines became aware that there was trouble, somewhere on the Moon.

The news spread slowly at first, for the Chief Administrator took a very poor view of unnecessary panic. So, still more strongly, did the Tourist Commissioner; nothing was worse for business than alerts and emergencies—even when, as happened in nine cases out of ten, they proved to be due to blown fuses, tripped cutouts, or over-sensitive alarms. But on a world like the Moon, it was necessary to be on one's toes. Better be scared by imaginary crises than fail to react to real ones.

It was several minutes before Commissioner Davis reluctantly admitted that this looked like a real one. *Selene*'s automatic beacon had failed to respond on one earlier occasion, but Pat Harris had answered as soon as he had been called on the cruiser's assigned frequency. This time, there was silence. *Selene* had not even replied to a signal sent out on the carefully guarded MOONCRASH band, reserved solely for emergencies. It was this news that brought the Commissioner hurrying from the Tourist Tower along the buried glideway into Clavius City.

At the entrance to the Traffic Control centre, he met the Chief Engineer, Earthside. That was a bad sign; it meant that someone thought that rescue operations would be necessary. The two men looked at each other gravely, each obsessed by the same thought.

"I hope you don't need me," said Chief Engineer Lawrence. "Where's the trouble? All I know is that a MOONCRASH signal's gone out. What ship is it?"

"It's not a ship. It's *Selene*; she's not answering, from the Sea of Thirst."

"My God—if anything's happened to her out there, we can only reach her with the dust-skis. I always said we should have two cruisers operating, before we started taking out tourists."

"That's what I argued—but Finance vetoed the idea. They said we couldn't have another until *Selene* proved she could make a profit."

"I hope she doesn't make headlines instead," said Lawrence grimly. "You know what *I* think about bringing tourists to the Moon."

The Commissioner did, very well; it had long been a bone of contention between them. For the first time, he wondered if the Chief Engineer might have a point.

It was, as always, very quiet in Traffic Control. On the great wall-maps the green and amber lights flashed continuously, their routine messages unimportant against the clamour of that single, flaring red. At the Air, Power and Radiation Consoles the duty officers sat like guardian angels, watching over the safety of one-quarter of a world.

"Nothing new," reported the Ground Traffic officer. "We're still completely in the dark. All we know is that they're *somewhere* out in the Sea."

He traced a circle on the large-scale map.

"Unless they're fantastically off-course, they must be in that general area. On the 19.00 hours check they were within a kilometre of their planned route. At 20.00, their signal had vanished, so whatever happened took place in that sixty minutes."

"How far can *Selene* travel in an hour?" someone asked.

"Flat out, a hundred and twenty kilometres," replied the Commissioner. "But she normally cruises at well under a hundred. You don't hurry on a sight-seeing tour."

He stared at the map, as if trying to extract information from it by the sheer intensity of his gaze.

"If they're out in the Sea, it won't take long to find them. Have you sent out the dust-skis?"

"No, sir; I was waiting for authorisation."

Davis looked at the Chief Engineer, who outranked anyone on this side of the Moon except Chief Administrator Olsen himself. Lawrence nodded slowly.

"Send them out," he said. "But don't expect results in a hurry. It will take a while to search several thousand square kilometres—especially at night. Tell them to work over the route from the last reported position, one ski on either side of it, so that they sweep the widest possible band."

When the order had gone out, Davis asked unhappily: "What do you think could have happened?"

"There are only a few possibilities. It must have been sudden, because there was no message from them. That usually means an explosion."

The Commissioner paled; there was always the chance of sabotage, and no one could ever guard against that. Because of their vulnerability, space-vehicles, like aircraft before them, were an irresistible attraction to a certain type of criminal. Davis thought of the Venus-bound liner *Argo*, which had been destroyed with two hundred men, women and children aboard—because a maniac had a grudge against a passenger who scarcely knew him.

"And then there's collision," continued the Chief Engineer. "She could have run into an obstacle."

"Harris is a very careful driver," said the Commissioner. "He's done this trip scores of times."

"Everyone can make mistakes; it's easy to misjudge your distance when you're driving by earthlight."

Commissioner Davis barely heard him; he was thinking of all the arrangements he might have to make, if the worst came to the worst. He'd better start by getting the Legal Branch to check the indemnity forms. If any relatives started suing the Tourist Commission for a few million dollars, that would undo his entire publicity campaign for the next year—even if he won.

The Ground Traffic officer gave a nervous cough.

"If I might make a suggestion," he said to the Chief Engineer. "We could call Lagrange. The astronomers up there may be able to see something."

"At night?" asked Davis sceptically. "From fifty thousand kilometres up?"

"Easily, if her searchlights are still burning. It's worth trying."

"Excellent idea," said the Chief Engineer. "Do that right away."

He should have thought of that himself, and wondered if there were any other possibilities he had overlooked. This was not the first occasion he had been forced to pit his wits against this strange and beautiful world, so breath-taking in her moments of magic—so deadly at her times of peril. She would never be wholly tamed, as Earth had been, and perhaps that was just as well. For it was the lure of the untouched wilderness, and the faint but ever-present hint of danger, that now brought the tourists as well as the explorers across the gulfs of space. He would prefer to do without the tourists—but they helped to pay his salary.

And now he had better start packing. This whole crisis might evaporate, and *Selene* might turn up again quite unaware of the panic she had caused. But he did not think this would happen, and his fear deepened to certainty as the minutes passed. He would give her another hour; then he would take the sub-orbital shuttle to Port Roris and to the realm of his waiting enemy, the Sea of Thirst.

When the PRIORITY RED signal reached Lagrange, Thomas Lawson, Ph.D., was fast asleep. He resented the interruption; though one needed only two hours' sleep in twenty-four when living under zero gravity, it seemed a little unfair to lose even that. Then he grasped the meaning of the message, and was fully awake. At last it looked as if he would be doing something useful here.

Tom Lawson had never been very happy about this assignment; he had wanted to do scientific research, and the atmosphere aboard Lagrange II was much too distracting. Balanced here between Earth and Moon, in a cosmic tight-rope act made possible by one of the obscurer consequences of the Law of Gravitation, the satellite was an astronautical maid-of-all-work. Ships passing in both directions took their fixes from it, and used it as a message centre —though there was no truth in the rumour that they stopped to pick up mail. Lagrange was also the relay station for almost all lunar radio traffic, for the whole Earthward-facing side of the Moon lay spread beneath it.

A hundred-centimetre telescope had been designed to look at objects billions of times further away than the Moon, but it was admirably suited for this job. From so close at hand, even with the low power, the view was superb. Tom seemed to be hanging in space immediately above the Sea of Rains, looking down upon the jagged peaks of the Appenines as they glittered in the morning light. Though he had only a sketchy knowledge of the Moon's geography, he could recognise at a glance the great craters of Archimedes and Plato, Aristillus and Eudoxus, the dark scar of the Alpine Valley, and the solitary pyramid of Pico, casting its long shadow across the plain.

But the daylight region did not concern him; what he sought lay in the darkened crescent where the sun had not yet risen. In some ways, that might make his task simpler. A signal lamp—even a hand-torch—would be easily visible down there in the night. He checked the map co-ordinates, and punched the control buttons. The burning mountains drifted out of his field of view, and only blackness remained, as he stared into the lunar night that had just swallowed more than twenty men and women.

At first he could see nothing—certainly no winking signal light, flashing its appeal to the stars. Then, as his eyes grew more sensitive, he could see that this land was not wholly dark. It was glimmering with a ghostly phosphorescence as it lay bathed in the earthlight, and the longer he looked, the more details he could see.

There were the mountains to the east of Rainbow Bay, waiting for the dawn that would strike them soon. And there—my God, what was that star shining in the darkness? His hopes soared, then swiftly crashed. That was only the lights of Port Roris, where even now men would be waiting anxiously for the results of his survey.

Within a few minutes, he had convinced himself that a visual search was useless. There was not the slightest chance that he could see an object no bigger than a bus, down there in that faintly luminous landscape. In the daytime, it would have been different; he could have spotted *Selene* at once by the long shadow she cast across the Sea. But the human eye was not sensitive enough to make this search by the light of the waning Earth, from a height of fifty thousand kilometres.

This did not worry Dr. Lawson. He had scarcely expected to see anything, on this first visual survey. It was a century and a half since astronomers had had to rely upon their eyesight; today, they had far more delicate weapons— a whole armoury of light-amplifiers and radiation-detectors. One of these, Tom Lawson was certain, would be able to find *Selene*.

He would not have been so sure of this, had he known that she was no longer upon the surface of the Moon.

CHAPTER IV

W H E N *Selene* C A M E to rest, both crew and passengers were still too stricken by astonishment to utter a sound. Captain Harris was the first to recover, perhaps because he was the only one who had any idea of what had happened.

It was a cave-in, of course; they were not rare, though none had ever been recorded in the Sea of Thirst. Deep down in the Moon, something had given way; possibly the infinitesimal weight of *Selene* had itself triggered the collapse. As Harris rose shakily to his feet, he wondered what line of talk he had better use to the passengers. He could hardly pretend that everything was under control and that they'd be on their way again in five minutes; on the other hand, panic was liable to set in if he revealed the true seriousness of the situation. Sooner or later he would have to, but until then it was essential to maintain confidence.

He caught Miss Wilkins' eye as she stood at the back of the cabin, behind the expectantly waiting passengers. She was very pale, but quite composed; he knew that he could rely on her, and flashed her a reassuring smile.

"We seem to be in one piece," he began in an easy, conversational style. "We've had a slight accident, as you'll gather, but things could be worse." (How? a part of his mind asked him. Well, the hull could have been fractured. . . . So you want to prolong the agony? He shut off the interior monologue by an effort of will.) "We've been caught in a landslip—a Moonquake, if you like. There's certainly no need to be alarmed; even if we can't get out under our own power, Port Roris will soon have someone here. Meanwhile, I know that Miss Wilkins was just going to serve refreshments, so I suggest you all relax while I—ah—do whatever proves necessary."

That seemed to have gone over quite well. With a silent sigh of relief, he turned back to the controls. As he did so, he noticed one of the passengers light a cigarette.

It was an automatic reaction, and one that he felt very much like sharing. He said nothing; that would have destroyed the atmosphere his little speech had created. But he caught the man's eye just long enough for the message to go home; the cigarette had been stubbed out before he resumed his seat.

As he switched on the radio, Pat heard the babble of conversation start up behind him. When a group of people was talking together, you could gather their mood even if you could not hear the individual words. He could detect annoyance, excitement, even amusement—but as yet, very little fear. Probably those who were speaking did not realise the full danger of the situation; the ones who did were silent.

And so was the ether. He searched the wave-bands from end to end, and found only a faint crackle from the electrified dust that had buried them. It was just as he had expected; this deadly stuff, with its high metallic content, was an almost perfect shield. It would pass neither radio waves nor sound; wi en he tried to transmit, he would be like a man shouting from the bottom of a well that was packed with feathers.

He switched the beacon to the high-powered emergency setting, so that it automatically broadcast a distress signal on the MOONCRASH band. If anything got through, this would; there was no point in trying to call Port Roris himself, and his fruitless efforts would merely upset the passengers. He left the receiver operating on *Selene*'s assigned frequency, in case of any reply; but he knew that it was useless. No one could hear them; no one could speak to them. As far as they were concerned, the rest of the human race might not exist.

He did not brood over this setback for very long; he had expected it, and there was too much else to do. With the utmost care, he checked all the instruments and gauges. Everything appeared to be perfectly normal, except that the temperature was just a shade high. That also was to be expected, now that the dust blanket was shielding them from the cold of space.

His greatest worry concerned the thickness of that blanket, and the pressure it was exerting on the boat. There must be thousands of tons of the stuff above *Selene*—and her hull had been designed to withstand pressure from within, not from without. If she went deep, she might be cracked like an eggshell.

How deep the cruiser was, he had no idea. When he had caught his last glimpse of the stars, she was about ten metres below the surface, and she might have been carried down much further by the suction of the dust. It would be advisable—even though it would increase their oxygen consumption —to put up the internal pressure and thus take some of the strain off the hull.

Very slowly, so that there would be no tell-tale popping of ears to alarm any-one, he boosted the cabin pressure by twenty per cent. When he had finished, he felt a little happier. He was not the only one, for as soon as the pressure gauge had stabilised at its new level a quiet voice said over his shoulders: "I think that was a very good idea."

He twisted round to see what busy-body was spying on him, but his angry protest died unborn. On his first quick inspection, Harris had recognised none of the passengers; now, however, he could tell that there was something vaguely familiar about the stocky, grey-haired man who had come forward to the driver's position.

"I don't want to intrude, Captain—you're the skipper here. But I thought I'd better introduce myself in case I can help. I'm Commodore Hansteen."

Harris stared, slack-jawed, at the man who had led the first expedition to Pluto, who had probably landed on more virgin planets and moons than any explorer in history. All he could say to express his astonishment was, "You weren't down on the passenger list!"

The Commodore smiled.

"My alias is Hanson. Since I retired, I've been trying to do a little sight-seeing without quite so much responsibility. And now that I've shaved off my beard, no one ever recognises me."

"I'm very glad to have you here," said Harris with deep feeling. Already some of the weight seemed to have lifted from his shoulders; the Commodore would be a tower of strength in the difficult hours—or days—that lay ahead.

"If you don't mind," continued Hansteen, with that same careful politeness. "I'd appreciate an evaluation. To put it bluntly, how long can we last?"

"Oxygen's the limiting factor, as usual. We've enough for about seven days, assuming that no leaks develop. So far, there are no signs of any."

"Well, that gives us time to think. What about food and water?"

"We'll be hungry, but we won't starve. There's an emergency reserve of compressed food, and of course the air-purifiers will produce all the water we need. So there's no problem there."

"Power?"

"Plenty, now that we're not using our motors."

"I notice that you haven't tried to call Base."

"It's useless; the dust blankets us completely. I've put the beacon on emergency—that's our only hope of getting a signal through, and it's a slim one."

"So they'll have to find us in some other way. How long do you think it will take them?"

"That's extremely difficult to say. The search will begin as soon as our 20.00 hours transmission is missed, and they'll know our general area. But we may have gone down without leaving any trace—you've seen how this dust obliterates everything. And even when they *do* find us——"

"—how will they get us out?"

"Exactly."

Skipper of twenty-seat dust-cruiser and Commodore of Space stared at each other in silence, as their minds circled the same problem. Then, cutting across the low murmur of conversation, they heard a very English voice call out: "I say, Miss—this is the first decent cup of tea I've drunk on the Moon. I thought no one could make it here; my congratulations."

The Commodore chuckled quietly.

"He ought to thank *you*, not the stewardess," he said, pointing to the pressure gauge.

Pat smiled rather wanly in return. That was true enough; now that he had put up the cabin pressure, water must be boiling at nearly its normal, sea-level temperature back on Earth. At last they could have some hot drinks—not the usual tepid ones. But it did seem a somewhat extravagant way to make tea, not unlike the reputed Chinese method of roasting pig by burning down the entire house.

"Our big problem," said the Commodore (and Pat did not in the least resent that "our"), "is to maintain morale. I think it's important, therefore, for you to give a pep-talk about the search procedure that must be starting now. But don't be *too* optimistic; you mustn't give the impression that someone will be knocking on the door inside half an hour. That might make it difficult if—well, if we have to wait several days."

"It won't take me long to describe the MOONCRASH organisation," said Pat. "And, frankly, it wasn't planned to deal with a situation like this. When a ship's down on the Moon, it can be spotted very quickly from one of the satellites—either Lagrange II above Earthside, or Lagrange I over Farside. But I doubt if they can help us now; as I said, we've probably gone down without leaving a trace."

"That's hard to believe. When a ship sinks on Earth, it always leaves *something* behind—bubbles, oil-slicks, floating wreckage."

"None of those apply to us. And I can't think of any way we could send something up to the surface—however far away that is."

"So we just have to sit and wait."

"Yes," agreed Pat. He glanced at the oxygen reserve indicator. "And there's one thing we can be sure of—we can only wait a week."

Fifty thousand kilometres above the Moon, Tom Lawson laid down the last of his photographs. He had gone over every square millimetre of the prints with a magnifying glass; their quality was excellent—the electronic image intensifier, millions of times more sensitive than the human eye, had revealed details clearly, as it was already daylight down there on the faintly glimmering plain. He had even spotted one of the dust-skis—or, more accurately, the long shadow it cast in the Earthlight. Yet there was no trace of *Selene*; the Sea was as smooth and unruffled as it had been before the coming of Man. And as it would be, in all probability, ages after he had gone.

Tom hated to admit defeat, even in matters far less important than this. He believed that all problems could be solved if they were tackled in the right way, with the right equipment. This was a challenge to his scientific ingenuity; the fact that there were many lives involved was immaterial. Dr. Tom Lawson had no great use for human beings, but he did respect the Universe. This was a private fight between him and It.

He considered the situation with a coldly critical intelligence. Now, how would the great Holmes have tackled the problem? (It was characteristic of Tom that one of the few men he really admired had never existed.) He had eliminated the open Sea, so that left only one possibility. The dust-cruiser must have come to grief along the coast or near the mountains, probably in the region known as—he checked the charts—Crater Lake. That made good sense; an accident was much more likely here than out on the smooth, unobstructed plain.

He looked at the photographs again, this time concentrating on the mountains. At once, he ran into a new difficulty. There were scores of isolated crags and boulders along the edge of the Sea—any one of which might be the missing cruiser. Worse still, there were many areas that he could not survey at all, because his view was blocked by the mountains themselves. From his vantage point, the Sea of Thirst was far around the curve of the Moon and his view of it was badly foreshortened. Crater Lake itself, for instance, was completely invisible to him, hidden by its mountain walls. That area could only be investigated by the dust-skis, working at ground level; even Tom Lawson's god-like eminence was useless here.

He had better call Earthside and give them his interim report.

'Lawson, Lagrange II," he said, when Communications had put him through. "I've searched the Sea of Thirst—there's nothing in the open plain. Your boat must have gone aground near the edge."

"Thank you," said an unhappy voice. "You're quite sure of that?"

"Absolutely. I can see your dust-skis, and they're only a quarter the size of *Selene*."

"Anything visible along the edge of the Sea?"

"There's too much small-scale detail to make a search possible; I can see fifty—oh, a hundred—objects that might be the right size. As soon as the sun rises I'll be able to examine them more closely. But it's night down there now, remember."

"We appreciate your help: let us know if you find anything else."

Down in Clavius City, the Tourist Commissioner heard Lawson's report with resignation. That settled it; the next-of-kin had better be notified. It was unwise, if not impossible, to maintain secrecy any longer.

He turned to the Traffic Control Officer and asked: "Is that passenger list in yet?"

"Just coming over the Telefax from Port Roris. Here you are." As he handed over the flimsy sheet he said inquisitively: "Anyone important aboard?"

"*All* tourists are important," said the Commissioner coldly, without looking up. Then, in almost the same breath, he added. "Oh, my God!"

"What's the matter?"

"Commodore Hansteen's aboard."

"*What*? I didn't know he was on the Moon."

"We've kept it quiet. We thought it was a good idea to have him on the Tourist Board, now that he's retired. He wanted to have a look around, *incognito*, before he made up his mind."

There was a shocked silence as the two men considered the irony of the situation. Here was one of the greatest heroes of space—lost as an ordinary tourist in some stupid accident in Earth's back-yard, the Moon. . . .

"That may be very bad luck for the Commodore," said the Traffic Controller at last. "But it's good luck for the passengers—if they're still alive."

"They'll need all the luck they can get, now the Observatory can't help us," said the Commissioner.

He was right on the first point, but wrong on the second. Dr. Tom Lawson still had a few tricks up his sleeve.

And so did Father Vincent Ferraro, S. J., a scientist of a very different kind. It was a pity that he and Tom Lawson were never to meet; the resulting fireworks would have been quite interesting. Father Ferraro believed in God and Man; Dr. Lawson believed in neither.

The priest had started his scientific career as a geophysicist, then switched worlds and became a selenophysicist—though that was a name he used only in his more pedantic moments. No man alive had a greater knowledge of the Moon's interior, gleaned from batteries of instruments strategically placed over the entire surface of the satellite.

Those instruments had just produced some rather interesting results. At 19 hours 35 minutes 47 seconds G.M.T., there had been a major quake in the general area of the Bay of Rainbows; that was a little surprising, for the area was an unusually stable one, even for the tranquil Moon. Father Ferraro set his computers to work pin-pointing the focus of the disturbance, and also instructed them to search for any other anomalous instrument readings. He left them at this task while he went to lunch, and it was here that his colleagues told him about the missing *Selene*.

No electronic computer can match the human brain at associating apparently irrelevant facts. Father Ferraro only had time for one spoonful of soup before he had put two and two together and had arrived at a perfectly reasonable but disastrously misleading answer.

CHAPTER V

"—AND THAT, LADIES and gentlemen, is the position," concluded Commodore Hansteen. "We're in no immediate danger, and I haven't the slightest doubt that we'll be located quite soon. Until then, we have to make the best of it."

He paused, and swiftly scanned the upturned, anxious faces. Already he had noted the possible trouble spots—that little man with the nervous tic, the acidulous, prune-faced lady who kept twisting her handkerchief in knots. Maybe they'd neutralise each other, if he could get them to sit together. . . .

"Captain Harris and I—he's the boss, I'm only acting as his adviser—have worked out a plan of action. Food will be simple and rationed, but will be adequate, especially as you won't be engaged in any physical activity. We would like to ask some of the ladies to help Miss Wilkins—she'll have a lot of extra work, and could do with some assistance. Our biggest problem, frankly, is going to be boredom. By the way, did anyone bring any books?"

There was much scrabbling in handbags and baskets. The total haul consisted of assorted lunar guides—including six copies of the official handbook; a current best-seller *The Orange and the Apple*, whose unlikely theme was a romance between Nell Gwyn and Sir Isaac Newton; a Harvard Press edition of *Shane*, with scholarly annotations by a professor of English; an introduction to the logical positivism of Auguste Comte; and a week-old copy of the *New York Times*, Earth edition. It was not much of a library, but with careful rationing it would help to pass the hours that lay ahead.

"I think we'll form an Entertainments Committee to decide how we'll use this material, though I don't know how it will deal with Monsieur Comte. Meanwhile, now that you know what our situation is, are there any questions—any points you'd like Captain Harris or myself to explain in more detail?"

"There's one thing I'd like to ask, sir," said the English voice that had made the complimentary remarks about the tea. "Is there the slightest chance that we'll *float* up? I mean—if this stuff is like water, won't we bob up sooner or later, like a cork?"

That floored the Commodore completely. He looked at Pat and said wryly: "That's one for you, Mr. Harris. Any comment?"

Pat shook his head.

"I'm afraid it won't work. True, the air inside the hull must make us very buoyant, but the resistance of this dust is enormous. We *may* float up eventually —in a few thousand years."

The Englishman, it seemed, was not easily discouraged.

"I noticed that there was a space-suit in the airlock. Could anyone get out and *swim* up? Then the search party will know where we are."

Captain Harris stirred uneasily. He was the only one qualified to wear that suit, which was purely for emergency use.

"I'm almost sure it's impossible," he answered. "I doubt if a man could move against the resistance—and of course he'd be absolutely blind. How would he know which way was up? And how would you close the outer door after him? Once the dust had flooded in, there would be no way of clearing it. You certainly couldn't pump it out again."

He could have said more, but decided to leave it at that. They might yet be reduced to such desperate expedients, if there was no sign of rescue by the end of the week. But that was a nightmare that must be kept firmly at the back of his mind, for to dwell too long upon it could only sap his courage.

"If there are no more questions," said Hansteen, "I suggest we introduce ourselves. Whether we like it or not, we have to get used to each other's company, so let's find out who we are. I'll go round the room and perhaps each of you in turn will give your name, occupation and home-town. You first, sir."

"Robert Bryan, civil engineer, retired—Kingston, Jamaica."

"Irving Schuster, Attorney at Law, Chicago—and my wife, Myra."

"Nihal Jayawardene, Professor of Zoology, University of Ceylon, Peradeniya."

As the roll-call continued, Pat Harris once again found himself grateful for the one piece of luck in this desperate situation. By character, training and experience Commodore Hansteen was a born leader of men: already he was beginning to weld this random collection of individuals into a unit, to build up that indefinable *esprit de corps* that transforms a mob into a team. These things he had learned while his little fleet—the first ever to venture beyond the orbit of Neptune, almost three billion miles from the Sun—had hung poised week upon week in the emptiness between the planets. Pat Harris, who was thirty years younger and had never been away from the Earth-Moon system, felt no resentment at the change of command that had tacitly taken place. It was nice of the Commodore to say that he was still the boss, but he knew better.

"Duncan McKenzie, physicist, Mount Stromlo Observatory, Canberra."

"Pierre Blanchard, cost accountant, Clavius City, Earthside."

"Phyllis Morley, journalist, London."

"Karl Johansen, nucleonics engineer, Tsiolkovski Base, Farside."

That was the lot; quite a collection of talent, though not an unusual one, for the people who came to the Moon always had something out of the ordinary—even if it was only money. But all the skill and experience now locked up in *Selene* could not, so it seemed to Harris, do anything to help them in their present situation.

That was not quite true, as Commodore Hansteen was now about to prove. He knew, as well as any man alive, that they would be fighting boredom as well as fear. They had been thrown upon their own resources; in an age of universal entertainment and communications, they had suddenly been cut off from the rest of the human race. Radio, TV, Telefax newsheets, movies, telephone—all these things meant no more to them than to the people of the Stone Age. They were like some ancient tribe gathered round the camp fire, in a wilderness that held no other men. Even on the Pluto run, thought Commodore Hansteen, they had never been as lonely as this. They had had a fine library and had been well stocked with every possible form of canned entertainment, and could talk by tight beam to the inner planets whenever they wished. But on *Selene*, there was not even a pack of cards. . . .

That was an idea. "Miss Morley! As a journalist, I imagine you have a note-book?"

"Why, yes, Commodore."

"Fifty-two blank sheets in it still?"

"I think so."

"Then I must ask you to sacrifice them. Please cut them out and mark a pack of cards on them. No need to be artistic—as long as they're legible, and the lettering doesn't show through the back."

"How are you going to shuffle paper cards?" asked somebody.

"A good problem for our Entertainments Committee to solve. Anyone who thinks they have talent in this direction?"

"I used to be on the stage," said Myra Schuster, rather hesitantly. Her husband did not look at all pleased at this revelation, but it delighted the Commodore.

"Excellent! Though we're a little cramped for space, I was hoping we might be able to put on a play."

Now Mrs. Schuster looked as unhappy as her husband.

"It was rather a long time ago," she said, "and I—I never did much talking."

There were several chuckles, and even the Commodore had difficulty in keeping a straight face. Looking at Mrs. Schuster, on the wrong side both of fifty years and a hundred kilos, it was a little hard to imagine her as—he suspected—a chorus girl.

"Never mind," he said, "it's the spirit that counts. Who will help Mrs. Schuster?"

"I've done some amateur theatricals," said Professor Jayawardene. "Mostly Brecht and Ibsen, though."

That final "though" indicated recognition of the fact that something a little lighter would be appreciated here—say one of the decadent but amusing comedies of the 1980s, which had invaded the airways in such numbers with the collapse of TV censorship.

There were no more volunteers for this job, so the Commodore moved Mrs. Schuster and Professor Jayawardene into adjacent seats and told them to start programme-planning. It seemed unlikely that such an ill-assorted pair would produce anything useful, but one never knew. The main thing was to keep everyone busy—either on tasks of their own, or co-operating with others.

"We'll leave it at that for the moment," concluded Hansteen. "If you have any bright ideas, please give them to the Committee. Meanwhile, I suggest you stretch your legs and get to know each other. Everyone's announced his job and home-town; many of you must have common interests or know the same friends. You'll have plenty of things to talk about." And plenty of time too, he added silently.

He was conferring with Pat in the pilot's cubicle when they were joined by Dr. McKenzie, the Australian physicist. He looked very worried—even more so than the situation merited.

"There's something I want to tell you, Commodore," he said urgently. "If I'm right, that seven days' oxygen reserve doesn't mean a thing. There's a much more serious danger."

"What's that?"

"Heat." The Australian indicated the outside world with a wave of his hand. "We're blanketed by this stuff, and it's about the best insulator you can have. On the surface, the heat our machines and bodies generated could escape into space, but down here it's trapped. That means we'll get hotter and hotter— until we cook."

"My God," said the Commodore. "I never thought of that. How long do you think it will take?"

"Give me half an hour, and I can make a fair estimate. My guess is—not much more than a day."

The Commodore felt a wave of utter helplessness sweep over him. There was a horrible sickness at the pit of his stomach, like the second time he had been in free fall. (Not the first—he had been ready for it then. But on the second trip, he had been over-confident.) If this estimate was right, all their hopes were blasted. They were slim enough in all conscience, but given a week there was a slight chance that something might be done. With only a day, it was out of the question. Even if they were found in that time, they could never be rescued.

"You might check the cabin temperature," continued McKenzie. "That will give us some indication."

Hansteen walked to the control panel and glanced at the maze of dials and indicators.

"I'm afraid you're right," he said. "It's gone up two degrees already."

"Over a degree an hour. That's about what I figured."

The Commodore turned to Harris, who had been listening to the discussion with growing alarm.

"Is there anything we can do to increase the cooling? How much reserve power has our air-conditioning gear got?"

Before Harris could answer, the physicist intervened.

"That won't help us," he said a little impatiently. "All that our refrigeration does is to pump heat out of the cabin and radiate it away. But that's exactly what it *can't* do now, because of the dust around us. If we try to run the cooling plant faster it will make matters worse."

There was a gloomy silence that lasted until the Commodore said: "Please check those calculations, and let me have your best estimate as soon as you can. And for heaven's sake don't let this go beyond the three of us."

He felt suddenly very old. He had been almost enjoying his unexpected last command; and now it seemed that he would have it only for a day.

At that very moment, though neither party knew the fact, one of the searching dust-skis was passing overhead. Built for speed, efficiency and cheapness, not for the comfort of tourists, it bore little resemblance to the sunken *Selene*. It was, in fact, no more than an open sledge with seats for pilot and one passenger—each wearing space-suits—and with a canopy overhead to give protection from the sun. A simple control panel, motor and twin fans at the rear, storage racks for tools and equipment—that completed the inventory. A ski going about its normal work usually towed at least one carrier sledge behind it, sometimes two or three, but this one was travelling light. It had zigzagged back and forth across several hundred square kilometres of the Sea, and had found absolutely nothing.

Over the suit intercom, the driver was talking to his companion.

"What do *you* think happened to them, George? I don't believe they're here."

"Where else can they be? Kidnapped by Outsiders?"

"I'm almost ready to buy that," was the half-serious answer. Sooner or later, all astronauts believed, the human race would meet intelligence from elsewhere. That meeting might still be far in the future, but meanwhile the hypothetical "Outsiders" were part of the mythology of space, and got the blame for everything that could not be explained in any other way.

It was easy to believe in them when you were with a mere handful of companions on some strange, hostile world where the very rocks and air (if there *was* air) was completely alien. Then nothing could be taken for granted, and the experience of a thousand Earth-bound generations might be useless. As ancient man had peopled the unknown around him with gods and spirits, so *Homo astronauticus* looked over his shoulder when he landed upon each new world, wondering who or what was here already. For a few brief centuries Man had imagined himself the lord of the universe, and those primeval hopes and fears had been buried in his subconscious. But now they were stronger than ever, and with good reason, as he looked into the shining face of the heavens, and thought of the power and knowledge that must be lurking there.

"Better report to Base," said George. "We've covered our area, and there's no point in going over it again. Not until sunrise, anyway—we'll have a much better chance of finding something then. This damned Earthlight gives me the creeps."

He switched on the radio, and gave the ski's call-sign.

"Duster Two calling Traffic Control—over."

"Port Roris Traffic Control here. Found anything?"

"Not a trace. What's new from your end?"

"We don't think she's out in the Sea. The Chief Engineer wants to speak to you."

"Right; put him on."

"Hello, Duster Two. Lawrence here. Plato Observatory's just reported a quake near the Mountains of Inaccessibility. It took place at 19.35, which is near enough the time when *Selene* should have been in Crater Lake. They suggest she's been caught in an avalanche somewhere in that area. So head for the mountains and see if you can spot any recent slides or rockfalls."

"What's the chance, sir," asked the dust-ski pilot anxiously, "that there may be more quakes?"

"Very small, according to the Observatory. They say it will be thousands of years before anything like this happens again, now that the stresses have been relieved."

"I hope they're right. I'll radio when I get to Crater Lake; that should be in about twenty minutes."

But it was only fifteen minutes before Duster Two destroyed the last hopes of the waiting listeners.

"Duster Two calling. This is it, I'm afraid. I've not reached Crater Lake yet—I'm still heading up the gorge. But the Observatory was right about the quake; there have been several slides, and we had difficulty in getting past some of them. There must be ten thousand tons of rock in the one I'm looking at now; if Selene's under that lot, we'll never find her. And it won't be worth the trouble of looking."

The silence in Traffic Control lasted so long that the ski called back: "Hello, Base—did you receive me?"

"Receiving you," said the Chief Engineer in a tired voice. "See if you can find *some* trace of them; I'll send Duster One in to help. Are you sure there's no chance of digging them out?"

"It might take weeks, even if we could locate them. I saw one slide three hundred metres long. If you tried to dig, the rock would probably start moving again."

"Be very careful. Report every fifteen minutes, whether you find anything or not."

Lawrence turned away from the microphone, physically and mentally exhausted. There was nothing more that he could do—or, he suspected, that anyone could do. Trying to compose his thoughts, he walked over to the southwards-facing observation window, and stared into the face of the crescent Earth.

It was hard to believe that she was fixed there in the southern sky—that though she hung so close to the horizon, she would neither rise nor set in a million years. However long one lived here, one never really accepted this fact, which violated all the racial wisdom of mankind.

On the other side of that gulf (already so small to a generation that had never known the time when it could not be crossed) ripples of shock and grief would soon be spreading. Thousands of men and women were involved, directly or indirectly, because the Moon had stirred briefly in her sleep.

Lost in his thoughts, it was some time before Lawrence realised that the Port signals officer was trying to attract his attention.

"Excuse me, sir—you've not called Duster One. Shall I do it now?"

"What? Oh yes—go ahead. Send him to help Two in Crater Lake. Tell him we've called off the search in the Sea of Thirst."

CHAPTER VI

THE NEWS THAT the search had been called off reached Lagrange II when Tom Lawson, red-eyed from lack of sleep, had almost completed the modifications to the hundred-centimetre telescope. He had been racing against time, and now it seemed that all his efforts had been wasted. *Selene* was not in the Sea of Thirst at all, but in a place where he could never have found her —hidden from him by the ramparts of Crater Lake, and for good measure buried by a few thousand tons of rock.

Tom's first reaction was not one of sympathy for the victims, but of anger at his wasted time and effort. Those YOUNG ASTRONOMER FINDS MISSING TOURISTS headlines would never flash across the news-screens of the inhabited worlds. As his private dreams of glory collapsed, he cursed for a good thirty seconds, with a fluency that would have astonished his colleagues. Then, still furious, he started to dismantle the equipment he had begged, borrowed and stolen from the other projects on the satellite.

It would have worked, he was sure of that. The theory had been quite sound —indeed, it was based on almost a hundred years of practice. Infra-red reconnaissance dated back to at least as early as the Second World War, when it was used to locate camouflaged factories by their tell-tale heat.

Though *Selene* had left no visible track across the Sea, she must surely have left an infra-red one. Her fans had stirred up the relatively warm dust a foot or so down, scattering it across the far colder surface layers. An eye that could see by the rays of heat could track her path for hours after she had passed. There would have been just time, Tom calculated, to make such an infra-red survey before the Sun rose and obliterated all traces of the faint heat-trail through the cold lunar night.

But, obviously, there was no point in trying now.

It was well that no one aboard *Selene* could have guessed that the search in the Sea of Thirst had been abandoned, and that the dust-skis were concentrating their efforts inside Crater Lake. And it was well, also, none of the passengers knew of Dr. McKenzie's predictions.

The physicist had drawn, on a piece of home-made graph-paper, the expected rise of temperature. Every hour he noted the reading of the cabin thermometer and pin-pointed it on the curve. The agreement with theory was depressingly good; in twenty hours, 110 degrees Fahrenheit would be passed, and the first deaths from heat-stroke would be occurring. Whatever way he looked at it, they had barely a day to live. In these circumstances, Commodore Hansteen's efforts to maintain morale seemed no more than an ironic jest. Whether he failed or succeeded, it would be all the same by the day after tomorrow.

Yet was that true? Though their only choice might lie between dying like men and dying like animals, surely the first was better. It made no difference, even if *Selene* remained undiscovered until the end of time, so that no one ever knew how her occupants passed their final hours. This was beyond logic or reason; but so, for that matter, was almost everything that was really important in the shaping of man's lives and deaths.

Commodore Hansteen was well aware of that, as he planned the programme for the dwindling hours that lay ahead. Some men are born to be leaders, and he was one of them. The emptiness of his retirement had been suddenly filled; for the first time since he had left the bridge of his flagship *Centaurus*, he felt whole again.

As long as his little crew was busy, he need not worry about morale. It did not matter what they were doing, provided they thought it interesting or important. That poker game, for instance, took care of the Space Administration accountant, the retired civil engineer, and the two executives on vacation from New York. One could tell at a glance that they were all poker-fanatics; the problem would be to stop them playing, not to keep them occupied.

Most of the other passengers had split up into discussion groups, talking quite cheerfully among themselves. The Entertainments Committee was still in session, with Professor Jayawardene making occasional notes while Mrs. Schuster reminisced about her days in burlesque, despite the attempts of her husband to shut her up. The only person who seemed a little apart from it all was Miss Morley, who was writing slowly and carefully, using a very minute hand, in what was left of her notebook. Presumably, like a good journalist she was keeping a diary of their adventure; Commodore Hansteen was afraid that it would be briefer than she suspected, and that not even those few pages would be filled. And if they were, he doubted that anyone would ever read them.

He glanced at his watch, and was surprised to see how late it was. By now, he should have been on the other side of the Moon, back in Clavius City. He had a lunch engagement at the Lunar Hilton, and after that a trip to—but there was no point in thinking about a future that could never exist. The brief present was all that would ever concern him now.

It would be as well to get some sleep, before the temperature became unbearable. *Selene* had never been designed as a dormitory—or a tomb, for that matter—but it would have to be turned into one now. This involved some research and planning, and a certain amount of damage to Tourist Commission property. It took him twenty minutes to ascertain all the facts; then, after a brief conference with Captain Harris, he called for attention.

"Ladies and gentlemen," he said, "we've all had a busy day, and I think most of us will be glad to get some sleep. This presents a few problems, but I've been doing some experimenting and have discovered that with a little encouragement the centre arm-rests between the seats come out. They're not supposed to, but I doubt if the Commission will sue us. That means that ten of us can stretch out across the seats; the rest will have to use the floor.

"Another point. As you will have noticed, it's becoming rather warm, and will continue to do so for some time. Therefore I advise you to take off all unnecessary clothing; comfort is much more important than modesty." ("And survival," he added silently, "is much more important than comfort"—but it would be some hours yet before it came to that.)

"We'll turn off the main cabin lights, and as we don't want to be in complete darkness we'll leave on the emergency lighting at low power. One of us will remain on watch at all times in the skipper's seat; Mr. Harris is working out a roster of two-hour shifts. Any questions or comments?"

There were none, and the Commodore breathed a sigh of relief. He was afraid that someone would be inquisitive about the rising temperature, and was not quite sure how he would have answered. His many accomplishments did not include the gift of lying, and he was anxious that the passengers should have as untroubled a sleep as was possible in the circumstances. Barring a miracle, it would be their last.

Miss Wilkins, who was beginning to lose a little of her professional smartness, took round final drinks for those who needed them. Most of the passengers had already begun to remove their outer clothing; the more modest ones waited until the main lights went off. In the dim red glow, the interior of *Selene* now had a fantastic appearance—one which would have been utterly inconceivable when she left Port Roris a few hours before. Twenty-two men and women, most of them stripped down to their underclothing, lay sprawled across the seats or along the floor. A few lucky ones were already snoring, but for most, sleep would not come as easily as that.

Captain Harris had chosen a position at the very rear of the cruiser; in fact, he was not in the cabin at all, but in the tiny airlock-kitchen. It was a good vantage point; now that the communicating door had been slid back, he could look the whole length of the cabin and keep an eye on everyone inside it.

He folded his uniform into a pillow, and lay down on the unyielding floor. It was six hours before his watch was due, and he hoped he could get some sleep before then.

Sleep! The last hours of his life were ticking away, yet he had nothing better to do. How well do condemned men sleep, he wondered, in the night that will end with the gallows?

He was so desperately tired that even this thought brought no emotion. The last thing he saw, before consciousness slipped away, was Dr. McKenzie taking yet another temperature reading and carefully plotting it on his chart, like an astrologer casting a horoscope.

Fifteen metres above—a distance that could be covered in a single stride under this low gravity—morning had already come. There is no twilight on the Moon, but for many hours the sky had held the promise of dawn. Stretching far ahead of the sun was the glowing pyramid of the Zodiacal Light, so seldom seen on Earth. With infinite slowness it edged its way above the horizon, growing brighter and brighter as the moment of sunrise approached. Now it had merged into the opalescent glory of the corona—and now, a million times more brilliant than either, a thin thread of fire began to spread along the horizon as the Sun made its reappearance after fifteen days of darkness. It would take more than an hour for it to lift itself clear of the skyline, so slowly did the Moon turn on its axis, but the night had already ended.

A tide of ink was swiftly ebbing from the Sea of Thirst, as the fierce light of dawn swept back the darkness. Now the whole drab expanse of the Sea was raked with almost horizontal rays; had there been anything showing above its surface, this grazing light would have thrown its shadow for hundreds of metres, revealing it at once to any who were searching.

But there were no searchers here: Duster One and Duster Two were busy on their fruitless quest in Crater Lake, fifteen kilometres away. They were still in darkness; it would be another two days before the sun rose above the surrounding peaks, though their summits were already blazing with the dawn. As the hours passed, the sharp-edged line of light would creep down the flanks of the mountains—sometimes moving no faster than a man could walk—until the sun climbed high enough for its rays to strike into the crater.

But man-made light was already shining here, flashing among the rocks as the searchers photographed the slides that had come sweeping silently down the mountains when the Moon trembled in its sleep. Within an hour, those photographs would have reached Earth; in another two, all the inhabited worlds would have seen them.

It would be very bad for the tourist business.

When Captain Harris awoke, it was already much hotter. Yet it was not the now oppressive heat that had interrupted his sleep, a good hour before he was due to go on watch.

Though he had never spent a night aboard her, Pat knew all the sounds that *Selene* could make. When the motors were not running, she was almost silent; one had to listen carefully to notice the sussuration of the air pumps and the low throb of the cooling plant. Those sounds were still there, as they had been before he went to sleep. They were unchanged; but they had been joined by another.

It was a barely audible whisper, so faint that for a moment he could not be sure if he was imagining it. That it should have called to his subconscious mind across the barriers of sleep seemed quite incredible; even now that he was awake, he could not identify it, or decide from which direction it came.

Then, abruptly, he knew why it had awakened him. In a second, the sogginess of sleep had vanished. He got quickly to his feet, and pressed his ear against the airlock door; for that mysterious sound was coming from *outside* the hull.

Now he could hear it, faint but distinct, and it set his skin crawling with apprehension. There could be no doubt; it was the sound of countless dust-grains whispering past *Selene*'s walls like a ghostly sand-storm. What did it mean? Was the Sea once more on the move? If so, would it take *Selene* with it? Yet there was not the slightest vibration or sense of motion in the cruiser itself; only the outside world was rustling past. . . .

Very quietly, being careful not to disturb his sleeping companions, Pat tiptoed into the darkened cabin. It was Dr. McKenzie's watch; the scientist was hunched up in the pilot's seat, staring out through the blinded windows. He turned round as Pat approached, and whispered: "Anything wrong at your end?"

"I don't know—come and see."

Back in the galley, they pressed their ears against the outer door, and listened for a long time to the mysterious crepitation. Presently McKenzie said: "The dust's moving all right—but I don't see why. That gives us another puzzle to worry about."

"Another?"

"Yes; I don't understand what's happening to the temperature. It's still going up, but nothing like as fast as it should."

The physicist seemed really annoyed that his calculations had proved incorrect, but to Pat this was the first piece of good news since the disaster.

"Don't look so miserable about it; we all make mistakes. And if this one gives us a few more days to live, I'm certainly not complaining."

"But I *couldn't* have made a mistake—the maths is elementary. We know how much heat twenty-two people generate, and it must go somewhere."

"They won't produce so much heat when they're sleeping; maybe that explains it."

"You don't think I'd overlook anything so obvious as that!" said the scientist testily. "It helps, but it isn't enough. There's some other reason why we're not getting as hot as we should."

"Let's just accept the fact and be thankful," said Pat. "Meanwhile, what about this noise?"

With obvious reluctance, McKenzie switched his mind to the new problem.

"The dust's moving, but we aren't, so it's probably merely a local effect. In fact, it only seems to be happening at the back of the cabin. I wonder if that has any significance." He gestured to the bulkhead behind them. "What's on the other side of this?"

"The motors, oxygen reserve, cooling equipment . . ."

"*Cooling* equipment! Of course! I remember noticing that when I came aboard. Our radiator fins are back there, aren't they?"

"That's right."

"*Now* I see what's happened. They've got so hot that the dust is circulating, like any liquid that's heated. There's a dust-fountain outside, and it's carrying away our surplus heat. With any luck, the temperature will stabilise now. We won't be comfortable, but we can survive."

In the crimson gloom, the two men looked at each other with a dawning hope. Then Pat said slowly: "I'm sure that's the explanation. Perhaps our luck's beginning to turn."

He glanced at his watch, and did a quick mental calculation.

"The sun's rising over the Sea about now. Base will have the dust-skis out looking for us, and they must know our approximate position. Ten to one they'll find us in a few hours."

"Should we tell the Commodore?"

"No, let him sleep. He's had a harder day than any of us. This news can wait until morning."

When McKenzie had left him, Pat tried to resume his interrupted sleep. But he could not do so; he lay with his eyes open in the faint red glow, wondering at this strange turn of fate. The dust which had swallowed and then had threatened to broil them had now come to their aid, as its convection currents swept their surplus heat up to the surface. Whether those currents would continue to flow when the rising sun smote the Sea with its full fury, he could not guess.

Outside the wall, the dust still whispered past, and suddenly Pat was reminded of an antique hour-glass he had once been shown as a child. When you turned it over, sand poured through a narrow construction into the lower chamber, and its rising level marked the passage of the minutes and the hours.

Before the invention of clocks, myriads of men must have had their days divided by such falling grains of sand. But none until now, surely, had ever had his life-span metered out by a fountain of rising dust.

CHAPTER VII

IN CLAVIUS CITY, Chief Administrator Olsen and Tourist Commissioner Davis had just finished conferring with the Legal Department. It had not been a cheerful occasion; much of the time had been spent discussing the waivers of responsibility which the missing tourists had signed before they boarded *Selene*. Commissioner Davis had been much against this when the trips were started, on the grounds that it would scare away customers, but the Administration's lawyers had insisted. Now he was very glad that they had had their way.

He was glad, also, that the Port Roris authorities had done the job properly; matters like this were sometimes treated as unimportant formalities and quietly ignored. There was a full list of signatures for *Selene*'s passengers—with one possible exception that the lawyers were still arguing about.

The incognito Commodore had been listed as R. S. Hanson, and it looked very much as if this was the name he had actually signed. The signature was, however, so illegible that it might well have been "Hansteen"; until a facsimile was radioed from Earth, no one would be able to decide this point. It was probably unimportant; as the Commodore was travelling on official business, the Administration was bound to accept some responsibility for him. And for all the other passengers, it was responsible morally, if not legally.

Above all, it had to make an effort to find them and give them a decent burial. This little problem had been placed squarely in the lap of Chief Engineer Lawrence, who was still at Port Roris.

He had seldom tackled anything with less enthusiasm. While there was a chance that the *Selene*'s passengers were still alive, he would have moved heaven, Earth and Moon to get at them. But now that they must be dead, he saw no point in risking men's lives to locate them and dig them out. Personally, he could hardly think of a better place to be buried, than among these eternal hills.

That they were dead, Chief Engineer Robert Lawrence did not have the slightest doubt; all the facts fitted together too perfectly. The quake had occurred at just about the time *Selene* should have been leaving Crater Lake, and the gorge was now half-blocked with slides. Even the smallest of those would have crushed her like a paper toy, and those aboard would have perished within seconds as the air gushed out. If, by some million to one chance, she had escaped being smashed, her radio signals would have been received; the tough little automatic beacon had been built to take any reasonable punishment, and if *that* was out of action, it must have been some crack-up. . . .

The first problem would be to locate the wreck; that might be fairly easy, even if it was buried beneath a million tons of rubble. There were prospecting instruments and a whole range of metal detectors that could do the trick. And when the hull was cracked, the air inside would have rushed out into the lunar near-vacuum; even now, hours later, there would be traces of carbon dioxide and oxygen that might be spotted by one of the gas detectors used for pin-pointing space-ship leaks. As soon as the dust-skis came back to base for servicing and recharging, he'd get them fitted with leak detectors and would send them sniffing round the rock-slides.

No—*finding* the wreck might be simple; it was getting it out that might be impossible. He wouldn't guarantee that the job could be done for a hundred million. (And he could just see the C.A.'s face if he mentioned a sum like that.) For one thing, it was a physical impossibility to bring heavy equipment into the area—the sort of equipment needed to move thousands of tons of rubble. The flimsy little dust-skis were useless; to shift those rock-slides one would have to float moondozers across the Sea of Thirst, and import whole shiploads of gelignite to blast a road through the mountains. The whole idea was absurd; he could understand the Administration's point of view, but he was damned if he would let his overworked Engineering Division get saddled with such a Sisyphean task.

As tactfully as possible—for the Chief Administrator was not the sort of man who liked to take "no" for an answer—he began to draft his report. Summarised, it might have read: "(A) The job's almost certainly impossible. (B) If it can be done at all it will cost millions and may involve further loss of life. (C) It's not worth doing anyway." But because such bluntness would make him unpopular, and he had to give his reasons, the report ran to over three thousand words.

When he had finished dictation he paused to marshall his ideas, could think of nothing further, and added: "Copies to Chief Administrator, Moon; Chief Engineer, Farside; Supervisor, Traffic Control; Tourist Commissioner; Central Filing. Classify as Confidential."

He pressed the Transcription key. Within twenty seconds all twelve pages of his report, impeccably typed and punctuated, with several grammatical slips corrected, had emerged from the office Telefax. He scanned it rapidly, in case the Electrosecretary had made mistakes. She did this occasionally (all Electrosecs were "she"), especially during rush periods when she might be taking dictation from a dozen sources at once. In any event, no wholly sane machine could cope with all the eccentricities of a language like English, and every wise executive checked his final draft before he sent it out. Many were the hilarious disasters that had overtaken those who had left it all to electronics.

Lawrence was half-way through this task when the telephone rang.

"Lagrange II on the line, sir," said the operator—a human one, as it happened. "A Doctor Lawson wants to speak to you."

Lawson? Who the devil's that? the C.E.E. asked himself. Then he remembered; that was the astronomer who was making the telescopic search. Surely someone had told him that it was useless. . . .

The Chief Engineer had never had the dubious privilege of meeting Dr. Lawson. He did not know that the astronomer was a very neurotic and very brilliant young man—and, what was more important in this case, a very stubborn one.

Lawson had just begun to dismantle the infra-red scanner when he stopped to consider his action. Since he had practically completed the blasted thing, he might as well test it, out of sheer scientific curiosity. Tom Lawson prided himself, rightly, as a practical experimenter; this was something unusual in an age when most so-called astronomers were really mathematicians who never went near an observatory.

He was now so tired that only sheer cussedness kept him going. If the scanner had not worked first time, he would have postponed testing it until he had some sleep. But by the good luck that is occasionally the reward of skill, it *did* work; only a few minor adjustments were needed before the image of the Sea of Thirst began to build up upon the viewing screen.

It appeared line by line, like an old-fashioned TV picture, as the infra-red detector scanned back and forth across the face of the Moon. The light patches indicated relatively warm areas, the dark ones, regions of cold. Almost all the Sea of Thirst was dark, except for a brilliant band where the rising sun had already touched it with fire. But in that darkness, as Tom looked closely, he could see some very faint tracks, glimmering as feebly as the paths of snails through some moonlit garden back on Earth.

Beyond doubt, there was the heat-trail of *Selene*; and there also, much fainter, were the zigzags of the dust-skis that even now were searching for her. All the trails converged towards the Mountains of Inaccessibility and there vanished beyond his field of view.

He was much too tired to examine them closely, and in any event it no longer mattered, for this merely confirmed what was already known. His only satisfaction, which was of some importance to him, lay in the proof that another piece of Lawson-built equipment had obeyed his will. For the record, he photographed the screen—then staggered to bed to catch up with his arrears of sleep.

Three hours later he awoke from a restless slumber. Despite his extra hour in bed, he was still tired, but something was worrying him and would not let him sleep. As the faint whisper of moving dust had disturbed Pat Harris in the sunken *Selene*, so also, fifty thousand kilometres away, Tom Lawson was recalled from sleep by a trifling variation from the normal. The mind has many watchdogs; sometimes they bark unnecessarily, but a wise man never ignores their warning.

Still bleary-eyed, Tom Lawson left the cluttered little cell that was his private cabin aboard Lagrange, hooked himself on to the nearest moving belt, and drifted along the gravityless corridors until he had reached the Observatory. He exchanged a surly good-morning (though it was now late in the satellite's arbitrary afternoon) with those of his colleagues who did not see him in time to take avoiding action. Then, thankful to be alone, he settled down among the instruments that were the only things he loved.

He ripped the photograph out of the one-shot camera where it had been lying all night, and looked at it for the first time. It was then that he saw the stubby trail emerging from the Mountains of Inaccessibility, and ending a very short distance away in the Sea of Thirst.

He must have seen it last night when he looked at the screen—but he had not noticed it. For a scientist, that was a serious, almost an unforgivable lapse and Tom Lawson felt very angry with himself. He had let his preconceived ideas affect his powers of observation.

What did it mean? He examined the area closely with a magnifier. The trail ended in a small, diffuse dot, which he judged to be about two hundred metres across. It was very odd—almost as if *Selene* had emerged from the mountains, and then taken off like a spaceship.

Tom's first theory was that she had blown to pieces, and that this smudge of heat was the aftermath of the explosion. But in that case, there would have been plenty of wreckage, most of it light enough to float on the dust. The skis could hardly have missed it when they passed through this area—as the thin, distinctive track of one showed it had indeed done.

There had to be some other explanation, yet the alternative seemed absurd. It was almost impossible to imagine that anything as large as *Selene* could sink without trace in the Sea of Thirst, merely because there had been a quake in that neighbourhood. He certainly could not call the Moon, on the evidence of a single photograph and say "You're looking in the wrong place." Though he pretended that the opinion of others meant nothing to him, Tom was terrified of making a fool of himself. Before he could advance this fantastic theory, he would have to get more evidence.

Through the telescope, the Sea was now a flat and featureless glare of light. Visual observation merely confirmed what he had proved before sunrise; there was nothing more than a few centimetres high projecting above the dust surface. The infra-red scanner was no greater help: the heat trails had vanished completely, wiped out hours ago by the sun.

Tom adjusted the instrument for maximum sensitivity, and searched the area where the trail had ended. Perhaps there was some lingering trace that could be picked up even now—some faint smudge of heat that still persisted, strong enough to be detected even in the warmth of the lunar morning. For the sun was still low, and its rays had not yet attained the murderous power they would possess at noon.

Was it imagination? He had the gain turned full up, so that the instrument was on the verge of instability. From time to time, at the very limit of its detecting power, he thought he could see a tiny glimmer of heat, in the exact area where last night's track had ended.

It was all infuriatingly inconclusive—not at all the sort of evidence that a scientist needed, especially when he was going to stick his neck out. If he said nothing, no one would ever know—but all his life he would be haunted by doubts. Yet if he committed himself, he might raise false hopes, become the laughing-stock of the Solar System, or be accused of seeking personal publicity.

He could not have it both ways; he would have to make a decision. With great reluctance, knowing that he was taking a step from which there could be no turning back, he picked up the Observatory phone.

"Lawson here," he said. "Get me Luna Central—Priority."

CHAPTER VIII

ABOARD *Selene*, BREAKFAST had been adequate but hardly inspiring. There were several complaints from passengers who thought that crackers and compressed meat, a dab of honey and a glass of tepid water, scarcely constituted a good meal. But the Commodore had been adamant: "We don't know how long this has got to last us," he said, "and I'm afraid we can't have hot meals. There's no way of preparing them, and it's too warm in the cabin already. Sorry, no more tea or coffee. And frankly, it won't do any of us much harm to cut down on the calories for a few days." That came out before he remembered Mrs. Schuster, and he hoped that she wouldn't take it as a personal affront. Ungirdled after last night's general clothes-shedding, she now looked rather like a good-natured hippopotamus, as she lay sprawled over a seat and a half.

"The sun's just risen overhead," continued Hansteen, "the search-parties will be out, and it's only a matter of time before they locate us. It's been suggested that we have a sweepstake on that; Miss Morley, who's keeping the log, will collect your bets.

"Now about our programme for the day. Professor Jayawardene—perhaps you'll let us know what the Entertainments Committee has arranged."

The Professor was a small, bird-like person whose gentle dark eyes seemed much too large for him. It was obvious that he had taken the task of entertainment very seriously, for his delicate brown hand clutched an impressive sheaf of notes.

"As you know," he said, "my speciality is the theatre—but I'm afraid that doesn't help us very much. It would be nice to have a play-reading, and I thought of writing out some parts; unfortunately, we're too short of paper to make that possible. So we'll have to think of something else.

"There's not much reading matter on board, and some of it is rather specialised. But we do have two novels—a University edition of one of the classic westerns, *Shane*, and this new historical romance, *The Orange and the Apple*. The suggestion is that we form a panel of readers and go through them. Has anyone any objection—or any better ideas?"

"We want to play poker," said a firm voice from the rear.

"But you can't play poker *all* the time," protested the Professor, thus showing a certain ignorance of the non-academic world. The Commodore decided to go to his rescue.

"The reading need not interfere with the poker," he said. "Besides, I suggest you take a break now and then. Those cards won't last much longer."

"Well, which book shall we start on first? And any volunteers as readers? I'll be quite happy to do so, but we want some variety——"

"I object to wasting our time on *The Orange and the Apple*," said Miss Morley. "It's utter trash, and most of it is—er—near-pornography."

"How do *you* know?" asked David Barrett, the Englishman who had commended the tea. The only answer was an indignant sniff. Professor Jayawardene looked very unhappy, and glanced at the Commodore for support. He did not get any; Hansteen was studiously looking the other way. If the passengers relied on him for everything, that would be fatal; as far as possible, he wanted them to stand on their own feet.

"Very well," said the Professor. "To prevent any argument, we'll start with *Shane*."

There were several protesting cries of: "We want *The Orange and the Apple*!" but, surprisingly, the Professor stood firm: "It's a very long book," he said. "I really don't think we'll have time to finish it before we're rescued." He cleared his throat, looked around the cabin to see if there were any further objections, and then started to read in an extremely pleasant though rather sing-song voice.

" 'Introduction—the Role of the Western in the Age of Space. By Karl Adams, Professor of English. Being based on the 2037 Kingsley Amis Seminars in Criticism at the University of Chicago.' "

The poker players were wavering; one of them was nervously examining the worn pieces of paper that served as cards. The rest of the audience had settled down, with looks of boredom or anticipation. Miss Wilkins was back in the airlock-galley, checking the provisions. The melodious voice continued:

" 'One of the most unexpected literary phenomena of our age has been the revival, after half a century of neglect, of the romance known as the "Western". These stories, set in a background extremely limited both in space and time— the United States of America, Earth, *circa* 1865–1900—were for a considerable period one of the most popular forms of fiction the world has ever known. Millions were written, almost all published in cheap magazines and shoddily-produced books, but out of those millions, a few have survived both as literature and as a record of an age—though we must never forget that the writers were describing an era that had passed long before they were born.

" 'With the opening up of the Solar System in the 1970s, the earth-based frontier of the American West seemed so ludicrously tiny that the reading public lost interest in it. This, of course, was as illogical as dismissing *Hamlet* on the grounds that events restricted to a small and draughty Danish castle could not possibly be of universal significance.

" 'During the last few years, however, a reaction has set in. I am creditably informed that Western stories are among the most popular reading matter in the libraries of the space-liners now plying between the planets. Let us see if we can discover the reason for this apparent paradox—this link between the Old West and the New Space.

" 'Perhaps we can best do this by divesting ourselves of all our modern scientific achievements, and imagining that we are back in the incredibly primitive world of 1870. Picture a vast, open plain, stretching away into the distance until it merges into a far-off line of misty mountains. Across that plain is crawling, with agonising slowness, a line of clumsy wagons. Around them ride men on horseback, bearing guns—for this is Indian territory.

" 'It will take those wagons longer to reach the mountains than a Star-class liner now requires to make the journey from Earth to Moon. The space of the prairie was just as great, therefore, to the men who challenged it as the space of the Solar System is to us. This is one of the links we have with the Western; there are others, even more fundamental. To understand them, we must first consider the role of the Epic in literature. . . .' "

It seemed to be going well, thought the Commodore. An hour would be long enough; at the end of that time Professor J. would be through the introduction and well into the story. Then they could switch to something else—preferably at an exciting moment in the narrative, so that the audience would be anxious to get back to it.

Yes, the second day beneath the dust had started smoothly, with everyone in good heart. But how many days were there still to go?

The answer to that question depended upon two men who had taken an instant dislike to each other even though they were fifty thousand kilometres apart. As he listened to Dr. Lawson's account of his discoveries, the Chief Engineer found himself torn in opposing directions. The astronomer had a most unfortunate method of approach, especially for a youngster who was addressing a very senior official more than twice his age. He talks to me, thought Lawrence —at first more amused than angry—as if I'm a retarded child, who has to have everything explained to him in words of one syllable.

When Lawson had finished, the C.E.E. was silent for a few seconds, examining the photographs that had come over the Telefax while they were talking. The earlier one, taken before sunrise, was certainly suggestive—but it was not enough to prove the case, in his opinion. And the one taken after dawn showed nothing at all on the reproduction he had received; there might have been something on the original print, but he would hate to take the word of this unpleasant young man for it.

"This is very interesting, Dr. Lawson," he said at last. "It's a great pity, though, that you didn't continue your observations when you took the first photos. Then we might have had something more conclusive."

Tom bridled instantly at this criticism, despite—or perhaps because of—the fact that it was well founded.

"If you think that anyone else could have done better——" he snapped.

"Oh, I'm not suggesting that," said Lawrence, anxious to keep the peace. "But where do we go from here? The spot you indicate may be fairly small, but its position is uncertain by at least half a kilometre. There may be nothing visible on the surface, even in daylight. Is there any way we can pin-point it more accurately?"

"There's one very obvious method. Use this same technique at ground level. Go over the area with an infra-red scanner. That will locate any hot-spot, even if it's only a fraction of a degree warmer than its surroundings."

"A good idea," said Lawrence, "I'll see what can be arranged, and will call you back if I need any further information. Thank you very much—Doctor."

He hung up quickly, and wiped his brow. Then he immediately put through another call to the satellite.

"Lagrange II? Chief Engineer, Earthside, here. Give me the Director, please.

"Professor Kotelnikov? This is Lawrence; I'm fine, thanks. I've been talking to your Dr. Lawson—no, he hasn't done anything, except nearly make me lose my temper. He's been looking for our missing dust-cruiser, and he thinks he's found her. What I'd like to know is—how competent is he?"

In the next five minutes, the Chief Engineer learned a good deal about young Dr. Lawson; rather more, in fact, than he had any right to know, even over a confidential circuit. When Professor Kotelnikov had paused for breath he interjected sympathetically: "I can understand why you put up with him; poor kid —I thought orphanages like that went out with Dickens and the twentieth century. A good thing it *did* burn down; do you suppose he set fire to it? No, don't answer that—you've told me he's a first-class observer, and that's all I want to know. Thanks a lot—see you down here someday?"

In the next half-hour, Lawrence made a dozen calls to points all over the Moon. At the end of that time, he had accumulated a large amount of information; now he had to act on it.

At Plato Observatory, Father Ferraro thought the idea was perfectly plausible. In fact, he had already suspected that the focus of the quake was under the Sea of Thirst rather than the Mountains of Inaccessibility, but couldn't prove it because the Sea had such a damping effect on all vibrations. No—a complete set of soundings had never been made; it would be very tedious and time-consuming. He'd probed it himself in a few places with telescopic rods, and had always hit bottom at less than forty metres. His guess for the average depth was under ten metres, and it was much more shallow round the edges.

No, he didn't have an infra-red detector, but the astronomers on Farside might be able to help.

Sorry—no i.r. detector at Dostoievsky. Our work is all in the ultra-violet. Try Verne.

Oh yes, we used to do some work in the infra-red, a couple of years back— taking spectograms of giant red stars. But do you know what—there were enough traces of lunar atmosphere to interfere with the readings so the whole programme was shifted out into space. Try Lagrange. . . .

It was at this point that Lawrence called Traffic Control for the shipping schedules from Earth, and found that he was in luck. But the next move would cost a lot of money, and only the Chief Administrator could authorise it.

That was one good thing about Olsen; he never argued with his technical staff over matters that were in their province. He listened carefully to Lawrence's story, and went straight to the main point.

"If this theory is true," he said, "there's a chance that they may still be alive, after all."

"More than a chance; I'd say it's quite likely. We know the Sea is shallow, so they can't be very deep. The pressure on the hull would be fairly low; it may still be intact."

"So you want this fellow Lawson to help with the search."

The Chief Engineer gave a gesture of resignation.

"He's about the last person I *want*," he answered. "But I'm afraid we've got to have him."

CHAPTER IX

THE SKIPPER OF the cargo-liner *Auriga* was furious, and so was his crew—but there was nothing they could do about it. Ten hours out from Earth and five hours from the Moon they were ordered to stop at Lagrange, with all the waste of speed and extra computing that that implied. And to make matters worse, they were being diverted from Clavius City to that miserable dump Port Roris, practically on the other side of the Moon. The ether crackled with messages cancelling dinners and assignations all over the southern hemisphere.

Not far from full, the mottled silver disc of the Moon, its eastern limb wrinkled with easily visible mountains, formed a dazzling background to Lagrange II as *Auriga* came to rest a hundred kilometres Earthwards of the station. She was allowed no closer; the interference produced by her equipment, and the glare of her jets, had already affected the sensitive recording instruments on the satellite. Only old-fashioned chemical rockets were permitted to operate in the immediate neighbourhood of Lagrange; plasma drives and fusion plants were strictly taboo.

Carrying one small case full of clothing, and one large case full of equipment, Tom Lawson entered the liner twenty minutes after departure from Lagrange; the shuttle pilot had refused to hurry, despite urgings from *Auriga.* The new passenger was greeted without warmth as he came aboard; he would have been received quite differently had anyone known his mission. The Chief Administrator, however, had ruled that it should be kept secret for the present; he did not wish to raise false hopes among the relatives of the lost passengers. The Tourist Commissioner had wanted an immediate release, maintaining that it would prove that they were doing their best, but Olsen had said firmly: "Wait until he produces results—*then* you can give something to your friends in the news agencies."

The order was already too late. Aboard *Auriga*, Maurice Spenser, Bureau Chief of Interplanet News, was on his way to take up his duties in Clavius City. He was not sure if this was a promotion or demotion from Peking, but it would certainly be a change.

Unlike all the other passengers, he was not in the least annoyed by the change of course. The delay was in the firm's time, and as an old newsman he always welcomed the unusual, the break in the established routine. It was certainly odd for a Moon-bound liner to waste several hours and an unimaginable amount of energy to stop at Lagrange, just to pick up a dour-faced young man with a couple of pieces of baggage. And why the diversion from Clavius to Port Roris? "Top-level instructions from Earth," said the skipper, and seemed to be telling the truth when he disowned all further knowledge. It was a mystery, and mysteries were Spenser's business. He made one shrewd guess at the reason, and was right—or almost right—first time.

It must be something to do with that lost dust-cruiser there had been such a fuss about, just before he left Earth. This scientist from Lagrange must have some information about her, or must be able to assist in the search. But why the secrecy? Perhaps there was some scandal or mistake that the Lunar Administration was trying to hush up; the simple and wholly creditable reason never occurred to Spenser.

He avoided speaking to Lawson during the remainder of the brief trip, and was amused to note that the few passengers who tried to strike up a conversation were quickly rebuffed. Spenser bided his time, and that time came thirty minutes before landing.

It was hardly an accident that he was sitting next to Lawson when the order came to fasten seat-belts for deceleration. With the fifteen other passengers, they sat in the tiny, blacked-out lounge, looking at the swiftly approaching Moon. Projected on a viewing screen from a lens in the outer hull, the image seemed sharper and more brilliant even than in real life. It was as if they were inside an old-fashioned *camera obscura;* the arrangement was very much safer than having an actual observation window—a structural hazard which spaceship designers fought against tooth and nail.

That dramatically expanding landscape was a glorious and unforgettable sight, yet Spenser could give it only half his attention. He was watching the man beside him, his intense aquiline features barely visible in the reflected light from the screen.

"Isn't it somewhere down there," he said, in his most casual tone of voice, "that the boat-load of tourists has just been lost?"

"Yes," said Tom, after a considerable delay.

"I don't know my way about the Moon. Any idea where they're supposed to be?"

Even the most uncooperative of men, Spenser had long ago discovered, could seldom resist giving information if you made it seem that they were doing you a favour, and gave them a chance of airing their superior knowledge. The trick worked in nine cases out of ten; it worked now with Tom Lawson.

"They're down there," he said, pointing to the centre of the screen. "Those are the Mountains of Inaccessibility—that's the Sea of Thirst all round them."

Spenser stared, in entirely unsimulated awe, at the sharply etched blacks and whites of the mountains towards which they were falling. He hoped the pilot —human or electronic—knew his job; the ship seemed to be coming in very fast. Then he realised that they were drifting towards the flatter territory on the left of the picture; the mountains and the curious grey area surrounding them, were sliding away from the centre of the screen.

"Port Roris, Tom volunteered unexpectedly, pointing to a barely visible black mark on the far left. "That's where we're landing."

"Well, I'd hate to come down in those mountains," said Spenser, determined to keep the conversation on target. "They'll never find the poor devils, if they're lost in that wilderness. Anyway, aren't they supposed to be buried under an avalanche?"

Tom gave a superior laugh.

"They're *supposed* to be," he said.

"Why—isn't that true?"

A little belatedly, Tom remembered his instructions.

"Can't tell you anything more," he replied in that same smug, cock-sure voice.

Spenser dropped the subject; he had already learned enough to convince him of one thing.

Clavius City would have to wait; he had better hang on at Port Roris for a while.

He was even more certain of this, when his envious eyes saw Dr. Tom Lawson cleared through Quarantine, Custom, Immigration and Exchange Control in three minutes flat.

Had any eavesdropper been listening to the sounds inside *Selene*, he would have been very puzzled. The cabin was reverberating unmelodiously to the sound of twenty-one voices, in almost as many keys, singing "Happy Birthday to You".

When the din had subsided, Commodore Hansteen called out: "Anyone else besides Mrs. Williams just remembered that it's his or her birthday? We know, of course, that some ladies like to keep it quiet when they reach a certain age——"

There were no volunteers, but David McKenzie raised his voice above the general laughter.

"There's a funny thing about birthdays—I used to win bets at parties with it. Knowing that there are three hundred and sixty-five days in the year—how large a group of people would you think was needed before you had a fifty-fifty chance that two of them shared the same birthday?"

After a brief pause while the audience considered the question, someone answered: "Why, half of the three hundred and sixty-five, I suppose. Say a hundred and eighty."

"That's the obvious answer—and it's completely wrong. If you have a group of more than twenty-four people, the odds are better than even that two of them have the same birthday."

"That's ridiculous! Twenty-four days out of three sixty-five *can't* give those odds."

"Sorry—it does. And if there are more than forty people, nine times out of ten two of them will have the same birthday. There's a sporting chance that it might work with the twenty-two of us. What about trying it, Commodore?"

"Very well—I'll go round the room, and ask each one of you for his date of birth."

"Oh, no," protested McKenzie. "People cheat, if you do it that way. The dates must be written down, so that nobody knows anyone else's birthday."

An almost blank page from one of the tourist guides was sacrificed for this purpose, and torn up into twenty-two slips. When they were collected and read, to everyone's astonishment and McKenzie's gratification—it turned out that both Pat Harris and Robert Bryant had been born on 23rd May.

"Pure luck!" said a sceptic, thus igniting a brisk mathematical argument among half a dozen of the male passengers. The ladies were quite uninterested; either because they did not care for mathematics, or preferred to ignore birthdays.

When the Commodore decided that this had gone on long enough, he rapped for attention.

"Ladies and gentlemen!" he called. "Let's get on with the next item on our programme. I'm pleased to say that the Entertainment Committee, consisting of Mr. Schuster and Professor Jaya-er, Professor J.—has come up with an idea that should give us some amusement. They suggest that we set up a court and cross-examine everybody here in turn. The object of the court is to find an answer to this question—why did we come to the Moon in the first place? Of course, some people may not want to be examined—for all I know, half of you may be on the run from the police, or your wives. You're at liberty to refuse to give evidence, but don't blame us if we draw the worst possible conclusions if you do. Well, what do you think of the idea?"

It was received with fair enthusiasm in some quarters, and ironic groans of disapproval in others, but as there was no determined opposition the Commodore went ahead. Almost automatically, he was elected President of the

Court; equally automatic was Irving Schuster's appointment as General Counsel.

The front-right pair of seats had been reversed so that it faced towards the rear of the cruiser; this would serve as the bench, shared by President and Counsel alike. When everyone had settled down, and the Clerk of the Court (*viz.* Pat Harris) had called for order, the President made a brief address.

"We are not yet engaged in criminal proceedings," he said, keeping his face straight with some difficulty. "This is purely a court of enquiry. If any witness feels that he is being intimidated by my learned colleagues, he can appeal to the Court. Will the Clerk call the first witness?"

"Er—your honour—who *is* the first witness?" said the Clerk, reasonably enough.

It took ten minutes of discussion between the Court, learned counsel and argumentative members of the public to settle this important point. Finally it was decided to have a ballot, and the first name to be produced was David Barrett's.

Smiling slightly, the witness came forward and took his stand in the narrow space before the bench.

Irving Schuster, looking and feeling none too legal in vest and underpants, cleared his throat impressively.

"Your name is David Barrett?"

"That is correct."

"Your occupation?"

"Agricultural engineer, retired."

"Mr. Barrett—will you tell this court exactly why you have come to the Moon."

"I was curious to see what it was like here and I had the time and money."

Irving Schuster looked at Barrett obliquely through his thick glasses; he had always found this to have an unsettling effect on witnesses. To wear spectacles was almost a sign of eccentricity in this age, but doctors and lawyers—especially the older ones—still patronised them; indeed, they had come to symbolise the legal and medical professions.

" 'You were curious to see what it was like,' " Schuster quoted. "That's no explanation. *Why* were you curious?"

"I am afraid that question is so vaguely worded that I cannot answer it. Why does one do anything?"

Commodore Hansteen relaxed with a smile of pleasure. This was just what he wanted—to get the passengers arguing and talking freely about something that would be of mutual interest to them all, but would arouse no passions or controversy. (It might do that, of course, but it was up to him to keep order in Court.)

"I admit," continued Counsel, "that my question might have been more specific. I will try to reframe it."

He thought for a moment, shuffling his notes. They consisted merely of sheets from one of the tourist guides; he had scribbled a few lines of questioning in the margins, but they were really for effect and reassurance. He had never liked to stand up in court without something in his hand; there were times when a few seconds of imaginary consultation were priceless.

"Would it be fair to say that you were attracted by the moon's scenic beauties?"

"Yes, that was part of the attraction. I had seen the tourist literature and movies, of course, and wondered if the reality would live up to it."

"And has it done so?"

"I would say," was the dry answer, "that it has exceeded my expectations."

There was general laughter from the rest of the company. Commodore Hansteen rapped loudly on the back of his seat.

"Order!" he called. "If there are any disturbances, I shall have to clear the Court!"

This, as he had intended, started a much louder round of laughter, which he let run its natural course. When the mirth had died down, Schuster continued in his most "Where were you on the night of the twenty-second?" tone of voice:

"This is very interesting, Mr. Barrett. You have come all the way to the Moon, at considerable expense, to look at the view. Tell me—have you ever seen the Grand Canyon?"

"No; have you?"

"Your Honour!" appealed Schuster. "The witness is being unresponsive."

Hansteen looked severely at Mr. Barrett, who did not seem in the least abashed.

"*You* are not conducting this enquiry, Mr. Barrett. Your job is to answer questions, not to ask them."

"I beg the Court's pardon, my Lord," replied the witness.

"Er—am I 'My Lord'?" said Hansteen uncertainly, turning to Schuster. "I thought I was 'Your Honour'."

The lawyer gave the matter several seconds of solemn thought.

"I suggest—Your Honour—that each witness uses the procedure to which he is accustomed in his country. As long as due deference is shown to the court, that would seem to be sufficient."

"Very well—proceed."

Schuster turned to his witness once more.

"I would like to know, Mr. Barrett, why you found it necessary to visit the Moon while there was so much of Earth that you hadn't seen. Can you give us any valid reason for this illogical behaviour?"

It was a good question, just the sort that would interest everyone, and Barrett was now making a serious attempt to answer it.

"I've seen a fair amount of Earth," he said slowly, in his precise English accent—almost as great a rarity now as Schuster's spectacles. "I've stayed at the Hotel Everest, been to both Poles, even gone to the bottom of the Calypso Deep. So I know something about our planet; let's say it had lost its capacity to surprise me. The Moon, on the other hand, was completely new—a whole world less than twenty-four hours away. I couldn't resist the novelty."

Hansteen listened to the slow and careful analysis with only half his mind; he was unobtrusively examining the audience while Barrett spoke. By now he had formed a good picture of *Selene*'s crew and passengers, and had decided who could be relied upon—and who would give trouble, if conditions became bad.

The key man, of course, was Captain Harris. The commodore knew his type well; he had met it so often in space—and more often still at such training establishments as Astrotech. (Whenever he made a speech there, it was to a front row of freshly scrubbed and barbered Pat Harrises.) Pat was a competent but unambitious youngster with mechanical interests who had been lucky enough to find a job that suited him perfectly, and which made no greater demands upon him than care and courtesy. (Attractive lady passengers, Hansteen was quite certain, would have no complaints on the latter score.) He would be loyal, conscientious and unimaginative, would do his duty as he saw it, and in the end would die gamely without making a fuss. That was a virtue not possessed by many far abler men, and it was one they would need badly aboard the cruiser, if they were still here five days from now.

Miss Wilkins, the stewardess, was almost as important as the captain in the scheme of things; she was certainly not the stereotyped space-hostess image, all vapid charm and frozen smile. She was, Hansteen had already decided, a young lady of character and considerable education—but so, for that matter, were many space-hostesses he had known.

Yes, he was lucky with the crew; and what about the passengers? They were considerably above average, of course; otherwise they would not have been on the Moon in the first place. There was an impressive reservoir of brains and talent here inside *Selene*, but the irony of the situation was that neither brains nor talent could help them now. What was needed was character, fortitude—or in a blunter word, bravery.

Few men in this age ever knew the need for physical bravery. From birth to death, they never came face to face with danger. The men and women aboard *Selene* had no training for what lay ahead, and he could not keep them occupied much longer with games and amusements.

Some time in the next twelve hours, he calculated, the first cracks would appear. By then it would be obvious that something was holding up the search parties, and that if they found the cruiser at all, the discovery might be too late.

Commodore Hansteen glanced swiftly round the cabin. Apart from their scanty clothing and slightly unkempt appearance, all these twenty-one men and women were still rational, self-controlled members of society.

Which, he wondered, would be the first to go?

CHAPTER X

DR. TOM LAWSON, so Chief Engineer Lawrence had decided, was an exception to the old saying, "To know all is to forgive all." The knowledge that the astronomer had passed a loveless, institutionalised childhood and had escaped from his origins by prodigies of pure intellect, at the cost of all other human qualities, helped one to understand him—but not to like him. It was singular bad luck, though Lawrence, that he was the only scientist within three hundred thousand kilometres who happened to have an infra-red detector, and knew how to use it.

He was now sitting in the observer's seat of Duster Two, making the final adjustments to the crude but effective lash-up he had contrived. A camera tripod had been fixed on the roof of the ski, and the detector had been mounted on this, in such a way that it could pan in any direction.

It seemed to be working, but that was hard to tell in this small, pressurised hangar, with a confused jumble of heat sources all around it. The real test could come only out in the Sea of Thirst.

"It's ready," said Lawson presently to the Chief Engineer. "Let me have a word with the man who's going to run it."

The C.E.E. looked at him thoughtfully, still trying to make up his mind. There were strong arguments for and against what he was considering now, but whatever he did, he must not let his personal feelings intrude. The matter was far too important for that.

"You can wear a space-suit, can't you?" he asked Lawson.

"I've never worn one in my life. They're only needed for going outside—and we leave that to the engineers."

"Well, now you have a chance of learning," said the C.E.E., ignoring the jibe. (If it was a jibe; much of Lawson's rudeness, he decided, was indifference to the social graces rather than defiance of them.) "There's not much to it, when you're riding a ski. You'll be sitting still in the observer's seat and the auto-regulator takes care of oxygen, temperature and the rest. There's only one problem——"

"What's that?"

"How are you for claustrophobia?"

Tom hesitated, not liking to admit any weakness. He had passed the usual space tests, of course, and suspected—quite rightly—that he had had a very close call on some of the psych ratings. Obviously he was not an acute claustrophobe, or he could never have gone aboard a ship. But a space-ship and a space-suit were two very different things.

"I can take it," he said at last.

"Don't fool yourself if you can't," Lawrence insisted. "I think you should come with us, but I'm not trying to bully you into false heroics. All I ask is that you make up your mind before we leave the hangar. It may be a little too late to have second thoughts, when we're twenty kilometres out to Sea."

Tom looked at the ski and bit his lip. The idea of skimming across that infernal lake of dust in such a flimsy contraption seemed crazy—but these men did it every day. And if anything went wrong with the detector, there was at least a slight chance that he could fix it.

"Here's a suit that's your size," said Lawrence. "Try it on—it may help you to make up your mind."

Tom struggled into the flaccid yet crinkly garment, closed the front zipper, and stood, still helmetless, feeling rather a fool. The oxygen flask that was buckled to his harness seemed absurdly small, and Lawrence noticed his anxious glance.

"Don't worry; that's merely the four-hour reserve. You won't be using it at all—the main supply's on the ski. Mind your nose—here comes the helmet."

He could tell, by the expressions of those around him, that this was the moment that separated the men from the boys. Until that element was seated, you were still part of the human races; afterwards, you were alone, in a tiny mechanical world of your own. There might be other men only centimetres away, but you had to peer at them through thick plastic, talk to them by radio. You could not even touch them, except through double layers of artificial skin. Someone had once written that it was very lonely to die in a space-suit; for the first time, Tom realised how true that must be.

The Chief Engineer's voice sounded suddenly, reverberantly from the tiny speakers set in the side of the helmet.

"The only control you need worry about is the intercom—that's the panel on your right. Normally you'll be connected to your pilot; the circuit will be live all the time you're both on the ski, so you can talk to each other whenever you feel like it. But as soon as you disconnect, you'll have to use radio—as you're doing now to listen to me. Press your TRANSMIT button and talk back."

"What's that red Emergency button for?" asked Tom, after he had obeyed this order.

"You won't need it—I hope. That actuates a homing beacon and sets up a radio racket until someone comes to find you. Don't touch any of the gadgets on the suit without instructions from us—especially that one."

"I won't," promised Tom. "Let's go."

He walked, rather clumsily—for he was used neither to the suit nor the lunar gravity—over to Duster Two and took his place in the observer's seat. A single umbilical cord, plugged inappropriately into the right hip, connected the suit to the ski's oxygen communications and power. The vehicle could keep him alive, though hardly comfortable, for three or four days at a pinch.

The little hangar was barely large enough for the two dust-skis, and it took only a few minutes for the pumps to exhaust its air. As the suit stiffened around him, Tom felt a touch of panic. The Chief Engineer and the two pilots were watching, and he did not wish to give them the satisfaction of thinking that he was afraid. No man could help feeling tense when, for the first time in his life, he went into vacuum.

The clamshell doors pivoted open; there was a faint tug of ghostly fingers as the last vestige of air gushed out, plucking feebly at his suit before it dispersed into the void. And then, flat and featureless, the empty grey of the Sea of Thirst stretched out to the horizon.

For a moment it seemed impossible that here, only a few metres away, was the reality behind the images he had studied from far out in space. (Who was looking through the hundred-centimetre telescope now? Was one of his colleagues watching, even at this moment, from his vantage point high above the Moon?) But this was no picture painted on a screen by flying electrons; *this* was the real thing, the strange, amorphous stuff that had swallowed twenty-two men and women without trace. And across which he, Tom Lawson, was about to venture on this insubstantial craft.

He had little time to brood. The ski vibrated beneath him as the fans started to spin; then, following Duster One, it glided slowly out on to the naked surface of the Moon.

The low rays of the rising sun smote them as soon as they emerged from the long shadow of the Port buildings. Even with the protection of the automatic filters, it was dangerous to look towards the blue-white fury in the eastern sky. No, Tom corrected himself, this is the Moon, not Earth; here the sun rises in the west. So we're heading north-east, into the Sinus Roris, along the track *Selene* followed and never retraced.

Now that the low domes of the Port were shrinking visibly towards the horizon, he felt something of the exhilaration and excitement of all forms of speed. The sensation lasted only for a few minutes, until no more landmarks could be seen and they were caught in the illusion of being poised at the very centre of an infinite plain. Despite the turmoil of the spinning fans, and the slow, silent fall of the dust parabolas behind them, they seemed to be motionless. Tom knew that they were travelling at a speed that would take them clear across the Sea in a couple of hours, yet he had to wrestle with the fear that they were lost light-years from any hope of salvation. It was at this moment that he began, a little late in the game, to feel a grudging respect for the men he was working with.

This was a good place to start checking his equipment. He switched on the detector, and set it scanning back and forth over the emptiness they had just crossed. With calm satisfaction, he noted the two blinding trails of light stretching behind them across the darkness of the Sea. This test, of course, was childishly easy; *Selene*'s fading thermal ghost would be a million times harder to spot against the waxing heat of dawn. But it was encouraging; if he had failed here, there would have been no point in continuing any further.

"How's it working?" said the Chief Engineer, who must have been watching from the other ski.

"Up to specification," replied Tom cautiously. "It seems to be behaving normally." He aimed the detector at the shrinking crescent of Earth; that was a slightly more difficult target, but not a really hard one, for it needed little sensitivity to pick up the gentle warmth of the mother world when it was projected against the cold night of space.

Yes, there it was—Earth in the far infra-red, a strange and at first glance baffling sight. For it was no longer a clean-cut, geometrically-perfect crescent, but a ragged mushroom with its stem lying along the Equator.

It took Tom a few seconds to interpret the picture. Both Poles had been chopped off—that was understandable, for they were too cold to be detected at this setting of the sensitivity. But why that bulge across the unilluminated night-side of the planet? Then he realised that he was seeing the warm glow of the tropical oceans, radiating back into the darkness the heat that they had stored during the day. In the infra-red, the Equatorial night was more brilliant than the Polar day.

It was a reminder of the fact, which no scientist should ever forget, that human senses perceived only a tiny, distorted picture of the Universe. Tom Lawson had never heard of Plato's analogy of the chained prisoners in the cave, watching shadows cast upon a wall and trying to deduce from them the realities of the external world. But here was a demonstration that Plato would have appreciated; for which Earth was "real"—the perfect crescent visible to the eye, the tattered mushroom glowing in the far infra-red—or neither?

The office was small, even for Port Roris—which was purely a transit station between Earthside and Farside, and a jumping-off point for tourists to the Sea of Thirst. (Not that any looked like jumping off in that direction for some time.) The port had had a brief moment of glory thirty years before, as the base used by one of the Moon's few successful criminals— Jerry Budker, who had made a small fortune dealing in fake pieces of Lunik II. He was hardly as exciting as Robin Hood or Billy the Kid, but he was the best that the Moon could offer.

Maurice Spenser was rather glad that Port Roris was such a quiet little one-dome town, though he suspected that it would not stay quiet much longer, especially when his colleagues at Clavius woke up to the fact that an I.N. Bureau Chief was lingering here unaccountably, and not hurrying southwards to the lights of the big (pop. 52,647) city. A guarded cable to Earth had taken care of his superiors, who would trust his judgment and would guess the story he was after. Sooner or later, the competition would guess it too—but by that time, he hoped to be well ahead.

The man he was conferring with was *Auriga*'s still-disgruntled skipper, who had just spent a complicated and unsatisfactory hour on the telephone with his agents at Clavius, trying to arrange transhipment of his cargo. McIver, McDonald, MacCathy and McCulloch, Ltd., seemed to think it was his fault that *Auriga* had put down at Roris; in the end he had hung up after telling them to sort it out with head office. As it was now early Sunday morning in Edinburgh, this should hold them for a while.

Captain Anson mellowed a little after the second whisky; a man who could find some Teacher's in Port Roris was worth knowing, and he asked Spenser how he had managed it.

"The power of the Press," said the other with a laugh. "A reporter never reveals his sources; if he did, he wouldn't stay in business for long."

He opened his briefcase, and pulled out a sheaf of maps and photos.

"I had an even bigger job getting these at such short notice—and I'd be obliged, Captain, if you would say nothing at all about this to anyone. It's extremely confidential, at least for the moment."

"Of course. What's it about—*Selene*?"

"So you guessed that, too? You're right—it may come to nothing, but I want to be prepared."

He spread one of the photos across the desk; it was a view of the Sea of Thirst, from the standard series issued by the Lunar Survey and taken from low-altitude reconnaissance satellites. Though this was an afternoon photograph, and the shadows thus pointed in the opposite direction, it was almost identical with the view Spenser had had just before landing. He had studied it so closely that he now knew it by heart.

"The Mountains of Inaccessibility," he said. "They rise very steeply out of the Sea to an altitude of almost two thousand metres. That dark oval is Crater Lake——"

"Where *Selene* was lost?"

"Where she may be lost: there's now some doubt about that. Our sociable young friend from Lagrange has evidence that she's actually gone down in the Sea of Thirst—round about this area. In that case, the people inside her may be alive. And in *that* case, Captain, there's going to be one hell of a salvage operation only a hundred kilometres from here. Port Roris will be the biggest news centre in the Solar System."

"Phew! So that's your game. But where do I come in?"

Once again Spenser placed his finger on the map.

"Right here, Captain. I want to charter your ship. And I want you to land me, with a cameraman and two hundred kilos of TV equipment—on the western wall of the Mountains of Inaccessibility."

"I have no further questions, your Honour," said Counsel Schuster, sitting down abruptly.

"Very well," replied Commodore Hansteen. "I must order the witness not to leave the jurisdiction of the Court."

Amid general laughter, David Barrett returned to his seat. He had put on a good performance; though most of his replies had been serious and thoughtful, they had been enlivened with flashes of humour and had kept the audience continuously interested. If all the other witnesses were equally forthcoming, that would solve the problem of entertainment, for as long as it had to be solved. Even if they used up all the memories of four life-times in every day —a complete impossibility, of course—someone would still be talking when the oxygen container gave its last gasp.

Hansteen looked at his watch; there was still an hour to go before their frugal lunch. They could revert to *Shane*, or start (despite Miss Morley's objections) on that preposterous historical novel. But it seemed a pity to break off now, while everyone was in a receptive mood.

"If you all feel the same way about it," said the Commodore, "I'll call another witness."

"I'll second that," was the quick reply from Barrett, who now considered himself safe from further inquisition. Even the poker players were in favour, so the Clerk of the Court pulled another name out of the coffee-pot in which the ballot papers had been mixed.

He looked at it with some surprise, and hesitated before reading it out.

"What's the matter?" said the Court. "Is it *your* name?"

"Er—no," replied the Clerk, glancing at learned Counsel with a mischievous grin. He cleared his throat and called: "Mrs. Myra Schuster!"

"Your Honour—I object!" Mrs. Schuster rose slowly, a formidable figure even though she had lost a kilogramme or two since leaving Port Roris. She pointed to her husband, who looked embarrassed and tried to hide behind his notes. "Is it fair for *him* to ask me questions?"

"I'm willing to stand down," said Irving Schuster, even before the Court could say "Objection sustained".

"I am prepared to take over the examination," said the Commodore, though his expression rather belied this. "But is there anyone else who feels qualified to do so?"

There was a short silence; then, to Hansteen's surprised relief, one of the poker players stood up.

"Though I'm not a lawyer, your Honour, I have some slight legal experience. I'm willing to assist."

"Very good, Mr. Harding. *Your* witness."

Harding took Schuster's place at the front of the cabin, and surveyed his captive audience. He was a well-built, tough-looking man who somehow did not fit his own description as a bank executive; Hansteen had wondered, fleetingly, if this was the truth.

"Your name is Myra Shuster?"

"Yes."

"And what, Mrs. Schuster, are you doing on the Moon?"

The witness smiled.

"That's an easy one to answer. They told me I'd weigh only twenty kilos here—so I came."

"For the record, *why* did you want to weigh twenty kilos?"

Mrs. Schuster looked at Harding as if he had said something very stupid.

"I used to be a dancer once," she said—and her voice was suddenly wistful, her expression faraway. "I gave that up, of course, when I married Irving."

"Why 'of course', Mrs. Schuster?"

The witness glanced at her husband, who stirred a little uneasily, looked as if he might raise an objection, but then thought better of it.

"Oh, he said it wasn't dignified. And I guess he was right—the kind of dancing *I* used to do."

This was too much for Mr. Schuster. He shot to his feet, ignoring the Court completely, and protested: "Really, Myra! There's no need——"

"Oh, vector it out, Irv!" she answered, the incongruously old-fashioned slang bringing back a faint whiff of the nineties. "What does it matter now? Let's stop acting and be ourselves. I don't mind these folk knowing that I used to dance at the 'Blue Asteroid'—*or* that you got me off the hook when the cops raided the place."

Irving subsided, spluttering, while the Court dissolved in a roar of laughter which His Honour did nothing to quell. This release of tensions was precisely what he had hoped for; when people were laughing, they could not be afraid.

And he began to wonder still more about Mr. Harding, whose casual yet shrewd questioning had brought this about. For a man who said he was not a lawyer, he was doing pretty well. It would be very interesting to see how he stood in the witness box—when it was Schuster's turn to ask the questions.

CHAPTER XI

A T L A S T T H E R E was something to break the featureless flatness of the Sea of Thirst. A tiny but brilliant splinter of light had edged itself above the horizon, and as the dust-skis raced forward it slowly climbed against the stars. Now it was joined by another—and a third. The peaks of the Inaccessible Mountains were rising over the edge of the Moon.

As usual, there was no way of judging their distance; they might have been small rocks a few paces away—or not part of the Moon at all, but a giant, jagged world, millions of kilometres out in space. In reality, they were fifty kilometres distant; the dust-skis would be there in half an hour.

Tom Lawson looked at them with thankfulness. Now there was something to occupy his eye and mind; he felt he would have gone crazy, staring at this apparently infinite plain for much longer. He was annoyed with himself for being so illogical; he knew the horizon was really very close and that the whole Sea was only a small part of the Moon's quite limited surface. Yet as he sat here in his space-suit, apparently getting nowhere, he was reminded of those horrible dreams in which you struggled with all your might to escape from some frightful peril—but remained stuck helplessly in the same place. Tom often had such dreams, and worse ones.

But now he could see that they were making progress, and that their long, black shadow was not frozen to the ground, as it sometimes seemed. He focused the detector on the rising peaks, and obtained a strong reaction. As he had expected, the exposed rocks were almost at boiling point where they faced the sun; though the lunar day had barely started, the mountains were already burning. It was much cooler down here at "Sea" level; the surface dust would not reach its maximum temperature until noon, still seven days away. That was one of the biggest points in his favour; though the day had already begun, he still had a sporting chance of detecting any faint source of heat before the full fury of the day had overwhelmed it.

Twenty minutes later, the mountains dominated the sky, and the skis slowed down to half-speed.

"We don't want to overrun their track," explained Lawrence. "If you look carefully, just below that double peak on the right, you'll see a dark vertical line. Got it?"

"Yes."

"That's the gorge leading to Crater Lake. The patch of heat you detected is three kilometres to the west of it, so it's still out of sight from here, below our horizon. Which direction do you want to approach from?"

Lawson thought this over. It would have to be from the north or the south. If he came in from the west, he would have those burning rocks in his field of view; the eastern approach was even more impossible, for that would be into the eye of the rising sun.

"Swing round to the north," he said. "And let me know when we're within two kilometres of the spot."

The skis accelerated once more; though there was no hope of detecting anything yet, he started to scan back and forth over the surface of the Sea. This whole mission was based upon one assumption—that the upper layers of dust were normally at a uniform temperature, and that any thermal disturbance was due to man. If this was wrong——

It was wrong. He had miscalculated completely. On the viewing screen, the Sea was a mottled pattern of light and shade—or rather, of warmth and cold-ness. The temperature differences were only fractions of a degree, but the picture was hopelessly confused. There was no possibility at all of locating any individual source of heat in that thermal maze.

Sick at heart, Tom Lawson looked up from the viewing screen and stared incredulously across the dust. To the unaided eye, it was still absolutely feature-less—the same unbroken grey it had always been. But by infra-red, it was as dappled as the sea during a cloudy day on Earth, when the waters are covered with shifting patterns of sunlight and shadow.

Yet there were no clouds here to cast their shadows on this arid sea; this dappling must have some other cause. Whatever it might be, Tom was too stunned to look for the scientific explanation. He had come all the way to the Moon, had risked neck and sanity on this crazy ride—and at the end of it all, some quirk of nature had ruined his carefully planned experiment. It was the worst possible luck, and he felt very sorry for himself.

Several minutes later, he got round to feeling sorry for the people aboard *Selene*.

"So," said the skipper of the *Auriga*, with exaggerated calm. "You would like to land on the Mountains of Inaccessibility. That's a verra interesting idea."

It was obvious to Spenser that Captain Anson had not taken him seriously; he probably thought he was dealing with a crazy newsman who had no concep-tion of the problems involved. That would have been correct twelve hours before, when the whole plan was only a vague dream in Spenser's mind. But now he had all the information at his finger-tips, and knew exactly what he was doing.

"I've heard you boast, Captain, that you could land this ship within a metre of any given point. Is that right?"

"Well—with a little help from the computer."

"That's good enough. Now take a look at this photograph."

"What is it? Glasgow on a wet Saturday night?"

"I'm afraid it's badly over-enlarged, but it shows all we want to know. It's a blow-up of this area—just below the western peak of the Mountains. I'll have a much better copy in a few hours, and an accurate contour map—Lunar Survey's drawing one now, working from the photos on their files. My point is that there's a wide ledge here—wide enough for a dozen ships to land. And it's fairly flat, at least at these points here—and here. So a landing would be no problem at all, from your point of view."

"No *technical* problem, perhaps. But have you any idea what it would cost?"

"That's my affair, Captain—or my network's. We think it may be worth while, if my hunch comes off."

Spenser could have said a good deal more, but it was bad business to show how much you needed someone else's wares. This might well be the news-story of the decade—the first space-rescue that had ever taken place literally under the eyes of the TV cameras. There had been enough accidents and disasters in space, heaven knows, but they had lacked all element of drama or suspense. Those involved had died instantly, or had been beyond all hope of rescue when their predicament was discovered. Such tragedies produced headlines, but not sustained, human-interest stories like the one he sensed here.

"There's not only the money," said the captain (though his tone implied that there were few matters of greater importance). "Even if the owners agree, you'll have to get special clearance from Space Control, Earthside."

"I know—someone is working on it now. That can be organised."

"And what about Lloyd's? Our policy doesn't cover little jaunts like this."

Spenser leaned across the table, and prepared to drop his city-buster.

"Captain," he said slowly, "Interplanet News is prepared to deposit a bond for the insured value of the ship—which I happen to know is a somewhat inflated Six Million Four Hundred and Twenty Five Thousand and Fifty Sterling Dollars."

Captain Anson blinked twice, and his whole attitude changed immediately. Then looking very thoughtful, he poured himself another drink.

"I never imagined I'd take up mountaineering at my time of life," he said. "But if you're fool enough to plonk down six million stollars—then my heart's in the highlands."

To the great relief of her husband, Mrs. Schuster's evidence had been interrupted by lunch. She was a talkative lady, and was obviously delighted at the first opportunity she had had in years of letting her hair down. Her career, such as it was, had not been particularly distinguished when fate and the

Chicago police had brought it to a sudden close—but she had certainly got around, and had known many of the great performers at the turn of the century. To not a few of the older passengers, her reminiscences brought back memories of their own youth, and faint echoes from the songs of the nineteen-nineties. At one point, without any protest from the Court, she led the entire company in a rendering of that durable favourite, *Spacesuit Blues*. As a morale-builder, the Commodore decided, Mrs. Schuster was worth her weight in gold—and that was saying a good deal.

After lunch (which some of the slower eaters managed to stretch to half an hour, by chewing each mouthful fifty times) book-reading was resumed, and the agitators for *The Orange and the Apple* finally got their way. The theme being English, it was decided that Mr. Barrett was the only man for the job; he protested with vigour, but all his objections were shouted down.

"Oh, very well,' he said reluctantly. "Here we go. Chapter One. Drury Lane. 1665. . . ."

The author certainly wasted no time. Within three pages, Sir Isaac Newton was explaining the law of gravitation to Mistress Gwyn, who had already hinted that she would like to do something in return. What form that appreciation would take, Pat Harris could readily guess, but duty called him. This entertainment was for the passengers; the crew had work to do.

"There's still one emergency locker I've not opened," said Miss Wilkins, as the airlock door thudded softly behind them, shutting off Mr. Barrett's carefully clipped accents. "We're low on crackers and jam, but the compressed meat is holding out."

"I'm not surprised," answered Pat. "Everyone seems to be getting sick of it. Let's see those inventory sheets."

The stewardess handed over the typed sheets, now much annotated with pencil marks.

"We'll start with this box. What's inside it?"

"Soap and paper towels."

"Well, we can't eat *them*. And this one?"

"Candy; I was saving it for the celebration—when they find us."

"That's a good idea, but I think you might break some of it out this evening. One piece for every passenger, as a nightcap. And this?"

"A thousand cigarettes."

"Make sure that no one sees them. I wish you hadn't told me." Pat grinned wryly at Sue and passed on to the next item. It was fairly obvious that food was not going to be a major problem, but they had to keep track of it. He knew the ways of Administration; after they were rescued, sooner or later some human or electronic clerk would insist on a strict accounting of all the food that had been used.

After they were rescued. Did he really believe that this was going to happen? They had been lost for more than two days, and there had not been the slightest sign that anyone was looking for them. He was not sure what signs there could be—but he had expected some.

He stood brooding in silence, until Sue asked anxiously:

"What's the trouble, Pat? Is something wrong?"

"Oh, no," he said sarcastically. "We'll be docking at Base in five minutes. It's been a pleasant trip, don't you think?"

Sue stared at him incredulously; then a flush spread over her cheeks, and her eyes began to brim with tears.

"I'm sorry," said Pat, instantly contrite. "I didn't mean that—it's been a big strain for us both, and you've been wonderful. I don't know what we'd have done without you, Sue."

She dabbed her nose with a handerchief, gave a brief smile and answered: "That's all right; I understand." They were both silent for a moment; then she added: "Do you really think we're going to get out of this?"

He gave a gesture of helplessness.

"Who can tell? Anyway, for the sake of the passengers, we've got to appear confident. We can be certain that the whole Moon's looking for us. I can't believe it will take much longer."

"But even if they find us—how are they going to get us out?"

Pat's eyes wandered to the external door, only a few centimetres away. He could touch it without moving from this spot; indeed, if he immobilised the safety interlock, he could open it, for it swung inwards. On the other side of that thin metal sheet were unknown tons of dust that would come pouring in, like water into a sinking ship, if there was the slightest crack through which they could enter. How far above them was the surface? That was a problem that had worried him ever since they had gone under, but there seemed no way of finding out.

Nor could he answer Sue's question. It was hard to think beyond the possibility of being found. The human race would not let them die, once it had discovered them alive. . . .

But this was wistful thinking, not logic. Hundreds of times in the past, men and women had been trapped as they were now, and all the resources of great nations had been unable to save them. There were the miners behind rockfalls, sailors in sunken submarines—and above all, astronauts in ships on wild orbits, beyond possibility of interception. Often they had been able to talk freely with their friends and relatives until the very end. That had happened only two years ago, when *Cassiopeia*'s main drive had jammed, and all her energies had been poured into hurling her away from the sun. She was out there now, heading towards Canopus, on one of the most precisely measured orbits of any space vehicle. The astronomers would be able to pin-point her to within a few thousand kilometres for the next million years. That must have been a great consolation to her crew, now in a tomb more permanent than any Pharaoh's.

Pat tore his mind away from this singularly profitless reverie. Their luck had not yet run out, and to anticipate disaster might be to invite it.

"Let's hurry up and finish this inventory. I want to hear how Nell is making out with Sir Isaac."

That was a much more pleasant train of thought, especially when you were standing so close to a very attractive and scantily-dressed girl. In a situation like this, thought Pat, women had one great advantage over men. Sue was still fairly smart, despite the fact that nothing much was left of her uniform in this tropical heat. But he—like all the men aboard *Selene*—felt scratchily uncomfortable with his three-day growth of beard, and there was absolutely nothing he could do about it.

Sue did not seem to mind the stubble, though, when he abandoned the pretence of work and moved up so close that his bristles rubbed against her cheek. On the other hand, she did not show any enthusiasm. She merely stood there, in front of the half-empty locker, as if she had expected this and was not in the least surprised. It was a disconcerting reaction, and after a few seconds Pat drew away.

"I suppose you think I'm an unscrupulous wolf," he said, "trying to take advantage of you like this."

"Not particularly," Sue answered. She gave a rather tired laugh. "It makes me glad to know that I'm not slipping. No girl ever minds a man *starting* to make approaches. It's when he won't stop that she gets annoyed."

"Do you want me to stop?"

"We're not in love, Pat. To me, that's rather important. Even now."

"Would it still be important if you knew we won't get out of this?"

Her forehead wrinkled in concentration.

"I'm not sure—but you said yourself, we've got to assume that they'll find us. If we don't, then we might as well give up right away."

"Sorry," said Pat. "I don't want you under those terms. I like you too much, for one thing."

"I'm glad to hear that; you know I've always enjoyed working with you— there were plenty of other jobs I could have transferred to."

"Bad luck for you," Pat answered, "that you didn't." His brief gust of desire, triggered by proximity, solitude, scanty clothing and sheer emotional strain, had already evaporated.

"Now you're being pessimistic again," said Sue. "You know—that's your big trouble. You let things get you down. And you won't assert yourself— anyone can push you around."

Pat looked at her with more surprise than annoyance.

"I'd no idea," he said, "that you'd been busy psyching me."

"I haven't. But if you're interested in someone, and work with him, how can you help learning about him?"

"Well, I don't believe that people push me around."

"No? Who's running this ship now?"

"If you mean the Commodore, that's different. He's a thousand times better qualified to take charge than I am. And he's been absolutely correct about it —he's asked my permission all along the line."

"He doesn't bother now. Anyway, that's not the whole point. Aren't you *glad* he's taken over?"

Pat thought about this for several seconds. Then he looked at Sue with grudging respect.

"Maybe you're right. I've never cared to throw my weight about, or assert my authority—if I have any. I guess that's why I'm driver of a moon-bus, not skipper of a space-liner. It's a little late to do anything about it now."

"You're not thirty yet."

"Thank you for those kind words. I'm thirty-two. We Harrises retain our youthful good looks well into old age. It's usually all we have left by then."

"Thirty-two—and no steady girl-friend?"

Ha! thought Pat—there are several things you don't know about me. But there was no point in mentioning Clarissa and her little apartment at Copernicus City, which now seemed so far away. (And how upset is Clarissa right now? he wondered. Which of the boys is busy consoling her? Perhaps Sue is right, after all. I don't have a *steady* girl-friend. I haven't had once since Yvonne, and that was five years ago. No, My God—*seven* years ago.)

"I believe there's safety in numbers," he said. "One of these days I'll settle down."

"Perhaps you'll still be saying that when you're forty—or fifty. There are so many spacemen like that. They haven't settled down when it's time to retire —and then it's too late. Look at the Commodore, for example."

"What about him? I'm beginning to get a little tired of the subject."

"He's spent all his life in space. He has no family, no children. Earth can't mean much to him—he's spent so little time there. He must have felt quite lost when he reached the age limit. This accident has been a godsend to him —he's really enjoying himself now."

"Good for him—he deserves it. I'll be happy if I've done a tenth as much as he has, when I've reached his age—which doesn't seem very likely at the moment."

Pat became aware that he was still holding the inventory sheets; he had forgotten all about them. They were a reminder of their dwindling resources, and he looked at them with distaste.

"Back to work," he said. "We have to think of the passengers."

"If we stay here much longer," replied Sue, "the passengers will start thinking of us."

She spoke more truthfully than she had guessed.

CHAPTER XII

Dr. LAWSON'S SILENCE, the Chief Engineer decided, had gone on long enough. It was high time to resume communication.

"Everything all right, Doctor?" he asked in his friendliest voice.

There was a short, angry bark—but the answer was directed at the universe, not at him.

"It won't work," Lawson answered bitterly. "The heat image is too confused. There are dozens of hot-spots, not just the one I was expecting."

"Stop your ski. I'll come over and have a look."

Duster Two slid to a halt; Duster One eased up beside it until the two vehicles were almost touching. Moving with surprising ease despite the encumbrance of his space-suit, Lawrence swung himself from one to the other and stood, gripping the supports of the overhead canopy, behind Lawson. He peered over the astronomer's shoulder at the image on the infra-red converter.

"I see what you mean; it's a mess. But why was it uniform when you took your photos?"

"It must be a sunrise effect. The Sea's warming up, and for some reason it's not heating at the same rate everywhere."

"Perhaps we can still make sense out of the pattern. I notice that there are some fairly clear areas—there must be an explanation for them. If we understood what's happening, it might help."

Tom Lawson stirred himself with a great effort. The brittle shell of his self-confidence had been shattered by this unexpected set-back, and he was very tired. He had had little sleep in the last two days, he had been hurried from satellite to space-ship to Moon to dust-ski, and after all that, his science had failed him.

"There could be a dozen explanations," he said dully. "This dust looks uniform, but there may be patches with different conductivities. And it must be deeper in some places than in others—that would alter the heat flow."

Lawrence was still staring at the pattern on the screen, trying to relate it to the visual scene around him.

"Just a minute," he said. "I think you've got something." He called to the pilot. "How deep is the dust round here?"

"Nobody knows; the Sea's never been sounded properly. But it's very shallow in these parts—we're near the northern edge. Sometimes we take out a fan blade on a reef."

"As shallow as that? Well, there's your answer. If there's rock only a few centimetres below us, anything could happen to the heat pattern. Ten to one you'll find the picture getting simpler again when we're clear of these shoals. This is only a local effect, caused by irregularities just underneath us."

"Perhaps you're right," said Tom, reviving slightly. "If Selene has sunk, she must be in an area where the dust's fairly deep. You're sure it's shallow here?"

"Let's find out; there's a twenty-metre probe on my ski."

A single section of the telescoping rod was enough to prove the point. When Lawrence drove it into the dust, it penetrated less than two metres before hitting an obstruction.

"How many spare fans have we got?" he asked thoughtfully.

"Four—two complete sets," answered the pilot. "But when we hit a rock, the cotter-pin shears through and the fans aren't damaged. Anyway, they're made of rubber; usually they just bend back. I've only lost three in the last year. Selene took out one the other day, and Pat Harris had to go outside and replace it. Gave the passengers some excitement."

"Right—let's start moving again. Head for the gorge; I've a theory that it continues out underneath the Sea, so the dust will be much deeper there. If it is, your picture should start getting simpler, almost at once."

Without much hope, Tom watched the patterns of light and shade flow across the screen. The skis were moving quite slowly now, giving him time to analyse the picture. They had travelled about two kilometres when he saw that Lawrence had been perfectly right.

The mottlings and dapplings had begun to disappear; the confused jumble of warmth and coolness was merging into uniformity. The screen was becoming a flat grey as the temperature variations smoothed themselves out; beyond question, the dust was swiftly deepening beneath them.

The knowledge that his equipment was effective once more should have gratified Tom, but it had almost the opposite result. He could think only of the hidden depths above which he was floating, supported on the most treacherous and unstable of mediums. Beneath him now there might be gulfs reaching far down into the Moon's mysterious heart; at any moment they might swallow the dust-ski, as already they had swallowed *Selene*.

He felt as if he were tight-rope walking across an abyss, or feeling his way along a narrow path through a quaking quicksand. All his life he had been uncertain of himself, and had known security and confidence only through his technical skills—never at the level of personal relations. Now the hazards of his present position were reacting upon those inner fears; he felt a desperate need for solidity—for something firm and stable to which he could cling.

Over there were the mountains, only three kilometres away—massive, eternal, their roots anchored in the Moon. He looked at the sunlit sanctuary of those high peaks as longingly as some Pacific castaway, helpless upon a drifting raft, might have stared at an island passing just beyond his reach.

With all his heart, he wished that Lawrence would leave this treacherous, insubstantial ocean of dust for the safety of the land. "Head for the mountains!" he found himself whispering. "Head for the mountains!"

There is no privacy in a space-suit—when the radio is switched on. Fifty metres away, Lawrence heard that whisper and knew exactly what it meant.

One does not become Chief Engineer for half a world without learning as much about men as about machines. I took a calculated risk, thought Lawrence, and it looks as if it hasn't come off. But I won't give in without a fight; perhaps I can still de-fuse this psychological time-bomb before it goes off. . . .

Tom Lawson never noticed the approach of the second ski; he was already too lost in his own nightmare. But suddenly he was being violently shaken— so violently that his forehead banged against the lower rim of his helmet. For a moment his vision was blinded by tears of pain; then, with anger—yet at the same time with an inexplicable feeling of relief—he found himself looking straight into the determined eyes of Chief Engineer Lawrence, and listening to his voice reverberate from the suit speakers.

"That's enough of this nonsense," said the C.E.E. "And I'll trouble you not to be sick in one of our space-suits. Every time that happens it costs us five hundred stollars to put it back into commission—and even then it's never quite the same again."

"I wasn't going to be sick——" Lawson managed to mutter. Then he realised that the truth was much worse, and felt grateful to Lawrence for his tact. Before he could add anything more, the other continued, speaking firmly but more gently: "No one else can hear us, Tom—we're on the suit circuit now. So listen to me, and don't get mad. I know a lot about you, and I know you've had a hell of a rough deal from life. But you've got a brain—a damn' good brain—so don't waste it by behaving like a scared kid. Sure—we're all scared kids at some time or other—but this isn't the time for it. There are twenty-two lives depending on you. In five minutes, we'll settle this business one way or the other. So keep your eye on that screen, and forget about everything else. I'll get you out of here all right—don't you worry about *that*."

Lawrence slapped the suit—gently, this time—without taking his eyes off the young scientist's stricken face. Then, with a vast feeling of relief, he saw Lawson slowly relax.

For a moment the astronomer sat quite motionless, obviously in full control of himself but apparently listening to some inner voice. What was it telling him? wondered Lawrence. Perhaps that he was part of mankind, even though it had condemned him to that unspeakable orphans' home when he was a child. Perhaps that, somewhere in the world, there might be a person who could care for him, and who would break through the ice that had encrusted his heart. . . .

It was a strange little tableau, here on this mirror-smooth plain, between the Inaccessible Mountains and the rising sun. Like ships becalmed in a dead and stagnant sea, Duster One and Duster Two floated side by side, their pilots playing no part in the conflict of wills that had just taken place, though they were dimly aware of it. No one watching from a distance could have guessed the issues that had been at stake, the lives and destinies that had trembled in the balance; and the two men involved would never talk of it again.

Indeed, they were already concerned with something else. For in the same instant, they had both become aware of a highly ironic situation.

All the time they had been standing here, so intent upon their own affairs that they had never looked at the screen of the infra-red scanner, it had been patiently holding the picture they sought.

When Pat and Sue had completed their inventory and emerged from the airlock-cum-kitchen, the passengers were still far back in Restoration England. Sir Isaac's brief physics lecture had been followed, as might easily have been predicted, by a considerably longer anatomy lesson from Nell Gwyn. The audience was thoroughly enjoying itself, especially as Barrett's English accent was now going full blast.

" 'Forsooth, Sir Isaac, you are indeed a man of great knowledge. Yet, me-thinks, there is much that a woman might teach you.'

" 'And what is that, my pretty maid?'

"Mistress Nell blushed shyly.

" 'I fear,' she sighed, 'that you have given your life to the things of the mind. You have forgotten, Sir Isaac, that the body, also, has much strange wisdom.'

" 'Call me "Ike" '. said the sage huskily, as his clumsy fingers tugged at the fastenings of her blouse.

" 'Not here—in the palace!' Nell protested, making no effort to hold him at bay. 'The King will be back soon!'

" 'Do not alarm yourself, my pretty one. Charles is roistering with that scribbler Pepys. We'll see naught of him tonight——' "

If we ever get out of here thought Pat, we must send a letter of thanks to the seventeen-year-old schoolgirl on Mars who is supposed to have written this nonsense. She's keeping everyone amused, and that's all that maters now.

No; there was someone who was definitely *not* amused. He became uncomfortably aware that Miss Morley was trying to catch his eye. Recalling his duties as skipper, he turned towards her and gave her a reassuring but rather strained smile.

She did not return it; if anything, her expression became even more forbidding. Slowly and quite deliberately, she looked at Sue Wilkins and then back at him.

There was no need for words. She had said, as clearly as if she had shouted it at the top of her voice: "I know what *you've* been doing, back there in the airlock."

Pat felt his face flame with indignation—the righteous indignation of a man who had been unjustly accused. For a moment he sat frozen in his seat, while the blood pounded in his cheeks. Then he muttered to himself: "I'll show the old bitch."

He rose to his feet, gave Miss Morley a smile of poisonous sweetness, and said just loudly enough for her to hear: "Miss Wilkins! I think we've forgotten something. Will you come back to the airlock?"

As the door closed behind them once more, interrupting the narration of an incident that threw the gravest possible doubts upon the paternity of the Duke of St. Albans, Sue Wilkins looked at him in puzzled surprise.

"Did you see that?" he said, still boiling.

"See what?"

"Miss Morley——"

"Oh," interrupted Susan. "Don't worry about her, poor thing. She's been eyeing you ever since we left Base. You know what her trouble is."

"What?" asked Pat, already uncomfortably sure of the answer.

"I suppose you could call it ingrowing virginity. It's a common complaint, and the symptoms are always the same. There's only one cure for it."

The ways of love are strange and tortuous. Only ten minutes ago, Pat and Sue had left the airlock together, mutually agreed to remain in a state of chaste affection. But now the improbable combination of Miss Morley and Nell Gwyn, and the feeling that one might as well be hanged for a sheep as for a lamb—as well as, perhaps, the instinctive knowledge of their bodies that, in the long run, love was the only defence against death—had combined to overwhelm them. For a moment they stood motionless in the tiny, cluttered space of the galley; then, neither knowing who moved first, they were in each other's arms.

Sue had time to whisper only one phrase before Pat's lips silenced her.

"Not *here*," she whispered, "in the palace!"

CHAPTER XIII

CHIEF ENGINEER LAWRENCE stared into the faintly glowing screen, trying to read its message. Like all engineers and scientists, he had spent an appreciable fraction of his life looking at the images painted by speeding electrons, recording events too large or too small, too bright or too faint, for human eyes to see. It was more than a hundred years since the cathode ray tube had placed the invisible world firmly in man's grasp; already he had forgotten that it had ever been beyond his reach.

Two hundred metres away, according to the infra-red scanner, a patch of slightly greater warmth was lying on the face of this dusty desert. It was almost perfectly circular, and quite isolated; there were no other sources of heat in the entire field of view. Though it was much smaller than the spot that Lawson had photographed from Lagrange, it was in the right area. There could be little doubt that it was the same thing.

There was no proof, however, that it was what they were looking for. It could have several explanations; perhaps it marked the site of an isolated peak, jutting up from the depths almost to the surface of the Sea. There was only one way to find out.

"You stay here," said Lawrence. "I'll go forward on Duster One. Tell me when I'm at the exact centre of the spot."

"D'you think it will be dangerous?"

"It's not very likely, but there's no point in us both taking a risk."

Very slowly, Duster One glided across to that enigmatically glowing patch—so obvious to the infra-red scanner, yet wholly invisible to the eye.

"A little to the left," Tom ordered. "Another few metres—we're nearly there—whoa!"

Lawrence stared at the grey dust upon which his vehicle was floating. At first sight, it seemed as featureless as any other portion of the Sea; then, as he looked more closely, he saw something that raised the goose-pimples on his skin.

When examined very carefully, as he was examining it now, the dust showed an extremely fine pepper-and-salt pattern. *That pattern was moving; the surface of the Sea was creeping very slowly towards him, as if blown by an invisible wind.*

Lawrence did not like it at all. On the Moon, one learned to be wary of the abnormal and the unexplained; it usually meant that something was wrong— or soon would be. This slowly crawling dust was both uncanny and disturbing; if a boat had sunk here once already, anything as small as a ski might be in even greater danger.

"Better keep away," he advised Duster Two. "There's something odd here— I don't understand it." Carefully, he described the phenomenon to Lawson, who thought it over and answered almost at once: "You say it looks like a fountain in the dust? That's exactly what it is. We already know there's a source of heat here—it's powerful enough to stir up a convection current."

"What could do that? It can't be *Selene*."

He felt a wave of disappointment sweep over him. It was all a wild-goose chase, as he had feared from the beginning. Some pocket of radioactivity, or an outburst of hot gases released by the quake, had fooled their instruments, and dragged them to this desolate spot. And the sooner they left it the better— it might still be dangerous.

"Just a minute," said Lawson. "A vehicle with a fair amount of machinery and twenty-two passengers—that must produce a good deal of heat. Three or four kilowatts, at least. If this dust is in equilibrium, that might be enough to start a fountain."

Lawrence thought this was very unlikely, but he was now willing to grasp at the slimmest straw. He picked up the thin metal probe, and thrust it vertic-ally into the dust. At first it penetrated with almost no resistance, but as the telescopic extensions added to its length it became harder and harder to move. By the time he had the full twenty metres out, it needed all his strength to push it downwards.

The upper end of the probe disappeared into the dust; he had hit nothing— but he had scarcely expected to succeed on this first attempt. He would have to do the job scientifically, and lay out a search pattern.

After a few minutes of cruising back and forth, he had criss-crossed the area with parallel bands of white tape, five metres apart, Like an old-time farmer planting potatoes, he started to move along the first of the tapes, driving his probe into the dust. It was a slow job, for it had to be done conscientiously. He was like a blind man, feeling in the dark with a thin, flexible wand. If what he sought was beyond the reach of his wand, he would have to think of something else. But he would deal with that problem when he came to it.

He had been searching for about ten minutes when he became careless. It required both hands to operate the probe, especially when it neared the limit of its extension. He was pushing with all his strength, leaning over the edge of the ski, when he slipped and fell headlong into the dust.

Pat was conscious of the changed atmosphere immediately he emerged from the airlock. The reading from *The Orange and the Apple* had finished some time ago, and a heated argument was now in progress. It stopped when he walked into the cabin, and there was an embarrassing silence while he surveyed the scene. Some of the passengers looked at him out of the corners of their eyes, whilst the others pretended he wasn't there.

"Well, Commodore," he said, "what's the trouble?"

"There's a feeling," Hansteen answered, "that we're not doing all we could to get out. I've explained that we have no alternative but to wait until someone finds us—but not everybody agrees."

It was bound to come sooner or later, thought Pat. As time ran out, and there was no sign of rescue, nerves would begin to snap, tempers get frayed. There would be calls for action—*any* action; it was against human nature to sit still and do nothing in the face of death.

"We've been through this over and over again," he said wearily. "We're at least ten metres down, and even if we opened the airlock no one could get up to the surface against the resistance of the dust."

"Can you be sure of that?" someone asked.

"Quite sure," Pat answered. "Have you ever tried to swim through sand? You won't get very far."

"What about trying the motors?"

"I doubt if they'd budge us a centimetre. And even if they did, we'd move forward—not up."

"We could all go to the rear; our weight might bring the nose up."

"It's the strain on the hull I'm worried about," said Pat.

"Suppose I did start the motors—it would be like butting into a brick wall. Heaven knows what damage it might do."

"But there's a chance it might work; isn't that worth the risk?"

Pat glanced at the Commodore, feeling a little annoyed that he had not come to his support. Hansteen stared straight back at him, as if to say "I've handled this so far—now it's your turn." Well, that was fair enough—especially after what Sue had just said. It was time he stood on his own feet, or at least proved that he could do so.

"The danger's too great," he said flatly. "We're perfectly safe here for at least another four days. Long before then, we'll be found. So why risk everything on a million to one chance? If it was our last resort, I'd say yes—but not now."

He looked round the cabin, challenging anyone to disagree with him. As he did so, he could not help meeting Miss Morley's eye, nor did he attempt to avoid it. Nevertheless, it was with as much surprise as embarrassment that he heard her say: "Perhaps the Captain is in no hurry to leave. I notice that we haven't seen much of him lately—*or* of Miss Wilkins."

Why, you prune-faced bitch, thought Pat. Just because no man in his right senses——

"Hold it, Harris," said the Commodore, in the nick of time. "*I'll* deal with this."

It was the first time that Hansteen had really asserted himself; until now he had run things easily and quietly, or stood in the background and let Pat get on with the job. But now they were hearing the authentic voice of authority, like a trumpet call across a battlefield. This was no retired astronaut speaking; it was a Commodore of Space.

"Miss Morley," he said, "that was a very foolish and uncalled-for remark. Only the fact that we are all under considerable strain can possibly excuse it. I think you should apologise to the Captain."

"It's true," she said stubbornly. "Ask him to deny it."

Commodore Hansteen had not lost his temper in thirty years, and had no intention of losing it now. But he knew when to pretend to lose it, and in this case little stimulation was necessary. He was not only angry with Miss Morley; he was annoyed with Pat, and felt that he had let him down. Of course, there might be nothing at all in Miss Morley's accusation, but Pat and Sue had certainly spent a devil of a long time over a simple job. There were occasions when the appearance of innocence was almost as important as the thing itself; he remembered an old Chinese proverb: "Do not stoop to tie your laces in your neighbour's melon-patch."

"I don't give a damn," he said in his most blistering voice, "about the relations, if any, between Miss Wilkins and the Captain. That's their own affair, and as long as they do their jobs efficiently we've no right to interfere. Are you suggesting that Captain Harris is *not* doing his job?"

"Well—I wouldn't say that."

"Then please don't say anything. We have enough problems on our hands already, without manufacturing any more."

The other passengers had sat listening with that mixture of embarrassment and enjoyment which most men feel when they overhear a quarrel in which they have no part. Though, in a very real sense, this did concern everyone aboard *Selene*, for it was the first challenge to authority, the first sign that discipline was cracking. Until now, this group had been welded into a harmonious whole, but now a voice had been raised against the Elders of the Tribe.

Miss Morley might be a neurotic old maid, but she was also a tough and determined one. The Commodore saw, with understandable qualms, that she was getting ready to answer him.

No one would ever know just what she intended to say; for at that moment, Mrs. Schuster let loose a shriek altogether in keeping with her dimensions.

When a man falls on the Moon, he usually has time to do something about it, for his nerves and muscles are designed to deal with a sixfold greater gravity. Yet when Chief Engineer Lawrence toppled off the ski, the distance was so short that he had no time to react. Almost at once, he hit the dust—and was engulfed in darkness.

He could see absolutely nothing, except for a very faint fluorescence from the illuminated instrument panel inside his suit. With extreme caution, he began to feel around in the softly-resisting, half-fluid substance in which he was floundering, seeking some solid object for support. There was nothing; he could not even guess which direction was up.

A mind-sapping despair, which seemed to drain his body of all its strength, almost overwhelmed him. His heart was thumping with that erratic beat that heralds the approach of panic, and the final overthrow of reason. He had seen other men become screaming struggling animals, and knew that he was moving swiftly to join them.

There was just enough left of his rational mind to remember that only a few minutes ago he had saved Lawson from this same fate, but he was not in a position to appreciate the irony. He had to concentrate all his remaining strength of will on regaining control of himself, and checking the thumping in his chest that seemed about to tear him to pieces.

And then, loud and clear in his helmet speaker, came a sound so utterly unexpected that the waves of panic ceased to batter against the island of his soul. It was Tom Lawson—laughing.

The laughter was brief, and it was followed by an apology.

"I'm sorry, Mr. Lawrence—I couldn't help it. You look so funny there, waving your legs in the sky."

The Chief Engineer froze in his suit. His fear vanished instantly, to be replaced by anger. He was furious with Lawson—but much more furious with himself.

Of course he had been in no danger; in his inflated suit, he was like a balloon floating upon water, and equally incapable of sinking. Now that he knew what had happened, he could sort matters out by himself. He kicked purposefully with his legs, paddled with his hands, and rolled round his centre of gravity— and vision returned as the dust streamed off his helmet. He had sunk, at the most, ten centimetres, and the ski had been within reach all the time. It was a remarkable achievement to have missed it completely while he was flailing around like a stranded octopus.

With as much dignity as he could muster, he grabbed the ski and pulled himself aboard. He did not trust himself to speak, for he was still breathless from his unnecessary exertions, and his voice might betray his recent panic. And he was still angry; he would not have made such a fool of himself in the days when he was working constantly out on the lunar surface. Now he was out of touch; why the last time he had worn a suit had been for his annual proficiency check, and then he had never even stepped outside the airlock.

Back on the ski, as he continued with his probing, his mixture of fright and anger slowly evaporated. It was replaced by a mood of thoughtfulness, as he realised how closely—whether he liked it or not—the events of the last half hour had linked him with Lawson. True, the astronomer had laughed when he was floundering in the dust—but he must have been an irresistibly funny sight. And Lawson had actually apologised for his mirth. A short time ago, both laughter and apology would have been equally unthinkable.

Then Lawrence forgot everything else; for his probe hit an obstacle, fifteen metres down.

CHAPTER XIV

WHEN MRS. SCHUSTER screamed, Commodore Hansteen's first reaction was: "My God—the woman's going to have hysterics." Half a second later, he needed all his will-power not to join her.

From outside the hull, where there had been no sound for three days except the whispering of the dust, there was a noise at last. It was unmistakable, and so was its meaning. Something metallic was scraping along the hull.

Instantly, the cabin was filled with shouts, cheers and cries of relief. With considerable difficulty, Hansteen managed to make himself heard.

"They've found us," he said, "but they may not know it. If we work together, they'll have a better chance of spotting us. Pat—you try the radio. The rest of us will rap on the hull—the old Morse V-sign—DIT DIT DIT DAH. Come on—all together!"

Selene reverberated with a ragged volley of dots and dashes, which slowly became synchronised into one resounding tattoo.

"Hold it!" said Hansteen a minute later. "Everyone listen carefully!"

After the noise, the silence was uncanny—even unnerving. Pat had switched off the air-pumps and fans, so that the only sound aboard the cruiser was the beating of twenty-two hearts.

The silence dragged on and on. Could that noise, after all, have been nothing but some contraction or expansion of *Selene*'s own hull? Or had the rescue party—if it *was* a rescue party—missed them and passed on across the empty face of the Sea?

Abruptly, the scratching came again. Hansteen checked the renewed enthusiasm with a wave of his hand.

"*Listen*, for God's sake," he entreated. "Let's see if we can make anything of it."

The scratching lasted only for a few seconds before being followed once again by that agonising silence. Presently someone said quietly, more to break the suspense than to make any useful contribution, "That sounded like a wire being dragged past. Maybe they're trawling for us."

"Impossible," answered Pat. "The resistance would be too great, especially at this depth. It's more likely to be a rod probing up and down."

"Anyway," said the Commodore, "there's a search party within a few metres of us. Give them another tattoo. Once again—altogether—"

DIT DIT DIT DAH. . . .

DIT DIT DIT DAH. . . .

Through *Selene*'s double hull and out into the dust throbbed the fateful opening rhythm of the Fifth Symphony, as a century earlier it had pulsed across Occupied Europe. In the pilot's seat, Pat Harris was saying again and again, with desperate urgency "*Selene* calling—are you receiving Over", and then listening out for an eternal fifteen seconds before he repeated the transmission. But the ether remained as silent as it had been ever since the dust had swallowed them up.

Aboard *Auriga*, Maurice Spenser looked anxiously at the clock.

"Dammit," he said, "the skis should have been there long ago. When was their last message?"

"Twenty-five minutes ago," said the ship's communications officer. "The half-hourly report should be coming in soon, whether they've found anything or not."

"Sure you're still on the right frequency?"

"You stick to your business and I'll stick to mine," retorted the indignant radioman.

"Sorry," replied Spenser, who had learned long ago when to apologise quickly. "I'm afraid my nerves are jumping."

He rose from his seat, and started to make a circuit of *Auriga*'s little control room. After he had bumped himself painfully against an instrument panel—he had not yet grown accustomed to lunar gravity, and was beginning to wonder if he ever would—he got himself under control once more.

This was the worst part of his job, the waiting until he knew whether or not he had a story. Already, he had incurred a small fortune in expenses. They would be nothing compared with the bills that would soon be accumulating, if he gave Captain Anson the order to go ahead. But in that event his worries would be over, for he would have his scoop.

"Here they are," said the communications officer suddenly. "Two minutes ahead of time. Something's happened."

"I've hit something," said Lawrence tersely, "but I can't tell what it is."

"How far down?" asked Lawson and both pilots simultaneously.

"About fifteen metres. Take me two metres to the right—I'll try again."

He withdrew the probe, then drove it in again when the ski had moved to the new position.

"Still there," he reported, "and at the same depth. Take me on another two metres."

Now the obstacle was gone—or was too deep for the probe to reach.

"Nothing there—take me back in the other direction."

It would be a slow and tiring job, charting the outlines of whatever lay buried down there. By such tedious methods, two centuries ago, men began to sound the oceans of Earth, lowering weighted lines to the sea bed and then hauling them up again. It was a pity, thought Lawrence, that he had no echo-sounder that would operate here, but he doubted if either acoustic or radio waves could penetrate through more than a few metres of the dust.

What a fool—he should have thought of that before! *That* was what had happened to *Selene*'s radio signals. If she had been swallowed by the dust, it would have blanketed and absorbed her transmission. But at this range, if he really was sitting on top of the cruiser . . .

Lawrence switched his receiver to the MOONCRASH band—and there she was, yelling at the top of her robot voice. The signal was piercingly strong—quite good enough, he would have thought, to have been picked up by Lagrange or Port Roris. Then he remembered that his metal probe was still resting on the submerged hull; it would give radio waves an easy path to the surface.

He sat listening to that train of pulses for a good fifteen seconds before he plucked up enough courage for the next move. He had never really expected to find anything, and even now his search might be in vain. That automatic beacon would call for weeks, like a voice from the tomb, long after *Selene*'s occupants were dead.

Then, with an abrupt, angry gesture that defied the fates to do their worst, Lawrence switched to the cruiser's own frequency—and was almost deafened by Pat Harris shouting: "*Selene* calling—*Selene* calling. Do you receive me? Over."

"This is Duster One," he answered. "C.E.E. speaking. I'm fifteen metres above you. Are you all O.K.? Over."

It was a long time before he could make any sense of the reply, the background of shouting and cheering was so loud. That in itself was enough to tell him that all the passengers were alive, and in good spirits. Listening to them, indeed, one might almost have imagined that they were holding some drunken celebration. In their joy at being discovered, at making contact with the human race, they thought that their troubles were over.

"Duster One calling Port Roris Control," said Lawrence, while he waited for the tumult to die down. "We've found *Selene* and established radio contact. Judging by the noise that's going on inside, everyone's quite O.K. She's fifteen metres down, just where Dr. Lawson indicated. I'll call you back in a few minutes. Out."

At the speed of light, waves of relief and happiness would now be spreading over the Moon, the Earth, the inner planets, bringing a sudden lifting of the hearts to billions of people. On streets and slideways, in buses and space-ships, perfect strangers would turn to each other and say "Have you heard? They've found *Selene*."

In all the Solar System, indeed, there was only one man who could not whole-heartedly share the rejoicing. As he sat on his ski, listening to those cheers from underground and looking at the crawling pattern in the dust, Chief Engineer Lawrence felt far more scared and helpless than the men and women trapped beneath his feet. He knew that he was facing the greatest battle in his life.

CHAPTER XV

FOR THE FIRST time in twenty-four hours, Maurice Spenser was relaxing. Everything that could be done had been done. Men and equipment were already moving towards Port Roris (lucky about Jules Braques being at Clavius —he was one of the best cameramen in the business, and they'd often worked together). Captain Anson was doing sums with the computer and looking thoughtfully at contour maps of the mountains. The crew (all six) had been rounded up from the bars (all three) and informed that there was yet another change of route. On Earth, at least a dozen contracts had been signed and telefaxed, and large sums of money had already changed hands. The financial wizards of Interplanet News would be calculating, with scientific precision, just how much they could charge the other agencies for the story without driving them to charter ships of their own, not that this was at all likely, for Spenser had too great a lead. No competitor could possibly reach the Mountains in less than forty-eight hours; he would be there in six.

Yes, it was very pleasant to take it easy, in the calm and confident assurance that everything was under control and going the way you wanted. It was these interludes that made life worth living, and Spenser knew how to make the most of them. They were his panacea against ulcers—still, after a hundred years, the occupational disease of the communications industry.

It was typical of him, however, that he was relaxing on the job. He was lying, a drink in one hand, a plate of sandwiches by the other, in the small observation lounge of the Embarkation Building. Through the double sheets of glass he could see the tiny dock from which *Selene* had sailed three days ago. (There was no escaping from those maritime words, inappropriate though they were to this situation.) It was merely a strip of concrete stretching for twenty metres out into the uncanny flatness of the dust; lying most of its length, like a giant concertina, was the flexible tube through which the passengers could walk from the Port into the cruiser. Now open to vacuum, it was deflated and partly collapsed—a most depressing sight, Spenser could not help thinking.

He glanced at his watch, then at that unbelievable horizon. (If he had been asked to guess, he would have said that it was at least a hundred kilometres away, not two or three.) A few minutes later, a reflected glint of sunlight caught his eye. There they were, climbing up over the edge of the Moon. They would be here in five minutes, out of the airlock in ten. Plenty of time to finish that last sandwich.

Doctor Lawson showed no signs of recognition when Spenser greeted him; that was not surprising, for their previous brief conversation had been in almost total darkness.

"Doctor Lawson? I'm Bureau Chief of Interplanet News. Permission to record?"

"Just a minute," interrupted Lawrence. "I know the Interplanet man. *You're* not Joe Leonard. . . ."

"Correct; I'm Maurice Spenser—I took over from Joe last week. He has to get used to Earth gravity again—otherwise he'll be stuck here for life."

"Well, you're damn' quick off the mark. It was only an hour ago that we radioed."

Spenser thought it best not to mention that he had already been here the better part of a day.

"I'd still like to know if I can record," he repeated. He was very conscientious about this; some newsmen took a chance and went ahead without permission; but if you were caught you lost your job. As a Bureau Chief he had to keep the rules laid down to safeguard his profession—and the public.

"Not now, if you don't mind," said Lawrence. "I've fifty things to organise, but Doctor Lawson will be glad to talk to you—he did most of the work and deserves all the credit. You can quote me on *that*."

"Er—thank you," mumbled Tom, looking very embarrassed.

"Right—see you later," said Lawrence. "I'll be at the Local Engineer's office, living on pills. But you might as well get some sleep."

"Not until I've finished with you," corrected Spenser, grabbing Tom and aiming him in the direction of the hotel.

The first person they met in the ten-metre square foyer was Captain Anson.

"I've been looking for you, Mr. Spenser," he said. "The Space-workers' Union is making trouble. You know there's a ruling about time-off between trips. Well, it seems that——"

"*Please*, Captain—not now. Take it up with Interplanet's legal department—call Clavius 1234—ask for Harry Dantzig—he'll straighten it out."

He propelled the unresisting Tom Lawson up the stairs (it was odd to find an hotel without elevators, but they were unnecesary on a world where you weighed only a dozen or so kilos) and into his suite.

Apart from its excessively small size, and complete absence of windows, the suite might have been in any cheap hotel on Earth. The simple chairs, couch and table were manufactured from the very minimum of material—most of it fibreglass, for quartz was common on the Moon. The bathroom was perfectly conventional (that was a relief, after those tricky free-fall toilets) but the bed had a slightly disconcerting appearance. Some visitors from Earth found it difficult to sleep under a sixth of a gravity, and for their benefit an elastic sheet could be stretched across the bed and held in place by light springs. The whole arrangement had a distinct flavour of strait-jackets and padded cells.

Another cheerful little touch was the notice behind the door, which announced in English, Russian and Mandarin that

THE HOTEL IS INDEPENDENTLY PRESSURISED. IN THE EVENT OF A DOME FAILURE, YOU WILL BE PERFECTLY SAFE. SHOULD THIS OCCUR, PLEASE REMAIN IN YOUR ROOM AND AWAIT FURTHER INSTRUCTIONS. THANK YOU.

Spenser had read that notice several times. He still thought that the basic information could have been conveyed in a more confident, light-hearted manner. The wording lacked charm.

And that, he decided, was the whole trouble on the Moon. The struggle against the forces of Nature was so fierce that no energy was left for gracious living. This was most noticeable in the contrast between the superb efficiency of the technical services, and the easygoing, take-it-or-leave-it attitude one met in all the other walks of life. If you complained about the telephone, the plumbing, the air (especially the air!) it was fixed within minutes. But just try to get quick service in a restaurant or bar. . . .

"I know you're very tired," Spenser began, "but I'd like to ask a few questions. You don't mind being recorded, I hope?"

"No," said Tom, who had long passed the stage of caring one way or the other. He was slumped in a chair, mechanically sipping the drink Spenser had poured out, but obviously not tasting it.

"This is Maurice Spenser, Interplanet News, talking with Doctor Thomas Lawson. Now, doctor, all we know at the moment is that you and Mr. Lawrence, Chief Engineer, Earthside, have found *Selene*, and that the people inside are safe, just how you—hell and damnation!"

He caught the slowly falling glass without spilling a drop, then eased the sleeping astronomer over to the couch. Well, he couldn't grumble; this was the only item that hadn't worked according to plan. And even this might be to his advantage; for no one else could find Lawson—still less interview him—while he was sleeping it off in what the Hotel Roris, with a fine sense of humour, called its luxury suite.

In Clavius City, the Tourist Commissioner had finally managed to convince everyone that he had not been playing favourites. His relief at hearing of *Selene*'s discovery had quickly abated when Reuter's, TIME-SPACE, Triplanetary Publications and Lunar News phoned him in rapid succession to ask just how Interplanet had managed to break the story first. It had been on the wires, in fact, even before it had reached Administration headquarters, thanks to Spenser's thoughtful monitoring of the dust-ski radios.

Now that it was obvious what had happened, the suspicions of all the other news-services had been replaced by frank admiration for Spenser's luck and enterprise. It would be a little while yet before they realised that he had an even bigger trick up his capacious sleeve.

The Communications Centre at Clavius had seen many dramatic moments, but this was one of the most unforgettable. It was, thought Commissioner Davis, almost like listening to voices from beyond the grave. A few hours ago, all these men and women were presumed dead—yet here they were, fit and cheerful, lining up at that buried microphone to relay messages of reassurance to their friends and relatives. Thanks to the probe which Lawrence had left as marker and antenna, that fifteen-metre blanket of dust could no longer cut the cruiser off from the rest of mankind.

The impatient reporters had to wait until there was a break in *Selene*'s transmission before they could get their interview. Miss Wilkins was now speaking, dictating messages that were being handed to her by the passengers. The cruiser must have been full of people scribbling telegraphese on the backs of torn-up guide-books, trying to condense the maximum amount of information into the minimum number of words. None of this material, of course, could be quoted or reproduced; it was all private and the Postmaster-Generals of three planets would descend in their combined wrath upon any reporter foolish enough to use it. Strictly speaking, they should not even be listening-in on this circuit, as the Communications Officer had several times pointed out with increasing degrees of indignation.

".... tell Martha, Jan and Ivy not to worry about me, I'll be home soon. Ask Tom how the Ericson deal went, and let me know when you call back. My love to you all—George. End of message. Did you get that? *Selene* calling—over."

"Lunar Central calling *Selene*. Yes, we have it all down—we'll see that the messages get delivered and will relay the answers as soon as they come in. Now can we speak to Captain Harris? Over."

There was a brief pause, during which the background noises in the cruiser could be clearly heard—the sound of voices, slightly reverberant in this enclosed space, the ·creak of a chair, a muffled "Excuse me". Then——

"Captain Harris calling Central. Over."

Commissioner Davis took the mike.

"Captain Harris—this is the Tourist Commissioner. I know that you all have messages you wish to send, but the news-services are here and are very anxious to have a few words with you. First of all, could you give me a brief description of conditions inside *Selene*? Over."

"Well, it's very hot, and we aren't wearing many clothes. But I don't suppose we can grumble about the heat, as it helped you to find us; anyway, we've grown used to it.

"The air's still good, and we have enough food and water, though the menu is—let's say it's monotonous. What more do you want to know? Over."

"Ask him about morale—how are the passengers taking it?— are there any signs of strain?" said the representative of Triplanetary Publications. The Tourist Commissioner relayed the question, rather more tactfully. It seemed to cause slight embarrassment at the other end of the line.

"Everyone's behaved very well," said Pat, just a little too hastily. "Of course, we all wonder how long it will take you to get us out. Can you give any ideas on that? Over."

"Chief Engineer Lawrence is in Port Roris now, planning rescue operations," Davis answered. "As soon as he has an estimate, we'll pass it on. Meanwhile, how are you occupying your time? Over."

Pat told him, thereby enormously multiplying the sale of *Shane* and, less happily, giving a boost to the flagging fortunes of *The Orange and the Apple*. He also gave a brief account of the court proceedings—now terminated *sine die*.

"That must have been amusing entertainment," said Davis. "But now you won't have to rely on your own resources. We can send you anything you want —music, plays, discussions. Just give the word—we'll fix it. Over."

Pat took his time in answering this. The radio link had already transformed their lives, had brought them hope and put them in touch with their loved ones. Yet in a way, he was almost sorry that their seclusion was ended. The heart-warming sense of solidarity, which even Miss Morley's outburst had scarcely ruffled, was already a fading dream. They no longer formed a single group, united in the common cause of survival. Now their lives had diverged again into a score of independent aims and ambitions. Humanity had swallowed them up once more, as the ocean swallows a rain-drop.

CHAPTER XVI

CHIEF ENGINEER LAWRENCE did not believe that committees ever achieved anything. His views were well known on the Moon, for shortly after the last biannual visit of the Lunar Board of Survey a notice had appeared on his desk conveying the information: A BOARD IS LONG, HARD AND NARROW. IT IS MADE OF WOOD.

But he approved of this committee, because it fulfilled his somewhat stringent requirements. He was chairman; there were no minutes, no secretary, no agenda. Best of all, he could ignore or accept its recommendations as he pleased. He was the man in charge of rescue operations, unless the Chief Administrator chose to sack him—which he would do only under extreme pressure from Earth. The committee existed merely to provide ideas and technical knowledge; it was his private Brains Trust.

Only half of its dozen members were physically present; the rest were scattered over Moon, Earth and space. The soil physics expert on Earth was at a disadvantage, for owing to the finite speed of radio waves he would always be a second and a half in arrears—and by the time his comments could get to the Moon, almost three seconds would have passed. He had accordingly been asked to make notes and to save up his views until the end, only interrupting if it was absolutely necessary. As many people had discovered, after setting up lunar conference calls at great expense, nothing hamstrung a brisk discussion more effectively than that three-second time-lag.

"For the benefit of the newcomers," said Lawrence, when the roll-call had been completed, "I'll brief you on the situation. *Selene* is fifteen metres down, on a level keel. She's undamaged, with all her equipment functioning, and the twenty-two people inside her are still in good spirits. They have enough oxygen for ninety hours—*that's* the dead-line we have to keep in mind.

"For those of you who don't know what *Selene* looks like, here's a one-in-twenty scale model." He lifted the model from the table, and turned it slowly in front of the camera. "She's just like a bus, or a small aircraft; the only thing unique is her propulsion system, which employ these wide-bladed, variable-pitch fans.

"Our great problem, of course, is the dust. If you've never seen it, you can't imagine what it's like. Any ideas you may have about sand or other materials on Earth won't apply here; this stuff is more like a liquid. Here's a sample of it."

Lawrence picked up a tall vertical cylinder, the lower third of which was filled with an amorphous grey substance. He tilted it—and the stuff began to flow. It moved more quickly than syrup, more slowly than water, and it took a few seconds for its surface to become horizontal again after it had been disturbed. No one could ever have guessed, by looking at it, that it was not a fluid.

"This cylinder is sealed," explained Lawrence, "with a vacuum inside, so the dust is showing its normal behaviour. In air, it's quite different; it's much stickier, and behaves rather like very fine sand or talcum powder. I'd better warn you—it's impossible to make a synthetic sample that has the properties of the real thing; it takes a few billion years of desiccation to produce the genuine article. If you want to do some experimenting, we'll ship you as much dust as you like; heaven knows, we can spare it.

"A few other points. *Selene* is three kilometres from the nearest solid land —the Mountains of Inaccesibility. There may be several hundred metres of dust beneath her, though we're not sure of that. Nor can we be quite sure that there will be no more cave-ins, though the geologists think it's very unlikely.

"The only way we can reach the site is by dust-ski. We've two units, and another one is being shipped round from Farside. They can carry or tow up to five tons of equipment; the largest single item we could put on a sledge would be about two tons. So we can't bring any really heavy gear to the site.

"Well, that's the position. We have ninety hours. Any suggestions? I've some ideas of my own, but I'd like to hear yours first."

There was a long silence while the members of the committee, scattered over a volume of space almost four hundred thousand kilometres across, brought their various talents to bear on the problem. Then the Chief Engineer, Farside, spoke from somewhere in the neighbourhood of Joliot-Curie.

"It's my hunch that we can't do anything effective in ninety hours; we'll have to build special equipment, and that always takes time. So—we have to get an air-line down to *Selene*. Where's her umbilical connection?"

"Behind the main entrance—at the rear. I don't see how you can get a line there and couple it up, fifteen metres down. Besides, everything will be clogged with dust."

"I've a better idea," someone interjected. "Drive a pipe down through the roof."

"You'll need two pipes," pointed out another speaker. "One to pump in oxygen, the other to suck out the foul air."

"That means using a complete air-purifier. And we won't even need it, if we can get those people out inside the ninety hours."

"Too big a gamble. Once the air supply is secure, we can take our time, and the ninety-hour deadline won't worry us."

"I accept that point," said Lawrence. "In fact, I've several men working on those lines right now. The next question is—do we try to raise the cruiser with everyone inside, or do we get the passengers out individually? Remember, there's only one space-suit aboard her."

"Could we sink a shaft to the door, and couple it to the airlock?" asked one of the scientists.

"Same problem as with the air-hose. Even worse, in fact, since the coupling would be so much bigger."

"What about a coffer-dam large enough to go round the whole cruiser? We could sink it round her, then dig out the dust."

"You'd need tons of piles and shorings. And don't forget—the dam would have to be sealed off at the bottom. Otherwise the dust would flow back into it, just as fast as we took it out of the top."

"Can you pump the stuff?" asked someone else.

"Yes, with the right kind of impeller. But you can't suck it, of course. It has to be lifted. A normal pump just cavitates."

"This dust," grumbled the Port Roris Assistant Engineer, "has the worst properties of solids and liquids, with none of their advantages. It won't flow when you want it to; it won't stay put when you want it to."

"Can I make a point?" said Father Ferraro, speaking from Plato. "This word 'dust' is highly misleading. What we have here is a substance that can't exist on Earth, so there's no name for it in our language. The last speaker was quite correct; sometimes you have to think of it as a non-wetting liquid, rather like mercury, but much lighter. At other times it's a flowing solid, like pitch—except that it moves much more rapidly, of course."

"I think that's a question for Earth," said Lawrence. "Dr. Evans—would you like to comment?"

Everyone waited for the three seconds which, as always, seemed very much longer. Then the physicist answered, quite as clearly as if he were in the same room: "I've been wondering about that. There might be organic binders—glue, if you like—that would make it stick together so that it could be handled more easily. Would plain water be any use? Have you tried that?"

"No, but we will, answered Lawrence, scribbling a note.

"Is the stuff magnetic?" asked the Traffic Control Officer.

"That's a good point," said Lawrence. "Is it, Father?"

"Slightly; it contains a fair amount of meteoric iron. But I don't think that helps us at all. A magnetic field would pull out the ferrous material, but it couldn't affect the dust as a whole."

"Anyway, we'll try," Lawrence made another note. It was his hope—though a faint one—that out of this clash of minds would come some bright ideas, some apparently far-fetched but fundamentally sound conception, that would solve his problem. And it was his, whether he liked it or not. He was responsible, through his various deputies and departments, for every piece of technical equipment on this side of the Moon. Especially when something went wrong with it.

"I'm very much afraid," said the Clavius Traffic Control Officer, "that your biggest headache will be logistics. Every piece of equipment has to be ferried out on the skis, and they take at least two hours for the round trip—more, if they're towing a heavy load. Before you even start operating, you'll have to build some kind of working platform—like a raft—that you can leave on the site. It may take a day to get that in position, and much longer to get all your equipment out to it."

"Including temporary living quarters," added someone. "The workmen will have to stay on the site."

"That's straightforward; as soon as we fix a raft, we can inflate an igloo on it."

"Better than that; you won't even need a raft. An igloo will float by itself."

"Getting back to this raft," said Lawrence, "we want strong, collapsible units that can be bolted together on the site. Any ideas?"

"Empty fuel tanks?"

"Too big and fragile. Maybe Tech Stores has something."

So it went on; the Brains Trust was in session. Lawrence would give it another half-hour, then he would decide on his plan of action.

One could not spend too much time talking, when the minutes were ticking away and many lives were at stake. Yet hasty and ill-conceived schemes were worse than useless, for they would absorb materials and skills that might tilt the balance between failure and success.

At first sight, it seemed such a straightforward job. There was *Selene*, within a hundred kilometres of a well-equipped base. Her position was known exactly, and she was only fifteen metres down. But that fifteen metres presented Lawrence with some of the most baffling problems of his entire career.

It was a career which, he knew very well, might soon terminate abruptly. For it would be very hard to explain his failure, if those twenty-two men and women died.

It was a great pity that not a single witness saw *Auriga* coming down, for it was a glorious sight. A space-ship landing or taking off is one of the most impressive spectacles that man has yet contrived—excluding some of the more exuberant efforts of the nuclear engineers. And when it occurs on the Moon, in slow motion and uncanny silence, it has a dream-like quality which no one who has seen it can ever forget.

Captain Anson saw no point in trying any fancy navigation, especially as someone else was paying for the gas. There was nothing in the Master's Handbook about flying a space-liner a hundred kilometres—a *hundred* kilometres, indeed!—though no doubt the mathematicians would be delighted to work out a trajectory, based on the Calculus of Variations, using the very minimum amount of fuel. Anson simply blasted straight up for a thousand kilometres (thus qualifying for deep-space rates under Interplanetary Law, though he would tell Spenser about this later) and came down again on a normal vertical approach, with final radar guidance. The ship's computer and the radar monitored each other, and both were monitored by Captain

Anson. Any one of the three could have done the job, so it was really quite simple and safe—though it did not look it.

Especially to Maurice Spenser, who began to feel a great longing for the soft green hills of Earth as those desolate peaks clawed up at him. Why had he talked himself into this? Surely there were cheaper ways of committing suicide. . . .

The worst part was the free-fall between the successive braking periods. Suppose the rockets failed to fire on command, and the ship continued to plunge moonwards, slowly but inexorably accelerating until it crashed? It was no use pretending that this was a stupid or childish fear, because it had happened more than once.

It was not, however, going to happen to *Auriga*. The unbearable fury of the braking jets was already splashing over the rocks, blasting skywards the dust and cosmic debris that had not been disturbed in thrice a billion years. For a moment the ship hovered in delicate balance only centimetres off the ground; then, almost reluctantly, the spears of flame that supported her retracted into their scabbards. The widely-spaced legs of the undercarriage made contact, their pads tilted according to the contours of the ground, and the whole ship rocked slightly for a second as the shock-absorbers neutralised the residual energy of Impact.

For the second time inside twenty-four hours, Maurice Spenser had landed on the Moon. That was a claim that very few men could make.

"Well," said Captain Anson, as he got up from the control board. "I hope you're satisfied with the view. It's cost you plenty—and there's still that little matter of overtime. According to the Space-workers' Union——"

"Have you no soul, Captain? Why bother me with such trivia at a time like this? But if I may say so without being charged any extra—that was a very fine landing."

"Oh, it's all part of the day's work," replied the skipper, though he could not conceal slight signs of pleasure. "By the way—would you mind initialling the log here, against the time of landing."

"What's *that* for?" asked Spenser suspiciously.

"Proof of delivery. The log's our prime legal document."

"It seems a little old-fashioned, having a written one," said Spenser. "I thought everything was done by nucleonics these days."

"Traditions of the service," replied Anson. "Of course, the ship's flight-recorders are running all the time we're under power, and the trip can always be reconstructed from them. But only the skipper's log gives the little details that make one voyage different from another—like 'Twins born to one of the steerage passengers this morning' or 'At six bells, sighted the White Whale off the starboard bow'."

"I take it back, Captain," said Spenser. "You *do* have a soul, after all." He added his signature to the log, then moved over to the observation window to examine the view.

The control cabin, a hundred and fifty metres above the ground, had the only direct-vision windows in the ship, and the view through them was superb.

Behind him, to the north, were the upper ramparts of the Mountains of Inaccessibility, ranging across half the sky. That name was no longer appropriate, thought Spenser; *he* had reached them, and while the ship was here it might even be possible to do some useful scientific research, such as collecting rock samples. Quite apart from the news value of being in such an outlandish place, he was genuinely interested in what might be discovered here. No man could ever become so *blasé* that the promise of the unknown and the unexplored completely failed to move him.

In the other direction, he could look across at least forty kilometres of the Sea of Thirst, which spanned more than half his field of view in a great arc of immaculate flatness. But what he was concerned with was less than five kilometres away, and two below.

Clearly visible in a low-powered pair of binoculars was the metal rod that Lawrence had left as a marker, and through which *Selene* was now linked with the world. The sight was not impressive—just a solitary spike jutting from an endless plain—yet it had a stark simplicity that appealed to Spenser. It would make a good opening; it symbolised the loneliness of man in this huge and hostile universe that he was attempting to conquer. In a few hours, this plain would be very far from lonely, but until then that rod would serve to set the scene, while the commentators discussed the rescue plans and filled in the time with appropriate interviews. That was not his problem; the unit at Clavius and the studios back on Earth could handle it in their stride. He had just one job now—to sit here in his eagle's nest, and to see that the pictures kept coming in. With the big zoom lens, thanks to the perfect clarity of this airless world, he could almost get closeups even from here, when the action started.

He glanced into the south-west, where the sun was lifting itself so sluggishly up the sky. Almost two weeks of daylight, as Earth counted time, still lay ahead. No need, then, to worry about the lighting. The stage was set.

CHAPTER XVII

CHIEF ADMINISTRATOR OLSEN seldom made public gestures; he preferred to run the Moon quietly and efficiently behind the scenes, leaving amiable extroverts like the Tourist Commissioner to face the newsmen. His rare appearances were, therefore, all the more impressive—as he intended them to be.

Though millions were watching him, the twenty-two men and women he was really addressing could not see him at all, for it had not been thought necessary to fit *Selene* with vision circuits. But his voice was sufficiently reassuring; it told them everything that they wanted to know.

"Hello, *Selene*," he began, "I want to tell you that all the resources of the Moon are now being mobilised for your aid. The engineering and technical staffs of my administration are working round the clock to help you.

"Mr. Lawrence, Chief Engineer, Earthside, is in charge, and I have complete confidence in him. He's now at Port Roris, where the special equipment needed for the operation is being assembled. It's been decided—and I'm sure you'll agree with this—that the most urgent task is to make certain that your oxygen supply can be maintained. For this reason, we plan to sink pipes to you; that can be done fairly quickly, and then we can pump down oxygen—as well as food and water, if necessary. So as soon as the pipes are installed, you'll have nothing more to worry about. It may still take a little time to reach you and get you out, but you'll be quite safe. You only have to sit and wait for us.

"Now I'll get off the air, and let you have this channel back so that you can talk to your friends. I'm sorry about the inconvenience and strain you've undergone, but that's all over now. We'll have you out in a day or two. Good luck!"

A burst of cheerful conversation broke out aboard *Selene* as soon as Administrator Olsen's broadcast finished. It had had precisely the effect he had intended; the passengers were already thinking of this whole episode as an adventure which would give them something to talk about for the rest of their lives. Only Pat Harris seemed a little unhappy.

"I wish," he told Commodore Hansteen, "the C.A. hadn't been quite so confident. On the Moon, remarks like that always seem to be tempting fate."

"I know exactly how you feel," the Commodore answered. "But you can hardly blame him—he's thinking of our morale."

"Which is fine, I'd say—especially now that we can talk to our friends and relatives."

"That reminds me; there's one passenger who hasn't received or sent any messages. What's more, he doesn't show the slightest interest in doing so."

"Who's that?"

Hansteen dropped his voice still further.

"The New Zealander, Radley. He just sits quietly in the corner over there. I'm not sure why, but he worries me."

"Perhaps the poor fellow has no one on Earth he wants to speak to."

"A man with enough money to go to the Moon must have *some* friends," replied Hansteen. Then he grinned; it was almost a boyish grin, that flickered swiftly across his face, softening its wrinkles and crow's feet. "That sounds very cynical—I didn't mean it that way. But I suggest we keep an eye on Mr. Radley."

"Have you mentioned him to Sue—er, Miss Wilkins?"

"She pointed him out to *me*."

I should have guessed that, thought Pat admiringly; not much gets past her. Now that it seemed he might have a future, after all, he had begun to think very seriously about Sue—and about what she had said to him. In his life he had been in love with five or six girls—or so he could have sworn at the time —but this was something different. He had known Sue over a year and from the start had felt attracted to her, but until now it had never come to anything.

What were her real feelings? he wondered. Did she regret that moment of shared passion, or did it mean nothing to her? She might argue—and so might he, for that matter—that what had happened in the airlock was no longer relevant; it was merely the action of a man and a woman who thought that only a few hours of life remained to them. They had not been themselves. . . .

But perhaps they had been; perhaps it was the real Pat Harris, the real Susan Wilkins, that had finally emerged from disguise, revealed by the strain and anxiety of the past few days. He wondered how he could be sure of this, but even as he did so, he knew that only time could give the answer. If there was a clear-cut, scientific test that could tell you when you were in love, Pat had not yet come across it.

The dust that lapped—if that was the word—against the quay from which *Selene* had departed four days ago was only a couple of metres deep, but for this test no greater depth was needed. If the hastily built equipment worked here, it would work out in the open Sea.

Lawrence watched from the Embarkation Building as his space-suited assistants bolted the framework together. It was made, like ninety per cent of the structures on the Moon, from slotted aluminium strips and bars. In some ways, thought Lawrence, the Moon was an engineer's paradise. The low gravity, the total absence of rust or corrosion—indeed, of weather itself, with its unpredictable winds and rains and frosts—removed at once a whole range of problems that plagued all terrestrial enterprises. But to make up for that, of course, the Moon had a few specialities of its own—like the two-hundred-below-zero nights, and the dust that they were fighting now.

The light framework of the raft rested upon a dozen large metal drums, which carried the prominently stencilled words: "Contents Ethyl Alcohol. Please return when empty to No. 3 Dispatching Centre, Copernicus." Their contents now were a very high grade of vacuum; each drum could support a weight of two lunar tons before sinking.

Now the raft was rapidly taking shape. Be sure to have plenty of spare nuts and bolts, Lawrence told himself. He had seen at least six dropped in the dust, which had instantly swallowed them. And there went a wrench; make an order that all tools *must* be tied to the raft even when in use, however inconvenient that might be. . . .

Fifteen minutes—not bad, considering that the men were working in vacuum and therefore hampered by their suits. The raft could be extended in any direction as required, but this would be enough to start with. This first section alone could carry over twenty tons, and it would be some time before they unloaded that weight of equipment on the site.

Satisfied with this stage of the project, Lawrence left the Embarkation Building while his assistants were still dismantling the raft. Five minutes later (that was one advantage of Port Roris—you could get anywhere in five minutes) he was in the local engineering depot. What he found here was not quite so satisfactory.

Supported on a couple of trestles was a two-metre-square mock-up of

Selene's roof—an exact copy of the real thing, made from the same materials. Only the outer sheet of aluminised fabric that served as a sun-shield was missing; it was so thin and flimsy that it would not affect the test.

The experiment was an absurdly simple one, involving only three ingredients —a pointed crowbar, a sledge-hammer, and a frustrated engineer who, despite strenuous efforts, had not yet succeeded in hammering the bar through the roof.

Anyone with a *little* knowledge of lunar conditions would have guessed at once why he had failed. The hammer, obviously, had only a sixth of its terrestrial weight; therefore—equally obviously—it was that much less effective.

The reasoning would have been completely false. One of the hardest things for the layman to understand was the difference between weight and mass, and the inability to do so had led to countless accidents. For weight was an arbitrary characteristic; you could change it by moving from one world to another. On Earth, that hammer would weigh six times as much as it did here; on the Sun, it would be almost two hundred times heavier—and in space it would weigh nothing at all.

But in all three places, and indeed throughout the universe, its mass or inertia would be exactly the same, and the impact it would produce when stopped, would be constant through all space and time. On a nearly gravityless asteroid, where it weighed less than a feather, that hammer would pulverise a rock just as effectively as on Earth.

"What's the trouble?" said Lawrence.

"The roof's too springy," explained the engineer, rubbing the sweat from his brow. "The crowbar just bounces back every time it's hit."

"I see. But will that happen when we're using a fifteen-metre pipe, with dust packed all around it? That may absorb the recoil."

"Perhaps—but look at this."

They kneeled beneath the mock-up and inspected the under-side of the roof. Chalk lines had been drawn upon it to indicate the position of the electric wiring, which had to be avoided at all costs.

"This fibreglass is so tough, you can't make a clean hole through it. When it does yield, it splinters and tears. See—it's already begun to star. I'm afraid that if we try this brute-force approach, we'll crack the roof."

"And we can't risk that," Lawrence agreed. "Well, drop the idea. If we can't pile-drive, we'll have to bore. Use a drill, screwed on the end of the pipe so it can be detached easily. How are you getting on with the rest of the plumbing?"

"Almost ready—it's all standard equipment. We should be finished in two or three hours."

"I'll be back in two," said Lawrence. He did not add, as some men would have done, "I want it finished by then." His staff was doing its utmost, and one could neither bully nor cajole trained and devoted men into working faster than their maximum. Jobs like this could not be rushed, and the deadline for *Selene*'s oxygen supply was still three days away. In a few hours, if all went well, it would have been pushed into the indefinite future.

Unfortunately, all was going very far from well.

Commodore Hansteen was the first to recognise the slow, insidious danger that was creeping up on them. He had met it once before, when he had been wearing a faulty space-suit on Ganymede—an incident he had no wish to recall, but had never really forgotten.

"Pat," he said quietly, making sure that no one could overhear. "Have you noticed any difficulty in breathing?"

Pat looked startled, then answered, "Yes, now that you mention it. I'd put it down to the heat."

"So did I at first. But I know these symptoms—especially the quick breathing. We're running into carbon dioxide poisoning."

"But that's ridiculous—we should be all right for another three days—unless something has gone wrong with the air-purifiers."

"I'm afraid it has. What system do we use to get rid of the CO_2?"

"Straight chemical absorption. It's a very simple, reliable set-up; we've never had any trouble with it before."

"Yes, but it's never had to work under these conditions before. I think the heat may have knocked out the chemicals. Is there any way we can check them?"

Pat shook his head.

"No; the access hatch is on the outside of the hull."

"Sue, my dear," said a tired voice which they hardly recognised as belonging to Mrs. Schuster, "do you have anything to fix a headache?"

"If you do," said another passenger, "I'd like some as well."

Pat and the Commodore looked at each other gravely. The classic symptoms were developing with text-book precision.

"How long would you guess?" said Pat very quietly.

"Two or three hours at the most. And it will be at least six before Lawrence and his men can get here."

It was then that Pat knew, without any further argument, that he was genuinely in love with Susan. For his first reaction was not fear for his own safety, but anger and grief that, after having endured so much, she would have to die within sight of rescue.

CHAPTER XVIII

WHEN TOM LAWSON woke up in that strange hotel room, he was not even sure who he was, still less where he was. The fact that he had some weight was his first reminder that he was no longer on Lagrange—but he was not heavy enough for Earth. Then it was not a dream; he was on the Moon, and he really had been out into that deadly Sea of Thirst.

And he had helped to find *Selene*; twenty-two men and women now had a chance of life, thanks to his skill and science. After all the disappointments and frustrations, his adolescent dreams of glory were about to come true. Now the world would have to make amends to him for its indifference and neglect.

The fact that society had provided him with an education which, a century earlier, only a few men could afford, did nothing to alleviate Tom Lawson's grudge against it. Such treatment was automatic in this age, when every child was educated to the level that his intelligence and aptitudes permitted. Now that civilisation needed all the talent that it could find, merely to maintain itself, any other educational policy would have been suicide. Tom Lawson gave no thanks to society for providing the environment in which he had obtained his doctor's degree; it had acted in its own self-interest.

Yet this morning he did not feel quite so bitter about life or so cynical about human beings. Success and recognition are great emollients, and he was on his way to achieving both. But there was more to it than that; he had glimpsed a deeper satisfaction. Out there on Duster Two, when his fears and uncertainties had been about to overwhelm him, he had made contact with another human being, and had worked in successful partnership with a man whose skill and courage he could respect.

It was only a tenuous contact, and like others in the past it might lead nowhere. A part of his mind, indeed, hoped that it would, so that he could once again assure himself that all men were selfish, sadistic scoundrels. Tom could no more escape from his early boyhood than Charles Dickens, for all his success and fame, could escape the shadows of the blacking factory that had both metaphorically and literally darkened his youth. But he had made a fresh beginning—though he still had very far to go before he became a fully-paid-up member of the human race.

When he had showered and tidied himself, he noticed the message that Spenser had left lying on the table. "Make yourself at home," it said. "I've had to leave in a hurry. Mike Graham is taking over from me—call him at 3443 as soon as you're awake."

I'm hardly likely to call him *before* I'm awake, thought Tom, whose excessively logical mind loved to seize on such loosenesses of speech. But he obeyed Spenser's request, heroically resisting the impulse to order breakfast first.

When he got through to Mike Graham, he discovered that he had slept through a very hectic six hours in the history of Port Roris, that Spenser had taken off in *Auriga* for the Sea of Thirst—and that the town was full of newsmen from all over the Moon, most of them looking for Dr. Lawson.

"Stay right where you are," said Graham, whose name and voice were both vaguely familiar to Tom; he must have seen him on those rare occasions that he tuned in to lunar telecasts. "I'll be over in five minutes."

"I'm starving," protested Tom.

"Call Room Service and order anything you like—it's on us, of course—but don't go outside the suite."

Tom did not resent being pushed around in this somewhat cavalier fashion;

it meant, after all, that he was now an important piece of property. He was much more annoyed by the fact that, as anyone in Port Roris could have told him, Mike Graham arrived long before Room Service. It was a hungry astronomer who now faced Mike's miniature telecamera and tried to explain, for the benefit of—as yet—only two hundred million viewers, exactly how he had been able to locate *Selene*.

Thanks to the transformation wrought by hunger and his recent experiences, he made a first-class job of it. A few days ago, had any TV reporter managed to draw Lawson in front of a camera to explain the technique of infra-red detection, he would have been swiftly and contemptuously blinded by science. Tom would have given a no-holds-barred lecture full of such terms as quantum efficiency, black-body radiation and spectral sensitivity that would have convinced his audience that the subject was extremely complex (which was true enough) and wholly impossible for the layman to understand (which was quite false).

But now he carefully and fairly patiently—despite the occasional urgent proddings of his stomach—answered Mike Graham's questions in terms that most of his viewers could understand. To the large section of the astronomical community which Tom had scarred at some time or other, it was a revelation. Up in Lagrange II, Professor Kotelnikov summarised the feelings of all his colleagues when, at the end of the performance, he paid Tom the ultimate compliment. "Quite frankly," he said in tones of incredulous disbelief, "I would never have recognised him."

It was something of a feat to have squeezed six men into *Selene*'s airlock, but—as Pat had demonstrated—it was the only place where one could hold a private conference. The other passengers doubtless wondered what was happening; they would soon know.

When Hansteen had finished, his listeners looked understandably worried, but not particularly surprised; they were intelligent men, and must have already guessed the truth.

"I'm telling you first," explained the Commodore, "because Captain Harris and I decided you were all level-headed—and tough enough to give us help if we need it. I hope to God we won't, but there may be trouble when I make my announcement."

"And if there is?" said Harding.

"If anyone makes a fuss—jump on them," answered the Commodore briefly. "But be as casual as you can when we go back into the cabin. Don't look as if you're expecting a fight; that's the best way to start one, our job is to damp out panic before it spreads."

"Do you think it's fair," said Dr. McKenzie, "not to give an opportunity to —well, send out some last messages?"

"We thought of that, but it would take a long time and would make everyone completely depressed. We want to get this through as quickly as possible. The sooner we act, the better our chance."

"Do you really think we have one?" asked Barrett.

"Yes," said Hansteen, "though I'd hate to quote the odds. No more questions? Bryan? Johanson? Right—let's go."

As they marched back into the cabin, and took their places, the remaining passengers looked at them with curiosity and growing alarm. Hansteen did not keep them in suspense.

"I've some grave news," he said, speaking very slowly. "You must all have noticed difficulty in breathing and several of you have complained about headaches.

"Yes, I'm afraid it's the air. We still have plenty of oxygen—that's not our problem. But we can't get rid of the carbon dioxide we exhale; it's accumulating inside the cabin. Why, we don't know; my guess is that the heat has knocked out the chemical absorbers. But the explanation hardly matters, for there's nothing we can do about it." He had to stop and take several deep breaths before he could continue.

"So we have to face this situation. Your breathing difficulties will get steadily worse; so will your headaches. I won't attempt to fool you. The rescue team can't possibly reach us in under six hours, and we can't wait that long."

There was a stifled gasp from somewhere in the audience; Hansteen avoided looking for its source. A moment later there came a stertorous snore from Mrs. Schuster; at another time it would have been funny, but not now. She was one of the lucky ones; she was already peacefully, if not quietly, unconscious.

The Commodore refilled his lungs; it was tiring to talk for any length of time.

"If I couldn't offer you some hope," he continued, "I would have said nothing. But we do have one chance and we have to take it soon. It's not a very pleasant one, but the alternative is much worse. Miss Wilkins—please hand me the sleep-tubes."

There was a deathly silence—not even interrupted by Mrs. Schuster—as the stewardess handed over a small metal box. Hansteen opened it, and took out a white cylinder the size and shape of a cigarette.

"You probably know," he continued, "that all space vehicles are compelled by law to carry these in their medicine chests. They are quite painless, and will knock you out for ten hours. That may mean all the difference between life and death—for man's respiration rate is cut by more than fifty per cent when he's unconscious. So our air will last twice as long as it would otherwise do. Long enough, we hope, for Port Roris to reach us.

"Now, it's essential for at least one person to remain awake to keep in touch with the rescue team. And to be on the safe side, we should have two. One of them must be the Captain; I think that goes without argument."

"And I suppose the other should be you?" said an all-too-familiar voice.

"I'm really very sorry for you, Miss Morley," said Commodore Hansteen, without the slightest sign of resentment—for there was no point, now, in making an issue of a matter that had already been settled. "Just to remove any possible misconceptions——"

Before anyone quite realised what had happened, he had pressed the cylinder to his forearm.

"I'll hope to see you all—ten hours from now," he said, very slowly but distinctly, as he walked to the nearest seat. He had barely reached it when he slumped quietly into oblivion.

It's all your show now, Pat told himself as he got to his feet. For a moment he thought like addressing a few well-chosen words to Miss Morley; then he realised that to do so would spoil the dignity of the Commodore's exit.

"I'm the captain of this vessel," he said in a firm, low voice. "And from now on, what I say goes."

"Not with *me*," retorted the indomitable Miss Morley. "I'm a paying passenger and I have my rights. I've not the slightest intention of using one of those things."

The blasted woman seemed unsnubbable; Pat was also compelled to admit that she had guts. He had a brief, nightmare glimpse of the future that her words suggested. Ten hours alone with Miss Morley, and no one else to talk to. . . .

He glanced at the five trouble-shooters. The nearest to Miss Morley was the Jamaican civil engineer, Robert Bryan. He looked ready and willing to move into action, but Pat still hoped that unpleasantness could be avoided.

"I don't wish to argue about rights," he said, "but if you were to look at the small print on your tickets you'd discover that, in an emergency, I'm in absolute charge here. In any event, this is for your own good, and your own comfort. I'd much rather be asleep than awake, while we wait for the rescue team to get here."

"That goes for me too," said Professor Jayawardene unexpectedly. "As the Commodore said, it will conserve the air, so it's our only chance. Miss Wilkins —will you give me one of those things?"

The calm logic of this helped to lower the emotional temperature; so did the Professor's smooth, obviously comfortable slide into unconsciousness. Two down and eighteen to go, murmured Pat under his breath.

"Let's waste no more time," he said aloud. "As you can see, these shots are entirely painless. There's a microjet hypodermic inside each cylinder, and you won't even feel a pin-prick."

Sue Wilkins was already handing out the innocent-looking little tubes, and several of the passengers had used them immediately. There went the Schusters—Irving, with a reluctant and touching tenderness, had pressed the tube against the arm of his sleeping wife—and the enigmatic Mr. Radley. That left fifteen. Who would be next?

Now Sue had come to Miss Morley. This was it, thought Pat. If she was *still* determined to make a fuss . . .

He might have guessed it.

"I thought I made it *quite* clear that I don't want one of those things. Please take it away."

Robert Bryan began to inch forward—but it was the sardonic, English voice of David Barrett that did the trick.

"What *really* worries the good lady, Captain," he said, obviously placing his barb with relish, "is that you may take advantage of her in her helpless condition."

For a few seconds Miss Morley sat speechless with fury, while her cheeks turned a bright crimson.

"I've never been so insulted in my——" she began.

"Nor have *I*, madam," interjected Pat, completing her demoralisation. She looked round the circle of faces—most of them solemn, but several grinning, even at a time like this—and realised that there was only one way out.

As she slumped in her seat, Pat breathed a vast sigh of relief. After that little episode, the rest should be easy.

Then he saw that Mrs. Williams, whose birthday had been celebrated in such spartan style only a few hours before, was staring in a kind of frozen trance at the cylinder in her hand. The poor woman was obviously terrified, and no one could blame her. In the next seat, her husband had already collapsed; it was a little ungallant, Pat thought, to have gone first and left his wife to fend for herself.

Before he could take any action, Sue had moved forward.

"I'm so sorry, Mrs. Williams—I made a mistake—I gave you an empty one. Perhaps you'll let me have it back. . . ."

The whole thing was done so neatly that it looked like a conjuring trick. Sue took—or seemed to take—the tube from the unresisting fingers, but as she did so she must have jolted it against Mrs. Williams. The lady never knew what had happened; she quietly folded up and joined her husband.

Half the company was unconscious now; on the whole, thought Pat, there had been remarkably little fuss. Commodore Hansteen had been too much of a pessimist; the riot squad had not been necessary, after all.

Then, with a slight sinking feeling, he noticed something that made him change his mind. It looked as if, as usual, the Commodore had known exactly what he was doing. Miss Morley was not going to be the only difficult customer.

It was at least two years since Lawrence had been inside an igloo; there was a time, in the days when he had been a junior engineer out on construction, when he had known what it was like to be surrounded by rigid walls. Since those days, of course, there had been many improvements in design; it was now no particular hardship to live in a home that would fold up into a small trunk.

This was one of the latest models—a Goodyear Mark Twenty—and it could sustain six men for an indefinite period, as long as they were supplied with power, water, food and oxygen. The igloo would provide everything else—even entertainment, for it had a built-in microlibrary of books, music and video. This was no extravagant luxury, though the auditors queried it with great regularity. In space, boredom could be a killer. It might take longer than, say, a leak in an airline—but it could be just as effective, and was sometimes much messier.

Lawrence stooped slightly to enter the airlock. In some of the old models, he remembered, you practically had to go down on hands and knees. He waited for the "pressure equalised" signal, then stepped into the hemispherical main chamber.

It was like being inside a balloon; indeed, that was exactly where he was. He could see only part of the interior, for it had been divided into several compartments by movable screens. (Another modern refinement; in *his* day, the only privacy was that given by the curtain across the toilet.) Overhead, three metres above the floor, were the lights and the air-conditioning grille, suspended from the ceiling by elastic webbing. Against the curved wall stood collapsible metal racks, only partly erected. From the other side of the nearest screen came the sound of a voice reading from an inventory, while every few seconds another interjected "Check".

Lawrence stepped around the screen and found himself in the dormitory section of the igloo. Like the wall-racks, the double-bunks had not been fully erected; it was merely necessary to see that all the bits and pieces were in their place, for as soon as the inventory was completed everything would be packed and rushed to the site.

Lawrence did not interrupt the two storemen as they continued their careful stocktaking. This was one of those unexciting but vital jobs—of which there were so many on the Moon—upon which lives could depend. A mistake here could be a sentence of death for someone, sometime in the future.

When the checkers had come to the end of a sheet, Lawrence said, "Is this the largest model you have in stock?"

"The largest that's serviceable," was the answer. "We have a twelve-man Mark Nineteen, but there's a slow leak in the outer envelope that has to be fixed."

"How long will that take?"

"Only a few minutes. But then there's a twelve-hour inflation test before we're allowed to check it out."

This was one of those times when the man who made the rules had to break them.

"We can't wait to make the full test. Put on a double patch and take a leak-reading, if it's inside the standard tolerance, get the igloo checked out right away. I'll authorise the clearance."

The risk was trivial, and he might need that big dome in a hurry. Somehow, he had to provide air and shelter for twenty-two men and women out there on the Sea of Thirst. They couldn't all wear space-suits, from the time they left *Selene* until they were ferried back to Port Roris.

There was a "beep-beep" from the communicator behind his left ear. He flicked the switch at his belt and acknowledged the call.

"C.E.E. speaking."

"Messages from *Selene*, sir," said a clear, tiny voice. "Very urgent—they're in trouble."

CHAPTER XIX

UNTIL NOW, PAT had scarcely noticed the man who was sitting with folded arms in window seat 3D, and had to think twice to remember his name. It was something like Builder—that was it, *Baldur*, Hans Baldur. He had looked the typical quiet tourist who never gave any trouble.

He was still quiet, but no longer typical—for he was remaining stubbornly conscious. At first sight he appeared to be ignoring everything around him, but the twitching of a cheek muscle betrayed his tenseness.

"What are you waiting for, Mr. Baldur?" asked Pat, in the most neutral tone that he could manage. He felt very glad of the moral and physical support ranged behind him; Baldur did not look exceptionally strong, but he was certainly more than Pat's moonborn muscles could have coped with—if it came to that.

Baldur shook his head, and remained staring out of the window for all the world as if he could see something there beside his own reflection.

"You can't make me take that stuff, and I'm not going to," he said, in heavily accented English.

"I don't want to force you to do anything," answered Pat. "But can't you see it's for your own good—and for the good of everyone else? What possible objection do you have?"

Baldur hesitated and seemed to be struggling for words.

"It's—it's against my principles," he said. "Yes, that's it. My religion won't allow me to take injections."

Pat knew vaguely that there were people with such scruples. Yet he did not for a moment believe that Baldur was one of them. The man was lying, but why?

"Can I make a point?" said a voice behind Pat's back.

"Of course, Mr. Harding," he answered, welcoming anything that might break this *impasse*.

"You say you won't permit any injections, Mr. Baldur," continued Harding, in tones that reminded Pat of his cross-examination of Mrs. Schuster. (How long ago *that* seemed!) "But I can tell that you weren't born on the Moon. No one can miss going through Quarantine—so, how did you get here without taking the usual shots?"

The question obviously left Baldur extremely agitated.

"That's no business of yours," he snapped.

"Quite true," said Harding pleasantly. "I'm only trying to be helpful." He stepped forward and reached out his left hand. "I don't suppose you'd let me see your Interplanetary Vaccination Certificate?"

That was a damn silly thing to ask, thought Pat. No human eye could read the magnetically inscribed information on an IVC. He wondered if this would occur to Baldur, and if so, what he would do about it.

He had no time to do anything. He was still staring, obviously taken by surprise, at Harding's open palm when his interrogator moved his other hand so swiftly that Pat never saw exactly what happened. It was like Sue's conjuring trick with Mrs. Williams—but far more spectacular, and also much deadlier. As far as Pat could judge, it involved the side of the hand and the base of the neck—and it was not, he was quite sure, the kind of skill he ever wished to acquire.

"That will hold him for fifteen minutes," said Harding in a matter-of-fact voice, as Baldur crumpled up in his seat. "Can you give me one of those tubes? Thanks." He pressed the cylinder against the unconscious man's arm; there was no sign that it had any additional effect.

The situation, thought Pat, had got somewhat out of his control. He was grateful that Harding had exercised his singular skills, but was not entirely happy about them.

"Now what was all that?" he asked, a little plaintively.

Harding rolled up Baldur's left sleeve, and turned the arm over to reveal the fleshy underside. The skin was covered with literally hundreds of almost invisible pin-pricks.

"Know what that is?" he said quietly.

Pat nodded. Some had taken longer to make the trip than others, but by now all the vices of weary old Earth had reached the Moon.

"You can't blame the poor devil for not giving his reasons. He's been conditioned against using the needle; judging from the state of those scars, he started his cure only a few weeks ago. Now it's psychologically impossible for him to accept an injection; I hope I've not given him a relapse, but that's the least of his worries."

"How did he ever get through Quarantine?"

"Oh, there's a special section for people like this; the doctor's don't talk about it, but the customers get temporary deconditioning under hypnosis. There are more of them than you might think; a trip to the Moon's highly recommended as part of the cure. It gets you away from your original environment."

There were quite a few other questions that Pat would have liked to ask Harding, but they had already wasted several minutes. Thank heaven all the remaining passengers had gone under. That last demonstration of judo, or whatever it was, must have encouraged any stragglers.

"You won't need me any more," said Sue, with a small, brave smile. "Goodbye, Pat—wake me when it's over."

"I will," he promised, lowering her gently into the space between the seatrows. "Or not at all," he added, when he saw that her eyes were closed.

He remained bending over her for several seconds before he regained enough control to face the others. There were so many things he wanted to tell her—but now the opportunity was gone, perhaps for ever.

Swallowing to overcome the dryness in his throat, he turned to the five survivors. There was still one more problem to deal with, and David Barrett summed it up for him.

"Well, Captain," he said. "Don't leave us in suspense. Which of us do you want to keep you company?"

One by one, Pat handed over five of the sleep-tubes.

"Thank you for your help," he said, "I know this is a little melodramatic, but it's the neatest way. Only four of those will work."

"I hope mine will," said Barrett, wasting no time. It did. A few seconds later, Harding, Bryan and Johanson followed the Englishman into oblivion.

"Well," said Dr. McKenzie, "I seem to be odd man out. I'm flattered by your choice—or did you leave it to luck?"

"Before I answer that question," replied Pat, "I'd better let Port Roris know what's happened."

He walked to the radio and gave a brief survey of the situation. There was a shocked silence from the other end; a few minutes later, Chief Engineer Lawrence was on the line.

"You did the best thing, of course," he said, when Pat had repeated his story in more detail. "Even if we hit no snags, we can't possibly reach you in under five hours. Will you be able to hold out until then?"

"The two of us, yes," answered Pat. We can take turns using the space-suit breathing circuit. It's the passengers I'm worried about."

"The only thing you can do is to check their respiration, and give them a blast of oxygen if they seem distressed. We'll do our damnedest from this end. Anything more you want to say?"

Pat thought for a few seconds.

"No," he said, a little wearily. "I'll call you again on each quarter hour. Selene out."

He got to his feet—slowly, for the strain and the CO_2 poisoning were now beginning to tell heavily upon him—and said to McKenzie: "Right, Doc—give me a hand with that space-suit."

"I'm ashamed of myself. I'd forgotten all about that."

"And I was worried because some of the other passengers might have remembered. They must all have seen it, when they came in through the airlock. It just goes to prove how you can overlook the obvious."

It took them only five minutes to detach the absorbent canisters and the twenty-four hours oxygen supply from the suit; the whole breathing circuit had been designed for quick-release, in case it was ever needed for artificial respiration. Not for the first time, Pat blessed the skill, ingenuity and foresight that had been lavished on Selene. There were some things that had been overlooked, or that might have been done a little better—but not many.

Their lungs aching, the only two men still conscious aboard the cruiser stood staring at each other across the grey metal cylinder that held another day of life. Then, simultaneously, each said: "You go first."

They laughed without much humour at the hackneyed situation, then Pat answered; "I won't argue" and placed the mask over his face.

Like a cool sea breeze after a dusty summer day; like a wind from the mountain pine-forests stirring the stagnant air in some deep lowlands valley—so the flow of oxygen seemed to Pat. He took four slow, deep breaths, and exhaled to the fullest extent, to sweep the carbon dioxide out of his lungs. Then, like a pipe of peace, he handed the breathing kit over to McKenzie.

Those four breaths had been enough to invigorate him, and to sweep away the cobwebs that had been gathering in his brain. Perhaps it was partly psychological—could a few cubic centimetres of oxygen have had so profound an effect?—but whatever the explanation, he felt a new man. Now he could face the five—or more—hours of waiting—hours that lay ahead.

Ten minutes later, he felt another surge of confidence. All the passengers seemed to be breathing as normally as could be expected—very slowly, but steadily. He gave each one a few seconds of oxygen, then called Base again.

"*Selene* here," he said. "Captain Harris reporting. Dr. McKenzie and I both feel quite fit now, and none of the passengers seem distressed. I'll remain listening out, and will call you again on the half-hour."

"Message received. But hold on a minute—several of the news agencies want to speak to you."

"Sorry," Pat answered. "I've given all the information there is, and I've twenty unconscious men and women to look after. *Selene* out."

That was only an excuse, of course, and a feeble one at that; he was not even sure why he had made it. He felt, in a sudden and uncharacteristic burst of rancour: "Why, a man can't even die in peace nowadays!" Had he known about that waiting camera, only five kilometres away, his reaction might have been even stronger.

"You still haven't answered my question, Captain," said Dr. McKenzie patiently.

"What question? Oh—*that*. No, it wasn't luck. The Commodore and I both thought you'd be the most useful man to have awake. You're a scientist, you spotted the overheating danger before anyone else did, and you kept quiet about it when we asked you."

"Well, I'll try to live up to your expectations. I certainly feel more alert than I've done for hours. It must be the oxygen we're sniffing; the big question is —how long will it last?"

"Between the two of us, twelve hours—plenty of time for the skis to get here. But we may have to give most of it to the others, if they show signs of distress. I'm afraid it's going to be a very close thing."

They were both sitting cross-legged on the floor, just beside the pilot's position, with the oxygen bottle between them. Every few minutes they would take turns with the inhaler—but only two breaths at a time. I never imagined, Pat told himself, that I should ever get involved in the Number One *cliché* of the TV Space Operas. But it had occurred in real life too often to be funny any more—especially when it was happening to you.

Both Pat and McKenzie—or almost certainly one of them—could survive if they abandoned the other passengers to their fate. Trying to keep these twenty men and women alive, they might also doom themselves.

The situation was one in which logic warred against conscience. But it was nothing new; certainly it was not peculiar to the age of space. It was as old as Mankind, for countless times in the past, lost or isolated groups had faced death through lack of water, food or warmth. Now it was oxygen that was in short supply, but the principle was just the same.

Some of those groups had left no survivors; others, a handful who would spend the rest of their lives in self-justification. What must George Pollard, late captain of the whaler *Essex*, have thought as he walked the streets of Nantucket, with the taint of cannibalism upon his soul? That was a two-hundred-year-old story of which Pat had never heard; he lived on a world too busy making its own legends to import those of Earth. As far as he was concerned, he had already made his choice—and he knew, without asking, that McKenzie would agree with him. Neither was the sort of man who would fight over the last bubble of oxygen in the tank. But if it *did* come to a fight——

"What are you smiling at?" asked McKenzie.

Pat relaxed; there was something about this burly Australian scientist that he found very reassuring. Hansteen gave him the same impression, but McKenzie was a very much younger man. There were some people you knew that you could trust, whom you were certain would never let you down. He had that feeling about McKenzie.

"If you want to know," he said, putting down the oxygen mask, "I was thinking that I wouldn't have much of a chance if you decided to keep the bottle for yourself."

McKenzie looked a little surprised, then he too grinned.

"I thought all you Moonborn were sensitive about that," he said.

"*I've* never felt that way," Pat answered. "After all, brains are more important than muscles. I can't help being bred in a gravity field a sixth of yours. Anyway, how could you tell I was Moonborn?"

"Well, it's partly your build. You all have that same tall, slender physique. And there's your skin colour—the u.v. lamps never seem to give you the same tan as natural sunlight."

"It's certainly tanned *you*," retorted Pat with a grin. "At night, you must be a menace to navigation. Incidentally, how did you get a name like McKenzie?"

Having had little contact with the racial tensions which were not yet wholly extinct on Earth, Pat could make such remarks without embarrassment—indeed, without even realising that they might cause embarrassment.

"My grandfather had it bestowed on him by a missionary when he was baptised. I'm very doubtful if it has any—ah—genetic significance. To the best of my knowledge, I'm a full-blooded abo."

"Abo?"

"Aboriginal. We were the people occupying Australia before the whites came along. The subsequent events were somewhat depressing."

Pat's knowledge of terrestrial history was vague; like most residents of the Moon, he tended to assume that nothing of great importance had ever happened before 8th November 1967, when the fifteenth anniversary of the Russian Revolution had been so spectacularly celebrated.

"I suppose there was war?"

"You could hardly call it that. We had spears and boomerangs—they had guns. Not to mention T.B. and V.D., which were much more effective. It took us about a hundred and fifty years to get over the impact; it's only in the last century—since about 1940—that our numbers started going up again. Now there are about a hundred thousand of us—*almost* as many as when your ancestors came."

McKenzie delivered this information with an ironic detachment that took any personal sting out of it, but Pat thought that he had better disclaim responsibility for the misdeeds of his terrestrial predecessors.

"Don't blame me for what happened on Earth," he said. "I've never been there, and I never will—I couldn't face that gravity. But I've looked at Australia plenty of times through the telescope. I have some sentimental feeling for the place—my parents took off from Woomera."

"And my ancestors named it; a woomer's a booster stage for spears."

"Are any of your people," asked Pat, choosing his words with care, "still living in primitive conditions? I've heard that's still true, in some parts of Asia."

"The old tribal life's gone. It went very quickly, when the African nations in the U.N. started bullying Australia. Often quite unfairly, I might add—for I'm an Australian first, and an aboriginal second. But I must admit that my white countrymen were often pretty stupid; they must have been, to think that *we* were stupid! Why, way into the last century some of them still thought we were Stone Age savages. Our technology was Stone Age, all right—but we weren't."

There seemed nothing incongruous to Pat about this discussion, beneath the surface of the Moon, of a way of life so distant both in space and time. He and McKenzie would have to entertain each other, keep an eye on their twenty unconscious companions, and fight off sleep, for at least five more hours. This was as good a way as any of doing it.

"If your people weren't in the Stone Age, Doc—and just for the sake of argument I'll grant that *you* aren't—how did the whites get that idea?"

"Sheer stupidity, with the help of a preconceived bias. It's an easy assumption that if a man can't count, write, or speak good English, he must be unintelligent. I can give you a perfect example from my own family. My grandfather—the first McKenzie—lived to see the year 2000, but he never learned to count beyond ten. And his description of a total eclipse of the Moon was 'Kerosene lamp bilong Jesus Christ he bugger-up finish altogether.'

"Now, I can write down the differential equations of the Moon's orbital motion, but I don't claim to be brighter than grandfather. If we'd been switched in time, he might have been the better physicist. Our opportunities were different—that's all. Grandfather never had occasion to learn to count, and I never had to raise a family in the desert—which was a highly skilled, full-time job."

"Perhaps," said Pat thoughtfully, "we could do with some of your grandfather's skills here. For that's what we're trying to do now—survive in a desert."

"I suppose you could put it that way, though I don't think that boomerang and fire-stick would be much use to us. Maybe we could use some magic— but I'm afraid I don't know any, and I doubt if the tribal gods could make it from Arnhem Land."

"Do you ever feel sorry," asked Pat, "about the break-up of your people's way of life?"

"How could I? I scarcely knew it; I was born in Brisbane, and had learned to run an electronic computer before I ever saw a corroboree——"

"A what?"

"Tribal religious dance—and half the participants in *that* were taking degrees in cultural anthropology. I've no romantic illusion about the simple life and the noble savage. My ancestors were fine people and I'm not ashamed of them, but geography had trapped them in a dead-end. After the struggle for sheer existence, they had no energy left for a civilisation. In the long run, it was a good thing that the white settlers arrived, despite their charming habit of selling us poisoned flour when they wanted our land."

"They did *that*?"

"They certainly did. But why are you surprised? That was a good hundred years before Belsen."

Pat thought this over for a few minutes. Then he looked at his watch and said, with a distinct expression of relief: "Time I reported to Base again. Let's have a quick look at the passengers first."

CHAPTER XX

THERE WAS NO time now, Lawrence realised, to worry about inflatable igloos and the other refinements of gracious living in the Sea of Thirst. All that mattered was getting those air-pipes down into the cruiser; the engineers and technicians would just have to sweat it out in the suits until the job was finished. Their ordeal would not last for long. If they could not manage inside five or six hours, they could turn round and go home again, and leave *Selene* to the world after which she was named.

In the workshops of Port Roris, unsung and unrecorded miracles of improvisation were now being achieved. A complete air-conditioning plant, with its liquid oxygen tanks, humidity and carbon dioxide absorbers, temperature and pressure regulators, had to be dismantled and loaded on to a sledge. So did a small drilling rig, hurled by shuttle rocket from the Geophysics Division at Clavius. So did the specially designed plumbing, which now had to work at the first attempt, for there would be no opportunity for modifications.

Lawrence did not attempt to drive his men; he knew it was unnecessary.

He kept in the background, checking the flow of equipment from stores and workshop out to the skis, and trying to think of every snag that could possibly arise. What tools would be needed? Were there enough spares? Was the raft being loaded on to the skis last, so that it could be off-loaded first? Would it be safe to pump oxygen into *Selene* before connecting up the exhaust line? These, and a hundred other details—some trivial, some vital—passed through his mind. Several times he called Pat to ask for technical information, such as the internal pressure and temperature, whether the cabin relief valve had blown-off yet (it hadn't, probably it was jammed with dust) and advice on the best spots to drill through the roof. And each time Pat answered with increasing slowness and difficulty.

Despite all attempts to contact him, Lawrence resolutely refused to speak to the newsmen now swarming round Port Roris and jamming half the sound and vision circuits between Earth and Moon. He had issued one brief statement explaining the position and what he intended doing about it; the rest was up to the administrative people. It was their job to protect him so that he could get on with his work undisturbed; he had made that quite clear to the Tourist Commissioner, and had hung up before Davis could argue with him.

He had no time, of course, even to glance at the TV coverage himself, though he had heard that Doctor Lawson was rapidly establishing a reputation as a somewhat prickly personality. That, he presumed, was the work of the Interplanet News man into whose hands he had dumped the astronomer; the fellow should be feeling quite happy about it.

The fellow was feeling nothing of the sort. High on the ramparts of the Inaccessible Mountains, whose title he had so convincingly refuted, Maurice Spenser was heading swiftly towards that ulcer he had avoided all his working life. He had spent a hundred stollars to get *Auriga* here—and now it looked as if there would be no story after all.

It would all be over before the skis could arrive; the suspense-packed, breathtaking rescue operations that would keep billions glued to their screens was never going to materialise. Few people could have resisted watching twenty-two men and women snatched from death; but no one would want to see an exhumation.

That was Spenser's cold-blooded analysis of the situation from the newscaster's viewpoint, but as a human being he was equally unhappy. It was a terrible thing to sit here on the mountain, only five kilometres away from impending tragedy, yet able to do absolutely nothing to avert it. He felt almost ashamed of every breath he took, knowing that those people down there were suffocating. Time and again he had wondered if there was anything that *Auriga* could do to help (the news value of this did not, of course, escape him) but now he was sure that she could only be a spectator. That implacable Sea ruled out all possibility of aid.

He had covered disasters before; but this time he felt uncommonly like a ghoul.

It was very peaceful now, aboard *Selene*—so peaceful that one had to fight against sleep. How pleasant it would be, thought Pat, if he could join the others, dreaming happily all around him. He envied them—and sometimes felt jealous of them. Then he would take a few draughts from the dwindling store of oxygen, and reality would close in upon him as he recognised his peril.

A single man could never have remained awake, or kept an eye on twenty unconscious men and women, feeding them oxygen whenever they showed signs of respiratory distress. He and McKenzie had acted as mutual watch-dogs; several times each had dragged the other back from the verge of sleep. There would have been no difficulty had there been plenty of oxygen, but that one bottle was becoming rapidly exhausted. It was maddening to know that there were still many kilograms of liquid oxygen in the cruiser's main tanks, but there was no way in which they could use it. The automatic system was metering it through the evaporators and into the cabin, where it was at once contaminated by the now almost unbearable atmosphere.

Pat had never known time to move so slowly. It seemed quite incredible that only four hours had passed since he and McKenzie had been left to guard their sleeping companions. He could have sworn that they had been here for days, talking quietly together, calling Port Roris every fifteen minutes, check-ing pulses and respiration, and doling out oxygen with a miserly hand.

But nothing lasts for ever. Over the radio, from the world which neither man really believed he would ever see again, came the news they had been waiting for.

"We're on the way," said the weary but determined voice of Chief Engineer Lawrence. "You only have to hang on for another hour—we'll be on top of you by then. How are you feeling?"

"Very tired," said Pat slowly. "But we can make it."

"And the passengers?"

"Just the same."

"Right—I'll call you every ten minutes. Leave your receiver on, volume high. This is Med Division's idea—they don't want to risk you falling asleep."

The blare of brass thundered across the face of the Moon, then echoed on past the Earth and out into the far reaches of the Solar System. Hector Berlioz could never have dreamed that, two centuries after he had composed it, the soul-stirring rhythm of his Rákóczy March would bring hope and strength to men fighting for their lives on another world.

As the music reverberated round the cabin, Pat looked at Dr. McKenzie with a wan smile.

"It may be old-fashioned," he said, "but it's working."

The blood was pounding in his veins, his foot was tapping with the beat of the music. Out of the lunar sky, flashing down from space, had come the tramp of marching armies, the thunder of cavalry across a thousand battle-fields, the call of bugles that had once summoned nations to meet their destiny. All gone, long ago, and that was well for the world. But they left behind them much that was fine and noble—examples of heroism and self-sacrifice, proofs that men could still hold on when their bodies should have passed the limits of physical endurance.

As his lungs laboured in the stagnant air, Pat Harris knew that he had need of such inspiration from the past—if he was to survive the endless hour that lay ahead.

Aboard the tiny, cluttered deck of Duster One, Chief Engineer Lawrence heard the same music, and reacted in the same fashion. His little fleet was indeed going into battle, against the enemy that Man would face to the end of time. As he spread across the universe from planet to planet and sun to sun, the forces of nature would be arrayed against him in ever new and un-expected ways. Even Earth, after all these aeons, still had many traps for the unwary, and on a world that men had known for only a lifetime, death lurked in a thousand innocent disguises. Whether or not the Sea of Thirst was robbed of its prey, Lawrence was sure of one thing—tomorrow there would be a fresh challenge.

Each ski was towing a single sledge, piled high with equipment which looked heavier and more impressive than it really was; most of the load was merely the empty drums upon which the raft would float. Everything not absolutely essential had been left behind; as soon as Duster One had dumped its cargo, Lawrence would send it straight back to Port Roris for the next load. Then he would be able to maintain a shuttle service between the site and Base, so that if he wanted anything quickly he would never have to wait more than an hour for it. This, of course, was taking the optimistic view; by the time he got to *Selene*, there might be no hurry at all. . . .

As the Port buildings dropped swiftly below the skyline, Lawrence ran through the procedure with his men. He had intended to do a full-dress re-hearsal before sailing, but that was another plan that had had to be abandoned through lack of time. The first countdown would be the only one that mattered.

"Jones, Sikorsky, Coleman, Matsui—when we arrive at the marker, you're to unload the drums and lay them out in the right pattern. As soon as that's done, Bruce and Hodges will fix the cross-members. Be very careful not to drop any of the nuts and bolts, and keep all your tools tied to you. If you accidentally fall off, don't panic; you can only sink a few centimetres. I know.

"Sikorski, Jones—you give a hand with the flooring, as soon as the raft framework's fixed. Coleman, Matsui—immediately there's enough working space, start laying out the air-pipes and the plumbing. Greenwood, Renaldi —you're in charge of the drilling operation——"

So it went on, point by point. The greatest danger, Lawrence knew, was that his men would get in each other's way as they worked in this confined space. A single trifling accident, and the whole effort would be wasted. One of Lawrence's private fears, which had been worrying him ever since they left Port Roris, was that some vital tool had been left behind. And there was an even worse nightmare—that the twenty-two men and women in *Selene* might die within minutes of rescue, because the only wrench that could make the final connection had been dropped overboard. . . .

On the Inaccessible Mountains, Maurice Spenser was staring through his binoculars and listening to the radio voices calling across the Sea of Thirst. Every ten minutes Lawrence would speak to *Selene*, and each time the pause before the reply would be a little longer. But Harris and McKenzie were still clinging to consciousness, thanks to sheer will-power and, presumably, the musical encouragement they were getting from Clavius City.

"What's that psychologist disc-jockey pumping into them now?" asked Spenser. On the other side of the control cabin, the ship's radio officer turned up the volume—and the Valkyries rode above the Mountains of Inaccessibility.

"I don't believe," grumbled Captain Anson, "that they've played anything later than the nineteenth century."

"Oh, yes they have," corrected Jules Braque, as he made some infinitesimal adjustment to his camera. "They did Khatchaturian's *Sabre Dance* just now. That's only a hundred years old."

"Time for Duster One to call again," said the radio officer. The cabin became instantly silent.

Right on the second, the dust-ski signal came in. The expedition was now so close that *Auriga* could receive it directly, without benefit of the relay from Lagrange.

"Lawrence calling *Selene*. We'll be over you in ten minutes. Are you O.K.?"

Again that agonising pause; this time it lasted almost five seconds. Then——

"*Selene* answering. No change here."

That was all. Pat Harris was not wasting his remaining breath.

"Ten minutes," said Spenser. "They should be in sight now. Anything on the screen?"

"Not yet," answered Jules, zooming out to the horizon and panning slowly along its empty arc; there was nothing above it but the black night of space.

The Moon, thought Jules, certainly presented some headaches to the cameraman. Everything was soot or whitewash; there were no nice, soft half-tones. And, of course, there was that eternal dilemma of the stars, though that was an aesthetic problem, rather than a technical one.

The public expected to see stars in the lunar sky even during the daytime, because they were there. But the fact was that the human eye could not normally see them; during the day, the eye was so desensitised by the glare that the sky appeared an empty, absolute black. If you wanted to see the stars, you had to look for them through blinkers that cut off all other light; then your pupils would slowly expand, and one by one the stars would come out until they filled the field of view. But as soon as you looked at anything else—*phut*, out they went. The human eye could look at the daylight stars, or the daylight landscape; it could never see both at once.

But the TV camera could, if desired, and some directors preferred it to do so. Others argued that this falsified reality; it was one of those problems that had no correct answer. Jules sided with the realists, and kept the Star Gate circuit switched off unless the studio asked for it.

At any moment, he would have some action for Earth. Already the news networks had taken flashes—general views of the mountains, slow pans across the Sea, close-ups of that lonely marker sticking through the dust. But before long, and perhaps for hours on end, his camera might well be the eyes of several billion people. This feature was either going to be a bust—or the biggest story of the year.

He fingered the talisman in his pocket. Jules Braque, Member of the Society of Motion Picture and Television Engineers, would have been very displeased had anyone accused him of carrying a lucky charm. On the other hand, he would have been very hard put to explain why he never brought out his little toy until the story he was covering was safely on the air.

"Here they are!" yelled Spenser, his voice revealing the strain under which he had been labouring. He lowered his binoculars and glanced at the camera. "You're too far off to the right!"

Jules was already panning. On the monitor screen, the geometrical smoothness of the far horizon had been broken at last; two tiny, twinkling stars had appeared on that perfect arc dividing Sea and space. The dust-skis were coming up over the face of the Moon.

Even with the longest focus of the zoom lens, they looked small and distant. That was the way Jules wanted it; he was anxious to give the impression of loneliness, emptiness. He shot a quick glance at the ship's main screen, now tuned to the Interplanet Channel. Yes, they were carrying him.

He reached into his pocket, pulled out a small diary, and laid it on top of the camera. He lifted the cover, which locked into position just short of the vertical—and immediately became alive with colour and movement. At the same time a faint gnat-sized voice started to tell him that this was a special programme of the Interplanet News Service, Channel One Oh Seven—and We Will Now Be Taking You Over To The Moon.

On the tiny screen was the picture he was seeing directly on his monitor. No—not *quite* the same picture. This was the one he had captured two and a half seconds ago; he was looking that far into the past. In those two and a half million microseconds—to change to the time-scale of the electronic engineer—this scene had undergone many adventures and transformations. From his camera it had been piped to *Auriga*'s transmitter, and beamed straight up to Lagrange, fifty thousand kilometres overhead. There it had been snatched out of space, boosted a few hundred times, and sped Earthwards to be caught by one or other of the satellite relays. Then down through the ionosphere—that last hundred kilometres the hardest of all—to the Interplanet Building, where its adventures really began, as it joined the ceaseless flood of sounds and sights and electrical impulses which informed and amused a substantial fraction of the human race.

And here it was again, after passing through the hands of programme directors and special effects departments and engineering assistants—right back where it started, broadcast over the whole of Earthside from the high-power transmitter in Lagrange II, and over the whole of Farside from Lagrange I. To span the single hand's breadth from Jules' TV camera to his pocket-diary receiver, that image had travelled three quarters of a million kilometres.

He wondered if it was worth the trouble. Men had been wondering that ever since television was invented.

L AWRENCE SPOTTED *Auriga* while he was still fifteen kilometres away; he could scarcely have failed to do so, for she was a conspicuous object, as the sunlight glistened from her plastic and metal.

"What the devil's that?" he asked himself, and answered the question at once. It was obviously a ship, and he remembered hearing vague rumours that some news-network had chartered a flight to the mountains. That was not his business, though at one time he himself had looked into the question of landing equipment there, to cut out this tedious haul across the Sea. Unfortunately, the plan wouldn't work. There was no safe landing-point within five hundred metres of "sea"-level; the ledge that had been so convenient for Spenser was at too great an altitude to be of use.

The Chief Engineer was not sure that he liked the idea of having his every move watched by long-focus lenses up in the hills—not that there was anything he could do about it. He had already vetoed an attempt to put a camera on his ski—to the enormous relief, though Lawrence did not know it, of Interplanet News, and the extreme frustration of the other services. Then he realised that it might well be useful having a ship only a few kilometres away. It would provide an additional information channel, and perhaps they could utilise its services in some other way. It might even provide hospitality until the igloos could be ferried out.

Where was the marker? Surely it should be in sight by now! For an uncomfortable moment Lawrence thought that it had fallen down and disappeared into the dust. That would not stop them finding *Selene*, of course, but it might delay them five or ten minutes at a time when every second was vital.

He breathed a sigh of relief; he had overlooked the thin shaft against the blazing background of the mountains. His pilot had already spotted their goal and had changed course slightly to head towards it.

The skis coasted to a halt on either side of the marker, and at once erupted into activity. Eight space-suited figures started unshipping roped bundles and large cylindrical drums at a great speed, according to the prearranged plan. Swiftly, the raft began to take shape as its slotted metal framework was bolted into position round the drums, and the light fibreglass flooring was laid across it.

No construction job in the whole history of the Moon had ever been carried out in such a blaze of publicity, thanks to the watchful eye in the mountains. But once they had started work, the eight men on the skis were totally unconscious of the millions looking over their shoulders. All that mattered to them now was getting that raft in position, and fixing the jigs which would guide the hollow, life-bearing drills down to their target.

Every five minutes, or less, Lawrence spoke to *Selene*, keeping Pat and McKenzie informed of progress. The fact that he was also informing the anxiously waiting world scarcely crossed his mind.

At last, in an incredible twenty minutes, the drill was ready, its first five-metre section poised like a harpoon ready to plunge into the Sea. But this harpoon was designed to bring life, not death.

"We're coming down," said Lawrence. "The first section's going in now."

"You'd better hurry," whispered Pat. "I can't hold out much longer."

He seemed to be moving in a fog; he could not remember a time when it was not there. Apart from the dull ache in his lungs, he was not really uncomfortable—merely incredibly, unbelievably tired. He was now no more than a robot, going about a task whose meaning he had long ago forgotten, if indeed he had ever known it. There was a wrench in his hand; he had taken it out of the tool kit hours ago, knowing that it would be needed. Perhaps it would remind him of what he had to do, when the time came.

From a great distance, it seemed, he heard a snatch of conversation that was obviously not intended for him; someone had forgotten to switch channels.

"We should have fixed it so that the drill could be unscrewed from this end. Suppose he's too weak to do it?"

"We had to take the risk; the extra fittings would have delayed us at least an hour. Give me that——"

Then the circuit went dead; but Pat had heard enough to make him angry—or as angry as a man could be, in his half-stupefied condition. He'd show them—he and his good pal Doctor Mac——. Mac what? He could no longer remember the name.

He turned slowly round in his swivelling seat and looked back along the Golgotha-like shambles of the cabin. For a moment he could not find the physicist among the other tumbled bodies; then he saw that he was kneeling beside Mrs. Williams, whose dates of birth and death now looked like being very close together. McKenzie was holding the oxygen mask over her face, quite unaware of the fact that the tell-tale hiss of gas from the cylinder had ceased, and the gauge had long ago reached zero.

"We're almost there," said the radio. "You should hear us hit at any minute."

So soon? thought Pat. But, of course, a heavy tube would slice down through the dust almost as quickly as it could be lowered. He thought it was very clever of him to deduce this.

Bang! Something had hit the roof. But where?

"I can hear you," he whispered. "You've reached us."

"We know," answered the voice. "We can feel the contact. But you have to do the rest. Can you tell where the drill's touching? Is it in a clear section of the roof, or is it over the wiring? We'll raise and lower it several times, to help you locate it."

Pat felt rather aggrieved at this; it seemed terribly unfair that he should have to decide such a complicated matter.

Knock, knock went the drill against the roof. He couldn't for the life of him (why did that phrase seem so appropriate?) locate the exact position of the sound. Well, they had nothing to lose. . . .

"Go ahead," he murmured. "You're in the clear." He had to repeat it twice before they understood his words.

Instantly—they were quick off the pad up there—the drill started whirring against the outer hull. He could hear the sound very distinctly, more beautiful than any music.

The bit was through the first obstacle in less than a minute. He heard it race, then stop as the motor was cut. Then the operator lowered it the few centimetres to the inner hull, and started it spinning again.

The sound was much louder now, and could be pin-pointed exactly. It came, Pat was mildly disconcerted to note, from very close to the main cable conduit, along the centre of the roof. If it went through *that* . . .

Slowly and unsteadily he got to his feet and walked over to the source of the sound. He had just reached it when there was a shower of dust from the ceiling, a sudden spitting of electricity—and the main lights went out.

Luckily, the emergency lighting remained on. It took Pat's eyes several seconds to adapt to the dim red glow; then he saw that a metal tube was protruding through the roof. It moved slowly downwards until it had travelled half a metre into the cabin; and there it stopped.

The radio was talking in the background, saying something that he knew was very important. He tried to make sense of it as he fitted the wrench around the bit-head, and tightened the screw-adjustment.

"*Don't* undo the bit until we tell you," said that remote voice. "We had no time to fit a non-return valve—the pipe's open to vacuum at this end. We'll tell you as soon as we're ready. I repeat—*don't remove the bit until we say so.*"

Pat wished the man would stop bothering him; he knew exactly what to do. If he leaned with all his might on the handle of the wrench—so—the drill-head would come off and he'd be able to breathe again.

Why wasn't it moving? He tried once more.

"My God," said the radio. "Stop that! We're not ready! You'll lose all your air!"

Just a minute, thought Pat, ignoring the distraction. There's something wrong here. A screw can turn *this* way—or *that* way. Suppose I'm tightening it up, when I should be doing the opposite?

This was horribly complicated. He looked at his right hand, then his left; neither seemed to help. (Nor did that silly man shouting on the radio.) Well, he could try the other way and see if that was better.

With great dignity, he performed a complete circuit of the tube, keeping one arm wrapped around it. As he fell on the wrench from the other side, he grabbed it with both hands to keep himself from collapsing. For a moment he rested against it, head bowed.

"Up periscope," he mumbled. Now what on Earth did that mean? He had no idea, but he had heard it somewhere and it seemed appropriate.

He was still puzzling over the matter when the drill-head started to unscrew beneath his weight, very easily and smoothly.

Fifteen metres above, Chief Engineer Lawrence and his assistants stood for a moment almost paralysed with horror. This was something that no one could ever have imagined; they had thought of a hundred other accidents, but not *this.*

"Coleman—Matsui!" snapped Lawrence. "Connect up that oxygen line, for God's sake!"

Even as he shouted at them, he knew that it would be too late. There were two connections still to be made, before the oxygen circuit was closed. And, of course, they were screw-threads, not quick-release couplings. Just one of those little points that normally wouldn't matter in a thousand years, but now made all the difference between life and death.

Like Samson at the mill, Pat trudged round and round the pipe, pushing the handle of the wrench before him. It offered no opposition, even in his present feeble state; by now the bit had unscrewed more than two centimetres —surely it would fall off in a few more seconds. . . .

Ah—almost there. He could hear a faint hissing, that grew steadily as the bit unwound. That would be oxygen rushing into the cabin, of course. In a few seconds, he would be able to breathe again, and all his troubles would be over.

The hiss had deepened to an ominous whistling, and for the first time Pat began to wonder if he was doing precisely the right thing. He stopped, looked thoughtfully at the wrench, and scratched his head. His slow mental processes could find no fault with his actions; if the radio had given him orders then, he might have obeyed, but it had abandoned the attempt.

Well, back to work (it was years since he'd had a hangover like this). He started to push on the wrench once more—and fell flat on his face as the drill came loose.

In the same instant, the cabin reverberated with a screaming roar, and a gale started all the loose papers fluttering like autumn leaves. A mist of condensation formed as the air, chilled by its sudden expansion, dumped its moisture in a thick fog. When Pat turned over on his back, conscious at last of what had happened, he was almost blinded by the mist around him.

That screen meant only one thing to a trained spaceman, and his automatic reactions had taken over now. He must find some flat object that could be slid over the hole—anything would do, if it was fairly strong.

He looked wildly around him in the crimson fog, which was already thining as it was sucked into space. The noise was deafening; it seemed incredible that so small a pipe could make such a scream.

Staggering over his unconscious companions, clawing his way from seat to seat, he had almost abandoned hope when he saw the answer to his prayer. There lay a thick volume, open face downwards on the floor where it had been dropped. Not the right way to treat books, he thought, but he was glad that someone had been careless. He might never have seen it otherwise.

When he reached the shrieking orifice that was sucking the life out of the cruiser, the book was literally torn from his hands and flattened against the end of the pipe. The sound died instantly, as did the gale. For a moment Pat stood swaying like a drunken man; then he quietly folded at the knees and pitched on to the floor.

CHAPTER XXII

T HE REALLY UNFORGETTABLE moments of TV are those which no one expects, and for which neither cameras nor commentators are prepared. For the last thirty minutes, the raft had been the site of feverish but controlled activity—then, without warning, it had erupted.

Impossible though that was, it seemed as if a geyser had spouted from the Sea of Thirst. Automatically, Jules tracked that ascending column of mist as it drove towards the stars (they were visible now; the director had asked for them). As it rose, it expanded like some strange, attenuated plant—or like a thinner, feebler version of the mushroom cloud that had terrorised two generations of mankind.

It lasted only for a few seconds, but in that time it held unknown millions frozen in front of their screens, wondering how a waterspout could possibly have reared itself from this arid sea. Then it collapsed and died, still in the same uncanny silence in which it had been born.

To the men on the raft that geyser of moisture-laden air was equally silent but they felt its vibration as they struggled to get the last coupling into place. They would have managed, sooner or later, even if Pat had not cut off the flow, for the forces involved were quite trivial. But there "later" might have been too late. Perhaps, indeed, it already was. . . .

"Calling *Selene*! Calling *Selene*!" shouted Lawrence. "Can you hear me?"

There was no reply; the cruiser's transmitter was not operating; he could not even hear the sounds her mike should be picking up inside the cabin.

"Connections ready, sir," said Coleman. "Shall I turn on the oxygen generator?"

It won't do any good, thought Lawrence, if Harris has managed to screw that damned bit back into place. I can only hope he's merely stuffed something into the end of the tube, and that we can blow it out. . . .

"O.K.," he said. "Let her go—all the pressure you can get."

With a sudden bang, the battered copy of *The Orange and the Apple* was blasted away from the pipe to which it had been vacuum-clamped. Out of the open orifice gushed an inverted fountain of gas, so cold that its outline was visible in ghostly swirls of condensing water vapour.

For several minutes the oxygen geyser roared without producing any effect. Then Pat Harris slowly stirred, tried to get up, and was knocked back to the ground by the concentrated jet. It was not a particularly powerful jet, but it was stronger than he was in his present state.

He lay with the icy blast playing across his face, enjoying its refreshing coolness almost as much as its breathability. In a few seconds he was completely alert—though he had a splitting headache—and aware of all that had happened in the last half-hour.

He nearly fainted again when he remembered unscrewing the bit, and fighting that gusher of escaping air. But this was no time to worry about past mistakes; all that mattered now was that he was alive—and with any luck would stay so.

He picked up the still unconscious McKenzie like a limp doll, and laid him beneath the oxygen blast. Its force was much weaker now, as the pressure inside the cruiser rose back to normal; in a few more minutes it would be only a gentle zephyr.

The scientist revived almost at once, and looked vaguely round him.

"Where am I?" he said, not very originally. "Oh—they got through to us. Thank God I can breathe again. What's happened to the lights?"

"Don't worry about that—I'll soon fix them. We must get everyone under this jet as quickly as we can, and flush some oxygen into their lungs. Can you give artificial respiration?"

"I've never tried."

"It's very simple—wait until I find the medicine chest."

When Pat had collected the resuscitator, he demonstrated on the nearest subject, who happened to be Irving Schuster.

"Push the tongue out of the way and slip the tube down the throat. Now squeeze this bulb—slowly. Keep up a natural breathing rhythm. Got the idea?"

"Yes, but how long shall I do it?"

"Five or six deep breaths should be enough, I'd guess; we're not trying to revive them, after all—we just want to get the stale air out of their lungs. You take the front half of the cabin—I'll do the rear."

"But there's only one resuscitator."

Pat grinned, without much humour.

"It's not necessary," he answered, bending over his next patient.

"Oh," said McKenzie. "I'd forgotten *that*."

It was hardly chance that Pat had headed straight to Sue, and was now blowing into her lips in the ancient—and highly effective—mouth-to-mouth method. But to do him justice, he wasted no time on her when he found that she was breathing normally.

He was just starting on his third subject when the radio gave another despairing call.

"Hello, *Selene*—is there anyone there?"

Pat took a few seconds off to grab the mike.

"Harris calling—we're O.K. We're applying artificial respiration to the passengers. No time to say more—we'll call you later. I'll remain on receive. Tell us what's happening."

"Thank God you're O.K.—we'd given you up. You gave us a hell of a fright when you unscrewed that drill."

Listening to the Chief Engineer's voice while he blew into the peacefully sleeping Mr. Radley, Pat had no wish to be reminded of that incident. He knew that, whatever happened, he would never live it down. Yet it had probably been for the best; most of the bad air had been syphoned out of *Selene* in that hectic minute or so of decompression. It might even have lasted longer than that, for it would have taken two or three minutes for a cabin of this size to lose much of its air, through a tube only four centimetres in diameter.

"Now listen," continued Lawrence, "because you've been overheating badly, we're letting you have your oxygen just as cold as we think it's safe. Call us back if it gets too chilly, or too dry.

"In five or ten minutes we'll be sinking the second pipe to you, so that we'll have a complete circuit and can take over your entire air-conditioning load. We'll aim this pipe for the rear of the cabin, just as soon as we've towed the raft a few metres.

"We're moving now. Call you back in a minute."

Pat and the doctor did not relax until they had pumped the foul air from the lungs of all their unconscious companions. Then, very tired, yet feeling the calm joy of men who see some great ordeal approach its triumphant end, they slumped to the floor and waited for the second drill to come through the roof.

Ten minutes later, they heard it bang against the outer hull, just forward of the airlock. When Lawrence called to check its position, Pat confirmed that this time it was clear of obstructions. "And don't worry," he added. "I won't touch that drill until you tell me."

It was now so cold that he and McKenzie had put on their outer clothing once more, and had draped blankets over the sleeping passengers. But Pat did not call a halt; as long as they were not in actual distress, the colder the better. They were driving back the deadly heat that had almost cooked them—and, even more important, their own air-purifiers would probably start working again, now that the temperature had dropped so drastically.

When that second pipe came through the roof, they would be doubly safeguarded. The men on the raft could keep them supplied with air indefinitely, and they would also have several hours—perhaps a day's—reserve of their own. They might still have a long wait here beneath the dust, but the suspense was over.

Unless, of course, the Moon arranged some fresh surprises.

"Well, Mr. Spenser," said Captain Anson, "looks as if you've got your story."

Spenser felt almost as exhausted, after the strain of the last hours, as any of the men out on the raft, two kilometres below him. He could see them there on the monitor, on medium close-up. They were obviously relaxing—as well as men could relax, when they were wearing space-suits.

Five of them, indeed, appeared to be trying to get some sleep, and were tackling the problem in a startling but sensible manner. They were lying beside the raft, half-submerged in the dust, rather like floating rubber dolls. It had not occurred to Spenser that a space-suit was much too buoyant to sink in this stuff. By getting off the raft, the five technicians were not only providing themselves with an incomparably luxurious couch; they were leaving a greatly enlarged working space for their companions.

The three remaining members of the team were moving slowly around, adjusting and checking equipment—especially the rectangular bulk of the air-purifier and the big lox spheres coupled to it. At maximum optical and electronic zoom, the camera could get within ten metres of all this gear—almost close enough to read the gauges. Even at medium magnification, it was easy to spot the two pipes going over the side and leading down to the invisible *Selene*.

This relaxed and peaceful scene made a startling contrast with that of an hour ago. But there was nothing more to be done here, until the next batch of equipment arrived. Both of the skis had gone back to Port Roris; that was where all the activity would now be taking place, as the engineering staff tested and assembled the gear which, they hoped, would enable them to reach *Selene*. It would be another day at least before that was ready. Meanwhile—barring accidents—the Sea of Thirst would continue to bask undisturbed in the morning sun, and the camera would have no new scenes to throw across space.

From one and a half light seconds away, the voice of the programme director back on Earth spoke inside *Auriga*'s control cabin.

"Nice work, Maurice, Jules. We'll keep taping the picture in case anything breaks at your end, but we don't expect to carry it live until the 06.00 News-spot."

"How's it holding up?"

"Supernova rating. And there's a new angle—every crackpot inventor who ever tried to patent a new paperclip is crawling out of the woodwork with ideas. We're rounding up a batch of them at 06.15; it should be good fun."

"Who knows—perhaps one of them may have something."

"Maybe, but I doubt it. The sensible ones won't come near our programme, when they see the treatment the others are getting."

"Why—what are you doing to them?"

"Their ideas are being analysed by your scientist friend Dr. Lawson. We've had a dummy run with him; he skins them alive."

"Not *my* friend," protested Spenser. "I've only met him twice. The first time I got ten words out of him; the second time, he fell asleep on me."

"Well, he's developed since then, believe it or not. You'll see him in—oh, forty-five minutes."

"I can wait. Anyway, I'm only interested in what Lawrence plans to do. Has he made a statement? You should be able to get at him, now the pressure's off."

"He's still furiously busy and won't talk. We don't think the Engineering Department has made up its mind yet, anyhow; they're testing all sorts of gadgets at Port Roris, and ferrying in equipment from all over the Moon. We'll keep you in touch if we learn anything new."

It was a paradoxical fact, which Spenser took completely for granted, that when you were covering a story like this you often had no idea of the big picture. Even when you were in the centre of things, as he was now. He had started the ball rolling, but now he was no longer in control. It was true that he and Jules were providing the most important video coverage—or would be, when the action shifted back here—but the pattern was being shaped at the news centres on Earth and in Clavius City. He almost wished he could leave Jules and hurry back to headquarters.

That was impossible, of course, and even if he did so, he would soon regret it. For this was not only the biggest scoop of his career; it was, he suspected, the last time he would ever be able to cover a story out in the field. By his own success, he would have doomed himself irrevocably to an office chair—or, at best, a comfortable little viewing booth behind the banked monitor screens at Clavius Central.

CHAPTER XXIII

I T W A S S T I L L very quiet aboard *Selene*, but the quietness was now that of sleep, not of death. Before long, all these people would be waking, to greet a day few of them could really have expected to see.

Pat Harris was standing somewhat precariously on the back of a seat, mending the break in the overhead lighting circuit. It was fortunate that the drill had not been five millimetres to the left; then it would have taken out the radio as well, and the job would have been very much worse.

"Throw in Number Three circuit-breaker, Doc," he called, winding up his insulating tape. "We should be in business now."

The main lights came on, blindingly brilliant after the crimson gloom. At the same time, there was a sudden, explosive sound, so unexpected and alarming that it shocked Pat off his unstable perch.

Before he reached the floor, he identified it. It was a sneeze.

The passengers were starting to waken—and he had, perhaps, slightly overdone the refrigeration, for the cabin was now extremely cold.

He wondered who would be the first to return to consciousness. Sue, he hoped, because then they would be able to talk together without interruption, at least for a little while. After what they had been through together, he did not regard Dave McKenzie's presence as any interference—though perhaps Sue could hardly be expected to see it that way.

Beneath the covering of blankets, the first figure was stirring. Pat hurried forward to give assistance; then he paused, and said under his breath: "Oh, *no*!"

Well, you couldn't win all the time, and a captain had to do his duty, come what may. He bent over the scrawny figure that was struggling to rise, and said solicitously: "How do you feel, Miss Morley?"

To have become a TV property was at once the best and the worst thing that could have happened to Dr. Lawson. It had built up his self-confidence, by convincing him that the world which he had always affected to despise was really interested in his special knowledge and abilities. (He did not realise how quickly he might be dropped again, as soon as the *Selene* incident was finished.) It had given him an outlet for expressing his genuine devotion to astronomy, somewhat stultified by living too long in the exclusive society of astronomers. And it was also earning him satisfactory quantities of money.

But the programme in which he was now involved might almost have been designed to confirm his old view that the men who weren't brutes were mostly fools. This, however, was hardly the fault of Interplanet News, which could not resist a feature that was a perfect fill-in for the long periods when nothing would be happening out at the raft.

The fact that Lawson was on the Moon and his victims were on Earth presented only a minor technical problem, which the TV technicians had solved long ago. The programme could not go out live; it had to be taped beforehand, and those annoying two-and-a-half second pauses while the radio waves flashed from planet to satellite and back again had to be sliced out. They would upset the performers—nothing could be done about *that*—but by the time a skilled editor had anachronised the tape, the listener would be unable to tell that he was hearing a discussion that spanned almost four hundred thousand kilometres.

Chief Engineer Lawrence heard the programme as he lay flat on his back in the Sea of Thirst, staring up into the empty sky. It was the first chance of resting he had had for more hours than he could remember, but his mind was too active to let him sleep. In any event, he had never acquired the knack of sleeping in a suit, and saw no need to learn it now, for the first of the igloos was already on the way from Port Roris. When that arrived, he would be able to live in well-earned, and much-needed, comfort.

Despite all the claims of the manufacturers, no one can function efficiently in a space-suit for more than twenty-four hours—for several obvious reasons, and several that are not so obvious. There is, for example, that baffling complaint known as spaceman's itch, affecting the small of the back—or even less accessible spots—after a day's incarceration in a suit. The doctors claim that it is purely psychological, and several heroic spacemedicos have worn suits for a week or more to prove it. The demonstration had done nothing to affect the incidence of the disease.

The mythology of space-suits is a vast, complex and frequently ribald subject, with a nomenclature all of its own. No one is quite sure why one famous model of the 1970s was known as the Iron Maiden, but any astronaut will gladly explain why the 2010's Mark XIV was called the Chamber of Horrors. There seems little truth, however, in the theory that it was designed by a sadistic female engineer, determined to inflict a diabolical revenge upon the opposite sex.

But Lawrence was reasonably at ease in his model, as he listened to these enthusiastic amateurs put forward their ideas. It was just possible—though very unlikely—that one of these uninhibited thinkers might come up with an idea that could be of practical use. He had seen it happen before, and was prepared to listen to suggestions rather more patiently than Dr. Lawson— who, it was obvious, would never learn to suffer fools gladly.

He had just demolished an amateur engineer from Sicily, who wanted to blow the dust away by means of strategically-placed air-jets. The scheme was typical of those put forward; even where there was no fundamental scientific flaw, most of these ideas fell to pieces when examined quantitatively. You *could* blow the dust away—if you had an unlimited supply of air. While the voluble flow of Italian-English was proceeding, Lawson had been doing some rapid calculations. "I estimate, Signor Gusalli," he said, "that you would need at least five tons of air a minute to keep open a hole large enough to be useful. It would be quite impossible to ship such quantities out to the site."

"Ah, but you could collect the air and use it over and over again!"

"Thank *you*, Signor Gusalli," cut in the firm voice of the master of ceremonies. "Now we have Mr. Robertson from London, Ontario. What's your plan, Mr. Robertson?"

"I suggest freezing."

"Just a minute," protested Lawson. "How can you freeze dust?"

"First I'd saturate it with water. Next I'd sink cooling pipes and turn the whole mass into ice. That would hold the dust in place, and then it would be easy to drill through it."

"It's an interesting idea," admitted Tom, rather reluctantly. "At least it's not as crazy as some that we've had. But the amount of water needed would be impossibly large. Remember, the cruiser is fifteen metres down——"

"What's that in feet?" said the Canadian, in a tone of voice that made it clear that he was one of the hardcore anti-metric school.

"Fifty feet—as I'm sure you know perfectly well. Now you'd have to deal with a column at least a metre across—a yard, to you—so that would involve—ah—approximately fifteen times ten squared times ten to the fourth cubic centimetres which gives—why, of course, fifteen tons of water. But this assumes no wastage at all; you'd really need several times as much as this. It might come to as much as a hundred tons. And how much do you think all the freezing gear would weigh?"

Lawrence was quite impressed. Unlike many scientists he had known, Tom had a firm grasp of practical realities, and was also a rapid calculator. Usually when an astronomer or a physicist did a quick computation, his first attempt was out by a factor of anything from ten to a hundred. As far as Lawrence could judge, Tom was always right the first time.

The Canadian refrigeration enthusiast was still putting up a fight when he was dragged off the programme, to be replaced by an African gentleman who wanted to use the opposite technique—heat. He planned to use a huge concave mirror focusing sunlight on the dust and fusing it into an immobile mass.

It was obvious that Tom was keeping his temper only with the utmost difficulty; the solar furnace advocate was one of those stubborn, self-taught "experts" who refused to admit that he could possibly make an error in his calculations. The argument was getting really violent when a voice from much closer at hand cut across the programme.

"The skis are coming, Mr. Lawrence."

Lawrence rolled into a sitting position and climbed aboard the raft. If anything was already in sight, that meant it was practically on top of him. Yes, there was Duster One—and also Duster Three, which had made a difficult and expensive trip from the Lake of Drought, the Sea's smaller equivalent on Farside. That journey was a saga in itself, that would remain for ever unknown except to the handful of men involved.

Each ski was towing two sledges, piled high with equipment. As they drew alongside the raft, the first item to be unloaded was the large packing-case containing the igloo. It was always fascinating to watch one being inflated, and Lawrence had never anticipated the spectacle more eagerly. (Yes, he definitely had spaceman's itch.) The process was completely automatic; one broke a seal, turned two separate levers—as a safeguard against the disastrous possibility of accidental triggering—and then waited.

Lawrence did not have to wait for long. The sides of the box fell flat, revealing a tightly-packed, convoluted mass of silvery fabric. It stirred and struggled like some living creature; Lawrence had once seen a moth emerging from the chrysalis, with its wings still crumpled, and the two processes bore an uncanny similarity. The insect, however, had taken an hour to reach its full size and splendour, but the igloo took three minutes.

As the air-generator pumped an atmosphere into the flaccid envelope, it expanded and stiffened in sudden jerks, followed by slow periods of consolidation. Now it was a metre high, and was spreading outwards rather than upwards. When it had reached the limits of its extension, it started to go upwards again, and the airlock popped away from the main dome. The whole operation, one felt, should be accompanied by laborious wheezings and puffings; it seemed quite wrong that it was happening in utter silence.

Now the structure had nearly reached its final dimensions, and it was obvious that "igloo" was the only possible name for it. Though they had been designed to provide protection against a very different—though almost equally hostile—environment, the snowhouses of the Eskimos had been of exactly the same shape. The technical problem had been similar; so was the solution.

It took considerably longer to install the fittings than to inflate the igloo, for all the equipment—bunks, chairs, tables, cupboards, electronic gear—had to be carried in through the airlock. Some of the larger items barely made it, having been designed with only centimetres to spare. But at last there was a radio call from inside the dome. "We're open for business!" it said. "Come on in!"

Lawrence wasted no time in accepting the invitation. He began to undo the fittings of his suit while he was still in the outer section of the two-stage airlock, and had the helmet off as soon as he could hear voices from inside the dome, reaching him through the thickening atmosphere.

It was wonderful to be a free man again—to be able to wriggle, scratch, move without encumbrance, talk to your fellows face to face. The coffin-sized shower removed the stink of the space-suit and made him feel fit for human society once more. Then he put on a pair of shorts—all that one ever wore in an igloo—and sat down to a conference with his assistants.

Most of the material he had ordered had come in this consignment; the rest would be arriving on Duster Two in the course of the next few hours. As he checked the supply lists, he felt himself much more the master of the situation. Oxygen was assured—barring catastrophe. Water had been getting short down there; well, he could supply that easily enough. Food was a little more difficult, though it was merely a matter of packing. Central Catering had already supplied samples of chocolate, compressed meat, cheese and even elongated French rolls—all packed into cylinders three centimetres wide. Presently he would shoot them down the air-pipes, and give morale in *Selene* a big boost.

But this was less important than the recommendations of his Brains Trust, embodied in a dozen blueprints and a terse six-page memorandum. Lawrence read it extremely carefully, nodding agreement from time to time. He had already come to the same general conclusions, and he could see no way of escaping from them.

Whatever happened to her passengers, *Selene* had made her last voyage.

CHAPTER XXIV

THE GALE THAT had swept through *Selene* seemed to have carried away with it more than the stagnant air. When he looked back on their first days beneath the dust, Commodore Hansteen realised that there had often been a hectic, even hysterical, mood aboard, after the initial shock had worn off. Trying to keep up their spirits, they had sometimes gone too far in the direction of false gaiety and childish humour.

Now that was all past, and it was easy to see why. The fact that a rescue team was at work only a few metres away was part of the explanation, but only part of it. The spirit of tranquillity that they now shared came from their encounter with death; after that, nothing could be quite the same again. The petty dross of selfishness and cowardice had been burned out of them.

No one knew this better than Hansteen; he had watched it happen many times before, whenever a ship's company faced peril in the far reaches of the Solar System. Though he was not philosophically inclined, he had had plenty of time to think in space. He had sometimes wondered if the real reason why men sought danger was that only thus could they find the companionship and solidarity which they unconsciously craved.

He would be sorry to say good-bye to all these people—yes, even to Miss Morley, who was now as agreeable and considerate as her temperament would allow. The fact that he could think that far ahead was the measure of his confidence; one could never be certain, of course, but the situation now seemed completely under control. No one knew exactly how Chief Engineer Lawrence intended to get them out, but that problem was now merely a choice between alternative methods. From now on, their imprisonment was an inconvenience, not a danger.

It was not even a hardship, since those food cylinders had started popping down the air-tubes. Though there had never been any risk of starvation, the diet had grown extremely monotonous, and water had been rationed for some time. Now several hundred litres had been pumped down, to refill the almost empty tanks.

It was strange that Commodore Hansteen, who usually thought of everything, never asked himself the simple question, "Whatever happened to all the water we started with?" Though he had more immediate problems on his mind, the sight of that extra mass being taken aboard should have set him worrying. But it never did, until it was much too late.

Pat Harris and Chief Engineer Lawrence were equally to blame for the oversight. It was the one flaw in a beautifully executed plan. And one flaw, of course, was all that was needed.

The Engineering Division of Earthside was still working swiftly, but no longer in a desperate race against the clock. There was time now to construct mock-ups of the cruiser, to sink them in the Sea off Port Roris, and to try various ways of entering them. Advice—sensible and otherwise—was still pouring in, but no one took any notice of it. The approach had been decided, and would not be modified now, unless it ran into unexpected obstacles.

Twenty-four hours after the igloo had been set up, all the special gear had been manufactured and shipped out to the site. It was a record that Lawrence hoped he would never have to break, and he was very proud of the men who had made it possible. The Engineering Division seldom got the credit it deserved: like the air, everyone took it for granted—forgetting that the engineers supplied that air.

Now that he was ready to go into action, Lawrence was quite willing to start talking—and Maurice Spenser was more than willing to accommodate him. This was the moment he had been waiting for.

As far as he could remember, it was also the first time that there had ever been a TV interview with camera and subject five kilometres apart. At this fantastic magnification, of course, the image was a little fuzzy, and the slightest vibration in *Auriga*'s cabin set it dancing on the screen. For this reason, everyone aboard the ship was motionless, and all non-essential machinery had been switched off.

Chief Engineer Lawrence was standing on the edge of the raft, his space-suited figure braced against the small crane that had been swung over the side. Hanging from the jib was a large concrete cylinder, open at both ends—the first section of the tube that was now being lowered into the dust.

"After a lot of thought," said Lawrence for the benefit of that distant camera—but above all, for the benefit of the men and women fifteen metres beneath him, "we've decided that this is the best way to tackle the problem. This cylinder is called a caisson"—he pronounced it "kasoon"—"and it will sink easily under its own weight; the sharp lower edge will cut through the dust like a knife through butter.

"We have enough sections to reach the cruiser; when we've made contact, and the tube is sealed at the bottom—its pressure against the roof will ensure that—we'll start scooping out the dust. As soon as that's done, we'll have an open shaft like a small well, right down to *Selene*.

"That will be half the battle, but only half. Then we'll have to connect the shaft to one of our pressurised igloos, so that when we cut through the cruiser's roof there's no loss of air. But I think—I hope—that these are fairly straight-forward problems."

He paused for a minute, wondering if he should touch on any of the other details that made this operation so much trickier than it looked. Then he decided not to; those who understood could see with their own eyes—and the others would not be interested, or would think he was boasting. This blaze of publicity (about half a billion people were watching, so the Tourist Commissioner had reported) did not worry him so long as things went well. But if they did not. . . .

He raised his arm and signalled to the crane-operator.

"Lower away!"

Slowly, the cylinder settled into the dust until its full four-metre length had vanished, except for a narrow ring just protruding above the surface. It had gone down smoothly and easily; Lawrence hoped that the remaining sections would be equally obliging.

One of the engineers was carefully going along the rim of the caisson with a spirit-level, to check that it was sinking vertically. Presently he gave the thumbs-up signal, which Lawrence acknowledged in the same manner. There had been a time when, like any regular spacehog, he could carry out an extended and fairly technical conversation by sign-language alone. This was an essential skill of the trade, for radio sometimes failed and there were occasions when one did not wish to clutter up the limited number of channels available.

"Ready for Number Two!" he said.

Now this would be tricky. The first section had to be held rigid, while the second was bolted to it without altering the alignment. One really needed two cranes for this job, but a framework of I-beams, supported a few centimetres above the surface of the dust, could carry the load when the crane was otherwise engaged.

No mistakes now, for God's sake! he breathed silently. Number Two Section swung off the sledge that had brought it from Port Roris, and three of the technicians man-handled it into the vertical. This was the sort of job where the distinction between weight and mass was vital. That swinging cylinder weighed relatively little—but its momentum was the same as it would be on Earth, and it could pulp a man if it managed to trap him on one of those sluggish oscillations. And that was something else peculiar to the Moon—the slow-motion movement of this suspended mass. In this gravity, a pendulum took two and a half times as long to complete its cycle as it would do on Earth. This was something that never looked quite right, except to a man who had been born here.

Now the second section was upended and mated to the first one. They were clamped together, and once again Lawrence gave the order to lower away.

The resistance of the dust was increasing, but the caisson continued to sink smoothly under its own weight.

"Eight metres gone," said Lawrence, "that means we're just past the half-way mark. Number Three Section coming up."

After this, there would only be one more—though Lawrence had provided a spare section, just in case. He had a hearty respect for the Sea's ability to swallow equipment. So far, only a few nuts and bolts had been lost, but if that piece of caisson slipped from the hook, it would be gone in a flash. Though it might not sink very far, especially if it hit the dust broadside-on, it would be effectively out of reach even if it was only a couple of metres down. They had no time to waste salvaging their own salvage gear.

There went Number Three, its last section moving with almost imperceptible slowness. But it was still moving; in a few minutes, with any luck at all, they would be knocking on the cruiser's roof.

"Twelve metres down," said Lawrence. "We're only three metres above you now, Selene. You should be able to hear us at any minute."

Indeed they could, and the sound was wonderfully reassuring. More than ten minutes ago Hansteen had noticed the vibration of the oxygen inlet pipe as the caisson scraped against it. You could tell when it stopped, and when it started moving again.

There was that vibration once more, accompanied this time by a delicate shower of dust from the roof. The two air-pipes had now been drawn up so that about twenty centimetres of their lengths projected through the ceiling, and the quick-drying cement which was part of the emergency kit of all space vehicles had been smoothed around their point of entry. It seemed to be working loose, but that impalpable rain of dust was far too slight to cause alarm. Nevertheless, Hansteen thought that he had better mention it to the skipper, who might not have noticed.

"Funny," said Pat, looking up at the projecting pipe. "That cement should hold, even if the pipe is vibrating."

He climbed up on a seat, and examined the air-pipe more closely. For a moment he said nothing; then he stepped down, looking puzzled and annoyed —and more than a little worried.

"What's the trouble?" Hansteen asked quietly. He knew Pat well enough now to read his face like an open book.

"That pipe's pulling through the roof," he said. "Someone up on the raft's being mighty careless—it's shortened by at least a centimetre since I fixed that plaster." Then Pat stopped, suddenly aghast. "My God," he whispered. "Suppose it's our own fault—*suppose we're still sinking.*"

"What if we are?" said the Commodore, quite calmly. "You'd expect the dust to continue settling beneath our weight—that doesn't mean we're in danger. Judging by that pipe, we've gone down one centimetre in twenty-four hours. They can always give us some more tubing if we need it."

Pat laughed, a little shamefacedly.

"Of course—that's the answer. I should have thought of it before. We've probably been sinking slowly all the time, but this is the first chance we've had of proving it. Still, I'd better report to Mr. Lawrence—it may affect his calculations."

Pat started to walk towards the front of the cabin; but he never made it.

CHAPTER XXV

IT HAD TAKEN Nature a million years to set the trap that had snared *Selene* and dragged her down into the Sea of Thirst. The second time, she was caught in a trap that she had made herself.

Because her designers had no need to watch every gram of excess weight, or plan for journeys lasting more than a few hours, they had never equipped *Selene* with those ingenious but unadvertised arrangements whereby space-ships recycle all their water supply. She did not have to conserve her resources in the miserly manner of deep-space vehicles; the small amount of water normally used and produced aboard, she simply dumped.

Over the past five days, several hundred kilos of liquid and vapour had left *Selene*, to be instantly absorbed by the thirsty dust. Many hours ago, the dust in the immediate neighbourhood of the waste vents had become saturated and had turned into mud. Dripping downward through scores of channels, it had honey-combed the surrounding Sea. Silently, patiently, the cruiser had been washing away her own foundations. The gentle nudge of the approaching caisson had done the rest.

Up on the raft, the first intimation of disaster was the flashing of the red warning-light on the air-purifier, synchronised with the howling of a radio-klaxon across all the space-suit wavebands. The howl ceased almost immediately, as the technician in charge punched the cut-off button, but the red light continued to flash.

A glance at the dials was enough to show Lawrence the trouble. The air-pipes—both of them—were no longer connected to *Selene*. The purifier was pumping oxygen into the Sea through one pipe and, worse still, sucking in dust through the other. Lawrence wondered how long it would take to clean out the filters, but wasted no further time upon that thought. He was too busy calling *Selene*.

There was no answer. He tried all the cruiser's frequencies, without receiving even a whisper of a carrier wave. The Sea of Thirst was as silent to radio as it was to sound.

"They're finished," he said; "it's all over. It was a near thing, but we just couldn't make it. And all we needed was another hour. . . ."

What could have happened? He thought dully. Perhaps the hull had col-lapsed under the weight of the dust. No—that was very unlikely; the internal air-pressure would have prevented that. It must have been another subsidence; he was not sure, but he thought that there had been a slight tremor underfoot. From the beginning he had been aware of this danger, but could see no way of guarding against it. This was a gamble they had all taken, and *Selene* had lost.

Even as *Selene* started to fall, something told Pat that this was quite dif-ferent from the first cave-in. It was much slower, and there were scrunching, squishing noises from outside the hull which, even in that desperate moment, struck Pat as being unlike any sounds that dust could possibly make.

Overhead, the oxygen pipes were tearing loose. They were not sliding out smoothly, for the cruiser was going down stern first, tilting towards the rear. With a crack of splintering fibreglass, the pipe just ahead of the airlock-galley ripped through the roof and vanished from sight. Immediately, a thick jet of dust sprayed into the cabin, and fanned out in a choking cloud where it hit the floor.

Commodore Hansteen was nearest, and got there first. Tearing off his shirt, he swiftly wadded it into a ball and rammed it into the aperture. The dust spurted in all directions as he struggled to block the flow; he had almost suc-ceeded when the forward pipe ripped loose—and the main lights went out as, for the second time, the cable conduit was wrenched away.

"I'll take it!" shouted Pat. A moment later, also shirtless, he was trying to stem the torrent pouring in through the hole.

He had sailed the Sea of Thirst a hundred times—yet never before had he touched its substance with his naked skin. The grey powder sprayed into his nose and eyes, half choking and wholly blinding him. Though it was as bone-dry as the dust from a Pharaoh's tomb—dryer than this, indeed, for it was a million times older than the Pyramids—it had a curiously soapy feeling. As he fought against it, Pat found himself thinking: "If there is one death worse than being drowned—it's being buried alive."

When the jet weakened to a thin trickle, he knew that he had avoided that fate—for the moment. The pressure produced by fifteen metres of dust, under the low lunar gravity, was not difficult to overcome—though it would have been another story if the holes in the roof had been much larger.

Pat shook the dust from his head and shoulders, and cautiously opened his eyes. At least he could see again; thank heaven for the emergency lighting, dim though it was. The Commodore had already plugged his leak, and was now calmly sprinkling water from a paper cup to lay the dust. The technique was remarkably effective, and the few remaining clouds quickly collapsed into patches of mud.

Hansteen looked up and caught Pat's eye.

"Well, Captain," he said. "Any theories?"

There were times, thought Pat, when the Commodore's Olympian self-control was almost maddening. He would like to see him break, just once. No —that was not really true. His feeling was merely a flash of envy, even of jealousy—understandable, but quite unworthy of him. He should be ashamed of it, and he was.

"I don't know *what's* happened," he said. "Perhaps the people on top can tell us."

It was an uphill walk to the pilot's position, for the cruiser was now tilted at about thirty degrees to the horizontal. As Pat took his seat in front of the radio, he felt a kind of despairing numbness that surpassed anything he had known since their original entombment. It was a sense of resignation—an almost superstitious belief that the Gods were fighting against them, and that further struggle was useless.

He felt sure of this when he switched on the radio and found that it was completely dead. The power was off; when that oxygen pipe had ripped out the roof cable-conduit, it had done a thorough job.

Pat swivelled slowly round in his seat. Twenty-one men and women were looking at him, awaiting his news. But twenty of them he did not see, for Susan was watching him, and he was conscious only of the expression on her face. It held anxiety and readiness—but even now, no hint of fear. As Pat looked at her, his own feelings of despair seemed to dissolve away. He felt a surge of strength, even of hope.

"I'm damned if I know what's happened," he said. "But I'm sure of this— we're not done for yet, by several lightyears. We may have sunk a little further, but our friends on the raft will soon catch up with us. This will mean a slight delay—that's all. There's certainly nothing to worry about."

"I don't want to be an alarmist, Captain," said Barrett, "but suppose the raft has sunk as well? What then?"

"We'll know as soon as I get the radio fixed," replied Pat, glancing anxiously at the wires dangling from the roof cable-duct. "And until I get this spaghetti sorted out, you'll have to put up with the emergency lighting."

"I don't mind," said Mrs. Schuster. "I think it's rather cute."

Bless you, Mrs. S., said Pat to himself. He glanced quickly round the cabin; though it was hard to see all their expressions in this dim lighting, the passengers seemed calm enough.

They were not quite so calm a minute later; that was all the time it took to discover that nothing could be done to repair the lights or radio. The wiring had been ripped out far down inside the conduit, beyond reach of the simple tools available here.

"This is rather more serious," reported Pat. "We won't be able to communicate, unless they lower a microphone to make contact with us."

"That means," said Barrett, who seemed to like looking on the dark side of things, "that they've lost touch with us. They won't understand why we're not answering. Suppose they assume that we're all dead—and abandon the whole operation?"

The thought had flashed through Pat's mind, but he had dismissed it almost at once.

"You've heard Chief Engineer Lawrence on the radio," he answered. "He's not the sort of man who'd give up until he had absolute proof that we're no longer alive. You needn't worry on *that* score."

"What about our air?" asked Professor Jayawardene anxiously. "We're back on our own resources again."

"It should last for several hours now the absorbers have been regenerated. Those pipes will be in place before then," answered Pat, with slightly more confidence than he felt. "Meanwhile, we'll have to be patient and provide our own entertainment again. We did it for three days; we should be able to manage for a couple of hours."

He glanced around the cabin, looking for any signs of disagreement, and saw that one of the passengers was rising slowly to his feet. It was the very last person he would have expected—quiet little Mr. Radley, who had uttered perhaps a dozen words during the entire trip.

Pat still knew no more about him than that he was an accountant, and came from New Zealand—the only country on Earth still slightly isolated from the rest of the world by virtue of its position. It could be reached, of course, as quickly as any other spot on the planet, but it was the end of the line, not a way-station to somewhere else. As a result, the New Zealanders still proudly preserved much of their individuality. They claimed with a good deal of truth, to have salvaged all that was left of English culture, now that the British Isles had been absorbed into the Atlantic Community.

"You want to say something, Mr. Radley?" asked Pat.

Radley looked round the dim-lit cabin, rather like a schoolmaster about to address a class.

"Yes, Captain," he began. "I have a confession to make. I am very much afraid this is all my fault."

When Chief Engineer Lawrence broke off his commentary, Earth knew within two seconds that something had gone wrong—though it took several minutes for the news to reach Mars and Venus. But what had happened, no one could guess from the picture on the screen. For a few seconds there had been a flurry of frantic but meaningless activity, but now the immediate crisis seemed to be over. The space-suited figures were huddled together, obviously in conference—and with their telephone circuits plugged in, so that no one could overhear them. It was very frustrating to watch that silent discussion, and to have no idea of what it was about.

During those long minutes of agonising suspense, while the studio was trying to discover what was happening, Jules did his best to keep the picture alive. It was an extremely difficult job, handling such a static scene from a single camera position. Like all cameramen, Jules hated to be pinned down in one spot. This site was perfect—but it was fixed, and he was getting rather tired of it. He had even asked if the ship could be moved, but as Captain Anson put it, "I'm damned if I'll go hopping back and forth over the mountains. This is a space-ship, not a—chamois."

So Jules had to ring the changes on pans and zooms, though he used the latter with discretion, because nothing upset viewers more quickly than being hurled back and forth through space, or watching scenery explode in their faces. If he used the power-zoom flat out, Jules could sweep across the Moon at about fifty thousand kilometres an hour—and several million viewers would get motion sickness.

At last that urgent, soundless conference was breaking up; the men on the raft were unplugging their telephones. Now, perhaps, Lawrence would answer the radio calls that had been bombarding him for the last five minutes. . . .

"My God," said Spenser. "I don't believe it! Do you see what they're doing?"

"Yes," said Captain Anson, "and I don't believe it either. But it looks as if they're abandoning the site."

Like lifeboats leaving a sinking ship, the two dust-skis, crowded with men, were pulling away from the raft.

CHAPTER XXVI

P ERHAPS IT WAS well that *Selene* was now out of radio contact; it would hardly have helped morale if her occupants had known that the skis, heavily overloaded with passengers, were heading away from the site. But at the moment no one in the cruiser was thinking of the rescue effort; Radley was holding the centre of the dimly-lit stage.

"What do you mean—this is all *your* fault?" asked Pat in the baffled silence that followed the New Zealander's statement. Only baffled as yet; not hostile, because no one could take such a remark seriously.

"It's a long story, Captain," said Radley, speaking in a voice which, though it was oddly unemotional, had undertones that Pat could not identify. It was almost like listening to a robot, and gave Pat an unpleasant feeling somewhere in the middle of his spine. "I don't mean to say that I *deliberately* caused this to happen. But I'm afraid it is deliberate, and I'm sorry to have involved you all. You see—*they* are after me."

This is all we need, thought Pat. We really seem to have the odds stacked against us. In this small company we've got a neurotic spinster, a drug addict —and now a maniac. What other freaks are going to reveal themselves, before we're finished?

Then he realised the unfairness of his judgment. The truth was that he had been very lucky. Against Radley, Miss Morley, and Hans Baldur (who had given no trouble after that single, never-mentioned incident) he had the Commodore, Dr. McKenzie, the Schusters, little Professor Jayawardene, David Barrett—and all the others who had done as they were asked, without making a fuss. He felt a sudden surge of affection—even of love—towards them all, for giving him their active or passive support.

And especially to Sue, who was already one jump ahead of him, as she always seemed to be. There she was, moving unobtrusively about her duties at the back of the cabin. Pat doubted if anyone noticed—certainly Radley did not—as she opened the medicine chest and palmed one of those cigarette-sized cylinders of oblivion. If this fellow gave trouble, she would be ready.

At the moment, trouble seemed the furthest thing from Radley's mind. He appeared to be completely self-possessed and perfectly rational; there was no mad gleam in his eye, or any other of the *clichés* of insanity. He looked exactly what he was—a middle-aged New Zealand accountant taking a holiday on the Moon.

"This is very interesting, Mr. Radley," said Commodore Hansteen in a carefully neutral voice, "but please excuse our ignorance. Who are 'they', and why should they be after you?"

"I am sure, Commodore, that you've heard of Flying Saucers?"

Flying *what*? Pat asked himself. Hansteen seemed better informed than he was.

"Yes, I have," he answered a little wearily. "I've come across them in old books on astronautics. They were quite a craze, weren't they, about eighty years ago?"

He realised that "craze" was an unfortunate word to use, and was relieved when Radley took no offence.

"Oh," he answered, "they go back much further than *that*, but it was only in the last century that people started to take notice of them. There's an old manuscript from an English abbey dated 1290 that describes one in detail— and that isn't the earliest report, by any means. More than ten thousand Flying Saucer sightings have been recorded prior to the twentieth century."

"Just a minute," interrupted Pat. "What the devil do you mean by 'Flying Saucer'? I've never heard of them."

"Then I'm afraid, Captain, that your education has been neglected," answered Radley in a sorrowful voice. "The term 'Flying Saucer' came into general use after 1947 to describe the strange, usually disc-shaped vehicles that have been investigating our planet for centuries. Some people prefer to use the phrase Unidentified Flying Objects."

That aroused a few faint memories in Pat's mind. Yes, he had heard that term in connection with the hypothetical Outsiders. But there was no concrete evidence, of course, that alien space-vessels had ever entered the Solar System.

"Do you *really* believe," said one of the other passengers sceptically, "that there are visitors from space hanging round the Earth?"

"Much more than that," answered Radley. "They've often landed and made contact with human beings. Before we came here, they had a base on Farside, but they destroyed it when the first survey rockets started taking close-ups."

"How do you know all this?" asked someone else. Radley seemed quite indifferent to the scepticism of his audience; he must have grown used to this response long ago. He radiated a kind of inner faith which, however ill-founded it might be, was oddly convincing. His insanity had exalted him into the realm beyond reason, and he was quite happy there.

"We have—contacts," he answered with an air of great importance. "A few men and women have been able to establish telepathic communication with the Saucer people. So we know a good deal about them."

"How is it that no one else does?" asked another disbeliever. "If they're really out there, why haven't our astronomers and space-pilots seen them?"

"Oh, but they have," Radley answered with a pitying smile, "and they're keeping quiet. There's a conspiracy of silence among the scientists; they don't like to admit that there are intelligences out in space so much superior to ours. So when a pilot does report a saucer, they make fun of him. Now, of course, every astronaut keeps quiet when he meets one."

"Have *you* ever met one, Commodore?" asked Mrs. Schuster, obviously half convinced. "Or are you in the—what did Mr. Radley call it—conspiracy of silence?"

"I'm very sorry to disappoint you," said Hansteen. "You'll have to take my word for it that all the space-ships I've ever met have been on Lloyd's Register."

He caught Pat's eye, and gave a little nod that said, "Let's go and talk this over in the airlock." Now that he was quite convinced that Radley was harmless, he almost welcomed this interlude. It had, very effectively, taken the passengers' minds off the situation in which they now found themselves. If Radley's brand of insanity could keep them entertained, then good luck to it.

"Well, Pat," said Hansteen, when the airlock door had sealed them off from the argument, "what do you think of him?"

"Does he *really* believe that nonsense?"

"Oh yes—every word of it. I've met his type before."

The Commodore knew a good deal about Radley's peculiar obsession; no one whose interests in astronautics dated back to the twentieth century could fail to do so. As a young man, he had even read some of the original writings on the subject—works of such brazen fraudulence or childish naïveté that they had shaken his belief that men were rational beings. That such a literature could ever have flourished was a disturbing thought—though it was true that

most of these books had been published in that psychotic era, the Frantic
Fifties.

"This is a very peculiar situation," complained Pat. "At a time like *this*
—all the passengers are arguing about Flying Saucers."

"I think it's an excellent idea," answered the Commodore. "What else would
you suggest they do?" Let's face it—we've got to sit here and wait, until
Lawrence starts knocking on the roof again."

"If he's still here. Barrett may be right—perhaps the raft has sunk."

"I think that's very unlikely—the disturbance was only a slight one. How
far would you imagine we went down?"

Pat thought this over. Looking back on the incident, it seemed to have lasted
a long time. The fact that he had been in virtual darkness, and had been
fighting that jet of dust, still further confused his memory. He could only
hazard a guess.

"I'd say—ten metres."

"Nonsense! The whole affair only lasted a couple of seconds. I doubt if
we dropped more than two or three metres."

Pat found this very hard to believe, but he hoped that the Commodore was
right. He knew that it was extremely difficult to judge weak accelerations,
particularly when one was under stress. Hansteen was the only man aboard
who could have had any experience of this; his verdict was probably correct
—and was certainly encouraging.

"They may never have felt a thing on the surface," continued Hansteen,
"and they're probably wondering why they can't contact us. Are you sure
there's nothing we can do about the radio?"

"Quite sure; the whole terminal block's come loose at the end of the cable
conduit. There's no way of reaching it from inside the cabin."

"Well, I suppose that's that. We might as well go back and let Radley try
to convert us—if he can."

Jules had tracked the overcrowded skis for a hundred metres before he
realised that they were not as overcrowded as they should have been. They
carried seven men—and there were eight on the site.

He panned swiftly back to the raft, and by the good luck or precognition
that separates the brilliant cameraman from the merely adequate one, he
arrived there just as Lawrence broke his radio silence.

"C.E.E. calling," he said, sounding as tired and frustrated as would any
man who had just seen his carefully-laid plans demolished. "Sorry for the
delay, but as you'll have gathered we have an emergency. There appears to
have been another cave-in; how deep it was, we don't know—but we've lost
physical contact with *Selene*, and she's not answering our radio.

"In case there's another subsidence, I've ordered my men to stand by a
few hundred metres away. The danger's very slight—we hardly felt that last
tremor—but there's no point in taking chances. I can do everything that's
necessary for the moment without any help.

"I'll call again in a few minutes. C.E.E. out."

With the eyes of millions upon him, Lawrence crouched at the edge of the raft, reassembling the probe with which he had first located the cruiser. He had twenty metres to play with; if she had gone deeper than that, he would have to think of something else.

The rod sank into the dust, moving more and more slowly as it approached the depth where *Selene* had rested. There was the original mark—fifteen point one five metres—just disappearing through the surface. The probe continued to move, like a lance piercing into the body of the Moon. How much further? whispered Lawrence to himself, in the murmurous silence of his space-suit.

The anticlimax was almost laughable, except that this was no laughing matter. The probe penetrated an extra metre and a half—a distance he could comfortably span without straining his arms.

Far more serious was the fact that *Selene* had not sunk evenly, as Lawrence discovered after a few additional probings. She was much lower at the stern, being now tilted at an angle of about thirty degrees. That alone was enough to wreck his plan; he had relied upon the caisson making a flush contact with the horizontal roof.

He put that problem aside for the moment; there was a more immediate one. Now that the cruiser's radio was silent—and he had to pray that it was a simple power failure—how could he tell if the people were still alive? They would hear his probe, but there was no way in which they could communicate with him.

But of course there was. The easiest and most primitive means of all, that could be so readily overlooked after a century and a half of electronics. . . .

Lawrence got to his feet and called the waiting skis.

"You can come back," he said. "There's no danger. She only sank a couple of metres."

He had already forgotten the watching millions. Though his new plan of campaign had still to be drawn up, he was going into action again.

CHAPTER XXVII

WHEN PAT AND the Commodore returned to the cabin, the debate was still going full blast. Radley, who had said so little until now, was certainly making up for lost time. It was as if some secret spring had been touched, or he had been absolved from an oath of secrecy. That was probably the explanation; now that he was convinced that his mission was discovered, he was only too happy to talk about it.

Commodore Hansteen had met many such believers—indeed, it was in sheer self-defence that he had waded through the turgid literature of the subject. The approach was almost always the same; first would be the suggestion that, "Surely, Commodore, you've seen some very strange things during your years in space?" Then, when his reply was unsatisfactory, there would be a guarded —and sometimes not so guarded—hint that he was either afraid or unwilling to speak. It was a waste of energy denying the charge; in the eyes of the faithful, that only proved that he was part of the conspiracy.

The other passengers had no such bitter experience to warn them, and Radley was evading their points with effortless ease. Even Schuster, for all his legal training, was unable to pin him into a corner; his efforts were as futile as trying to convince a paranoic that he was not really being persecuted.

"Does it seem *reasonable*," Schuster argued, "that if thousands of scientists know this, not one of them will let the cat out of the bag? You can't keep a secret that big! It would be like trying to hide the Washington Monument!"

"Oh, there have been attempts to reveal the truth," Radley answered. "But the evidence has a way of being mysteriously destroyed—as well as the men who wanted to reveal it. They can be utterly ruthless when it's necessary."

"But you said that—*they*—have been in contact with human beings. Isn't that a contradiction?"

"Not at all. You see, the forces of good and evil are at work in the Universe, just as they are on Earth. Some of the Saucer people want to help us—others to exploit us. The two groups have been struggling together for thousands of years. Sometimes the conflict involves Earth; that is how Atlantis was destroyed."

Hansteen was unable to resist a smile. Atlantis always got into the act sooner or later—or if not Atlantis, then Lemuria or Mu. They all appealed to the same type of unbalanced, mystery-mongering mentality.

The whole subject had been thoroughly investigated by a group of psychologists during——if Hansteen remembered correctly—the 1970s. They had concluded that around the mid-twentieth century a substantial percentage of the population was convinced that the world was about to be destroyed, and that the only hope lay in intervention from space. Having lost faith in themselves, men had sought salvation in the sky.

The Flying Saucer religion flourished among the lunatic fringe of mankind for almost exactly ten years; then it had abruptly died out, like an epidemic that had run its course. Two factors, the psychologists had decided, were responsible for this: the first was sheer boredom—the second was the International Geophysical Year, that had heralded Man's own entry into space.

In the eighteen months of the IGY, the sky was watched and probed by more instruments, and more trained observers, than in the whole of previous history. If there had been celestial visitors poised above the atmosphere, this concentrated scientific effort would have revealed them. It did nothing of the sort; and when the first manned vehicles started leaving Earth, the Flying Saucers were still more conspicuous by their absence.

For most men, that settled the matter. The thousands of unidentified flying objects that had been seen over the centuries had some natural cause, and with better understanding of meterology and astronomy there was no lack of reasonable explanations. As the Age of Space dawned, restoring Man's confidence in his own destiny, the world lost interest in Flying Saucers.

It is seldom, however, that a religion dies out completely, and a small body of the faithful kept the cult alive with fantastic "revelations", accounts of meetings with extra-terrestrials, and claims of telepathic contacts. Even when, as frequently happened, the current prophets were proved to have faked the evidence, the devotees never wavered. They needed their gods in the sky, and would not be deprived of them.

"You still haven't explained to us," Mr. Schuster was now saying, "why the Saucer people should be after *you*. What have you done to annoy them?"

"I was getting too close to some of their secrets, so they have used this opportunity to eliminate me."

"I should have thought they could have found less elaborate ways."

"It is foolish to imagine that our limited minds can understand their mode of thinking. But this would seem like an accident; no one would suspect that it was deliberate."

"A good point. Since it makes no difference now, could you tell us what secret you were after? I'm sure we'd all like to know."

Hansteen shot a quick glance at Irving Schuster. The lawyer had struck him as a rather solemn, humourless little man; irony seemed somewhat out of character.

"I'd be glad to tell you," answered Radley. "It really starts back in 1953, when an American astronomer named O'Neill observed something very remarkable on the eastern border of the Mare Crisium.

"Other astronomers, of course, laughed at him—but less prejudiced ones confirmed the existence of the bridge. Within a few years, however, it had vanished. Obviously, our interest had alarmed the saucer people, and they had dismantled it."

That "obvious", Hansteen told himself, was a perfect example of Saucerite logic—the daring *non sequitur* that left the normal mind helplessly floundering several jumps behind. He had never heard of O'Neill's Bridge, but there had been a score of examples of mistaken observations in the astronomical records. The Martian canals were the classic case; honest observers had reported them for years, but they simply did not exist—at least as the fine spider-web that Lowell and others had drawn. Did Radley think that someone had filled in the canals, between the time of Lowell and the securing of the first clear photographs of Mars? He was quite capable of it, Hansteen was sure.

Presumably, O'Neill's Bridge had been a trick of the lighting, or of the Moon's perpetually shifting shadows—but such a simple explanation was not, of course, good enough for Radley. And in any event, what was the man doing here, a couple of thousand kilometres from the Mare Crisium?

Someone else had thought of that, and had put the same question. As usual, Radley had a convincing answer at the tip of his tongue.

"I'd hoped," he said, "to divert their suspicions by behaving like an ordinary tourist. Because the evidence I was looking for lay on the western hemisphere, I went east. I planned to get to Mare Crisium by going across Farside; there were several places there that I wanted to look at, too. But they were too clever for me. I should have guessed that I'd be spotted by one of their agents —they can take human form, you know. Probably they've been following me ever since I landed on the Moon."

"I'd like to know," said Mrs. Schuster, who seemed to be taking Radley with ever-increasing seriousness, "what they're going to do to us now."

"I wish I could tell you, ma'am," answered Radley. "We know that they have caves deep down inside the Moon, and almost certainly that's where we're being taken. As soon as they saw that the rescuers were getting close, they stepped in again. I'm afraid we're too deep for anyone to reach us now."

That's quite enough of this nonsense, said Pat to himself. We've had our comic relief, and now this madman is starting to depress people. But how can we shut him up?

Insanity was rare on the Moon, as in all frontier societies. Pat did not know how to deal with it—especially this confident, curiously persuasive variety. There were moments when he almost wondered if there might be something in Radley's delusion; in other circumstances, his natural healthy scepticism would have protected him, but now, after these days of strain and suspense, his critical faculties were dimmed. He wished there was some neat way of breaking the spell that this glib-tongued maniac was undoubtedly casting.

Half-ashamed of the thought, he remembered the quick *coup de grâce* that had put Hans Baldur so neatly to sleep. Without intending to do so—at least, to his conscious knowledge—he caught Harding's eye. To his alarm there was an immediate response; Harding nodded slightly, and rose slowly to his feet. No! said Pat—but only to himself. I don't mean *that*—leave the poor lunatic alone—*what sort of man are you, anyway?*

Then he relaxed, very slightly. Harding was not attempting to move from his seat, four places from Radley. He was merely standing there, looking at the New Zealander with an unfathomable expression. It might even have been pity, but in this dim lighting Pat could not be sure.

"I think it's time to make my contribution," he said. "At least *one* of the things our friend was telling you is perfectly true. He has been followed—but not by Saucerites. By me.

"For an amateur, Wilfred George Radley, I'd like to congratulate you. It's been a fine chase—from Christchurch to Astrograd to Clavius to Tycho to Ptolemy to Plato to Port Roris—and to here, which I guess is the end of the trail, in more ways than one."

Radley did not seem in the least perturbed. He merely inclined his head in an almost regal gesture of acknowledgement, as if he recognised Harding's existence, but did not wish to pursue his acquaintance.

"As you may have guessed," continued Harding. "I'm a detective. Most of the time I specialise in fraud. Quite interesting work, though I seldom have a chance of talking about it. I'm quite grateful for this opportunity.

"I've no interest—well, no professional interest—in Mr. Radley's peculiar beliefs. Whether they're true or not doesn't affect the fact that he's a very smart accountant, earning a good salary back in N.Z. Though not one good enough to pay for a month on the Moon.

"But that was no problem—because, you see, Mr. Radley was senior accountant at the Christchurch branch of Universal Travel Cards, Incorporated. The system is supposed to be fool-proof and double-checked, but somehow he managed to issue himself a card—Q Category, good for unlimited travel anywhere in the Solar System, for hotel and restaurant billings, for cashing cheques up to five hundred dollars on demand. There aren't many Q Cards around, and they're handled as if they're made of plutonium.

"Of course, people have tried to get away with this sort of thing before; clients are always losing their cards, and enterprising characters have a fine time with them for a few days before they're caught. But only a few days; the UTC central billing system is very efficient—it has to be. There are several safeguards against unauthorised use, and until now the longest run anyone's had was a week."

"Nine days," Radley unexpectedly interjected.

"Sorry—*you* should know. Nine days, then. But Radley had been on the move for almost three weeks before we spotted him. He'd taken his annual leave, and told the office he'd be vacationing quietly on the North Island. Instead, he went to Astrograd and then on to the Moon, making history in the process. For he's the first man—and we hope the last one—to leave Earth entirely on credit.

"We still want to know exactly how he did it. How did he bypass the automatic checking circuits? Did he have an accomplice in the computer programming section? And similar questions of absorbing interest to UTC, Inc. I hope, Radley, you'll let down your hair with me, just to satisfy my curiosity. I think it's the least you can do in the circumstances.

"Still, we know *why* you did it—why you threw up a good job to go on a spree that was bound to land you in jail. We guessed the reason, of course, as soon as we found you were on the Moon. UTC knew all about your hobby, but it didn't affect your efficiency. They took a gamble, and it's been an expensive one."

"I'm very sorry," Radley replied, not without dignity. "The firm's always treated me well, and it did seem a shame. But it was in a good cause, and if I could have found my evidence——"

But at that point everyone, except Detective Inspector Harding, lost interest in Radley and his saucers. The sound that they had all been anxiously waiting for had come a last.

Lawrence's probe was scratching against the roof.

CHAPTER XXVIII

I SEEM TO have been here for half a life-time, thought Maurice Spenser —yet the sun is still low in the west, where it rises on this weird world, and it's still three days to noon. How much longer am I going to be stuck on this mountain-top, listening to Captain Anson's tall stories of the spaceways, and watching that distant raft with its twin igloos?

It was a question that no one could answer. When the caisson had started to descend, it had looked as if another twenty-four hours would see the job finished. But now they were back where they had started—and to make matters worse, all the visual excitement of the story was over. Everything that would happen from now on would be hidden deep in the Sea, or would take place behind the walls of an igloo. Lawrence still stubbornly refused to allow a camera out on the raft, and Spenser could hardly blame him. The Chief Engineer had been unlucky once, when his commentary had blown up in his face, and was not going to risk it happening again.

Yet there was no question of *Auriga* abandoning the site which she had reached at such expense. If all went well, there was one dramatic scene still to come. And if all went badly, there would be a tragic one. Sooner or later, those dust-skis would be heading back to Port Roris—with or without the men and women they had come to save. Spenser was not going to miss the departure of that caravan, whether it took place under the rising or the setting sun, or beneath the fainter light of the unmoving Earth.

As soon as he had re-located *Selene*, Lawrence had started drilling again. On the monitor screen, Spenser could see the thin shaft of the oxygen supply-tube making its second descent into the dust. Why was Lawrence bothering to do this, he wondered, if he was not sure whether anyone was still alive aboard *Selene*? And how was he going to check this, now that the radio had failed?

That was a question that millions of people were asking themselves, as they watched the pipe sink down into the dust, and perhaps many of them thought of the right answer. Yet oddly enough, it never occurred to anyone aboard *Selene*—not even to the Commodore.

As soon as they heard that heavy thump against the roof, they knew at once that this was no sounding-rod, delicately probing the Sea. When, a minute later, there came the unmistakable whirr of a drill chewing its way through fibreglass, they felt like condemned men who had been granted a last-minute reprieve.

This time, the drill missed the cable conduit—not that it mattered now. The passengers watched, almost hypnotised, as the grinding sound grew louder and the first flakes planed down from the ceiling. When the head of the drill appeared and descended twenty centimetres into the cabin, there was a brief but heart-felt burst of cheering.

Now what? said Pat to himself. We can't talk to them; how will I know when to unscrew the drill? I'm not going to make *that* mistake a second time. . . .

Startlingly loud in this tense, expectant silence, the metal tube resonated with the DIT DIT DIT DAH which, surely, not one of *Selene*'s company would forget, however long he lived. Pat replied at once, banging out an answering "V" with a pair of pliers. Now they know we're alive, he thought. He had never really believed that Lawrence would assume that they were dead and abandon them, yet at the same time there was that always haunting doubt.

The tube signalled again, this time much more slowly. It was a nuisance having to learn Morse—in this age, it seemed such an anachronism, and many were the bitter protests among pilots and space-engineers at the waste of effort. In your whole life-time, you might need it only once.

But that was the point. You would *really* need it then.

DIT DIT DAH, rapped the tube, DAH DIT . . . DIT DIT DIT . . . DAH DIT DAH DIT . . . DIT DAH DIT . . . DIT . . . DIT DAH DAH.

Then, so that there would be no mistake, it started to repeat the word— but both Pat and the Commodore, rusty though they were, had got the message.

"They're telling us to unscrew the drill," said Pat. "Well, here we go."

The brief rush of air gave everyone a moment of unnecessary panic as the pressure equalised. Then the pipe was open to the upper world, and twenty-two anxious men and women waited for the first breath of oxygen to come gushing down it.

Instead, the tube spoke. Out of the open orifice came a voice hollow and sepulchral, but perfectly clear. It was so loud, and so utterly unexpected, that a gasp of surprise came from the company. Probably not more than half a dozen of these men and women had ever heard a speaking tube; they had grown up in the belief that only through electronics could the voice be sent across space. This antique revival was as much a novelty to them as a telephone would have been to an ancient Greek.

"This is Chief Engineer Lawrence speaking. Can you hear me?"

Pat cupped his hands over the opening, and answered slowly: "Hearing you loud and clear. How do you receive us?"

"Very clear—are you all right?"

"Yes—what's happened?"

"You've dropped a couple of metres—no more than that. We hardly noticed anything up here, until the pipes came adrift. How's your air?"

"Still good—but the sooner you start supplying us, the better."

"Don't worry—we'll be pumping again as soon as we get the dust out of the filters, and can rush out another drill-head from Port Roris. The one you've just unscrewed was the only spare—it was lucky we had that."

So it will be at least an hour, Pat told himself, before their air supply could be secured again. That, however, was not the problem that now worried him. He knew how Lawrence had hoped to reach them—and he realised that the plan would not work, now that *Selene* was no longer on an even keel.

"How are you going to get at us?" he asked bluntly.

There was only the briefest of hesitations before Lawrence answered.

"I've not worked out the details, but we'll add another section to the caisson and continue it down until it reaches you. Then we'll start scooping out the dust until we get to the bottom. That will take us to within a few centimetres of you; we'll cross that gap somehow. But there's one thing I want you to do first."

"What's that?"

"I'm ninety per cent sure that you won't settle again—but if you're going to, I'd rather you did it now. I want you all to jump up and down together for a couple of minutes."

"Will that be safe?" asked Pat doubtfully. "Suppose this pipe tears out again?"

"Then you can plug it again. Another small hole won't matter—but another subsidence will, if it happens when we're trying to make a man-sized opening in the roof."

Selene had seen some strange sights, but this was undoubtedly the strangest. Twenty-two men and women were solemnly jumping up and down in unison, rising to the ceiling and then pushing themselves back as vigorously as possible to the floor. All the while Pat kept a careful watch on that pipe leading to the upper world; after a minute's strenuous exertions on the part of her passengers, *Selene* had moved downwards by less than two centimetres.

He reported this to Lawrence, who received the news with thankfulness. Now that he was reasonably sure that *Selene* would not shift again, he was confident that he could get these people out. Exactly how, he was not yet certain, but the plan was beginning to form in his mind.

It took shape over the next twelve hours, in conferences with his Brains Trust and experiments on the Sea of Thirst. The Engineering Division had learned more about the dust in the last week than during the whole of its previous existence; it was no longer fighting in the dark against a largely unknown opponent. It understood which liberties could be taken—and which could not.

Despite the speed with which the changed plans were drawn up, and the necessary hardware constructed, there was no undue haste and certainly no carelessness. For this was another operation that had to work first time; if it failed, then at the very least the caisson would have to be abandoned and a new one sunk. And at the worst—those aboard *Selene* would be drowned in dust.

"It's a pretty problem," said Tom Lawson, who liked pretty problems—and not much else. "The lower end of the caisson's wide open to the dust, because it's resting against *Selene* at only one point, and the tilt of the roof prevents it from sealing. Before we can pump out the dust, we have to close that gap.

"Did I say 'pump'? That was a mistake. You can't pump the stuff; it has to be lifted. And if we tried that as things are now, it would flow in just as fast at the bottom of the tube as we took it out of the top."

Tom paused and grinned sardonically at his multi-million audience, as if challenging it to solve the problem he had outlined. He let his viewers stew in their own thoughts for a while, then picked up the model lying on the studio table. Though it was an extremely simple one, he was rather proud of it, for he had made it himself. No one could have guessed, from the other side of the camera, that it was only cardboard sprayed with aluminium paint.

"This tube," he said, "represents a short section of the caisson that's now leading down to *Selene*—and which, as I said, is full of dust. Now *this*"—with the other hand, he picked up a stubby cylinder, closed at one end—"fits snugly inside the caisson, like a piston. It's very heavy, and will try to sink under its own weight. But it can't do so, of course, while the dust is trapped underneath it."

Tom turned the piston until its flat end was towards the camera. He pressed his forefinger against the centre of the circular face, and a small trapdoor opened.

"This acts as a valve; when it's open, dust can flow through and the piston can sink down the shaft. As soon as it reaches the bottom, the valve will be closed by a signal from above. That will seal off the caisson, and we can start scooping out the dust.

"It sounds very simple, doesn't it? We'll, it's not. There are about fifty problems I haven't mentioned. For example, as the caisson is emptied, it will try to float up to the surface with a lift of a good many tons. Chief Engineer Lawrence has worked out an ingenious system of anchors to hold it down.

"You'll realise, of course, that even when this tube has been emptied of dust, there will still be that wedge-shaped gap between its lower end and *Selene*'s roof. How Mr. Lawrence proposes to deal with that, I don't know. And please don't send *me* any more suggestions; we've already had enough half-baked ideas on this programme to last a life-time.

"This—piston gadget—isn't just theory. The engineers here have built and tested it during the last twelve hours, and it's now in action. If I can make any sense of the signals the man's waving at me, I think we're now going over to the Sea of Thirst, to find what's happening on the raft."

The temporary studio in the Hotel Roris faded from a million screens; in its place was the picture that, by this time, must have been familiar to most of the human race.

There were now three igloos of assorted sizes on or around the raft; as the sunlight glinted from their reflecting outer surfaces, they looked like giant drops of mercury. One of the dust-skis was parked beside the largest dome; the other two were in transit, still shuttling supplies from Port Roris.

Like the mouth of a well, the caisson projected from the Sea. Its rim was only twenty centimetres above the dust, and the opening seemed much too narrow for a man to enter. It would, indeed, have been a very tight fit for anyone wearing a space-suit—but the crucial part of this operation would be done without suits.

At regular intervals, a cylindrical grab was disappearing into the well, to be hauled back to the surface a few seconds later by a small but powerful crane.

On each withdrawal, the grab would be swung clear of the opening, and would disgorge its contents back into the Sea. For an instant a grey dunce's cap of dust would stand in momentary balance on the level plain; then it would collapse in slow motion, vanishing completely before the next load had emerged from the shaft. It was a conjuring trick being carried out in broad daylight, and it was fascinating to watch. More effectively than a thousand words of description, it told the viewers all that they needed to know about the Sea of Thirst.

The grab was taking longer on its journeys now, as it plunged deeper into the dust. And at last there came the moment when it emerged only half-full, and the way to *Selene* was open—except for that road-block at the end.

CHAPTER XXIX

"WE'RE STILL IN very good spirits," said Pat, into the microphone that had now been lowered down the air-shaft. "Of course, we had a bad shock after that second cave-in, when we lost contact with you—but now we're sure you'll soon have us out. We can hear the grab at work, as it scoops up the dust, and it's wonderful to know that help is so close. We'll never forget," he added, a little awkwardly, "the efforts that so many people have made to help us, and whatever happens we'd like to thank them. All of us are quite sure that everything possible has been done.

"And now I'll hand over the mike, as several of us have messages we want to send. With any luck at all, this will be the last broadcast from *Selene*."

As he gave the microphone to Mrs. Williams, he realised that he might have phrased that last remark a little better; it could be interpreted in two ways. But now that rescue was so close at hand, he refused to admit the possibility of further set-backs. They had been through so much that, surely, nothing more would happen to them now.

Yet he knew that the final stage of the operation would be the most difficult, and the most critical, of all. They had discussed it endlessly during the last few hours, ever since Chief Engineer Lawrence had explained his plans to them. There was little else to talk about now that—by common consent —the subject of Flying Saucers was vetoed.

They could have continued with the book readings, but somehow both *Shane* and *The Orange and the Apple* had lost their appeal. No one could concentrate on anything now except the prospects of rescue, and the renewal of life that lay before them when they had rejoined the human race.

From overhead, there was a sudden, heavy thump. That could mean only one thing; the grab had reached the bottom of the shaft, and the caisson was clear of dust. Now it could be coupled to one of the igloos and pumped full of air.

It took more than an hour to complete the connection and make all the necessary tests. The specially modified Mark Nineteen igloo, with a hole in its floor just large enough to accommodate the protruding end of the caisson, had to be positioned and inflated with the utmost care. The lives of *Selene*'s passengers, and also those of the men attempting to rescue them, might depend upon this air seal.

Not until Chief Engineer Lawrence was thoroughly satisfied did he strip off his space-suit and approach that yawning hole. He held a floodlight above the opening and looked down into the shaft, which seemed to dwindle away to infinity. Yet it was just seventeen metres to the bottom; even in this low gravity, an object would take only five seconds to fall that distance.

Lawrence turned to his assistants; each was wearing a space-suit, but with the face-plate open. If anything went wrong, those plates could be snapped shut in a fraction of a second, and the men inside would probably be safe. But for Lawrence there would be no hope at all—nor for the twenty-two aboard *Selene*.

"You know exactly what to do," he said. "If I want to come up in a hurry, all of you pull on the rope ladder together. Any questions?"

There was none; everything had been thoroughly rehearsed. With a nod to his men and a chorus of "Good lucks" in return, Lawrence lowered himself into the shaft.

He let himself fall most of the way, checking his speed from time to time by grabbing at the ladder. On the Moon it was quite safe to do this; well, *almost* safe. Lawrence had seen men killed because they had forgotten that even this gravity field could accelerate one to a lethal speed in less than ten seconds.

This was like Alice's fall into Wonderland (so much of Carroll might have been inspired by space-travel) but there was nothing to see on the way down except the blank concrete wall, so close that Lawrence had to squint to focus upon it. And then, with the slightest of bumps, he had reached the bottom.

He squatted down on the little metal platform, the size and shape of a manhole cover, and examined it carefully. The trapdoor-valve that had been open during the piston's descent through the dust was leaking very slightly, and a trickle of grey powder was creeping round the seal. It was nothing to worry about, but Lawrence could not help wondering what would happen if the valve opened under the pressure from beneath. How fast would the dust rise up the shaft, like water in a well? Not as fast, he was quite certain, as he could go up that ladder. . . .

Beneath his feet now, only centimetres away, was the roof of the cruiser, sloping down into the dust at that maddening thirty degrees. His problem now was to mate the horizontal end of the shaft with the sloping roof of the cruiser—and to do it so well that the coupling would be dust-tight.

He could see no flaw in the plan; nor did he expect to, for it had been devised by the best engineering brains on Earth and Moon. It even allowed for the possibility that *Selene* might shift again, by a few centimetres, while he was working here. But theory was one thing—and as he knew all too well, practice was another.

There were six large thumbscrews spaced round the circumference of the metal disc on which Lawrence was sitting, and he started to turn them one by one, like a drummer tuning his instrument. Connected to the lower side of the platform was a short piece of concertina-like tubing, almost as wide as the caisson, and now folded flat. It formed a flexible coupling large enough for a man to crawl through, and was now slowly opening as Lawrence turned the screws.

One side of the corrugated tube had to stretch through forty centimetres to reach the sloping roof; the other had to move scarcely at all. Lawrence's chief worry had been that the resistance of the dust would prevent the concertina from opening, but the screws were easily overcoming the pressure.

Now none of them could be tightened any further; the lower end of the coupling must be flush against *Selene*'s roof, and sealed to it, he hoped, by the rubber gasket round its rim. How tight that seal was, he would very soon know.

Automatically checking his escape route, Lawrence glanced up the shaft. He could see nothing past the glare of the floodlight hanging two metres above his head, but the rope ladder stretching past it was extremely reassuring.

"I've let down the connector," he shouted to his invisible colleagues. "It seems to be flush against the roof. Now I'm going to open the valve."

Any mistake now, and the whole shaft would be flooded, perhaps beyond possibility of further use. Slowly and gently, Lawrence released the trapdoor which had allowed the dust to pass through the piston while it was descending. There was no sudden upwelling; the corrugated tube beneath his feet was holding back the Sea.

Lawrence reached through the valve—and his fingers felt the roof of *Selene*, still invisible beneath the dust but now only a hand's-breadth away. Few achievements in all his life had ever given him such a sense of satisfaction. The job was still far from finished—*but he had reached the cruiser.* For a moment he crouched in his little pit, feeling as some old-time miner must have done when the first nugget of gold gleamed in the lamp-light.

He banged three times on the roof; immediately, his signal was returned. There was no point in striking up a Morse conversation, for if he wished, he could talk directly through the microphone circuit, but he knew the psychological effect that his tapping would have. It would prove to the men and women in *Selene* that rescue was now only centimetres away.

Yet there were still major obstacles to be demolished, and the next one was the manhole cover on which he was sitting—the face of the piston itself. It had served its purpose, holding back the dust while the caisson was being emptied, but now it had to be removed before anyone could escape from *Selene*. This had to be done, however, without disturbing the flexible coupling that it had helped to place in position.

To make this possible, the circular face of the piston had been built so that it could be lifted out, like a saucepan lid, when eight large bolts were unscrewed. It took Lawrence only a few minutes to deal with these and to attach a rope to the now loose metal disc; then he shouted "Haul away!"

A fatter man would have had to climb the shaft while the circular lid came up after him, but Lawrence was able to squeeze against the wall while the metal plate, moving edgeways, was hoisted past him. There goes the last line of defence, he told himself, as the disc vanished overhead. Now it would be impossible to seal the shaft again, if the coupling failed and the dust started to pour in.

"Bucket!" he shouted. It was already on its way down.

Forty years ago, thought Lawrence, I was playing on a Californian beach with bucket and spade, making castles in the sand. Now here I am on the Moon—Chief Engineer, Earthside, no less—shovelling in even deadlier earnest, with the whole human race looking over my shoulder.

When the first load was hoisted up, he had exposed a considerable area of *Selene's* roof. The volume of dust trapped inside the coupling-tube was quite small, and two more bucketfuls disposed of it.

Before him now was the aluminised fabric of the sun-shield, which had long ago crumpled under the pressure. Lawrence cut it away without difficulty —it was so fragile that he could tear it with his bare hands—and exposed the slightly roughened fibreglass of the outer hull. To cut through that with a small power saw would be easy; it would also be fatal.

For by this time *Selene's* double hull had lost its integrity; when the roof had been damaged, the dust would have flooded into the space between the two walls. It would be waiting there, under pressure, to come spurting out as soon as he made his first incision. Before he could enter *Selene*, that thin but deadly layer of dust would have to be immobilised.

Lawrence rapped briskly against the roof; as he had expected, the sound was muffled by the dust. What he did not expect was to receive an urgent, frantic tattoo in reply.

This, he could tell at once, was no reassuring "I'm O.K." signal from inside the cruiser. Even before the men overhead could relay the news to him, Lawrence had guessed that the Sea of Thirst was making one final bid to keep its prey.

Because Karl Johanson was a nucleonics engineer, had a sensitive nose, and happened to be sitting at the rear of the bus, he was the one who spotted the approach of disaster. He remained quite still for a few seconds, nostrils twitching, then said, "Excuse me" to his companion in the aisle seat, and strolled quietly to the washroom. He did not wish to cause alarm if there was no need, especially when rescue seemed so near. But in his professional lifetime he had learned, through more examples than he cared to remember, never to ignore the smell of burning insulation.

He was in the washroom for less than fifteen seconds; when he emerged he was walking quickly, but not quickly enough to cause panic. He went straight to Pat Harris, who was deep in conversation with Commodore Hansteen, and interrupted them without ceremony.

"Captain," he said in a low, urgent voice. "We're on fire. Go and check in the toilet. I've not told anyone else."

In a second, Pat was gone, and Hansteen with him. In space, as on the sea, no one stopped to argue when he heard the word "Fire". And Johanson was not the sort of man to raise a false alarm; like Pat, he was a Lunar Administration tech, and had been one of those whom the Commodore had selected for his riot squad.

The toilet was typical of that on any small vehicle of land, sea, air or space; one could touch every wall without changing position. But the rear wall, immediately above the washbowl, could no longer be touched at all. The fibreglass was blistered with heat, and was buckling and bulging even while the horrified spectators looked at it.

"My God!" said the Commodore. "That will be through in a minute. What's causing it?"

But Pat had already gone. He was back a few seconds later, carrying the cabin's two small fire-extinguishers under his arms.

"Commodore," he said, "go and report to the raft. Tell them we may only have a few minutes. I'll stay here in case it breaks through."

Hansteen did as he was told. A moment later Pat heard his voice calling the message into the microphone, and the sudden turmoil among the passengers that followed. Almost immediately the door opened again, and he was joined by McKenzie.

"Can I help?" asked the scientist.

"I don't think so," Pat answered, holding the extinguisher at the ready. He felt a curious numbness, as if this was not really happening to him, but was all a dream from which he would soon awaken. Perhaps by now he had passed beyond fear; having surmounted one crisis after another, all emotion had been wrung out of him. He could still endure, but he could no longer react.

"What's causing it?" asked McKenzie, echoing the Commodore's unanswered question and immediately following it with another. "What's behind this bulkhead?"

"Our main power supply. Twenty heavy-duty cells."

"How much energy in them?"

"Well, we started with five thousand kilowatt-hours. We probably still have half of it."

"There's your answer. Something's shorting out our power supply. It's probably been burning up ever since the overhead wiring got ripped out."

The explanation made sense, if only because there was no other source of energy aboard the cruiser. She was completely fire-proof, so could not support an ordinary combustion. But there was enough electrical energy in her powercells to drive her at full speed for hours on end, and if this dissipated itself in raw heat the results would be catastrophic.

Yet this was impossible; such an overload would have tripped the circuitbreakers at once—unless, for some reason, they had jammed.

They had not, as McKenzie reported after a quick check in the airlock.

"All the breakers have jumped," he said. "The circuits are as dead as mutton. I don't understand it."

Even in this moment of peril, Pat could hardly refrain from smiling. McKenzie was the eternal scientist; he might be about to die, but he would insist on knowing how. If he was being burned at the stake—and a similar fate might well be in store—he would ask his executioners, "What kind of wood are you using?"

The folding door creased inwards as Hansteen came back to report.

"Lawrence says he'll be through in ten minutes," he said. "Will that wall hold until then?"

"God knows," answered Pat. "It may last for another hour—it may go in the next five seconds. Depends how the fire's spreading."

"Aren't there automatic fire-fighting appliances in that compartment?"

There's no point in having them—this is our pressure bulkhead, and there's normally vacuum on the other side. That's the best fire-fighter you can get."

"That's it!" exclaimed McKenzie. "Don't you see? The whole compartment's flooded. When the roof tore, the dust started to work its way in. It's shorting all the electrical equipment."

Pat knew, without further discussion, that McKenzie was right. By now all the sections normally open to space must be packed with dust. It would have poured in through the broken roof, flowed along the gap between the double-hull, slowly accumulated around the open bus-bars in the power compartment. And then the pyrotechnics would have started: there was enough meteoric iron in the dust to make it a good conductor. It would be arcing and shorting in there like a thousand electric fires.

"If we sprinkled water on that wall," said the Commodore, "would it help matters—or would it crack the fibreglass?"

"I think we should try it," answered McKenzie, "but very carefully—not too much at a time." He filled a plastic cup—the water was already hot—and looked enquiringly at the others. As there were no objections, he began to splash a few drops on the slowly blistering surface.

The cracklings and poppings that resulted were so terrifying that he stopped at once. It was too big a risk; with a metal wall it would have been a good idea, but this non-conducting plastic would shatter under the thermal stresses.

"There's nothing we can do in here," said the Commodore. "Even those extinguishers won't help much. We'd better get out and block off this whole compartment. The door will act as a fire-wall, and give us some extra time."

Pat hesitated. The heat was already almost unbearable, but it seemed cowardice to leave. Yet Hansteen's suggestion made excellent sense; if he stayed here until the fire broke through, he would probably be gassed at once by the fumes.

"Right—let's get out," he agreed. "We'll see what kind of barricade we can build behind this door."

He did not think they would have much time to do it; already he could hear, quite distinctly, a frying, blistering sound from the wall that was holding the inferno at bay.

CHAPTER XXX

THE NEWS THAT *Selene* was on fire made no difference at all to Lawrence's actions. He could not move any faster than he was doing now; if he attempted it, he might make a mistake, just when the trickiest part of the entire job was coming up. All he could do was to forge ahead, and hope that he would beat the flames.

The apparatus now being lowered down the shaft looked like an overgrown grease-gun, or a giant version of those syringes used to put icing on wedding-cakes. This one held neither grease nor icing, but an organic silicon compound under great pressure. At the moment it was liquid; it would not remain so for long.

Lawrence's first problem was to get the liquid between the double hull, without letting the dust escape. Using a small rivet-gun, he fired seven hollow bolts into *Selene*'s outer skin one in the centre of the exposed circle, the other six evenly spaced around its circumference.

He connected the syringe to the centre bolt, and pressed the trigger. There was a slight hiss as the fluid rushed through the hollow bolt, its pressure opening a tiny valve in the bullet-shaped nose. Working very swiftly, Lawrence moved from bolt to bolt, shooting equal charges of fluid through each. Now the stuff would have spread out almost evenly between the two hulls, in a ragged pancake more than a metre across. No—not a pancake—a *soufflé*, for it would have started to foam as soon as it escaped from the nozzle.

And a few seconds later, it would have started to set, under the influence of the catalyst injected with it. Lawrence looked at his watch; in five minutes, that foam would be rock-hard, though as porous as pumice—which, indeed, it would very closely resemble. There would be no chance of more dust entering this section of the hull; what was already there was frozen in place.

There was nothing he could do to shorten that five minutes; the whole plan depended upon the foam setting to a known consistency. If his timing and positioning had been faulty, or the chemists back at Base had made an error, the people aboard *Selene* were already as good as dead.

He used the waiting period to tidy up the shaft, sending all the equipment back to the surface. Soon only Lawrence himself was left at the bottom, with no tools at all but his bare hands. If Maurice Spenser could have smuggled his camera into this narrow space—and he would have signed any reasonable contract with the Devil to have done so—his viewers would have been quite unable to guess at Lawrence's next move.

They would have been still more baffled, when what looked like a child's hoop was slowly lowered down the shaft. But this was no nursery toy; it was the key that would open *Selene*.

Susan had already marshalled the passengers to the front, and now much higher, end of the cabin. They were all standing there in a tightly-packed group, looking anxiously at the ceiling and straining their ears for every encouraging sound.

Encouragement, thought Pat, was what they needed now. And he needed it more than any of them, for he alone knew—unless Hansteen or McKenzie had guessed it—the real magnitude of the danger they were facing.

The fire was bad enough, and could kill them if it broke through into the cabin. But it was slow-moving, and they could fight it, even if only for a while. Against explosion, however, they could do nothing.

For *Selene* was a bomb, and the fuse was already lit. The stored-up energy in the power-cells that drove her motors and all her electrical devices could escape as raw heat, but it could not detonate. That was not true, unfortunately, of the liquid oxygen tanks. . . .

They must still hold many litres of the fearfully cold, violently reactive element. When the mounting heat ruptured those tanks, there would be both a physical and a chemical explosion. A small one, it was true—perhaps equivalent to a hundred kilogrammes of T.N.T. But that would be quite enough to smash *Selene* to pieces.

Pat saw no point in mentioning this to Hansteen, who was already planning his barricade. Seats were being unscrewed from the rows near the front of the cabin, and jammed between the rear row and the toilet door. It looked as if the Commodore was preparing for an invasion rather than a fire—as indeed he was. The fire itself, because of its nature, might not spread beyond the power-cell compartment, but as soon as that cracked and blistered wall finally gave way, the dust would come flooding through.

"Commodore," said Pat, "while you're doing this, I'll start organising the passengers. We can't have twenty people trying to get out at once."

That was a nightmare prospect that had to be avoided at all costs. Yet it would be hard to avoid panic—even in this well-disciplined community—if a single narrow tunnel was the only means of escape from a rapidly approaching death.

Pat walked to the front of the cabin; on Earth that would have been a steep uphill climb, but here a thirty-degree slope was barely noticeable. He looked at the anxious faces ranged in front of him and said: "We're going to be out of here very soon. When the ceiling opens, a rope ladder will be dropped down. The ladies will go first, then the men—all in alphabetical order. Don't bother to use your feet. Remember how little you weigh here, and go up hand over hand, as quickly as you can. But don't crowd the person in front; you should have plenty of time, and it will take you only a few seconds to reach the top.

"Susan, please sort everyone out in the right order. Harding, Bryan, Johanson, Barrett—I'd like you to stand by as you did before. We may need your help——"

He did not finish the sentence. There was a kind of soft, muffled explosion from the rear of the cabin—nothing spectacular, the popping of a paper bag would have made more noise. But it meant that the wall was down—while the ceiling, unfortunately, was still intact.

On the other side of the roof, Lawrence laid his hoop flat against the fibreglass and started to fix it in position with quick-drying cement. The ring was almost as wide as the little well in which he was crouching; it came to within a few centimetres of the corrugated walls. Though it was perfectly safe to handle, he treated it with exaggerated care. He had never acquired that easy familiarity with explosives that characterises those who have to live with them.

The ring-charge he was tamping in place was a perfectly conventional specimen of the art, involving no technical problems. It would make a neat, clean cut of exactly the desired width and thickness, doing in a thousandth of a second a job that would have taken a quarter of an hour with a power-saw. That was what Lawrence had first intended to use; now he was very glad that he had changed his mind. It seemed most unlikely that he would have a quarter of an hour.

How true that was, he learned while he was still waiting for the foam to set. "The fire's through into the cabin!" yelled a voice from overhead.

Lawrence looked at his watch. For a moment it seemed as if the second-hand was motionless, but that was an illusion he had experienced all his life. The watch had not stopped; it was merely that Time, as usual, was not going at the speed he wished. Until this moment it had been passing too swiftly; now, of course, it was crawling on leaden feet.

The foam should be rock-hard in another thirty seconds. Far better to leave it a little longer than to risk shooting too soon, while it was still plastic.

He started to climb the rope ladder, without haste, trailing the thin detonating wires behind him. His timing was perfect. When he had emerged from the shaft, uncrimped the short-circuit he had put for the sake of safety at the end of the wires, and connected them to the exploder, there were just ten seconds to go.

"Tell them we're starting to count down from ten," he said.

As Pat raced downhill to help the Commodore—though just what he could do now, he had very little idea—he heard Sue calling in an unhurried voice: "Miss Morley, Mrs. Schuster, Mrs. Williams . . ." How ironic it was that Miss Morley would once again be the first, this time by virtue of alphabetical accident. She could hardly grumble about the treatment she was getting now.

And then a second and much grimmer thought flashed through Pat's mind. *Suppose Mrs. Schuster got stuck in the tunnel* and blocked the exit. Well, they could hardly leave her until last. No, she'd go up all right; she had been a deciding factor in the tube's design, and since then she had lost several kilos. . . .

At first glance, the outer door of the toilet still seemed to be holding. Indeed, the only sign that anything had happened was a slight wisp of smoke curling past the hinges. For a moment Pat felt a surge of relief; why, it might take the fire half an hour to burn through the double thickness of fibreglass, and long before that——

Something was tickling his bare feet. He had moved automatically aside before his conscious mind said, "*What's that?*"

He looked down. Though his eyes were now accustomed to the dim emergency lighting, it was some time before he realised that a ghostly grey tide was pouring beneath that barricaded door—and that the panels were already bulging inwards under the pressure of tons of dust. It could be only a matter of minutes before they collapsed; even if they held, it might make little difference. That silent, sinister tide had risen above his ankles even while he was standing here.

Pat did not attempt to move, or to speak to the Commodore, who was standing equally motionless a few centimetres away. For the first time in his life—and now, it might well be, for the last—he felt an emotion of sheer, overwhelming hate. In that moment, as its million dry and delicate feelers brushed against his bare legs, it seemed to Pat that the Sea of Thirst was a conscious, malignant entity that had been playing with them like a cat with a mouse. Every time, he told himself, we thought we were getting the situation under control, it was preparing a new surprise. We were always one move behind, and now it is tired of its little game; we no longer amuse it. Perhaps Radley was right, after all. . . .

The loudspeaker dangling from the air-pipe roused him from his fatalistic reverie.

"We're ready!" it shouted. "Crowd at the end of the bus and cover your faces. I'll count down from ten.

"TEN——"

We're already at the end of the bus, thought Pat. We don't need all that time. We may not even have it.

"NINE"

I'll bet it doesn't work, anyway. The Sea won't let it, if it thinks we have a chance of getting out.

"EIGHT"

A pity, though, after all this effort. A lot of people have half killed themselves trying to help us. They deserved better luck.

"SEVEN"

That's supposed to be a lucky number, isn't it? Perhaps we may make it, after all. Some of us.

"SIX"

Let's pretend. It won't do much harm now. Suppose it takes—oh fifteen seconds to get through——

"FIVE"

—and of course to let down the ladder again—they probably rolled that up for safety——

"FOUR"

—and assuming that someone goes out every three seconds—no, let's make it five to be on the safe side——

"THREE"

—that will be twenty-two times five which is one thousand and, no, that's ridiculous, I've forgotten how to do simple arithmetic——

"TWO"

—say one hundred and something seconds which must be the best part of two minutes and that's still plenty of time for those lox tanks to blow us all to kingdom come——

"ONE"

ONE! And I haven't even covered my face; maybe I should lie down even if I have to swallow this filthy stinking dust——

There was a sudden, sharp *crack* and a brief puff of air; that was all. It was disappointingly anticlimatic, but the explosives experts had known their job, as is highly desirable that explosives experts should. The energy of the charge had been precisely calculated and focused; there was barely enough left over to ripple the dust that now covered almost half the floor-space of the cabin.

Time seemed to be frozen; for an age, nothing happened. Then there was a slow and beautiful miracle, breathtaking because it was so unexpected, yet so obvious if one had stopped to think about it.

A ring of brilliant white light appeared among the crimson shadows of the ceiling. It grew steadily thicker and brighter—then, quite suddenly, expanded into a complete and perfect circle as the section of the roof fell away. The light pouring down was only that of a single glow-tube twenty metres above, but to eyes that had seen nothing but dim redness for hours it was more glorious than any sunrise.

The ladder came through almost as soon as the circle of roofing hit the floor. Miss Morley, poised like a sprinter, was gone in a flash. Mrs. Schuster followed—a little more slowly, but still at a speed of which no one could complain—it was like an eclipse, only a few stray beams of light now filtered down that radiant road to safety. It was dark again, as if after that brief glimpse of dawn the night had returned with redoubled gloom. Mrs. Williams was only a second later.

Now the men were starting to go—Baldur first, probably blessing his position in the alphabet. There were only a dozen left in the cabin, when the barricaded door finally ripped from its hinges, and the pent-up avalanche burst forth.

The first wave of dust caught Pat while he was half-way up the slope of the cabin. Light and impalpable though it was, it slowed his movements until it seemed that he was struggling to wade through glue. It was fortunate that the moist and heavy air had robbed it of some of its power, for otherwise it would have filled the cabin with choking clouds. Pat sneezed and coughed and was partly blinded, but he could still breathe.

In the foggy gloom he could hear Sue counting—"Fifteen, Sixteen, Seventeen—Eighteen, Nineteen——" as she marshalled the passengers to safety. He had intended her to go with the other women, but she was still down here, shepherding her charges. Even as he struggled against the cloying quicksand that had now risen almost to his waist, he felt for Susan a love so great that it seemed to burst his heart. Now he had no possible doubt. Real love was a perfect balance of desire and tenderness. The first had been there for a long time, and now the second had come in full measure.

"Twenty—that's *you*, Commodore—quickly!"

"Like hell it is, Susan," said the Commodore. "Up you go." Pat could not see what happened—he was still partly blinded by the dust and the darkness—but he guessed that Hansteen must have literally thrown Sue through the roof. Neither his age nor his years in space had yet robbed him of his earthborn strength.

"Are you there, Pat?" he called. "I'm on the ladder."

"Don't wait for me—I'm coming."

That was easier said than done; it felt as if a million soft yet determined fingers were clutching at him, pulling him back into the rising flood. He gripped one of the seat-backs—now almost hidden beneath the dust—and pulled himself towards the beckoning light.

Something whipped against his face; instinctively, he reached out to push it aside—then realised that it was the end of the rope-ladder. He hauled upon it with all his might, and slowly, reluctantly, the Sea of Thirst relaxed its grip upon him.

Before he entered the shaft, he had one last glimpse of the cabin. The whole of the rear was now submerged by that crawling tide of grey; it seemed unnatural, and doubly sinister, that it rose in such a geometrically perfect plane, without a single ripple to furrow its surface. A metre away—this was something Pat knew he would remember all his life, though he could not imagine why—a solitary paper cup was floating sedately on the rising tide, like a toy boat upon a peaceful lake. In a few minutes it would reach the ceiling and be overwhelmed, but for the moment it was still bravely defying the dust.

And so were the emergency lights; they would continue to burn for days, even when each one was encapsulated in utter darkness.

Now the dimlit shaft was around him; he was climbing as quickly as his muscles would permit, but he could not overtake the Commodore. There was a sudden flood of light from above as Hansteen cleared the mouth of the shaft, and involuntarily Pat looked downwards to protect his eyes from the glare. The dust was already rising swiftly behind him, still unrippled, still smooth and placid . . . and inexorable.

Then he was straddling the low mouth of the caisson, in the centre of a fantastically overcrowded igloo. All around him, in various stages of exhaustion and dishevelment, were his fellow passengers; helping them were four space-suited figures and one man without a suit, whom he assumed was Chief Engineer Lawrence. How strange it was to see a new face, after all these days. . . .

"Is everyone out?" Lawrence asked anxiously.

"Yes," said Pat. "I'm the last man." Then he added "I hope", for he realised that in the darkness and confusion someone might have been left behind. Suppose Radley had decided not to face the music back in New Zealand. . . .

No—he was here with the rest of them. Pat was just starting to do a count of heads when the plastic floor gave a sudden jump—and out of the open well shot a perfect smoke-ring of dust. It hit the ceiling, rebounded, and disintegrated before anyone could move.

"What the devil was *that*?" said Lawrence.

"Our lox tank," answered Pat. "Good old bus—she lasted just long enough."

And then, to his helpless horror, the skipper of *Selene* burst into tears.

CHAPTER XXXI

"I STILL DON'T think those flags are a good idea," said Pat as the cruiser pulled away from Port Roris. "They look so phoney, when you know they're in vacuum."

Yet he had to admit that the illusion was excellent, for the lines of pennants draped around the Embarkation building were stirring and fluttering in a non-existent breeze. It was all done by springs and electric motors, and would be very confusing to the viewers back on Earth.

This was a big day for Port Roris, and indeed for the whole Moon. He wished that Sue could be here, but she was hardly in proper shape for the trip. Very literally; as she had remarked when he kissed her good-bye that morning: "I don't see how women could ever have had babies on Earth. Fancy carrying all this weight around, in six times our gravity."

Pat turned his mind away from his impending family, and pushed *Selene II* up to full speed. From the cabin behind him came the "Ohs!" and "Ahs!" of the thirty-two passengers, as the grey parabolas of dust soared against the sun like monochrome rainbows. This maiden voyage was in daylight; the travellers would miss the Sea's magical phosphorescence, the night ride up the canyon to Crater Lake, the green glories of the motionless Earth. But the novelty and excitement of the journey were the main attractions; thanks to her ill-fated predecessor, *Selene II* was one of the best-known vehicles in the Solar System.

It was proof of the old saying that there is no such thing as bad publicity. Now that the advance bookings were coming in, the Tourist Director was very glad that he had taken his courage in both hands and insisted on more passenger space. At first he had had to fight to get a new *Selene* at all; "Once bitten, twice shy," the Chief Administrator had said, and had capitulated only when Father Ferraro and the Geophysics Division had proved beyond reasonable doubt, that the Sea would not stir again for another million years.

"Hold her on that course," said Pat to his co-pilot. "I'll go back and talk to the customers."

He was still young enough, and vain enough, to savour the admiring glances as he walked back into the passenger cabin. Everyone aboard would have read of him or seen him on TV; in fact, the very presence of these people here was an implicit vote of confidence. Pat knew well enough that others shared the credit, but he had no false modesty about the role he had played during the last hours of *Selene I*. His most valued possession was the little golden model of the cruiser that had been a wedding present to Mr. and Mrs. Harris "From all on the last voyage, in sincere appreciation". That was the only testimonial that counted, and he desired no other.

He had walked half-way down the cabin, exchanging a few words with a passenger here and there, when he suddenly stopped dead in his tracks.

"Hello, Captain," said an unforgotten voice. "You seem surprised to see me."

Pat made a quick recovery and flashed his most dazzling official smile.

"It's certainly an unexpected pleasure, Miss Morley. I had no idea you were on the Moon."

"It's rather a surprise to me—I owe it to the story I wrote about *Selene I*. I'm covering this trip for *Life Interplanetary*."

"I only hope," said Pat, "that it will be a little less exciting than last time. By the way, are you in touch with any of the others? Dr. McKenzie and the Schusters wrote a few weeks ago, but I've often wondered what happened to poor little Radley after Harding marched him off."

"Nothing—except that he lost his job. Universal Travel Cards decided that if they prosecuted, everyone would sympathise with Radley, and it would also give other people the same idea. He makes a living, I believe, lecturing to his fellow-cultists about 'What I found on the Moon'. And I'll make you a prediction, Captain Harris."

"What's that?"

"Some day, he'll get back to the Moon."

"I rather hope he does. I never did discover just what he expected to find in the Mare Crisium."

They both laughed; then Miss Morley said: "I hear you're giving up this job."

Pat looked slightly embarrassed.

"That's true," he admitted. "I'm transferring to the Space Service. *If* I can pass the tests."

He was by no means sure that he could, yet he knew that he had to make the effort. Driving a moon-bus had been an interesting and enjoyable job, but it was also a dead-end—as both Sue and the Commodore had now convinced him. And there was another reason. . . .

He had often wondered how many other lives had been changed or diverted when the Sea of Thirst had yawned beneath the stars. No one who had been aboard *Selene I* could fail to be marked by the experience, in most cases for the better. The fact that he was now having this friendly talk with Miss Morley was sufficient proof of that.

It must also have had a profound effect on the men who had been involved in the rescue effort—especially Doctor Lawson and Chief Engineer Lawrence.

Pat had seen Lawson many times, giving his irascible TV talks on scientific subjects; he was grateful to the astronomer, but found it impossible to like him. It seemed, however, that some millions of people did.

As for Lawrence, he was hard at work on his memoirs, provisionally entitled "A Man About the Moon"—and wishing to God he'd never signed the contract. Pat had already helped him on the *Selene* chapters, and Sue was reading the typescript while waiting for the baby.

"If you'll excuse me," said Pat, remembering his duties as skipper, "I must attend to the other passengers. But please look us up next time you're in Clavius City."

"I will," promised Miss Morley, slightly taken aback but obviously somewhat pleased.

Pat continued his progress to the rear of the cabin, exchanging a greeting here, answering a question there. Then he reached the airlock-galley and closed the door behind him—and was instantly alone.

There was more room here than in *Selene I*'s little airlock, but the basic design was the same. No wonder that memories came flooding back; that might have been the space-suit whose oxygen he and McKenzie had shared while all the rest were sleeping; that could have been the wall against which he had pressed his ear, and heard in the night the whisper of the ascending dust. And this whole chamber, indeed, could have been where he had first known Sue, in the literal and biblical sense.

There was one innovation in this new model—the small window in the outer door. He pressed his face against it, and stared across the speeding surface of the Sea.

He was on the shadowed side of the cruiser, looking away from the sun, into the dark night of space. And presently, as his vision adjusted itself to that darkness, he could see the stars. Only the brighter ones, for there was enough stray light to desensitise his eyes, but there they were—and there also was Jupiter, most brilliant of all the planets next to Venus.

Soon he would be out there, far from his native world. The thought exhilarated and terrified him, but he knew he had to go.

He loved the Moon, but it had tried to kill him: never again could he be wholly at ease out upon its open surface. Though deep space was still more hostile and unforgiving, as yet it had not declared war upon him. With his own world, from now on, there could never be more than an armed neutrality.

The door of the cabin opened, and the stewardess entered with a tray of empty cups. Pat turned away from the window, and from the stars. The next time he saw them, they would be a million times brighter.

He smiled at the neatly uniformed girl, and waved his hand around the little galley.

"This is all yours, Miss Johnson," he said. "Look after it well."

Then he walked back to the controls to take *Selene II* on his last voyage, and her maiden one, across the Sea of Thirst.

RENDEZVOUS
WITH RAMA

CONTENTS

CHAPTER I

Spaceguard

SOONER OR LATER it was bound to happen. On 30th June 1908, Moscow escaped destruction by three hours and four thousand kilometres—a margin invisibly small by the standards of the universe. Again, on 12th February 1947, yet another Russian city had a still narrower escape, when the second great meteorite of the twentieth century detonated less than four hundred kilometres from Vladivostok, with an explosion rivalling that of the newly-invented uranium bomb.

In those days, there was nothing that men could do to protect themselves against the last random shots in the cosmic bombardment that had once scarred the face of the Moon. The meteorites of 1908 and 1947 had struck uninhabited wilderness; but by the end of the twenty-first century, there was no region left on Earth that could be safely used for celestial target practice. The human race had spread from pole to pole. And so, inevitably...

At 09.46 GMT on the morning of 11th September, in the exceptionally beautiful summer of the year 2077, most of the inhabitants of Europe saw a dazzling fireball appear in the eastern sky. Within seconds it was brighter than the sun, and as it moved across the heavens—at first in utter silence—it left behind it a churning column of dust and smoke.

Somewhere above Austria it began to disintegrate, producing a series of concussions so violent that more than a million people had their hearing permanently damaged. They were the lucky ones.

Moving at fifty kilometres a second, a thousand tons of rock and metal impacted on the plains of northern Italy, destroying in a few flaming moments the labour of centuries. The cities of Padua and Verona were wiped from the face of the earth; and the last glories of Venice sank forever beneath the sea as the waters of the Adriatic came thundering landwards after the hammer-blow from space.

Six hundred thousand people died, and the total damage was more than a trillion dollars. But the loss to art, to history, to science—to the whole human race, for the rest of time—was beyond all computation. It was as if a great war had been fought and lost in a single morning; and few could draw much pleasure from the fact that, as the dust of destruction slowly settled, for months the whole world witnessed the most splendid dawns and sunsets since Krakatoa.

After the initial shock, mankind reacted with a determination and a unity that no earlier age could have shown. Such a disaster, it was realised, might not occur again for a thousand years—but it might occur tomorrow. And the next time, the consequences could be even worse.

Very well; *there would be no next time.*

A hundred years earlier a much poorer world, with far feebler resources, had squandered its wealth attempting to destroy weapons launched, suicidally, by mankind against itself. The effort had never been successful, but the skills acquired then had not been forgotten. Now they could be used for a far nobler purpose, and on an infinitely vaster stage. No meteorite large enough to cause catastrophe would ever again be allowed to breach the defences of Earth.

So began Project SPACEGUARD. Fifty years later—and in a way that none of its designers could ever have anticipated—it justified its existence.

CHAPTER II

Intruder

By THE YEAR 2130, the Mars-based radars were discovering new asteroids at the rate of a dozen a day. The SPACEGUARD computers automatically calculated their orbits, and stored away the information in their enormous memories, so that every few months any interested astronomer could have a look at the accumulated statistics. These were now quite impressive.

It had taken more than a hundred and twenty years to collect the first thousand asteroids, since the discovery of Ceres, largest of these tiny worlds, on the very first day of the nineteenth century. Hundreds had been found and lost and found again; they existed in such swarms that one exasperated astronomer had christened them "vermin of the skies". He would have been appalled to know that SPACEGUARD was now keeping track of half a million.

Only the five giants—Ceres, Pallas, Juno, Eunomia and Vesta—were more than two hundred kilometres in diameter; the vast majority were merely oversized boulders that would fit into a small park. Almost all moved in orbits that lay beyond Mars; only the few that came far enough sunwards to be a possible danger to Earth were the concern of SPACEGUARD. And not one in a thousand of these, during the entire future history of the solar system, would pass within a million kilometres of Earth.

The object first catalogued as 31/439, according to the year and the order of its discovery, was detected while still outside the orbit of Jupiter. There was nothing unusual about its location; many asteroids went beyond Saturn before turning once more towards their distant master, the sun. And Thule II, most far-ranging of all, travelled so close to Uranus that it might well be a lost moon of that planet.

But a first radar contact at such a distance was unprecedented; clearly, 31/439 must be of exceptional size. From the strength of the echo, the computers deduced a diameter of at least forty kilometres; such a giant had not been discovered for a hundred years. That it had been overlooked for so long seemed incredible.

Then the orbit was calculated, and the mystery was resolved—to be replaced by a greater one. 31/439 was not travelling on a normal asteroidal path, along an ellipse which it retraced with clockwork precision every few years. It was a lonely wanderer between the stars, making its first and last visit to the solar system—for it was moving so swiftly that the gravitational field of the sun could never capture it. It would flash inwards past the orbits of Jupiter, Mars, Earth, Venus and Mercury, gaining speed as it did so, until it rounded the sun and headed out once again into the unknown.

It was at this point that the computers started flashing their "Hi there! We have something interesting" sign, and for the first time 31/439 came to the attention of human beings. There was a brief flurry of excitement at SPACEGUARD Headquarters, and the interstellar vagabond was quickly dignified by a name instead of a mere number. Long ago, the astronomers had exhausted Greek and Roman mythology; now they were working through the Hindu pantheon. And so 31/439 was christened Rama.

For a few days, the news media made a fuss of the visitor, but they were badly handicapped by the sparsity of information. Only two facts were known about Rama—its unusual orbit, and its approximate size. Even this was merely an educated guess, based upon the strength of the radar echo. Through the telescope, Rama still appeared as a faint, fifteenth magnitude star—much too small to show a visible disc. But as it plunged in towards the heart of the solar system, it would grow brighter and larger, month by month; before it vanished forever, the orbiting observatories would be able to gather more precise information about its shape and size. There was plenty of time, and perhaps during the next few years some space-ship on its ordinary business might be routed close enough to get good photographs. An actual rendezvous was most unlikely; the energy cost would be far too great to permit physical contact with an object cutting across the orbits of the planets at more than a hundred thousand kilometres an hour.

So the world soon forgot about Rama; but the astronomers did not. Their excitement grew with the passing months, as the new asteroid presented them with more and more puzzles.

First of all, there was the problem of Rama's light curve. It didn't have one.

All known asteroids, without exception, showed a slow variation in their brilliance, waxing and waning with a period of a few hours. It had been recognised for more than two centuries that this was an inevitable result of their spin, and their irregular shape. As they toppled end over end along their orbits the reflecting surfaces they presented to the sun were continually changing, and their brightness varied accordingly.

Rama showed no such changes. Either it was not spinning at all or it was perfectly symmetrical. Both explanations seemed equally unlikely.

There the matter rested for several months, because none of the big orbiting telescopes could be spared from their regular job of peering into the remote depths of the universe. Space astronomy was an expensive hobby, and time on a large instrument could easily cost a thousand dollars a minute. Dr. William Stenton would never have been able to grab the Farside two-hundred-metre reflector for a full quarter of an hour, if a more important programme had not been temporarily derailed by the failure of a fifty cent capacitor. One astronomer's bad luck was his good fortune.

Bill Stenton did not know what he had caught until the next day, when he was able to get computer time to process his results. Even when they were finally flashed on his display screen, it took him several minutes to understand what they meant.

The sunlight reflected from Rama was not, after all, absolutely constant in its intensity. There was a very small variation—hard to detect, but quite unmistakable, and extremely regular. Like all the other asteroids, Rama was indeed spinning. But whereas the normal "day" for an asteroid was several hours, Rama's was only four *minutes*.

Dr. Stenton did some quick calculations, and found it hard to believe the results. At its equator, this tiny world must be spinning at more than a thousand kilometres an hour; it would be rather unhealthy to attempt a landing anywhere except at the Poles. The centrifugal force at Rama's equator must be powerful enough to flick any loose objects away from it at an acceleration of almost one gravity. Rama was a rolling stone that could never have gathered any cosmic moss; it was surprising that such a body had managed to hold itself together, and had not long ago shattered into a million fragments.

An object forty kilometres across, with a rotation period of only four minutes—where did that fit into the astronomical scheme of things? Dr. Stenton was a somewhat imaginative man, a little too prone to jump to conclusions. He now jumped to one which gave him a very uncomfortable few minutes indeed.

The only specimen of the celestial zoo that fitted this description was a collapsed star. Perhaps Rama was a dead sun—a madly spinning sphere of neutronium, every cubic centimetre weighing billions of tons. . . .

At this point, there flashed briefly through Dr. Stenton's horrified mind the memory of that timeless classic, H. G. Wells' *The Star*. He had first read it as a very small boy, and it had helped to spark his interest in astronomy. Across more than two centuries of time, it had lost none of its magic and terror. He would never forget the images of hurricanes and tidal waves, of cities sliding into the sea, as that other visitor from the stars smashed into Jupiter and then fell sunwards past the Earth. True, the star that old Wells described was not cold, but incandescent, and wrought much of its destruction by heat. That scarcely mattered; even if Rama was a cold body, reflecting only the light of the sun, it could kill by gravity as easily as by fire.

Any stellar mass intruding into the solar system would completely distort the orbits of the planets. The Earth had only to move a few million kilometres sunwards—or starwards—for the delicate balance of climate to be destroyed. The Antarctic icecap could melt and flood all low-lying land; or the oceans could freeze and the whole world be locked in an eternal winter. Just a nudge in either direction would be enough. . . .

Then Dr. Stenton relaxed and breathed a sigh of relief. This was all nonsense; he should be ashamed of himself.

Rama could not possibly be made of condensed matter. No star-sized mass could penetrate so deeply into the solar system without producing disturbances which would have betrayed it long ago. The orbits of all the planets would have been affected; that, after all, was how Neptune, Pluto and Persephone had been discovered. No, it was utterly impossible for an object as massive as a dead sun to sneak up unobserved.

In a way, it was a pity. An encounter with a dark star would have been quite exciting.

While it lasted. . . .

CHAPTER III

Rama and Sita

THE EXTRAORDINARY MEETING of the Space Advisory Council was brief and stormy. Even in the twenty-second century, no way had yet been discovered of keeping elderly and conservative scientists from occupying crucial administrative positions. Indeed, it was doubted if the problem ever would be solved.

To make matters worse, the current Chairman of the SAC was Professor (Emeritus) Olaf Davidson, the distinguished astrophysicist. Professor Davidson was not very much interested in objects smaller than galaxies, and never bothered to conceal his prejudices. And though he had to admit that ninety per cent of his science was now based upon observations from space-borne instruments, he was not at all happy about it. No less than three times during his distinguished career, satellites specially launched to prove one of his pet theories had done precisely the opposite.

The question before the Council was straightforward enough. There was no doubt that Rama was an unusual object—but was it an important one? In a few months it would be gone forever, so there was little time in which to act. Opportunities missed now would never recur.

At rather a horrifying cost, a space-probe soon to be launched from Mars to beyond Neptune could be modified and sent on a high-speed trajectory to meet Rama. There was no hope of a rendezvous; it would be the fastest fly-by on record, for the two bodies would pass each other at two hundred thousand kilometres an hour. Rama would be observed intensively for only a few minutes—and in real close-up for less than a second. But with the right instrumentation, that would be long enough to settle many questions.

Although Professor Davidson took a very jaundiced view of the Neptune probe, it had already been approved and he saw no point in sending more good money after bad. He spoke eloquently on the follies of asteroid-chasing, and the urgent need for a new high-resolution interferometer on the Moon to prove the newly-revived Big Bang theory of creation, once and for all.

That was a grave tactical error, because the three most ardent supporters of the Modified Steady State Theory were also members of the Council. They secretly agreed with Professor Davidson that asteroid-chasing was a waste of money; nevertheless . . .

He lost by one vote.

Three months later the space-probe, rechristened Sita, was launched from Phobos, the inner moon of Mars. The flight time was seven weeks, and the instrument was switched to full power only five minutes before interception. Simultaneously, a cluster of camera pods was released, to sail past Rama so that it could be photographed from all sides.

The first images, from ten thousand kilometres away, brought to a halt the activities of all mankind. On a billion television screens, there appeared a tiny, featureless cylinder, growing rapidly second by second. By the time it had doubled its size, no one could pretend any longer that Rama was a natural object.

Its body was a cylinder so geometrically perfect that it might have been turned on a lathe—one with centres fifty kilometres apart. The two ends were quite flat, apart from some small structures at the centre of one face, and were twenty kilometres across; from a distance, when there was no sense of scale, Rama looked almost comically like an ordinary domestic boiler.

Rama grew until it filled the screen. Its surface was a dull, drab grey, as colourless as the Moon, and completely devoid of markings except at one point. Halfway along the cylinder there was a kilometre-wide stain or smear, as if something had once hit and splattered, ages ago.

There was no sign that the impact had done the slightest damage to Rama's spinning walls; but this mark had produced the slight fluctuation in brightness that had led to Stenton's discovery.

The images from the other cameras added nothing new. However, the trajectories their pods traced through Rama's minute gravitational field gave one other vital piece of information—the mass of the cylinder.

It was far too light to be a solid body. To nobody's great surprise, it was clear that Rama must be hollow.

The long-hoped-for, long-feared encounter had come at last. Mankind was about to receive its first visitor from the stars.

CHAPTER IV

Rendezvous

COMMANDER NORTON REMEMBERED those first TV trans-
missions, which he had replayed so many times, during the final minutes of
the rendezvous. But there was one thing no electronic image could possibly
convey—and that was Rama's overwhelming size.

He had never received such an impression when landing on a natural body
like the Moon or Mars. Those were worlds, and one expected them to be big.
Yet he had also landed on Jupiter VIII, which was slightly larger than Rama
—and that had seemed quite a small object.

It was very easy to resolve the paradox. His judgment was wholly altered
by the fact that this was an artifact, millions of times heavier than anything
that Man had ever put into space. The mass of Rama was at least ten million
million tons; to any spaceman, that was not only an awe-inspiring, but a
terrifying thought. No wonder that he sometimes felt a sense of insignificance,
and even depression, as that cylinder of sculptured, ageless metal filled more
and more of the sky.

There was also a sense of danger here, that was wholly novel to his experience. In every earlier landing he had known what to expect; there was
always the possibility of accident, but never of surprise. With Rama, surprise
was the only certainty.

Now *Endeavour* was hovering less than a thousand metres above the North
Pole of the cylinder, at the very centre of the slowly turning disc. This end
had been chosen because it was the one in sunlight; as Rama rotated, the
shadows of the short, enigmatic structures near the axis swept steadily across
the metal plain. The northern face of Rama was a gigantic sundial, measuring
out the swift passage of its four-minute day.

Landing a five thousand ton space-ship at the centre of a spinning disc was
the least of Commander Norton's worries. It was no different from docking
at the axis of a large space-station; *Endeavour*'s lateral jets had already given
her a matching spin, and he could trust Lieutenant Joe Calvert to put her
down as gently as a snowflake, with or without the aid of the nav computer.

"In three minutes," said Joe, without taking his eyes from the display,
"we'll know if it's made of antimatter."

Norton grinned, as he recalled some of the more hair-raising theories about
Rama's origin. If that unlikely speculation was true, in a few seconds there
would be the biggest bang since the solar system was formed. The total
annihilation of ten thousand tons would, briefly, provide the planets with a
second sun.

Yet the mission profile had allowed even for this remote contingency;
Endeavour had squirted Rama with one of her jets from a safe thousand
kilometres away. Nothing whatsoever had happened when the expanding

cloud of vapour arrived on target—and a matter-antimatter reaction involving even a few milligrams would have produced an awesome firework display.

Norton, like all space commanders, was a cautious man. He had looked long and hard at the northern face of Rama, choosing the point of touchdown. After much thought, he had decided to avoid the obvious spot—the exact centre, on the axis itself. A clearly marked circular disc, a hundred metres in diameter, was centred on the Pole, and Norton had a strong suspicion that this must be the outer seal of an enormous airlock. The creatures who had built this hollow world must have had some way of taking their ships inside. This was the logical place for the main entrance, and Norton thought it might be unwise to block the front door with his own vessel.

But this decision generated other problems. If *Endeavour* touched down even a few metres from the axis, Rama's rapid spin would start her sliding away from the Pole. At first, the centrifugal force would be very weak, but it would be continuous and inexorable. Commander Norton did not relish the thought of his ship slithering across the polar plain, gaining speed minute by minute until it was slung off into space at a thousand kilometres an hour when it reached the edge of the disc.

It was possible that Rama's minute gravitational field—about one thousandth of Earth's—might prevent this from happening. It would hold *Endeavour* against the plain with a force of several tons, and if the surface was sufficiently rough the ship might stay near the Pole. But Commander Norton had no intention of balancing an unknown frictional force against a quite certain centrifugal one.

Fortunately, Rama's designers had provided an answer. Equally spaced around the polar axis were three low, pillbox-shaped structures, about ten metres in diameter. If *Endeavour* touched down between any two of these, the centrifugal drift would fetch her up against them and she would be held firmly in place, like a ship glued against a quayside by the incoming waves.

"Contact in fifteen seconds," said Joe. As he tensed himself above the duplicate controls, which he hoped he would not have to touch, Commander Norton became acutely aware of all that had come to focus on this instant of time. This, surely, was the most momentous landing since the first touch-down on the Moon, a century and a half ago.

The grey pillboxes drifted slowly upwards outside the control port. There was the last hiss of a reaction jet, and a barely perceptible jar.

In the weeks that had passed, Commander Norton had often wondered what he would say at this moment. But now that it was upon him, History chose his words, and he spoke almost automatically, barely aware of the echo from the past:

"Rama Base. *Endeavour* has landed."

As recently as a month ago, he would never have believed it possible. The ship had been on a routine mission, checking and emplacing asteroid warning beacons, when the order had come. *Endeavour* was the only space-craft in the solar system which could possibly make a rendezvous with the intruder before it whipped round the sun and hurled itself back towards the stars. Even so, it had been necessary to rob three other ships of the Solar Survey, which were now drifting helplessly until tankers could refuel them. Norton feared that it would be a long time before the skippers of *Calypso*, *Beagle* and *Challenger* would speak to him again.

Even with all this extra propellant, it had been a long, hard chase; Rama was already inside the orbit of Venus when *Endeavour* caught up with her. No other ship could ever do so; this privilege was unique, and not a moment of the weeks ahead was to be wasted. A thousand scientists on Earth would have cheerfully mortgaged their souls for this opportunity; now they could only watch over the TV circuits, biting their lips and thinking how much better *they* could do the job. They were probably right, but there was no alternative. The inexorable laws of celestial mechanics had decreed that *Endeavour* was the first, and the last, of all Man's ships that would ever make contact with Rama.

The advice he was continually receiving from Earth did little to alleviate Norton's responsibility. If split-second decisions had to be made, no one could help him; the radio time-lag to Mission Control was already ten minutes, and increasing. He often envied the great navigators of the past, before the days of electronic communications, who could interpret their sealed orders without continual monitoring from headquarters. When *they* made mistakes, no one ever knew.

Yet at the same time, he was glad that some decisions could be delegated to Earth. Now that *Endeavour*'s orbit had coalesced with Rama's they were heading sunwards like a single body; in forty days they would reach perihelion, and pass within twenty million kilometres of the sun. That was far too close for comfort; long before then, *Endeavour* would have to use her remaining fuel to nudge herself into a safer orbit. They would have perhaps three weeks of exploring time, before they parted from Rama forever.

After that, the problem would be Earth's. *Endeavour* would be virtually helpless, speeding on an orbit which could make her the first ship to reach the stars—in approximately fifty thousand years. There was no need to worry, Mission Control had promised. Somehow, regardless of cost, *Endeavour* would be refuelled—even if it proved necessary to send tankers after her, and abandon them in space once they had transferred every gram of propellant. Rama was a prize worth any risk, short of a suicide mission.

And, of course, it might even come to that. Commander Norton had no illusions on this score. For the first time in a hundred years an element of total uncertainty had entered human affairs. Uncertainty was one thing that neither scientists nor politicians could tolerate. If that was the price of resolving it, *Endeavour* and her crew would be expendable.

CHAPTER V

First EVA

Rama was as silent as a tomb—which, perhaps, it was. No radio signals, on any frequency; no vibrations that the seismographs could pick up, apart from micro-tremors undoubtedly caused by the sun's increasing heat; no electrical currents; no radio-activity. It was almost ominously quiet; one might have expected that even an asteroid would be noisier.

What did we expect? Norton asked himself. A committee of welcome? He was not sure whether to be disappointed or relieved. The initiative, at any rate, appeared up to him.

His orders were to wait for twenty-four hours, then to go out and explore. Nobody slept much that first day; even the crew members not on duty spent their time monitoring the ineffectually probing instruments, or simply looking out of the observation ports at the starkly geometrical landscape. Is this world alive? they asked themselves, over and over again. Is it dead? Or is it merely sleeping?

On the first EVA, Norton took only one companion—Lieut.-Commander Karl Mercer, his tough and resourceful life-support officer. He had no intention of getting out of sight of the ship, and if there was any trouble, it was unlikely that a larger party would be safer. As a precaution, however, he had two more crew members, already suited up, standing by in the airlock.

The few grams of weight that Rama's combined gravitational and centrifugal fields gave them were neither help nor hindrance; they had to rely entirely on their jets. As soon as possible, Norton told himself, he would string a cat's-cradle of guide ropes between the ship and the pillboxes, so that they could move around without wasting propellants.

The nearest pillbox was only ten metres from the airlock, and Norton's first concern was to check that the contact had caused no damage to the ship. *Endeavour*'s hull was resting against the curving wall with a thrust of several tons, but the pressure was evenly distributed. Reassured, he began to drift around the circular structure, trying to determine its purpose.

Norton had travelled only a few metres when he came across an interruption in the smooth, apparently metallic wall. At first, he thought it was some peculiar decoration, for it seemed to serve no useful function. Six radial grooves, or slots, were deeply recessed in the metal, and lying in them were six crossed bars like the spokes of a rimless wheel, with a small hub at the centre. But there was no way in which the wheel could be turned, as it was embedded in the wall.

Then he noticed, with growing excitement, that there were deeper recesses at the ends of the spokes, nicely shaped to accepting a clutching hand (claw? tentacle?). If one stood *so*, bracing against the wall, and pulled on the spoke so . . .

Smooth as silk, the wheel slid out of the wall. To his utter astonishment—for he had been virtually certain that any moving parts would have become vacuum-welded ages ago—Norton found himself holding a spoked wheel. He might have been the captain of some old windjammer standing at the helm of his ship.

He was glad that his helmet sunshade did not allow Mercer to read his expression.

He was startled, but also angry with himself; perhaps he had already made his first mistake. Were alarms now sounding inside Rama, and had his thoughtless action already triggered some implacable mechanism?

But *Endeavour* reported no change; its sensors still detected nothing but faint thermal crepitations and his own movements.

"Well, Skipper—are you going to turn it?"

Norton thought once more of his instructions. "Use your own discretion, but proceed with caution." If he checked every single move with Mission Control, he would never get anywhere.

"What's your diagnosis, Karl?" he asked Mercer.

"It's obviously a manual control for an airlock—probably an emergency back-up system in case of power failure. I can't imagine *any* technology, however advanced, that wouldn't take such precautions."

"And it would be fail-safe," Norton told himself. "It could only be operated if there was no possible danger to the system. . . ."

He grasped two opposing spokes of the windlass, braced his feet against the ground, and tested the wheel. It did not budge.

"Give me a hand," he asked Mercer. Each took a spoke; exerting their utmost strength, they were unable to produce the slightest movement.

Of course, there was no reason to suppose that clocks and corkscrews on Rama turned in the same direction as they did on Earth. . . .

"Let's try the other way," suggested Mercer.

This time, there was no resistance. The wheel rotated almost effortlessly through a full circle. Then, very smoothly, it took up the load.

Half a metre away, the curving wall of the pillbox started to move, like a slowly opening clamshell. A few particles of dust, driven by wisps of escaping air, streamed outwards like dazzling diamonds as the brilliant sunlight caught them.

The road to Rama lay open.

CHAPTER VI

Committee

IT HAD BEEN a serious mistake, Dr. Bose often thought, to put the United Planets Headquarters on the Moon. Inevitably, Earth tended to dominate the proceedings—as it dominated the landscape beyond the dome. If they *had* to build here, perhaps they should have gone to Farside, where that hypnotic disc never shed its rays. . . .

But, of course, it was much too late to change, and in any case there was no real alternative. Whether the colonies liked it or not, Earth would be the cultural and economic overlord of the solar system for centuries to come.

Dr. Bose had been born on Earth, and had not emigrated to Mars until he was thirty, so he felt that he could view the political situation fairly dispassionately. He knew now that he would never return to his home planet, even though it was only five hours away by shuttle. At 115, he was in perfect health, but he could not face the reconditioning needed to accustom him to three times the gravity he had enjoyed for most of his life. He was exiled forever from the world of his birth; not being a sentimental man, this had never depressed him unduly.

What did depress him sometimes was the need for dealing, year after year, with the same familiar faces. The marvels of medicine were all very well, and certainly he had no desire to put back the clock—but there were men around this conference table with whom he had worked for more than half a century. He knew exactly what they would say and how they would vote on any given subject. He wished that, some day, one of them would do something totally unexpected—even something quite crazy.

And probably they felt exactly the same way about him. . . .

The Rama committee was still manageably small, though doubtless that would soon be rectified. His six colleagues—the UP representatives for Mercury, Earth, Luna, Ganymede, Titan and Triton—were all present in the flesh. They had to be; electronic diplomacy was not possible over solar system distances. Some elder statesmen, accustomed to the instantaneous communications which Earth had long taken for granted, had never reconciled themselves to the fact that radio waves took minutes, or even hours, to journey across the gulfs between the planets. "Can't you scientists do something about it?" they had been heard to complain bitterly, when told that face-to-face conversation was impossible between Earth and any of its remoter children. Only the Moon had that barely acceptable one-and-a-half-second delay—with all the political and psychological consequences which it implied. Because of this fact of astronomical life, the Moon—and *only* the Moon—would always be a suburb of Earth.

Also present in person were three of the specialists who had been co-opted to the Committee. Professor Davidson, the astronomer, was an old acquaintance; today, he did not seem his usual irascible self. Dr. Bose knew nothing of the infighting that had preceded the launch of the first probe to Rama, but the professor's colleagues had not let him forget it.

Dr. Thelma Price was familiar through her numerous television appearances, though she had first made her reputation fifty years ago during the archaeological explosion that had followed the draining of that vast marine museum, the Mediterranean.

Dr. Bose could still recall the excitement of that time, when the lost treasures of the Greeks, Romans and a dozen other civilisations were restored to the light of day. That was one of the few occasions when he was sorry to be living on Mars.

The exobiologist, Carlisle Perera, was another obvious choice; so was Dennis Solomons, the science historian. Dr. Bose was slightly less happy about the presence of Conrad Taylor, the celebrated anthropologist, who had made his reputation by uniquely combining scholarship and eroticism in his study of puberty rites in late twentieth-century Beverly Hills.

No one, however, could possibly have disputed the right of Sir Lewis Sands to be on the committee. A man whose knowledge was matched only by his urbanity, Sir Lewis was reputed to lose his composure only when called the Arnold Toynbee of his age.

The great historian was not present in person; he stubbornly refused to leave Earth, even for so momentous a meeting as this. His stereo image, indistinguishable from reality, apparently occupied the chair to Dr. Bose's right; as if to complete the illusion, someone had placed a glass of water in front of him. Dr. Bose considered that this sort of technological *tour de force* was an unnecessary gimmick, but it was surprising how many undeniably great men were childishly delighted to be in two places at once. Sometimes this electronic miracle produced comic disasters: he had been at one diplomatic reception where somebody had tried to walk through a stereogram—and discovered, too late, that it was the real person. And it was even funnier to watch projections trying to shake hands. . . .

His Excellency the Ambassador for Mars to the United Planets called his wandering thoughts to order, cleared his throat, and said: "Gentlemen, the committee is now in session. I think I am correct in saying that this is a gathering of unique talents, assembled to deal with a unique situation. The directive that the Secretary-General has given us is to evaluate that situation, and to advise Commander Norton when necessary."

This was a miracle of over-simplification, and everyone knew it. Unless there was a real emergency, the Committee might never be in direct contact with Commander Norton—if, indeed, he ever heard of its existence. For the Committee was a temporary creation of the United Planets' Science Organisation, reporting through its Director to the Secretary-General. It was true that the Space Survey was part of the UP—but on the *Operations*, not the Science side. In theory, this should not make much difference; there was no reason why the Rama Committee—or anyone else for that matter—should not call up Commander Norton and offer helpful advice.

But Deep Space Communications are expensive. *Endeavour* could be contacted only through PLANETCOM, which was an autonomous corporation, famous for the strictness and efficiency of its accounting. It took a long time to establish a line of credit with PLANETCOM; somewhere, someone was working on this; but at the moment, PLANETCOM's hard-hearted computers did not recognise the existence of the Rama Committee.

"This Commander Norton," said Sir Robert Mackay, the Ambassador for Earth. "He has a tremendous responsibility. What sort of person is he?"

"I can answer that," said Professor Davidson, his fingers flying over the keyboard of his memory pad. He frowned at the screenful of information, and started to make an instant synopsis.

"William Tsien Norton, born 2077, Brisbane, Oceana. Educated Sydney, Bombay, Houston. Then five years at Astrograd, specialising in propulsion. Commissioned 2102. Rose through usual ranks—Lieutenant on the Third Persephone expedition, distinguished himself during fifteenth attempt to establish base on Venus . . . um . . . um . . . exemplary record . . . dual citizenship, Earth and Mars . . . wife and one child in Brisbane, wife and *two* in Port Lowell, with option on third. . . ."

"Wife?" asked Taylor innocently.

"No, child of course," snapped the Professor, before he caught the grin on the other's face. Mild laughter rippled round the table, though the overcrowded terrestrials looked more envious than amused. After a century of determined effort, Earth had still failed to get its population below the target of one billion. . . .

". . . appointed commanding officer Solar Survey Research Vessel *Endeavour*. First voyage to retrograde satellites of Jupiter . . . um, that was a tricky one . . . on asteroid mission when ordered to prepare for this operation . . . managed to beat deadline. . . ."

The professor cleared the display and looked up at his colleagues.

"I think we were extremely lucky, considering that he was the only man available at such short notice. We might have had the usual run-of-the-mill captain." He sounded as if he was referring to the typical peg-legged scourge of the spaceways, pistol in one hand and cutlass in the other.

"The record only proves that he's competent," objected the Ambassador from Mercury (population: 112,500 but growing). "How will he react in a wholly novel situation like this?"

On Earth, Sir Lewis Sands cleared his throat. A second and a half later, he did so on the Moon.

"Not exactly a novel situation," he reminded the Hermian, "even though it's three centuries since it last occurred. If Rama is dead, or unoccupied—and so far all the evidence suggests that it is—Norton is in the position of an archaeologist discovering the ruins of an extinct culture." He bowed politely to Dr. Price, who nodded in agreement. "Obvious examples are Schliemann at Troy or Mouhot at Angkor Vat. The danger is minimal, though of course accident can never be completely ruled out."

"But what about the booby traps and trigger mechanisms these Pandora people have been talking about?" asked Dr. Price.

"Pandora?" asked the Hermian Ambassador quickly. "What's that?"

"It's a crackpot movement," explained Sir Robert, with as much embarrassment as a diplomat was ever likely to show, "which is convinced that Rama is a grave potential danger. A box that shouldn't be opened, you know." He doubted if the Hermian *did* know: classical studies were not encouraged on Mercury.

"Pandora—paranoia," snorted Conrad Taylor. "Oh, of course, such things are *conceivable*, but why should any intelligent race want to play childish tricks?"

"Well, even ruling out such unpleasantness," Sir Robert continued, "we still have the much more ominous possibility of an active, inhabited Rama. Then the situation is one of an encounter between two cultures—at very different technological levels. Pizzaro and the Incas. Peary and the Japanese. Europe and Africa. Almost invariably, the consequences have been disastrous —for one or both parties. I'm not making any recommendations: I'm merely pointing out precedents."

"Thank you, Sir Robert," replied Dr. Bose. It was a mild nuisance, he thought, having two "Sirs" on one small committee; in these latter days, knighthood was an honour which few Englishmen escaped. "I'm sure we've all thought of these alarming possibilities. But if the creatures inside Rama are —er—malevolent—will it really make the slightest difference what we do?"

"They might ignore us if we go away."

"What—after they've travelled billions of miles and thousands of years?"

The argument had reached the take-off point, and was now self-sustaining. Dr. Bose sat back in his chair, said very little, and waited for the consensus to emerge.

It was just as he had predicted. Everyone agreed that, once he had opened the first door, it was inconceivable that Commander Norton should not open the second.

CHAPTER VII

Two Wives

IF HIS WIVES ever compared his videograms, Commander Norton thought with more amusement than concern, it would involve him in a lot of extra work. Now, he could make one long 'gram and dupe it, adding only brief personal messages and endearments before shooting the almost identical copies off to Mars and Earth.

Of course, it was highly unlikely that his wives ever would do such a thing; even at the concessionary rates allowed to space-men's families, it would be expensive. And there would be no point in it; his families were on excellent terms with each other, and exchanged the usual greetings on birthdays and anniversaries. Yet, on the whole, perhaps it was just as well that the girls had never met, and probably never would. Myrna had been born on Mars and so could not tolerate the high gravity of Earth. And Caroline hated even the twenty-five minutes of the longest possible terrestrial journey.

"Sorry I'm a day late with this transmission," said the Commander after he had finished the general-purpose preliminaries, "but I've been away from the ship for the last thirty hours, believe it or not. . . .

"Don't be alarmed—everything is under control, going perfectly. It's taken us two days, but we're almost through the airlock complex. We could have done it in a couple of hours, if we'd known what we do now. But we took no chances, sent remote cameras ahead, and cycled all the locks a dozen times to make sure they wouldn't seize up behind us—*after* we'd gone through. . . .

"Each lock is a simple revolving cylinder with a slot on one side. You go in through this opening, crank the cylinder round a hundred and eighty degrees —and the slot then matches up with another door so that you can step out of it. Or float, in this case.

"The Ramans really made sure of things. There are three of these cylinder-locks, one after the other just inside the outer hull and below the entry pill-box. I can't imagine how even one would fail, unless someone blew it up with explosives, but if it did, there would be a second back-up, and then a third. . . .

"And *that's* only the beginning. The final lock opens into a straight corridor, almost half a kilometre long. It looks clean and tidy, like everything else we've seen; every few metres there are small ports that probably held lights, but now everything is completely black and, I don't mind telling you, scary. There are also two parallel slots, about a centimetre wide, cut in the walls and running the whole length of the tunnel. We suspect that some kind of shuttle runs inside these, to tow equipment—or people—back and forth. It would save us a lot of trouble if we could get it working. . . .

"I mentioned that the tunnel was half a kilometre long. Well, from our seismic soundings we knew that's about the thickness of the shell, so obviously we were almost through it. And at the end of the tunnel we weren't surprised to find another of those cylindrical airlocks.

"Yes, *and* another. *And* another. These people seem to have done everything in threes. We're in the final lock chamber now, awaiting the O.K. from Earth before we go through. The interior of Rama is only a few metres away. I'll be a lot happier when the suspense is over.

"You know Jerry Kirchoff, my Exec, who's got such a library of *real* books that he can't afford to emigrate from Earth? Well, Jerry told me about a situation just like this, back at the beginning of the twenty-first—no, twentieth century. An archaeologist found the tomb of an Egyptian king, the first one that hadn't been looted by robbers. His workmen took months to dig their way in, chamber by chamber, until they came to the final wall. Then they broke through the masonry, and he held out a lantern and pushed his head inside. He found himself looking into a whole roomful of treasure—incredible stuff, gold and jewels. . . .

"Perhaps this place is also a tomb; it seems more and more likely. Even now, there's still not the slightest sound, or hint of any activity. Well, tomorrow we should know."

Commander Norton switched the recorder to HOLD. What else, he wondered, should he say about the work before he began the separate personal messages to his families? Normally, he never went into so much detail, but these circumstances were scarcely normal. This might be the last 'gram he would ever send to those he loved; he owed it to them to explain what he was doing.

By the time they saw these images, and heard these words, he would be inside Rama—for better or for worse.

CHAPTER VIII

Through the Hub

NEVER BEFORE HAD Norton felt so strongly his kinship with that long dead Egyptologist. Not since Howard Carter had first peered into the tomb of Tutankhamen could any man have known a moment such as this—yet the comparison was almost laughably ludicrous.

Tutankhamen had been buried only yesterday—not even four thousand years ago; Rama might be older than mankind. That little tomb in the Valley of the Kings could have been lost in the corridors through which they had already passed, yet the space that lay beyond this final seal was at least a million times greater. And as for the treasure it might hold—that was beyond imagination.

No one had spoken over the radio circuits for at least five minutes; the well-trained team had not even reported verbally when all the checks were complete. Mercer had simply given him the O.K. sign and waved him towards the open tunnel. It was as if everyone realised that this was a moment for History, not to be spoiled by unnecessary small-talk. That suited Commander Norton, for at the moment he too had nothing to say. He flicked on the beam of his flashlight, triggered his jets, and drifted slowly down the short corridor, trailing his safety line behind him. Only seconds later, he was inside.

Inside *what*? All before him was total darkness; not a glimmer of light was reflected back from the beam. He had expected this, but he had not really believed it. All the calculations had shown that the far wall was tens of kilometres away; now his eyes told him that this was indeed the truth. As he drifted slowly into that darkness, he felt a sudden need for the reassurance of his safety line, stronger than any he had ever experienced before, even on his very first EVA. And that was ridiculous; he had looked out across the light-years and the megaparsecs without vertigo; why should he be disturbed by a few cubic kilometres of emptiness?

He was still queasily brooding over this problem when the momentum damper at the end of the line braked him gently to a halt, with a barely perceptible rebound. He swept the vainly-probing beam of the flashlight down from the nothingness ahead, to examine the surface from which he had emerged.

He might have been hovering over the centre of a small crater, which was itself a dimple in the base of a much larger one. On either side rose a complex of terraces and ramps—all geometrically precise and obviously artificial—which extended for as far as the beam could reach. About a hundred metres away he could see the exit of the other two airlock systems, identical with this one.

And that was all. There was nothing particularly exotic or alien about the scene: in fact, it bore a considerable resemblance to an abandoned mine. Norton felt a vague sense of disappointment; after all this effort, there should have been some dramatic, even transcendental revelation. Then he reminded himself that he could see only a couple of hundred metres. The darkness beyond his field of view might yet contain more wonders than he cared to face.

He reported briefly to his anxiously-waiting companions, then added: "I'm sending out the flare—two minutes' delay. Here goes."

With all his strength, he threw the little cylinder straight upwards—or outwards—and started to count seconds as it dwindled along the beam. Before he had reached the quarter-minute it was out of sight; when he had got to a hundred he shielded his eyes and aimed the camera. He had always been good at estimating time; he was only two seconds off when the world exploded with light. And this time, there was no cause for disappointment.

Even the millions of candlepower of the flare could not light up the whole of this enormous cavity, but now he could see enough to grasp its plan and appreciate its titanic scale. He was at one end of a hollow cylinder at least ten kilometres wide, and of indefinite length. From his viewpoint at the central axis he could see such a mass of detail on the curving walls surrounding him that his mind could not absorb more than a minute fraction of it; he was looking at the landscape of an entire world by a single flash of lightning, and he tried by a deliberate effort of will to freeze the image in his mind.

All round him, the terraced slopes of the "crater" rose up until they merged into the solid wall that rimmed the sky. No—that impression was false; he must discard the instincts both of the Earth and of space, and reorientate himself to a new system of co-ordinates.

He was not at the lowest point of this strange, inside-out world, but the highest. From here, all directions were *down*, not up. If he moved away from this central axis, towards the curving wall which he must no longer think of as a wall, gravity would steadily increase. When he reached the inside surface of the cylinder, he could stand upright on it at any point, feet towards the stars and head towards the centre of the spinning drum. The concept was familiar enough; since the earliest dawn of spaceflight, centrifugal force had been used to simulate gravity. It was only the scale of this application which was so overwhelming, so shocking. The largest of all space-stations, Syncsat Five, was less than two hundred metres in diameter. It would take some little while to grow accustomed to one a hundred times that size.

The tube of landscape which enclosed him was mottled with areas of light and shade that could have been forests, fields, frozen lakes or towns; the distance, and the fading illumination of the flare, made identification impossible. Narrow lines that could be highways, canals, or well-trained rivers formed a faintly visible geometrical network; and far along the cylinder, at the very limit of vision, was a band of deeper darkness. It formed a complete circle, ringing the interior of this world, and Norton suddenly recalled the myth of Oceanus, the sea which, the ancients believed, surrounded the Earth.

Here, perhaps, was an even stranger sea—not circular, but *cylindrical*. Before it became frozen in the interstellar night, did it have waves and tides and currents—and fish?

The flare guttered and died; the moment of revelation was over. But Norton knew that as long as he lived these images would be burned on his mind. Whatever discoveries the future might bring, they could never erase this first impression. And History could never take from him the privilege of being the first of all mankind to gaze upon the works of an alien civilisation.

CHAPTER IX

Reconnaissance

"WE HAVE NOW launched five long-delay flares down the axis of the cylinder, and so have a good photo-coverage of its full length. All the main features are mapped; though there are very few that we can identify, we've given them provisional names.

"The interior cavity is fifty kilometres long and sixteen wide. The two ends are bowl-shaped, with rather complicated geometries. We've called ours the Northern Hemisphere and are establishing our first base here at the axis.

"Radiating away from the central hub, 120 degrees apart, are three ladders that are almost a kilometre long. They all end at a terrace or ring-shaped plateau, that runs right round the bowl. And leading on from *that*, continuing the direction of the ladders, are three enormous stairways, which go all the way down to the plain. If you imagine an umbrella with only three ribs, equally spaced, you'll have a good idea of this end of Rama.

"Each of those ribs is a stairway, very deep near the axis and then slowly flattening out as it approaches the plain below. The stairways—we've called them Alpha, Beta, Gamma—aren't continuous, but break at five more circular terraces. We estimate there must be between twenty and thirty thousand steps ... presumably they were only used for emergencies, since it's inconceivable that the Ramans—or whatever we're going to call them—had no better way of reaching the axis of their world.

"The Southern Hemisphere looks quite different; for one thing, it has no stairways, and no flat central hub. Instead, there's a huge spike—kilometres long—jutting along the axis, with six smaller ones around it. The whole arrangement is very odd, and we can't imagine what it means.

"The fifty-kilometre-long cylindrical section between the two bowls we've called the Central Plain. It may seem crazy to use the word 'plain' to describe something so obviously curved, but we feel it's justified. It will appear flat to us when we get down there—just as the interior of a bottle must seem flat to an ant crawling round inside it.

"The most striking feature of the Central Plain is the ten-kilometre-wide dark band running completely round it at the half-way mark. It looks like ice, so we've christened it the cylindrical sea. Right out in the middle there's a large oval island, about ten kilometres long and three wide, and covered with tall structures. Because it reminds us of Old Manhattan, we've called it New York. Yet I don't think it's a city; it seems more like an enormous factory or chemical processing plant.

"But there are some cities—or at any rate, towns. At least six of them; if they were built for human beings, they could each hold about fifty thousand people. We've called them Rome, Peking, Paris, Moscow, London, Tokyo. ... They are linked with highways and something that seems to be a rail system.

"There must be enough material for centuries of research in this frozen carcass of a world. We've four thousand square kilometres to explore, and only a few weeks to do it in. I wonder if we'll ever learn the answer to the two mysteries that have been haunting me ever since we got inside; who were they—*and what went wrong*?"

The recording ended. On Earth and Moon, the members of the Rama Committee relaxed, then started to examine the maps and photographs spread in front of them. Though they had already studied these for many hours, Commander Norton's voice added a dimension which no pictures could convey. He had actually been there—had looked with his own eyes across this extraordinary inside-out world, during the brief moments while its age-long night had been illuminated by the flares. And he was the man who would lead any expedition to explore it.

"Dr. Perera, I believe you have some comments to make?"

Ambassador Bose wondered briefly if he should have first given the floor to Professor Davidson, as senior scientist and the only astronomer. But the old cosmologist still seemed to be in a mild state of shock, and was clearly out of his element. All his professional career, he had looked upon the universe as an arena for the titanic impersonal forces of gravitation, magnetism, radiation; he had never believed that life played an important role in the scheme of things, and regarded its appearance on Earth, Mars and Jupiter as an accidental aberration.

But now there was proof that life not only existed outside the solar system, but had scaled heights far beyond anything that man had achieved, or could hope to reach for centuries to come. Moreover, the discovery of Rama challenged another dogma that Professor Olaf had preached for years. When pressed, he would reluctantly admit that life probably did exist in other star systems—but it was absurd, he had always maintained, to imagine that it could ever cross the interstellar gulfs. . . .

Perhaps the Ramans had indeed failed, if Commander Norton was correct in believing that their world was now a tomb. But at least they had attempted the feat, on a scale which indicated a high confidence in the outcome. If such a thing had happened once, it must surely have happened many times in this Galaxy of a hundred thousand million suns . . . and someone, somewhere, would eventually succeed.

This was the thesis which, without proof but with considerable arm-waving, Dr. Carlisle Perera had been preaching for years. He was now a very happy man, though also a most frustrated one. Rama had spectacularly confirmed his views—but he could never set foot inside it, or even see it with his own eyes. If the devil had suddenly appeared and offered him the gift of instantaneous teleportation, he would have signed the contract without bothering to look at the small print.

"Yes, Mr. Ambassador, I think I have some information of interest. What we have here is undoubtedly a 'Space Ark'. It's an old idea in the astronautical literature; I've been able to trace it back to the British physicist J. D. Bernal, who proposed this method of interstellar colonisation in a book published in 1929—yes, two hundred years ago. And the great Russian pioneer Tsiolkovski put forward somewhat similar proposals even earlier.

"If you want to go from one star system to another you have a number of choices. Assuming that the speed of light is an absolute limit—and that's *still* not completely settled, despite anything you may have heard to the contrary"—there was an indignant sniff, but no formal protest from Professor Davidson—"you can make a fast trip in a small vessel, or a slow journey in a giant one.

"There seems no technical reason why space-craft cannot reach ninety per cent, or more, of the speed of light. That would mean a travel time of five to ten years between neighbouring stars—tedious, perhaps, but not impracticable, especially for creatures whose life-spans might be measured in centuries. One can imagine voyages of this duration, carried out in ships not much larger than ours.

"But perhaps such speeds are impossible, with reasonable payloads; remember, you have to carry the fuel to slow down at the end of the voyage, even if you're on a one-way trip. So it may make more sense to take your time—ten thousand, a hundred thousand years. . . .

"Bernal and others thought this could be done with mobile worldlets a few kilometres across, carrying thousands of passengers on journeys that would last for generations. Naturally, the system would have to be rigidly closed, recycling all food, air and other expendables. But, of course, that's just how the Earth operates—on a slightly larger scale.

"Some writers suggested that these Space Arks should be built in the form of concentric spheres; others proposed hollow, spinning cylinders so that centrifugal force could provide artificial gravity—exactly what we've found in Rama——"

Professor Davidson could not tolerate this sloppy talk.

"No such thing as centrifugal *force*. It's an engineer's phantom. There's only inertia."

"You're quite right, of course," admitted Perera, "though it might be hard to convince a man who'd just been slung off a carousel. But mathematical rigour seems unnecessary——"

"Hear, hear," interjected Dr. Bose, with some exasperation. "We all know what you mean, or think we do. Please don't destroy our illusions."

"Well, I was merely pointing out that there's nothing conceptually novel about Rama, though its size is startling. Men have imagined such things for two hundred years.

"Now I'd like to address myself to another question. Exactly how long has Rama been travelling through space?

"We now have a very precise determination of its orbit and its velocity. Assuming that it's made no navigational changes, we can trace its position back for millions of years. We expected that it would be coming from the direction of a near-by star—but that isn't the case at all.

"It's more than *two hundred thousand years* since Rama passed near any star, and that particular one turns out to be an irregular variable—about the most unsuitable sun you could imagine for an inhabited solar system. It has a brightness range of over fifty to one; any planets would be alternately baked and frozen every few years."

"A suggestion," put in Dr. Price. "Perhaps that explains everything. Maybe this was once a normal sun and became unstable. That's why the Ramans had to find a new one."

Dr. Perera admired the old archaeologist, so he let her down lightly. But what would *she* say, he wondered, if he started pointing out the instantly obvious in her own speciality. . . .

"We did consider that," he said gently. "But if our present theories of stellar evolution are correct, this star could *never* have been stable—could never have had life-bearing planets. So Rama has been cruising through space for at least two hundred thousand years, and perhaps for more than a million.

"Now it's cold and dark and apparently dead, and I think I know why. The Ramans may have had no choice—perhaps they were indeed fleeing from some disaster—but they miscalculated.

"No closed ecology can be one hundred per cent efficient; there is always waste, loss—some degradation of the environment, and build-up of pollutants. It may take billions of years to poison and wear out a planet—but it will happen in the end. The oceans will dry up, the atmosphere will leak away. . . .

"By our standards, Rama is enormous—yet it is still a very tiny planet.

My calculations, based on the leakage through its hull, and some reasonable guesses about the rate of biological turnover, indicate that its ecology could only survive for about a thousand years. At the most, I'll grant ten thousand. . . .

"That would be long enough, at the speed Rama is travelling, for a transit between the closely-packed suns in the heart of the Galaxy. But not out here, in the scattered population of the spiral arms. Rama is a ship which exhausted its provisions before it reached its goal. It's a derelict, drifting among the stars.

"There's just one serious objection to this theory, and I'll raise it before anybody else does. Rama's orbit is aimed so accurately at the solar system that coincidence seems ruled out. In fact, I'd say it's now heading much too close to the sun for comfort; *Endeavour* will have to break away long before perihelion, to avoid overheating.

"I don't pretend to understand this. Perhaps, there may be some form of automatic terminal guidance still operating, steering Rama to the nearest suitable star ages after its builders are dead.

"And they *are* dead; I'll stake my reputation on that. All the samples we've taken from the interior are absolutely sterile—we've not found a single micro-organism. As for the talk you may have heard about suspended animation, you can ignore it. There are fundamental reasons why hibernation techniques will only work for a very few centuries—and we're dealing with time spans a thousand-fold longer.

"So the Pandorans and their sympathisers have nothing to worry about. For my part, I'm sorry. It would have been wonderful to have met another intelligent species.

"But at least we have answered one ancient question. We are not alone. The stars will never again be the same to us."

CHAPTER X

Descent into Darkness

COMMANDER NORTON WAS sorely tempted—but, as Captain, his first duty was to his ship. If anything went badly wrong on this initial probe, he might have to run for it.

So that left his second officer, Lieut.-Commander Mercer, as the obvious choice. Norton willingly admitted that Karl was better suited for the mission. *The* authority on life-support systems, Mercer had written some of the standard text-books on the subject. He had personally checked out innumerable types of equipment, often under hazardous conditions, and his biofeedback control was famous. At a moment's notice he could cut his pulse-rate by fifty per cent, and reduce respiration to almost zero for up to ten minutes. These useful little tricks had saved his life on more than one occasion.

Yet despite his great ability and intelligence, he was almost wholly lacking in imagination. To him the most dangerous experiments or missions were simply jobs that had to be done. He never took unnecessary risks, and had no use at all for what was commonly regarded as courage.

The two mottoes on his desk summed up his philosophy of life. One asked WHAT HAVE YOU FORGOTTEN? The other said HELP STAMP OUT BRAVERY. The fact that he was widely regarded as the bravest man in the Fleet was the only thing that ever made him angry.

Given Mercer, that automatically selected the next man—his inseparable companion Lieut. Joe Calvert. It was hard to see what the two had in common; the lightly-built, rather highly strung navigating officer was ten years younger than his stolid and imperturbable friend, who certainly did not share his passionate interest in the art of the primitive cinema.

But no one can predict where lightning will strike, and years ago Mercer and Calvert had established an apparently stable liaison. That was common enough; much more unusual was the fact that they also shared a wife back on Earth, who had borne each of them a child. Commander Norton hoped that he could meet her one day; she must be a very remarkable woman. The triangle had lasted for at least five years, and still seemed to be an equilateral one.

Two men were not enough for an exploring team; long ago it had been found that three was the optimum—for if one man was lost, two might still escape where a single survivor would be doomed. After a good deal of thought, Norton had chosen Technical Sergeant Willard Myron. A mechanical genius who could make anything work—or design something better if it wouldn't— Myron was the ideal man to identify alien pieces of equipment. On a long Sabbatical from his regular job as Associate Professor at Astrotech, the Sergeant had refused to accept a commission on the grounds that he did not wish to block the promotion of more deserving career officers. No one took this explanation very seriously and it was generally agreed that Will rated zero for ambition. He might make it to Space Sergeant, but would never be a full professor. Myron, like countless NCOs before him, had discovered the ideal compromise between power and responsibility.

As they drifted through the last airlock and floated out along the weightless axis of Rama, Lieut. Calvert found himself, as he so often did, in the middle of a movie flashback. He sometimes wondered if he should attempt to cure himself of this habit, but he could not see that it had any disadvantages. It could make even the dullest situations interesting and—who could tell?—one day it might save his life. He would remember what Fairbanks or Connery or Hiroshi had done in similar circumstances....

This time, he was about to go over the top, in one of the early-twentieth-century wars; Mercer was the sergeant, leading a three-man patrol on a night raid into no-man's-land. It was not too difficult to imagine that they were at the bottom of an immense shell-crater, though one that had somehow become neatly tailored into a series of ascending terraces. The crater was flooded with light from three widely spaced plasma-arcs, which gave an almost shadowless illumination over the whole interior. But beyond that—over the rim of the most distant terrace—was darkness and mystery.

In his mind's eye, Calvert knew perfectly well what lay there. First there was the flat circular plain over a kilometre across. Trisecting it into three equal parts, and looking very much like broad railroad tracks, were three wide ladders, their rungs recessed into the surface so that they would provide no obstruction to anything sliding over it. Since the arrangement was completely symmetrical, there was no reason to choose one ladder rather than another; that nearest to Airlock Alpha had been selected purely as a matter of convenience.

Though the rungs of the ladders were uncomfortably far apart, that presented no problem. Even at the rim of the hub, half a kilometre from the axis, gravity was still barely one thirtieth of Earth's. Although they were carrying almost a hundred kilos of equipment and life-support gear, they would still be able to move easily hand-over-hand.

Commander Norton and the back-up team accompanied them along the guide ropes that had been stretched from Airlock Alpha to the rim of the crater; then, beyond the range of the floodlights, the darkness of Rama lay before them. All that could be seen in the dancing beams of the helmet lights was the first few hundred metres of the ladder, dwindling away across a flat and otherwise featureless plain.

And now, Karl Mercer told himself, I have to make my first decision. Am I going *up* that ladder, or *down* it?

The question was not a trivial one. They were still essentially in zero gravity, and the brain could select any reference system it pleased. By a simple effort of will, Mercer could convince himself that he was looking out across a horizontal plain, or up the face of a vertical wall, or over the edge of a sheer cliff. Not a few astronauts had experienced grave psychological problems by choosing the wrong co-ordinates when they started on a complicated job.

Mercer was determined to go head-first, for any other mode of locomotion would be awkward; moreover, this way he could more easily see what was in front of him. For the first few hundred metres, therefore, he would imagine he was climbing upwards; only when the increasing pull of gravity made it impossible to maintain the illusion would he switch his mental directions one hundred and eighty degrees.

He grasped the first rung and gently propelled himself along the ladder. Movement was as effortless as swimming along the sea bed—more so, in fact, for there was no backward drag of water. It was so easy that there was a temptation to go too fast, but Mercer was much too experienced to hurry in a situation as novel as this.

In his earphones, he could hear the regular breathing of his two companions. He needed no other proof that they were in good shape, and wasted no time in conversation. Though he was tempted to look back, he decided not to risk it until they had reached the platform at the end of the ladder.

The rungs were spaced a uniform half-metre apart, and for the first portion of the climb Mercer missed the alternate ones. But he counted them carefully, and at around two hundred noticed the first distinct sensations of weight. The spin of Rama was starting to make itself felt.

At rung four hundred, he estimated that his apparent weight was about five kilos. This was no problem, but it was now getting hard to pretend that he was climbing, when he was being firmly dragged *upwards*.

The five hundredth rung seemed a good place to pause. He could feel the muscles in his arms responding to the unaccustomed exercise, even though Rama was now doing all the work and he had merely to guide himself.

"Everything O.K., Skipper," he reported. "We're just passing the half-way mark. Joe, Will—any problems?"

"I'm fine—what are you stopping for?" Joe Calvert answered.

"Same here," added Sergeant Myron. "But watch out for the Coriolis force. It's starting to build up."

So Mercer had already noticed. When he let go of the rungs he had a distinct tendency to drift off to the right. He knew perfectly well that this was merely the effect of Rama's spin, but it seemed as if some mysterious force was gently pushing him away from the ladder.

Perhaps it was time to start going feet-first, now that "down" was beginning to have a physical meaning. He would run the risk of a momentary disorientation.

"Watch out—I'm going to swing round."

Holding firmly on to the rung, he used his arms to twist himself round a hundred and eighty degrees, and found himself momentarily blinded by the lights of his companions. Far above them—and now it really *was* above—he could see a fainter glow along the rim of the sheer cliff. Silhouetted against it were the figures of Commander Norton and the back-up team, watching him intently. They seemed very small and far away, and he gave them a reassuring wave.

He released his grip, and let Rama's still feeble pseudo-gravity take over. The drop from one rung to the next required more than two seconds; on Earth, in the same time, a man would have fallen thirty metres.

The rate of fall was so painfully slow that he hurried things up a trifle by pushing with his hands, gliding over spans of a dozen rungs at a time, and checking himself with his feet whenever he felt he was travelling too fast.

At rung seven hundred, he came to another halt and swung the beam of his helmet-lamp downwards; as he had calculated, the beginning of the stairway was only fifty metres below.

A few minutes later, they were on the first step. It was a strange experience, after months in space, to stand upright on a solid surface, and to feel it pressing against one's feet. Their weight was still less than ten kilograms, but that was enough to give a feeling of stability. When he closed his eyes, Mercer could believe that he once more had a real world beneath him.

The ledge or platform from which the stairway descended was about ten metres wide, and curved upwards on each side until it disappeared into the darkness. Mercer knew that it formed a complete circle and that if he walked along it for five kilometres he would come right back to his starting-point, having circumnavigated Rama.

At the fractional gravity that existed here, however, real walking was impossible; one could only bound along in giant strides. And therein lay danger.

The stairway that swooped down into the darkness, far below the range of their lights, would be deceptively easy to descend. But it would be essential to hold on to the tall handrail that flanked it on either side; too bold a step might send an incautious traveller arching far out into space. He would hit the surface again perhaps a hundred metres lower down; the impact would be harmless, but its consequences might not be—for the spin of Rama would have moved the stairway off to the left. And so a falling body would hit against the smooth curve that swept in an unbroken arc to the plain almost seven kilometres below.

That, Mercer told himself, would be a hell of a toboggan ride; the terminal speed, even in this gravity, could be several hundred kilometres an hour. Perhaps it would be possible to apply enough friction to check such a headlong descent; if so, this might even be the most convenient way to reach the inner surface of Rama. But some very cautious experimenting would be necessary first.

"Skipper," reported Mercer, "there were no problems getting down the ladder. If you agree, I'd like to continue towards the next platform. I want to time our rate of descent on the stairway."

Norton replied without hesitation.

"Go ahead." He did not need to add, "Proceed with caution."

It did not take Mercer long to make a fundamental discovery. It was impossible at least at this one-twentieth-of-a-gravity level, to walk down the stairway in the normal manner. Any attempt to do so resulted in a slow-motion dream-like movement that was intolerably tedious; the only practical way was to ignore the steps, and to use the handrail to pull oneself downwards.

Calvert had come to the same conclusion.

"This stairway was built to walk *up*, not down!" he exclaimed. "You can use the steps when you're moving against gravity, but they're just a nuisance in this direction. It may not be dignified, but I think the best way down is to slide along the handrail."

"That's ridiculous," protested Sergeant Myron. "I can't believe the Ramans did it this way."

"I doubt if they ever used this stairway—it's obviously only for emergencies. They must have had some mechanical transport system to get up here. A funicular, perhaps. That would explain those long slots running down from the hub."

"I always assumed they were drains—but I suppose they could be both. I wonder if it ever rained here?"

"Probably," said Mercer. "But I think Joe is right, and to hell with dignity. Here we go."

The handrail—presumably it *was* designed for something like hands—was a smooth, flat, metal bar supported on widely-spaced pillars a metre high. Commander Mercer straddled it, carefully gauged the braking power he could exert with his hands, and let himself slide.

Very sedately, slowly picking up speed, he descended into the darkness, moving in the pool of light from his helmet lamp. He had gone about fifty metres when he called the others to join him.

None would admit it, but they all felt like boys again, sliding down the banisters. In less than two minutes, they had made a kilometre descent in safety and comfort. Whenever they felt they were going too fast, a tightened grip on the handrail provided all the braking that was necessary.

"I hope you enjoyed yourselves," Commander Norton called when they stepped off at the second platform. "Climbing back won't be quite so easy."

"That's what I want to check," replied Mercer, who was walking experimentally back and forth, getting the feel of the increased gravity. "It's already a tenth of a gee here—you really notice the difference."

He walked—or, more accurately, glided—to the edge of the platform, and shone his helmet light down the next section of the stairway. As far as his beam could reach, it appeared identical with the one above—though careful examination of photos had shown that the height of the steps steadily decreased with the rising gravity. The stair had apparently been designed so that the effort required to climb it was more or less constant at every point in its long curving sweep.

Mercer glanced up towards the hub of Rama, now almost two kilometres above him. The little glow of light, and the tiny figures silhouetted against it, seemed horribly far away. For the first time, he was suddenly glad that he could not see the whole length of this enormous stairway. Despite his steady nerves and lack of imagination, he was not sure how he would react if he could see himself like an insect crawling up the face of a vertical saucer more than sixteen kilometres high—and with the upper half overhanging above him. Until this moment, he had regarded the darkness as a nuisance; now he almost welcomed it.

"There's no change of temperature," he reported to Commander Norton. "Still just below freezing. But the air-pressure is up, as we expected—around three hundred millibars. Even with this low oxygen content, it's almost breathable; further down there will be no problems at all. That will simplify exploration enormously. What a find—the first world on which we can walk without breathing gear! In fact, I'm going to take a sniff."

Up on the Hub, Commander Norton stirred a little uneasily. But Mercer, of all men, knew exactly what he was doing. He would already have made enough tests to satisfy himself.

Mercer equalised pressure, unlatched the securing clip of his helmet, and opened it a crack. He took a cautious breath; then a deeper one.

The air of Rama was dead and musty, as if from a tomb so ancient that the last trace of physical corruption had disappeared ages ago. Even Mercer's ultra-sensitive nose, trained through years of testing life-support systems to and beyond the point of disaster, could detect no recognisable odours. There was a faint metallic tang, and he suddenly recalled that the first men on the Moon had reported a hint of burnt gunpowder when they repressurised the lunar module. Mercer imagined that the moon-dust-contaminated cabin on Eagle must have smelled rather like Rama.

He sealed the helmet again, and emptied his lungs of the alien air. He had extracted no sustenance from it; even a mountaineer acclimatised to the summit of Everest would die quickly here. But a few kilometres further down, it would be a different matter.

What else was there to do here? He could think of nothing, except the enjoyment of the gentle, unaccustomed gravity. But there was no point in growing used to that, since they would be returning immediately to the weightlessness of the hub.

"We're coming back, Skipper," he reported. "There's no reason to go further—until we're ready to go *all* the way."

"I agree. We'll be timing you, but take it easy."

As he bounded up the steps, three or four at a stride, Mercer agreed that Calvert had been perfectly correct; these stairs were built to be walked *up*, not down. As long as one did not look back, and ignored the vertiginous steepness of the ascending curve, the climb was a delightful experience. After about two hundred steps, however, he began to feel some twinges in his calf muscles, and decided to slow down. The others had done the same; when he ventured a quick glance over his shoulder, they were considerably further down the slope.

The climb was wholly uneventful—merely an apparently endless succession of steps. When they stood once more on the highest platform, immediately beneath the ladder, they were barely winded, and it had taken them only ten minutes. They paused for another ten, then started on the last vertical kilometre.

Jump—catch hold of a rung—jump—catch—jump—catch . . . it was easy, but so boringly repetitious that there was danger of becoming careless. Half-way up the ladder they rested for five minutes: by this time their arms as well as their legs had begun to ache. Once again, Mercer was glad that they could see so little of the vertical face to which they were clinging; it was not too difficult to pretend that the ladder only extended just a few metres beyond their circle of light, and would soon come to an end.

Jump—catch a rung—jump—then, quite suddenly, the ladder *really* ended. They were back at the weightless world of the axis, among their anxious friends. The whole trip had taken under an hour, and they felt a sense of modest achievement.

But it was much too soon to feel pleased with themselves. For all their efforts, they had traversed less than an eighth of that cyclopean stairway.

CHAPTER XI

Men, Women and Monkeys

SOME WOMEN, COMMANDER NORTON had decided long ago, should not be allowed aboard ship; weightlessness did things to their breasts that were too damn distracting. It was bad enough when they were motionless; but when they started to move, and sympathetic vibrations set in, it was more than any warm-blooded male should be asked to take. He was quite sure that at least one serious space accident had been caused by acute crew distraction, after the transit of a well-upholstered lady officer through the control cabin.

He had once mentioned this theory to Surgeon-Commander Laura Ernst, without revealing who had inspired his particular train of thought. There was no need; they knew each other much too well. On Earth, years ago, in a moment of mutual loneliness and depression, they had once made love. Probably they would never repeat the experience (but could one ever be *quite* sure of that?) because so much had changed for both of them. Yet whenever the well-built surgeon oscillated into the Commander's cabin he felt a fleeting echo of an old passion, she knew that he felt it, and everyone was happy.

"Bill," she began, "I've checked our mountaineers, and here's my verdict. Karl and Joe are in good shape—all indications normal for the work they've done. But Will shows signs of exhaustion and body-loss—I won't bother about the details. I don't believe he's been getting all the exercise he should, and he's not the only one. There's been some cheating in the centrifuge; if there's any more, heads will roll. Please pass the word."

"Yes, Ma'am. But there's some excuse. The men have been working very hard."

"With their brains and fingers, certainly. But not with their bodies—not *real* work in kilogram-metres. And that's what we'll be dealing with, if we're going to explore Rama."

"Well, can we?"

"Yes, if we proceed with caution. Karl and I have worked out a very conservative profile—based on the assumption that we can dispense with breathing gear below Level Two. Of course, that's an incredible stroke of luck, and changes the whole logistics picture. I still can't get used to the idea of a world with oxygen. . . . So we only need to supply food and water and thermo-suits, and we're in business. Going down will be easy; it looks as if we can slide most of the way, on that very convenient banister."

"I've got Chips working on a sled with parachute braking. Even if we can't risk it for crew, we can use it for stores and equipment."

"Fine; *that* should do the trip in ten minutes; otherwise it will take about an hour.

"Climbing up is harder to estimate; I'd like to allow six hours, including two one-hour rest periods. Later, as we get experience—*and* develop some muscles—we may be able to cut this back considerably."

"What about psychological factors?"

"Hard to assess, in such a novel environment. Darkness may be the biggest problem."

"I'll establish searchlights on the Hub. Besides its own lamps, any party down there will always have a beam playing on it."

"Good—that should be a great help."

"One other point: should we play safe and send a party only half-way down the stair—and back—or should we go the whole way on the first attempt?"

"If we had plenty of time, I'd be cautious. But time is short, and I can see no danger in going all the way—and looking around when we get there."

"Thanks, Laura—that's all I want to know. I'll get the Exec. working on the details. And I'll order all hands to the centrifuge—twenty minutes a day at half a gee. Will that satisfy you?"

"No. It's point six gee down there in Rama, and I want a safety margin. Make it three-quarters——"

"Ouch!"

"—for ten minutes——"

"I'll settle for that——"

"—*twice* a day."

"Laura, you're a cruel, hard woman. But so be it. I'll break the news just before dinner. That should spoil a few appetites."

It was the first time that Commander Norton had ever seen Karl Mercer slightly ill at ease. He had spent the fifteen minutes discussing the logistics problems in his usual competent manner, but something was obviously worrying him. His captain, who had a shrewd idea of what it was, waited patiently until he brought it out.

"Skipper," Karl said at length, "are you *sure* you should lead this party? If anything goes wrong, I'm considerably more expendable. And I've been further inside Rama than anyone else—even if only by fifty metres."

"Granted. But it's time the commander led his troops, and we've decided that there's no greater risk on this trip than on the last. At the first sign of trouble, I'll be back up that stairway fast enough to qualify for the Lunar Olympics."

He waited for any further objections, but none came, though Karl still looked unhappy. So he took pity on him and added gently: "And I bet Joe will beat me to the top."

The big man relaxed, and a slow grin spread across his face. "All the same, Bill, I wish you'd taken someone else."

"I wanted *one* man who'd been down before, and we can't both go. As for Herr Doktor Professor Sergeant Myron, Laura says he's two kilos overweight. Even shaving off that moustache didn't help."

"Who's your number three?"

"I still haven't decided. That depends on Laura."

"She wants to go herself."

"Who doesn't? But if she turns up at the top of her own fitness list, I'll be very suspicious."

As Lieut.-Commander Mercer gathered up his papers and launched himself out of the cabin, Norton felt a brief stab of envy. Almost all the crew—about eighty-five per cent, by his minimum estimate—had worked out some sort of emotional accommodation. He had known ships where the captain had done the same, but that was not his way. Though discipline aboard the *Endeavour* was based very largely on the mutual respect between highly trained and intelligent men and women, the commander needed something more to underline his position. His responsibility was unique, and demanded a certain degree of isolation, even from his closest friends. Any liaison could be damaging to morale, for it was almost impossible to avoid charges of favouritism. For this reason, affairs spanning more than two degrees of rank were firmly discouraged; but apart from this, the only rule regulating shipboard sex was "So long as they don't do it in the corridors and frighten the simps".

There were four superchimps aboard *Endeavour*, though strictly speaking the name was inaccurate, because the ship's non-human crew was not based on chimpanzee stock. In zero gravity, a prehensile tail is an enormous advantage, and all attempts to supply these to humans had turned into embarrassing failures. After equally unsatisfactory results with the great apes, the Superchimpanzee Corporation had turned to the monkey kingdom.

Blackie, Blondie, Goldie and Brownie had family trees whose branches included the most intelligent of the Old and New World monkeys, plus synthetic genes that had never existed in nature. Their rearing and education had probably cost as much as that of the average space-man, and they were worth it. Each weighed less than thirty kilos and consumed only half the food and oxygen of a human being, but each could replace 2.75 men for housekeeping, elementary cooking, tool-carrying and dozens of other routine jobs.

That 2.75 was the Corporation's claim, based on innumerable time-and-motion studies. The figure, though surprising and frequently challenged, appeared to be accurate, for simps were quite happy to work fifteen hours a day and did not get bored by the most menial and repetitious tasks. So they freed human beings for human work; and on a space-ship, that was a matter of vital importance.

Unlike the monkeys who were their nearest relatives *Endeavour*'s simps were docile, obedient and uninquisitive. Being cloned, they were also sexless, which eliminated awkward behavioural problems. Carefully house-trained vegetarians, they were very clean and didn't smell; they would have made perfect pets, except that nobody could possibly have afforded them.

Despite these advantages, having simps on board involved certain problems. They had to have their own quarters—inevitably labelled "The Monkey House". Their little mess-room was always spotless, and was well equipped with TV, games equipment and programmed teaching machines. To avoid accidents, they were absolutely forbidden to enter the ship's technical areas; the entrances to all these were colour-coded in red, and the simps were conditioned so that it was psychologically impossible for them to pass these visual barriers.

There was also a communications problem. Though they had an equivalent IQ of 60, and could understand several hundred words of English, they were unable to talk. It had proved impossible to give useful vocal chords either to apes or monkeys, and they therefore had to express themselves in sign language.

The basic signs were obvious and easily learned, so that everyone on board ship could understand routine messages. But the only man who could speak fluent Simpish was their handler—Chief Steward McAndrews.

It was a standing joke that Sergeant Ravi McAndrews *looked* rather like a simp—which was hardly an insult, for with their short, tinted pelts and graceful movements they were very handsome animals. They were also affectionate, and everyone on board had his favourite; Commander Norton's was the aptly-named Goldie.

But the warm relationship which one could so easily establish with simps created another problem, often used as a powerful argument against their employment in space. Since they could only be trained for routine, low-grade tasks, they were worse than useless in an emergency; they could then be a danger to themselves and to their human companions. In particular, teaching them to use space-suits had proved impossible, the concepts involved being quite beyond their understanding.

No one liked to talk about it, but everybody knew what had to be done if a hull was breached or the order came to abandon ship. It had happened only once; then the simp handler had carried out his instructions more than adequately. He was found with his charges, killed by the same poison. Thereafter, the job of euthing was transferred to the chief medical officer, who it was felt would have less emotional involvement.

Norton was very thankful that this responsibility, at least, did not fall upon the captain's shoulders. He had known men he would have killed with far fewer qualms than he would Goldie.

CHAPTER XII

The Stairway of the Gods

IN THE CLEAR, cold atmosphere of Rama, the beam of the searchlight was completely invisible. Three kilometres down from the central hub, the hundred-metre-wide oval of light lay across a section of that colossal stairway. A brilliant oasis in the surrounding darkness, it was sweeping slowly towards the curved plain still five kilometres below; and in its centre moved a trio of ant-like figures, casting long shadows before them.

It had been, just as they had hoped and expected, a completely uneventful descent. They had paused briefly at the first platform, and Norton had walked a few hundred metres along the narrow, curving ledge before starting the slide down to the second level. Here they had discarded their oxygen gear, and revelled in the strange luxury of being able to breathe without mechanical aids. Now they could explore in comfort, freed from the greatest danger that confronts a man in space, and forgetting all worries about suit integrity and oxygen reserve.

By the time they had reached the fifth level, and there was only one more section to go, gravity had reached almost half its terrestrial value. Rama's centrifugal spin was at last exerting its real strength; they were surrendering themselves to the implacable force which rules every planet, and which can exert a merciless price for the smallest slip. It was still very easy to go down-wards; but the thought of the return, up those thousands upon thousands of steps, was already beginning to prey upon their minds.

The stairway had long ago ceased its vertiginous downward plunge and was now flattening out towards the horizontal. The gradient was now only about 1 in 5; at the beginning, it had been 5 in 1. Normal walking was now both physically, and psychologically, acceptable; only the lowered gravity reminded them that they were not descending some great stairway on Earth. Norton had once visited the ruins of an Aztec temple, and the feelings he had then experienced came echoing back to him—amplified a hundred times. Here was the same sense of awe and mystery, and the sadness of the irrevocably vanished past. Yet the scale here was so much greater, both in time and space, that the mind was unable to do it justice; after a while, it ceased to respond. Norton wondered if, sooner or later, he would take even Rama for granted.

And there was another respect in which the parallel with terrestrial ruins failed completely. Rama was hundreds of times older than any structure that had survived on Earth—even the Great Pyramid. *But everything looked absolutely new; there was no sign of wear and tear.*

Norton had puzzled over this a good deal, and had arrived at a tentative explanation. Everything that they had so far examined was part of an emer-gency back-up system, very seldom put to actual use. He could not imagine that the Ramans—unless they were physical fitness fanatics of the kind not uncommon on Earth—ever walked up and down this incredible stairway, or its two identical companions completing the invisible Y far above his head. Perhaps they had only been required during the actual construction of Rama, and had served no purpose since that distant day. That theory would do for the moment, yet it did not feel right. There was something wrong, some-where. . . .

They did not slide for the last kilometre but went down the steps two at a time in long, gentle strides; this way, Norton decided, they would give more exercise to muscles that would soon have to be used. And so the end of the stairway came upon them almost unawares; suddenly, there were no more steps—only a flat plain, dull grey in the now weakening beam of the hub searchlight, fading away into the darkness a few hundred metres ahead.

Norton looked back along the beam, towards its source upon the axis more than eight kilometres away. He knew that Mercer would be watching through the telescope, so he waved to him cheerfully.

"Captain here," he reported over the radio. "Everyone in fine shape—no problems. Proceeding as planned."

"Good," replied Mercer. "We'll be watching."

There was a brief silence; then a new voice cut in. "This is the Exec., on board ship. Really, Skipper, this isn't good enough. You know the news services have been screaming at us for the last week. I don't expect deathless prose, but can't you do better than that?"

"I'll try," Norton chuckled. "But remember there's nothing to see yet. It's like—well, being on a huge, darkened stage, with a single spotlight. The first few hundred steps of the stairway rise out of it until they disappear into the darkness overhead. What we can see of the plain looks perfectly flat—the curvature's too small to be visible over this limited area. And that's about it."

"Like to give any impressions?"

"Well, it's still very cold—below freezing—and we're glad of our thermo-suits. And *quiet* of course; quieter than anything I've ever known on Earth, or in space, where there's always some background noise. Here, every sound is swallowed up; the space around us is so enormous that there aren't any echoes. It's weird, but I hope we'll get used to it."

"Thanks, Skipper. Anyone else—Joe, Boris?"

Lieut. Joe Calvert, never at a loss for words, was happy to oblige.

"I can't help thinking that this is the first time—*ever*—that we've been able to walk on another world, breathing its natural atmosphere—though I suppose 'natural' is hardly the word you can apply to a place like this. Still, Rama must resemble the world of its builders; our own space-ships are all miniature earths. Two examples are damned poor statistics, but does this mean that all intelligent life-forms are oxygen eaters? What we've seen of their work suggests that the Ramans were humanoid, though perhaps about fifty per cent taller than we are. Wouldn't you agree, Boris?"

Is Joe teasing Boris? Norton asked himself. I wonder how he's going to react? . . .

To all his shipmates, Boris Rodrigo was something of an enigma. The quiet, dignified communications officer was popular with the rest of the crew, but he never entered fully into their activities and always seemed a little apart—marching to the music of a different drummer.

As indeed he was, being a devout member of the Fifth Church of Christ, Cosmonaut. Norton had never been able to discover what had happened to the earlier four, and he was equally in the dark about the Church's rituals and ceremonies. But the main tenet of its faith was well known: it believed that Jesus Christ was a visitor from space, and had constructed an entire theology on that assumption.

It was perhaps not surprising that an unusually high proportion of the Church's devotees worked in space in some capacity or other. Invariably, they were efficient, conscientious and absolutely reliable. They were universally respected and even liked, especially as they made no attempt to convert others. Yet there was also something slightly spooky about them; Norton could never understand how men with advanced scientific and technical training could possibly believe some of the things he had heard Christers state as incontrovertible facts.

As he waited for Lieut. Rodrigo to answer Joe's possibly loaded question, the commander had a sudden insight into his own hidden motives. He had chosen Boris because he was physically fit, technically qualified, and completely dependable. At the same time, he wondered if some part of his mind had not selected the lieutenant out of an almost mischievous curiosity. How would a man with such religious beliefs react to the awesome reality of Rama? Suppose he encountered something that confounded his theology . . . or, for that matter, confirmed it?

But Boris Rodrigo, with his usual caution, refused to be drawn.

"They were certainly oxygen breathers, and they *could* be humanoid. But let's wait and see. With any luck, we should discover what they were like. There may be pictures, statues—perhaps even bodies, over in those towns. If they are towns."

"And the nearest is only eight kilometres away," said Joe Calvert hopefully.

Yes, thought the commander, but it's also eight kilometres back—and then there's that overwhelming stairway to climb again. Can we take the risk?

A quick sortie to the "town" which they had named Paris had been among the first of his contingency plans, and now he had to make his decision. They had ample food and water for a stay of twenty-four hours; they would always be in full view of the back-up team on the Hub, and any kind of accident seemed virtually impossible on this smooth, gently curving, metal plain. The only foreseeable danger was exhaustion; when they got to Paris, which they could do easily enough, could they do more than take a few photographs and perhaps collect some small artifacts, before they had to return?

But even such a brief foray would be worth it; there was so little time, as Rama hurtled sunwards towards a perihelion too dangerous for *Endeavour* to match.

In any case, part of the decision was not his to make. Up in the ship, Dr. Ernst would be watching the outputs of the bio-telemetering sensors attached to his body. If she turned thumbs-down, that would be that.

"Laura, what do you think?"

"Take thirty minutes' rest, and a five hundred calorie energy module. Then you can start."

"Thanks, doc," interjected Joe Calvert. "Now I can die happy. I always wanted to see Paris. Montmartre, here we come."

CHAPTER XIII

The Plain of Rama

AFTER THOSE INTERMINABLE stairs, it was a strange luxury to walk once more on a horizontal surface. Directly ahead, the ground was indeed completely flat; to right and left, at the limits of the floodlit area, the rising curve could just be detected. They might have been walking along a very wide, shallow valley; it was quite impossible to believe that they were really crawling along the inside of a huge cylinder, and that beyond this little oasis of light the land rose up to meet—no, to *become*—the sky.

Though they all felt a sense of confidence and subdued excitement, after a while the almost palpable silence of Rama began to weigh heavily upon them. Every footstep, every word, vanished instantly into the unreverberant void; after they had gone little more than half a kilometre, Lieut. Calvert could stand it no longer.

Among his minor accomplishments was a talent now rare, though many thought not rare enough—the art of whistling. With or without encouragement he could reproduce the themes from most of the movies of the last two hundred years. He started appropriately with "Heigh-ho, heigh-ho, 'tis off to work we go", found that he couldn't stay down comfortably in the bass with Disney's marching dwarves, and switched quickly to "River Kwai". Then he progressed, more or less chronologically, through half a dozen epics, culminating with the theme from Sid Krassman's famous late-twentieth-century *Napoleon*.

It was a good try, but it didn't work, even as a morale-builder. Rama needed the grandeur of Bach or Beethoven or Sibelius or Tuan Sun, not the trivia of popular entertainment. Norton was on the point of suggesting that Joe save his breath for later exertions, when the young officer realised the inappropriateness of his efforts. Thereafter, apart from an occasional consultation with the ship, they marched on in silence. Rama had won this round.

On his initial traverse, Norton had allowed for one detour. Paris lay straight ahead, half-way between the foot of the stairway and the shore of the Cylindrical Sea, but only a kilometre to the right of their track was a very prominent, and rather mysterious, feature which had been christened the Straight Valley. It was a long groove or trench, forty metres deep and a hundred wide, with gently sloping sides; it had been provisionally identified as an irrigation ditch or canal. Like the Stairway itself, it had two similar counterparts, equally spaced around the curve of Rama.

The three valleys were almost ten kilometres long, and stopped abruptly just before they reached the Sea—which was strange, if they were intended to carry water. And on the other side of the Sea the pattern was repeated: three more ten-kilometre trenches continued on to the South Polar region.

They reached the end of the Straight Valley after only fifteen minutes' comfortable walking, and stood for a while staring thoughtfully into its depths. The perfectly smooth walls sloped down at an angle of sixty degrees; there were no steps or footholds. Filling the bottom was a sheet of flat, white material that looked very much like ice. A specimen could settle a good many arguments; Norton decided to get one.

With Calvert and Rodrigo acting as anchors and playing out a safety rope, he rappelled slowly down the steep incline. When he reached the bottom, he fully expected to find the familiar slippery feel of ice underfoot, but he was mistaken. The friction was too great; his footing was secure. This material was some kind of glass or transparent crystal; when he touched it with his fingertips, it was cold, hard and unyielding.

Turning his back to the searchlight and shielding his eyes from its glare, Norton tried to peer into the crystalline depths, as one may attempt to gaze through the ice of a frozen lake. But he could see nothing; even when he tried the concentrated beam of his own helmet-lamp, he was no more successful. This stuff was translucent, but not transparent. If it was a frozen liquid, it had a melting-point very much higher than water.

He tapped it gently with the hammer from his geology kit; the tool rebounded with a dull, unmusical "clunk". He tapped harder, with no more result, and was about to exert his full strength when some impulse made him desist.

It seemed most unlikely that he could crack this material; but what if he did? He would be like a vandal, smashing some enormous plate-glass window. There would be a better opportunity later, and at least he had discovered valuable information. It now seemed more unlikely than ever that this was a canal; it was simply a peculiar trench that stopped and started abruptly, but led nowhere. And if at any time it had carried liquid, where were the stains, the encrustations of dried-up sediment, that one would expect? Everything was bright and clean, as if the builders had left only yesterday. . . .

Once again he was face to face with the fundamental mystery of Rama, and this time it was impossible to evade it. Commander Norton was a reasonably imaginative man, but he would never have reached his present position if he had been liable to the wilder flights of fancy. Yet now, for the first time, he had a sense—not exactly of foreboding, but of anticipation. Things were not what they seemed; there was something very, very odd about a place that was simultaneously brand new—and a million years old.

Very thoughtfully, he began to walk slowly along the length of the little valley, while his companions, still holding the rope that was attached to his waist, followed him along the rim. He did not expect to make any further discoveries, but he wanted to let his curious emotional state run its course. For something else was worrying him; and it had nothing to do with the inexplicable newness of Rama.

He had walked no more than a dozen metres when it hit him like a thunderbolt.

He knew this place. *He had been here before.* Even on Earth, or some familiar planet, that experience is disquieting, though it is not particularly rare. Most men have known it at some time or other, and usually they dismiss it as the memory of a forgotten photograph, a pure coincidence—or, if they are mystically inclined, some form of telepathy from another mind, or even a flash-back from their own future.

But to recognise a spot which *no* other human being can possibly have seen— that is quite shocking. For several seconds, Commander Norton stood rooted to the smooth crystalline surface on which he had been walking, trying to straighten out his emotions. His well-ordered universe had been turned upside down, and he had a dizzying glimpse of those mysteries at the edge of existence which he had successfully ignored for most of his life.

Then, to his immense relief, common sense came to the rescue. The disturbing sensation of *déjà-vu* faded out, to be replaced by a real and identifiable memory from his youth.

It was true—he had once stood between such steeply sloping walls, watching them drive into the distance until they seemed to converge at a point indefinitely far ahead. But they had been covered with neatly trimmed grass; and underfoot had been broken stone, not smooth crystal.

It had happened thirty years ago, during a summer vacation in England. Largely because of another student (he could remember her face—but he had forgotten her name) he had taken a course of industrial archaeology, then very popular among science and engineering graduates. They had explored abandoned coal-mines and cotton mills, climbed over ruined blast-furnaces and steam-engines, goggled unbelievingly at primitive (and still dangerous) nuclear reactors, and driven priceless turbine-powered antiques along restored motor roads.

Not everything that they saw was genuine; much had been lost during the centuries, for men seldom bother to preserve the commonplace articles of everyday life. But where it was necessary to make copies, they had been reconstructed with loving care.

And so young Bill Norton had found himself bowling along, at an exhilarating hundred kilometres an hour, while he furiously shovelled precious coal into the firebox of a locomotive that looked two hundred years old, but was actually younger than he was. The thirty-kilometre stretch of the Great Western Railway, however, was quite genuine, though it had required a good deal of excavating to get it back into commission.

Whistle screaming, they had plunged into a hillside and raced through a smoky, flame-lit darkness. An astonishingly long time later, they had burst out of the tunnel into a deep, perfectly straight cutting between steep grassy banks. The long-forgotten vista was almost identical with the one before him now.

"What it it, Skipper?" called Lieut. Rodrigo. "Have you found something?"

As Norton dragged himself back to present reality, some of the oppression lifted from his mind. There was mystery here—yes; but it might not be beyond human understanding. He had learned a lesson, though it was not one that he could readily impart to others. At all costs, he must not let Rama overwhelm him. That way lay failure—perhaps even madness.

"No," he answered, "there's nothing down here. Haul me up—we'll head straight to Paris."

CHAPTER XIV

Storm Warning

"I've called this meeting of the Committee," said His Excellency the Ambassador of Mars to the United Planets, "because Dr. Perera has something important to tell us. He insists that we get in touch with Commander Norton right away, using the priority channel we've been able to establish after, I might say, a good deal of difficulty. Dr. Perera's statement is rather technical, and before we come to it I think a summary of the present position might be in order; Dr. Price has prepared one. Oh yes—some apologies for absence. Sir Lewis Sands is unable to be with us because he's chairing a conference, and Dr. Taylor asks to be excused."

He was rather pleased about that last abstention. The anthropologist had rapidly lost interest in Rama, when it became obvious that it would present little scope for him. Like many others, he had been bitterly disappointed to find that the mobile worldlet was dead; now there would be no opportunity for sensational books and viddies about Raman rituals and behavioural patterns. Others might dig up skeletons and classify artifacts; *that* sort of thing did not appeal to Conrad Taylor. Perhaps the only discovery that would bring him back in a hurry would be some highly explicit works of art, like the notorious frescoes of Thera and Pompeii.

Thelma Price, the archaeologist, took exactly the opposite point of view. She preferred excavations and ruins uncluttered by inhabitants who might interfere with dispassionate, scientific studies. The bed of the Mediterranean had been ideal—at least until the city planners and landscape artists had started getting in the way. And Rama would have been perfect, except for the maddening detail that it was a hundred million kilometres away and she would never be able to visit it in person.

"As you all know," she began, "Commander Norton has completed one traverse of almost thirty kilometres, without encountering any problems. He explored the curious trench shown on your maps as the Straight Valley; its purpose is still quite unknown, but it's clearly important as it runs the full length of Rama—except for the break at the Cylindrical Sea—and there are two other identical structures 120 degrees apart round the circumference of the world.

"Then the party turned left—or east, if we adopt the North Pole convention —until they reached Paris. As you'll see from this photograph, taken by a telescope camera at the Hub, it's a group of several hundred buildings, with wide streets between them.

"Now *these* photographs were taken by Commander Norton's group when they reached the site. If Paris is a city, it's a very peculiar one. Note that none of the buildings have windows, or even doors! They are all plain rectangular structures, an identical thirty-five metres high. And they appear to have been extruded out of the ground—there are no seams or joints—look at this close-up of the base of a wall—there's a smooth transition into the ground.

"My own feeling is that this place is not a residential area, but a storage or supply depot. In support of that theory, look at this photo. . . .

"These narrow slots or grooves, about five centimetres wide, run along all the streets, and there's one leading to every building—going straight into the wall. There's a striking resemblance to the street-car tracks of the early twentieth century; they are obviously part of some transport system.

"We've never considered it necessary to have public transport direct to every house. It would be economically absurd—people can always walk a few hundred metres. But if these buildings are used for the storage of heavy materials, it would make sense."

"May I ask a question?" said the Ambassador for Earth.

"Of course, Sir Robert."

"Commander Norton couldn't get into a single building?"

"No; when you listen to his report, you can tell he was quite frustrated. At one time he decided that the buildings could only be entered from underground; then he discovered the grooves of the transport system, and changed his mind."

"Did he try to break in?"

"There was no way he could, without explosives or heavy tools. And he doesn't want to do that until all other approaches have failed."

"I have it!" Dennis Solomons suddenly interjected. "Cocooning!"

"I beg your pardon?"

"It's a technique developed a couple of hundred years ago," continued the science historian. "Another name for it is moth-balling. When you have something you want to preserve, you seal it inside a plastic envelope, and then pump in an inert gas. The original use was to protect military equipment between wars; it was once applied to whole ships. It's still widely used in museums that are short of storage space; no one knows what's inside some of the hundred-year-old cocoons in the Smithsonian basement."

Patience was not one of Carlisle Perera's virtues; he was aching to drop his bombshell, and could restrain himself no longer.

"*Please*, Mr. Ambassador! This is all very interesting, but I feel my information is rather more urgent."

"If there are no other points—very well, Dr. Perera."

The exobioligist, unlike Conrad Taylor, had not found Rama a disappointment. It was true that he no longer expected to find life—but sooner or later, he had been quite sure, some remains would be discovered of the creatures who had built this fantastic world. The exploration had barely begun, although the time available was horribly brief before *Endeavour* would be forced to escape from her present sun-grazing orbit.

But now, if his calculations were correct, Man's contact with Rama would be even shorter than he had feared. For one detail had been overlooked—because it was so large that no one had noticed it before.

"According to our latest information," Perera began, "one party is now on its way to the Cylindrical Sea, while Commander Norton has another group setting up a supply base at the foot of Stairway Alpha. When that's established, he intends to have at least two exploratory missions operating at all times. In this way he hopes to use his limited manpower at maximum efficiency.

"It's a good plan, but there may be no time to carry it out. In fact, I would advise an immediate alert, and a preparation for total withdrawal at twelve hours' notice. Let me explain. . . .

"It's surprising how few people have commented on a rather obvious anomaly about Rama. It's now well inside the orbit of Venus—yet the interior is still frozen. But the temperature of an object in direct sunlight at this point is about five hundred degrees!

"The reason, of course, is that Rama hasn't had time to warm up. It must have cooled down to near absolute zero—two hundred and seventy below—while it was in interstellar space. Now, as it approaches the sun, the outer hull is already almost as hot as molten lead. But the inside will stay cold, until the heat works its way through that kilometre of rock.

"There's some kind of fancy dessert with a hot exterior and ice-cream in the middle—I don't remember what it's called——"

"Baked Alaska. It's a favourite at UP banquets, unfortunately."

"Thank you, Sir Robert. That's the situation in Rama at the moment, but it won't last. All these weeks, the solar heat has been working its way through, and we expect a sharp temperature rise to begin in a few hours. *That's* not the problem; by the time we'll have to leave anyway, it will be no more than comfortably tropical."

"Then what's the difficulty?"

"I can answer in one word, Mr. Ambassador. *Hurricanes.*"

CHAPTER XV

The Edge of the Sea

THERE WERE NOW more than twenty men and women inside Rama —six of them down on the plain, the rest ferrying equipment and expendables through the airlock system and down the stairway. The ship itself was almost deserted, with the minimum possible staff on duty; the joke went around that *Endeavour* was really being run by the four simps and that Goldie had been given the rank of Acting-Commander.

For these first explorations, Norton had established a number of ground-rules; the most important dated back to the earliest days of man's space-faring. Every group, he had decided, must contain one person with prior experience. But not *more* than one. In that way, everybody would have an opportunity of learning as quickly as possible.

And so the first party to head for the Cylindrical Sea, though it was led by Surgeon-Commander Laura Ernst, had as its one-time veteran Lieut. Boris Rodrigo, just back from Paris. The third member, Sergeant Pieter Rousseau, had been with the back-up teams at the Hub; he was an expert on space reconnaissance instrumentation, but on this trip he would have to depend on his own eyes and a small portable telescope.

From the foot of Stairway Alpha to the edge of the Sea was just under fifteen kilometres—or an Earth-equivalent of eight under the low gravity of Rama. Laura Ernst, who had to prove that she lived up to her own standards, set a brisk pace. They stopped for thirty minutes at the mid-way mark, and made the whole trip in a completely uneventful three hours.

It was also quite monotonous, walking forward in the beam of the search-light through the anechoic darkness of Rama. As the pool of light advanced with them, it slowly elongated into a long, narrow ellipse; this foreshortening of the beam was the only visible sign of progress. If the observers up on the Hub had not given them continual distance checks, they could not have guessed whether they had travelled one kilometre, or five, or ten. They just plodded onwards through the million-year-old night, over an apparently seamless metal surface.

But at last, far ahead at the limits of the now weakening beam, there was something new. On a normal world, it would have been a horizon; as they approached, they could see that the plain on which they were walking came to an abrupt stop. They were nearing the edge of the Sea.

"Only a hundred metres," said Hub Control. "Better slow down."

That was hardly necessary, yet they had already done so. It was a sheer straight drop of fifty metres from the level of the plain to that of the Sea—if it was a sea, and not another sheet of that mysterious crystalline material. Although Norton had impressed upon everyone the danger of taking anything for granted in Rama, few doubted that the Sea was really made of ice. But for what conceivable reason was the cliff on the southern shore five hundred metres high, instead of the fifty here?

It was as if they were approaching the edge of the world; their oval of light, cut off abruptly ahead of them, became shorter and shorter. But far out on the curved screen of the Sea their monstrous foreshortened shadows had appeared, magnifying and exaggerating every movement. Those shadows had been their companions every step of the way, as they marched down the beam, but now that they were broken at the edge of the cliff they no longer seemed part of them. They might have been creatures of the Cylindrical Sea, waiting to deal with any intruders into their domain.

Because they were now standing on the edge of a fifty-metre cliff, it was possible for the first time to appreciate the curvature of Rama. But no one had ever seen a frozen lake bent upwards into a cylindrical surface; that was distinctly unsettling, and the eye did its best to find some other interpretation. It seemed to Dr. Ernst, who had once made a study of visual illusions, that half the time she was really looking at a *horizontally* curving bay, not a surface that soared up into the sky. It required a deliberate effort of will to accept the fantastic truth.

Only in the line directly ahead, parallel to the axis of Rama, was normalcy preserved. In this direction alone was there agreement between vision and logic. Here—for the next few kilometres at least—Rama looked flat, and *was* flat. . . . And out there, beyond their distorted shadows and the outer limit of the beam lay the island that dominated the Cylindrical Sea.

"Hub Control," Dr. Ernst radioed, "please aim your beam at New York."

The night of Rama fell suddenly upon them, as the oval of light went sliding out to sea. Conscious of the now invisible cliff at their feet, they all stepped back a few metres. Then, as if by some magical stage transformation, the towers of New York sprang into view.

The resemblance to old-time Manhattan was only superficial; this star-born echo of Earth's past possessed its own unique identity. The more Dr. Ernst stared at it, the more certain she became that it was not a city at all.

The real New York, like all of Man's habitations, had never been finished; still less had it been designed. *This* place, however, had an overall symmetry and pattern, though one so complex that it eluded the mind. It had been conceived and planned by some controlling intelligence—and then it had been completed, like a machine devised for some specific purpose. After that, there was no possibility of growth or change.

The beam of the searchlight slowly tracked along those distant towers and domes and interlocked spheres and criss-crossed tubes. Sometimes there would be a brilliant reflection as some flat surface shot the light back towards them; the first time this happened, they were all taken by surprise. It was exactly as if, over there on that strange island, someone was signalling to them. . . .

But there was nothing that they could see here that was not already shown in greater detail on photographs taken from the Hub. After a few minutes, they called for the light to return to them, and began to walk eastwards along the edge of the cliff. It had been plausibly theorised that, somewhere, there must surely be a flight of steps, or a ramp, leading down to the Sea. And one crewman, who was a keen sailor, had raised an interesting conjecture.

"Where there's a sea," Sergeant Ruby Barnes had predicted, "there must be docks and harbours—and ships. You can learn everything about a culture by studying the way it builds boats." Her colleagues thought this a rather restricted point of view, but at least it was a stimulating one.

Dr. Ernst had almost given up the search, and was preparing to make a descent by rope, when Lieut. Rodrigo spotted the narrow stairway. It could easily have been overlooked in the shadowed darkness below the edge of the cliff, for there was no guard-rail or other indication of its presence. And it seemed to lead nowhere; it ran down the fifty-metre vertical wall at a steep angle, and disappeared below the surface of the Sea.

They scanned the flight of steps with their helmet lights, could see no conceivable hazard, and Dr. Ernst got Commander Norton's permission to descend. A minute later, she was cautiously testing the surface of the Sea.

Her foot slithered almost frictionlessly back and forth. The material felt exactly like ice. It *was* ice.

When she struck it with her hammer, a familiar pattern of cracks radiated from the impact point, and she had no difficulty in collecting as many pieces as she wished. Some had already melted when she held up the sample holder to the light; the liquid appeared to be slightly turbid water, and she took a cautious sniff.

"Is that safe?" Rodrigo called down, with a trace of anxiety.

"Believe me, Boris," she answered, "if there are any pathogens around here that have slipped through my detectors, our insurance policies lapsed a week ago."

But Boris had a point. Despite all the tests that had been carried out, there was a very slight risk that this substance might be poisonous, or might carry some unknown disease. In normal circumstances, Dr. Ernst would not have taken even this minuscule chance. Now, however, time was short and the stakes were enormous. If it became necessary to quarantine *Endeavour*, that would be a very small price to pay for her cargo of knowledge.

"It's water, but I wouldn't care to drink it—it smells like an algae culture that's gone bad. I can hardly wait to get it to the lab."

"Is the ice safe to walk on?"

"Yes, solid as a rock."

"Then we can get to New York."

"Can we, Pieter? Have you ever tried to walk across four kilometres of ice?"

"Oh—I see what you mean. Just imagine what Stores would say, if we asked for a set of skates! Not that many of us would know how to use them, even if we had any aboard."

"And there's another problem," put in Boris Rodrigo. "Do you realise that the temperature is already above freezing? Before long, that ice is going to melt. How many space-men can swim four kilometres? Certainly not this one. . . ."

Dr. Ernst rejoined them at the edge of the cliff, and held up the small sample bottle in triumph.

"It's a long walk for a few c.c.s of dirty water, but it may teach us more about Rama than anything we've found so far. Let's head for home."

They turned towards the distant lights of the Hub, moving with the gentle, loping strides which had proved the most comfortable means of walking under this reduced gravity. Often they looked back, drawn by the hidden enigma of the island out there in the centre of the frozen sea.

And just once, Dr. Ernst thought she felt the faint suspicion of a breeze against her cheek.

It did not come again, and she quickly forgot all about it.

CHAPTER XVI

Kealakekua

"As you know perfectly well, Dr. Perera," said Ambassador Bose in tones of patient resignation, "few of us share your knowledge of mathematical meteorology. So please take pity on our ignorance."

"With pleasure," answered the exobiologist, quite unabashed. "I can explain it best by telling you what is going to happen inside Rama—very soon.

"The temperature is now about to rise, as the solar heat pulse reaches the interior. According to the latest information I've received, it's already above freezing point. The Cylindrical Sea will soon start to thaw; and unlike bodies of water on Earth, it will melt from the bottom upwards. That may produce some odd effects; but I'm much more concerned with the atmosphere.

"As it's heated, the air inside Rama will expand—and will attempt to rise towards the central axis. And this is the problem. At ground level, although it's apparently stationary, it's actually sharing the spin of Rama—over eight hundred kilometres an hour. As it rises towards the axis it will try to retain that speed—and it won't be able to do so, of course. The result will be violent winds and turbulence; I estimate velocities of between two and three hundred kilometres an hour.

"Incidentally, very much the same thing occurs on Earth. The heated air at the Equator—which shares the Earth's sixteen-hundred-kilometres-an-hour spin—runs into the same problem when it rises and flows north and south."

"Ah, the Trade Winds! I remember that from my geography lessons."

"Exactly, Sir Robert. Rama will have Trade Winds, with a vengeance. I believe they'll last only a few hours, and then some kind of equilibrium will be restored. Meanwhile, I should advise Commander Norton to evacuate—as soon as possible. Here is the message I propose sending."

With a little imagination, Commander Norton told himself, he could pretend that this was an improvised night camp at the foot of some mountain in a remote region of Asia or America. The clutter of sleeping pads, collapsible chairs and tables, portable power plant, lighting equipment, electrosan toilets, and miscellaneous scientific apparatus would not have looked out of place on Earth—especially as there were men and women working here without life-support systems.

Establishing Camp Alpha had been very hard work, for everything had had to be man-handled through the chain of airlocks, sledded down the slope from the Hub, and then retrieved and unpacked. Sometimes, when the braking parachutes had failed, a consignment had ended up a good kilometre away out on the plain. Despite this, several crew members had asked permission to make the ride; Norton had firmly forbidden it. In an emergency, however, he might be prepared to reconsider the ban.

Almost all this equipment would stay here, for the labour of carrying it back was unthinkable—in fact, impossible. There were times when Commander Norton felt an irrational shame at leaving so much human litter in this strangely immaculate place. When they finally departed, he was prepared to sacrifice some of their precious time to leave everything in good order. Improbable though it was, perhaps millions of years hence, when Rama shot through some other star system, it might have visitors again. He would like to give them a good impression of Earth.

Meanwhile, he had a rather more immediate problem. During the last twenty-four hours he had received almost identical messages from both Mars and Earth. It seemed an odd coincidence; perhaps they had been commiserating with each other, as wives who lived safely on different planets were liable to do under sufficient provocation. Rather pointedly, they had reminded him that even though he was now a great hero, he still had family responsibilities.

The Commander picked up a collapsible chair, and walked out of the pool of light into the darkness surrounding the camp. It was the only way he could get any privacy, and he could also think better away from the turmoil. Deliberately turning his back on the organised confusion behind him, he began to speak into the recorder slung around his neck.

"Original for personal file, dupes to Mars and Earth. Hello, darling—yes, I know I've been a lousy correspondent, but I haven't been aboard ship for a week. Apart from a skeleton crew, we're all camping inside Rama, at the foot of the stairway we've christened Alpha.

"I have three parties out now, scouting the plain, but we've made disappointingly slow progress, because everything has to be done on foot. If only we had some means of transport! I'd be very happy to settle for a few electric bicycles . . . they'd be perfect for the job.

"You've met my medical officer, Surgeon-Commander Ernst——" He paused uncertainly; Laura had met *one* of his wives, but which? Better cut that out——

Erasing the sentence, he began again.

"My MO, Surgeon-Commander Ernst, led the first group to reach the Cylindrical Sea, fifteen kilometres from here. She found that it was frozen water, as we'd expected—but you wouldn't want to drink it. Dr. Ernst says it's a dilute organic soup, containing traces of almost any carbon compound you care to name, as well as phosphates and nitrates and dozens of metallic salts. There's not the slightest sign of life—not even any dead micro-organisms. So we still know nothing about the biochemistry of the Ramans . . . though it was probably not wildly different from ours."

Something brushed lightly against his hair; he had been too busy to get it cut, and would have to do something about that before he next put on a space-helmet. . . .

"You've seen the viddies of Paris and the other towns we've explored on this side of the Sea . . . London, Rome, Moscow. It's impossible to believe that they were ever built for anything to *live* in. Paris looks like a giant storage depot. London is a collection of cylinders linked together by pipes connected to what are obviously pumping stations. Everything is sealed up, and there's no way of finding what's inside without explosives or lasers. We won't try these until there are no alternatives.

"As for Rome and Moscow——"

"Excuse me, Skipper. Priority from Earth."

What now? Norton asked himself. Can't a man get a few minutes to talk to his families?

He took the message from the Sergeant, and scanned it quickly, just to satisfy himself that it was not immediate. Then he read it again, more slowly.

What the devil was the Rama Committee? And why had he never heard of it? He knew that all sorts of associations, societies, and professional groups —some serious, some completely crackpot—had been trying to get in touch with him; Mission Control had done a good job of protection, and would not have forwarded this message unless it was considered important.

"Two-hundred-kilometre winds—probably sudden onset"—well, that was something to think about. But it was hard to take it too seriously, on this utterly calm night; and it would be ridiculous to run away like frightened mice, when they were just starting effective exploration.

Commander Norton lifted a hand to brush aside his hair, which had some-how fallen into his eyes again. Then he froze, the gesture uncompleted.

He *had* felt a trace of wind, several times in the last hour. It was so slight that he had completely ignored it; after all, he was the commander of a *space*-ship, not a sailing-ship. Until now the movement of air had not been of the slightest professional concern. What would the long-dead captain of that earlier *Endeavour* have done, in a situation such as this?

Norton had asked himself that question at every moment of crisis in the last few years. It was his secret, which he had never revealed to anyone. And like most of the important things in life, it had come about quite by accident.

He had been captain of *Endeavour* for several months before he realised that it was named after one of the most famous ships in history. True, during the last four hundred years there had been a dozen *Endeavours* of sea and two of space, but the ancestor of them all was the 370-ton Whitby collier that Captain James Cook, RN, had sailed round the world between 1768 and 1771.

With a mild interest that had quickly turned to an absorbing curiosity— almost an obsession—Norton had begun to read everything he could find about Cook. He was now probably the world's leading authority on the greatest explorer of all time, and knew whole sections of the *Journals* by heart.

It still seemed incredible that one man could have done so much, with such primitive equipment. But Cook had been not only a supreme navigator, but a scientist and—in an age of brutal discipline—a humanitarian. He treated his own men with kindness, which was unusual; what was quite unheard of was that he behaved in exactly the same way to the often hostile savages in the new lands he discovered.

It was Norton's private dream, which he knew he would never achieve, to retrace at least one of Cook's voyages around the world. He had made a limited but spectacular start, which would certainly have astonished the Captain, when he once flew a polar orbit directly above the Great Barrier Reef. It had been early morning on a clear day, and from four hundred kilometres up he had had a superb view of that deadly wall of coral, marked by its line of white foam along the Queensland coast.

He had taken just under five minutes to travel the whole two thousand kilometres of the Reef. In a single glance, he could span weeks of perilous voyaging for that first *Endeavour*. And through the telescope, he had caught a glimpse of Cooktown and the estuary where the ship had been dragged ashore for repairs, after her near-fatal encounter with the Reef.

A year later, a visit to the Hawaii Deep-Space Tracking station had given him an even more unforgettable experience. He had taken the hydrofoil to Kealakekua Bay, and as he moved swiftly past the bleak volcanic cliffs, he felt a depth of emotion that had surprised and even disconcerted him. The guide had led his group of scientists, engineers and astronauts past the glittering metal pylon that had replaced the earlier monument, destroyed by the Great Tsunami of '68. They had walked on for a few more yards across black, slippery lava to the small plaque at the water's edge. Little waves were breaking over it, but Norton scarcely noticed them as he bent down to read the words:

NEAR THIS SPOT

CAPTAIN JAMES COOK

WAS KILLED

FEBRUARY 14, 1779

ORIGINAL TABLET DEDICATED AUGUST 28, 1928

BY COOK SESQUICENTENNIAL COMMISSION.

REPLACED BY TRICENTENNIAL COMMISSION

FEBRUARY 14, 2079

That was years ago, and a hundred million kilometres away. But at moments like this, Cook's reassuring presence seemed very close. In the secret depths of his mind, he would ask: "Well, Captain—what is *your* advice?" It was a little game he played, on occasions when there were not enough facts for sound judgment, and one had to rely on intuition. That had been part of Cook's genius; he always made the right choice—until the very end, at Kealakekua Bay.

The Sergeant waited patiently, while his Commander stared silently out into the night of Rama. It was no longer unbroken, for at two spots about four kilometres away, the faint patches of light of exploring parties could be clearly seen.

In an emergency, I can recall them within the hour, Norton told himself. And that, surely, should be good enough.

He turned to the Sergeant. "Take this message. Rama Committee, care of Spacecom. Appreciate your advice and will take precautions. Please specify meaning of phrase 'sudden onset'. Respectfully, Norton, Commander, *Endeavour*."

He waited until the sergeant had disappeared towards the blazing lights of the camp, then switched on his recorder again. But the train of thought was broken, and he could not get back into the mood. The letter would have to wait for some other time.

It was not often that Captain Cook came to his aid when he was neglecting his duty. But he suddenly remembered how rarely and briefly poor Elizabeth Cook had seen her husband in sixteen years of married life. Yet she had borne him six children—and outlived them all.

His wives, never more than ten minutes away at the speed of light, had nothing to complain about. . . .

CHAPTER XVII

Spring

DURING THE FIRST "nights" on Rama, it had not been easy to sleep. The darkness and the mysteries it concealed were oppressive, but even more unsettling was the silence. Absence of noise is not a natural condition; all human senses require some input. If they are deprived of it, the mind manufactures its own substitutes.

And so many sleepers had complained of strange noises—even of voices—which were obviously illusions, because those awake had heard nothing. Surgeon-Commander Ernst had prescribed a very simple and effective cure; during the sleeping period, the camp was now lulled by gentle, unobtrusive background music.

This night, Commander Norton found the cure inadequate. He kept straining his ears into the darkness, and he knew what he was listening for. But though a very faint breeze did caress his face from time to time, there was no sound that could possibly be taken for that of a distant, rising wind. Nor did either of the exploring parties report anything unusual.

At last, around Ship's midnight, he went to sleep. There was always a man on watch at the communications console, in case of any urgent messages. No other precautions seemed necessary.

Not even a hurricane could have created the sound that did wake him, and the whole camp, in a single instant. It seemed that the sky was falling, or that Rama had split open and was tearing itself apart. First, there was a rending crack, then a long-drawn-out series of crystalline crashes like a million glass-houses being demolished. It lasted for minutes, though it seemed like hours; it was still continuing, apparently moving away into the distance, when Norton got to the message centre.

"Hub Control! What's happened?"

"Just a moment, Skipper. It's over by the Sea. We're getting the light on it."

Eight kilometres overhead, on the axis of Rama, the searchlight began to swing its beam out across the plain. It reached the edge of the Sea, then started to track along it, scanning around the interior of the world. A quarter of the way round the cylindrical surface, it stopped.

Up there in the sky—or what the mind still persisted in calling the sky—something extraordinary was happening. At first, it seemed to Norton that the Sea was boiling. It was no longer static and frozen in the grip of an eternal winter; a huge area, kilometres across, was in turbulent movement. And it was changing colour; a broad band of white was marching across the ice.

Suddenly a slab perhaps a quarter of a kilometre on a side began to tilt upwards like an opening door. Slowly and majestically, it reared into the sky, glittering and sparkling in the beam of the searchlight. Then it slid back and vanished beneath the surface, while a tidal wave of foaming water raced outwards in all directions from its point of submergence.

Not until then did Commander Norton fully realise what was happening. *The ice was breaking up.* All these days and weeks, the Sea had been thawing, far down in the depths. It was hard to concentrate because of the crashing roar that still filled the world and echoed round the sky, but he tried to think of a reason for so dramatic a convulsion. When a frozen lake or river thawed on Earth, it was nothing like this. . . .

But of course! It was obvious enough, now that it had happened. The Sea was thawing from *beneath* as the solar heat seeped through the hull of Rama. And when ice turns into water, it occupies less volume. . . .

So the Sea had been sinking below the upper layer of ice, leaving it unsupported. Day by day the strain had been building up; now the band of ice that encircled the equator of Rama was collapsing, like a bridge that had lost its central pier. It was splintering into hundreds of floating islands, that would crash and jostle into each other until they too melted. Norton's blood ran suddenly cold, when he remembered the plans that were being made to reach New York by sledge. . . .

The tumult was swiftly subsiding; a temporary stalemate had been reached in the war between ice and water. In a few hours, as the temperature continued to rise, the water would win and the last vestiges of ice would disappear. But in the long run, ice would be the victor, as Rama rounded the sun and set forth once more into the interstellar night.

Norton remembered to start breathing again; then he called the party nearest the Sea. To his relief, Lieut. Rodrigo answered at once. No, the water hadn't reached them. No tidal wave had come sloshing over the edge of the cliff. "So now we know," he added very calmly, "why there *is* a cliff." Norton agreed silently; but that hardly explains, he thought to himself, why the cliff on the southern shore is ten times higher. . . .

The Hub searchlight continued to scan round the world. The awakened Sea was steadily calming, and the boiling white foam no longer raced outwards from capsizing ice-floes. In fifteen minutes, the main disturbance was over.

But Rama was no longer silent; it had awakened from its sleep, and ever and again there came the sound of grinding ice as one berg collided with another.

Spring had been a little late, Norton told himself, but winter had ended. And there was that breeze again, stronger than ever. Rama had given him enough warnings; it was time to go.

As he neared the half-way mark, Commander Norton once again felt gratitude to the darkness that concealed the view above—and below. Though he knew that more than ten thousand steps still lay ahead of him, and could picture the steeply ascending curve in his mind's eye, the fact that he could see only a small portion of it made the prospect more bearable.

This was his second ascent, and he had learned from his mistakes on the first. The great temptation was to climb too quickly in this low gravity; every step was so easy that it was very hard to adopt a slow, plodding rhythm. But unless one did this, after the first few thousand steps strange aches developed in the thighs and calves. Muscles that one never knew existed started to protest, and it was necessary to take longer and longer periods of rest. Towards the end he had spent more time resting than climbing, and even then it was not enough. He had suffered painful leg-cramps for the next two days, and would have been almost incapacitated had he not been back in the zero-gravity environment of the ship.

So this time he had started with almost painful slowness, moving like an old man. He had been the last to leave the plain, and the others were strung out along the half-kilometre of stairway above him; he could see their lights moving up the invisible slope ahead.

He felt sick at heart at the failure of his mission, and even now hoped that this was only a temporary retreat. When they reached the Hub, they could wait until any atmospheric disturbances has ceased. Presumably, it would be a dead calm there, as at the centre of a cyclone, and they could wait out the expected storm in safety.

Once again, he was jumping to conclusions, drawing dangerous analogies from Earth. The meteorology of a whole world, even under steady-state conditions, was a matter of enormous complexity. After several centuries of study, terrestrial weather-forecasting was still not absolutely reliable. And Rama was not merely a completely novel system; it was also undergoing rapid changes, for the temperature had risen several degrees in the last few hours. Yet still there was no sign of the promised hurricane, though there had been a few feeble gusts from apparently random directions.

They had now climbed five kilometres, which in this low and steadily diminishing gravity was equivalent to less than two on Earth. At the third level, three kilometres from the axis, they rested for an hour, taking light refreshments and massaging leg muscles. This was the last point at which they could breathe in comfort; like old-time Himalayan mountaineers, they had left their oxygen supplies here, and now put them on for the final ascent.

An hour later, they had reached the top of the stairway—and the beginning of the ladder. Ahead lay the last, vertical kilometre, fortunately in a gravity field only a few per cent of Earth's. Another thirty-minute rest, a careful check of oxygen, and they were ready for the final lap.

Once again, Norton made sure that all his men were safely ahead of him, spaced out at twenty-metre intervals along the ladder. From now on, it would be a slow, steady haul, extremely boring. The best technique was to empty the mind of all thoughts and to count the rungs as they drifted by—one hundred, two hundred, three hundred, four hundred. . . .

He had just reached twelve hundred and fifty when he suddenly realised that something was wrong. The light shining on the vertical surface immediately in front of his eyes was the wrong colour—and it was much too bright.

Commander Norton did not even have time to check his ascent, or to call a warning to his men. Everything happened in less than a second.

In a soundless concussion of light, dawn burst upon Rama.

CHAPTER XVIII

Dawn

THE LIGHT WAS so brilliant that for a full minute Norton had to keep his eyes clenched tightly shut. Then he risked opening them, and stared through barely-parted lids at the wall a few centimetres in front of his face. He blinked several times, waited for the involuntary tears to drain away, and then turned slowly to behold the dawn.

He could endure the sight for only a few seconds; then he was forced to close his eyes again. It was not the glare that was intolerable—he could grow accustomed to that—but the awesome spectacle of Rama, now seen for the first time in its entirety.

Norton had known exactly what to expect; nevertheless the sight had stunned him. He was seized by a spasm of uncontrollable trembling; his hands tightened round the rungs of the ladder with the violence of a drowning man clutching at a lifebelt. The muscles of his forearms began to knot, yet at the same time his legs—already fatigued by hours of steady climbing—seemed about to give way. If it had not been for the low gravity, he might have fallen.

Then his training took over, and he began to apply the first remedy for panic. Still keeping his eyes closed and trying to forget the monstrous spectacle around him, he started to take deep, long breaths, filling his lungs with oxygen and washing the poisons of fatigue out of his system.

Presently he felt much better, but he did not open his eyes until he had performed one more action. It took a major effort of will to force his right hand to open—he had to talk to it like a disobedient child—but presently he manoeuvred it down to his waist, unclipped the safety belt from his harness, and hooked the buckle to the nearest rung. Now, whatever happened, he could not fall.

Norton took several more deep breaths; then—still keeping his eyes closed—he switched on his radio. He hoped his voice sounded calm and authoritative as he called: "Captain here. Is everyone O.K.?"

As he checked off the names one by one, and received answers—even if somewhat tremulous ones—from everybody, his own confidence and self-control came swiftly back to him. All his men were safe, and were looking to him for leadership. He was the commander once more.

"Keep your eyes closed until you're quite sure you can take it," he called. "The view is—overwhelming. If anyone finds that it's too much, keep on climbing without looking back. Remember, you'll soon be at zero gravity, so you can't possibly fall."

It was hardly necessary to point out such an elementary fact to trained space-men, but Norton had to remind himself of it every few seconds. The thought of zero gravity was a kind of talisman, protecting him from harm. Whatever his eyes told him, Rama could not drag him down to destruction on the plain eight kilometres below.

It became an urgent matter of pride and self-esteem that he should open his eyes once more and look at the world around him. But first, he had to get his body under control.

He let go of the ladder with *both* hands, and hooked his left arm under a rung. Clenching and unclenching his fists, he waited until the muscle cramps had faded away; then, when he felt quite comfortable, he opened his eyes and slowly turned to face Rama.

His first impression was one of blueness. The glare that filled the sky could not have been mistaken for sunlight; it might have been that of an electric arc. So Rama's sun, Norton told himself, must be hotter than ours. That should interest the astronomers....

And now he understood the purpose of those mysterious trenches, the Straight Valley and its five companions; they were nothing less than gigantic strip-lights. Rama had six linear suns, symmetrically ranged around its interior. From each, a broad fan of light was aimed across the central axis, to shine upon the far side of the world. Norton wondered if they could be switched alternately to produce a cycle of light and darkness, or whether this was a planet of perpetual day.

Too much staring at those blinding bars of light had made his eyes hurt again; he was not sorry to have a good excuse to close them for a while. It was not until then, when he had almost recovered from this initial visual shock, that he was able to devote himself to a much more serious problem.

Who, or what, had switched on the lights of Rama?

This world was sterile, by the most sensitive tests that man could apply to it. But now something was happening that could not be explained by the action of natural forces. There might not be life here, but there could be consciousness, awareness; robots might be waking after a sleep of aeons. Perhaps this outburst of light was an unprogrammed, random spasm—a last dying gasp of machines that were responding wildly to the warmth of a new sun, and would soon lapse again into quiescence, this time forever.

Yet Norton could not believe such a simple explanation. Bits of the jigsaw puzzle were beginning to fall into place, though many were still missing. The absence of all signs of wear, for example—the feeling of *newness*, as if Rama had just been created. . . .

These thoughts might have inspired fear, even terror. Somehow, they did nothing of the sort. On the contrary, Norton felt a sense of exhilaration—almost of delight. There was far more here to discover than they had ever dared to hope. "Wait," he said to himself, "until the Rama Committee hears about *this*!"

Then, with calm determination, he opened his eyes again and began a careful inventory of everything he saw.

First, he had to establish some kind of reference system. He was looking at the largest enclosed space ever seen by man, and needed a mental map to find his way around it.

The feeble gravity was very little help, for with an effort of will he could switch Up and Down in any direction he pleased. But some directions were psychologically dangerous; whenever his mind skirted these, he had to vector it hastily away.

Safest of all was to imagine that he was at the bowl-shaped bottom of a gigantic well, sixteen kilometres wide and fifty deep. The advantage of this image was that there could be no danger of falling further; nevertheless, it had some serious defects.

He could pretend that the scattered towns and cities, and the differently coloured and textured areas, were all securely fixed to the towering walls. The various complex structures that could be seen hanging from the dome overhead were perhaps no more disconcerting than the pendent candelabra in some great concert-hall on Earth. What was quite unacceptable was the Cylindrical Sea. . . .

There it was, half-way up the well-shaft—a band of water, wrapped completely round it, with no visible means of support. There could be no doubt that it *was* water; it was a vivid blue, flecked with brilliant sparkles from the few remaining ice-floes. But a vertical sea forming a complete circle twenty kilometres up in the sky was such an unsettling phenomenon that after a while he began to seek an alternative.

That was when his mind switched the scene through ninety degrees. Instantly, the deep well became a long tunnel, capped at either end. "Down" was obviously in the direction of the ladder and the stairway he had just ascended; and now with this perspective, Norton was at last able to appreciate the true vision of the architects who had built this place.

He was clinging to the face of a curving sixteen-kilometre-high cliff, the upper half of which overhung completely until it merged into the arched roof of what was now the sky. Beneath him, the ladder descended more than five hundred metres, until it ended at the first ledge or terrace. There the stairway began, continuing almost vertically at first in this low-gravity regime, then slowly becoming less and less steep until, after breaking at five more platforms, it reached the distant plain. For the first two or three kilometres he could see the individual steps, but thereafter they had merged into a continuous band.

The downward swoop of that immense stairway was so overwhelming that it was impossible to appreciate its true scale. Norton had once flown round Mount Everest, and had been awed by its size. He reminded himself that this stairway was as high as the Himalayas, but the comparison was meaningless.

And no comparison at all was possible with the other two stairways, Beta and Gamma, which slanted up into the sky and then curved far out over his head. Norton had now acquired enough confidence to lean back and glance up at them—briefly. Then he tried to forget that they were there. . . .

For too much thinking along those lines evoked yet a third image of Rama, which he was anxious to avoid at all costs. This was the viewpoint that regarded it once again as a vertical cylinder or well—but now he was at the *top*, not the bottom, like a fly crawling upside down on a domed ceiling, with a fifty-kilometre drop immediately below. Every time Norton found this image creeping up on him, it needed all his will-power not to cling to the ladder again in mindless panic.

In time, he was sure, all these fears would ebb. The wonder and strangeness of Rama would banish its terrors, at least for men who were trained to face the realities of space. Perhaps no one who had never left Earth, and had never seen the stars all around him, could endure these vistas. But if any men could accept them, Norton told himself with grim determination, it would be the captain and crew of *Endeavour*.

He looked at his chronometer. This pause had lasted only two minutes, but it had seemed a lifetime. Exerting barely enough effort to overcome his inertia and the fading gravitational field, he started to pull himself slowly up the last hundred metres of the ladder. Just before he entered the airlock and turned his back upon Rama, he made one final swift survey of the interior.

It had changed, even in the last few minutes; a mist was rising from the Sea. For the first few hundred metres the ghostly white columns were tilted sharply forward in the direction of Rama's spin; then they started to dissolve in a swirl of turbulence, as the uprushing air tried to jettison its excess velocity. The Trade Winds of this cylindrical world were beginning to etch their patterns in its sky; the first tropical storm in unknown ages was about to break.

CHAPTER XIX

A Warning from Mercury

I T   W A S   T H E   first time in weeks that every member of the Rama Committee had made himself available. Professor Solomons had emerged from the depths of the Pacific, where he had been studying mining operations along the mid-ocean trenches. And to nobody's surprise, Dr. Taylor had reappeared, now that there was at least a possibility that Rama held something more newsworthy than lifeless artifacts.

The Chairman had fully expected Dr. Carlisle Perera to be even more dogmatically assertive than usual, now that his prediction of a Raman hurricane had been confirmed. To His Excellency's great surprise, Perera was remarkably subdued, and accepted the congratulations of his colleagues in a manner as near to embarrassment as he was ever likely to achieve.

The exobiologist, in fact, was deeply mortified. The spectacular break-up of the Cylindrical Sea was a much more obvious phenomenon than the hurricane winds—yet he had completely overlooked it. To have remembered that hot air rises, but to have forgotten that hot ice contracts, was not an achievement of which he could be very proud. However, he would soon get over it, and revert to his normal Olympian self-confidence.

When the Chairman offered him the floor, and asked what further climatic changes he expected, he was very careful to hedge his bets.

"You must realise," he explained, "that the meteorology of a world as strange as Rama may have many other surprises. But if my calculations are correct, there will be no further storms, and conditions will soon be stable. There will be a slow temperature rise until perihelion—and beyond—but that won't concern us, as *Endeavour* will have had to leave long before then."

"So it should soon be safe to go back inside?"

"Er—probably. We should certainly know in forty-eight hours."

"A return is imperative," said the Ambassador for Mercury. "We have to learn everything we possibly can about Rama. The situation has now changed completely."

"I think we know what you mean, but would you care to elaborate?"

"Of course. Until now, we have assumed that Rama is lifeless—or at any rate uncontrolled. But we can no longer pretend that it is a derelict. Even if there are no life-forms aboard, it may be directed by robot mechanisms, programmed to carry out some mission—perhaps one highly disadvantageous to us. Unpalatable though it may be, we must consider the question of self-defence."

There was a babble of protesting voices, and the Chairman had to hold up his hand to restore order.

"Let His Excellency finish!" he pleaded. "Whether we like the idea or not, it should be considered seriously."

"With all due respect to the Ambassador," said Dr. Conrad Taylor in his most disrespectful voice, "I think we can rule out as naïve the fear of malevolent intervention. Creatures as advanced as the Ramans must have correspondingly developed morals. Otherwise, they would have destroyed themselves —as we nearly did in the twentieth century. I've made that quite clear in my new book *Ethos and Cosmos*. I hope you received your copy."

"Yes, thank you, though I'm afraid the pressure of other matters has not allowed me to read beyond the introduction. However, I'm familiar with the general thesis. We may have no malevolent intentions towards an ant-heap. But if we want to build a house on the same site. . . ."

"This is as bad as the Pandora Party! It's nothing less than interstellar xenophobia!"

"Please, *gentlemen*! This is getting us nowhere. Mr. Ambassador, you still have the floor."

The Chairman glared across three hundred and eighty thousand kilometres of space at Conrad Taylor, who reluctantly subsided, like a volcano biding its time.

"Thank you," said the Ambassador for Mercury. "The danger may be unlikely, but where the future of the human race is involved, we can take no chances. And, if I may say so, we Hermians may be particularly concerned. We may have more cause for alarm than anyone else."

Dr. Taylor snorted audibly, but was quelled by another glare from the Moon.

"Why Mercury, more than any other planet?" asked the Chairman.

"Look at the dynamics of the situation. Rama is already inside our orbit. It is only an assumption that it will go round the sun and head on out again into space. Suppose it carries out a braking manoeuvre? If it does so, this will be at perihelion, about thirty days from now. My scientists tell me that if the entire velocity change is carried out there, Rama will end up in a circular orbit only twenty-five million kilometres from the sun. From here, it could dominate the solar system."

For a long time nobody—not even Conrad Taylor—spoke a word. All the members of the committee were marshalling their thoughts about those difficult people the Hermians, so ably represented here by their Ambassador.

To most people, Mercury was a fairly good approximation of Hell; at least, it would do until something worse came along. But the Hermians were proud of their bizarre planet, with its days longer than its years, its double sunrises and sunsets, its rivers of molten metal. . . . By comparison, the Moon and Mars had been almost trivial challenges. Not until men landed on Venus (if they ever did) would they encounter an environment more hostile than that of Mercury.

And yet this world had turned out to be, in many ways, the key to the solar system. This seemed obvious in retrospect, but the Space Age had been almost a century old before the fact was realised. Now the Hermians never let anyone forget it.

Long before men reached the planet, Mercury's abnormal density hinted at the heavy elements it contained; even so, its wealth was still a source of astonishment, and had postponed for a thousand years any fears that the key metals of human civilisation would be exhausted. And these treasures were in the best possible place, where the power of the Sun was ten times greater than on frigid Earth.

Unlimited energy—unlimited metal; *that* was Mercury. Its great magnetic launchers could catapult manufactured products to any point in the solar system. It could also export energy, in synthetic transuranium isotopes or pure radiation. It had even been been proposed that Hermian lasers would one day thaw out gigantic Jupiter, but this idea had not been well received on the other worlds. A technology that could cook Jupiter had too many tempting possibilities for interplanetary blackmail.

That such a concern had ever been expressed said a good deal about the general attitude towards the Hermians. They were respected for their toughness and engineering skills, and admired for the way in which they had conquered so fearsome a world. But they were not liked, and still less were they completely trusted.

At the same time, it was possible to appreciate their point of view. The Hermians, it was often joked, sometimes behaved as if the Sun was their personal property. They were bound to it in an intimate love-hate relationship —as the Vikings had once been linked to the sea, the Nepalese to the Himalayas, the Eskimos to the tundra. They would be most unhappy if something came between them and the natural force that dominated and controlled their lives.

At last, the Chairman broke the long silence. He still remembered the sun of India, and shuddered to contemplate the sun of Mercury. So he took the Hermians very seriously indeed, even though he considered them uncouth technological barbarians.

"I think there is some merit in your argument, Mr. Ambassador," he said slowly. "Have you any proposals?"

"Yes, sir. Before we know what action to take, we must have the facts. We know the geography of Rama—if one can use that term—but we have no idea of its capabilities. And the key to the problem is this: does Rama have a propulsion system? *Can it change orbit?* I'd be very interested in Dr. Perera's views."

"I've given the subject a good deal of thought," answered the exobiologist. "Of course, Rama must have been given its original impetus by some launching device, but that could have been an external booster. If it does have onboard propulsion, we've found no trace of it. Certainly there are no rocket exhausts, or anything similar, anywhere on the outer shell."

"They could be hidden."

"True, but there would seem little point in it. And where are the propellant tanks, the energy sources? The main hull is solid—we've checked that with seismic surveys. The cavities in the northern cap are all accounted for by the airlock systems.

"That leaves the southern end of Rama, which Commander Norton has been unable to reach, owing to that ten-kilometre-wide band of water. There are all sorts of curious mechanisms and structures up on the South Pole—you've seen the photographs. What they are is anybody's guess.

"But I'm reasonably sure of this. If Rama does have a propulsion system, it's something completely outside our present knowledge. In fact, it would have to be the fabulous 'Space Drive' people have been talking about for two hundred years."

"You wouldn't rule that out?"

"Certainly not. If we can prove that Rama has a Space Drive—even if we learn nothing about its mode of operation—that would be a major discovery. At least we'd know that such a thing is possible."

"What *is* a Space Drive?" asked the Ambassador for Earth, rather plaintively.

"Any kind of propulsion system, Sir Robert, that doesn't work on the rocket principle. Anti-gravity—if it is possible—would do very nicely. At present, we don't know where to look for such a drive, and most scientists doubt if it exists."

"It doesn't," Professor Davidson interjected. "Newton settled *that*. You can't have action without reaction. Space drives are nonsense. Take it from me."

"You may be right," Perera replied with unusual blandness. "But if Rama doesn't have a Space Drive, it has no drive at all. There's simply no room for a conventional propulsion system, with its enormous fuel tanks."

"It's hard to imagine a whole world being pushed around," said Dennis Solomons. "What would happen to the objects inside it? Everything would have to be bolted down. Most inconvenient."

"Well, the acceleration would probably be very low. The biggest problem would be the water in the Cylindrical Sea. How would you stop that from . . ."

Perera's voice suddenly faded away, and his eyes glazed over. He seemed to be in the throes of incipient epileptic fit, or even a heart attack. His colleagues looked at him in alarm; then he made a sudden recovery, banged his fist on the table and shouted: "Of course! That explains everything! The southern cliff—*now* it makes sense!"

"Not to me," grumbled the Lunar Ambassador, speaking for all the diplomats present.

"Look at this longitudinal cross-section of Rama," Perera continued excitedly, unfolding his map. "Have you got your copies? The Cylindrical Sea is enclosed between two cliffs, which completely circle the interior of Rama. The one on the north is only fifty metres high. The southern one, on the other hand, is almost half a kilometre high. Why the big difference? No one's been able to think of a sensible reason.

"But suppose Rama *is* able to propel itself—accelerating so that the northern end is forward. The water in the Sea would tend to move back; the level at the south would rise—perhaps hundreds of metres. Hence the cliff. Let's see——"

Perera started scribbling furiously. After an astonishingly short time—it could not have been more than twenty seconds—he looked up in triumph.

"Knowing the height of those cliffs, we can calculate the maximum acceleration Rama can take. If it was more than two per cent of a gravity, the Sea would slosh over into the southern continent."

"A fiftieth of a gee? That's not very much."

"It is—for a mass of ten million megatons. And it's all you need for astronomical manoeuvring."

"Thank you very much, Dr. Perera," said the Hermian Ambassador. "You've given us a lot to think about. Mr. Chairman—can we impress on Commander Norton the importance of looking at the South Polar region?"

"He's doing his best. The Sea is the obstacle, of course. They're trying to build some kind of raft—so that they can at least reach New York."

"The South Pole may be even more important. Meanwhile, I am going to bring these matters to the attention of the General Assembly. Do I have your approval?"

There were no objections, not even from Dr. Taylor. But just as the committee members were about to switch out of circuit, Sir Lewis raised his hand. The old historian very seldom spoke; when he did, everyone listened.

"Suppose we do find that Rama is—*active*—and has these capabilities. There is an old saying in military affairs that capability does not imply intention."

"How long should we wait to find what its intentions are?" asked the Hermian. "When we discover them, it may be far too late."

"It is already too late. There is nothing we can do to affect Rama. Indeed, I doubt if there ever was."

"I do not admit that, Sir Lewis. There are many things we can do—if it proves necessary. But the time is desperately short. Rama is a cosmic egg, being warmed by the fires of the sun. It may hatch at any moment."

The Chairman of the Committee looked at the Ambassador for Mercury in frank astonishment. He had seldom been so surprised in his diplomatic career.

He would never have dreamed that a Hermian was capable of such a poetic flight of imagination.

CHAPTER XX

Book of Revelation

WHEN ONE OF his crew called him "Commander", or, worse still, "*Mister* Norton", there was always something serious afoot. He could not recall that Boris Rodrigo had ever before addressed him in such a fashion, so this must be doubly serious. Even in normal times, Lieut.-Commander Rodrigo was a very grave and sober person.

"What's the problem, Boris?" he asked when the cabin door closed behind them.

"I'd like permission, Commander, to use Ship Priority for a direct message to Earth."

This *was* unusual, though not unprecedented. Routine signals went to the nearest planetary relay—at the moment, they were working through Mercury —and even though the transit time was only a matter of minutes, it was often five or six hours before the message arrived at the desk of the person for whom it was intended. Ninety-nine per cent of the time, that was quite good enough; but in an emergency more direct, and much more expensive, channels could be employed, at the captain's discretion.

"You know, of course, that you have to give me a good reason. All our available bandwidth is already clogged with data transmissions. Is this a personal emergency?"

"No, Commander. It is much more important than *that*. I want to send a message to the Mother Church."

Uh-uh, said Norton to himself. How do I handle this?

"I'd be glad if you'll explain."

It was not mere curiosity that prompted Norton's request—though that was certainly present. If he gave Boris the priority he asked, he would have to justify his action.

The calm, blue eyes stared into his. He had never known Boris to lose control, to be other than completely self-assured. All the Cosmo-Christers were like this; it was one of the benefits of their faith, and it helped to make them good space-men. Sometimes, however, their unquestioning certainty was just a little annoying to those unfortunates who had not been vouchsafed the Revelation.

"It concerns the purpose of Rama, Commander. I believe I have discovered it."

"Go on."

"Look at the situation. Here is a completely empty, lifeless world—yet it is suitable for human beings. It has water, and an atmosphere we can breathe. It comes from the remote depths of space, aimed precisely at the solar system —something quite incredible, if it was a matter of pure chance. And it appears not only new; *it looks as if it has never been used*."

We've all been through this dozens of times, Norton told himself. What could Boris add to it?

"Our faith has told us to expect such a visitation though we do not know exactly what form it will take. The Bible gives hints. If this is not the Second Coming, it may be the Second Judgment; the story of Noah describes the first. I believe that Rama is a cosmic Ark, sent here to save—those who are worthy of salvation."

There was silence for quite a while in the Captain's cabin. It was not that Norton was at a loss for words; rather, he could think of too many questions, but he was not sure which ones it would be tactful to ask.

Finally he remarked, in as mild and non-committal a voice as he could manage: "That's a very interesting concept, and though I don't go along with your faith, it's a tantalisingly plausible one." He was not being hypocritical or flattering; stripped of its religious overtones, Rodrigo's theory was at least as convincing as half a dozen others he had heard. Suppose some catastrophe was about to befall the human race, and a benevolent higher intelligence knew all about it? That would explain everything, very neatly. However, there were still a few problems. . . .

"A couple of questions, Boris. Rama will be at perihelion in three weeks; then it will round the sun and leave the solar system just as fast as it came in. There's not much time for a Day of Judgment, or for shipping across those who are, er, selected—however *that's* going to be done."

"Very true. So when it reaches perihelion, Rama will have to decelerate and go into a parking orbit—probably one with aphelion at Earth's orbit. There it might make another velocity change, and rendezvous with Earth."

This was disturbingly persuasive. If Rama wished to remain in the solar system, it was going the right way about it. The most efficient way to slow down was to get as close to the sun as possible, and carry out the braking manoeuvre there. If there was any truth in Rodrigo's theory—or some variant of it—it would soon be put to the test.

"One other point, Boris. What's controlling Rama now?"

"There is no doctrine to advise on that. It could be a pure robot. Or it could be—a spirit. That would explain why there are no signs of biological life forms."

The Haunted Asteroid; why had that phrase popped up from the depths of memory? Then he recalled a silly story he had read years ago; he thought it best not to ask Boris if he had ever run into it. He doubted if the other's tastes ran to that sort of reading.

"I'll tell you what we'll do, Boris," said Norton, abruptly making up his mind. He wanted to terminate this interview before it got too difficult, and thought he had found a good compromise.

"Can you sum up your ideas in less than—oh, a thousand bits?"

"Yes, I think so."

"Well, if you can make it sound like a straightforward scientific theory, I'll send it, top priority, to the Rama Committee. Then a copy can go to your Church at the same time, and everyone will be happy."

"Thank you, Commander, I really appreciate it."

"Oh, I'm not doing this to save my conscience. I'd just like to see what the Committee makes of it. Even if I don't agree with you all along the line, you may have hit on something important."

"Well, we'll know at perihelion, won't we?"

"Yes. We'll know at perihelion."

When Boris Rodrigo had left, Norton called the bridge and gave the necessary authorisation. He thought he had solved the problem rather neatly; besides, just suppose that Boris *was* right.

He might have increased his chances of being among the saved.

CHAPTER XXI

After the Storm

A s THEY DRIFTED along the now familiar corridor of the Alpha
airlock complex, Norton wondered if they had let impatience overcome
caution. They had waited aboard *Endeavour* for forty-eight hours—two precious days—ready for instant departure if events should justify it. But nothing
had happened; the instruments left in Rama had detected no unusual activity.
Frustratingly, the television camera on the Hub had been blinded by a fog
which had reduced visibility to a few metres and had only now started to
retreat.

When they operated the final airlock door, and floated out into the cat's-
cradle of guide ropes around the Hub, Norton was struck first by the change
in the light. It was no longer harshly blue, but was much more mellow and
gentle, reminding him of a bright, hazy day on Earth.

He looked outwards along the axis of the world—and could see nothing
except a glowing, featureless tunnel of white, reaching all the way to those
strange mountains at the South Pole. The interior of Rama was completely
blanketed with clouds, and nowhere was a break visible in the overcast. The
top of the layer was quite sharply defined; it formed a smaller cylinder
inside the larger one of this spinning world, leaving a central core,
five or six kilometres wide, quite clear except for a few stray wisps of
cirrus.

The immense tube of cloud was lit from underneath by the six artificial
suns of Rama. The locations of the three on this northern continent were
clearly defined by diffuse strips of light, but those on the far side of the
Cylindrical Sea merged together into a continuous, glowing band.

What is happening down beneath those clouds? Norton asked himself. But
at least the storm, which had centrifuged them into such perfect symmetry
about the axis of Rama, had now died away. Unless there were some other
surprises, it would be safe to descend.

It seemed appropriate, on this return visit, to use the team that had made
the first deep penetration into Rama. Sergeant Myron—like every other member of *Endeavour*'s crew—now fully met Surgeon-Commander Ernst's physical
requirements; he even maintained, with convincing sincerity, that he was
never going to wear his old uniforms again.

As Norton watched Mercer, Calvert and Myron "swimming" quickly and
confidently down the ladder, he reminded himself how much had changed.
That first time they had descended in cold and darkness; now they were
going towards light and warmth. And on all earlier visits, they had been
confident that Rama was dead. That might yet be true, in a biological sense.
But something was stirring; and Boris Rodrigo's phrase would do as well as
any other. The spirit of Rama was awake.

When they had reached the platform at the foot of the ladder and were preparing to start down the stairway, Mercer carried out his usual routine test of the atmosphere. There were some things that he never took for granted; even when the people around him were breathing perfectly comfortably, without aids, he had been known to stop for an air check before opening his helmet. When asked to justify such excessive caution, he had answered: "Because human senses aren't good enough, that's why. You may think you're fine, but you could fall flat on your face with the next deep breath."

He looked at his meter, and said "Damn!"

"What's the trouble?" asked Calvert.

"It's broken—reading too high. Odd; I've never known that to happen before. I'll check it on my breathing circuit."

He plugged the compact little analyser into the test point on his oxygen supply, then stood in thoughtful silence for a while. His companions looked at him with anxious concern; anything that upset Karl was to be taken very seriously indeed.

He unplugged the meter, used it to sample the Rama atmosphere again, then called Hub Control.

"Skipper! Will you take a O_2 reading?"

There was a much longer pause than the request justified. Then Norton radioed back: "I think there's something wrong with my meter."

A slow smile spread across Mercer's face.

"It's up fifty per cent, isn't it?"

"Yes, what does that mean?"

"It means that we can all take off our masks. Isn't that convenient?"

"I'm not sure," replied Norton, echoing the sarcasm in Mercer's voice. "It seems too good to be true." There was no need to say any more. Like all space-men, Commander Norton had a profound suspicion of things that were too good to be true.

Mercer cracked his mask open a trifle, and took a cautious sniff. For the first time at this altitude, the air was perfectly breathable. The musty, dead smell had gone; so had the excessive dryness, which in the past had caused several respiratory complaints. Humidity was now an astonishing eighty per cent; doubtless the thawing of the Sea was responsible for this. There was a muggy feeling in the air, though not an unpleasant one. It was like a summer evening, Mercer told himself, on some tropical coast. The climate inside Rama had improved dramatically during the last few days....

And why? The increased humidity was no problem; the startling rise in oxygen was much more difficult to explain. As he recommenced the descent, Mercer began a whole series of mental calculations. He had not arrived at any satisfactory result by the time they entered the cloud layer.

It was a dramatic experience, for the transition was very abrupt. At one moment they were sliding downwards in clean air, gripping the smooth metal of the handrail so that they would not gain speed too swiftly in this quarter-of-a-gravity region. Then, suddenly, they shot into a blinding white fog, and visibility dropped to a few metres. Mercer put on the brakes so quickly that

Calvert almost bumped into him—and Myron *did* bump into Calvert, nearly knocking him off the rail.

"Take it easy," said Mercer. "Spread out so we can just see each other. And don't let yourself build up speed, in case I have to stop suddenly."

In eerie silence, they continued to glide downwards through the fog. Calvert could just see Mercer as a vague shadow ten metres ahead, and when he looked back, Myron was at the same distance behind him. In some ways, this was even spookier than descending in the complete darkness of the Raman night; then, at least, the searchlight beams had shown them what lay ahead. But *this* was like diving in poor visibility in the open sea.

It was impossible to tell how far they had travelled, and Calvert guessed they had almost reached the fourth level when Mercer suddenly braked again. When they had bunched together, he whispered: "Listen! Don't you hear something?"

"Yes," said Myron, after a minute. "It sounds like the wind."

Calvert was not so sure. He turned his head back and forth, trying to locate the direction of the very faint murmur that had come to them through the fog, then abandoned the attempt as hopeless.

They continued the slide, reached the fourth level, and started on towards the fifth. All the while the sound grew louder—and more hauntingly familiar. They were half-way down the fourth stairway before Myron called out: "Now do you recognise it?"

They would have identified it long ago, but it was not a sound they would ever have associated with any world except Earth. Coming out of the fog, from a source whose distance could not be guessed, was the steady thunder of falling water.

A few minutes later, the cloud ceiling ended as abruptly as it had begun. They shot out into the blinding glare of the Raman day, made more brilliant by the light reflected from the low-hanging clouds. There was the familiar curving plain—now made more acceptable to mind and senses, because its full circle could no longer be seen. It was not too difficult to pretend that they were looking along a broad valley, and that the upward sweep of the Sea was really an *outward* one.

They halted at the fifth and penultimate platform, to report that they were through the cloud cover and to make a careful survey. As far as they could tell, nothing had changed down there on the plain; but up here on the northern dome, Rama had brought forth another wonder.

So there was the origin of the sound they had heard. Descending from some hidden source in the clouds three or four kilometres away was a waterfall, and for long minutes they stared at it silently, almost unable to believe their eyes. Logic told them that on this spinning world no falling object could move in a straight line, but there was something horribly unnatural about a curving waterfall that curved sideways, to many kilometres away from the point directly below its source. . . .

"If Galileo had been born in this world," said Mercer at length, "he'd have gone crazy working out the laws of dynamics."

"I thought I knew them," Calvert replied, "and I'm going crazy anyway. Doesn't it upset you, Prof.?"

"Why should it?" said Sergeant Myron. "It's a perfectly straightforward demonstration of the Coriolis Effect. I wish I could show it to some of my students."

Mercer was staring thoughtfully at the globe-circling band of the Cylindrical Sea.

"Have you noticed what's happened to the water?" he said at last.

"Why—it's no longer so blue. I'd call it pea-green. What does that signify?"

"Perhaps the same thing that it does on Earth. Laura called the Sea an organic soup waiting to be shaken into life. Maybe that's exactly what's happened."

"In a couple of days! It took millions of years on Earth."

"Three hundred and seventy-five million, according to the latest estimate. So *that's* where the oxygen's come from. Rama's shot through the anerobic stage and has got to photosynthetic plants—in about forty-eight hours. I wonder what it will produce tomorrow?"

CHAPTER XXII

To Sail the Cylindrical Sea

WHEN THEY REACHED the foot of the stairway, they had another shock. At first, it appeared that something had gone through the camp, overturning equipment, even collecting smaller objects and carrying them away. But after a brief examination, their alarm was replaced by a rather shamefaced annoyance.

The culprit was only the wind; though they had tied down all loose objects before they left, some ropes must have parted during exceptionally strong gusts. It was several days before they were able to retrieve all their scattered property.

Otherwise, there seemed no major changes. Even the silence of Rama had returned, now that the ephemeral storms of spring were over. And out there at the edge of the Plain was a calm sea, waiting for the first ship in a million years.

"Shouldn't one christen a new boat with a bottle of champagne?"

"Even if we had any on board, I wouldn't allow such a criminal waste. Anyway, it's too late. We've already launched the thing."

"At least it does float. You've won your bet, Jimmy. I'll settle when we get back to Earth."

"It's got to have a name. Any ideas?'

The subject of these unflattering comments was now bobbing beside the steps leading down into the Cylindrical Sea. It was a small raft, constructed from six empty storage drums held together by a light metal framework. Building it, assembling it at Camp Alpha and hauling it on demountable wheels across more than ten kilometres of plain had absorbed the crew's entire energies for several days. It was a gamble that had better pay off.

The prize was worth the risk. The enigmatic towers of New York, gleaming there in the shadowless light five kilometres away, had taunted them ever since they had entered Rama. No one doubted that the city—or whatever it might be—was the real heart of this world. If they did nothing else, they must reach New York.

"We still don't have a name. Skipper—what about it?"

Norton laughed, then became suddenly serious.

"I've got one for you. Call it *Resolution*."

"Why?"

"That was one of Cook's ships. It's a good name—may she live up to it."

There was a thoughtful silence; then Sergeant Barnes, who had been principally responsible for the design, asked for three volunteers. Everyone present held up a hand.

"Sorry—we only have four life-jackets. Boris, Jimmy, Pieter—you've all done some sailing. Let's try her out."

No one thought it in the least peculiar that an Executive Sergeant was now taking charge of the proceedings. Ruby Barnes had the only Master's Certificate aboard, so that settled the matter. She had navigated racing trimarans across the Pacific, and it did not seem likely that a few kilometres of dead-calm water could present much of a challenge to her skills.

Ever since she had set eyes upon the Sea, she had been determined to make this voyage. In all the thousands of years that man had had dealings with the waters of his own world, no sailor had ever faced anything remotely like this. In the last few days a silly little jingle had been running through her mind, and she could not get rid of it. "To sail the Cylindrical Sea...." Well, that was precisely what she was going to do.

Her passengers took their places on the improvised bucket seats, and Ruby opened the throttle. The twenty-kilowatt motor started to whirr, the chain-drives of the reduction gear blurred, and *Resolution* surged away to the cheers of the spectators.

Ruby had hoped to get 15 k.p.h with this load, but would settle for anything over 10. A half-kilometre course had been measured along the cliff, and she made the round trip in five and a half minutes. Allowing for turning time, this worked out at 12 k.p.h; she was quite happy with that.

With no power, but with three energetic paddlers helping her own more skilful blade, Ruby was able to get a quarter of this speed. So even if the motor broke down, they could get back to shore in a couple of hours. The heavy-duty power cells could provide enough energy to circumnavigate the world; she was carrying two spares, to be on the safe side. And now that the fog had completely burned away, even such a cautious mariner as Ruby was prepared to put to sea without a compass.

She saluted smartly as she stepped ashore.

"Maiden voyage of *Resolution* successfully completed, sir. Now awaiting your instructions."

"Very good . . . Admiral. When will you be ready to sail?"

"As soon as stores can be loaded aboard, and the Harbour Master gives us clearance."

"Then we leave at dawn."

"Aye, aye, sir."

Five kilometres of water does not seem very much on a map; it is very different when one is in the middle of it. They had been cruising for only ten minutes, and the fifty-metre cliff facing the Northern Continent already seemed a surprising distance away. Yet, mysteriously, New York hardly appeared much closer than before. . . .

But most of the time they paid little attention to the land; they were still too engrossed in the wonder of the Sea. They no longer made the nervous jokes that had punctuated the start of the voyage; this new experience was too overwhelming.

Every time, Norton told himself, he felt that he had grown accustomed to Rama, it produced some new wonder. As *Resolution* hummed steadily forward, it seemed that they were caught in the trough of a gigantic wave— a wave which curved up on either side until it became vertical—then overhung until the two flanks met in a liquid arch sixteen kilometres above their heads. Despite everything that reason and logic told them, none of the voyagers could for long throw off the impression that at any minute those millions of tons of water would come crashing down from the sky.

Yet despite this, their main feeling was one of exhilaration; there was a sense of danger, without any *real* danger. Unless, of course, the Sea itself produced any more surprises.

That was a distinct possibility, for as Mercer had guessed, the water was now alive. Every spoonful contained thousands of spherical, single-celled micro-organisms, similar to the earliest forms of plankton that had existed in the oceans of Earth.

Yet they showed puzzling differences; they lacked a nucleus, as well as many of the other minimum requirements of even the most primitive terrestrial life forms. And although Laura Ernst—now doubling as research scientist as well as ship's doctor—had proved that they definitely generated oxygen, there were far too few of them to account for the augmentation of Rama's atmosphere. They should have existed in billions, not mere thousands.

Then she discovered that their numbers were dwindling rapidly, and must have been far higher during the first hours of the Raman dawn. It was as if there had been a brief explosion of life, recapitulating on a trillionfold swifter time-scale the early history of Earth. Now, perhaps, it had exhausted itself;

the drifting micro-organisms were disintegrating, releasing their stores of chemicals back into the Sea.

"If you have to swim for it," Dr. Ernst had warned the mariners, "keep your mouths closed. A few drops won't matter—if you spit them out right away. But all those weird organo-metallic salts add up to a fairly poisonous package, and I'd hate to have to work out an antidote."

This danger, fortunately, seemed very unlikely. *Resolution* could stay afloat if any two of her buoyancy tanks were punctured. (When told of this, Joe Calvert had muttered darkly: "Remember the *Titanic*!") And even if she sank, the crude but efficient life-jackets would keep their heads above water. Although Laura had been reluctant to give a firm ruling on this, she did not think that a few hours' immersion in the Sea would be fatal; but she did not recommend it.

After twenty minutes of steady progress, New York was no longer a distant island. It was becoming a real place, and details which they had seen only through telescopes and photo-enlargements were now revealing themselves as massive, solid structures. It was now strikingly apparant that the "city", like so much of Rama, was triplicated; it consisted of three identical, circular complexes or superstructures, rising from a long, oval foundation. Photographs taken from the Hub also indicated that each complex was *itself* divided into three equal components, like a pie sliced into 120-degree portions. This would greatly simplify the task of exploration; presumably they had to examine only one-ninth of New York to have seen the whole of it. Even this would be a formidable undertaking; it would mean investigating at least a square kilometre of buildings and machinery, some of which towered hundreds of metres into the air.

The Ramans, it seemed, had brought the art of triple-redundancy to a high degree of perfection. This was demonstrated in the airlock system, the stairways at the Hub, the artificial suns. And where it really mattered, they had even taken the next step. New York appeared to be an example of triple-triple redundancy.

Ruby was steering *Resolution* towards the central complex, where a flight of steps led up from the water to the very top of the wall or levee which surrounded the island. There was even a conveniently-placed mooring post to which boats could be tied; when she saw this, Ruby became quite excited. Now she would never be content until she found one of the craft in which the Ramans sailed their extraordinary sea.

Norton was the first to step ashore; he looked back at his three companions and said: "Wait here on the boat until I get to the top of the wall. When I wave, Pieter and Boris will join me. You stay at the helm, Ruby, so that we can cast off at a moment's notice. If anything happens to me, report to Karl and follow his instructions. Use your best judgment—but no heroics. Understood?"

"Yes, Skipper. Good luck!"

Commander Norton did not really believe in luck; he never got into a situation until he had analysed all the factors involved and had secured his line of retreat. But once again Rama was forcing him to break some of his cherished rules. Almost every factor here was unknown—as unknown as the Pacific and the Great Barrier Reef had been to his hero, three and a half centuries ago. . . . Yes, he could do with all the luck that happened to be lying around.

The stairway was a virtual duplicate of the one down which they had descended on the other side of the Sea; doubtless his friends over there were looking straight across at him through their telescopes. And "straight" was now the correct word; in this one direction, parallel to the axis of Rama, the Sea was indeed completely flat. It might well be the only body of water in the universe of which this was true, for on all other worlds, every sea or lake must follow the surface of a sphere, with equal curvature in all directions.

"Nearly at the top," he reported, speaking for the record and for his intently listening second-in-command, five kilometres away, "still completely quiet—radiation normal. I'm holding the meter above my head, just in case this wall is acting as a shield for anything. And if there are any hostiles on the other side, they'll shoot that first."

He was joking, of course. And yet—why take any chances, when it was just as easy to avoid them?

When he took the last step, he found that the flat-topped embankment was about ten metres thick; on the inner side, an alternating series of ramps and stairways led down to the main level of the city, twenty metres below. In effect, he was standing on a high wall which completely surrounded New York, and so was able to get a grandstand view of it.

It was a view almost stunning in its complexity, and his first act was to make a slow panoramic scan with his camera. Then he waved to his companions and radioed back across the Sea: "No sign of any activity—everything quiet. Come on up—we'll start exploring."

CHAPTER XXIII

N.Y., Rama

I T W A S N O T a city; it was a machine. Norton had come to that conclusion in ten minutes, and saw no reason to change it after they had made a complete traverse of the island. A city—whatever the nature of its occupants—surely had to provide some form of accommodation: there was nothing here of that nature, unless it was underground. And if that was the case, where were the entrances, the stairways, the elevators? He had not found anything that even qualified as a simple door. . . .

The closest analogy he had ever seen to this place on Earth was a giant chemical processing plant. However, there were no stockpiles of raw materials, or any indications of a transport system to move them around. Nor could he imagine where the finished product would emerge—still less what that product could possibly be. It was all very baffling, and more than a little frustrating.

"Anybody care to make a guess?" he said at last, to all who might be listening. "If this is a factory, what does it make? And where does it get its raw materials?"

"I've a suggestion, Skipper," said Karl Mercer, over on the far shore. "Suppose it uses the Sea. According to Doc, that contains just about anything you can think of."

It was a plausible answer, and Norton had already considered it. There could well be buried pipes leading to the Sea—in fact, there *must* be, for any conceivable chemical plant would require large quantities of water. But he had a suspicion of plausible answers; they were so often wrong.

"That's a good idea, Karl; but what does New York *do* with its seawater?"

For a long time, nobody answered from ship, Hub or northern plain. Then an unexpected voice spoke.

"That's easy, Skipper. But you're all going to laugh at me."

"No, we're not, Ravi. Go ahead."

Sergeant Ravi McAndrews, Chief Steward and Simp Master, was the last person on this ship who would normally get involved in a technical discussion. His IQ was modest and his scientific knowledge was minimal, but he was no fool and had a natural shrewdness which everyone respected.

"Well, it's a factory all right, Skipper, and maybe the Sea provides the raw material . . . after all, that's how it all happened on Earth, though in a different way. . . . I believe New York is a factory for making—Ramans."

Somebody, somewhere, snickered, but became quickly silent and did not identify himself.

"You know, Ravi," said his commander at last, "that theory is crazy enough to be true. And I'm not sure if I want to see it tested . . . at least, until I get back to the mainland."

This celestial New York was just about as wide as the island of Manhattan, but its geometry was totally different. There were few straight thoroughfares; it was a maze of short, concentric arcs, with radial spokes linking them. Luckily, it was impossible to lose one's bearings inside Rama; a single glance at the sky was enough to establish the north–south axis of the world.

They paused at almost every intersection to make a panoramic scan. When all these hundreds of pictures were sorted out, it would be a tedious but fairly straightforward job to construct an accurate scale model of the city. Norton suspected that the resulting jigsaw puzzle would keep scientists busy for generations.

It was even harder to get used to the silence here than it had been out on the plain of Rama. A city-machine should make some sound; yet there was not even the faintest of electric hums, or the slightest whisper of mechanical motion. Several times Norton put his ear to the ground, or to the side of a building, and listened intently. He could hear nothing except the pounding of his own blood.

The machines were sleeping: they were not even ticking over. Would they ever wake again, and for what purpose? Everything was in perfect condition, as usual. It was easy to believe that the closing of a single circuit, in some patient, hidden computer, would bring all this maze back to life.

When at last they had reached the far side of the city, they climbed to the top of the surrounding levee and looked across the southern branch of the Sea. For a long time Norton stared at the five-hundred-metre cliff that barred them from almost half of Rama—and, judging from their telescopic surveys, the most complex and varied half. From this angle, it appeared an ominous, forbidding black, and it was easy to think of it as a prison wall surrounding a whole continent. Nowhere along its entire circle was there a flight of stairways or any other means of access.

He wondered how the Ramans reached their southern land from New York. Probably there was an underground transport system running beneath the Sea, but they must also have aircraft as well; there were many open areas here in the city that could be used for landing. To discover a Raman vehicle would be a major accomplishment—especially if they could learn to operate it. (Though could any conceivable power-source still be functioning, after several hundred thousand years?) There were numerous structures that had the functional look of hangars or garages, but they were all smooth and windowless, as if they had been sprayed with sealant. Sooner or later, Norton had told himself grimly, we'll be forced to use explosives and laser beams. He was determined to put off this decision to the last possible moment.

His reluctance to use brute force was based partly on pride, partly on fear. He did not wish to behave like a technological barbarian, smashing what he could not understand. After all, he was an uninvited visitor in this world, and should act accordingly.

As for his fear—perhaps that was too strong a word; apprehension might be better. The Ramans seemed to have planned for everything; he was not anxious to discover the precautions they had taken to guard their property. When he sailed back to the mainland, it would be with empty hands.

CHAPTER XXIV

Dragonfly

LIEUTENANT JAMES PAK was the most junior officer on board *Endeavour*, and this was only his fourth mission into deep space. He was ambitious, and due for promotion; he had also committed a serious breach of regulations. No wonder, therefore, that he took a long time to make up his mind.

It would be a gamble; if he lost, he could be in deep trouble. He could not only be risking his career; he might even be risking his neck. But if he succeeded, he would be a hero. What finally convinced him was neither of these arguments; it was the certainty that, if he did nothing at all, he would spend the rest of his life brooding over his lost opportunity. Nevertheless, he was still hesitant when he asked the Captain for a private meeting.

What is it *this* time? Norton asked himself, as he analysed the uncertain expression on the young officer's face. He remembered his delicate interview with Boris Rodrigo; no, it wouldn't be anything like that. Jimmy was certainly not the religious type; the only interests he had ever shown outside his work were sport and sex, preferably combined.

It could hardly be the former, and Norton hoped it was not the latter. He had encountered most of the problems that a commanding officer could encounter in this department—except the classical one of an unscheduled birth during a mission. Though this situation was the subject of innumerable jokes, it had never happened yet; but such gross incompetence was probably only a matter of time.

"Well, Jimmy, what is it?"

"I have an idea, Commander. I know how to reach southern continent—even the South Pole."

"I'm listening. How do you propose to do it?"

"Er—by flying there."

"Jimmy, I've had at least five proposals to do that—more, if you count crazy suggestions from Earth. We've looked into the possibility of adapting our space-suit propulsors, but air drag would make them hopelessly inefficient. They'd run out of fuel before they could go ten kilometres."

"I know that. But I have the answer."

Lieut. Pak's attitude was a curious mixture of complete confidence and barely suppressed nervousness. Norton was quite baffled; what was the kid worried about? Surely he knew his commanding officer well enough to be certain that no reasonable proposal would be laughed out of court.

"Well, go on. If it works, I'll see your promotion is retroactive."

That little half-promise, half-joke didn't go down as well as he had hoped. Jimmy gave a rather sickly smile, made several false starts, then decided on an oblique approach to the subject.

"You know, Commander, that I was in the Lunar Olympics last year."

"Of course. Sorry you didn't win."

"It was bad equipment; I know what went wrong. I have friends on Mars who've been working on it, in secret. We want to give everyone a surprise."

"Mars? But I didn't know . . ."

"Not many people do—the sport's still new there; it's only been tried in the Xante Sportsdome. But the best aerodynamicists in the solar system are on Mars; if you can fly in *that* atmosphere, you can fly anywhere.

"Now, my idea was that if the Martians could build a good machine, with all their know-how, it would *really* perform on the Moon—where gravity is only half as strong."

"That seems plausible, but how does it help us?"

Norton was beginning to guess, but he wanted to give Jimmy plenty of rope.

"Well, I formed a syndicate with some friends in Lowell City. They've built a fully aerobatic flyer with some refinements that no one has ever seen before. In lunar gravity, under the Olympic dome, it should create a sensation."

"And win you the gold medal."

"I hope so."

"Let me see if I follow your train of thought correctly. A sky-bike that could enter the Lunar Olympics, at a sixth of a gravity, would be even more sensational inside Rama, with no gravity at all. You could fly it right along the axis, from the North Pole to the South—and back again."

"Yes—easily. The one-way trip would take three hours, non-stop. But of course you could rest whenever you wanted to, as long as you kept near the axis."

"It's a brilliant idea, and I congratulate you. What a pity sky-bikes aren't part of regular Space Survey equipment."

Jimmy seemed to have some difficulty in finding words. He opened his mouth several times, but nothing happened.

"All right, Jimmy. As a matter of morbid interest, and purely off the record, how did you smuggle the thing aboard?"

"Er—'Recreational Stores'."

"Well, you weren't lying. And what about the weight?"

"It's only twenty kilograms."

"*Only!* Still, that's not as bad as I thought. In fact, I'm astonished you can build a bike for that weight."

"Some have been only fifteen, but they were too fragile and usually folded up when they made a turn. There's no danger of *Dragonfly* doing that. As I said, she's fully aerobatic."

"*Dragonfly*—nice name. So tell me just how you plan to use her; then I can decide whether a promotion or a court martial is in order. Or both."

CHAPTER XXV

Maiden Flight

$D_{ragonfly}$ WAS CERTAINLY a good name. The long, tapering wings were almost invisible, except when the light struck them from certain angles and was refracted into rainbow hues. It was as if a soap-bubble had been wrapped round a delicate tracery of aerofoil sections; the envelope enclosing the little flyer was an organic film only a few molecules thick, yet strong enough to control and direct the movements of a 50 k.p.h. air flow.

The pilot—who was also the powerplant and the guidance system—sat on a tiny seat at the centre of gravity, in a semi-reclining position to reduce air resistance. Control was by a single stick which could be moved backwards and forwards, right and left; the only "instrument" was a piece of weighted ribbon attached to the leading edge, to show the direction of the relative wind.

Once the flyer had been assembled at the Hub, Jimmy Pak would allow no one to touch it. Clumsy handling could snap one of the single-fibre structural members, and those glittering wings were an almost irresistible attraction to prying fingers. It was hard to believe that there was *really* something there....

As he watched Jimmy climb into the contraption, Commander Norton began to have second thoughts. If one of those wire-sized struts snapped when *Dragonfly* was on the other side of the Cylindrical Sea, Jimmy would have no way of getting back—even if he was able to make a safe landing. They were also breaking one of the most sacrosanct rules of space exploration; a man was going *alone* into unknown territory, beyond all possibility of help. The only consolation was that he would be in full view and communication all the time; they would know exactly what had happened to him, if he did meet with disaster.

Yet this opportunity was far too good to miss; if one believed in fate or destiny, it would be challenging the gods themselves to neglect the only chance they might ever have of reaching the far side of Rama, and seeing at close quarters the mysteries of the South Pole. Jimmy knew what he was attempting, far better than anyone in the crew could tell him. This was precisely the sort of risk that had to be taken; if it failed, that was the luck of the game. You couldn't win them all....

"Now listen to me carefully, Jimmy," said Surgeon-Commander Ernst. "It's very important not to over-exert yourself. Remember, the oxygen level here at the axis is still very low. If you feel breathless at any time, stop and hyperventilate for thirty seconds—but no longer."

Jimmy nodded absent-mindedly as he tested the controls. The whole rudder-elevator assembly, which formed a single unit on an outrigger five metres behind the rudimentary cockpit, began to twist around; then the flap-shaped ailerons, half-way along the wing, moved alternately up and down.

"Do you want me to swing the prop?" asked Joe Calvert, unable to suppress memories of two-hundred-year-old war movies. "Ignition! Contact!" Probably no one except Jimmy knew what he was talking about, but it helped to relieve the tension.

Very slowly, Jimmy started to move the foot-pedals. The flimsy, broad fan of the airscrew—like the wing, a delicate skeleton covered with shimmering film—began to turn. By the time it had made a few revolutions, it had disappeared completely; and *Dragonfly* was on her way.

She moved straight outwards from the Hub, moving slowly along the axis of Rama. When she had travelled a hundred metres, Jimmy stopped pedalling; it was strange to see an obviously aerodynamic vehicle hanging motionless in mid-air. This must be the first time such a thing had ever happened, except possibly on a very limited scale inside one of the larger space stations.

"How does she handle?" Norton called.

"Response good, stability poor. But I know what the trouble is—no gravity. We'll be better off a kilometre lower down."

"Now wait a minute—is that safe?"

By losing altitude, Jimmy would be sacrificing his main advantage. As long as he stayed precisely on the axis, he—and *Dragonfly*—would be completely weightless. He could hover effortlessly, or even go to sleep if he wished. But as soon as he moved away from the central line around which Rama spun, the pseudo-weight of centrifugal force would reappear.

And so, unless he could maintain himself at this altitude, he would continue to lose height—and at the same time, *to gain weight.* It would be an accelerating process, which could end in catastrophe. The gravity down on the plain of Rama was twice that in which *Dragonfly* had been designed to operate. Jimmy might be able to make a safe landing; he could certainly never take off again.

But he had already considered all this, and he answered confidently enough: "I can manage a tenth of a gee without any trouble. And she'll handle more easily in denser air."

In a slow, leisurely spiral, *Dragonfly* drifted across the sky, roughly following the line of Stairway Alpha down towards the plain. From some angles, the little sky-bike was almost invisible; Jimmy seemed to be sitting in mid-air pedalling furiously. Sometimes he moved in spurts of up to thirty kilometres an hour; then he would coast to a halt, getting the feel of the controls, before accelerating again. And he was always very careful to keep a safe distance from the curving end of Rama.

It was soon obvious that *Dragonfly* handled much better at lower altitudes; she no longer rolled around at any angle, but stabilised so that her wings were parallel to the plain seven kilometres below. Jimmy completed several wide orbits, then started to climb upwards again. He finally halted a few metres above his waiting colleagues and realised, a little belatedly, that he was not quite sure how to land his gossamer craft.

"Shall we throw you a rope?" Norton asked half-seriously.

"No, Skipper—I've got to work this out myself. I won't have anyone to help me at the other end."

He sat thinking for a while, then started to ease *Dragonfly* towards the Hub with short bursts of power. She quickly lost momentum between each, as air drag brought her to rest again. When he was only five metres away, and the sky-bike was still barely moving, Jimmy abandoned ship. He let himself float towards the nearest safety line in the Hub webwork, grasped it, then swung around in time to catch the approaching bike with his hands. The manoeuvre was so neatly executed that it drew a round of applause.

"For my *next* act——" Joe Calvert began.

Jimmy was quick to disclaim any credit.

"That was messy," he said. "But now I know how to do it. I'll take a sticky-bomb on a twenty-metre line; then I'll be able to pull myself in wherever I want to."

"Give me your wrist, Jimmy," ordered the doctor, "and blow into this bag. I'll want a blood sample, too. Did you have any difficulty in breathing?"

"Only at this altitude. Hey, what do you want the blood for?"

"Sugar level; then I can tell how much energy you've used. We've got to make sure you can carry enough fuel for the mission. By the way, what's the endurance for sky-biking?"

"Two hours twenty-five minutes three point six seconds. On the Moon, of course—a two-kilometre circuit in the Olympic Dome."

"And you think you can keep it up for six hours?"

"Easily, since I can stop for a rest at any time. Sky-biking on the Moon is at least twice as hard as it is here."

"O.K., Jimmy—back to the lab. I'll give you a Go-No-Go as soon as I've analysed these samples. I don't want to raise false hopes—but I think you can make it."

A large smile of satisfaction spread across Jimmy Pak's ivory-hued countenance. As he followed Surgeon-Commander Ernst to the airlock, he called back to his companions: "Hands off, *please*! I don't want anyone putting his fist through the wings."

"I'll see to that, Jimmy," promised the Commander. "*Dragonfly* is off limits to *everybody*—including myself."

CHAPTER XXVI

The Voice of Rama

THE REAL MAGNITUDE of his adventure did not hit Jimmy Pak until he reached the coast of the Cylindrical Sea. Until now, he had been over known territory; barring a catastrophic structural failure, he could always land and walk back to base in a few hours.

That option no longer existed. If he came down in the Sea, he would probably drown, quite unpleasantly, in its poisonous waters. And even if he made a safe landing in the southern continent, it might be impossible to rescue him before *Endeavour* had to break away from Rama's sunward orbit.

He was also acutely aware that the foreseeable disasters were the ones most unlikely to happen. The totally unknown region over which he was flying might produce any number of surprises; suppose there were flying creatures here, who objected to his intrusion? He would hate to engage in a dog-fight with anything larger than a pigeon. A few well-placed pecks could destroy *Dragonfly*'s aerodynamics.

Yet, if there were no hazards, there would be no achievement—no sense of adventure. Millions of men would gladly have traded places with him now. He was going not only where no one had ever been before—but where no one would ever go again. In all of history, he would be the only human being to visit the southern regions of Rama. Whenever he felt fear brushing against his mind, he could remember that.

He had now grown accustomed to sitting in mid-air, with the world wrapped around him. Because he had dropped two kilometres below the central axis, he had acquired a definite sense of "up" and "down". The ground was only six kilometres below, but the arch of the sky was ten kilometres overhead. The "city" of London was hanging up there near the zenith; New York, on the other hand, was the right way up, directly ahead.

"*Dragonfly*," said Hub Control, "you're getting a little low. Twenty-two hundred metres from the axis."

"Thanks," he replied. "I'll gain altitude. Let me know when I'm back at twenty."

This was something he'd have to watch. There was a natural tendency to lose height—and he had no instruments to tell him exactly where he was. If he got too far away from the zero gravity of the axis, he might never be able to climb back to it. Fortunately, there was a wide margin for error, and there was always someone watching his progress through a telescope at the Hub.

He was now well out over the Sea, pedalling along at a steady twenty kilometres an hour. In five minutes, he would be over New York; already the island looked rather like a ship, sailing forever round and round the Cylindrical Sea.

When he reached New York, he flew a circle over it, stopping several times so that his little TV camera could send back steady, vibration-free images. The panorama of buildings, towers, industrial plants, power stations—or whatever they were—was fascinating but essentially meaningless. No matter how long he stared at its complexity, he was unlikely to learn anything. The camera would record far more details than he could possibly assimilate; and one day—perhaps years hence—some student might find in them the key to Rama's secrets.

After leaving New York, he crossed the other half of the Sea in only fifteen minutes. Though he was not aware of it, he had been flying fast over water, but as soon as he reached the south coast he unconsciously relaxed and his speed dropped by several kilometres an hour. He might be in wholly alien territory—but at least he was over land.

As soon as he had crossed the great cliff that formed the Sea's southern limit, he panned the TV camera completely round the circle of the world.

"Beautiful!" said Hub Control. "This will keep the map-makers happy. How are you feeling?"

"I'm fine—just a little fatigue, but no more than I expected. How far do you make me from the Pole?"

"Fifteen point six kilometres."

"Tell me when I'm at ten; I'll take a rest then. And make sure I don't get low again. I'll start climbing when I've five to go."

Twenty minutes later the world was closing in upon him; he had come
to the end of the cylindrical section, and was entering the southern dome.

He had studied it for hours through the telescopes at the other end of
Rama, and had learned its geography by heart. Even so, that had not fully
prepared him for the spectacle all around him.

In almost every way the southern and northern ends of Rama differed
completely. Here was no triad of stairways, no series of narrow, concentric
plateaus, no sweeping curve from hub to plain. Instead, there was an immense
central spike, more than five kilometres long, extending along the axis. Six
smaller ones, half this size, were equally spaced around it; the whole assembly
looked like a group of remarkably symmetrical stalactites, hanging from the
roof of a cave. Or, inverting the point of view, the spires of some Cambodian
temple, set at the bottom of a crater. . . .

Linking these slender, tapering towers, and curving down from them to
merge eventually in the cylindrical plain, were flying buttresses that looked
massive enough to bear the weight of a world. And this, perhaps, was their
function, if they were indeed the elements of some exotic drive units, as some
had suggested.

Lieutenant Pak approached the central spike cautiously, stopped pedalling
while he was still a hundred metres away, and let *Dragonfly* drift to rest.
He checked the radiation level, and found only Rama's very low background.
There might be forces at work here which no human instruments could detect,
but that was another unavoidable risk.

"What can you see?" Hub Control asked anxiously.

"Just Big Horn—it's absolutely smooth—no markings—and the point's so
sharp you could use it as a needle. I'm almost scared to go near it."

He was only half joking. It seemed incredible that so massive an object
should taper to such a geometrically perfect point. Jimmy had seen collections
of insects impaled upon pins, and he had no desire for his own *Dragonfly* to
meet a similar fate.

He pedalled slowly forward until the spike had flared out to several metres
in diameter, then stopped again. Opening a small container, he rather gingerly
extracted a sphere about as big as a baseball, and tossed it towards the spike.
As it drifted away, it played out a barely visible thread.

The sticky-bomb hit the smoothly curving surface—and did not rebound.
Jimmy gave the thread an experimental twitch, then a harder tug. Like a
fisherman hauling in his catch, he slowly wound *Dragonfly* across to the tip
of the appropriately christened "Big Horn", until he was able to put out his
hand and make contact with it.

"I suppose you could call this some kind of touch-down," he reported to
Hub Control. "It feels like glass—almost frictionless, and slightly warm. The
sticky-bomb worked fine. Now I'm trying the mike . . . let's see if the suction
pad holds as well . . . plugging in the leads . . . anything coming through?"

There was a long pause from the Hub; then Control said disgustedly:
"Not a damn thing, except the usual thermal noises. Will you tap it with a
piece of metal? Then at least we'll find if its hollow."

"O.K. Now what?"

"We'd like you to fly along the spike, making a complete scan every half-kilometre, and looking out for anything unusual. Then, if you're sure it's safe, you might go across to one of the Little Horns. But only if you're certain you can get back to zero gee without any problems."

"Three kilometres from the axis—that's slightly above lunar gravity. *Dragonfly* was designed for that. I'll just have to work harder."

"Jimmy, this is the Captain. I've got second thoughts on that. Judging by your pictures, the smaller spikes are just the same as the big one. Get the best coverage of them you can with the zoom lens. I don't want you leaving the low-gravity region . . . unless you see something that looks very important. Then we'll talk it over."

"O.K., Skipper," said Jimmy, and perhaps there was just a trace of relief in his voice. "I'll stay close to Big Horn. Here we go again."

He felt he was dropping straight downwards into a narrow valley between a group of incredibly tall and slender mountains. Big Horn now towered a kilometre above him, and the six spikes of the Little Horns were looming up all around. The complex of buttresses and flying arches which surrounded the lower slopes was approaching rapidly; he wondered if he could make a safe landing somewhere down there in that Cyclopean architecture. He could no longer land on Big Horn itself, for the gravity on its widening slopes was now too powerful to be counteracted by the feeble force of the sticky-bomb.

As he came ever closer to the South Pole, he began to feel more and more like a sparrow flying beneath the vaulted roof of some great cathedral—though no cathedral ever built had been even one hundredth the size of this place. He wondered if it was indeed a religious shrine, or something remotely analogous, but quickly dismissed the idea. Nowhere in Rama had there been any trace of artistic expression; everything was purely functional. Perhaps the Ramans felt that they already knew the ultimate secrets of the universe, and were no longer haunted by the yearnings and aspirations that drove mankind.

That was a chilling thought, quite alien to Jimmy's usual not-very-profound philosophy; he felt an urgent need to resume contact, and reported his situation back to his distant friends.

"Say again, *Dragonfly*," replied Hub Control. "We can't understand you —your transmission is garbled."

"I repeat—I'm near the base of Little Horn Number Six, and am using the sticky-bomb to haul myself in."

"Understand only partially. Can you hear me?"

"Yes, perfectly. Repeat, perfectly."

"Please start counting numbers."

"One, two, three, four. . . ."

"Got part of that. Give us beacon for fifteen seconds, then go back to voice."

"Here it is."

Jimmy switched on the low-powered beacon which would locate him any-where inside Rama, and counted off the seconds. When he went over to voice again he asked plaintively: "What's happening? Can you hear me now?"

Presumably Hub didn't, because the controller then asked for fifteen seconds of TV. Not until Jimmy had repeated the question twice did the message get through.

"Glad you can hear us O.K., Jimmy. But there's something very peculiar happening at your end. Listen."

Over the radio, he heard the familiar whistle of his own beacon, played back to him. For a moment it was perfectly normal; then a weird distortion crept into it. The thousand-cycle whistle became modulated by a deep, throb-bing pulse so low that it was almost beneath the threshold of hearing; it was a kind of *basso-profundo* flutter in which each individual vibration could be heard. And the modulation was itself modulated; it rose and fell, rose and fell with a period of about five seconds.

Never for a moment did it occur to Jimmy that there was something wrong with his radio transmitter. This was from outside; though what it was, and what it meant, was beyond his imagination.

Hub Control was not much wiser, but at least it had a theory.

"We think you must be in some kind of very intense field—probably mag-netic—with a frequency of about ten cycles. It may be strong enough to be dangerous. Suggest you get out right away—it may only be local. Switch on your beacon again, and we'll play it back to you. Then you can tell when you're getting clear of the interference."

Jimmy hastily jerked the sticky-bomb loose and abandoned his attempt to land. He swung *Dragonfly* round in a wide circle, listening as he did so to the sound that wavered in his earphones. After flying only a few metres, he could tell that its intensity was falling rapidly; as Hub Control had guessed, it was extremely localised.

He paused for a moment at the last spot where he could hear it, like a faint throbbing deep in his brain. So might a primitive savage have listened in awestruck ignorance to the low humming of a giant power transformer. And even the savage might have guessed that the sound he heard was merely the stray leakage from colossal energies, fully controlled, but biding their time. . . .

Whatever this sound meant, Jimmy was glad to be clear of it. This was no place, among the overwhelming architecture of the South Pole, for a lone man to listen to the voice of Rama.

CHAPTER XXVII

Electric Wind

As JIMMY TURNED homewards, the northern end of Rama seemed incredibly far away. Even the three giant stairways were barely visible, as a faint Y etched on the dome that closed the world. The band of the Cylindrical Sea was a wide and menacing barrier, waiting to swallow him up if, like Icarus, his fragile wings should fail.

But he had come all this way with no problems, and though he was feeling slightly tired he now felt that he had nothing to worry about. He had not even touched his food or water, and had been too excited to rest. On the return journey, he would relax and take it easy. He was also cheered by the thought that the homeward trip could be twenty kilometres shorter than the outward one, for as long as he cleared the Sea, he could make an emergency landing anywhere in the northern continent. That would be a nuisance, because he would have a long walk—and much worse, would have to abandon *Dragonfly*—but it gave him a very comforting safety margin.

He was now gaining altitude, climbing back towards the central spike; Big Horn's tapering needle still stretched for a kilometre ahead of him, and sometimes he felt it was the axis on which this whole world turned.

He had almost reached the tip of Big Horn when he became aware of a curious sensation; a feeling of foreboding, and indeed of physical as well as psychological discomfort, had come over him. He suddenly recalled—and this did nothing at all to help—a phrase he had once come across: *"Someone is walking over your grave."*

At first, he shrugged it off, and continued his steady pedalling. He certainly had no intention of reporting anything as tenuous as a vague malaise to Hub Control, but as it grew steadily worse he was tempted to do so. It could not possibly be psychological; if it was, his mind was much more powerful than he realised. For he could, quite literally, feel his skin beginning to crawl. . . .

Now seriously alarmed, he stopped in mid-air and began to consider the situation. What made it all the more peculiar was the fact that this depressed heavy feeling was not completely novel; he had known it before, but could not remember where.

He looked around him. Nothing had changed. The great spike of Big Horn was a few hundred metres above, with the other side of Rama spanning the sky beyond that. Eight kilometres below lay the complicated patchwork of the southern continent, full of wonders that no other man would ever see. In all the utterly alien yet now familiar landscape, he could find no cause for his discomfort.

Something was tickling the back of his hand; for a moment, he thought an insect had landed there, and brushed it away without looking. He had only half-completed the swift motion when he realised what he was doing and checked himself, feeling slightly foolish. Of course, no one had ever seen an insect in Rama. . . .

He lifted his hand, and stared at it, mildly puzzled because the tickling sensation was still there. It was then that he noticed that every individual hair was standing straight upright. All the way up his forearm it was the same—and so it was with his head, when he checked with an exploring hand.

So *that* was the trouble. He was in a tremendously powerful electric field; the oppressed, heavy sensation he had felt was that which sometimes precedes a thunderstorm on Earth.

The sudden realisation of his predicament brought Jimmy very near to panic. Never before in his life had he been in real physical danger. Like all space-men, he had known moments of frustration with bulky equipment, and times when, owing to mistakes or inexperience, he had wrongly believed he was in a perilous situation. But none of these episodes had lasted more than a few minutes, and usually he was able to laugh at them almost at once.

This time there was no quick way out. He felt naked and alone in a suddenly hostile sky, surrounded by titanic forces which might discharge their furies at any moment. *Dragonfly*—already fragile enough—now seemed more insubstantial than the finest gossamer. The first detonation of the gathering storm would blast her to fragments.

"Hub Control," he said urgently. "There's a static charge building up around me, I think there's going to be a thunderstorm at any moment."

He had barely finished speaking when there was a flicker of light behind him; by the time he had counted ten, the first crackling rumble arrived. Three kilometres—that put it back around the Little Horns. He looked towards them and saw that every one of the six needles seemed to be on fire. Brush discharges, hundreds of metres long, were dancing from their points, as if they were giant lightning conductors.

What was happening back there could take place on an even larger scale near the tapering spike of Big Horn. His best move would be to get as far as possible from this dangerous structure, and to seek clear air. He started to pedal again, accelerating as swifty as he could without putting too great a strain on *Dragonfly*. At the same time he began to lose altitude; even though this would mean entering the region of higher gravity, he was now prepared to take such a risk. Eight kilometres was much too far from the ground for his peace of mind.

The ominous black spike of Big Horn was still free of visible discharges, but he did not doubt that tremendous potentials were building up there. From time to time the thunder still reverberated behind him, rolling round and round the circumference of the world. It suddenly occurred to Jimmy how strange it was to have such a storm in a perfectly clear sky; then he realised that this was not a meteorological phenomenon at all. In fact, it might be only a trivial leakage of energy from some hidden source, deep in the southern cap of Rama. But why *now*? And, even more important—*what next*?

He was now well past the tip of Big Horn, and hoped that he would soon be beyond the range of any lightning discharges. But now he had another problem; the air was becoming turbulent, and he had difficulty in controlling

Dragonfly. A wind seemed to have sprung up from nowhere, and if conditions became much worse the bike's fragile skeleton would be endangered. He pedalled grimly on, trying to smooth out the buffeting by variations in power and movements of his body. Because *Dragonfly* was almost an extension of himself, he was partly successful; but he did not like the faint creaks of protest that came from the main spar, nor the way in which the wings twisted with every gust.

And there was something else that worried him—a faint rushing sound, steadily growing in strength, that seemed to come from the direction of Big Horn. It sounded like gas escaping from a valve under great pressure, and he wondered if it had anything to do with the turbulence which he was battling. Whatever its cause, it gave him yet further grounds for disquiet.

From time to time he reported these phenomena, rather briefly and breathlessly, to Hub Control. No one there could give him any advice, or even suggest what might be happening; but it was reassuring to hear the voices of his friends, even though he was now beginning to fear that he would never see them again.

The turbulence was still increasing. It almost felt as if he was entering a jet stream—which he had once done, in search of a record, while flying a high-altitude glider on Earth. But what could possibly create a jet stream inside Rama?

He had asked himself the right question; as soon as he had formulated it, he knew the answer.

The sound he had heard was the electric wind carrying away the tremendous ionisation that must be building up around Big Horn. Charged air was spraying out along the axis of Rama, and more air was flowing into the low-pressure region behind. He looked back at that gigantic and now doubly threatening needle, trying to visualise the boundaries of the gale that was blowing from it. Perhaps the best tactic would be to fly by ear, getting as far as possible away from the ominous hissing.

Rama spared him the necessity of choice. A sheet of flame burst out behind him, filling the sky. He had time to see it split into six ribbons of fire, stretching from the tip of Big Horn to each of the Little Horns. Then the concussion reached him.

CHAPTER XXVIII

Icarus

J I M M Y P A K H A D barely time to radio: "The wing's buckling—I'm going to crash—I'm going to crash!" when *Dragonfly* started to fold up gracefully around him. The left wing snapped cleanly in the middle, and the outer section drifted away like a gently falling leaf. The right wing put up a more complicated performance. It twisted round at the root, and angled back so sharply that its tip became entangled in the tail. Jimmy felt that he was sitting in a broken kite, slowly falling down the sky.

Yet he was not quite helpless; the airscrew still worked, and while he had power there was still some measure of control. He had perhaps five minutes in which to use it.

Was there any hope of reaching the Sea? No—it was much too far away. Then he remembered that he was still thinking in terrestrial terms; though he was a good swimmer, it would be hours before he could possibly be rescued, and in that time the poisonous waters would undoubtedly have killed him. His only hope was to come down on land; the problem of the sheer southern cliff he would think about later—if there was any "later".

He was falling very slowly, here in this tenth-of-a-gravity zone, but would soon start to accelerate as he got further away from the axis. However, air-drag would complicate the situation, and would prevent him from building up too swift a rate of descent. *Dragonfly*, even without power, would act as a crude parachute. The few kilograms of thrust he could still provide might make all the difference between life and death; that was his only hope.

Hub had stopped talking; his friends could see exactly what was happening to him and knew that there was no way their words could help. Jimmy was now doing the most skilful flying of his life; it was too bad, he thought with grim humour, that his audience was so small, and could not appreciate the finer details of his performance.

He was going down in a wide spiral, and as long as its pitch remained fairly flat his chances of survival were good. His pedalling was helping to keep *Dragonfly* airborne, though he was afraid to exert maximum power in case the broken wings came completely adrift. And every time he swung southwards, he could appreciate the fantastic display that Rama had kindly arranged for his benefit.

The streamers of lightning still played from the tip of Big Horn down to the lesser peaks beneath, but now the whole pattern was rotating. The six-pronged crown of fire was turning against the spin of Rama, making one revolution every few seconds. Jimmy felt that he was watching a giant electric motor in operation, and perhaps that was not hopelessly far from the truth.

He was half-way down to the plain, still orbiting in a flat spiral, when the firework display suddenly ceased. He could feel the tension drain from the sky and knew, without looking, that the hairs on his arms were no longer straining upright. There was nothing to distract or hinder him now, during the last few minutes of his fight for life.

Now that he could be certain of the general area in which he must land, he started to study it intently. Much of this region was a checkerboard of totally conflicting environments, as if a mad landscape gardener had been given a free hand and told to exercise his imagination to the utmost. The squares of the checkerboard were almost a kilometre on a side, and though most of them were flat he could not be sure if they were solid, their colours and textures varied so greatly. He decided to wait until the last possible minute before making a decision—if indeed he had any choice.

When there were a few hundred metres to go, he made a last call to the Hub. "I've still got some control—will be down in half a minute—will call you then."

That was optimistic, and everyone knew it. But he refused to say good-bye; he wanted his comrades to know that he had gone down fighting, and without fear.

Indeed, he felt very little fear, and this surprised him, for he had never thought of himself as a particularly brave man. It was almost as if he was watching the struggles of a complete stranger, and was not himself personally involved. Rather, he was studying an interesting problem in aerodynamics, and changing various parameters to see what would happen. Almost the only emotion he felt was a certain remote regret for lost opportunities—of which the most important was the forthcoming Lunar Olympics. One future at least was decided; *Dragonfly* would never show her paces on the Moon.

A hundred metres to go; his ground speed seemed acceptable, but how fast was he falling? And here was one piece of luck—the terrain was completely flat. He would put forth all his strength in a final burst of power, starting—NOW!

The right wing, having done its duty, finally tore off at the roots. *Dragonfly* started to roll over, and he tried to correct by throwing the weight of his body against the spin. He was looking directly at the curving arch of landscape sixteen kilometres away when he hit.

It seemed altogether unfair and unreasonable that the sky should be so hard.

CHAPTER XXIX

First Contact

WHEN JIMMY PAK returned to consciousness, the first thing he became aware of was a splitting headache. He almost welcomed it; at least it proved that he was still alive.

Then he tried to move, and at once a wide selection of aches and pains brought themselves to his attention. But as far as he could tell, nothing seemed to be broken.

After that, he risked opening his eyes, but closed them at once when he found himself staring straight into the band of light along the ceiling of the world. As a cure for a headache, that view was not recommended.

He was still lying there, regaining his strength and wondering how soon it would be safe to open his eyes, when there was a sudden crunching noise from close at hand. Turning his head very slowly towards the source of the sound, he risked a look—and almost lost consciousness again.

Not more than five metres away, a large crab-like creature was apparently dining on the wreckage of poor *Dragonfly*. When Jimmy recovered his wits he rolled slowly and quietly away from the monster, expecting at every moment to be seized by its claws, when it discovered that more appetising fare was available. However, it took not the slightest notice of him; when he had increased their mutual separation to ten metres, he cautiously propped himself up in a sitting position.

From this greater distance, the thing did not appear quite so formidable. It had a low, flat body about two metres long and one wide, supported on six triple-jointed legs. Jimmy saw that he was mistaken in assuming that it had been eating *Dragonfly*; in fact, he could not see any sign of a mouth. The creature was actually doing a neat job of demolition, using scissor-like claws to chop the sky-bike into small pieces. A whole row of manipulators, which looked uncannily like tiny human hands, then transferred the fragments to a steadily growing pile on the animal's back.

But *was* it an animal? Though that had been Jimmy's first reaction, now he had second thoughts. There was a purposefulness about its behaviour which suggested fairly high intelligence; he could see no reason why any creature of pure instincts should carefully collect the scattered pieces of his sky-bike—unless, perhaps, it was gathering material for a nest.

Keeping a wary eye on the crab, which still ignored him completely, Jimmy struggled to his feet. A few wavering steps demonstrated that he could still walk, though he was not sure if he could outdistance those six legs. Then he switched on his radio, never doubting that it would still be operating. A crash that *he* could survive would not even have been noticed by its solid-state electronics.

"Hub Control," he said softly. "Can you receive me?"

"Thank God! Are you O.K.?"

"Just a bit shaken. Take a look at this."

He turned his camera towards the crab, just in time to record the final demolition of *Dragonfly*'s wing.

"What the devil is it—and why is it chewing up your bike?"

"Wish I knew. It's finished with *Dragonfly*. I'm going to back away, in case it wants to start on me."

Jimmy slowly retreated, never taking his eyes off the crab. It was now moving round and round in a steadily widening spiral, apparently searching for fragments it might have overlooked, and so Jimmy was able to get an overall view of it for the first time.

Now that the initial shock had worn off, he could appreciate that it was quite a handsome beast. The name "crab" which he had automatically given it was perhaps a little misleading; if it had not been so impossibly large, he might have called it a beetle. Its carapace had a beautiful metallic sheen; in fact, he would almost have been prepared to swear that it *was* metal.

That was an interesting idea. Could it be a robot, and not an animal? He stared at the crab intently with this thought in mind, analysing all the details of its anatomy. Where it should have had a mouth was a collection of manipulators that reminded Jimmy strongly of the multipurpose knives that are the delight of all red-blooded boys; there were pinchers, probes, rasps, and even something that looked like a drill. But none of this was decisive. On Earth, the insect world had matched all these tools, and many more. The animal-or-robot question remained in perfect balance in his mind.

The eyes, which might have settled the matter, left it even more ambiguous. They were so deeply recessed in protective hoods that it was impossible to tell whether their lenses were made of crystal or jelly. They were quite expressionless, and of a startlingly vivid blue. Though they had been directed towards Jimmy several times, they had never shown the slightest flicker of interest. In his perhaps biased opinion, that decided the level of the creature's intelligence. An entity —robot or animal—which could ignore a human being could not be very bright.

It had now stopped its circling, and stood still for a few seconds, as if listening to some inaudible message. Then it set off, with a curious rolling gait, in the general direction of the Sea. It moved in a perfectly straight line at a steady four or five kilometres an hour, and had already travelled a couple of hundred metres before Jimmy's still slightly shocked mind registered the fact that the last sad relics of his beloved *Dragonfly* were being carried away from him. He set off in hot and indignant pursuit.

His action was not wholly illogical. The crab was heading towards the Sea— and if any rescue was possible, it would only be from this direction. Moreover, he wanted to discover what the creature would do with its trophy; that should reveal something about its motivation and intelligence.

Because he was still bruised and stiff, it took Jimmy several minutes to catch up with the purposefully moving crab. When he had done so, he followed it at a respectful distance, until he felt sure that it did not resent his presence. It was then that he noticed his water-flask and emergency ration pack among the debris of *Dragonfly*, and instantly felt both hungry and thirsty.

There, scuttling away from him at a remorseless five kilometres an hour, was the only food and drink in all this half of the world. Whatever the risk, he had to get hold of it.

He cautiously closed in on the crab, approaching from right rear. While he kept station with it, he studied the complicated rhythm of its legs, until he could anticipate where they would be at any moment. When he was ready, he muttered a quick "Excuse *me*", and shot swiftly in to grab his property. Jimmy had never dreamed that he would one day have to exercise the skills of a pickpocket, and was delighted with his success. He was out again in less than a second, and the crab never slackened its steady pace.

He dropped back a dozen metres, moistened his lips from the flask, and started to chew a bar of meat concentrate. The little victory made him feel much happier; now he could even risk thinking about his sombre future.

While there was life, there was hope; yet he could imagine no way in which he could possibly be rescued. Even if his colleagues crossed the Sea, how could he reach them, half a kilometre below? "We'll find a way down *somehow*," Hub Control had promised. "That cliff can't go right round the world, without a break anywhere." He had been tempted to answer "Why not?", but had thought better of it.

One of the strangest things about walking inside Rama was that you could always see your destination. Here, the curve of the world did not hide—it *revealed*. For some time Jimmy had been aware of the crab's objective; up there in the land which seemed to rise before him was a half-kilometre-wide pit. It was one of three in the southern continent; from the Hub, it had been impossible to see how deep they were. All had been named after prominent lunar craters, and he was approaching Copernicus. The name was hardly appropriate, for there were no surrounding hills and no central peaks. This Copernicus was merely a deep shaft or well, with perfectly vertical sides.

When he came close enough to look into it, Jimmy was able to see a pool of ominous, leaden-green water at least half a kilometre below. This would put it just about level with the Sea, and he wondered if they were connected.

Winding down the interior of the well was a spiral ramp, completely recessed into the sheer wall, so that the effect was rather like that of rifling in an immense gun-barrel. There seemed to be a remarkable number of turns; not until Jimmy had traced them for several revolutions, getting more and more confused in the process, did he realise that there was not one ramp but *three*, totally independent and 120 degrees apart. In any other background than Rama, the whole concept would have been an impressive architectural *tour de force*.

The three ramps led straight down into the pool and disappeared beneath its opaque surface. Near the water-line Jimmy could see a group of black tunnels or caves; they looked rather sinister, and he wondered if they were inhabited. Perhaps the Ramans were amphibious. . . .

As the crab approached the edge of the well, Jimmy assumed that it was going to descend one of the ramps—perhaps taking the wreckage of *Dragonfly* to some entity who would be able to evaluate it. Instead, the creature walked straight to the brink, extended almost half its body over the gulf without any sign of hesitation, though an error of a few centimetres would have been disastrous—and gave a brisk shrug. The fragments of *Dragonfly* went fluttering down into the depths; there were tears in Jimmy's eyes as he watched them go. So much, he thought bitterly, for *this* creature's intelligence.

Having disposed of the garbage, the crab swung around and started to walk towards Jimmy, standing only about ten metres away. Am I going to get the same treatment? he wondered. He hoped the camera was not too unsteady as he showed Hub Control the rapidly approaching monster. "What do you advise?" he whispered anxiously, without much hope that he would get a useful answer. It was some small consolation to realise that he was making history, and his mind raced through the approved patterns for such a meeting. Until now, all of these had been purely theoretical. He would be the first man to check them in practice.

"Don't run until you're sure it's hostile," Hub Control whispered back at him. Run where? Jimmy asked himself. He thought he could out-distance the thing in a hundred-metre sprint, but had a sick certainty that it could wear him down over the long haul.

Slowly, Jimmy held up his outstretched hands. Men had been arguing for two hundred years about this gesture; would every creature, everywhere in the universe, interpret this as "See—no weopons"? But no one could think of anything better.

The crab showed no reaction whatsoever, nor did it slacken its pace. Ignoring Jimmy completely, it walked straight past him and headed purposefully into the south. Feeling extremely foolish, the acting representative of *Homo sapiens* watched his First Contact stride away across the Raman plain, totally indifferent to his presence.

He had seldom been so humiliated in his life. Then Jimmy's sense of humour came to his rescue. After all, it was no great matter to have been ignored by an animated garbage truck. It would have been worse if it had greeted him as a long-lost brother. . . .

He walked back to the rim of Copernicus, and stared down into its opaque waters. For the first time, he noticed that vague shapes—some of them quite large—were moving slowly back and forth beneath the surface. Presently one of them headed towards the nearest spiral ramp, and something that looked like a multi-legged tank started on the long ascent. At the rate it was going, Jimmy decided, it would take almost an hour to get here; if it was a threat, it was a very slow-moving one.

Then he noticed a flicker of much more rapid movement, near those cave-like openings down by the water-line. Something was travelling very swiftly along the ramp, but he could not focus clearly upon it, or discern any definite shape. It was as if he was looking at a small whirlwind or "dust-devil", about the size of a man. . . .

He blinked and shook his head, keeping his eyes closed for several seconds. When he opened them again, the apparition was gone.

Perhaps the impact had shaken him up more than he had realised; this was the first time he had ever suffered from visual hallucinations. He would not mention it to Hub Control.

Nor would he bother to explore those ramps, as he had half-thought of doing. It would obviously be a waste of energy.

The spinning phantom he had merely imagined seeing had nothing to do with his decision.

Nothing at all; for, of course, Jimmy did not believe in ghosts.

CHAPTER XXX

The Flower

JIMMY'S EXERTIONS HAD made him thirsty, and he was acutely conscious of the fact that in all this land there was no water that a man could drink. With the contents of his flask, he could probably survive a week—but for what purpose? The best brains of Earth would soon be focused on his problem; doubtless Commander Norton would be bombarded with suggestions. But he could imagine no way in which he could lower himself down the face of that half-kilometre cliff. Even if he had a long enough rope, there was nothing to which he could attach it.

Nevertheless, it was foolish—and unmanly—to give up without a struggle. Any help would have to come from the Sea, and while he was marching towards it he could carry on with his job as if nothing had happened. No one else would ever observe and photograph the varied terrain through which he must pass, and that would guarantee a posthumous immortality. Though he would have preferred many other honours, that was better than nothing.

He was only three kilometres from the Sea as poor *Dragonfly* could have flown, but it seemed unlikely that he could reach it in a straight line; some of the terrain ahead of him might prove too great an obstacle. That was no problem, however, as there were plenty of alternative routes. Jimmy could see them all, spread out on the great curving map that swept up and away from him on either side.

He had plenty of time; he would start with the most interesting scenery, even if it took him off his direct route. About a kilometre away towards the right was a square that glittered like cut glass—or a gigantic display of jewellery. It was probably this thought that triggered Jimmy's footsteps. Even a doomed man might reasonably be expected to take some slight interest in a few thousand square metres of gems.

He was not particularly disappointed when they turned out to be quartz crystals, millions of them, set in a bed of sand. The adjacent square of the checkerboard was rather more interesting, being covered with an apparently random pattern of hollow metal columns, set very close together and ranging in height from less than one to more than five metres. It was completely impassable; only a tank could have crashed through that forest of tubes.

Jimmy walked between the crystals and the columns until he came to the first cross-roads. The square on the right was a huge rug or tapestry made of woven wire; he tried to prise a strand loose, but was unable to break it. On the left was a tessellation of hexagonal tiles, so smoothly inlaid that there were no visible joints between them. It would have appeared a continuous surface, had the tiles not been coloured all the hues of the rainbow. Jimmy spent many minutes trying to find two adjacent tiles of the same colour, to see if he could then distinguish their boundaries, but he could not find a single example of such a coincidence.

As he did a slow pan right around the cross-roads, he said plaintively to Hub Control: "What do *you* think this is? I feel I'm trapped in a giant jigsaw puzzle. Or is this the Raman Art Gallery?"

"We're as baffled as you, Jimmy. But there's never been any sign that the Ramans go in for art. Let's wait until we have some more examples before we jump to any conclusions."

The two examples he found at the next cross-roads were not much help. One was completely blank—a smooth, neutral grey, hard but slippery to the touch. The other was a soft sponge, perforated with billions upon billions of tiny holes. He tested it with his foot, and the whole surface undulated sickeningly beneath him like a barely stabilised quicksand.

At the next cross-roads he encountered something strikingly like a ploughed field—except that the furrows were a uniform metre in depth, and the material of which they were made had the texture of a file or rasp. But he paid little attention to this, because the square adjacent to it was the most thought-provoking of all that he had so far met. At last there was something that he could understand; and it was more than a little disturbing.

The entire square was surrounded by a fence, so conventional that he would not have looked at it twice had he seen it on Earth. There were posts—apparently of metal—five metres apart, with six strands of wire strung taut between them.

Beyond this fence was a second, identical one—and beyond that, a third. It was another typical example of Raman redundancy; whatever was penned inside this enclosure would have no chance of breaking out. There was no entrance —no gates that could be swung open to drive in the beast, or beasts, that were presumably kept here. Instead, there was a single hole, like a smaller version of Copernicus, in the centre of the square.

Even in different circumstances, Jimmy would probably not have hesitated, but now he had nothing to lose. He quickly scaled all three fences, walked over to the hole, and peered into it.

Unlike Copernicus, this well was only fifty metres deep. There were three tunnel exits at the bottom, each of which looked large enough to accommodate an elephant. And that was all.

After staring for some time, Jimmy decided that the only thing that made sense about the arrangement was for the floor down there to be an elevator. But *what* it elevated he was never likely to know; he could only guess that it was quite large, and possibly quite dangerous.

During the next few hours, he walked more than ten kilometres along the edge of the Sea, and the checkerboard squares had begun to blur together in his memory. He had seen some that were totally enclosed in tent-like structures of wire mesh, as if they were giant bird-cages. There were others which seemed to be pools of congealed liquid, full of swirl-patterns; however, when he tested them gingerly, they were quite solid. And there was one so utterly black that he could not even see it clearly; only the sense of touch told him that anything was there.

Yet now there was a subtle modulation into something he could understand. Ranging one after the other towards the south was a series of—no other word would do—*fields*. He might have been walking past an experimental farm on Earth; each square was a smooth expanse of carefully levelled earth, the first he had ever seen in the metallic landscapes of Rama.

The great fields were virgin, lifeless—waiting for crops that had never been planted. Jimmy wondered what their purpose could be, since it was incredible that creatures as advanced as the Ramans would engage in any form of agriculture; even on Earth, farming was no more than a popular hobby and a source of exotic luxury foods. But he could swear that these were potential farms, immaculately prepared. He had never seen earth that looked so clean; each square was covered with a great sheet of tough, transparent plastic. He tried to cut through it to obtain a sample, but his knife could barely scratch the surface.

Further inland were other fields, and on many of them were complicated constructions of rods and wires, presumably intended for the support of climbing plants. They looked very bleak and desolate, like leafless trees in the depths of winter. The winter they had known must have been long and terrible indeed, and these few weeks of light and warmth might be only a brief interlude before it came again.

Jimmy never knew what made him stop and look more closely into the metal maze to the south. Unconsciously, his mind must have been checking every detail around him; it had noticed, in this fantastically alien landscape, something even more anomalous.

About a quarter of a kilometre away, in the middle of a trellis of wires and rods, glowed a single speck of colour. It was so small and inconspicuous that it was almost at the limit of visibility; on Earth, no one would have looked at it twice. Yet undoubtedly one of the reasons he had noticed it now was because it reminded him of Earth. . . .

He did not report to Hub Control until he was sure that there was no mistake, and that wishful thinking had not deluded him. Not until he was only a few metres away could he be completely sure that life as he knew it had intruded into the sterile, aseptic world of Rama. For blooming here in lonely splendour at the edge of the southern continent was a flower.

As he came closer, it was obvious to Jimmy that something had gone wrong. There was a hole in the sheathing that, presumably, protected this layer of earth from contamination by unwanted life-forms. Through this break extended a green stem, about as thick as a man's little finger, which twined its way up through the trellis-work. A metre from the ground it burst into an efflorescence of bluish leaves, shaped more like feathers than the foliage of any plant known to Jimmy. The stem ended, at eye-level, in what he had first taken to be a single flower. Now he saw, with no surprise at all, that it was actually three flowers tightly packed together.

The petals were brightly coloured tubes about five centimetres long; there were at least fifty in each bloom and they glittered with such metallic blues, violets and greens, that they seemed more like the wings of a butterfly than anything in the vegetable kingdom. Jimmy knew practically nothing about botany, but he was puzzled to see no trace of any structures resembling petals or stamens. He wondered if the likeness to terrestrial flowers might be a pure coincidence; perhaps this was something more akin to a coral polyp. In either case, it would seem to imply the existence of small, airborne creatures to serve either as fertilising agents—or as food.

It did not really matter. Whatever the scientific definition, to Jimmy this was a flower. The strange miracle, the un-Raman-like accident, of its existence here reminded him of all that he would never see again; and he was determined to possess it.

That would not be easy. It was more than ten metres away, separated from him by a lattice-work made of thin rods. They formed a cubic pattern, repeated over and over again, less than forty centimetres on a side. Jimmy would not have been flying sky-bikes unless he had been slim and wiry, so he knew he could crawl through the interstices of the grid. But getting out again might be quite a different matter; it would certainly be impossible for him to turn around, so he would have to retreat backwards.

Hub Control was delighted with his discovery, when he had described the flower and scanned it from every available angle. There was no objection when he said: "I'm going after it." Nor did he expect there to be; his life was now his own, to do with as he pleased.

He stripped off all his clothes, grasped the smooth metal rods, and started to wriggle into the framework. It was a tight fit; he felt like a prisoner escaping through the bars of his cell. When he had inserted himself completely into the lattice he tried backing out again, just to see if there were any problems. It was considerably more difficult, since he now had to use his outstretched arms for pushing instead of pulling, but he saw no reason why he should get helplessly trapped.

Jimmy was a man of action and impulse, not of introspection. As he squirmed uncomfortably along the narrow corridor of rods, he wasted no time asking himself just why he was performing so quixotic a feat. He had never been interested in flowers in his whole life, yet now he was gambling his last energies to collect one.

It was true that this specimen was unique, and of enormous scientific value. But he really wanted it because it was his last link with the world of life and the planet of his birth.

Yet when the flower was within his grasp, he had sudden qualms. Perhaps it was the only flower that grew in the whole of Rama; was he justified in picking it?

If he needed any excuse, he could console himself with the thought that the Ramans themselves had not included it in their plans. It was obviously a freak, growing ages too late—or too soon. But he did not really require an excuse, and his hesitation was only momentary. He reached out, grasped the stem, and gave a sharp jerk.

The flower came away easily enough; he also collected two of the leaves, then started to back slowly through the lattice. Now that he had only one free hand, progress was extremely difficult, even painful, and he soon had to pause to regain his breath. It was then that he noticed that the feathery leaves were closing, and the headless stem was slowly unwinding itself from its supports. As he watched with a mixture of fascination and dismay, he saw that the whole plant was steadily retreating into the ground, like a mortally injured snake crawling back into its hole.

I've murdered something beautiful, Jimmy told himself. But then Rama had killed him. He was only collecting what was his rightful due.

CHAPTER XXXI

Terminal Velocity

COMMANDER NORTON HAD never yet lost a man, and he had no intention of starting now. Even before Jimmy had set off for the South Pole, he had been considering ways of rescuing him in the event of accident; the problem, however, had turned out to be so difficult that he had found no answer. All that he had managed to do was to eliminate every obvious solution.

How does one climb a half-kilometre vertical cliff, even in reduced gravity? With the right equipment—and training—it would be easy enough. But there were no piton-guns aboard *Endeavour*, and no one could think of any other practical way of driving the necessary hundreds of spikes into that hard, mirror surface.

He had glanced briefly at more exotic solutions, some frankly crazy. Perhaps a simp, fitted with suction pads, could make the ascent. But even if this scheme was practical, how long would it take to manufacture and test such equipment—and to train a simp to use it? He doubted if a man would have the necessary strength to perform the feat.

Then there was more advanced technology. The EVA propulsion units were tempting, but their thrust was too small, since they were designed for zero-gee operation. They could not possibly lift the weight of a man, even against Rama's modest gravity.

Could an EVA thruster be sent up on automatic control, carrying only a rescue line? He had tried out this idea on Sergeant Myron, who had promptly shot it down in flames. There were, the engineer pointed out, severe stability problems; they might be solved, but it would take a long time—much longer than they could afford.

What about balloons? There seemed a faint possibility here, if they could devise an envelope and a sufficiently compact source of heat. This was the only approach that Norton had not dismissed, when the problem suddenly ceased to be one of theory, and became a matter of life and death, dominating the news in all the inhabited worlds.

While Jimmy was making his trek along the edge of the Sea, half the crackpots in the solar system were trying to save him. At Fleet Headquarters, all the suggestions were considered, and about one in a thousand was forwarded to *Endeavour*. Dr. Carlisle Perera's arrived twice—once via the Survey's own network, and once by PLANETCOM, RAMA PRIORITY. It had taken the scientist approximately five minutes of thought and one millisecond of computer time.

At first, Commander Norton thought it was a joke in very poor taste. Then he saw the sender's name and the attached calculations, and did a quick double-take.

He handed the message to Karl Mercer.

"What do you think of this?" he asked, in as non-committal a tone of voice as he could manage.

Karl read it swiftly, then said, "Well I'm damned! He's right, of course."

"Are you *sure*?"

"He was right about the storm, wasn't he? We should have thought of this; it makes me feel a fool."

"You have company. The next problem is—how do we break it to Jimmy?"

"I don't think we should . . . until the last possible minute. That's how I'd prefer it, if I was in his place. Just tell him we're on the way."

Though he could look across the full width of the Cylindrical Sea, and knew the general direction from which *Resolution* was coming, Jimmy did not spot the tiny craft until it had already passed New York. It seemed incredible that it could carry six men—and whatever equipment they had brought to rescue him.

When it was only a kilometre away, he recognised Commander Norton, and started waving. A little later the skipper spotted him, and waved back.

"Glad to see you're in good shape, Jimmy," he radioed. "I promised we wouldn't leave you behind. Now do you believe me?"

Not quite, Jimmy thought; until this moment he had still wondered if this was all a kindly plot to keep up his morale. But the Commander would not have crossed the Sea just to say good-bye; he must have worked out *something*.

"I'll believe you, Skipper," he said, "when I'm down there on the deck. *Now* will you tell me how I'm going to make it?"

Resolution was now slowing down, a hundred metres from the base of the cliff; as far as Jimmy could tell, she carried no unusual equipment—though he was not sure what he had expected to see.

"Sorry about that, Jimmy—but we didn't want you to have too many things to worry about."

Now *that* sounded ominous; what the devil did he mean?

Resolution came to a halt, fifty metres out and five hundred below; Jimmy had almost a bird's-eye view of the Commander as he spoke into his microphone.

"This is it, Jimmy. You'll be perfectly safe, but it will require nerve. We know you've got plenty of that. *You're going to jump.*"

"Five hundred metres!"

"Yes, but at only half a gee."

"So—have you ever fallen two hundred and fifty on Earth?"

"Shut up, or I'll cancel your next leave. You should have worked this out for yourself . . . it's just a question of terminal velocity. In this atmosphere, you can't reach more than ninety kilometres an hour—whether you fall two hundred or two thousand metres. Ninety's a little high for comfort, but we can trim it some more. This is what you'll have to do, so listen carefully . . ."

"I will," said Jimmy. "It had better be good."

He did not interrupt the Commander again, and made no comment when Norton had finished. Yes, it made sense, and was so absurdly simple that it would take a genius to think of it. And, perhaps, someone who did not expect to do it himself. . . .

Jimmy had never tried high-diving, or made a delayed parachute drop, which would have given him some psychological preparation for this feat. One could tell a man that it was perfectly safe to walk a plank across an abyss —yet even if the structural calculations were impeccable, he might still be unable to do it. Now Jimmy understood why the Commander had been so evasive about the details of the rescue. He had been given no time to brood, or to think of objections.

"I don't want to hurry you," said Norton's persuasive voice from half a kilometre below. "But the sooner the better."

Jimmy looked at his precious souvenir, the only flower in Rama. He wrapped it very carefully in his grimy handkerchief, knotted the fabric, and tossed it over the edge of the cliff.

It fluttered down with reassuring slowness, but it also took a very long time, getting smaller, and smaller, and smaller, until he could no longer see it. But then *Resolution* surged forward, and he knew that it had been spotted.

"Beautiful!" exclaimed the Commander enthusiastically. "I'm sure they'll name it after you. O.K.—we're waiting. . . ."

Jimmy stripped off his shirt—the only upper garment anyone ever wore in this now tropical climate—and stretched it thoughtfully. Several times on his trek he had almost discarded it; now it might help to save his life.

For the last time, he looked back at the hollow world he alone had explored, and the distant, ominous pinnacles of the Big and Little Horns. Then, grasping the shirt firmly with his right hand, he took a running jump as far out over the cliff as he could.

Now there was no particular hurry; he had a full twenty seconds in which to enjoy the experience. But he did not waste any time, as the wind strengthened around him and *Resolution* slowly expanded in his field of view. Holding his shirt with both hands, he stretched his arms above his head, so that the rushing air filled the garment and blew it into a hollow tube.

As a parachute, it was hardly a success; the few kilometres an hour it subtracted from his speed was useful, but not vital. It was doing a much more important job—keeping his body vertical, so that he would arrow straight into the sea.

He still had the impression that he was not moving at all, but that the water below was rushing up towards him. Once he had committed himself, he had no sense of fear; indeed, he felt a certain indignation against the skipper for keeping him in the dark. Did he *really* think that he would be scared to jump, if he had to brood over it too long?

At the very last moment, he let go of his shirt, took a deep breath, and grabbed his mouth and nose with his hands. As he had been instructed, he stiffened his body into a rigid bar, and locked his feet together. He would enter the water as cleanly as a falling spear. . . .

"It will be just the same," the Commander had promised, "as stepping off a diving board on Earth. Nothing to it—*if* you make a good entry."

"And if I don't?" he had asked.

"Then you'll have to go back and try again."

Something slapped him across the feet—hard, but not viciously. A million slimy hands were tearing at his body; there was a roaring in his ears, a mounting pressure—and even though his eyes were tightly closed, he could tell that darkness was falling as he arrowed down into the depths of the Cylindrical Sea.

With all this strength, he started to swim upwards towards the fading light. He could not open his eyes for more than a single blink; the poisonous water felt like acid when he did so. He seemed to have been struggling for ages, and more than once he had a nightmare fear that he had lost his orientation and was really swimming downwards. Then he would risk another quick glimpse, and every time the light was stronger.

His eyes were still clenched tightly shut when he broke water. He gulped a precious mouthful of air, rolled over on his back, and looked around.

Resolution was heading towards him at top speed; within seconds, eager hands had grabbed him and dragged him aboard.

"Did you swallow any water?" was the Commander's anxious question.

"I don't think so."

"Rinse out with this, anyway. That's fine. How do you feel?"

"I'm not really sure. I'll let you know in a minute. Oh ... thanks, everybody." The minute was barely up when Jimmy was only too sure how he felt.

"I'm going to be sick," he confessed miserably. His rescuers were incredulous.

"In a dead calm—on a flat sea?" protested Sergeant Barnes, who seemed to regard Jimmy's plight as a direct reflection on her skill.

"I'd hardly call it *flat*," said the Commander, waving his arm around the band of water that circled the sky. "But don't be ashamed—you may have swallowed some of that stuff. Get rid of it as quickly as you can."

Jimmy was still straining, unheroically and unsuccessfully, when there was a sudden flicker of light in the sky behind them. All eyes turned towards the South Pole, and Jimmy instantly forgot his sickness. The Horns had started their firework display again.

There were the kilometre-long streamers of fire, dancing from the central spike to its smaller companions. Once again they began their stately rotation, as if invisible dancers were winding their ribbons around an electric maypole. But now they began to accelerate, moving faster and faster until they blurred into a flickering cone of light.

It was a spectacle more awe-inspiring than any they had yet seen here, and it brought with it a distant crackling roar which added to the impression of overwhelming power. The display lasted for about five minutes; then it stopped as abruptly as if someone had turned a switch.

"I'd like to know what the Rama Committee make of *that*," Norton muttered to no one in particular. "Has anyone here got any theories?"

There was no time for an answer, because at that moment Hub Control called in great excitement.

"*Resolution*! Are you O.K.? Did you feel that?"

"Feel *what*?"

"We think it was an earthquake—it must have happened the minute those fireworks stopped."

"Any damage?"

"I don't think so. It wasn't really violent—but it shook us up a bit."

"We felt nothing at all. But we wouldn't, out here in the Sea."

"Of course, silly of me. Anyway, everything seems quiet now . . . until next time."

"Yes, until the next time," Norton echoed. The mystery of Rama was steadily growing; the more they discovered about it, the less they understood.

There was a sudden shout from the helm.

"Skipper—look—up there in the sky!"

Norton lifted his eyes, swiftly scanning the circuit of the Sea. He saw nothing, until his gaze had almost reached the zenith, and he was staring at the other side of the world.

"My God," he whispered slowly, as he realised that the "next time" was already almost here.

A tidal wave was racing towards them, down the eternal curve of the Cylindrical Sea.

CHAPTER XXXII

The Wave

YET EVEN IN that moment of shock, Norton's first concern was for his ship.

"*Endeavour*!" he called. "Situation report!"

"All O.K., Skipper," was the reassuring answer from the Exec. "We felt a slight tremor, but nothing that could cause any damage. There's been a small change of attitude—the bridge says about point two degrees. They also think the spin rate has altered slightly—we'll have an accurate reading on that in a couple of minutes."

So it's beginning to happen, Norton told himself, and a lot earlier than we expected; we're still a long way from perihelion, and the logical time for an orbit change. But some kind of trim was undoubtedly taking place—and there might be more shocks to come.

Meanwhile, the effects of this first one were all too obvious, up there on the curving sheet of water which seemed perpetually falling from the sky. The wave was still about ten kilometres away, and stretched the full width of the Sea from northern to southern shore. Near the land, it was a foaming wall of white, but in deeper water it was a barely visible blue line, moving much faster than the breakers on either flank. The drag of the shoreward shallows was already bending it into a bow, with the central portion getting further and further ahead.

"Sergeant," said Norton urgently. "This is *your* job. What can we do?"

Sergeant Barnes had brought the raft completely to rest, and was studying the situation intently. Her expression, Norton was relieved to see, showed no trace of alarm—rather a certain zestful excitement, like a skilled athlete about to accept a challenge.

"I wish we had some soundings," she said. "If we're in deep water, there's nothing to worry about."

"Then we're all right. We're still four kilometres from shore."

"I hope so, but I want to study the situation."

She applied power again, and swung *Resolution* around until it was just under way, heading directly towards the approaching wave. Norton judged that the swiftly moving central portion would reach them in less than five minutes, but he could also see that it presented no serious danger. It was only a racing ripple a fraction of a metre high, and would scarcely rock the boat. The walls of foam lagging far behind it were the real menace.

Suddenly, in the very centre of the Sea, a line of breakers appeared. The wave had clearly hit a submerged wall, several kilometres in length, not far below the surface. At the same time, the breakers on the two flanks collapsed, as they ran into deeper water.

Anti-slosh plates, Norton told himself. Exactly the same as in *Endeavour*'s own propellant tanks—but on a thousand-fold greater scale. There must be a complex pattern of them all around the Sea, to damp out any waves as quickly as possible. The only thing that matters now is: are we right on top of one?

Sergeant Barnes was one jump ahead of him. She brought *Resolution* to a full stop and threw out the anchor. It hit bottom at only five metres.

"Haul it up!" she called to her crewmates. "We've got to get away from here!"

Norton agreed heartily; but in which direction? The Sergeant was headed full speed *towards* the wave, which was now only five kilometres away. For the first time, he could hear the sound of its approach—a distant, unmistakable roar which he had never expected to hear inside Rama. Then it changed in intensity; the central portion was collapsing once more—and the flanks were building up again.

He tried to estimate the distance between the submerged baffles, assuming that they were spaced at equal intervals. If he was right, there should be one more to come; if they could station the raft in the deep water between them, they would be perfectly safe.

Sergeant Barnes cut the motor, and threw out the anchor again. It went down thirty metres without hitting bottom.

"We're O.K.," she said, with a sigh of relief. "But I'll keep the motor running."

Now there were only the lagging walls of foam along the coast; out here in the central Sea it was calm again, apart from the inconspicuous blue ripple still speeding towards them. The Sergeant was just holding *Resolution* on course towards the disturbance, ready to pour on full power at a moment's notice.

Then, only two kilometres ahead of them, the Sea started to foam once more. It humped up in white-maned fury, and now its roaring seemed to fill the world. Upon the sixteen-kilometre-high wave of the Cylindrical Sea, a smaller ripple was superimposed, like an avalanche thundering down a mountain slope. And that ripple was quite large enough to kill them.

Sergeant Barnes must have seen the expressions on the faces of her crewmates. She shouted above the roar: "What are you scared about? I've ridden bigger ones than this." That was not quite true; nor did she add that her earlier experience had been in a well-built surf-boat, not an improvised raft. "But if we *have* to jump, wait until I tell you. Check your life-jackets."

She's magnificent, though the Commander—obviously enjoying every minute, like a Viking warrior going into battle. And she's probably right—unless we've miscalculated badly.

The wave continued to rise, curving upwards and over. The slope above them probably exaggerated its height, but it looked enormous—an irresistible force of nature that would overwhelm everything in its path.

Then, within seconds, it collapsed, as if its foundations had been pulled out from underneath it. It was over the submerged barrier, in deep water again. When it reached them a minute later *Resolution* merely bounced up and down a few times before Sergeant Barnes swung the raft around and set off at top speed towards the north.

"Thanks, Ruby—that was splendid. But will we get home before it comes round for the second time?"

"Probably not; it will be back in about twenty minutes. But it will have lost all its strength then; we'll scarcely notice it."

Now that the wave had passed, they could relax and enjoy the voyage—though no one would be completely at ease until they were back on land. The disturbance had left the water swirling round in random eddies, and had also stirred up a most peculiar acidic smell—"Like crushed ants", as Jimmy aptly put it. Though unpleasant, the odour caused none of the attacks of sea-sickness that might have been expected; it was something so alien that human physiology could not respond to it.

A minute later, the wave front hit the next underwater barrier, as it climbed away from them and up the sky. This time, seen from the rear, the spectacle was unimpressive and the voyagers felt ashamed of their previous fears. They began to feel themselves masters of the Cylindrical Sea.

The shock was therefore all the greater when, not more than a hundred metres away, something like a slowly rotating wheel began to rear up out of the water. Glittering metallic spokes, five metres long, emerged dripping from the sea, spun for a moment in the fierce Raman glare, and splashed back into the water. It was as if a giant starfish with tubular arms had broken the surface.

At first sight, it was impossible to tell whether it was an animal or a machine. Then it flopped over and lay half-awash, bobbing up and down in the gentle aftermath of the wave.

Now they could see that there were nine arms, apparently jointed, radiating from a central disc. Two of the arms were broken, snapped off at the outer point. The others ended at a complicated collection of manipulators that reminded Jimmy very strongly of the crab he had encountered. The two creatures came from the same line of evolution—or the same drawingboard.

At the middle of the disc was a small turret, bearing three large eyes. Two were closed, one open—and even that appeared to be blank and unseeing. No one doubted that they were watching the death-throes of some strange monster, tossed up to the surface by the submarine disturbance that had just passed.

Then they saw that it was not alone. Swimming round it, and snapping at its feebly moving limbs, were two small beasts like overgrown lobsters. They were efficiently chopping up the monster, and it did nothing to resist, though its own claws seemed quite capable of dealing with the attackers.

Once again, Jimmy was reminded of the crab that had demolished *Dragon-fly*. He watched intently as the one-sided conflict continued, and quickly confirmed his impression.

"Look, Skipper," he whispered. "Do you see—they're not eating it. They don't even have any mouths. *They're simply chopping it to pieces.* That's exactly what happened to *Dragonfly*."

"You're right. They're dismantling it—like—like a broken machine." Norton wrinkled his nose. "But no dead machine ever smelled like that!"

Then another thought struck him.

"My God—suppose they start on us! Ruby, get us back to shore as quickly as you can!"

Resolution surged forward with reckless disregard for the life of her power cells. Behind them, the nine spokes of the great starfish—they could think of no better name for it—were clipped steadily shorter, and presently the weird tableau sank back into the depths of the Sea.

There was no pursuit, but they did not breathe comfortably again until *Resolution* had drawn up to the landing stage and they had stepped thankfully ashore. As he looked back across that mysterious and now suddenly sinister band of water, Commander Norton grimly determined that no one would ever sail it again. There were too many unknowns, too many dangers....

He looked back upon the towers and ramparts of New York, and the dark cliff of the continent beyond. They were safe now from inquisitive man.

He would not tempt the gods of Rama again.

CHAPTER XXXIII

Spider

FROM NOW ON, Norton had decreed, there would always be at least three people at Camp Alpha, and one of them would always be awake. In addition, all exploring parties would follow the same routine. Potentially dangerous creatures were on the move inside Rama, and though none had shown active hostility, a prudent commander would take no chances.

As an extra safeguard, there was always an observer up on the Hub, keeping watch through a powerful telescope. From this vantage point, the whole interior of Rama could be surveyed, and even the South Pole appeared only a few hundred metres away. The territory round any group of explorers was to be kept under regular observation; in this way, it was hoped to eliminate any possibility of surprise. It was a good plan—and it failed completely.

After the last meal of the day, and just before the 22.00 hour sleep period, Norton, Rodrigo, Calvert and Laura Ernst were watching the regular evening news telecast specially beamed to them from the transmitter at Inferno, Mercury. They had been particularly interested in seeing Jimmy's film of the southern continent, and the return across the Cylindrical Sea—an episode which had excited all viewers. Scientists, news commentators, and members of the Rama Committee had given their opinions, most of them contradictory. No one could agree whether the crab-like creature Jimmy had encountered was an animal, a machine, a genuine Raman—or something that fitted none of these categories.

They had just watched, with a distinctly queasy feeling, the giant starfish being demolished by its predators when they discovered that they were no longer alone. There was an intruder in the camp.

Laura noticed it first. She froze in sudden shock, then said: "Don't move, Bill. Now look slowly to the right."

Norton turned his head. Ten metres away was a slender-legged tripod surmounted by a spherical body no larger than a football. Set around the body were three large, expressionless eyes, apparently giving 360 degrees of vision, and trailing beneath it were three whiplike tendrils. The creature was not quite as tall as a man, and looked far too fragile to be dangerous, but that did not excuse their carelessness in letting it sneak up on them unawares. It reminded Norton of nothing so much as a three-legged spider, or daddy-long-legs, and he wondered how it had solved the problem—never challenged by any creature on Earth—of tripedal locomotion.

"What do you make of it, Doc?" he whispered, turning off the voice of the TV newscaster.

"Usual Raman three-fold symmetry. I don't see how it could hurt us, though those whips might be unpleasant—and they could be poisonous, like a coelenterate's. Sit tight and see what it does."

After regarding them impassively for several minutes, the creature suddenly moved—and now they could understand why they had failed to observe its arrival. It was *fast*, and it covered the ground with such an extraordinary spinning motion that the human eye and mind had real difficulty in following it.

As far as Norton could judge—and only a high-speed camera could settle the matter—each leg in turn acted as a pivot around which the creature whirled its body. And he was not sure, but it also seemed to him that every few "steps" it reversed its direction of spin, while the three whips flickered over the ground like lightning as it moved. Its top speed—though this also was very hard to estimate—was at least thirty kilometres an hour.

It swept swiftly round the camp, examining every item of equipment, delicately touching the improvised beds and chairs and tables, communication gear, food containers, Electrosans, cameras, water tanks, tools—there seemed to be nothing that it ignored, except the four watchers. Clearly, it was intelligent enough to draw a distinction between humans and their inanimate property; its actions gave the unmistakable impression of an extremely methodical curiosity or inquisitiveness.

"I wish I could examine it!" Laura exclaimed in frustration, as the creature continued its swift pirouette. "Shall we try to catch it?"

"How?" Calvert asked, reasonably enough.

"You know—the way primitive hunters bring down fast-moving animals with a couple of weights whirling around at the end of a rope. It doesn't even hurt them."

"That I doubt," said Norton. "But even if it worked, we can't risk it. We don't know how intelligent this creature is—and a trick like that could easily break its legs. Then we would be in real trouble—from Rama, Earth and everyone else."

"But I've got to have a specimen!"

"You may have to be content with Jimmy's flower—unless one of these creatures co-operates with you. Force is out. How would you like it if something landed on Earth and decided that *you* would make a nice specimen for dissection?"

"I don't want to dissect it," said Laura, not at all convincingly. "I only want to examine it.'

"Well, alien visitors might have the same attitude towards you, but you could have a very uncomfortable time before you believed them. We must make no move that could possibly be regarded as threatening."

He was quoting from Ship's Orders, of course, and Laura knew it. The claims of science had a lower priority than those of space-diplomacy.

In fact, there was no need to bring in such elevated considerations; it was merely a matter of good manners. They were all visitors here, and had never even asked permission to come inside. . . .

The creature seemed to have finished its inspection. It made one more high-speed circuit of the camp, then shot off at a tangent—towards the stairway.

"I wonder how it's going to manage the steps?" Laura mused. Her question was quickly answered; the spider ignored them completely, and headed up the gently sloping curve of the ramp without slackening its speed.

"Hub Control," said Norton. "You may have a visitor shortly; take a look at the Alpha Stairway Section Six. And incidentally, thanks a lot for keeping such a good watch on us."

It took a minute for the sarcasm to sink in; then the Hub observer started to make apologetic noises.

"Er—I can just see *something*, Skipper, now you tell me it's there. But what is it?"

"Your guess is as good as mine," Norton answered, as he pressed the *General Alert* button. "Camp Alpha calling all stations. We've just been visited by a creature like a three-legged spider, with very thin legs, about two metres high, small spherical body, travels very fast with a spinning motion. Appears harmless but inquisitive. It may sneak up on you before you notice it. Please acknowledge."

The first reply came from London, fifteen kilometres to the east.

"Nothing unusual here, Skipper."

The same distance to the west, Rome answered, sounding suspiciously sleepy.

"Same here, Skipper. Uh, just a moment . . ."

"What is it?"

"I put my pen down a minute ago—it's gone! What—oh!"

"Talk sense!"

"You won't believe this, Skipper. I was making some notes—you know I like writing, and it doesn't disturb anybody—I was using my favourite ball-point, it's nearly two hundred years old—well, now it's lying on the ground, about five metres away! I've got it—thank goodness—it isn't damaged."

"And how do you suppose it got there?"

"Er—I may have dozed off for a minute. It's been a hard day."

Norton sighed, but refrained from comment; there were so few of them, and they had so little time in which to explore a world. Enthusiasm could not always overcome exhaustion, and he wondered if they were taking unnecessary risks. Perhaps he should not split his men up into such small groups, and try to cover so much territory. But he was always conscious of the swiftly passing days, and the unsolved mysteries around them. He was becoming more and more certain that something was about to happen, and that they would have to abandon Rama even before it reached perihelion—the moment of truth when any orbit change must surely take place.

"Now listen, Hub, Rome, London—everyone," he said. "I want a report at every half-hour through the night. We must assume that from now on we may expect visitors at any time. Some of them may be dangerous, but at all costs we have to avoid incidents. You all know the directives on this subject."

That was true enough; it was part of their training—yet perhaps none of them had ever really believed that the long-theorised "physical contact with intelligent aliens" would occur in their lifetimes—still less that they would experience it themselves.

Training was one thing, reality another; and no one could be sure that the ancient, human instincts of self-preservation would not take over in an emergency. Yet it was essential to give every entity they encountered in Rama the benefit of the doubt, up to the last possible minute—and even beyond.

Commander Norton did not want to be remembered by history as the man who started the first interplantary war.

Within a few hours there were hundreds of the spiders, and they were all over the plain. Through the telescope, it could be seen that the southern continent was also infested with them—but not, it seemed, the island of New York.

They took no further notice of the explorers, and after a while the explorers took little notice of them—though from time to time Norton still detected a predatory gleam in his Surgeon-Commander's eye. Nothing would please her better, he was sure, than for one of the spiders to have an unfortunate accident, and he would not put it past her to arrange such a thing in the interests of science.

It seemed virtually certain that the spiders could not be intelligent; their bodies were far too small to contain much in the way of brains, and indeed it was hard to see where they stored all the energy to move. Yet their behaviour was curiously purposeful and co-ordinated; they seemed to be everywhere, but they never visited the same place twice. Norton frequently had the impression that they were *searching* for something. Whatever it was, they did not seem to have discovered it.

They went all the way up to the central Hub, still scorning the three great stairways. How they managed to ascend the vertical sections, even under almost zero gravity, was not clear; Laura theorised that they were equipped with suction pads.

And then, to her obvious delight, she got her eagerly desired specimen. Hub Control reported that a spider had fallen down the vertical face and was lying, dead or incapacitated, on the first platform. Laura's time up from the plain was a record that would never be beaten.

When she arrived at the platform, she found that, despite the low velocity of impact, the creature had broken all its legs. Its eyes were still open, but it showed no reactions to any external tests. Even a fresh human corpse would have been livelier, Laura decided; as soon as she got her prize back to *Endeavour*, she started to work with her dissecting kit.

The spider was so fragile that it almost came to pieces without her assistance. She disarticulated the legs, then started on the delicate carapace, which split along three great circles and opened up like a peeled orange.

After some moments of blank incredulity—for there was nothing that she could recognise or identify—she took a series of careful photographs. Then she picked up her scalpel.

Where to start cutting? She felt like closing her eyes, and stabbing at random, but that would not have been very scientific.

The blade went in with practically no resistance. A second later, Surgeon-Commander Ernst's most unladylike yell echoed the length and breadth of *Endeavour.*

It took an annoyed Sergeant McAndrews a good twenty minutes to calm down the startled simps.

CHAPTER XXXIV

His Excellency Regrets . . .

"As you are all aware, gentlemen," said the Martian ambassador, "a great deal has happened since our last meeting. We have much to discuss—and to decide. I'm therefore particularly sorry that our distinguished colleague from Mercury is not here."

That last statement was not altogether accurate. Dr. Bose was not particularly sorry that H.E. the Hermian Ambassador was absent. It would have been much more truthful to say that he was worried. All his diplomatic instincts told him that something was happening, and though his sources of information were excellent, he could gather no hints as to what it might be.

The Ambassador's letter of apology had been courteous and entirely uncommunicative. His Excellency had regretted that urgent and unavoidable business had kept him from attending the meeting, either in person or by video. Dr. Bose found it very hard to think of anything more urgent—or more important—than Rama.

"Two of our members have statements to make. I would first like to call on Professor Davidson."

There was a rustle of excitement among the other scientists on the committee. Most of them had felt that the astronomer, with his well-known cosmic viewpoint, was not the right man to be Chairman of the Space Advisory Council. He sometimes gave the impression that the activities of intelligent life were an unfortunate irrelevance in the majestic universe of stars and galaxies, and that it was bad manners to pay too much attention to it. This had not endeared him to exobiologists such as Dr. Perera, who took exactly the opposite view. To them, the only purpose of the Universe was the production of intelligence, and they were apt to talk sneeringly about purely astronomical phenomena. "Mere dead matter" was one of their favourite phrases.

"Mr. Ambassador," the scientist began, "I have been analysing the curious behaviour of Rama during the last few days, and would like to present my conclusions. Some of them are rather startling."

Dr. Perera looked surprised, then rather smug. He strongly approved of anything that startled Professor Davidson.

"First of all, there was the remarkable series of events when that young lieutenant flew over the southern hemisphere. The electrical discharges themselves, though spectacular, are not important; it is easy to show that they contained relatively little energy. But they coincided with a change in Rama's rate of spin, and its attitude—that is, its orientation in space. *This* must have involved an enormous amount of energy; the discharges which nearly cost Mr.—er—Pak his life were merely a minor by-product—perhaps a nuisance that had to be minimised by those giant lightning conductors at the south pole.

"I draw two conclusions from this. When a space-craft—and we must call Rama a space-craft, despite its fantastic size—makes a change of attitude, that usually means it is about to make a change of orbit. We must therefore take seriously the views of those who believe that Rama may be preparing to become another planet of our sun, instead of going back to the stars.

"If this is the case, *Endeavour* must obviously be prepared to cast off—is that what space-ships do?—at a moment's notice. She may be in very serious danger while she is still physically attached to Rama. I imagine that Commander Norton is already well aware of this possibility, but I think we should send him an additional warning."

"Thank you very much, Professor Davidson. Yes—Dr. Solomons?"

"I'd like to comment on that," said the science historian. "Rama seems to have made a change of spin *without* using any jets or reaction devices. This leaves only two possibilities, it seems to me.

"The first one is that it has internal gyroscopes, or their equivalent. They must be enormous; where are they?

"The second possibility—which would turn all our physics upside down—is that it has a reactionless propulsion system. The so-called Space Drive, which Professor Davidson doesn't believe in. If this is the case, Rama may be able to do almost anything. We will be quite unable to anticipate its behaviour, even on the gross physical level."

The diplomats were obviously somewhat baffled by this exchange, and the astronomer refused to be drawn. He had gone out on enough limbs for one day.

"I'll stick to the laws of physics, if you don't mind, until I'm forced to give them up. If we've not found any gyroscopes in Rama, we may not have looked hard enough, or in the right place."

Ambassador Bose could see that Dr. Perera was getting impatient. Normally, the exobiologist was as happy as anyone else to engage in speculation; but now, for the first time, he had some solid facts. His long-impoverished science had become wealthy overnight.

"Very well—if there are no other comments—I know that Dr. Perera has some important information."

"Thank you, Mr. Ambassador. As you've all seen, we have at last obtained a specimen of a Raman life-form, and have observed several others at close quarters. Surgeon-Commander Ernst, *Endeavour*'s medical officer, has sent a full report on the spider-like creature she dissected.

"I must say at once that some of her results are baffling, and in any other circumstances I would have refused to believe them.

"The spider is definitely organic, though its chemistry differs from ours in many respects—it contains considerable quantities of light metals. Yet I hesitate to call it an animal, for several fundamental reasons.

"In the first place, it seems to have no mouth, no stomach, no gut—no method of ingesting food! Also no air intakes, no lungs, no blood, no reproductive system. . . .

"You may wonder what it *has* got. Well, there's a simple musculature, controlling its three legs and the three whiplike tendrils or feelers. There's a brain—fairly complex, mostly concerned with the creature's remarkably developed tri-ocular vision. But eighty per cent of the body consists of a honeycomb of large cells, and this is what gave Dr. Ernst such an unpleasant surprise when she started her dissection. If she'd been luckier she might have recognised it in time, because it's the one Raman structure that *does* exist on Earth—though only in a handful of marine animals.

"Most of the spider is simply a battery, very much like that found in electric cells and rays. But in this case, it's apparently not used for defence. *It's the creature's source of energy.* And that is why it has no provisions for eating and breathing; it doesn't need such primitive arrangements. And incidentally, this means that it would be perfectly at home in a vacuum. . . .

"So we have a creature which, to all intents and purposes, is nothing more than a mobile eye. It has no organs of manipulation; those tendrils are much too feeble. If I had been given its specifications, I would have said it was merely a reconnaissance device.

"Its behaviour certainly fits that description. All the spiders ever do is to run around and look at things. That's all they *can* do. . . .

"But the other animals are different. The crab, the starfish, the sharks—for want of better words—can obviously manipulate their environment and appear to be specialised for various functions. I assume that they are also electrically powered since, like the spider, they appear to have no mouths.

"I'm sure you'll appreciate the biological problems raised by all this. Could such creatures evolve naturally? I really don't think so. They appear to be *designed* like machines, for specific jobs. If I had to describe them, I would say that they are robots—biological robots—something that has no analogy on Earth.

"If Rama is a space-ship, perhaps they are part of its crew. As to how they are born—or created—that's something I can't tell you. But I can guess that the answer's over there in New York. If Commander Norton and his men can wait long enough, they may encounter increasingly more complex creatures, with unpredictable behaviour. Somewhere along the line they may meet the Ramans themselves—the real makers of this world.

"And when *that* happens, gentlemen, there will be no doubt about it at all. . . ."

CHAPTER XXXV

Special Delivery

C OMMANDER NORTON WAS sleeping soundly when his personal communicator dragged him away from happy dreams. He had been holidaying with his family on Mars, flying past the awesome, snow-capped peak of Nix Olympica—mightiest volcano in the solar system. Little Billie had started to say something to him; now he would never know what it was.

The dream faded; the reality was his executive officer, up on the ship.

"Sorry to wake you, Skipper," said Lieut.-Commander Kirchoff. "Triple A priority from Headquarters."

"Let me have it," Norton answered sleepily.

"I can't. It's in code—Commander's Eyes Only."

Norton was instantly awake. He had received such a message only three times in his whole career, and on each occasion it had meant trouble.

"Damn!" he said. "What do we do now?"

His Exec. did not bother to answer. Each understood the problem perfectly; it was one that Ship's Orders had never anticipated. Normally, a commander was never more than a few minutes away from his office and the Code Book in his personal safe. If he started now, Norton might get back to the ship—exhausted—in four or five hours. That was not the way to handle a Class AAA Priority.

"Jerry," he said at length. "Who's on the switchoard?"

"No one; I'm making the call myself."

"Recorder off?"

"By an odd breach of regulations, yes."

Norton smiled. Jerry was the best Exec. he had ever worked with. He thought of everything.

"O.K. You know where my key is. Call me back."

He waited as patiently as he could for the next ten minutes, trying—without much success—to think of other problems. He hated wasting mental effort; it was very unlikely that he could out-guess the message that was coming, and he would know its contents soon enough. *Then* he could start worrying effectively.

When the Exec. called back, he was obviously speaking under considerable strain.

"It's not really *urgent*, Skipper—an hour won't make any difference. But I prefer to avoid radio. I'll send it down by messenger."

"But *why*—oh, very well—I trust your judgment. Who will carry it through the airlocks?"

"I'm going myself; I'll call you when I reach the Hub."

"Which leaves Laura in charge."

"For one hour, at the most. I'll get right back to the ship."

A medical officer did not have the specialised training to be acting commander, any more than a commander could be expected to do an operation. In
emergencies, both jobs had sometimes been successfully switched; but it was
not recommended. Well, one order had already been broken tonight. . . .

"For the record, you never leave the ship. Have you woken Laura?"

"Yes. She's delighted with the opportunity."

"Lucky that doctors are used to keeping secrets. Oh—have you sent the
acknowledgement?"

"Of course, in your name."

"Then I'll be waiting."

Now it was quite impossible to avoid anxious anticipations. "Not *really*
urgent—but I prefer to avoid radio. . . ."

One thing was certain. The Commander was not going to get much more
sleep this night.

CHAPTER XXXVI

Biot Watcher

SERGEANT PIETER ROUSSEAU knew why he had volunteered for
this job; in many ways, it was a realisation of a childhood dream. He had
become fascinated by telescopes when he was only six or seven years old,
and much of his youth had been spent collecting lenses of all shapes and sizes.
These he had mounted in cardboard tubes, making instruments of ever-increasing power until he was familiar with the moon and planets, the nearer space-
stations, and the entire landscape within thirty kilometres of his home.

He had been lucky in his place of birth, among the mountains of Colorado;
in almost every direction, the view was spectacular and inexhaustible. He had
spent hours exploring, in perfect safety, the peaks which every year took their
toll of careless climbers. Though he had seen much, he had imagined even
more; he had liked to pretend that over each crest of rock, beyond the reach
of his telescope, were magic kingdoms full of wonderful creatures. And so for
years he had avoided visiting the places his lenses brought to him, because
he knew that the reality could not live up to the dream.

Now, on the central axis of Rama, he could survey marvels beyond the
wildest fantasies of his youth. A whole world lay spread out before him—a
small one, it was true, yet a man could spend an entire life-time exploring four
thousand square kilometres, even when it was dead and changeless.

But now life, with all its infinite possibilities, had come to Rama. If the
biological robots were not living creatures, they were certainly very good
imitations.

No one knew who invented the word "biot"; it seemed to come into instant
use, by a kind of spontaneous generation. From his vantage point on the Hub,

Pieter was Biot-Watcher-in-Chief, and he was beginning—so he believed—to understand some of their behaviour patterns.

The Spiders were mobile sensors, using vision—and probably touch—to examine the whole interior of Rama. At one time there had been hundreds of them rushing around at high speed, but after less than two days they had disappeared; now it was quite unusual to see even one.

They had been replaced by a whole menagerie of much more impressive creatures; it had been no minor task, thinking of suitable names for them. There were the Window Cleaners, with large padded feet, who were apparently polishing their way the whole length of Rama's six artificial suns. Their enormous shadows, cast right across the diameter of the world, sometimes caused temporary eclipses on the far side.

The crab that had demolished *Dragonfly* seemed to be a Scavenger. A relay chain of identical creatures had approached Camp Alpha and carried off all the debris that had been neatly stacked on the outskirts; they would have carried off everything else if Norton and Mercer had not stood firm and defied them. The confrontation had been anxious but brief; thereafter, the Scavengers seemed to understand what they were allowed to touch, and arrived at regular intervals to see if their services were required. It was a most convenient arrangement, and indicated a high degree of intelligence—either on the part of the Scavangers themselves, or some controlling entity elsewhere.

Garbage disposal on Rama was very simple; everything was thrown into the Sea, where it was, presumably, broken down into forms that could be used again. The process was rapid; *Resolution* had disappeared overnight, to the great annoyance of Ruby Barnes. Norton had consoled her by pointing out that it had done its job magnificently—and he would never have allowed anyone to use it again. The Sharks might not be as discriminating as the Scavengers.

No astronomer discovering an unknown planet could have been happier than Pieter when he spotted a new type of biot and secured a good photo of it through his telescope. Unfortunately, it seemed that all the interesting species were over at the South Pole, where they were performing mysterious tasks round the Horns. Something that looked like a centipede with suction pads could be seen from time to time exploring Big Horn itself, while round the lower peaks Pieter had caught a glimpse of a burly creature that could have been a cross between a hippopotamus and a bulldozer. And there was even a double-necked giraffe, which apparently acted as a mobile crane.

Presumably Rama, like any ship, required testing, checking and repairing after its immense voyage. The crew was already hard at work; when would the passengers appear?

Biot classifying was not Pieter's main job; his orders were to keep watch on the two or three exploring parties that were always out, to see that they did not get into trouble, and to warn them if anything approached. He alternated every six hours with anyone else who could be spared, though more than once he had been on duty for twelve hours at a stretch. As a result, he now knew the geography of Rama better than any man who would ever live. It was as familiar to him as the Colorado mountains of his youth.

When Jerry Kirchoff emerged from Airlock Alpha, Pieter knew at once that something unusual was happening. Personnel transfers never occurred during the sleeping period, and it was now past midnight by Mission Time. Then Pieter remembered how short-handed they were, and was shocked by a much more startling irregularity.

"Jerry—who's in charge of the ship?"

"*I* am," said the Exec. coldly, as he flipped open his helmet. "You don't think I'd leave the bridge while I'm on watch, do you?"

He reached into his suit carry-all, and pulled out a small can still bearing the label: CONCENTRATED ORANGE JUICE: TO MAKE FIVE LITRES.

"You're good at this, Pieter. The skipper is waiting for it."

Pieter hefted the can, then said, "I hope you've put enough mass inside it —sometimes they get stuck on the first terrace."

"Well, you're the expert."

That was true enough. The Hub observers had had plenty of practice, sending down small items that had been forgotten or were needed in a hurry. The trick was to get them safety past the low-gravity region, and then to see that the Coriolis Effect did not carry them too far away from the Camp during the eight-kilometre roll downhill.

Pieter anchored himself firmly, grasped the can, and hurled it down the face of the cliff. He did not aim directly towards Camp Alpha, but almost thirty degrees away from it.

Almost immediately, air resistance robbed the can of its initial speed, but then the pseudo-gravity of Rama took over and it started to move downwards at a constant velocity. It hit once near the base of the ladder, and did a slow-motion bounce which took it clear of the first terrace.

"It's O.K. now," said Pieter. "Like to make a bet?"

"No," was the prompt reply. "You know the odds."

"You're no sportsman. But I'll tell you now—it will stop within three hundred metres of the Camp."

"That doesn't sound very close."

"You might try it some time. I once saw Joe miss by a couple of kilometres."

The can was no longer bouncing; gravity had become strong enough to glue it to the curving face of the North Dome. By the time it had reached the second terrace it was rolling along at twenty or thirty kilometres an hour, and had reached very nearly the maximum speed that friction would allow.

"Now we'll have to wait," said Pieter, seating himself at the telescope, so that he could keep track of the messenger. "It will be there in ten minutes. Ah, here comes the skipper—I've got used to recognising people from this angle—now he's looking up at us."

"I believe that telescope gives you a sense of power."

"Oh, it does. I'm the only person who knows everything that's happening in Rama. At least, I *thought* I did," he added plaintively, giving Kirchoff a reproachful look.

"If it will keep you happy, the skipper found he'd run out of tooth-paste."

After that, conversation languished; but at last Pieter said: "Wish you'd taken that bet... he's only got to walk fifty metres... now he sees it... mission complete."

"Thanks, Pieter—a very good job. Now you can go back to sleep."

"Sleep! I'm on watch until 04.00."

"Sorry—you *must* have been sleeping. Or how else could you have dreamed all this?"

SPACE SURVEY HQ TO COMMANDER SSS ENDEAVOUR. PRIORITY AAA. CLASSIFICATION YOUR EYES ONLY. NO PERMANENT RECORD.
SPACEGUARD REPORTS ULTRA HIGH SPEED VEHICLE APPARENTLY LAUNCHED MERCURY TEN TO TWELVE DAYS AGO ON RAMA INTERCEPT. IF NO ORBIT CHANGE ARRIVAL PREDICTED DATE 322 DAYS 15 HOURS. MAY BE NECESSARY YOU EVACUATE BEFORE THEN. WILL ADVISE FURTHER.   C IN C.

Norton read the message half a dozen times to memorise the date. It was hard to keep track of time inside Rama; he had to look at his calendar watch to see that it was now Day 315. That might leave them only one week....

The message was chilling, not only for what it said, but for what it implied. The Hermians had made a clandestine launch—that in itself a breach of Space Law. The conclusion was obvious; their "vehicle" could only be a missile.

But *why*? It was inconceivable—well, almost inconceivable—that they would risk endangering *Endeavour*, so presumably he would receive ample warning from the Hermians themselves. In an emergency, he could leave at a few hours' notice, though he would do so only under extreme protest, at the direct orders of the Commander-in-Chief.

Slowly, and very thoughtfully, he walked across to the improvised life-support complex and dropped the message into a Electrosan. The brilliant flare of laser light bursting out through the crack beneath the seat-cover told him that the demands of Security were satisfied. It was too bad, he told himself, that all problems could not be disposed of, so swiftly and hygienically.

CHAPTER XXXVII

Missile

THE MISSILE WAS still five million kilometres away when the glare of its plasma braking jets became clearly visible in *Endeavour*'s main telescope. By that time the secret was already out, and Norton had reluctantly ordered the second and perhaps final evacuation of Rama; but he had no intention of leaving until events gave him no alternative.

When it had completed its braking manoeuvre, the unwelcome guest from Mercury was only fifty kilometres from Rama, and apparently carrying out a survey through its TV cameras. These were clearly visible—one fore and one aft—as were several small omni-antennas and one large directional dish, aimed steadily at the distant star of Mercury. Norton wondered what instructions were coming down that beam, and what information was going back.

Yet the Hermians could learn nothing that they did not already know; all that *Endeavour* had discovered had been broadcast throughout the solar system. This space-craft—which had broken all speed records to get here—could only be an extension of its makers' will, an instrument of their purpose. That purpose would soon be known, for in three hours the Hermian ambassador to the United Planets would be addressing the General Assembly.

Officially, the missile did not exist. It bore no identification marks, and was not radiating on any standard beacon frequency. This was a serious breach of law, but even SPACEGUARD had not yet issued a formal protest. Everyone was waiting, with nervous impatience, to see what Mercury would do next.

It had been three days since the missile's existence—and origin—had been announced; all that time, the Hermians had remained stubbornly silent. They could be very good at that, when it suited them.

Some psychologists had claimed that it was almost impossible to understand fully the mentality of anyone born and bred on Mercury. Forever exiled from Earth by its three-times-more-powerful gravity, Hermians could stand on the Moon and look across the narrow gap to the planet of their ancestors—even of their own parents—but they could never visit it. And so, inevitably, they claimed that they did not want to.

They pretended to despise the soft rains, the rolling fields, the lakes and seas, the blue skies—all the things that they could know only through recordings. Because their planet was drenched with such solar energy that the daytime temperature often reached six hundred degrees, they affected a rather swaggering toughness that did not bear a moment's serious examination. In fact, they tended to be physically weak, since they could only survive if they were totally insulated from their environment. Even if he could have tolerated the gravity, a Hermian would have been quickly incapacitated by a hot day in any equatorial country on Earth.

Yet in matters that really counted, they *were* tough. The psychological pressures of that ravening star so close at hand, the engineering problems of tearing into a stubborn planet and wrenching from it all the necessities of life —these had produced a spartan and in many ways highly admirable culture. You could rely on the Hermians; if they promised something, they would do it—though the bill might be considerable. It was their own joke that, if the sun ever showed signs of going nova, they would contract to get it under control—once the fee had been settled. It was a non-Hermian joke that any child who showed signs of interest in art, philosophy or abstract mathematics was ploughed straight back into the hydroponic farms. As far as criminals and psychopaths were concerned, this was not a joke at all. Crime was one of the luxuries that Mercury could not afford.

Commander Norton had been to Mercury once, had been enormously impressed—like most visitors—and had acquired many Hermian friends. He had fallen in love with a girl in Port Lucifer, and had even contemplated signing a three-year contract, but parental disapproval of anyone from outside the orbit of Venus had been too strong. It was just as well.

"Triple A message from Earth, Skipper," said the bridge. "Voice and back-up text from Commander-in-Chief. Ready to accept?"

"Check and file text; let me have the voice."

"Here it comes."

Admiral Hendrix sounded calm and matter-of-fact, as if he was issuing a routine fleet order, instead of handling a situation unique in the history of space. But then, he was not ten kilometres from the bomb.

"C-in-C to Commander, *Endeavour*. This is a quick summary of the situation as we see it now. You know that the General Assembly meets at 14.00 and you'll be listening to the proceedings. It is possible that you may then have to take action immediately, without consultation; hence this briefing.

"We've analysed the photos you have sent us; the vehicle is a standard space-probe, modified for high-impulse and probably laser-riding for initial boost. Size and mass are consistent with fusion bomb in the 500 to 1,000 megaton range; the Hermians use up to 100 megatons routinely in their mining operations, so they would have had no difficulty in assembling such a warhead.

"Our experts also estimate that this would be the minimum size necessary to assure destruction of Rama. If it was detonated against the thinnest part of the shell—underneath the Cylindrical Sea—the hull would be ruptured and the spin of the body would complete its disintegration.

"We assume that the Hermians, if they are planning such an act, will give you ample time to get clear. For your information, the gamma-ray flash from such a bomb could be dangerous to you up to a range of a thousand kilometres.

"But that is not the most serious danger. The fragments of Rama, weighing tons and spinning off at almost a thousand kilometres an hour, could destroy you at an *unlimited* distance. We therefore recommend that you proceed along the spin axis, since no fragments will be thrown off in that direction. Ten thousand kilometres should give an adequate safety margin.

"This message cannot be intercepted; it is going by multiple-pseudo-random routing, so I can talk in clear English. Your reply may not be secure, so speak with discretion and use code when necessary. I will call you immediately after the General Assembly discussion. Message concluded. C-in-C, out."

CHAPTER XXXVIII

General Assembly

ACCORDING TO THE history books—though no one could really believe it—there had been a time when the old United Nations had 172 members. The United Planets had only seven; and that was sometimes bad enough. In order of distance from the Sun, they were Mercury, Earth, Luna, Mars, Ganymede, Titan and Triton.

The list contained numerous omissions and ambiguities which presumably the future would rectify. Critics never tired of pointing out that most of the United Planets were not planets at all, but satellites. And how ridiculous that the four giants, Jupiter, Saturn, Uranus and Neptune were not included. . . .

But no one lived on the Gas Giants, and quite possibly no one ever would. The same might be true of the other major absentee, Venus. Even the most enthusiastic of planetary engineers agreed that it would take centuries to tame Venus; meanwhile the Hermians kept their eyes on her, and doubtless brooded over long-range plans.

Separate representation for Earth and Luna had also been a bone of contention; the other members argued that it put too much power in one corner of the solar system. But there were more people on the Moon than all the other worlds except Earth itself—and it *was* the meeting place of the UP. Moreover, Earth and Moon hardly ever agreed on anything, so they were not likely to constitute a dangerous bloc.

Mars held the asteroids in trust—except for the Icarian group (supervised by Mercury) and a handful with perihelions beyond Saturn—and thus claimed by Titan. One day the larger asteroids, such as Pallas, Vesta, Juno and Ceres, would be important enough to have their own ambassadors, and membership of the UP would then reach double figures.

Ganymede represented not only Jupiter—and therefore more mass than all the rest of the solar system put together—but also the remaining fifty or so Jovian satellites, if one included temporary captures from the asteroid belt (the lawyers were still arguing over this). In the same way, Titan took care of Saturn, its rings and the other thirty-plus satellites.

The situation for Triton was even more complicated. The large moon of Neptune was the outermost body in the solar system under permanent habitation; as a result, its ambassador wore a considerable number of hats. He represented Uranus and its eight moons (none yet occupied); Neptune and its other three satellites; Pluto and its solitary moon; and lonely, moonless Persephone. If there were planets beyond Persephone, they too would be Triton's responsibility. And as if that was not enough, the Ambassador for the Outer Darkness, as he was sometimes called, had been heard to ask plaintively: "What about comets?" It was generally felt that this problem could be left for the future to solve.

And yet, in a very real sense, that future was already here. By some definitions, Rama *was* a comet; they were the only other visitors from the interstellar deeps, and many had travelled on hyperbolic orbits even closer to the Sun than Rama's. Any space-lawyer could make a very good case out of that—and the Hermian Ambassador was one of the best.

"We recognise His Excellency the Ambassador for Mercury."
As the delegates were arranged counter-clockwise in order of distance from the sun, the Hermian was on the President's extreme right. Up to the very last minute, he had been interfacing with his computer; now he removed the synchronising spectacles which allowed no one else to read the message on the display screen. He picked up his sheaf of notes, and rose briskly to his feet.
"Mr. President, distinguished fellow delegates, I would like to begin with a brief summary of the situation which now confronts us."
From some delegates, that phrase "a brief summary" would have evoked silent groans among all listeners; but everyone knew that Hermians meant exactly what they said.
"The giant spaceship, or artificial asteroid, which has been christened Rama was detected over a year ago, in the region beyond Jupiter. At first it was believed to be a natural body, moving on a hyperbolic orbit which would take it round the sun and on to the stars.
"When its true nature was discovered, the Solar Survey Vessel *Endeavour* was ordered to rendezvous with it. I am sure we will all congratulate Commander Norton and his crew for the efficient way in which they have carried out their unique assignment.
"At first, it was believed that Rama was dead—frozen for so many hundreds of thousands of years that there was no possibility of revival. This may still be true, in a strictly biological sense. There seems general agreement, among those who have studied the matter, that no living organism of any complexity can survive more than a very few centuries of suspended animation. Even at absolute zero, residual quantum effects eventually erase too much cellular information to make revival possible. It therefore appeared that, although Rama was of enormous archaeological importance, it did not present any major astropolitical problems.
"It is now obvious that this was a very naïve attitude, though even from the first there were some who pointed out that Rama was too precisely aimed at the Sun for pure chance to be involved.
"Even so, it might have been argued—indeed, it was argued—that here was an experiment that had failed. Rama had reached the intended target, but the controlling intelligence had not survived. This view also seems very simple-minded; it surely underestimates the entities we are dealing with.
"What we failed to take into account was the possibility of *non*-biological survival. If we accept Dr. Perera's very plausible theory, which certainly fits all the facts, the creatures who have been observed inside Rama did not exist until a short time ago. Their patterns, or templates, were stored in some central information bank, and when the time was ripe they were manufactured from

available raw materials—presumably the metallo-organic soup of the Cylindrical Sea. Such a feat is still somewhat beyond our own ability, but does not present any theoretical problems. We know that solid state circuits, unlike living matter, can store information without loss, for indefinite periods of time.

"So Rama is now in full operating condition, serving the purpose of its builders—whoever they may be. From our point of view, it does not matter if the Ramans themselves have all been dead for a million years, or whether they too will be re-created, to join their servants, at any moment. With or without them, their will is being done—and will continue to be done.

"Rama has now given proof that its propulsion system is still operating. In a few days, it will be at perihelion, where it would logically make any major orbit change. We may therefore soon have a new planet—moving through the solar space over which my government has jurisdiction. Or it may, of course, make additional changes and occupy a final orbit at any distance from the sun. It could even become a satellite of a major planet—such as Earth. . . .

"We are therefore, fellow delegates, faced with a whole spectrum of possibilities, some of them very serious indeed. It is foolish to pretend that these creatures *must* be benevolent, and will not interfere with us in any way. If they come to our solar system, they need something from it. Even if it is only scientific knowledge—consider how that knowledge may be used. . . .

"What confronts us now is a technology hundreds—perhaps thousands—of years in advance of ours, and a *culture* which may have no points of contact whatsoever. We have been studying the behaviour of the biological robots—the biots—inside Rama, as shown on the films that Commander Norton has relayed, and we have arrived at certain conclusions which we wish to pass on to you.

"On Mercury we are perhaps unlucky in having no indigenous life-forms to observe. But, of course, we have a complete record of terrestrial zoology, and we find in it one striking parallel with Rama.

"This is the termite colony. Like Rama, it is an artificial world with a controlled environment. Like Rama, its functioning depends upon a whole series of specialised biological machines—workers, builders, farmers—*warriors*. And although we do not know if Rama has a Queen, I suggest that the island known as New York serves a similar function.

"Now, it would obviously be absurd to press this analogy too far; it breaks down at many points. But I put it to you for this reason.

"What degree of co-operation or understanding would ever be possible between human beings and termites? When there is no conflict of interest, we tolerate each other. But when either needs the other's territory or resources, no quarter is given.

"Thanks to our technology and our intelligence, we can always win, if we are sufficiently determined. But sometimes it is not easy, and there are those who believe that, in the long run, final victory may yet go to the termites. . . .

"With this in mind, consider now the appalling threat that Rama may—I do not say *must*—present to human civilisation. What steps have we taken to counter it, if the worst eventuality should occur? None whatsoever; we have merely talked and speculated and written learned papers.

"Well, my fellow delegates, Mercury has done more than this. Acting under the provisions of Clause 34 of the Space Treaty of 2057, which entitled us to take any steps necessary to protect the integrity of our solar space, we have despatched a high-energy nuclear device to Rama. We will indeed be happy if we never have to utilise it. But now, at least, we are not helpless—as we were before.

"It may be argued that we have acted unilaterally, without prior consultation. We admit that. But does anyone here imagine—with all respect, Mister President—that we could have secured any such agreement in the time available? We consider that we are acting not only for ourselves, but for the whole human race. All future generations may one day thank us for our foresight.

"We recognised that it would be a tragedy—even a crime—to destroy an artifact as wonderful as Rama. If there is any way in which this can be avoided, *without risk to humanity,* we will be very happy to hear of it. We have not found one, and time is running out.

"Within the next few days, before Rama reaches perihelion, the choice will have to be made. We will, of course, give ample warning to *Endeavour*—but we would advise Commander Norton always to be ready to leave at an hour's notice. It is conceivable that Rama may undergo further dramatic transformations at any moment.

"That is all, Mister President, fellow delegates. I thank you for your attention. I look forward to your co-operation."

CHAPTER XXXIX

Command Decision

"WELL, ROD, HOW do the Hermians fit into your theology?"

"Only too well, Commander," replied Rodrigo with a humourless smile. "It's the age-old conflict between the forces of good and the forces of evil. And there are times when men have to take sides in such a conflict."

I thought it would be something like that, Norton told himself. This situation must have been a shock to Boris, but he would not have resigned himself to passive acquiescence. The Cosmo-Christers were very energetic, competent people. Indeed, in some ways they were remarkably like the Hermians.

"I take it you have a plan, Rod."

"Yes, Commander. It's really quite simple. We merely have to disable the bomb."

"Oh. And how do you propose to do that?"

"With a small pair of wire-cutters."

If this had been anyone else, Norton would have assumed that they were joking. But not Boris Rodrigo.

"Now just a minute! It's bristling with cameras. Do you suppose the Hermians will just sit and watch you?"

"Of course; that's all they *can* do. When the signal reaches them, it will be far too late. I can easily finish the job in ten minutes."

"I see. They certainly *will* be mad. But suppose the bomb is booby-trapped so that interference sets it off?"

"That seems very unlikely; what would be the purpose? This bomb was built for a specific deep-space mission, and it will be fitted with all sorts of safety devices to prevent detonation *except* on a positive command. But that's a risk I'm prepared to take—and it can be done without endangering the ship. I've worked everything out."

"I'm sure you have," said Norton. The idea was fascinating—almost seductive in its appeal; he particularly liked the idea of the frustrated Hermians, and would give a good deal to see their reactions when they realised—too late—what was happening to their deadly toy.

But there were other complications, and they seemed to multiply as Norton surveyed the problem. He was facing by far the most difficult, and the most crucial, decision in his entire career.

And that was a ridiculous understatement. He was faced with the most difficult decision *any* commander had ever had to make; the future of the entire human race might well depend upon it. For just suppose the Hermians were right?

When Rodrigo had left, he switched on the DO NOT DISTURB sign; he could not remember when he had last used it, and was mildly surprised that it was working. Now, in the heart of his crowded, busy ship, he was completely alone —except for the portrait of Captain James Cook, gazing at him down the corridors of time.

It was impossible to consult with Earth; he had already been warned that any messages might be tapped—perhaps by relay devices on the bomb itself. That left the whole responsibility in his hands.

There was a story he had heard somewhere about a President of the United States—was it Roosevelt or Perez?—who had a sign on his desk saying "The buck stops here". Norton was not quite certain what a buck was, but he knew when one had stopped at his desk.

He could do nothing, and wait until the Hermians advised him to leave. How would that look in the histories of the future? Norton was not greatly concerned with posthumous fame or infamy, yet he would not care to be remembered forever as the accessory to a cosmic crime—which it had been in his power to prevent.

And the plan was flawless. As he had expected, Rodrigo had worked out every detail, anticipated every possibility—even the remote danger that the bomb might be triggered when tampered with. If that happened, *Endeavour* could still be safe, behind the shield of Rama. As for Lieutenant Rodrigo himself, he seemed to regard the possibility of instant apotheosis with complete equanimity.

Yet, even if the bomb was successfully disabled, that would be far from the end of the matter. The Hermians might try again—unless some way could be found of stopping them. But at least weeks of time would have been bought; Rama would be far past perihelion before another missile could possibly reach it. By then, hopefully, the worst fears of the alarmists might have been disproved. Or the reverse. . . .

To act, or not to act—that was the question. Never before had Commander Norton felt such a close kinship with the Prince of Denmark. Whatever he did, the possibilities for good and evil seemed in perfect balance. He was faced with the most morally difficult of all decisions. If his choice was wrong, he would know very quickly. But if he was correct—he might never be able to prove it. . . .

It was no use relying any further on logical arguments and the endless mapping of alternative futures. That way, one could go round and round in circles forever. The time had come to listen to his inner voices.

He returned the calm, steady gaze across the centuries.

"I agree with you, Captain," he whispered. "The human race has to live with its conscience. Whatever the Hermians argue, survival is not everything."

He pressed the call button for the bridge circuit and said slowly, "Lieutenant Rodrigo—I'd like to see you."

Then he closed his eyes, hooked his thumbs in the restraining straps of his chair, and prepared to enjoy a few moments of total relaxation.

It might be some time before he would experience it again.

CHAPTER XL

Saboteur

THE SCOOTER HAD been stripped of all unnecessary equipment; it was now merely an open framework holding together propulsion, guidance and life-support systems. Even the seat for the second pilot had been removed, for every kilogram of extra mass had to be paid for in mission time.

That was one of the reasons, though not the most important, why Rodrigo had insisted on going alone. It was such a simple job that there was no need for any extra hands, and the mass of a passenger would cost several minutes of flight time. Now the stripped-down scooter could accelerate at over a third of a gravity; it could make the trip from *Endeavour* to the bomb in four minutes. That left six to spare; it should be sufficient.

Rodrigo looked back only once when he had left the ship; he saw that, as planned, it had lifted from the central axis and was thrusting gently away across the spinning disc of the North Face. By the time he reached the bomb, it would have placed the thickness of Rama between them.

He took his time, flying over the polar plain. There was no hurry here, because the bomb's cameras could not yet see him, and he could therefore conserve fuel. Then he drifted over the curving rim of the world—and there was the missile, glittering in sunlight fiercer even than that shining on the planet of its birth.

Rodrigo had already punched in the guidance instructions. He initiated the sequence; the scooter spun on its gyros, and came up to full thrust in a matter of seconds. At first the sensation of weight seemed crushing; then Rodrigo adjusted to it. He had, after all, comfortably endured twice as much inside Rama—and had been born under three times as much on Earth.

The huge, curving exterior wall of the fifty-kilometre cylinder was slowly falling away beneath him as the scooter aimed itself directly at the bomb. Yet it was impossible to judge Rama's size, since it was completely smooth and featureless—so featureless, indeed, that it was difficult to tell that it was spinning.

One hundred seconds into the mission; he was approaching the half-way point. The bomb was still too far away to show any details, but it was much brighter against the jet-black sky. It was strange to see no stars—not even brilliant Earth or dazzling Venus; the dark filters which protected his eyes against the deadly glare made that impossible. Rodrigo guessed that he was breaking a record; probably no other man had ever engaged in extra-vehicular work so close to the sun. It was lucky for him that solar activity was low.

At two minutes ten seconds the flip-over light started flashing, thrust dropped to zero, and the scooter spun through 180 degrees. Full thrust was back in an instant, but now he was decelerating at the same mad rate of three metres per second squared—rather better than that, in fact, since he had lost almost half his propellent mass. The bomb was twenty-five kilometres away; he would be there in another two minutes. He had hit a top speed of fifteen hundred kilometres an hour—which, for a space-scooter, was utter insanity, and probably another record. But this was hardly a routine EVA, and he knew precisely what he was doing.

The bomb was growing; and now he could see the main antenna, holding steady on the invisible star of Mercury. Along that beam, the image of his approaching scooter had been flashing at the speed of light for the last three minutes. There were still two to go, before it reached Mercury.

What would the Hermians do, when they saw him? There would be consternation, of course; they would realise instantly that he had made a rendezvous with the bomb several minutes before they even knew he was on the way. Probably some stand-by observer would call higher authority—that would take more time. But even in the worst possible case—even if the officer on duty had authority to detonate the bomb, and pressed the button immediately—it would take another five minutes for the signal to arrive.

Though Rodrigo was not gambling on it—Cosmo-Christers *never* gambled —he was quite sure that there would be no such instantaneous reaction. The Hermians would hesitate to destroy a reconnaissance vehicle from *Endeavour*, even if they suspected its motives. They would certainly attempt some form of communication first—and that would mean *more* delay.

And there was an even better reason; they would not waste a gigaton bomb on a mere scooter. Wasted it would be, if it was detonated twenty kilometres from its target. They would have to move it first. Oh, he had plenty of time . . . but he would still assume the very worst.

He would act as if the triggering impulse would arrive in the shortest possible time—just five minutes.

As the scooter closed in across the last few hundred metres, Rodrigo quockly matched the details he could now see with those he had studied in the photographs taken at long range. What had been only a collection of pictures became hard metal and smooth plastic—no longer abstract, but a deadly reality.

The bomb was a cylinder about ten metres long and three in diameter—by a strange coincidence, almost the same proportions as Rama itself. It was attached to the framework of the carrier vehicle by an open latticework of short I-beams. For some reason, probably to do with the location of the centre of mass, it was supported at *right angles* to the axis of the carrier, so that it conveyed an appropriately sinister hammer-head impression. It was indeed a hammer, one powerful enough to smash a world.

From each end of the bomb, a bundle of braided cables ran along the cylindrical side and disappeared through the latticework into the interior of the vehicle. All communication and control was here; there was no antenna of any kind on the bomb itself. Rodrigo had only to cut those two sets of cables and there would be nothing here but harmless, inert metal.

Although this was exactly what he had expected, it still seemed a little too easy. He glanced at his watch; it would be another thirty seconds before the Hermians, even if they had been watching when he rounded the edge of Rama, could know of his existence. He had an absolutely certain five minutes for uninterrupted work—and a ninety-nine per cent probability of much longer than that.

As soon as the scooter had drifted to a complete halt, Rodrigo grappled it to the missile framework so that the two formed a rigid structure. That took only seconds; he had already chosen his tools, and was out of the pilot's seat at once, only slightly hampered by the stiffness of his heavy-insulation suit.

The first thing he found himself inspecting was a small metal plate bearing the inscription:

DEPARTMENT OF POWER ENGINEERING
Section D,
47 Sunset Boulevard,
Vulcanopolis, 17464
For information apply to Mr. Henry K. Jones

Rodrigo suspected that, in a very few minutes, Mr. Jones might be rather busy.

The heavy wire-cutters made short work of the cable. As the first strands parted, Rodrigo gave scarcely a thought to the fires of hell that were pent up only centimetres away; if his actions triggered them, he would never know.

He glanced again at his watch; this had taken less than a minute, which meant that he was on schedule. Now for the back-up cable—and then he could head for home, in full view of the furious and frustrated Hermians.

He was just beginning to work on the second cable assembly when he felt a faint vibration in the metal he was touching. Startled, he looked back along the body of the missile.

The characteristic blue-violet glow of a plasma thruster in action was hovering round one of the attitude control jets. The bomb was preparing to move.

The message from Mercury was brief, and devastating. It arrived two minutes after Rodrigo had disappeared around the edge of Rama.

COMMANDER ENDEAVOUR FROM MERCURY SPACE CONTROL, INFERNO WEST. YOU HAVE ONE HOUR FROM RECEIPT OF THIS MESSAGE TO LEAVE VICINITY OF RAMA. SUGGEST YOU PROCEED MAXIMUM ACCELERATION ALONG SPIN AXIS. REQUEST ACKNOWLEDGEMENT. MESSAGE ENDS.

Norton read it with sheer disbelief, then anger. He felt a childish impulse to radio back that all his crew were inside Rama, and it would take hours to get everyone out. But that would achieve nothing—except perhaps to test the will and nerve of the Hermians.

And why, several days before perihelion, had they decided to act? He wondered if the mounting pressure of public opinion was becoming too great, and they decided to present the rest of the human race with a *fait accompli*. It seemed an unlikely explanation; such sensitivity would have been uncharacteristic.

There was no way in which he could recall Rodrigo, for the scooter was now in the radio shadow of Rama and would be out of contact until they were in line of sight again. That would not be until the mission was completed—or had failed.

He would have to wait it out; there was still plenty of time—a full fifty minutes. Meanwhile, he had decided on the most effective answer to Mercury. He would ignore the message completely, and see what the Hermians did next.

Rodrigo's first sensation, when the bomb started to move, was not one of physical fear; it was something much more devastating. He believed that the universe operated according to strict laws, which not even God Himself could disobey—much less the Hermians. No message could travel faster than light; he was five minutes ahead of anything that Mercury could do.

This could only be a coincidence—fantastic, and perhaps deadly, but no more than that. By chance, a control signal must have been sent to the bomb at about the time he was leaving *Endeavour*; while he was travelling fifty kilometres, it had covered eighty million.

Or perhaps this was only an automatic change of attitude, to counter over-heating somewhere in the vehicle. There were places where the skin temperature approached fifteen hundred degrees, and Rodrigo had been very careful to keep in the shadows as far as possible.

A second thruster started to fire, checking the spin given by the first. No, this was *not* a mere thermal adjustment. The bomb was re-orientating itself, to point towards Rama. . . .

Useless to wonder *why* this was happening, at this precise moment in time. There was one thing in his favour: the missile was a low acceleration device. A tenth of a gee was the most that it could manage. He could hang on.

He checked the grapples attaching the scooter to the bomb framework, and re-checked the safety line on his own suit. A cold anger was growing in his mind, adding to his determination. Did this manoeuvre mean that the Hermians were going to explode the bomb without warning, giving *Endeavour* no chance to escape? That seemed incredible—an act not only of brutality but of folly, calculated to turn the rest of the solar system against them. And what would have made them ignore the solemn promise of their own ambassador? Whatever their plan, they would not get away with it.

The second message from Mercury was identical with the first, and arrived ten minutes later. So they had extended the deadline—Norton still had one hour. And they had obviously waited until a reply from *Endeavour* could have reached them before calling him again.

Now there was another factor; by this time they must have seen Rodrigo, and would have had several minutes in which to take action. Their instructions could already be on the way. They could arrive at any second.

He should be preparing to leave. At any moment, the sky-filling bulk of Rama might become incandescent along the edges, blazing with a transient glory that would far outshine the sun.

When the main thrust came on, Rodrigo was securely anchored. Only twenty seconds later, it cut off again. He did a quick mental calculation; the delta vee could not have been more than fifteen kilometres an hour. The bomb would take over an hour to reach Rama; perhaps it was only moving in close to get a quicker reaction. If so, that was a wise precaution; but the Hermians had left it too late.

Rodrigo glanced at his watch, though by now he was almost aware of the time without having to check. On Mercury, they would now be seeing him heading purposefully towards the bomb, and less than two kilometres away from it. They could have no doubt of his intentions, and would be wondering if he had already carried them out.

The second set of cables went as easily as the first; like any good workman, Rodrigo had chosen his tools well. The bomb was disarmed; or, to be more accurate, it could no longer be detonated by remote command.

Yet there was one other possibility, and he could not afford to ignore it. There were no external contact fuses, but there might be internal ones, armed by the shock of impact. The Hermians still had control over their vehicle's movement, and could crash it into Rama whenever they wished. Rodrigo's work was not yet completely finished.

Five minutes from now, in that control room somewhere on Mercury, they would see him crawling back along the exterior of the missile, carrying the modestly-sized wire-cutters that had neutralised the mightiest weapon ever built by man. He was almost tempted to wave at the camera, but decided that it would seem undignified; after all, he was making history, and millions would watch this scene in the years to come. Unless, of course, the Hermians destroyed the recording in a fit of pique; he would hardly blame them.

He reached the mounting of the long-range antenna, and drifted hand-over-hand along it to the big dish. His faithful cutters made short work of the multiplex feed system, chewing up cables and laser wave guides alike. When he made the last snip, the antenna started to swing slowly around; the unexpected movement took him by surprise, until he realised that he had destroyed its automatic lock on Mercury. Just five minutes from now, the Hermians would lose all contact with their servant. Not only was it impotent; now it was blind and deaf.

Rodrigo climbed slowly back to the scooter, released the shackles, and swung it round until the forward bumpers were pressing against the missile, as close as possible to its centre of mass. He brought thrust up to full power, and held it there for twenty seconds.

Pushing against many times its own mass, the scooter responded very sluggishly. When Rodrigo cut the thrust back to zero, he took a careful reading of the bomb's new velocity vector.

It would miss Rama by a wide margin—and it could be located again with precision at any future time. It was, after all, a very valuable piece of equipment.

Lieutenant Rodrigo was a man of almost pathological honesty. He would not like the Hermians to accuse him of losing their property.

CHAPTER XLI

Hero

"DARLING," BEGAN NORTON, "this nonsense has cost us more than a day, but at least it's given me a chance to talk to you.

"I'm still in the ship, and she's heading back to station at the polar axis. We picked up Rod an hour ago, looking as if he'd just come off duty after a quiet watch. I suppose neither of us will ever be able to visit Mercury again, and I'm wondering if we're going to be treated as heroes or villains when we get back to Earth. But *my* conscience is clear; I'm sure we did the right thing. I wonder if the Ramans will ever say 'thank you'.

"We can stay here only two more days; unlike Rama, we don't have a kilometre-thick skin to protect us from the sun. The hull's already developing dangerous hot-spots and we've had to put out some local screening. I'm sorry —I didn't want to bore you with my problems. . . .

"So there's time for just one more trip into Rama, and I intend to make the most of it. But don't worry—I'm not taking any chances."

He stopped the recording. That, to say the least, was stretching the truth. There was danger and uncertainty about every moment inside Rama; no man could ever feel really at home there, in the presence of forces beyond his understanding. And on this final trip, now that he knew they would never return and that no future operations would be jeopardised, he intended to press his luck just a little further.

"In forty-eight hours, then, we'll have completed this mission. What happens then is still uncertain; as you know, we've used virtually all our fuel getting into this orbit. I'm still waiting to hear if a tanker can rendezvous with us in time to get back to Earth, or whether we'll have to make planet-fall at Mars. Anyway, I should be home by Christmas. Tell Junior I'm sorry I can't bring a baby biot; there's no such animal. . . .

"We're all fine, but we're very tired. I've earned a long leave after all this, and we'll make up for lost time. Whatever they say about me, you can claim you're married to a hero. How many wives have a husband who saved a world?"

As always, he listened carefully to the tape before duping it, to make sure that it was applicable to both his families. It was strange to think that he did not know which of them he would see first; usually, his schedule was determined at least a year in advance, by the inexorable movements of the planets themselves.

But that was in the days before Rama; now nothing would ever be the same again.

CHAPTER XLII

Temple of Glass

"IF WE TRY it," said Karl Mercer, "do you think the biots will stop us?"

"They may; that's one of the things I want to find out. Why are you looking at me like that?"

Mercer gave his slow, secret grin, which was liable to be set off at any moment by a private joke he might or might not share with his shipmates.

"I was wondering, Skipper, if you think you own Rama. Until now, you've vetoed any attempt to cut into buildings. Why the switch? Have the Hermians given you ideas?"

Norton laughed, then suddenly checked himself. It was a shrewd question, and he was not sure if the obvious answers were the right ones.

"Perhaps I have been ultra-cautious—I've tried to avoid trouble. But this is our last chance; if we're forced to retreat, we won't have lost much."

"Assuming that we retreat in good order."

"Of course. But the biots have never shown hostility; and except for the spiders, I don't believe there's anything here that can catch us—if we do have to run for it."

"*You* may run, Skipper, but I intend to leave with dignity. And incidentally, I've decided why the biots are so polite to us."

"It's a little late for a new theory."

"Here it is, anyway. They think we're Ramans. They can't tell the difference between one oxy-eater and another."

"I don't believe they're *that* stupid."

"It's not a matter of stupidity. They've been programmed for their particular jobs, and we simply don't come into their frame of reference."

"Perhaps you're right. We may find out—as soon as we start to work on London."

Joe Calvert had always enjoyed those old bank-robbery movies, but he had never expected to be involved in one. Yet this was, essentially, what he was doing now.

The deserted streets of "London" seemed full of menace, though he knew that was only his guilty conscience. He did not *really* believe that the sealed and windowless structures ranged all around them were full of watchful inhabitants, waiting to emerge in angry hordes as soon as the invaders laid a hand on their property. In fact, he was quite certain that this whole complex—like all the other towns—was merely some kind of storage area.

Yet a second fear, also based on innumerable ancient crime dramas, could be better grounded. There might be no clanging alarm bells and screaming sirens, but it was reasonable to assume that Rama would have some kind of warning system. How otherwise did the biots know when and where their services were needed?

"Those without goggles, turn your backs," ordered Sergeant Myron. There was a smell of nitric oxide as the air itself started to burn in the beam of the laser torch, and a steady sizzling as the fiery knife sliced towards secrets that had been hidden since the birth of man.

Nothing material could resist this concentration of power, and the cut proceeded smoothly at a rate of several metres a minute. In a remarkably short time, a section large enough to admit a man had been sliced out.

As the cutaway section showed no sign of moving, Myron tapped it gently —then harder—then banged on it with all his strength. It fell inwards with a hollow, reverberating crash.

Once again, as he had done during that very first entrance into Rama,

Norton remembered the archaeologist who had opened the old Egyptian tomb. He did not expect to see the glitter of gold; in fact, he had no preconceived ideas at all, as he crawled through the opening, his flashlight held in front of him.

A Greek temple made of glass—that was his first impression. The building was filled with row upon row of vertical crystalline columns, about a metre wide and stretching from floor to ceiling. There were hundreds of them, marching away into the darkness beyond the reach of his light.

Norton walked towards the nearest column, and directed his beam into its interior. Refracted as through a cylindrical lens, the light fanned out on the far side to be focused and refocused, getting fainter with each repetition, in the array of pillars beyond. He felt that he was in the middle of some complicated demonstration in optics.

"Very pretty," said the practical Mercer, "but what does it mean? Who needs a forest of glass pillars?"

Norton rapped gently on one column. It sounded solid, though more metallic than crystalline. He was completely baffled, and so followed a piece of useful advice he had heard long ago: "When in doubt, say nothing and move on."

As he reached the next column, which looked exactly like the first, he heard an exclamation of surprise from Mercer.

"I could have sworn this pillar was empty—now there's something inside it."

Norton glanced quickly back.

"Where?" he said. "I don't see anything."

He followed the direction of Mercer's pointing finger. It was aimed at nothing; the column was still completely transparent.

"You can't see it?" said Mercer incredulously. "Come around this side. Damn—now I've lost it!"

"What's going on here?" demanded Calvert. It was several minutes before he got even the first approximation to an answer.

The columns were not transparent from every angle or under all illuminations. As one walked around them, objects would suddenly flash into view, apparently embedded in their depths like flies in amber—and would then disappear again. There were dozens of them, all different. They looked absolutely real and solid, yet many seemed to occupy the identical volume of space.

"Holograms," said Calvert. "Just like a museum on Earth."

That was the obvious explanation, and therefore Norton viewed it with suspicion. His doubts grew as he examined the other columns, and conjured up the images stored in their interiors.

Hand-tools (though for huge and peculiar hands), containers, small machines with keyboards that appeared to have been made for more than five fingers, scientific instruments, startlingly conventional domestic utensils, including knives and plates which apart from their size would not have attracted a second glance on any terrestrial table . . . they were all there, with hundreds of less identifiable objects, often jumbled up together in the same pillar. A museum, surely, would have some logical arrangement, some segregation of related items. This seemed to be a completely random collection of hardware.

They had photographed the elusive images inside a score of the crystal pillars when the sheer variety of items gave Norton a clue. Perhaps this was not a collection, but a *catalogue*, indexed according to some arbitrary but perfectly logical system. He thought of the wild juxtapositions that any dictionary or alphabetised list will give, and tried the idea on his companions.

"I see what you mean," said Mercer. "The Ramans might be equally surprised to find us putting—ah—camshafts next to cameras."

"Or books beside boots," added Calvert, after several seconds' hard thinking. One could play this game for hours, he decided, with increasing degrees of impropriety.

"That's the idea," replied Norton. "This may be an indexed catalogue for 3-D images—templates—solid blueprints, if you like to call them that."

"For what purpose?"

'Well, you know the theory about the biots . . . the idea that they don't exist until they're needed and then they're created—synthesised—from patterns stored somewhere?"

"I see," said Mercer slowly and thoughtfully. "So when a Raman needs a left-handed blivet, he punches out the correct code number, and a copy is manufactured from the pattern in here."

"Something like that. But please don't ask me about the practical details."

The pillars through which they had been moving had been steadily growing in size, and were now more than two metres in diameter. The images were correspondingly larger; it was obvious that, for doubtless excellent reasons, the Ramans believed in sticking to a one-to-one scale. Norton wondered how they stored anything *really* big, if this was the case.

To increase their rate of coverage, the four explorers had now spread out through the crystal columns and were taking photographs as quickly as they could get their cameras focused on the fleeting images. This was an astonishing piece of luck, Norton told himself, though he felt that he had earned it; they could not possibly have made a better choice than this Illustrated Catalogue of Raman Artifacts. And yet, in another way, it could hardly have been more frustrating. There was nothing actually *here*, except impalpable patterns of light and darkness; these apparently solid objects did not really exist.

Even knowing this, more than once Norton felt an almost irresistible urge to laser his way into one of the pillars, so that he could have something material to take back to Earth. It was the same impulse, he told himself wryly, that would prompt a monkey to grab the reflection of a banana in a mirror.

He was photographing what seemed to be some kind of optical device when Calvert's shout started him running through the pillars.

"Skipper—Karl—Will—look at *this*!"

Joe was prone to sudden enthusiasms, but what he had found was enough to justify any amount of excitement.

Inside one of the two-metre columns was an elaborate harness, or uniform, obviously made for a vertically-standing creature, much taller than a man. A very narrow central metal band apparently surrounded the waist, thorax, or some division unknown to terrestrial zoology. From this rose three slim columns, tapering outwards and ending in a perfectly circular belt, an impressive metre in diameter. Loops equally spaced along it could only be intended to go round upper limbs or arms. *Three* of them. . . .

There were numerous pouches, buckles, bandoliers from which tools (or weapons?) protruded, pipes and electrical conductors, even small black boxes that would have looked perfectly at home in an electronics lab on Earth. The whole arrangement was almost as complex as a space-suit, though it obviously provided only partial covering for the creature wearing it.

And was that creature a Raman? Norton asked himself. We'll probably never know; but it must have been intelligent—no mere animal could cope with all that sophisticated equipment.

"About two and a half metres high," said Mercer thoughtfully, "not counting the head—whatever *that* was like."

"With three arms—and presumably three legs. The same plan as the Spiders, on a much more massive scale. Do you suppose that's a coincidence?"

"Probably not. We design robots in our own image; we might expect the Ramans to do the same."

Joe Calvert, unusually subdued, was looking at the display with something like awe.

"Do you suppose they know we're here?" he half-whispered.

"I doubt it," said Mercer. "We've not even reached their threshold of consciousness—though the Hermians certainly had a good try."

They were still standing there, unable to drag themselves away, when Pieter called from the Hub, his voice full of urgent concern.

"Skipper—you'd better get outside."

"What is it—biots heading this way?"

"No—something much more serious. *The lights are going out.*"

CHAPTER XLIII

Retreat

W HEN HE HASTILY emerged from the hole they had lasered, it seemed to Norton that the six suns of Rama were as brilliant as ever. Surely, he thought, Pieter must have made a mistake . . . that's not like him at all. . . .

But Pieter had anticipated just this reaction.

"It happened so slowly," he explained apologetically, "that it was a long time before I noticed any difference. But there's no doubt about it—I've taken a meter reading. The light level's down forty per cent."

"Now, as his eyes readjusted themselves after the gloom of the glass temple, Norton could believe him. The long day of Rama was drawing to its close.

It was still as warm as ever, yet Norton felt himself shivering. He had known this sensation once before, during a beautiful summer day on Earth. There had been an inexplicable weakening of light as if darkness was falling from the air, or the sun had lost its strength—though there was not a cloud in the sky. Then he remembered; a partial eclipse was in progress.

"This is it," he said grimly. "We're going home. Leave all the equipment behind—we won't need it again."

Now, he hoped, one piece of planning was about to prove its worth. He had selected London for this raid because no other town was so close to a stairway; the foot of Beta was only four kilometres away.

They set off at the steady, loping trot which was the most comfortable mode of travelling at half a gravity. Norton set a pace which, he estimated, would get them to the edge of the plain without exhaustion, and in the minimum time. He was acutely aware of the eight kilometres they would still have to climb when they had reached Beta, but he would feel much safer when they had actually started the ascent.

The first tremor came when they had almost reached the stairway. It was very slight, and instinctively Norton turned towards the south, expecting to see another display of fireworks around the Horns. But Rama never seemed to repeat itself exactly; if there were any electrical discharges above those needle-sharp mountains, they were too faint to be seen.

"Bridge," he called, "did you notice that?"

"Yes, Skipper—very small shock. Could be another attitude change. We're watching the rate gyro—nothing yet. Just a minute! Positive reading! Can just detect it—less than a microradian per second, but holding."

So Rama was beginning to turn, though with almost imperceptible slowness. Those earlier shocks might have been a false alarm—but this, surely, was the real thing.

"Rate increasing—five microrad. Hello, did you feel *that* shock?"

"We certainly did. Get all ship's systems operational. We may have to leave in a hurry."

"Do you expect an orbit change already? We're still a long way from perihelion."

"I don't think Rama works by our text-books. Nearly at Beta. We'll rest there for five minutes."

Five minutes was utterly inadequate, yet it seemed an age. For there was now no doubt that the light was failing, and failing fast.

Though they were all equipped with flashlights, the thought of darkness here was now intolerable; they had grown so psychologically accustomed to the endless day that it was hard to remember the conditions under which they had first explored this world. They felt an overwhelming urge to escape—to get out into the light of the sun, a kilometre away on the other side of these cylindrical walls.

"Hub Control!" called Norton. "Is the searchlight operating? We may need it in a hurry."

"Yes, Skipper. Here it comes."

A reassuring spark of light started to shine eight kilometres above their heads. Even against the now fading day of Rama, it looked surprisingly feeble; but it had served them before, and would guide them once again if they needed it.

This, Norton was grimly aware, would be the longest and most nerve-wracking climb they had ever done. Whatever happened, it would be impossible to hurry; if they over-exerted themselves, they would simply collapse somewhere on that vertiginous slope, and would have to wait until their protesting muscles permitted them to continue. By this time, they must be one of the fittest crews that had ever carried out a space mission; but there were limits to what flesh and blood could do.

After an hour's steady plodding they had reached the fourth section of the stairway, about three kilometres from the plain. From now on, it would be much easier; gravity was already down to a third of Earth value. Although there had been minor shocks from time to time, no other unusual phenomena had occurred, and there was still plenty of light. They began to feel more optimistic, and even to wonder if they had left too soon. One thing was certain, however; there was no going back. They had all walked for the last time on the plain of Rama.

It was while they were taking a ten-minute rest on the fourth platform that Joe Calvert suddenly exclaimed:

"What's that noise, Skipper?"

"Noise?—I don't hear anything."

"High-pitched whistle—dropping in frequency, you *must* hear it."

"Your ears are younger than mine—oh, now I do."

The whistle seemed to come from everywhere. Soon it was loud, even piercing, and falling swiftly in pitch. Then it suddenly stopped.

A few seconds later it came again, repeating the same sequence. It had all the mournful, compelling quality of a lighthouse siren sending out its warnings into the fog-shrouded night. There was a message here, and an urgent one. It was not designed for their ears, but they understood it. Then, as if to make doubly sure, it was reinforced by the lights themselves.

They dimmed almost to extinction, then started to flash. Brilliant beads, like ball lightning, raced along the six narrow valleys that had once illuminated this world. They moved from both Poles towards the Sea in a synchronised, hypnotic rhythm which could have only one meaning. "To the Sea!" the lights were calling, "To the Sea!" And the summons was hard to resist; there was not a man who did not feel a compulsion to turn back, and to seek oblivion in the waters of Rama.

"Hub Control!" Norton called urgently. "Can you see what's happening?"

The voice of Pieter came back to him; he sounded awed, and more than a little frightened.

"Yes, Skipper. I'm looking across at the southern continent. There are still scores of biots over there—including some big ones. Cranes, Bulldozers—lots of Scavengers. And they're all rushing back to the Sea faster than I've ever seen them move before. There goes a Crane—right over the edge! Just like

Jimmy, but going down a lot quicker . . . it smashed to pieces when it hit . . . and here come the Sharks—they're tearing into it . . . ugh; it's not a pleasant sight. . . .

"Now I'm looking at the plain. Here's a Bulldozer that seems to have broken down . . . it's going round and round in circles. Now a couple of Crabs are tearing into it, pulling it to pieces . . . Skipper, I think you'd better get back right away."

"Believe me," Norton said with deep feeling, "we're coming just as quickly as we can."

Rama was battening down the hatches, like a ship preparing for a storm. That was Norton's overwhelming impression, though he could not have put it on a logical basis. He no longer felt completely rational; two compulsions were warring in his mind—the need to escape, and the desire to obey those bolts of lightning that still flashed across the sky, ordering him to join the biots in their march to the sea.

One more section of stairway—another ten-minute pause, to let the fatigue poisons drain from his muscles. Then on again—another two kilometres to go, but let's try not to think about that——

The maddening sequence of descending whistles abruptly ceased. At the same moment, the fireballs racing along the slots of the Straight Valleys stopped their seaward strobing; Rama's six linear suns were once more continuous bands of light.

But they were fading fast, and sometimes they flickered, as if tremendous jolts of energy were being drained from waning power sources. From time to time, there were slight tremors underfoot; the bridge reported that Rama was still swinging with imperceptible slowness, like a compass needle responding to a weak magnetic field. This was perhaps reassuring; it was when Rama *stopped* its swing that Norton would really begin to worry.

All the biots had gone, so Pieter reported. In the whole interior of Rama, the only movement was that of human beings, crawling with painful slowness up the curving face of the northern dome.

Norton had long since overcome the vertigo he had felt on that first ascent, but now a new fear was beginning to creep into his mind. They were so vulnerable here, on this endless climb from plain to Hub. Suppose that, when it had completed its attitude change, Rama started to accelerate?

Presumably its thrust would be along the axis. If it was in the northward direction, that would be no problem; they would be held a little more firmly against the slope which they were ascending. But if it was towards the south, they might be swept off into space, to fall back eventually on the plain far below.

He tried to reassure himself with the thought that any possible acceleration would be very feeble. Dr. Perera's calculations had been most convincing; Rama could not possibly accelerate at more than a fiftieth of a gravity, or the Cylindrical Sea would climb the southern cliff and flood an entire continent. But Perera had been in a comfortable study back on Earth, not with kilometres of overhanging metal apparently about to crash down upon his head. And perhaps Rama was designed for periodic flooding——

No, that was ridiculous. It was absurd to imagine that all these trillions of tons could suddenly start moving with sufficient acceleration to shake him loose. Nevertheless, for all the remainder of the ascent, Norton never let himself get far from the security of the handrail.

Lifetimes later, the stairway ended; only a few hundred metres of vertical, recessed ladder were left. It was no longer necessary to climb this section since one man at the Hub, hauling on a cable, could easily hoist another against the rapidly diminishing gravity. Even at the bottom of the ladder a man weighed less than five kilos; at the top, practically zero.

So Norton relaxed in the sling, grasping a rung from time to time to counter the feeble Coriolis force still trying to push him off the ladder. He almost forgot his knotted muscles, as he had his last view of Rama.

It was about as bright now as a full moon on Earth; the overall scene was perfectly clear, but he could no longer make out the finer details. The South Pole was now partially obscured by a glowing mist; only the peak of Big Horn protruded through it—a small, black dot, seen exactly head-on.

The carefully mapped but still unknown continent beyond the Sea was the same apparently random patchwork that it had always been. It was too fore-shortened, and too full of complex detail, to reward visual examination, and Norton scanned it only briefly.

He swept his eyes round the encircling band of the Sea, and noticed for the first time a regular pattern of disturbed water, as if waves were breaking over reefs set at geometrically precise intervals. Rama's manoeuvring was having some effect, but a very slight one. He was sure that Sergeant Barnes would have sailed forth happily under these conditions, had he asked her to cross the Sea in her lost *Resolution*.

New York, London, Paris, Moscow, Rome . . . he said farewell to all the cities of the northern continent, and hoped the Ramans would forgive him for any damage he had done. Perhaps they would understand that it was all in the cause of science.

Then, suddenly, he was at the Hub, and eager hands reached out to grab him, and to hurry him through the airlocks. His overstrained legs and arms were trembling so uncontrollably that he was almost unable to help himself, and he was content to be handled like a half-paralysed invalid.

The sky of Rama contracted above him, as he descended into the central crater of the Hub. As the door of the inner airlock shut off the view for ever, he found himself thinking: "How strange that night should be falling, now that Rama is closest to the sun!"

CHAPTER XLIV

Space Drive

A HUNDRED KILOMETRES was an adequate safety margin, Norton had decided. Rama was now a huge black rectangle, exactly broadside-on, eclipsing the sun. He had used this opportunity to fly *Endeavour* completely into shadow, so that the load could be taken off the ship's cooling systems and some overdue maintenance could be carried out. Rama's protective cone of darkness might disappear at any moment, and he intended to make as much use of it as he could.

Rama was still turning; it had now swung through almost fifteen degrees, and it was impossible to believe that some major orbit change was not imminent. On the United Planets, excitement had now reached a pitch of hysteria, but only a faint echo of this came to *Endeavour*. Physically and emotionally, her crew were exhausted; apart from a skeleton watch, everyone had slept for twelve hours after take-off from the North Polar Base. On doctor's orders, Norton himself had used electro-sedation; even so he had dreamed that he was climbing an infinite stairway.

The second day back on ship, everything had almost returned to normal; the exploration of Rama already seemed part of another life. Norton started to deal with the accumulated office work and to make plans for the future; but he refused the requests for interviews that had somehow managed to insinuate themselves into the Survey and even SPACEGUARD radio circuits. There were no messages from Mercury, and the UP General Assembly had adjourned its session, though it was ready to meet again at an hour's notice.

Norton was having his first good night's sleep, thirty hours after leaving Rama, when he was rudely shaken back to consciousness. He cursed groggily, opened a bleary eye at Karl Mercer—and then, like any good commander, was instantly wide awake.

"It's stopped turning?"

"Yes. Steady as a rock."

"Let's go to the bridge."

The whole ship was awake; even the simps knew that something was afoot, and made anxious, meeping noises until Sergeant McAndrews reassured them with swift hand-signals. Yet as Norton slipped into his chair and fastened the restraints round his waist, he wondered if this might be yet another false alarm.

Rama was now foreshortened into a stubby cylinder, and the searing rim of the sun had peeked over one edge. Norton jockeyed *Endeavour* gently back into the umbra of the artificial eclipse, and saw the pearly splendour of the corona reappear across a background of the brighter stars. There was one huge prominence, at least half a million kilometres high, that had climbed so far from the sun that its upper branches looked like a tree of crimson fire.

So now we have to wait, Norton told himself. The important thing is not to get bored, to be ready to react at a moment's notice, to keep all the instruments aligned and recording, no matter how long it takes. . . .

That was strange. The star field was shifting, almost as if he had actuated the Roll thrusters. But he had touched no controls, and if there had been any real movement, he would have sensed it at once.

"Skipper!" said Calvert urgently from the Nav. position, "we're rolling—look at the stars! *But I'm getting no instrument readings!*"

"Rate gyros operating?"

"Perfectly normal—I can see the zero jitter. But we're rolling several degrees a second!"

"That's impossible!"

"Of course it is—but look for yourself. . . ."

When all else failed, a man had to rely on eyeball instrumentation. Norton could not doubt that the star field was indeed slowly rotating—there went Sirius, across the rim of the port. Either the universe, in a reversion to pre-Copernican cosmology, had suddenly decided to revolve around *Endeavour*; or the stars were standing still, and the ship was turning.

The second explanation seemed rather more likely, yet it involved apparently insoluble paradoxes. If the ship was really turning at this rate, he would have *felt* it—literally by the seat of his pants, as the old saying went. And the gyros could not all have failed, simultaneously and independently.

Only one answer remained. Every atom of *Endeavour* must be in the grip of some force—and only a powerful gravitational field could produce this effect. At least, no other *known* field. . . .

Suddenly, the stars vanished. The blazing disc of the sun had emerged from behind the shield of Rama, and its glare had driven them from the sky.

"Can you get a radar reading? What's the doppler?"

Norton was fully prepared to find that this too was inoperative, but he was wrong.

Rama was under way at last, accelerating at the modest rate of 0.015 gravities. Dr. Perera, Norton told himself, would be pleased; he had predicted a maximum of 0.02. And *Endeavour* was somehow caught in its wake like a piece of flotsam, whirling round and round behind a speeding ship. . . .

Hour after hour, that acceleration held constant; Rama was falling away from *Endeavour* at steadily increasing speed. As its distance grew, the anomalous behaviour of the ship slowly ceased; the normal laws of inertia started to operate again. They could only guess at the energies in whose backwash they had been briefly caught, and Norton was thankful that he had stationed *Endeavour* at a safe distance before Rama had switched on its drive.

As to the nature of that drive, one thing was now certain, even though all else was mystery. There were no jets of gas, no beams of ions or plasma thrusting Rama into its new orbit. No one put it better than Sergeant-Professor Myron when he said, in shocked disbelief: "There goes Newton's Third Law."

It was Newton's Third Law, however, upon which *Endeavour* had to depend the next day, when she used her very last reserves of propellent to bend her own orbit outward from the sun. The change was slight, but it would increase her perihelion distance by ten million kilometres. That was the difference between running the ship's cooling system at ninety-five per cent capacity— and a certain fiery death.

When they had completed their own manoeuvre, Rama was two hundred thousand kilometres away, and difficult to see against the glare of the sun. But they could still obtain accurate radar measurements of its orbit; and the more they observed, the more puzzled they became.

They checked the figures over and over again, until there was no escaping from the unbelievable conclusion. It looked as if all the fears of the Hermians, the heroics of Rodrigo, and the rhetoric of the General Assembly, had been utterly in vain.

What a cosmic irony, said Norton as he looked at his final figures, if after a million years of safe guidance Rama's computers had made one trifling error —perhaps changing the sign of an equation from plus to minus.

Everyone had been so certain that Rama would lose speed, so that it could be captured by the sun's gravity and thus become a new planet of the solar system. It was doing just the opposite.

It was gaining speed—and in the worst possible direction.

Rama was falling ever more swiftly into the sun.

CHAPTER XLV

Phoenix

AS THE DETAILS of its new orbit became more and more clearly defined, it was hard to see how Rama could possibly escape disaster. Only a handful of comets had ever passed as close to the sun; at perihelion, it would be less than half a million kilometres above that inferno of fusing hydrogen. No solid material could withstand the temperature of such an approach; the tough alloy that comprised Rama's hull would start to melt at ten times that distance.

Endeavour had now passed its own perihelion, to everyone's relief, and was slowly increasing its distance from the sun. Rama was far ahead on its closer, swifter orbit, and already appeared well inside the outermost fringes of the corona. The ship would have a grandstand view of the drama's final stage.

Then, five million kilometres from the sun, and still accelerating, Rama started to spin its cocoon. Until now, it had been visible under the maximum power of *Endeavour*'s telescopes as a tiny bright star; suddenly it began to scintillate, like a star seen through horizon mists. It almost seemed as if it was disintegrating; when he saw the image breaking up, Norton felt a poignant sense of grief at the loss of so much wonder. Then he realised that Rama was still there, but that it was surrounded by a shimmering haze.

And then it was gone. In its place was a brilliant, star-like object, showing no visible disc—as if Rama had suddenly contracted into a tiny ball.

It was some time before they realised what had happened. Rama had indeed disappeared: it was now surrounded by a perfectly reflecting sphere, about a hundred kilometres in diameter. All that they could now see was the reflection of the sun itself, on the curved portion that was closest to them. Behind this protective bubble, Rama was presumably safe from the solar inferno.

As the hours passed, the bubble changed its shape. The image of the sun became elongated, distorted. The sphere was turning into an ellipsoid, its long axis pointed in the direction of Rama's flight. It was then that the first anomalous reports started coming in from the robot observatories, which, for almost two hundred years, had been keeping a permanent watch on the sun.

Something was happening to the solar magnetic field, in the region around Rama. The million-kilometre-long lines of force that threaded the corona, and drove its wisps of fiercely ionised gas at speeds which sometimes defied even the crushing gravity of the sun, were shaping themselves around that glittering ellipsoid. Nothing was yet visible to the eye, but the orbiting instruments reported every change in magnetic flux and ultra-violet radiation.

And presently, even the eye could see the changes in the corona. A faintly-glowing tube or tunnel, a hundred thousand kilometres long, had appeared high in the outer atmosphere of the sun. It was slightly curved, bending along the orbit which Rama was tracing, and Rama itself—or the protective cocoon around it—was visible as a glittering bead racing faster and faster down that ghostly tube through the corona.

For it was still gaining speed; now it was moving at more than two thousand kilometres a second, and there was no question of it ever remaining a captive of the sun. Now, at last, the Raman strategy was obvious; they had come so close to the sun merely to tap its energy at the source, and to speed themselves even faster on the way to their ultimate, unknown goal. . . .

And presently it seemed that they were tapping more than energy. No one could ever be certain of this, because the nearest observing instruments were thirty million kilometres away, but there were definite indications that matter was flowing from the sun *into Rama itself*, as if it was replacing the leakage and losses of ten thousand centuries in space.

Faster and faster Rama swept around the sun, moving now more swiftly than any object that had ever travelled through the solar system. In less than two hours, its direction of motion had swung through more than 90 degrees, and it had given a final, almost contemptuous proof of its total lack of interest in all the worlds whose peace of mind it had so rudely disturbed.

It was dropping out of the Ecliptic, down into the southern sky, far below the plain in which all the planets move. Though that, surely, could not be its ultimate goal, it was aimed squarely at the Greater Magellanic Cloud, and the lonely gulfs beyond the Milky Way.

CHAPTER XLVI

Interlude

"COME IN," SAID Commander Norton absent-mindedly at the quiet knock on his door.

"Some news for you, Bill. I wanted to give it first, before the crew gets into the act. And anyway, it's my department."

Norton still seemed far away. He was lying with his hands clasped under his head, eyes half shut, cabin light low—not really drowsing, but lost in some reverie or private dream.

He blinked once or twice, and was suddenly back in his body.

"Sorry, Laura—I don't understand. What's it all about?"

"Don't say you've forgotten!"

"Stop teasing, you wretched woman. I've had a few things on my mind recently."

Surgeon-Commander Ernst slid a captive chair across in its slots and sat down beside him.

"Though interplanetary crises come and go, the wheels of Martian bureaucracy grind steadily away. But I suppose Rama helped. Good thing you didn't have to get permission from the Hermians as well."

Light was dawning.

"Oh—Port Lowell has issued the permit!"

"Better than that—it's already been acted on." Laura glanced at the slip of paper in her hand. "Immediate," she read. "Probably right now, your new son is being conceived. Congratulations."

"Thank you. I hope he hasn't minded the wait."

Like every astronaut, Norton had been sterilised when he entered the service; for a man who would spend years in space, radiation-induced mutation was not a risk—it was a certainty. The spermatazoon that had just delivered its cargo of genes on Mars, two hundred million kilometres away, had been frozen for thirty years, awaiting its moment of destiny.

Norton wondered if he would be home in time for the birth. He had earned rest, relaxation—such normal family life as an astronaut could ever know. Now that the mission was essentially over, he was beginning to unwind, and to think once more about his own future, and that of both his families. Yes, it would be good to be home for a while, and to make up for lost time—in many ways. . . .

"This visit," protested Laura rather feebly, "was purely in a professional capacity."

"After all these years," replied Norton, "we know each other better than that. Anyway, you're off duty now."

"*Now* what are you thinking?" demanded Surgeon-Commander Ernst, very much later. "You're not becoming sentimental, I hope."

"Not about us. About Rama. I'm beginning to miss it."

"Thanks very much for the compliment."

Norton tightened his arms around her. One of the nicest things about weightlessness, he often thought, was that you could really hold someone all night, without cutting off the circulation. There were those who claimed that love at one gee was so ponderous that they could no longer enjoy it.

"It's a well-known fact, Laura, that men, unlike women, have *two*-track minds. But seriously—well, *more* seriously—I do feel a sense of loss."

"I can understand that."

"Don't be so clinical; that's not the only reason. Oh, never mind." He gave up. It was not easy to explain, even to himself.

He had succeeded beyond all reasonable expectation; what his men had discovered in Rama would keep scientists busy for decades. And, above all, he had done it without a single casualty.

But he had also failed. One might speculate endlessly, but the nature and the purpose of the Ramans was still utterly unknown. They had used the solar system as a refuelling stop—as a booster station—call it what you will, and had then spurned it completely, on their way to more important business. They would probably never even know that the human race existed; such monumental indifference was worse than any deliberate insult.

When Norton had glimpsed Rama for the last time, a tiny star hurtling outwards beyond Venus, he knew that part of his life was over. He was only fifty-five, but he felt he had left his youth down there on the curving plain, among mysteries and wonders now receding inexorably beyond the reach of man. Whatever honours and achievements the future brought him, for the rest of his life he would be haunted by a sense of anticlimax, and the knowledge of opportunities missed.

So he told himself; but even then, he should have known better.

And on far-off Earth, Dr. Carlisle Perera had as yet told no one how he had woken from a restless sleep with the message from his subconscious still echoing in his brain:

The Ramans do everything in threes.